ISABEL, ANACAONA &
COLUMBUS'S DEMISE

Yúcahu, the spirit of yucca and male fertility, also master of the sea, fatherless, and the most important spirit in Taíno daily life.

Praise for

ISABEL, ANACAONA & COLUMBUS'S DEMISE
1498-1502 Retold

"Deeply researched, devastating novel of the dawn of Caribbean colonialism... Like all of Rowen's principal characters, Anacaona is drawn from historical record, a savvy leader who expects and plans for betrayal...Rowen's storytelling prioritizes fidelity to the historical timeline, vividly capturing power shifts and what the major players thought and felt at each development. Dialogue is invented, but the chapters read like reported history...Violence is alluded to rather than relished, as the novel illuminates the drift of history and how a diverse array of leaders...arrived at decisions that shaped history."

—booklife

"Andrew Rowen's *Isabel, Anacaona & Columbus's Demise* is a wonderful reimagination of a consequence-heavy moment of world history, something like a chronicle of a holocaust foretold, slowly, methodically, and menacingly. Fascinating and compellingly written."

—Greg Grandin, *America, América: A New History of the New World*

"...the Spanish conquest of the Caribbean...is one of the most fascinating, and important, chapters in the encounter between the native people of the Americas and Europeans. This exciting retelling of the narrative brings the people on both sides to life in an excellent page-turner..."

—Samuel M. Wilson, *Hispaniola: Caribbean Chiefdoms in the Age of Columbus*

"Drawing on accurate, first-hand accounts, this book offers a window into our past, delving into the minds and thoughts of all the key players of the period. It vividly reveals the exploits and failures of the invaders and dispels numerous myths created by past historians, including the false narrative of Taino Indian docility. Mr. Rowen humanizes our Indigenous ancestors by neither romanticizing nor demonizing them. Instead, he shows just how complex our history is. Our ancestors were a people with great leaders and warriors!...I wholeheartedly endorse this book!"

—Kasike Atunwa Jorge Baracutay Estevez of the Higuayagua
Taino Luku Kairi tribe

"...an excellent and original account of the dramatic and momentous events that took place at the dawn of the conquest and colonization of the New World... moving and enlightening for any reader interested in understanding the origins of American history."

—**Manuel García Arévalo,** member of the Dominican Academy of History

"A refreshing, well-informed take on a less well-known period of history...a fresh, scholarly perspective on Christopher Columbus...With a plethora of controversial accounts of Columbus on offer, it's easy to feel discouraged when picking up a new title about the era in which he lived. However, in this work of historical fiction, Rowen brings a fresh, inviting viewpoint... This narrative has the same scholarly weight as his previous two works— *Encounters Unforeseen: 1492 Retold* and *Columbus and Caonabó: 1493-1498 Retold*—but can just as easily be read as a stand-alone...Over the course of the novel, Rowen's writing is clear and easy to read, despite the dense material, and can be enjoyed by laypeople looking for an engaging up-to-date perspective on this time period, or by scholars, who may appreciate the surface-level fictionalized narrative or a deep dive into the bibliographical contents...an enjoyable, educational read..."

—*Kirkus Reviews*

"The narrative perspective is varied. It includes the voices of mercurial, shrewd Columbus, diplomatic and pious Isabel, and Anacaona, a member of a ruling Taíno family who observes the arrival of the Spaniards with dread. The latter is tactical, using her feminine wiles to negotiate and protect her tribe. Columbus's favorite interpreter, Diego, is also given space...Their development is complex and compelling, as is that of secondary characters: Some settlers are escaping Spain's classist society; some marry Indigenous women and form meaningful attachments to their new communities. Others are exploitative and intolerant...An enthralling historical novel, *Isabel, Anacaona & Columbus's Demise* chronicles the ruinous progress of European colonialism."

—Foreword

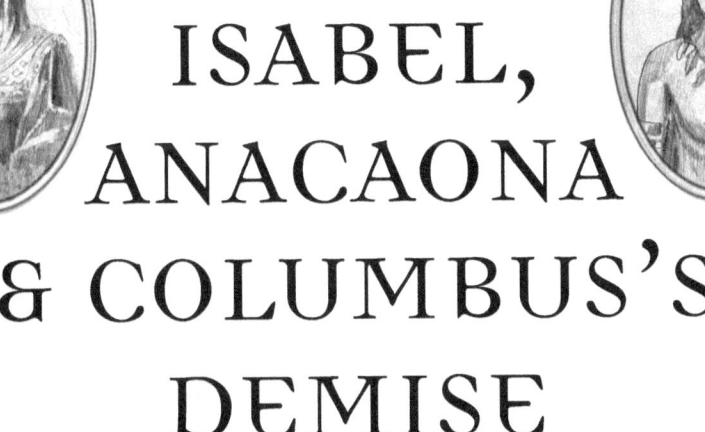

ISABEL,
ANACAONA
& COLUMBUS'S
DEMISE

1498~1502 Retold

Andrew Rowen

ALL PERSONS PRESS

NEW YORK, NEW YORK

All Persons Press
New York, New York
First published in 2025 by All Persons Press

Permissions and Credits on pages vi and xi-xiii.

Library of Congress Control Number: 2025910035

ISBN 978-0-9991961-6-8 Hardcover
ISBN 978-0-9991961-7-5 Trade Paperback
ISBN 978-0-9991961-8-2 eBook

Cover and Book Design by Glen Edelstein, Hudson Valley Book Design
Cover and Title Page Illustrations by Robert Hunt
Interior Maps and Illustrations by Boris De Los Santos

For Sam, Ben, and Hannah

CONTENTS

LIST OF MAPS
AND ILLUSTRATIONS

Stories are told from the perspective of the participants' probable knowledge of geography at the time of the story, and maps presented herein are from the sixteenth through eighteenth centuries, except those designated by an asterisk, which have been drawn by Boris De Los Santos. The sketches of Cacique Diego Colón, a Bayahibe bush, and Anacaona; the collage of Taínos panning for gold; and routes drawn on the historic maps are also by Boris De Los Santos.

HISTORICAL NOTE

This novel dramatizes the Spanish subjugation of the island Columbus named Española—known to its Taíno peoples as Haiti or Quisqueya—and the Taínos' resistance, accommodations, and submissions thereto during the last years of Columbus's governance and the initial rule of crown-appointed successors, from 1498 to 1502. The history is told through the eyes and intimate relationships of the principal protagonists, including the Taíno chieftains Behecchio, Mayobanex, and Guarionex; Columbus, his favorite Taíno interpreter, and the leader of the Spaniards who rebelled against him; and two of history's remarkable woman rulers, Spain's Queen Isabella and Haiti's Anacaona, Behecchio's sister.

The period presented is the least documented and studied of Española's brutal conquest. While often perceived today that the conquest was complete by 1498, Columbus and other Europeans then remained fearful the "Indians" could expel their invasion from the island, and many Taíno chieftains yet hoped to maintain their chiefdoms and civilization in some form of coexistence with the conquerors. Events depicted herein include Anacaona and Behecchio's struggle to so continue to rule their chiefdom of Xaraguá; the uneven steps Isabella and her husband Ferdinand took to limit the Indians' enslavement and abuse; and Columbus's governance of Española and tortured demise, culminating in Isabella and Ferdinand's decision to replace him. Focus includes the society Isabella wanted to establish in Española following that replacement and the organic origins of the cruel systems of *repartimiento* and *encomienda* through which Spanish monarchs would thereafter govern the Spanish American empire then being born. Scenes portray life in conquered Española and coexisting Haiti. While much of the action involves Columbus and other male protagonists, the novel's title reflects Isabella's direction of her conquest and Anacaona's resistance to it.

The novel is a sequel to—and readable independently from—*Encounters Unforeseen: 1492 Retold*, which portrays the lives of many of the same protagonists from youth through 1492, and *Columbus and Caonabó: 1493–1498 Retold*, which relates Columbus's first invasion of the island and the brief war of resistance mounted by Anacaona's husband, Chief Caonabó. As in these prior books, I have sought to portray the Taíno and European protagonists with commensurate stature and gravitas and to avoid the traditional Columbus- and European-centric focus of most accounts of the events, including those critical of Columbus. I present the protagonists' actions and thoughts as I believe they would have lived them day to day, seeking foremost historical validity through reliance on primary and anthropological sources (rather than inventing an overarching literary plot) and without expressing historical conclusions or moral judgments (which are left for the reader). I also continue to resist embellishing hero or villain in my interpretations of the historical record and fictionalizations of detail not found therein. For readers interested, the Sources section indicates the sources considered for each story and sometimes explains my reasoning and that of contrary interpretations.

The contemporary European accounts of what happened on Española from 1498 through 1502 are limited and typically quite partisan, infected with self-promotion and/or pro- or anti-Columbus sentiment. Columbus's own writings include journal entries relating the westward crossing of his third voyage, subsequent letters to Isabella and Ferdinand or their courtiers relating his perspective of events on the island and his removal, and communications to his lieutenants on Española and the Spaniards in rebellion against him. Views of the rebels—who took haven with Behecchio and Anacaona in Xaraguá—can be found principally in communications by their leader, Francisco Roldán, and their testimony in the partially preserved record of the investigation of Columbus by his successor in 1500. The incomplete record of this investigation, published in 2006, also contains testimony by Columbus's servants and supporters, including criticisms of him. There are less partisan sources, including reports by missionaries. Isabella and Ferdinand's proclamations and orders regarding the Indies define the policy established, providing insight into their thoughts. Considerable resort is made to the contemporary chronicles by Bartolomé de Las Casas, Peter Martyr d'Anghera, Gonzalo Fernández de Oviedo, and Columbus's son Ferdinand, all of whom make minor appearances in the novel.

The Taínos had no written language by which to leave their own account of the history, so Taíno voices must be reconstructed from the European primary sources. These sources do record actions—or, more typically, reactions—of Haiti's chieftains during the period, including attempts various chieftains made to influence or compromise the terms of conquest imposed on them. However, the European sources reflect limited knowledge of the Taíno perspective and often lack credibility, obviously reflecting a male conqueror's viewpoint and bias, including base presumptions regarding indigenous women's surrender to conquest. In part, I have relied on the analyses of anthropologists, archaeologists, and other experts to deduce a more complete and bias-free understanding of the Taíno and female side of the history. In instances, when believing portions of the European primary and secondary accounts not credible, I have contradicted them by presenting what I suspect more likely occurred, noting such in the Sources section. Much is unknown, and I have speculated as to the Taíno perspective of a range of important conditions or events—including the appropriateness of concubinage or marriage with the conquerors (the origin of mestizo society through which Taíno culture largely survived); the early Christian missionary efforts; and the horrific decline in the Taíno population that commenced in 1495 and continued apace during the period presented (due to European diseases, Spanish brutality, forced labor, collapse of the social system, and suicide).

All persons identified with proper names are historic except a few incidental characters given proper names to facilitate the narrative's readability, and these exceptions are noted in the Sources section. Historic Taínos known by baptized Christian names or with unknown names are given fictitious birth names—such as Bakako—which are also noted in the Sources section. Conversations are fictionalized when possible based on primary sources either recounting the conversation or indicating the views of the participants. The text occasionally quotes or paraphrases words from primary sources to best capture the participants' intent and fifteenth-century perspective; to preserve the novel style, these incorporations are not designated by quotation marks, but the Sources section indicates the chapters, sections, paragraphs, and/or dates of the sources relied on. Taíno words are italicized and translated when introduced and then compiled in the Glossary.

My earlier books set Isabella and Ferdinand's missionary effort in Española within the greater intellectual framework of their actions to Christianize their Spanish kingdoms through the Inquisition, the expulsion of the Jews, and the completion of the Reconquista. This book continues that framing, depicting their decisions regarding the missionary effort side by side with their actions to expel the Muslims, sometimes with the assistance of the same advisor, Archbishop Ximénez de Cisneros.

In worlds ruled largely by men, Isabella was admired and obeyed by her Christian subjects, as was Anacaona by her Taíno subjects. Isabella also was feared by her enemies and the peoples she conquered, and Anacaona's authority as her people's natural ruler was respected by those conquering for Isabella. The queen's legacies—including presiding at the birth of both modern Spain and Spanish America—are well known, and she steadfastly pursued them. The chief's struggle against conquest—and her fate to preside at the birth of mestizo society—are relatively unknown, and she made decisions without the experience of the next five centuries of European invasion, settlement, brutality, and treaty-breaking to guide her.

As this novel depicts, Isabella sincerely but ineffectively tried to curtail the enslavements and abuses by those who conquered on her behalf. Anacaona did succeed—with Behecchio and then alone—to preserve her chiefdom in coexistence with Isabella's conquest during the entirety of the period presented. While the conquest dwarfs the accomplishment, I hope to give the latter the recognition long overdue.

August 1, 2025   ANDREW ROWEN

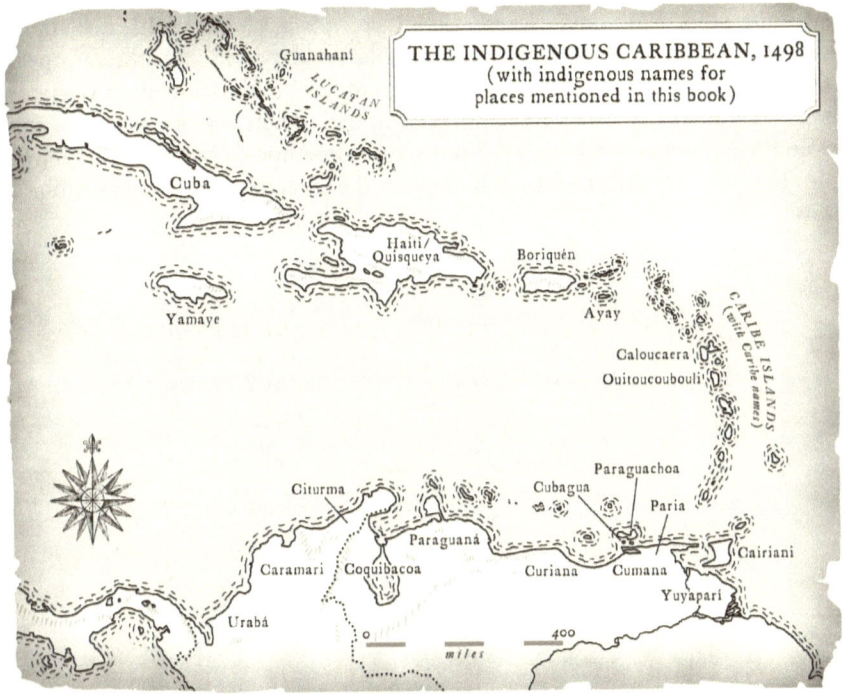

Caribbean Islands: Ayay (St. Croix); Boriquén (Puerto Rico); Caloucaera (Guadeloupe); Cairiani (Trinidad); Cuba (Cuba); Guanahaní (San Salvador); Haiti or Quisqueya (Haiti and Dominican Republic); Lucayan Islands (the Bahamas and Turks & Caicos); Ouitoucoubouli (Dominica); and Yamaye (Jamaica). South American coastline and islands (east to west): Venezuela—Yuyaparí (Orinoco River and delta), Paria (Paria Penisula), Paraguachoa (Margarita Island), Cubagua (Cubagua Island), Cumana, Curiana, Paraguaná, Coquibacoa; Colombia—Citurma, Caramari, Urabá (Gulf of Uraba). The South American coastline is marked for the boundaries of modern Venezuela and Colombia.

TAÍNO, CARIBE, INDIAN

Taíno civilization spread across modern eastern Cuba, Haiti, the Dominican Republic, Jamaica, Puerto Rico, and the Bahamas, although it's doubtful the Taínos conceived or used the word *Taíno* to refer to themselves as one people other than to distinguish themselves from Caribes. Caribes lived in the Lesser Antilles, i.e., Guadeloupe, Dominica, and nearby islands. Historically related peoples—Arawaks and mainland Caribes—lived with other peoples along the coastline of modern Venezuela and Colombia and in Trinidad.

Columbus believed he'd reached a place in or near the Indies on his first voyage (disembarking in the Bahamas, Cuba, Haiti, and the Dominican Republic), and in his journal of that voyage, he referred to the peoples he encountered as "Indians" (*Encounters Unforeseen*, chapter VIII, depicts his journal's first use of the word). That appellation persisted after the European realization that the Americas weren't the "Indies" and assumed an ethnic or racial connotation, as opposed to geographic. When a story herein is told from the European perspective, Taínos and sometimes other indigenous peoples typically are referred to as Indians in the fifteenth-century geographical sense.

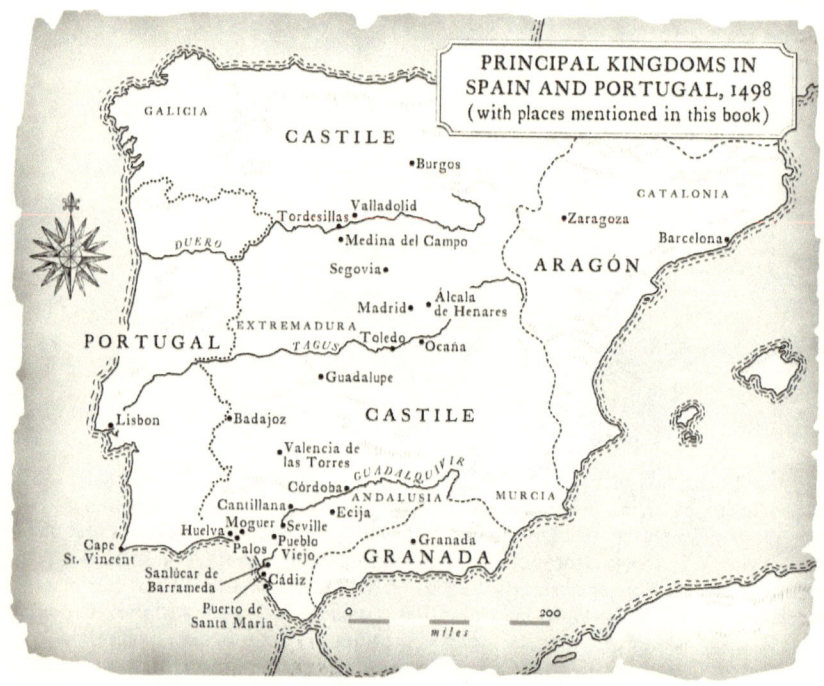

NAMES OF PEOPLE AND PLACES

Names of Spaniards and Portuguese are in Spanish and Portuguese, respectively. Columbus and his family's names are in Spanish, rather than Ligurian. Names of other Europeans sometimes are in English translation. Names of Taíno chieftains have spellings currently used by anthropologists, historians, and others writing in English.

Names of places typically are the English or Spanish version of the names that would have been used by the persons in the passage, usually with the modern spelling.

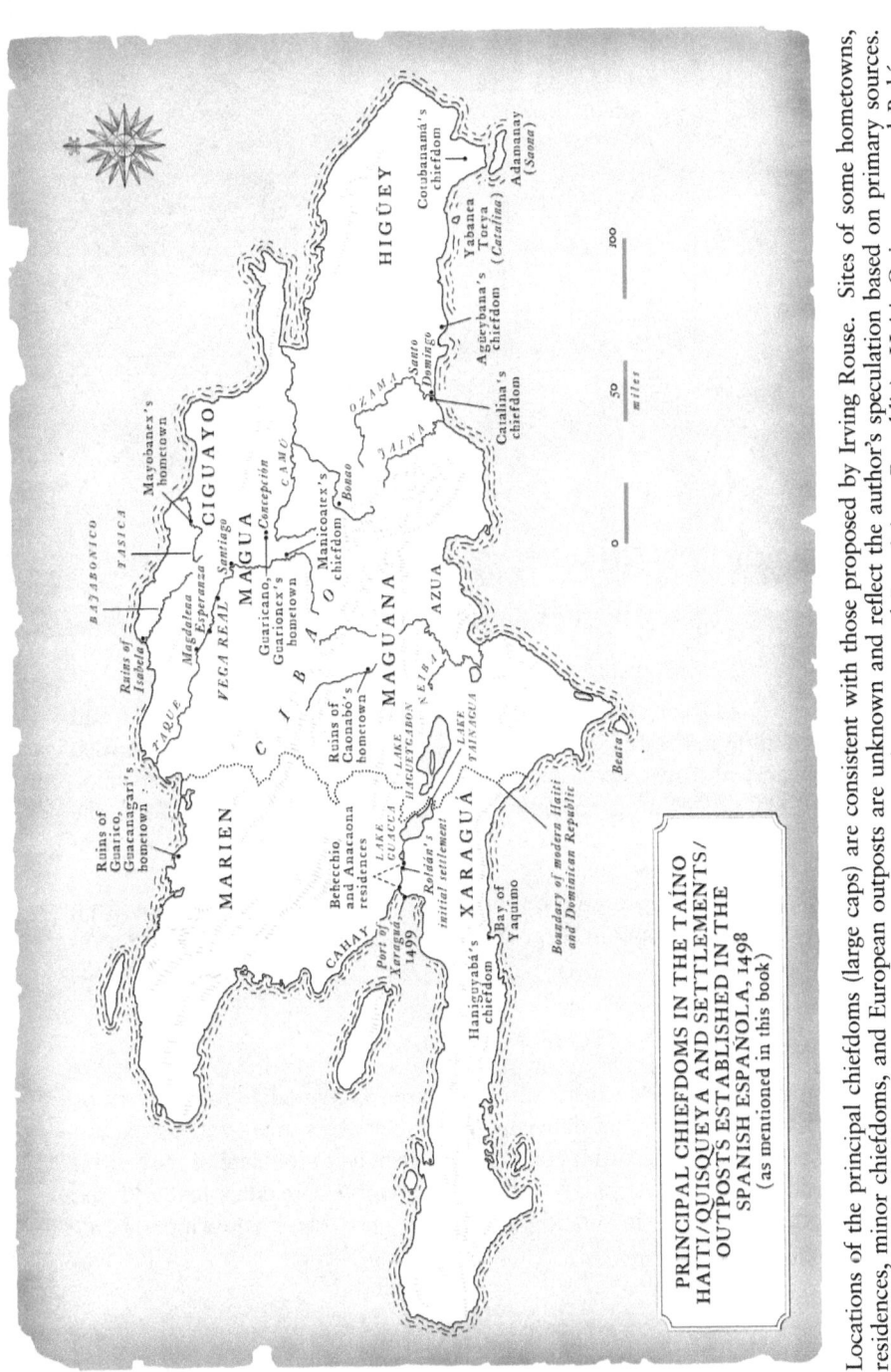

PRINCIPAL CHIEFDOMS IN THE TAÍNO
HAITI/QUISQUEYA AND SETTLEMENTS/
OUTPOSTS ESTABLISHED IN THE
SPANISH ESPAÑOLA, 1498
(as mentioned in this book)

Locations of the principal chiefdoms (large caps) are consistent with those proposed by Irving Rouse. Sites of some hometowns, residences, minor chiefdoms, and European outposts are unknown and reflect the author's speculation based on primary sources. There were three indigenous names for Española (the modern Haiti and Dominican Republic)—Haiti, Quisqueya, and Bohío—and Haiti is mostly used herein, including sometimes by Europeans. The map shows the boundary between modern Haiti and the Dominican Republic so readers can see that places identified in the indigenous Haiti are often within the modern Dominican Republic.

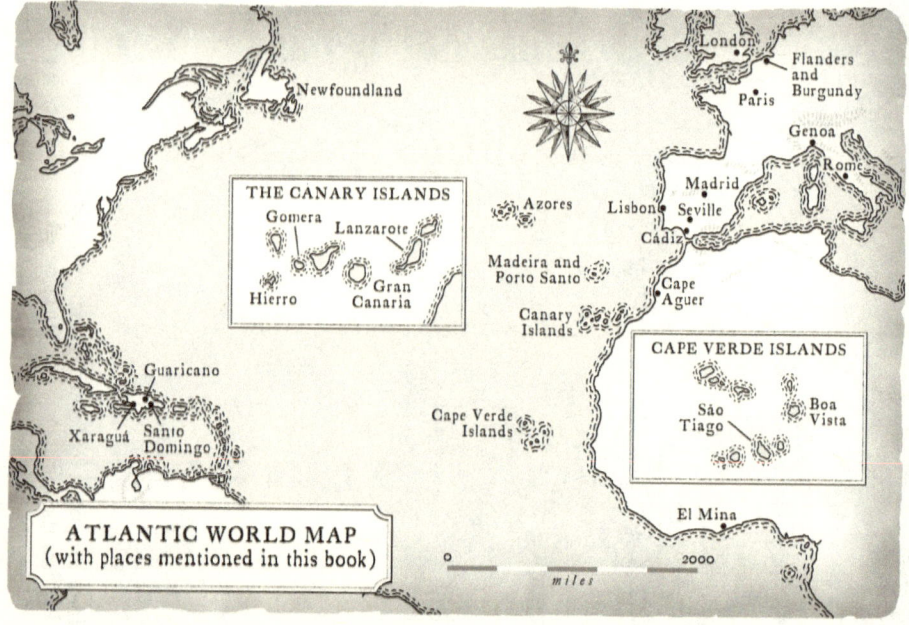

ATLANTIC WORLD MAP
(with places mentioned in this book)

TIME, DISTANCE, MONEY

While Taínos had their own measures of time and distance, for simplicity and uniformity, time and dates are based on Julius Caesar's calendar then used by Europeans, and distances are presented in modern US statutory miles. Columbus and other Europeans often measured distance in "leagues," and the text uses leagues when appropriate to the story, with one league equal to about 3.68 modern US statutory miles.

During the period presented, the Spanish *maravedí* was an accounting unit fixed to gold, not a coin. A gold ducat or castellano was said to represent 375 maravedís.

DATING OF STORIES

If the historical record indicates a specific or approximate date for an event or events central to a story, that date is noted in the story's title—without parentheses. If the historical record is conflicted or silent as to the date of the central events dramatized, the story's title indicates a possible date consistent with the context of other events—in parentheses. If history provides no guidance or context, the story is left undated.

FOOTNOTES

. . . are for historians and those inclined but need not be read to follow the story.

I

THE GUAMIQUINA RETURNS

ANACAONA,
Xaraguá, Haiti (Quisqueya), Spring 1498

Anacaona hovered anxiously at the rear of the gathering, spying from the veiled shadows of a doorway as her brother Behecchio entertained seventy pale men who'd trespassed into Xaraguá. All of them were seated beneath the spacious canopy that extended from his enormous chieftain's residence. Drums resounded, and in the great ballcourt beyond, women and girls wearing flower headbands sang and danced in choreographed unison, stately led by the most beautiful of Behecchio's wives, Guanahattabenecheuá.

The ceremony was performed only for the most important visitors, and Anacaona surmised the trespassers appreciated the distinction and honor. As expected, the dancers' nakedness also tempted them, and she gleaned that their leers and smirks betrayed a lack of respect for her civilization. Nakedness had been her peoples' choice and norm from time immemorial—save for *naguas* (loincloths) worn by married women. She scrutinized Behecchio's expressions to determine if he'd resolved to assassinate the entire band as they slept that night.

She was sadly and proudly torn by a fleeting vision of her husband, Caonabó, the late supreme *cacique* (chief) of Maguana. Years before, he'd recognized that the pale men who'd arrived on three vessels were an enemy people, and he'd massacred the three dozen of them initially stationed on the island (1492–1493). But the pale *guamiquina* (a people's leader) had soon returned to invade with many more vessels bearing over a thousand men (1493) and imprisoned him for waging war in opposition (1495). Following battles lost and enslavements, other supreme caciques on the island had surrendered to become vassals to the pale men's rulers, Fernando and Isabel, and agreed to the guamiquina's demand to deliver gold in tribute every three months (1495–1496). Yet Caonabó had refused such submission. So the guamiquina had hauled him across the sea to capitulate at those rulers' feet, and he'd perished on the journey (1496).

Anacaona stifled her memories and grimly eyed those assembled. Taíno women and men from the subjugated chiefdoms crowded among the pale men, the voluntariness of such union unbelievable. The pale men cradled on their laps their forbidding weapons, proven superior to Taíno spears and arrows in battle. As if theirs, they now called the island—known forever as Haiti or Quisqueya—*La Isla Española* (the Spanish Island). Behecchio's warriors lined the ball-court as an honor guard, proud yet bowed. They'd been vanquished in Caonabó's war, and the guamiquina's brother Bartolomé had then intruded to demand that Behecchio submit (1497).

As the dance concluded, Anacaona emerged from the doorway and raised her hand, signaling for the performers to bow and rest. In her early thirties, she was slender and supple, with long black hair that fell over her breasts and down her back, and while her cheeks no longer shimmered youthfully, her eyes and smile radiated a spark and command that enticed and confirmed her supreme rank. She wove gracefully through the gathering toward Behecchio, intending to listen as he parleyed with the pale men's leader, who sat beside him. Most pale men she passed wore necklaces with a *cemí* (a token of a spirit) depicting the cross upon which their Christ-spirit apparently had died—tiny replicas of the large wooden crosses they'd erected in the plazas and ballcourts of the subjugated chiefdoms. She was angered by the spirit's presence, certain that he'd assisted the pale men's conquest, as men alone couldn't inflict the horrific famine, plague, and death suffered in those chiefdoms (1495–1497). She knelt behind her brother as he and the pale leader shifted to face each other, surrounded by their counselors.

"I present myself as King Fernando and Queen Isabel's new leader on the island," Francisco Roldán announced, studying Behecchio's lean frame and piercing black eyes. "I have replaced the guamiquina and his brother, who violated the king and queen's trust." He paused while his Taíno manservant translated the Castilian into the chieftain's tongue. "Throughout Española, I've offered other caciques a better arrangement so that our peoples may live in peace, harmony, and friendship. Your Highness, I come to offer that relationship to you as well."

An Andalusian, Roldán had sailed on Admiral Cristóbal Colón's second voyage (1493), and although a commoner with little education, he'd risen to be appointed Española's chief magistrate by Colón himself. Despite that favor, he'd led his seventy men in rebellion against Colón's rule after Colón departed for Spain (1496–1497), claiming authority on behalf of Fernando and Isabel deriving from that appointment.

"I've already struck an understanding with Bartolomé," Behecchio replied sternly, extending a forefinger to command attention while stroking his necklace of creatures' teeth with the other hand. "He swore your people would stay out of Xaraguá—forever." Waiting for the interpreter's translation, he took stock of Roldán, judging the brawn and weathered skin were those of a soldier or laborer, not a ruler, and that the pale man's age approximated his own, mid-to-late thirties. "In return, I promised I wouldn't oppose your people's conquest of Haiti's other chiefdoms, and I agreed to deliver your caciques ransom in *cazabi* (cassava, a toasted bread made from yucca) and cotton every three months." He gazed imperiously about the crowd. "It was a peace treaty, not a pledge of friendship, and it entitles me to slay you and your men for coming here. To live in harmony, our peoples must live apart."

The assembly, both olive- and pale-skinned, hushed. The island's supreme caciques often bluffed and cajoled, just like European princes. Roldán held himself expressionless, his native boldness bolstered by his attainment of authority.

"Your Highness, hear me out," he said. "I offer to release you from the obligation to deliver cazabi, cotton, gold, or anything else to the guamiquina. He returns soon, and I'll protect you from him and his brother. I will even slay them if necessary to prevent them from reimposing that tribute. My men will defend you from their harsh rule."

Behecchio casually fondled the largest shark's tooth on his necklace and studied his warriors in the ballcourt. "What would you expect from me in return?" he asked, his tone inscrutable.

"My men intend to live in your kingdom," Roldán answered, skirting a request for permission. "You would provide us shelter, food, and assistance so that we may live peacefully among your people in friendship. You and your people will profit, as we have much to teach you about how to live."

Roldán's band listened breathlessly—securing a haven was critical. Famine in the conquered chiefdoms had stricken the conquerors and the conquered alike. Arrest and harsh punishment loomed inevitable when Colón returned from Spain and learned of their rebellion.

Behecchio glanced at Anacaona. It was as they'd expected. Caonabó's brother Manicoatex, now ruling Maguana, had sent word that he had accepted a similar offer from Roldán. Scouts and informants reported that other caciques subjugated by the guamiquina also had accepted.

"Why do your caciques Fernando and Isabel approve this offer?" Behecchio inquired. "They forsake their gold, and their other subjects on Haiti shall hunger. Just to favor you and your band?"

"Fernando and Isabel wish their people to live in harmony with yours, without excessive obligations on your behalf," Roldán blustered. His king and queen knew nothing of his rebellion, much less his undoing of tribute.

"Have those people come here of their own volition?" Behecchio demanded, pointing to the Taínos from other chiefdoms. Reports from Manicoatex and others warned that the assistance Roldán required included the labor of servants or slaves and the submission of women.

"They are friends and servants, all blessed to learn our customs and the singular truth of our Christian faith," Roldán responded. "I swear that you, your family, and your noblemen will continue to live as you always have, without the need to serve us. You must simply ensure that your subjects serve us. In return, you and your subjects will be safe from the guamiquina and free from tribute."

Anacaona recoiled, offended by the slight to Taíno spirits and the bald invitation that Behecchio sacrifice his subjects to maintain himself. But she was silent. Her turn would come.

"You come here with seventy men. Yet my informants estimate that the guamiquina and his brother command four hundred," Behecchio observed. "Why should I believe you are able to defend my people from him?"

"Few of those four hundred approve of the guamiquina's rule," Roldán asserted curtly, irritated by the naked heathen's challenge. "Perhaps only a few dozen would stand at his side if dangerous to do so. His promises of riches have proven false, and they are worse off for having followed him." A blush darkened his cheeks slightly.

Anacaona sensed a vulnerability, an indignation easily roiled, perhaps rooted in a jealousy of others' rank. Behecchio had enough information to decide. The consensus of other caciques who'd met this Roldán was clear enough. For them, Roldán's arrangement was preferable to the guamiquina's rule and tribute payments.

"I will consider your offer tonight," Behecchio indicated. He glared at Roldán and raised his voice. "But you must accept an absolute condition, just as Bartolomé did. I am—and I shall remain—the supreme ruler of Xaraguá and its peoples, never a vassal to you, your Fernando and Isabel, or any other person."

"Your Highness, I promise you that is my understanding," Roldán glibly assured—for the moment. His vassalage to Fernando and Isabel and service to their conquest dictated otherwise.

"My sister Anacaona shall sing for us," Behecchio flourished, as if warming. "She is Caonabó's widow," he added, marking abiding distrust.

Anacaona stood, and the assembly rustled, captivated. A shell necklace with *guanín* pendants hung about her neck, heralding her caciqual ancestry, and a black nagua stretched long and narrow from navel to ankle, shielding her womb and honoring her late husband.*

---

* Guanín being a composite of gold, copper, and silver, with a reddish hue.

She wore arm and leg bands finely inlaid with gold. In her youth, she'd been renowned as Haiti's most beautiful woman, and for years, her poetic composition and performance of *areítos* (songs, dances) had been acclaimed as the most perceptive, her sensuality and wit casting a spell that no man—olive or pale—could resist.

"It's my pleasure to offer you an areíto about my people and our spirits," she announced, disbelieving that Roldán felt any remorse for Caonabó's death yet smiling as if extending friendship. "My daughter shall accompany me."

She strode regally to the ballcourt, and a *nitaíno* (nobleman, lord) crowned her with a headdress, displaying an exotic rainbow of flowers from her private garden. A lone drumbeat commenced, quieting all, whereupon fourteen-year-old Higueymota—of marriageable age but unmarried—came to stand beside her. The daughter's prettiness and coquetry complemented the mother's elegance and aplomb. They sang, alternating verses.

"Two caves lay hidden in the wilds of Haiti's mountains, at the center of the universe," Higueymota began, as mother and daughter gracefully raised their arms to form circles above their heads. "In ages past, the Taíno peoples lived in one, and unimportant peoples lived in the other," Anacaona followed, lowering her arms so Higueymota's cave remained alone. "Long ago, we Taínos emerged to populate the world, canoeing the seas from island to island," Higueymota related, mother and daughter paddling their arms, ambling slowly to and fro.

"We lived in peace, both among ourselves and the unimportant peoples," Anacaona exclaimed. They halted abruptly. "We honored and obeyed our spirits, both friendly and destructive." Higueymota gazed to the heavens. "In return, we prospered, each man and woman aspiring to prosper in harmony with the prosperity of others, both giving to and receiving from others, without confrontation except when necessary." Anacaona embraced Higueymota for emphasis.

"Yúcahu, the friendly spirit of *yuca* (yucca), the sea, and fathers' fertility helps us farm and fish. His mother, Attabeira, provides water for crops, nourishment for those in need, and for mothers' fertility." Higueymota moved her arms as if hoeing, then twitched her fingers as if rain. "The destructive spirit Guabancex brings *hurikáns* (hurricanes), reminding that She and other spirits reign supreme above all mortal beings." Anacaona waved her arms wildly, her face contorted in fury.

"After death, the souls of those who have promoted peace and prosperity go to a place joyous and delectable, and the souls of tyrants go to a place dark and dreadful," mother and daughter exhorted in unison. Higueymota rose resplendent, while Anacaona fell to her knees in agony, staring directly at Roldán.

The drumbeat ceased, and mother and daughter held their final positions. Some in the crowd respectfully murmured approval, others were gingerly silent, and Roldán clapped conspicuously. Anacaona glanced warily at the Taíno women from other chiefdoms. The pallid glaze of their eyes, the absence of smiles, and the wan hunch of their shoulders exposed the obliteration of all pleasure, pride, and hope. The pale men couldn't have understood much, and she beseeched Yúcahu to make them understand and fear the soul's final judgment. She walked with Higueymota to sit down directly facing the pale leader and her brother.

"Magnificent, Your Highness!" Roldán declared, his gaze on Anacaona's face but flickering to her breasts.

"It's my honor to enchant you. Do you enjoy dance and poetry?"

"Of course, Your Highness."

"That delights me. Call me Anacaona, and my daughter Higuey-mota, so our friendship blossoms," she replied gayly, suspecting the man had no use for theater. "May we call you Francisco?"

"That would be my privilege."

The three chatted amiably for some moments. Mother and daughter learned of Roldán's admiration for Haiti's beaches, mountains, and forests and the cultivation of the land, and they nodded often and attentively, as if impressed with his insight. Roldán occasionally spoke haltingly in broken Taíno, dispensing with the need for the interpreter, and Anacaona recognized she'd underestimated his understanding of her people. When he was lulled by the discussion's triviality, she began her inquiry.

"Francisco, you must be of noble birth—tell me of your lineage and rank in your homeland."

"I am Christian and Castilian, liege to King Fernando and Queen Isabel, their chief magistrate commanding these men," Roldán said, offering no new information. No Spaniard thought he had a lineage to brag of, and he was cocksure that shouldn't concern a naked, heathen queen—to whom Christian or Castilian alone ought to signify nobility.

"How illustrious! When at home, do you often dine with your Fernando and Isabel?"

Roldán hesitated. His eyes had fallen to Higueymota's tender pubic hair, but he realized that Anacaona was more to be reckoned with than he'd anticipated. He'd never met his sovereigns, but he solemnly boasted, "They are the world's most powerful princes and very busy. Yet I am summoned to their chambers and partake at their table when the need arises."

"Marvelous!" Anacaona suspected by the pale man's exhale that he was pleased with a lie well delivered. She reached forward, warmly placing her hand on his. "Tell me of your wife and family. Do they attend your rulers, as well?"

Native American dance in Xaraguá. Taken from Pieter van der Aa, 1706. The John Carter Brown Library, portion of rec. no. 08984-016.

Roldán vacillated again, pondering why the queen was asking such questions, both smitten and daunted by her vitality. He hadn't decided how long he would remain in Española. "My Anacaona, I have never married." Anacaona sensed a slight quiver in his wrist and surmised another lie.

She reached forward to gently grasp a cemí depicting the Christ-spirit hanging from his neck, tenderly drawing it and him toward her, as if prelude to a kiss. "If you teach me of this spirit, would it please you that I teach you of our own? The spirits of whom we sang?"

"Your Highness, I would enjoy whatever you wish to share with me."

Pleasantries and compliments extended for a time, but no one was keen on small talk. Behecchio offered Roldán and his men such *bohíos* (houses or homes, made of wood and thatch) they wished for the night.

"If we fail to see eye to eye in the morning, I shall guarantee your people's safety as you depart Xaraguá for good," he warned.

"Your Highness, there is no other place we wish to go."

⊡   ⊡   ⊡

Roldán and his gang chose to spend the night in adjacent bohíos on the outskirts of the village, with swords unsheathed and cross-bowmen and a musketeer standing sentry, their two remaining horses saddled. That evening, he summoned the men to a clearing between the bohíos to discuss their reactions and plan.

Most were four-year veterans of Admiral Colón's second voyage, enlisted among the twelve hundred recruits sailing on its fleet of seventeen ships. A minority had arrived on resupply ships later dispatched. All were wizened from fighting "Indians"—as the Admiral had named the local peoples, believing their islands lay near the Indies. The battles had been engaged on open ground and to defend forts built in the subjugated chiefdoms (1495–1497). Spanish provisions and wine had long exhausted, so they'd been forced to subsist on the Indians' food—including cazabi, *mahisi* (corn), *hutia* (a cat-sized rodent), the native fish and fowl, and *chicha* (corn beer). They'd also endured bouts of local diseases that had stricken nearly all men of the second voyage, many mortally.

Mostly Castilian artisans, farmers, or soldiers, they were united in their contempt for the Admiral. He'd promised them fortune on a voyage to great civilizations where gold abounded and heathens timidly stood eager to serve. Instead, they'd suffered battle wounds, hunger, and disease. He also wasn't true nobility. He, Bartolomé, and their younger brother Diego weren't even Spanish, just Genoese weavers spinning lies, pressing excessive demands and inflicting cruel punishments upon them.

Roldán's gang also angered—they hadn't ventured to Española to starve and spill their blood simply to remain undistinguished, unempowered commoners, enduring unrewarded, ignominious servitude to others, be they Genoese weavers or the sovereigns' courtiers and noblemen in Spain who presumed their obeisance. They, rather than those courtiers, were building a new world and were due new entitlements therein. Estates of land. The service of heathens. Neither the Admiral, nor king and queen, had yet paid their salaries, and salaries couldn't compensate for the hardship, anyway.

Yet alongside their dreams for Española, the gang also sorely coveted the liberty to return to Spain, and they'd recognized their rebellion's gravity precluded that unless the sovereigns abandoned the Admiral or a trustworthy pardon were obtained. They'd sacked the conquest's former headquarters at Isabela and struggled unsuccessfully for a year to install Roldán as the Admiral's successor. Bartolomé, appointed by the Admiral as *Adelantado* (Spanish for frontier governor) in his absence, had barred them from entering the new headquarters established at Santo Domingo, whereupon—with horses raided from Isabela—they'd roamed and squatted in limbo for almost a year (1497–1498).

Bartolomé had repeatedly dangled promises of amnesty and pardon (1497), desperate to settle the rebellion before his brother returned, and Roldán and Bartolomé had parleyed multiple times. But Roldán had refused to settle, concluding the promised pardon a ruse prelude to incarceration and execution, and the two men's mutual distrust now was irreconcilable. That February, resupply ships arriving from Spain had brought news dashing the gang's hope for the Admiral's abandonment—the king and queen had reaffirmed their support for him and even authorized a third voyage.

"This is the best sanctuary—the food is plentiful, and the Indians are civil," Roldán told his men. His tall frame quivered and voice broke, his unquenchable hatred for Bartolomé transparent. "Its distance from Santo Domingo provides a barrier, protecting us from arrest."

"We must make Xaraguá ours," a rebel exclaimed.

"Its riches are ours, free from the Colóns' grasp," another cried.

"Death to them should they try to arrest us here!" a third shouted. "The women will be terrific to mount, the men easy to order about. We shall suffer no work or exertion."

Roldán relished the raw emotions he'd harnessed for his rebellion. But he signaled for the men to quiet down. "The chieftain hasn't confirmed that we may stay," he cautioned. "Do any of you doubt our safety here? Do we stay by force, if necessary?" Roldán had argued to Bartolomé that the Indians would become peaceful, productive servants were tribute eliminated, ignoring Bartolomé's admonishment that such elimination constituted treason to the king and would only embolden Indian resistance.

Most favored remaining, whether by persuasion or force. "Muskets and crossbows assure our safety, and the Lord is on our side," one proclaimed.

"These Indians are untrustworthy, urging idols and Satan to poison us, but we'll subdue them," another declared. "The chieftain's a coward, like all the rest. We'll do as we wish, and the Virgin will protect us."

Roldán turned to other followers, searching for other voices. A few were of notable birth in Spain or otherwise accomplished, with greater stakes drawing their return home. Others had grown accustomed to the service of the Indian women they'd brought with them, indentured as concubines and maids over the past two years. Most of these were pregnant. Some already had infants or young children.

"We'll be secure here," said Adrian de Múxica, a minor nobleman and one of the rebellion's ringleaders. "But when the Admiral returns, we must seek his pardon, regardless of our promise to protect this Behecchio from him."

"Pardon is essential," Roldán agreed. "If the Admiral pardons us, and we trust it enough to return to Spain, we can throw this chieftain overboard when we say goodbye—leaving his fate to tribute, enslavement, or such punishment the Admiral wishes."

"Any pardon by the Admiral will be hollow, a lie," Diego de Escobar warned. He'd sailed on both the first and second voyages, and the Admiral had entrusted him to command one of the forts along the Yaque River (1495–1497). But Escobar had been disillusioned by the Colóns' cruelties to Spaniards and Indians alike. "We must do our best to retain this chieftain's alliance and support, in case we are forced to remain indefinitely," he maintained. "We must treat these people better than the Genoese treat them."

"We must get along with these people," another rebel recommended, once an impoverished Andalusian farmer. "Even if pardoned, some of us may prefer being served by them here rather than serving a Castilian don at home. In Spain, my birthright is merely to sweat so others feast and idle."

"Our lordship of these Indians should be Christian," remarked an Andalusian artisan who'd grown affectionate to his concubine. "I have children here, and they and my woman must be fed. The food is here."

As the moon rose, Roldán drew the meeting to close, satisfied in the consensus that they remain in Xaraguá, even if that required hostilities. "Over the next weeks, I'll award each of you estates to live on," he promised.

Before sleeping, he prayed for his wife and daughter in Spain, Juana and Elvira. But he would dream of Anacaona's astonishing allure and Higueymota's ripe body. An intrigue or marriage with either could gain a multitude of servants and life as a prince of savages.

◻ ◻ ◻

As the pale men spoke, Anacaona and Behecchio met alone in the innermost sanctum of his enormous residence, his *caney* (a chieftain's home, made of wood and thatch) inland, a few miles west of Lake Guacca.* Embers in a stone fire circle glowed before them.

---

*Now known as Lake Trou Caïman, Haiti.

Gonzalo Fernández de Oviedo's sketches of a bohío and caney,
sixteenth century. Oviedo's *Historia General.*

Their caciqual family had ruled Xaraguá for decades, and as
their subjects, they had an abiding pride in Xaraguá's preeminence.
Their chiefdom was admired throughout the island for its abundant
crops, the civility of its daily life, and the beauty of its women. Its
people celebrated their culture, religion, history, and artistry itself.
Its location—nestled beside the great gulf on Haiti's western coast,
its eastern border buffered from the remainder of the island by mountains and desert—had long nurtured its distinctive society and polity.

Brother and sister had once opposed the guamiquina's invasion
of Haiti. Anacaona had assisted Caonabó in organizing a war alliance among the island's caciques to expel it, and essential to that,
Behecchio had proclaimed his support (1494–1495). Shocked,
they'd watched the pale men readily subjugate and impose the gold
tribute obligation in Guarionex's Magua and Guacanagarí's Marien,
and as Caonabó's wife, Anacaona had witnessed firsthand the pale
men's pillage and rape of Maguana. She'd returned to Xaraguá after
learning of her husband's death, and with Behecchio, observed the
ghastly famine and death engulfing the conquered chiefdoms (1496).
Food production had collapsed while villagers desperately searched
for gold to satisfy the tribute obligation, countless perishing en masse
from hunger, gruesome unknown diseases, or the pale men's cruelties,

and some committing suicide. They'd also witnessed the guamiquina and his brother break promises and treaties with caciques, including by slave raiding.

Pierre-François-Xavier de Charlevoix's map of Española/Haiti, 1731.
The John Carter Brown Library, portion of rec. no. 06296-3.

They had agreed to a truce with Bartolomé to save Xaraguá from conquest and the devastation of a similar collapse (1497). Bartolomé had been desperate to secure payments of cazabi to feed his famished men, and with the leverage of abundant crops, they'd rejected his demand for gold tribute. They'd offered cazabi and cotton instead—an obligation they felt their subjects could satisfy without jeopardizing Xaraguá's health—and demanded a promise that Xaraguá wouldn't be invaded. Anacaona had smitten Bartolomé's affection and desire, enticing a lustful relationship yet unconsummated and ambiguously tied to the guamiquina's sparing of the chiefdom.

"A boaster and liar," Behecchio judged Roldán. "I doubt he has any authority at all. But he may be able to protect us from the gua-miquina. Bartolomé hasn't been able to crush him."

"He hasn't the nobility worthy of a marriage alliance, and his leer and manners are even cruder than Bartolomé's," Anacaona reflected. "I doubt his rulers know of him, even less his promises to undo tribute." She paused, waiting for her brother's analysis, anticipating that the pale men's vigilance had brought him to abandon any thought of assassinating them as they slept.

"The guamiquina apparently returns, and as we've always known, he and Bartolomé may break their truce with us someday," Behecchio reasoned. "This Roldán proposes we break the truce first. If he can protect us from the guamiquina, we're free from the yoke and humiliation of payments, and Xaraguá remains beyond the guamiquina's conquest. If he can't, we will have squandered the truce, and the guamiquina will feel entitled to invade afresh."

"We shouldn't permit any pale men to live among us, even assuming they could protect us from the guamiquina," Anacaona rejoined. "These men may be the guamiquina's enemy, but they were among those who pillaged and raped other chiefdoms. We know they'll abuse villagers and *naborias* (servants, the servant class) if we allow them in." She raised the tenor and gravity of her voice. "The suffering and humiliation of the Taínos they've brought here is transparent. We can't so forsake our own subjects."

Behecchio shook his head. "Xaraguá's independence, our rule, and our people's safety are best preserved if the pale men fight among themselves. Supporting one band against another furthers that. We'll pray they massacre each other—the guamiquina and Roldán included—liberating the entire island."

They sat in silence for some moments, aware that both choices were perilous. Children of the same mother, they'd always been close friends and confidants. He admired her sharp intelligence and uncommon presence. She appreciated that he was exceptionally fit to lead, commanding the respect of their subjects, and as the most capable male heir in the caciqual family, was entitled to rule. Even though she'd always felt qualified to rule herself.

"Allowing this band to live in Xaraguá poses dangers," Behecchio admitted. "But there are only seventy of them. We must insist they reform their conduct."

"Caciques in the subjugated chiefdoms have already so insisted!" Anacaona replied, her disagreement unbridled. "Regardless, the pale men have overworked their villagers, abused and raped women, and indentured children and naborias as slaves. We agreed to the guamiquina's payments precisely to avoid that! The outcome of this

Roldán's proposal will be that our subjects suffer at the hands of his band while our rule is fortified against the guamiquina's."

"A few of our subjects may suffer the abuse of these seventy if we fail to restrain them." He was unbridled in return. "I seek the most prudent course to avoid the pale man's conquest of all our subjects! The well-being and safety of that multitude depend on the preservation of our rule."

Anacaona's frustration welled. Her brother underestimated the peril of living side by side with pale men. She bit her lip and turned to the enemy's spirit.

"The pale men have conquered in ways we don't understand," she warned. "Whether they profess peace and harmony or attack brutally, they bear their Christ-spirit on their chests and plant him throughout the subjugated chiefdoms. You saw and heard it today. Everywhere this spirit goes, he brings death. He allies in the guamiquina's conquest. If we admit these seventy men, we admit him too. Neither Yúcahu, Attabeira, nor Guabancex have prevailed over him."

Behecchio nodded, acknowledging that he valued her wisdom—especially of the spirits. But then he stiffened, grimacing.

"Ordering Roldán to leave also risks the bloodshed of Xaraguáns—in this very village." He caressed her cheek. "The guamiquina has led the conquest of our island. We must seize this opportunity to make his enemy our friend, as other caciques have done. We will accept the offer. Exhort our spirits to protect our people from the Christ-spirit. Smite Roldán at a distance—just as you did Bartolomé—or perhaps ask Higueymota to do so. Infiltrating his thoughts would be useful."

Anacaona was uncomfortable with the strategy, but she understood her brother had listened sincerely, and she resolved to make it work. She would relish deceiving Roldán to spy on him, much as she'd deceived Bartolomé for mercy. Bidding Higueymota do so troubled her.

She departed as the moon rose, choosing to sit alone in the serenity of her garden before retiring. It brimmed with blossoming flowers, trees, and shrubs collected from throughout Haiti and served as her haven to consult spirits, compose areítos, and hold audiences. She ambled past the sturdy magnolias that framed its entrance, the lilies that gracefully lined the bordering streambank, and the sublime orchids and brutal cacti arrayed within—all glistening silver in the moonlight—and knelt before the bayahibe bushes. Their limbs bore delicate flowers that shrouded the vicious needles of cactus trunks.

Sadly, tenderly, Anacaona sensed Caonabó's presence. He'd been gone three years, and his vision of driving the pale men from the island had shriveled. She invoked his counsel and reaffirmed her vow to avenge his death. Gazing at the bayahibes' pink petals, she explained that the guise of friendship underlay the new approach, and he cautioned her never to rely on friendship alone.

She also sensed the spirit Yúcahu guiding her eyes beneath the petals to the needles, reminding that she could lure an enemy to friendship. *Warm if friendship is reciprocated,* she understood. *Stab if not, and never truly befriend, with barbs ever vigilant and poised to preserve Xaraguá's civilization.*

ISABEL,
Toledo, Castile, April 29–May 1498

On Sunday, April 29, 1498, Queen Isabel sat on the dais below the towering altarpiece of Toledo's great cathedral, her kingdom's nobility crowding the pews and beyond. Her firstborn child stepped before Archbishop Ximénez de Cisneros at the altar to be recognized—by the Lord's design and authority—as heir to the Castilian throne.

Isabel overcame the angst in her heart and devoutly pledged to Him, as His chosen instrument in the struggle against Spain's enemies, that when she departed for His kingdom her daughter would carry her legacy forward. The noblemen's entitlements would continue to be honored, the well-being of her subjects further improved, their faith in Him purified and strengthened, and her dominions expanded in His name. Isabel imperiously listened as the nobility recited their oath accepting Princess Isabel, Queen of Portugal, as heir and swore they would obey her as queen and the husband standing at her side, Portugal's King Manoel, as king consort on Isabel's death.

One by one, prominent noblemen strutted to the altar to restate that oath and proffer homage and tidings to the queen, princess, and their non-Castilian husbands, and Isabel's thoughts drifted to her lineage. Fernando, King of Aragón and Castile, sat at her side, her husband of almost three decades, her partner in rule, and her love and closest confidant, their bond forged by triumphs and trials. In their youth, he'd labored indefatigably with her to crush contenders to her throne, and after her coronation, to sternly impose their joint rule, restore law and order in their subjects' daily lives, and raise their Spanish kingdoms to become a continental power (1469–1479). They'd then struggled to Christianize their kingdoms, establishing the Inquisition to punish conversos secretly practicing Judaism (1480), expelling the Jews who refused to convert (1492), and consummating the Reconquista, reconquering the emirate of Granada on Spain's southern coast from the Mohammedan infidel (1492).* They'd also boldly sought to expand her kingdoms overseas, subjugating the Canary Islands (1477–1496) and claiming the lands their Admiral Colón had found in the Indies. Their marriage terms had dictated the result just affirmed, that their child would inherit Castile, not him if surviving her. Isabel felt a tinge of remorse that he'd earned that throne on her death and a pang of anxiety for Castile in the absence of his rule.

Together, they'd conceived and nurtured five children past marriageable age, a long journey as dear to her as her other accomplishments—decades of love, discipline, instruction, anguish, and endless machinations over marriages plotted, agreed, and reneged. Isabel gazed at the altar cross, the image of Christ nailed and dying, and she was tormented by a resurgence of the pain that now lurked ever present. The previous October, the Lord had taken their only son, Prince Juan, then recognized as heir to the throne. In December, He'd taken Juan's own heir, miscarried by his young wife, Margarite.

Isabel admonished herself that the Lord's reasons were His own, often indiscernible, and that these deaths were reminders of His almighty power—perhaps even punishments for her own transgressions, for which her conscience bore a few concerns. Self-pity had no place. She diverted her eyes to Princess Isabel's womb, now seeded with child, and the pain subsided. *My Almighty, thank you for these blessings,* she prayed. *Watch over mother and grandchild.*

---

* Conversos being Christians who had converted from Judaism.

Isabel had a special love for her firstborn, the only child born before she'd become queen. After the child's birth, she had endured eight barren years (1470–1478), when she and the girl had shared a close companionship that the press of governing later made imprac-tical with her younger daughters, Juana, María, and Catalina. She studied Princess Isabel's regal demeanor while acknowledging the oath takers' flatteries and longed the princess would find the where-withal to rule in a world otherwise ruled by men. For years, she'd doubted the child's strength to do so. The princess had retreated into devotional seclusion upon the death of her first husband (1490), tor-mented by apocalyptical fears of demons and refusing her parents' entreaties to remarry.* But the princess finally had relented (1497), Manoel held genuine affection for her, and his kingdom—just as Fernando's Aragón—was less powerful than Castile, affording the princess the same leverage over her husband that Isabel had enjoyed over Fernando. *May motherhood and an able partner restore your strength and wits,* Isabel prayed for her daughter. *Bear a grandson to extend our dynasty throughout Hispania.*

Manoel and Princess Isabel brought the affirmation to conclusion by invoking the assembly to rise and cry, "Long live the Catholic Monarchs, Isabel and Fernando!" The archbishop and royal party led the procession through the church's cavernous nave onto its plaza abutting the archbishop's residence, where week-long festivities com-menced—banquets punctuated by toasts of fealty, private audiences affirming alliances and hatching schemes, and invocations of Christ and the Virgin to support all of it. Yet the noblemen recognized that the commemorations wouldn't rise to the triumphant glory of past celebrations—the succession wasn't a triumph and neither monarch was jubilant.

In their mid-forties, Isabel and Fernando stood in the plaza to receive their vassals' homage one by one, their finery designed to be the talk of courts throughout Christendom. Her amber gown was woven of the finest silk, embroidered with wools, and bedecked with gold and gems, and her shoes were similarly adorned. Her jewelry included venerated pieces worn by past Castilian kings and queens.

---

* Princess Isabel's first husband was Prince Afonso, son of Portugal's King João II, who was Manoel's cousin and predecessor.

Fernando was dressed in commensurate elegance, with a gem-studded leather doublet, silk breeches, and at his waist, an ornate battle-worn sword borne by past kings of Aragón. The diamonds of their crowns sparkled in the sunlight. None present could doubt the wealth and might of the Spanish kingdoms.

But Isabel's eyes and cheeks were puffed from tears, the once plump heartiness and radiant vigor of her bearing faded, her auburn hair paling, and whatever smiles she managed were forced. Fernando's youth was better preserved, his frame still slender and athletic, but his once piercing brown eyes now often shied away, and his imposing demeanor occasionally betrayed disinterest. Their suzerain flourishes were no longer effortless. The entire court knew to address them circumspectly, skirting issues troubling or upsetting.

Isabel steeled herself to stand some moments with Fernando, hailing and complimenting her vassals. But her thoughts wandered to memories of her past visits to Toledo. Spain's great, walled imperial city had towered on a steep hillside overlooking plains of farmland since the time of Romans and Visigoths. Prince Juan had received the successional oaths at the very altar from which they'd just come, and she'd delivered Juana close by in the royal alcazar's palace. She and Fernando had built the church of San Juan de los Reyes (Saint John of the Kings) on a promontory overlooking the river gorge circling the city to commemorate the defeat of usurpers coveting her throne, proclaiming and warning that her and her husband's rule was rooted unassailably in Spain's ancient dynastic history. Proudly, without guilt of conscience, she recalled that the city's streets had borne parades of conversos being led to penitence and punishment in the early years of her Inquisition, some to be burned at the stake. Its once large ghetto of Jews had vanished on their expulsion, those remaining within now blessedly converted to Christianity, their synagogues confiscated.

The memories didn't sustain her, and Isabel soon tired. Following a grand wave to the assembled and their boisterous acclaim, she departed by carriage up the steep street to the alcazar to observe afternoon prayer and other devotions, leaving Fernando to linger to reaffirm that they remained unbowed. Neither homage nor flattery would make her whole. Her chambermaids awaited her at the alcazar's gate, and they escorted her to her palace's private chambers and chapel to assist as she undressed. Joylessly, she put the gown, shoes, and jewelry aside and donned a simple black frock befit for mourning. She entered the dim chapel to sit at its only pew, whereupon the chambermaids departed, leaving her alone but for Him.

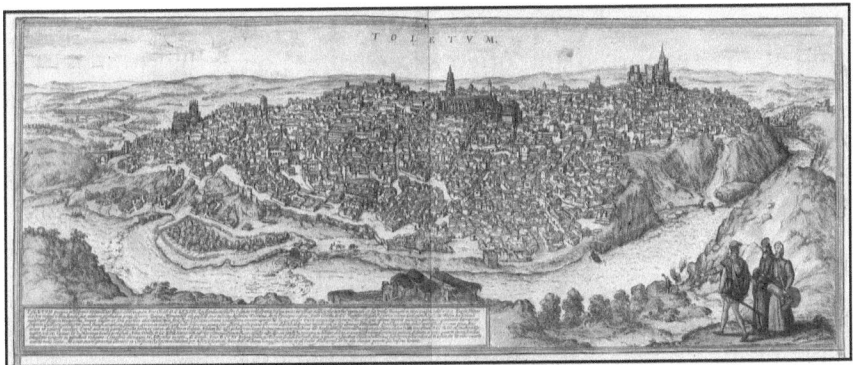

Toledo in the sixteenth century. Civitates Orbis Terrarum.

Isabel was soothed by the bare altar cross and, set beside it, the first altar paintings she'd commissioned to portray Christ's greatest moments on earth, depicting Christ in Castilian settings to show His intimate presence in her daily life.* Juan's death had reminded her of the importance of emulating Christ's life and that her own time was limited. Work remained to lionize her mark in the trajectory of Spain's and Christendom's historical ascendance. She began her prayers silently, awaiting His presence.

Almighty, give me the strength to perfect my dynasty, she beseeched, seeking a second chance, envisioning becoming the grandmother of a son and training a mother to nurture a king, as she had once done. *I shall guide my child and grandchild to pursue your perfection, to distinguish truth and falsehood,* she promised, excusing that a queen dressed opulently for the purpose of reigning, to instill love and fear, not for covetous vanity. *They will continue to purge the nobility and church of sin, and I shall exhort them to spread your Word throughout my kingdoms in preparation for Your return.* The Spanish monarchs were Christ's instruments in the holy struggle

---

* The paintings by Juan de Flandes and Michel Sittow, now known as the Retablo de Isabel la Católica.

against Satan, the vanguard responsible for readying the world for His second coming and ushering in the apocalyptical triumph of Christianity prophesied by Saint John the Evangelist.

Isabel soon felt her husband's hand on her shoulder, and he knelt beside her and crossed himself. Fernando also had tired of the ceremony, preferring to reserve his energy for the audiences that would follow. She warmed to his touch, grateful that his undaunted energy and ability reinforced and often exceeded her own, the combination of their efforts usually achieving her visions. She'd never forgiven the infidelity of his youth—the frolics with Aragón's noblewomen and Castilian tarts, with the birth of a few illegitimates—but it had run its course, his passion now simply their dynasty and its aggrandizement. She hadn't been entirely pure herself, once deceiving him at a critical juncture—crowning herself without his knowledge (1474), suspecting he'd attempt to claim Castile's crown for himself. But he'd long forgotten that. They glanced into each other's eyes.

"Our firstborn did well enough," she judged.

"You play the hand you're dealt," he responded.

□   □   □

In the cathedral plaza, the noblemen and churchmen feasted heartily and gossiped meanly, venting peeves and speculating what the king and queen had in mind.

"This bodes poorly. The princess is unstable," a duke whispered. "Some say she's cuckoo, still lamenting her first husband, insisting that the Jews cast a spell that threw him from his horse." Princess Isabel had consented to marry Manoel only after he agreed to punish the Jews by expelling them from Portugal.

"Her chambermaids say she's morbid, fixated she'll die in childbirth," a count confided. "See how thin she grows. They say she eats like a mouse."

"Let's pray she or the child survives to reign," a grandee advised. "Otherwise, we'll end up kneeling to an impudent Burgundian." Isabel and Fernando had wed Princess Juana to Archduke Philippe of Austria and Burgundy, son of Maximillian of Austria, the leader of the Holy Roman Empire (1496), calculating the alliance would counter French aggression. But Philippe had soon affronted Isabel and Fernando and all Spain's nobility by proclaiming himself the heir to the Castilian throne following Prince Juan's death.

"The king and queen warned Philippe to bite his tongue," a knight rejoined. "Let's trust they won't tolerate his swagger and guile."

Others discussed the sovereigns' great endeavors, and admiration was professed for all but one. The integration of the Granadan conquest had been a triumph, its illustrious capital city now brimming with forty thousand Christian families who'd settled there. The confiscations and bloodshed of the Inquisition's early years and the dislocations caused by the Jews' exodus had passed. While the pocketbooks, wounds, and gravestones of those trampled would never forgive, the daily life of those remaining in Spain—"true Christians" and conversos—had returned to peaceful, albeit distrustful, coexistence. While the sovereigns hadn't expelled Mohammedans—the Mudejar—from Spain, the morerías of Castile and Aragón and the predominantly Mohammedan Granada remained largely free of religious strife.* The Canarian conquests were nigh complete, and Castilian settlers were growing commerce there.

But Admiral Cristóbal Colón's discoveries had failed to contribute to the sovereigns' and their merchants' wealth. A clique of merchant noblemen mulled how long the sovereigns' patience would last.

"Colón's failed to produce the gold promised," a shipowner remarked. "His men have scoured Española for five years, and no ship has returned home in over a year. I say that means there's no gold to mine."

"Colón's resupply ships berthed mostly soldiers to fight the savages, hardly any miners at all, who knew better," a gem merchant related, referring to the two ships that had sailed to Española that February in advance of Colón's third voyage. "Those ships and the voyage set to sail are meant to bear some three hundred fresh settlers to better establish the place, but enlistment has been grossly short that number," he divulged. "No one wants to go to Española."

"Colón hasn't delivered a shortcut to Cathay's spices," a spice trader observed. "The island's nothing but a hellhole of naked heathens squatting in poverty."

---

* *Mudejar* refers to Muslims living in a Christian kingdom and vassal to its Christian sovereign. *Morería* refers to the neighborhood where they lived.

"It's worse than that. It's a death pit of disease, hunger, and blood-shed," a financier chided. "He promised the savages would be ser-vile, but they're hostile. There's nothing saleable to finance. Sooner or later, the king and queen will abandon the fiasco."

"That would squander an opportunity," rejoined an Andalu-sian slave trader of Canarians and Africans. "I could bring the entire business to profit if the king and queen blessed enslaving Indians. The Genoese has begged for it. I saw some of the specimens he hauled back. They're timid and intelligent, so they'd make excellent servants."

"You'd better hurry to convince the queen," the financier retorted. "Manoel may reach the Indies first and lock up the trade." King Manoel had insisted as a marriage condition that his kingdom retain the freedom to compete in foreign conquest and trade. He'd already dispatched five ships, sailing east rather than west, hoping that by circumventing Guinea (southern Africa) his men would arrive in the Indies' fabled civilizations before Colón (1497).

▫ ▫ ▫

When authorizing Cristóbal Colón's third voyage, Isabel and Fer-nando had resolved to cure Española's financial failure and depen-dence on resupply by abandoning the approach of crown ownership of its land and produce and incentivizing their subjects to settle on and establish it permanently, with stakes in the island's future prosperity and food production. Their third voyage instructions had directed Colón to enlist three hundred thirty persons on the crown payroll to reside in the Indies and authorized him to *repartir*—grant and distribute—hereditary and alienable land plots for building homes, farms, and vineyards so long as occupied for four years (1497). Grants were to be awarded based on the settler's status and service to the crown and the condition and quality of his person and lifestyle. To assist profitability, the sovereigns had pardoned criminals—other than heretics, sodomizers, ax murderers, and the like—who agreed to become residents without salary and directed courts and sheriffs that those sentenced to banishment be sent to Española.

Residents would be free to come and go from the island, so long as the minimum of three hundred thirty was maintained, and to keep or sell what they produced on the land or obtained in trade, although gold, other metals, and brazilwood remained the sovereigns'. Of the total, one hundred and forty were to be officers, soldiers, and laborers, sixty seaman and midshipmen, twenty gold miners, sixty farmers and vegetable gardeners, twenty artisans, and thirty women, to be available for Christian marriages and home-keeping. Colón also was directed to enlist monks and priests of good character.

Plowing and animal husbandry were to be introduced, residents would be furnished their germinal grain and livestock, and all eventually would use their salaries to purchase goods sold by merchants newly authorized to trade between Spain and Española. The crown would fund the settlers' initial housing and provisioning costs. Although the crown remained obligated for the salaries of men of the second voyage still on the island, most of them were expected to rush home to Spain on the ships bearing the newcomers. Colón had the discretion to increase the settlement population to five hundred— including second-voyage men remaining—and adjust the occupational headcount, provided the additional persons didn't require initial provisioning.

As the succession festivities petered into May, the sovereigns made time for audiences with crown officials. In Isabel's youth, courtiers regularly had spoken down to her—as if a woman and queen couldn't preside, deal, or trade, no less punish, attack, or invade. But they rarely condescended anymore, as she'd proven them wrong on all scores time and again over two decades. One morning, she and Fernando summoned to the alcazar the senior courtier they'd appointed jointly with Colón to organize, recruit, and administer the Indies' voyages and settlement.

Juan Rodríguez de Fonseca (b. 1451) hailed from an illustrious family that had supported Isabel's early claims to the Castilian throne and had served the sovereigns notably since, including as an administrator in the Reconquista and a diplomat in arranging Prince Juan's and Princess Juana's marriages. Isabel and Fernando had rewarded his competence and loyalty by ordination and promotion within the church, most recently by appointing him as Bishop of Badajoz. Never much passioned by the scriptures, the bishop's acumen was for organizing difficult undertakings and tending their income and expense ledgers. The sovereigns trusted him to oversee their mercurial admiral and guard that Española's wealth wasn't pilfered by the sailors and settlers—and admiral—who went there.

"What progress in arranging the Admiral's ships?" Fernando asked. "What's the financing?"

"Your Highnesses, as you know, two advance ships departed this February, bearing fresh supplies and over a hundred men," Fonseca replied. "Thus far, the Admiral has commissioned five of the remaining six, funded principally by loans from Seville's Genoese financiers. He's departed Seville for the port at Sanlúcar de Barrameda to review the ships' fittings and provisioning." Obtaining financing for the fleet's hire, supplies, and sailors' salaries had been an ordeal that dragged on for months, and pledges of Princess Isabel's dowry had been exacted as security. The sale into slavery of almost three hundred Indian captives brought on the last ships arriving from Española (1496) had provided a portion of the crown's direct funding.

"The Admiral relishes inviting his countrymen to participate," Fonseca observed, without mentioning that most other financiers had lost confidence in Colón. He and Colón hadn't seen eye to eye on many things, and by the spring of 1498, neither bothered to hide their disagreements and animosities from the sovereigns. He'd lost patience with Colón's endless promises of gold. "If he obeys my orders, the Admiral should sail from Sanlúcar within weeks, with or without the sixth ship."

"Do the recruits have the requisite experience in mining gold, planting gardens, and building towns and forts?" Fernando inquired.

"Do they understand they must also seed our faith, customs, and traditions, just as our settlers are doing in Granada and the Canaries?" Isabel added.

"It's roughly as we expected," Fonseca responded guardedly, concealing his pessimism. The sovereigns rarely accepted defeat. "He's mustered almost two hundred and thirty men in the seven ships arranged to date—so far, a bit short of the number we specified."

He pivoted to Fernando. "Half the hundred-plus men on the ships that sailed in February were soldiers, mostly crossbowmen, and more soldiers will berth on the ships about to sail. On the seven ships combined, some thirty true farmers have enlisted—half the number we instructed—and perhaps fifty laborers fit for construction, mining gold, or whatever else is required—again half the number expected. There are ten murderers, who can be sent to the mines without salary, and a handful of women, including among the murderers." He frowned in disappointment. "So far, the Admiral's recruited at least one experienced gold miner."

All three grimly paused, recalling the glorious departure of Colón's second voyage—seventeen ships brimming with twelve hundred men, all clamoring for Española's gold. The five ships preparing to sail were vacant in comparison, barren of pride and grandeur.

"Haven't peasant farmers understood that we will sponsor their homes, seed, and cattle?" Isabel grated. "Haven't their daughters understood that Española's safe and its settlers will make advantageous marriage partners?"

"Aren't our miners stirred they'll pocket a handsome share of the gold mined, not only their salaries?" Fernando stammered, jarred that he and Isabel had approved a miners' share of one-third, only to be ignored (1497).

"Your Highnesses, I believe your wishes, orders, and inducements have been published, proclaimed, and widely understood," Fonseca replied. "I suspect disillusionment with the Admiral and his failed assurances has diminished your subjects' appetites. But we will redouble our efforts to enlist more miners and farmers before he sails."

"How many friars sail?" Isabel demanded, keen that the spiritual not take second place.

"Your Highness, not many, so far," Fonseca replied wanly. "I know of three, including the Admiral's own chaplain." He refrained from disclosing that one of the other friars was a known drunkard.

"The Indians' conversion remains our priority," Isabel admonished. "Enlist more churchmen promptly."

Fernando folded his arms, mistrustful of the composition of those enlisted. "Are so many soldiers really necessary to defend against Indian attack?"

"It's the Admiral's judgment, but I believe so. Another of his broken promises—the Indians are neither friendly nor submissive."

Isabel and Fernando glanced at each other warily. On return from his first voyage, Colón had assured them the Indians wouldn't resist their conquest, and they'd expected the Indians' ready vassalage, not war or enslavements. Pope Alexander VI's bulls granting Isabel sovereignty over Colón's discoveries had imposed a duty to lead the conversion of the peoples subjugated (1493), and prior to the second voyage, they'd instructed Colón to compel their Spanish subjects to treat the Indians very well and lovingly and abstain from doing them any injury (1493). But since then, Colón repeatedly had requested authority to establish a general slave trade in Indians, and to their growing consternation, he or his brother had shipped enslaved captives home to Spain a number of times (1494–1496).

The papacy had long approved enslavement of nonresisting African heathens obtained in Manoel's Guinean possessions, but Pope Alexander's grant of Colón's discoveries to Isabel hadn't addressed Indian enslavement, casting doubt whether enslavement of nonresisting Indians could be reconciled with the duty of conversion. Many theologians believed enslavement of nonresisting, conquered heathens was forbidden, and Isabel and Fernando had honored that view in their Canarian conquest. Following the arrival home of Colón's first large captive shipment—five hundred fifty dispatched, two-thirds surviving the ocean crossing—the sovereigns had pronounced that a committee of theologians, lawyers, and other learned men would study the permissibility of Indian enslavement generally. Pending that determination, they'd directed Fonseca to sell the captives then and later sent into slavery conditionally, subject to manumission if enslavement was determined unlawful (1495). Indians had warred against their conquest (1495), and—as they had in the Canaries—they'd approved the sale of resisters into slavery (1496). But, suspiciously, the three hundred captives last sold had arrived from Española within mere months following that authorization. They certainly hadn't approved the offensive use of soldiers to slave raid.

"Remind the Admiral of our instruction that he treat the Indians as our vassals," Isabel commanded, her distrust and anger visible. Their third voyage instructions had directed Colón to lead the Indians to serve benignly under their sovereignty.

"Remind him also that the penalties he applies to Indians who fail tribute must be light—not enslavement," she remonstrated. The sovereigns had approved Cristóbal's imposition of tribute, envisioning their Indian vassals would contribute gold just as their Spanish vassals paid taxes and other levies (1497). They'd instructed him to place brass tokens about the necks of Indians who'd satisfied their obligation, facilitating the arrest and minor punishment of those who hadn't.

"Chasten him that we still haven't approved enslavement of Indians who accept our rule!" she exclaimed.

"Your Highness, I'll speak to him, bluntly," Fonseca assured. But he doubted that doing so would prevent enslavements. Colón would simply claim that all Indians he captured had resisted—as he'd probably done already! Fonseca also chafed that the sovereigns failed to understand. Española would fail without a slave trade. Their kingdoms' merchants pined for it! Exasperated, Fonseca welled with scorn for the sovereigns' reluctance to enslave Indians. Their own chambermaids included infidel enslaved during the Reconquista. Conquered infidel and heathen from Africa, the Balkans, the Canaries, and even the Holy Land toiled daily in their kingdoms. He asked himself, *Why not enslave Indians? Aren't all conquered peoples fit for slavery?*

Fonseca waited for Isabel to regain herself. He judged that the delay in resolving the issue of Indian enslavement and the funding of the pending voyage partly from the sale of Indian slaves belied Isabel's anguished protestation. He brooded over how long the purported committee of theologians had debated. *Three years studying! The sovereigns held the power to prohibit enslavement of Indians if they truly so wished—rather than passing the issue to the church. They certainly could have demanded a decision in months or weeks, if not days.*

"My bishop, you have much to address before the Admiral sails," Fernando said, breaking the silence. "But don't delay his departure. The Admiral has promised new discoveries in the southern oceans, and others race to claim them first. Ask him to write whether his brother has conquered all of Española." Colón had boasted that the Indians' gold payments would surge as the island's conquest was completed. "Tell him to remit all the gold tribute that's been collected to date."

Now calm, Isabel's long-standing affection for Colón stirred within her, dissipating the disappointment in his performance. She recalled he wasn't an adventurer simply weighing his own risk and reward. His faith was as absolute and true as her own, regardless of his open lust for nobility and riches. While bloated, his ego and vanity drove him first to prove a geographical theory he believed rooted in the holy scriptures—and upon which he'd risked his life. Much like herself, he'd surmounted decades of scorn by courtiers and experts who doubted him to prove them wrong.

"Tell the Admiral to write to us promptly about everything that's going on in Española," she directed courteously. "Has the morale of the men improved? Have their criticisms of his command subsided? How many Indians have been baptized? Are they contentedly paying our tribute?"

⊞   ⊞   ⊞

One evening toward the middle of May, as the Castilian succession ceremonies concluded and the court prepared to depart to conduct the same in Aragón, Isabel rode by carriage to the church of San Juan de los Reyes, accompanied by Ximénez de Cisneros (b. ca. 1436). She'd first chosen him as her confessor, then entrusted him to reform the Spanish church, and finally appointed him as Toledo's archbishop, Spain's most senior prelate, esteeming his rigorous devotion. In his youth, he'd sought the most austere Franciscan postings in rural communities to live alone as a hermit, seeking to achieve an ongoing communication with Christ by subsisting for years on bread, herbs, and water, donning but sackcloth, sleeping on straw, and scourging himself regularly. Now elderly, with a wasted frame, pallid complexion, and eyes shimmering ecstatic as if an ancient biblical prophet, he still retired to his monastic cell when not needed.

Queen and confessor entered the church and sat alone in the first pew, a few royal attendants and sentries standing watch by doorways.

Isabel studied the walls rising on either side, boldly emblazoned with her and Fernando's royal marks, and she was startled that she felt neither ennobled, proud, nor confident, but crestfallen and unsure. She shuddered, fearing for Princess Isabel's future, anguishing that her daughter dwelled on death rather than the joy of childbirth and ignored eating to prepare for it. She angered, piqued by the possibility that Princess Juana's husband might stand king consort to the Spanish thrones. She saddened, recalling the day she'd delivered Prince Juan and the tumultuous celebrations that had reverberated throughout Spain.

Cisneros studied the same walls and was inspired, sensing Christ's presence and indomitable power and justice. He held an unquenchable hatred of false religions, and with a selfless disregard for his own fate, burned with a duty and ambition to vanquish them and their earthly adherents. He relished that the church sat on the remains of the Jewish ghetto's marketplace and that its outer walls draped chains of Christians freed from the infidel during the Reconquista—warning Christ's enemies of the great battle and inevitable victory Saint John had foretold.

Marriage at Cana, with Saint John and his bride, likely also figuratively depicting Prince Juan and his bride Princess Margarite. Juan de Flandes, ca. 1497. The Metropolitan Museum of Art, object no. 1982.60.20.

"Take my confession," Isabel bid Cisneros, abhorring weakness. "I fear I begin to fall short of the saint's legacy. I mustn't wilt in the work of bringing Christ's word to my vassals, despite my misfortunes. Absolve me of faintheartedness in His service."

Cisneros was surprised. He had no doubt of her dedication, although the recent tragedies had sapped her energy.

"Your Highness, the Lord understands your dedication, which stands unmatched in all of Christendom," he comforted. "Absolution is unnecessary. But for your peace of mind, I absolve you." He reflected on what might be improved or strengthened in his queen. "Your Highness, remember that all means devoutly taken to bring souls to Christ are blessed and absolved."

MAYOBANEX, GUARIONEX, AND BARTOLOMÉ,
War in Ciguayo, May 1498

Mayobanex, the supreme cacique of the Ciguayo, stood in the small ballcourt of his highland village in the northern coastal mountains east of the pale men's settlement at Isabela, studying his friend of almost four decades approach. Guarionex's short stature and slender frame belied a soul of grand intellect and spirituality. Today, his gait was tired, his gaze fearful, and his clenched lips forlorn—his bearing wasted by the pillage of his chiefdom of Magua and his own humiliating downfall. But Mayobanex was certain his friend's soul hadn't been crushed.

Both shy of fifty, the two men embraced, encircled by their nitaínos and Guarionex's wives, children, and extended household. Weeks before, scouts had informed Mayobanex that Guarionex and the entourage had departed their hometown village, Guaricano. The family was exhausted from trekking through the mountainous rainforest, and Mayobanex's eldest wife escorted them to bohíos to recuperate. He and Guarionex sat alone, their conversation cloaked by the gurgle of the village river, the Yasica, as it coursed to the sea.

Ciguayo remained untouched by the guamiquina's invasion, but both men knew such fortune had ruptured. Scouts reported that the pale man called Adelantado was trespassing into Ciguayo's southern boundary with ninety foot soldiers and several horsemen, apparently in pursuit of Guarionex. Guarionex spoke forthrightly in Taíno, which Mayobanex understood, although not the Ciguayos' native tongue.*

"I've abandoned my chiefdom because I can no longer stomach commanding my subjects to pay tribute," he related. "Neither humility nor pride has worked in parleying with the guamiquina. He and his brother reciprocate compromise and accommodation with ill-treatment, violence, and enslavement, no matter how far I bend to accept their presence." He grimaced in shame. "You and Caonabó were correct. They are an intractable enemy whose word is worth nothing. Resistance is our people's only course. Bowing to the guamiquina and his caciques, Fernando and Isabel, will only lead to our people's extinction." To himself, Guarionex acknowledged more— that he'd failed his subjects, who no longer trusted his rule.

Mayobanex exhaled, jolted by the mention of extinction, alluding unmistakably to an event blazoned in their memories long ago. In his youth, Guarionex had participated in a venerated cohoba ceremony conducted by his father, during which Yúcahu predicted that those who remained after his father's death would rule for a brief time before a clothed people arrived to overcome them and kill them, and they would die of hunger.† The demise of Guarionex's rule fulfilled the prophecy's second step, and Guarionex's terror was apparent.

"Does Adelantado intend to war against me and my people?" Mayobanex asked, peering into Guarionex's eyes.

"I don't know," Guarionex admitted. "They come to seize me, to haul me home to restore the gold and cazabi payments I promised. The guamiquina returns to Haiti, thirsting to find the gold collected, and the pale men still starve for food." He shrugged. "Perhaps Adelantado simply wishes my head, fearing I'll convince you to war against them."

"What do you request of me and my people?" Mayobanex was grateful for the honesty and anxious their relationship was deeper than friendship. Years before, Guarionex had elevated their bond to

---

* Mayobanex's native language was Macorís. Peoples spoke different local languages throughout the Taíno Caribbean, but Taíno generally served as the lingua franca.
† Cohoba ceremonies invoked communication with Taíno spirits, assisted by inhalation of a narcotic powder. *Encounters Unforeseen*, chapter III, depicts the cohoba ceremony revealing the extinction prophecy. *Columbus and Caonabó*, chapter V, depicts Caonabó's cohoba ceremony exhorting war.

spiritual brotherhood and loyalty in a sacred areíto ceremony conferring Maguan ancestry upon Mayobanex, as if he'd been born
Maguan.

"Harbor me and my family from seizure," Guarionex replied,
mortified. "Otherwise, I'll perish when I refuse to do as Adelantado wishes, leaving the family destitute or worse." Guarionex had
advocated and practiced peaceful rule most of his life, but he eyed
his friend with admiration. Black charcoal and dye streaked Mayobanex's sinewy torso head to foot, and his hair—uncut for years—
fell to his buttocks, strewn wildly with parrot feathers. The fearsome
appearance was deliberate, customary for Ciguayan warriors. "I also
commend that you war against them, and I'd be honored to fight at
your side."

Mayobanex hesitated, alert his friend hadn't confided everything.
"Why haven't you made peace with the one called Roldán, as others
have done? They say he released Manicoatex and others from the
guamiquina's rule."

"Roldán and his band are no less an enemy than the guamiquina."

"You've met them?"

"They attacked and brutalized my people, just as Adelantado
did." Roldán's gang had squatted in Magua for months (1497).
"Manicoatex simply kneels at Roldán's feet rather than the guamiquina's, delivering Roldán the gold and food instead. Roldán took
a son and nephew hostage to compel that." He shut his eyes. "One of
Roldán's men raped one of my wives and goes unpunished."

Affronted, Mayobanex wrapped his arm about his friend's
shoulder, offering sympathy. Rape of a wife was an unconscionable
denigration. "I will consult others, and you'll have my answer in the
morning. You should rest."

"Perhaps the guamiquina's conquest will collapse one day," Guarionex reflected. "Your resoluteness might preserve our civilization."

Mayobanex retired to his caney to review Guarionex's plea with
his council, all of them accomplished warriors. Ciguayan military
prowess had been renowned on Haiti prior to the pale men's arrival,
particularly in repelling Caribe raiders, and Mayobanex and his
council had embraced Caonabó's war alliance wholeheartedly. But
the war had been fought in the interior, not on the northern coast,

and Ciguayans hadn't participated meaningfully (1495). Like others, they'd observed that the pale men's superior weaponry prevailed over overwhelming numbers of Taíno warriors.

"We must defend Guarionex from capture and our chiefdom from incursion," Mayobanex declared. "He is honorable and Taíno, an exemplary model of our island's peoples. He's always been Ciguayo's friend, and he opposes the pale men." A vision of the guamiquina—imperious and remorseless—flickered through Mayobanex's thoughts. The two men had met at the end of the guamiquina's first incursion (1493), parleying after an altercation among their peoples. "The guamiquina thirsts for conquest, and his brother violates our land. We must demonstrate that we defend our sovereignty."

All concurred, although reasoning varied. "They've never met us in battle, and we'll give them one they'll regret!" a younger nitaíno blustered.

"Our mountains provide an advantage that those vanquished lacked," an older nitaíno reasoned.

"We needn't defend Guarionex or fight his battles," a cacique admonished. "But we've always repelled invaders. The pale men are no exception."

Meanwhile, alone in the bohío provided his family, Guarionex confessed to his father and Yúcahu, assessing the tortured trail of his own judgments over the last five years. He'd been naive in believing that friendship could negate the prophecy and sought a peaceful accord with the guamiquina, refusing to join Caonabó's alliance (1494). He'd been gullible in expecting that compromises could dispel it and acquiesced in the construction of Fort Concepción near Guaricano in return for an assurance of no further incursions. He'd even sanctified that agreement by marrying one of his sisters to the guamiquina's Taíno slave Bakako, awarding brotherhood to the guamiquina himself through an areíto ceremony, and consenting to study the Christ-spirit (1495). He'd been a fool to burden his subjects with the crushing obligation of paying tribute, which had accelerated the prophecy rather than defeating it (1495). After the rout of an uprising he'd organized, he'd been shameless, groveling at Adelantado's feet before thousands of his subjects to recite an oath reaffirming his submission to Fernando and Isabel (1497).

Guarionex assured his father and the spirit that he was forever finished with bending before pale men. After a lifetime convinced that mutual compromise and reconciliation were the proper path among peoples, he implored Yúcahu, *The pale men's destruction remains the only course to undo your prophecy. Let it be done. Lead Mayobanex to understanding and victory.*

In the morning, the two chieftains met alone by the Yasica.

"Tonight, I dispatch six thousand warriors to slay Adelantado," Mayobanex advised resolutely, without hubris or fear. "Eight thousand remain with us, as a precaution."

❒ ❒ ❒

The Ciguayan prisoner's torture began at dusk in a mangrove marsh washed by the sea east of the Yasica's terminal estuary and ended a few hours later, when he succumbed to reveal that an army of six thousand Ciguayan warriors lay in ambush upstream on the river's western bank. But he divulged nothing of Guarionex's whereabouts, denying even awareness of the chieftain's presence in Ciguayo.

Adelantado Bartolomé Colón scrutinized his two enslaved Maguan interpreters—one apparently willing to betray Guarionex, the other openly relishing the pillage of Ciguayo—and concluded they'd dutifully extracted all the information obtainable. He ordered the prisoner bound, destined for slavery, and directed his ninety-some Christian Spaniards and a squadron of heathen Indian allies to bivouac by the estuary, with sentries posted. Mosquitoes and occasional rain beset all.

The Spaniards were exhausted from headlong marches, most from the new settlement at Santo Domingo on the southern coast, a few from Fort Concepción in the interior. The Taíno allies consisted of warriors whom Bartolomé had entreated to fight, drawn from Ciguayo's borderlands and either vengeful against the Ciguayo or afraid to deny him. In decades past, peoples from other chiefdoms had considered the Ciguayans bellicose and untrustworthy, prone to border skirmishes and encroachments of fishing and hunting grounds.

Bartolomé was the last to sleep, as indefatigable as any man could be, save for his older brother. He was ten years younger (b. ca. 1461), and his sturdy, tall frame resembled Cristóbal's, although slighter in height. His wit was as keen as Cristóbal's, his rigor sterner, with a harshness that rarely melted to reveal the courteousness and generosity Cristóbal could display. Despite exhaustion, Bartolomé slept fitfully, buffeted by rages and schemes as his mind clung to the tasks that thwarted him. Roldán's rebellion had hatched during his watch, and he'd failed to quell it. He'd spared Guarionex's life after the uprising in return for the chieftain's oath to collect tribute, but the chieftain had double-crossed him, mocking his authority. Magua's gold was critical for meeting the sovereigns' expectations, its cazabi for satisfying his men's hunger, and their collection was cornerstone to tribute's imposition throughout Española. Shackling Guarionex at Fort Concepción was urgent, both so he'd fulfill the oath and to warn that dereliction of tribute brought incarceration or worse.

When the moon dropped low, Bartolomé roused his men and bid his lieutenants to organize the Indian allies. Devoutly, he and Spaniards beseeched the Lord for victory and the Virgin for protection, and they and the Indian allies then tread softly inland along the Yasica's meander. A knife to his throat, the tortured Ciguayan prisoner occasionally revealed where Ciguayan warriors might lay in wait in tree line and underbrush on the opposite riverbank.

Bartolomé was keen that his men establish an undetected position across the river before sunrise, and his scouts reported that an upcoming riverbend was ideal. The floodplain beyond extended flatly into the distance, permitting the horsemen to charge and terrify the Indians, who'd never known horses and often perceived rider and beast as a single monster. After amassing his men at the river's curl, Bartolomé reiterated his prayers, and at twilight's first glimmer, ordered his crossbowmen and swordsmen to wade across.

Suddenly, the ghastly whoosh of arrows hailing from all points along the encircling riverbank and the horrific screech of war cries burst the pastoral hush, and Ciguayan warriors surged from thickets and reeds into the river, thrusting and hurling spears. Instantly, Bartolomé's musketeers fired their pistols, harquebuses (muskets), and falconets (small swivel cannons), horsemen bearing lances bolted forward, and a half dozen attack dogs were set loose. Spaniards and Ciguayans met waist deep in the water in brutal face-to-face combat.

The Ciguayans were astonished by the invaders' brawn, height, helmets, and body armor and repulsed by the invaders' bristling whiskers. They were terrified by the savagery of the unknown weapons and beasts and enraged by the invasion of their homeland. The Spaniards were staggered by the coordination of the heathens' attack and horrified by their demonic body paint and unshorn hair. They were stunned by the savagery capable of the crude weapons and enraged by the resistance to Christian domination.

Crossbowmen and swordsmen without armor or shields were decimated. Spearmen were ravaged by a potency they'd never experienced—bullets invisible, arrows shot from astounding distance, slashes of metals sharpened incredibly, and the speed, strength, bite, and tear of creatures enlisted in human warfare. Christian and Taíno blood streaked the river red, and corpses began to float downstream.

Bartolomé winced at the Indian ferocity, which surpassed his prior experience, with many of his men rapidly wounded, some mortally. But he invoked Christ to vanquish the heathens and rushed to midstream, brandishing his sword and exhorting his soldiers to pierce the onrush and surmount the opposite riverbank, confident the Indians' terror of the boom of gunshot, the horsemen, and the dogs would rout them, as it always had. Within minutes, Ciguayan casualties were so severe the warriors in the river retreated to the embankment, and Bartolomé shouted for his men to pursue and slay them on the floodplain. At dawn, he stood on the plain victorious, watching his horsemen gallop in pursuit of terrified Ciguayans, and he ordered those taken alive to be bound and held for enslavement.

Yet by evening, Bartolomé was disappointed. Scouts and Indian allies reported that the Ciguayan army hadn't been routed—it simply had regrouped in the forested hills beyond the floodplain. Engagement would become more difficult and dangerous and the charge of horsemen impossible. The next morning, Bartolomé took his forces inland, suspecting he might capture Guarionex in Mayobanex's hometown, some days' march distant. By nightfall, they arrived at a small mountain village deserted by its residents, and he commandeered it to serve as an interim headquarters. Hidden by forest and mountain ravines, Ciguayan warriors attacked his advance throughout the day, and after his forces settled into the village, long into the night.

Bartolomé was undaunted by challenge, failure, disobedience, and hostility, having assisted Cristóbal for over two decades. He'd helped Cristóbal seek royal sponsorship for the first voyage, suffered the rejections in Portugal and Spain for a decade, and even traveled alone to England only to be rejected by King Henry VII (1488). After reuniting with Cristóbal in Española, he'd served as Cristóbal's right hand in virtually all callings—as enforcer in disciplining unruly or indolent Spaniards (1494), as commander in fighting Indian armies (1495), as conqueror in instituting tribute (1495), and after Cristóbal's departure for Spain, as builder of Santo Domingo (1496), as slave raider (1496), and as executioner while crushing Guarionex's uprising (1497). Many thought him heartless and cruel, not just severe.

As his men suffered wounds, Bartolomé resolved to compose a clear message for Mayobanex, and over the next two days, his soldiers forayed from the village into the surrounding hills, luring Ciguayans into protracted skirmishes. Crossbows slayed from unassailable distances, metal swords hacked bare skin as breastplates, helmets, and shields deflected arrows and wooden spears, and dogs voraciously hurtled through thickets. Ciguayan warriors were hacked to pieces before their families. Bohíos were pillaged and burned, and warriors surrendering or caught were enslaved, as were their women and those children old enough for servitude. On the third day, after seizing almost fifty Ciguayan captives, at knife point Bartolomé ordered one of them to deliver the message and a request to Mayobanex, accompanied by the Maguan interpreter willing to betray Guarionex.

⊞   ⊞   ⊞

Nitaínos advised Mayobanex of the two messengers' arrival, and he received them in his ballcourt. He'd already been apprised of the message—Adelantado's advance inland, the battles, the bloodshed, and the enslavements. He turned to the Ciguayan, who appeared unwounded.

"How were you captured?" he asked contemptuously.

"They surrounded my bohío and seized me and my family," the messenger replied, trembling for his failure to defend them and Mayobanex's chiefdom through death.

"Where is your family now?" Mayobanex refrained from scorning the man's dishonor.

"The pale men have bound them as hostages."

Mayobanex turned to the Maguan. "Why do you bring messages on behalf of pale men?"

"Most of my family has perished by their hands." The Maguan squirmed fearfully. "I wish those remaining to survive."

Mayobanex didn't challenge that as a lie. He raised his eyebrows, ready to receive the request. "What does Adelantado wish to say?"

"He does not intend to make war upon you or our people," the Ciguayan responded. "He desires your friendship, demanding only that you deliver Guarionex to him, who will be punished."

"He counsels that your people not be drawn into conflict over matters unrelated to you," the Maguan explained. "If you surrender Guarionex, the guamiquina will count you as friend and protect and respect your territory. If you refuse, you will be made to repent. Your entire country will be devastated with fire and sword, and all you possess will be destroyed."

"Guarionex is a hero, virtuous in all respects, deserving of my protection," Mayobanex proclaimed imperiously, having anticipated the request. "Tell that to Adelantado. Tell him I don't enter into alliances with violent and perfidious men who shed the blood of innocents, such as the guamiquina and himself." He waved his hand brusquely, dispatching the messengers back to Adelantado.

◻ ◻ ◻

When he heard the response, in reply Bartolomé burned the village he'd taken as headquarters, as well as other nearby villages, and his men seized scores more villagers captive. The same two messengers were dispatched to Mayobanex again, inviting him to send trusted advisers to parley for peace.

Mayobanex was affronted by the brutality of the reply. He also despised the two messengers as traitors, to Guarionex and himself. But murmurs and whispers abounded among his nitaínos that defending Guarionex wasn't worth Ciguayan blood. Adelantado's reply, despite the savage slaughter of more innocents, reiterated an overture for peace that couldn't be ignored. Reluctantly, Mayobanex

consented to dispatch his most trusted nitaíno and two subordinate caciques to accompany the two messengers back to parley with
Adelantado.

Bartolomé met the emissaries at the smoldering remains of his village encampment, over a hundred captives bound in plain sight. He
knew enough Taíno to address the emissaries with gracious saluta-
tions, as if hailing a European prince, and he offered gifts of embroidered skull caps, honoring their nobility. Through the Maguan
interpreter, he spoke earnestly of friendship and peace, leaving the
murmurs and wails of the captives to speak for themselves. He courteously reiterated his prior offer. Tribute wasn't demanded or even
mentioned.

When the emissaries returned, Mayobanex dispatched runners
summoning his ten principal subordinate caciques from throughout
his chiefdom, and within days, they assembled to sit in his ballcourt,
together with their own subordinate caciques and countless nitaínos,
filling the space to capacity. Mayobanex understood that reluctance
to war with the pale men was widespread, and he rose to summarize
Adelantado's incursion—the deaths, the destruction of villages, and
the enslavements, including of women and children. He bid the emissaries recount their impressions of Adelantado's offer and sincerity,
as to which they expressed hope but no assurance. When they concluded, he imparted his own wisdom.

"My subjects, Guarionex has fought the pale men, who we all
know are evil. For that alone, he deserves our protection. I have
promised him sanctuary, honoring our longstanding brotherhood,
a promise and bond that our traditions counsel we must respect."
He spread his arms, inviting disagreement. "Do any disagree that we
should war to protect him?"

"*Matunherí* (supreme lord), I do," responded one of the ten subordinate caciques, esteemed by the crowd for his bravery in fighting Caribes.
"Our paramount duty is to our subjects and their well-being and safety.
It supersedes any obligation, moral or otherwise, to Guarionex. We must
admit that the pale men prevail in battles decisively. I strongly oppose war,
regardless of Guarionex's fate. We should hand him over."

"Guarionex has already lost his chiefdom," another of the ten
observed. "We've witnessed the dreadful course of his demise, as

well as Caonabó's defeat and the pillaging of both Maguana and Magua. Let's not delude ourselves that our warriors are so superior we'll prevail where others haven't." He stared at Mayobanex. "You dispatched six thousand upon Adelantado, yet he still advances upon us. We must surrender Guarionex."

"We must accept this offer without delay," a third declared. "This may be our last opportunity to strike a truce with the pale men that spares Ciguayo from their invasion."

Shouts of agreement cascaded through the assembly, and a few prominent nitaínos and *behiques* (shamans) rose to curse Guarionex. Mayobanex listened, waiting for the crowd finally to still, his expression impenetrable.

"My subjects, I understand your views on Guarionex, and we may agree to disagree. But he represents only the dispute of this moment." He scanned the assembly, seeking their understanding. "The last five years have shown, time and again, that the guamiquina, his brother, and their pale brethren are a false, insincere people who care nothing to honor their word. A truce struck now will be broken whenever they hunger for our pillage. We either spill our blood now or destine our children to spill theirs."

He paused, studying the anxious shifting of his most loyal men, vassals and friends for decades. Their consternation grew to grisly silence, as most disagreed, wishful a truce could lead to independence rather than subjugation. But their loyalty, esteem for his leadership, and apprehension of his severe discipline prevailed, and none rose to debate further.

"We shall remain at war," Mayobanex pronounced, signaling the assembly was over. He remained to mingle among the crowd, graciously hailing those who'd spoken and indicating to all that he valued their loyalty and expected it unquestioned thereafter. That evening, scores of cohoba ceremonies were organized to invoke the spirits' alliance for victory.

Mayobanex stole away for a few words with Guarionex, pledging that their fortunes would be shared through death. Guarionex shuddered, sorrowful that so many would die on his behalf yet unbowed that resistance remained the only course.

In the morning, Mayobanex decided not to send a response to Adelantado. The Ciguayan and Maguan messengers he despised had remained with Adelantado, and anticipating that Adelantado would soon dispatch them to learn his response, Mayobanex ordered the two beheaded. Adelantado would grasp the scorn, dare, and hostility intended. Ciguayans would understand their supreme cacique executed cowards and traitors.

CRISTÓBAL AND HOLY TRINITY,
Ocean Sea, May 30–July 31, 1498

On May 30, 1498, as the tide ebbed at Sanlúcar de Barrameda, Admiral Cristóbal Colón commanded that his six ships weigh anchor. He was weary and pained from two years of pleading to his sovereigns and quarreling with their courtiers. He was grim the ships weren't berthed to capacity and that his departure lacked cannon shot and fireworks, which had heralded his sailing five years earlier. He was ill, suffering twinges and severe cramps in his legs that sometimes forced him to bed.* His rage at the courtiers and that ingloriousness had exploded unbridled moments earlier, disgracing his noble comportment. While parting on the wharf, he'd slugged and kicked the worst of Bishop Fonseca's cabal, the sovereign's accountant charged with the Indies, who'd incessantly disparaged and vilified most everything Cristóbal was, did, or planned. Mortified, seething livid at enemies ever hounding and trembling forsaken as nigh friendless, he abruptly ceded command of his flagship to its pilot and descended to his cabin in the stern castle, retreating to the solace and haven of the Holy Trinity.

But the sanctity of the silver cross on his bed stand was slow to calm his fury. The accountant Briviesca's insolent backbiting had stirred the bitterest memories of his long struggle to discover the shortcut to the Indies across the Ocean Sea and govern the lands he'd possessed. Isabel and Fernando had kept him languishing impoverished for seven years before approving a voyage, their courtiers scorning him relentlessly, often to his face (1485–1491). After

---

* Contemporaries generally referred to the illness as "gout." Modern epidemiologists speculate other diagnoses, particularly reactive arthritis.

he'd found the route and proved the critics wrong, they'd simply regrouped to cast doubt at every hurdle and disappointment—the delay in locating Española's gold, the Indians' hostility, the illness and hunger of men under his command—deriding such as his fault or error, his incompetence, his broken promises, or most maliciously, his lies or crimes (1494–1498). The senior officers the sovereigns appointed to assist in Española's settlement had been disastrous, disobeying him and deserting the island in less than a year (1494). Even the sovereigns had grown fickle, dispatching a courtier to challenge his conduct, which had fueled the insolence of those he was expected to command (1495).*

Cristóbal struggled to restore himself and confessed to the Lord that his self-importance was a sinful vanity, disrespectful of the Lord's omnipotence. Yet he couldn't resist beseeching Him to punish his critics, whom he perceived numerous—including most Spaniards he knew. The worst were the second-voyage recruits who'd shirked his orders to build the settlement at Isabela—whining over deprivations that were expected when conquering unknown lands and maligning his nobility and Genoese heritage (1494–1495). Fonseca and Briviesca had no standing to cast judgments on him! They'd never captained a ship or crew, braved the ocean, or slept among dangerous peoples in distant lands. They tended ledgers in comfort, contemplating expenses, ignorant of the vast potential and glory of the Indies.

His flagship crossed the harbor bar, slipping into the swell of the Ocean Sea, and Cristóbal sensed a glimmer of rejuvenation. He'd returned to his native element, his conquest of it an honor forever unassailable, and resumed sole command of his destination, released from the strangle of courtiers. He stared at the cross and devoutly prayed. *I dedicate this voyage to you, the Holy Trinity. You have moved my sovereigns to approve it, and I shall be your messenger to increase the Faith.*

As his anger tempered, Cristóbal drew strength from recalling his decade-long study of the biblical prophets, having discovered first that they'd foretold his geographic theory (1485–1486), and

---

* The senior officers were the papal nuncio, Fray Bernardo Buil, and Pedro Margarite. The courtier was Juan Aguado.

years later, that they'd revealed his unique destiny as that messenger (1497–1498). The Jewish sage Esdras had predicted that water covered only one-seventh of the earth, and he'd triumphantly conceived his first voyage on the premise that the sailing distance from Spain west to the Indies was just that one-seventh. Isaiah and other scriptures had foretold not only Christ's resurrection, but that the Lord would choose a seafarer to evangelize peoples across the sea.* As the hull pounded cresting waves, he recalled verses of Isaiah's revelations that brought him serenity, giving meaning to his life's work.

The Lord will reach out his hand to reclaim his people, including from the islands of the sea, a verse pronounced, heralding the evangelization of the Indies he'd begun. *You that go down to the sea, sing his praise from the ends of the earth,* a verse directed mariners, a command he was fulfilling as no other had before. *In his law the islands will put their hope,* another verse declared, foretelling the baptism of the Indians. *The islands' sons will come, bearing their silver and gold. . . the Lord's glorious temple will be adorned,* verses confirmed, auguring Española's gold and its use—as he'd long exhorted—to reclaim Jerusalem from the infidel. *I have chosen you my servant from among the earth's chief men. . . Fear not. I will uphold you, and those incensed against you shall be ashamed, confounded, and perish,* verses reported the Lord's word. He was the chosen one and would be revenged.

Cristóbal stood, his confidence restored, and considered the verses of his life next to unfold. For the past two years, he'd dressed in the plain, brown habit of a Franciscan friar, proclaiming humble penitence rather than noble rank or a mariner's authority, seeking to emphasize to both supporters and detractors—and particularly Queen Isabel—that the evangelization of the Indies remained a sacrosanct glory despite financial and other setbacks. While many had scorned this attire, Isabel hadn't, and regardless of his critics, she and Fernando had publicly renewed their support for him, confirming both his title Admiral and the broad authorities and entitlements they'd awarded him at the time of the first voyage (1492 and 1497). He and his heirs remained the admiral, viceroy, and governor of all

---

* *Encounters Unforeseen,* chapter V, and *Columbus and Caonabó,* chapter XII, discuss the proof and his destiny.

the islands and mainland he or they discovered in perpetuity, and he possessed all of the executive, administrative, military, and judicial power therein, including to impose the death penalty. Critics begone!

The next verses demanded exercising these authorities to impose discipline and order on Española's peoples, both Spanish and Indian, as kindly or sternly as necessary. Cristóbal undressed, folded his habit into a chest, and slipped into a wool shirt, embroidered jerkin, and breeches, august and practical, befitting an admiral, viceroy, governor, mariner, and military general returning to work. His tall, sturdy build and graying hair accentuated that eminence.

His thoughts wandered to his heirs—his sons, already working as his eyes and ears at court—and the testamentary disposition he'd completed that February. Seventeen-year-old Diego, born of his deceased Portuguese wife, Filipa, and ten-year-old Fernando, born of his Castilian lover, Beatriz, now served at Isabel's invitation as her pages.* On death, the title Admiral and his authorities and financial entitlements would pass to Diego and his heirs, or failing that, Fernando and his heirs, with his brothers Bartolomé and Diego in line contingently and son Diego instructed to provide maintenance to all the lineage. Proudly, defiantly, the testament had declared what he'd long sublimated, that he'd come from and been born in Genoa, and while gracious and loyal to the sovereigns, it had expressed no love or concern for their countrymen. The next chapter would build his lineage's compounds and dynasty in the Indies—just as entitled and prophesied, part and parcel with building the sovereigns' forts and towns.

Cristóbal trembled, exasperated that the next chapter would also amass his lineage's riches, as well as the sovereigns'. For decades—even through the last two years—he'd scrounged for money to support himself, suffering the base frugality of a commoner regardless of his nobility, pandering ignominiously for the sovereigns' support or advances, loans, or charity from merchants notwithstanding the enormity of his accomplishments. For the first two voyages, the sovereigns had granted him a tenth of the profits from the Indies (1493)—but there had been none. In awarding the third, they'd recognized that he deserved something and agreed for three years to pay

---

* Filipa Moniz Perestrelo and Beatriz Enríquez de Arana.

him an eighth of revenues on top of any tenth (1497). He'd reviewed his financial entitlements jealously, compiling all the royal promises in a book, and his testament claimed he was due a quarter of the Indies revenues.* Whatever the calculation, in the next chapter he'd finally be rewarded for his singular vision, his extraordinary struggle, and the monumental triumph he'd brought the sovereigns.

With a firmness that concealed the pain in his legs, Cristóbal strode from his cabin and mounted the stern deck to resume command of his ship, fleet, and enterprise. The sea breeze invigorated him, and visions of a lifetime on the ocean washed through his thoughts. He'd sailed far more broadly and farther than any man he knew, both as a sailor and merchant's agent—east to Chios in the Orient (Scios, 1474), north to Thule in icy seas (Iceland, 1477), south to Mina, Portugal's gold and slave-trading settlement in Guinea (Ghana, 1482–1483), and countless shorter trips and expeditions in the Mediterranean and along the Iberian coast. His seminal voyage west across the Ocean Sea had made him the most renowned mariner alive (1492), and his exploration of the territory the Indians called Cuba had embellished that distinction (1494).

But the vastness of the Ocean Sea reminded him that it was sovereign to the mariners upon it and fate was the Lord's design. His grimness returned, tinged with desperation. Prophets could be wrong. His acclaim as the greatest mariner alive wasn't worth a whit—at least in the eyes of his sovereigns and their courtiers and subjects—if he failed to promptly make the Indies profitable.

⊡ ⊡ ⊡

The fleet coursed south toward Africa to avoid French warships reputed to be lurking off Cape St. Vincent (Portugal), as Spain's intermittent hostilities with France threatened to resume in their border provinces. Before dusk, Cristóbal commenced a journal reporting the fleet's course and other daily observations to Isabel and Fernando, just as on the prior two voyages. By evening, the ships veered southwest toward the first ports of call, the Portuguese island possessions Porto Santo and Madeira, 175 leagues distant.

---

* The book is known as the *Book of Privileges*.

From the stern deck, he evaluated his fleet's seaworthiness in the moonlight, studying his flagship—a nao—and the five smaller caravels plowing the sea before it, all six three-masted, mostly square-rigged, a few with a lateen sail at the bow or stern. They hauled the newly enlisted residents and supplies not dispatched in February, and as agreed with Isabel and Fernando, three would sail directly for Española and three would divert for exploration under his command before sailing there. The ships and crews were predominantly from Palos, Moguer, and Huelva, the small Andalusian ports where he'd requisitioned ships and crews for his first voyage. The ship owners, builders, and sailors there remained confident that fleets under his command wouldn't sink or perish, and as a captain he placed like trust in their workmanship and seamanship. The seventy-foot *Niña* of the first voyage still served, most recently as the lead ship of the two dispatched to Española in February, its fifth ocean crossing, having withstood the most brutal storms he'd ever encountered at sea (1493 and 1494).

The exploration's destination was the seas south of Española and Cuba, the vision and expectation a great coastline or mainland. Indians and Caribes encountered during the second voyage, as well as Indian guides and interpreters Cristóbal had enslaved on the prior voyages, had confirmed its existence. Portugal's King João II, Manoel's predecessor, had always envisioned it, and he'd negotiated the Treaty of Tordesillas with Isabel and Fernando hoping to preserve the landmass for Portugal, even if Cristóbal or other Spanish explorers discovered it first (1494). Under the treaty, Portugal was entitled to all lands found in the Ocean Sea lying east of a longitudinal line extending pole to pole 370 leagues west of the Cape Verde Islands, Castile entitled to those found west (1494).* Iberian geographers debated how the unknown coastline might fit with those known. Since Aristotle (384–322 BC) and Ptolemy (ca. AD 100–170), most educated Europeans had understood that the earth's principal landmass, terra firma, extended east from Portugal through the Holy Land to the Indies. The Ocean Sea filled the globe between Portugal's western tip and the Indies' eastern coast, dotted by islands, and Africa extended into the southern hemisphere below Europe and the

---

* *Columbus and Caonabó*, chapter V, discusses the treaty negotiations.

Indies. Some geographers speculated the unknown coastline was part of the Indies. Others envisioned a western extension of the Canary or Cape Verde islands. The possibility of lands entirely new and separate in the southern hemisphere couldn't be dismissed.

Despite the geographic uncertainty, based on Aristotle's and others' teachings and the exceptional mines in Portugal's Guinean settlements, Isabel, Fernando, and Manoel's courtiers believed that gold and gems were most likely to be found in the earth's equatorial and southern regions, fueling ambition to claim the coastline. Isabel and Fernando were anxious to ascertain that they hadn't forsaken a gold-rich possession by conceding the establishment of the Tordesillas line so far west. Manoel was keen to learn that they had. Cristóbal was instructed to find out.

That night, and on the following days, Cristóbal grew satisfied that his vessels were appropriately fit for the exploration and Española's resupply without significant alteration of riggings, rudders, or loads. The flagship, the *Santa María de Guia,* was small for a nao, facilitating navigating unknown coastal reefs and inlets on the exploration, with roughly the same capacity and maneuverability as the seventy-five-foot *Santa María* lost on the first voyage. It could load some one hundred tuns of wine and was equipped with a small captain's quarters in the stern castle for administering the fleet.* The two nimblest caravels would accompany it—the *Vaqueña,* with a seventy-tun capacity, which had been obtained from a mariner's widow in Palos just prior to sailing, and the *Correo,* with a sixty-tun capacity. While larger than the *Niña*'s fifty-three tuns, they both performed almost as tightly in tack before the wind. The three caravels for resupply were roughly the capacity of the *Vaqueña,* less efficient against the wind but with adequate maneuverability given that their route was now well traversed and largely downwind.

On June 7, the fleet anchored at Vila Baleira, Porto Santo's main town, nestled at the base of a grassland tucked between two volcanic peaks. Cristóbal again reflected on his dynasty and destiny. His deceased wife Filipa's family held hereditary title to the island, and after their marriage, he and Filipa had resided there while he'd established his business as a merchant's agent (1479–1484). His son

---
* About 250 gallons per tun.

Diego had been born there, and so had his dream to sail west across the Ocean Sea. He fondly recollected clambering down the cliffs on the island's northwest coast to beachheads where carved wood and perhaps bamboo cane had washed and puzzling from how far east they'd drifted. He brooded over his youthful innocence and the trials and humiliations he'd thereafter suffered realizing the dream.

Disembarking, Cristóbal was startled to learn that the townsfolk had fled inland, mistaking his fleet for a band of French corsairs. Bemused, he ordered the ships to sail for neighboring Madeira, the larger of the two islands, with thriving vineyards, orchards, and sugarcane plantations. As a young man, he'd spent time there, arranging shipments of sugar and other goods for Genoese merchants (1478). For six days, the fleet took on water, chickens and lambs to eat at sea, wood for cooking, and Madeira's acclaimed wine. Cristóbal reunited with old acquaintances and was gratified by their admiration for his attainment of nobility, the rarest of feats for one they'd known as a commoner.

By June 19, the fleet approached the Canary Island Gomera, 90 leagues south and remote in the Ocean Sea. Its port, San Sebastián, was compactly snuggled between volcanic ridges, and Cristóbal's gratification ebbed to visions of his anchorages there. The *Niña*, *Pinta*, and *Santa María* of the first voyage had bobbed tiny and fragile in the harbor, unknown and unheralded, and the seventeen ships of the second had filled the harbor to its brim a year later, grandiosely attesting to his fame. The mere six would float in testimony of his declining fortune.

His thoughts also drifted to a woman's lustful clutch. The town was home to his life's most tantalizing infatuation, the island's alluring governess and seductress, Beatriz de Bobadilla, a noblewoman who'd ignited his passion and ambition for a few heated months during her widowhood (1491). At the time, she'd returned to Spain to answer charges that she'd wrongfully massacred and enslaved Gomera's natives, and she'd since been engaged to and was living with the logical marriage partner for her rule of a Canary Island. Alonso de Lugo, whom Cristóbal had met at court, was Isabel and Fernando's conquistador for the Canaries. Cristóbal's musings on the couple were cut short when the fleet entered the harbor as a French corsair was departing with an abducted Spanish vessel, and he dispatched caravels to rescue it.

The next day, Cristóbal formally paid his respects to Beatriz and Alonso, attending a feast she hosted in her blockhouse. Beatriz was unashamed she'd conquered men since youth and pleased she'd picked a winner for her second marriage. Alonso bore no jealousy for a suitor he'd outmatched, and Cristóbal felt no great sadness or loss. Beatriz had been a failed gambit in his rise to nobility, and he no longer had passion for women. He'd achieved nobility without her or her island, and his zeal for his Indian dynasty and devotion to the Holy Trinity now eviscerated all other attachments. Alonso—as scheming and cruel as his Beatriz—thanked him for the rescue, and they spoke alone to compare notes on conquest, slavery, and jousting with the sovereigns' courtiers. Both men understood Cristóbal's fame far greater and his conquest of greater potential—if he ever could make it work.

Cristóbal returned to his flagship before sunset and summoned the captains of the caravels traveling directly to Española to receive his sailing directions, which had been kept secret until the last moment lest spies lurked. Their ships would split away to cross the Ocean Sea from Gomera, while he continued farther south to cross from King Manoel's Cape Verde Islands. He'd selected them—a royal courtier and two kinsmen—for well-proven loyalty, essential since they'd serve on Española beyond his supervision.

Alonso Sánchez de Carvajal, a gentleman, had worked on Isabel's staff during the Reconquista, risen to become a councilman in a recaptured Granadan town, and assisted with provisioning and sailed on the second voyage on the crown's behalf (1493). He'd then served on the five-member ruling council Cristóbal had established to govern Española while he explored Cuba (1494) and dutifully assisted Bartolomé in the gritty task of enforcing the men's discipline at Isabela. He expected to become Cristóbal's business partner. Giovanni Antonio Colombo was Cristóbal's first cousin, hailing from Genoa. Two years prior, he and two brothers had decided to split his expenses in traveling to meet Cristóbal in Spain so he could hitch the family to Cristóbal's rising fortunes. Giovanni had come through, becoming Cristóbal's butler (1497). Pedro de Arana was a brother of Beatriz de Arana, Cristóbal's former mistress and son Fernando's mother. His and Beatriz's cousin Diego had sailed on the first voyage and died in Española (1493). While Cristóbal had abandoned Beatriz, he still maintained close relations with her family.

"We'll sail before dawn and part at the neighboring island," Cristóbal instructed, seated on the stern deck. "From there, sail west by south for 850 leagues to Dominica, then west-northwest to the island the Indians call Boriquén (Puerto Rico). Course it to the south, and then continue west to Española, which you'll soon sight off the bow." The route resembled that of the second voyage, Dominica having been its first landfall, followed by stopovers north on Guadalupe and St. Croix—all three islands so named by Cristóbal—and then west to Boriquén and Española.[*]

"The wind and current will push you to Dominica," he explained proudly and definitively. His discovery that northeasterly winds and ocean currents coursed southwest from the Canaries to the Indies had been fundamental to the success of his prior voyages.[†]

"The flesh eaters live on the easternmost islands," Carvajal warned, referring to Caribes encountered on Guadalupe and St. Croix during the second voyage. "We must be vigilant there. They're hostile."

"But the Indians living on the islands farther west are more friendly, so long as you treat them respectfully," Cristóbal assured. "When you stop to resupply, offer the locals trinkets, and they usually will give you what you need. If you use force, they'll conceal their foodstuffs and grow insolent."

Pedro listened quietly, doubting Cristóbal, mindful that the Indian chieftain Caonabó had assassinated his cousin. Giovanni was impressed, perceiving his cousin's proficiency in dealing with foreign heathens as emblematic of the legendary know-how of Genoese merchants and explorers.

"You'll skirt Española's southern coast, passing the islands of Saona and Catalina. From there, it's 25 leagues to New Isabela," Cristóbal concluded, referring to the new settlement at Santo Domingo,

---

[*] The indigenous names for Dominica, Guadalupe (the Spanish spelling for the now French Guadeloupe), and St. Croix were Ouitoucoubouli, Caloucaera, and Ayay, respectively.
[†] The winds being the permanent trade winds.

which he'd never seen.* He'd informed Isabel and Fernando that the new settlement would continue her namesake after Isabela's abandonment, but men returning from Española reported that Bartolomé had named it for their father Domenico instead (1496).[†] Cristóbal was resolved to undo that—the royal, Spanish, and biblical names he typically conferred on discoveries and settlements, rather than those of own lineage, were due the sovereigns, politic, and reverent.

"Española's Christians are more trouble than its Indians," Cristóbal admonished Pedro and Giovanni. "Most are deceitful and mean-spirited, more hateful of my rule than the Indians. Only a few are trustworthy. Scrutinize who is friend or enemy." His voice rose. "Always give the Christians an incentive to serve us—duty to the sovereigns and the Lord alone aren't enough."

"Tell Bartolomé to gather all the gold amassed in New Isabela," Cristóbal ordered Carvajal. "None of it should remain at Isabela, Fort Concepción, or the mines he's established. When I arrive, I'll dispatch the entire yield to the sovereigns on the first ships sailing." Cristóbal and Carvajal's eyes met for an instant, both anxious that the yield might be meager. Before last departing Española, Cristóbal had written the sovereigns that tribute payments were threatened by a famine ravaging Española's Indian population (1495). But gold deposits had since been found near New Isabela (1496), and both men hoped the find would offset the deficiency in tribute.[‡]

Cristóbal dismissed the three captains and retired to his cabin to record in his journal. The sharp sways and fits in his mood veered optimistic and undaunted, just as he'd felt on the eve of departure from Gomera twice before. Contemplating the exploration, he prayed. *May our Lord guide me and grant that which serves Him, the king and queen, and the honor of Christendom, for I believe no man has yet taken this course and the sea is altogether unknown.*

◻   ◻   ◻

---

* The indigenous names for Saona and Catalina were Adamanay and Yabanea Toeya, respectively.

† *Columbus and Caonabó*, chapter X, discusses Santo Domingo's establishment.

‡ The deposits were named the San Cristóbal mines.

On June 21, the six ships departed San Sebastián and skirted Heirro by late afternoon, where the three bound for the unknown veered south for the initial 250-league journey to the Cape Verde Islands. Cristóbal suffered a new bout of leg cramps and rested the night in his cabin rather than standing watch. He was satisfied the two other ships were in salted hands, their captains just as fit for the unknown's treacheries as Carvajal, Colombo, and Arana were for Española's. Pedro de Terreros, his steward on both prior voyages, captained the *Vaqueña*, and Hernan Peréz Mateos of Palos, cousin to the renowned Pinzón mariners of the first voyage, captained the *Correo*. Pedro de Salcedo, his loyal page on both prior voyages, sat outside his cabin door, alert to call him back on deck if necessary.

After six days, the exploratory fleet anchored off the Cape Verde island Boa Vista (Good View), home to a large leper colony, thousands of sea turtles and goats, and a handful of King Manoel's Portuguese notaries. The lepers had come from Portugal and other European kingdoms, as turtle meat and blood—eaten and smeared over the skin daily—was thought curative of leprosy. The ships remained for a day of goat hunting, then sailed for the islands' main settlement on São Tiago (Saint James), arriving at the principal township Ribeira Grande (now Cidade Velha) within days. Cristóbal dispatched men ashore to find and purchase a deck load of the black cattle roaming there, believing the breed might thrive at roughly the same latitude in Española's tropical climate.

Ribeira Grande bustled with Manoel's African slave trade, replete with slave pens, auction blocks, a whipping post, and a transient and resident slave population large enough to support its own African church. The island had become a weigh station for Portuguese ships hauling slaves from the African kingdoms on Guinea's west coast to work in Madeira's sugar plantations and to be sold in Lisbon and other mainland ports. Cristóbal was impressed by the slave trade's vigor—the ships constantly arriving and departing, the town's merchants obviously thriving.

But São Tiago's heat was blistering, its skies thick with haze and fog, and Cristóbal had grown feverish, his legs pinching severely. Leading citizens came aboard to pay their respects, and he learned that five ships had passed through the prior year, coursing to circumvent

Guinea and attain the Indies by sailing east, led by one Vasco da Gama. Cristóbal pried intently, keen to evaluate his challenger. But the visitors knew little more.

◻   ◻   ◻

While Cristóbal's fleet watered at São Tiago, Isabel and Fernando's competitors racing to claim the Indies' trade and territory—son-in-law Manoel and England's King Henry VII—were making headway, confident of a Christian entitlement to claim Indies' territory not already possessed by Isabel and Fernando or other Christian princes. The Treaty of Tordesillas had expressly confirmed Manoel's exclusive right vis-a-vis Spain to circumnavigate Africa and claim Indies' lands sailing east. Henry didn't care what Portugal and Spain had agreed, and after reviewing Pope Alexander's bull awarding Cristóbal's discoveries to Castile, he'd taken the view that his kingdom was entitled to find a northern route west across the Ocean Sea to the Indies, and after landfall, claim heathen or infidel territory not yet conquered, no matter how far south.

Manoel's Vasco da Gama—a minor nobleman, bold and quick-tempered—had passed through São Tiago in July 1497, and unknown to Manoel and competitors, by late May 1498 three of his ships had reached the Indies. They'd harbored at Calicut (in India), a wealthy city-state ruled by a Hindu raja with a considerable Muslim merchant trading community and bountiful production of ginger, pepper, and cinnamon. From a mariner's perspective, the voyage had been extraordinary. South of São Tiago, da Gama had veered his ships southwest deeply into the Ocean Sea to locate southwesterly gales to drive them back east past the Cape of Good Hope, a three-month landless circuit spanning over 1,200 leagues, whereupon they'd traversed the African coastline north to Mombasa and Malindi and sailed across the Indian Sea.

But the journey had been less successful from trading and territory perspectives. Da Gama's men had skirmished with Muslim peoples encountered along the African coast, and he and the raja hadn't warmed to each other. Nevertheless, by July, da Gama and crew had made headway trading for spices and gems. Dear to Manoel's heart and ambition, some crewmen perceived that the raja was of an unknown Christian sect and deduced there were Christians in the Indies with whom a glorious alliance might be made to surround the infidel and drive them from Jerusalem. More feasibly and profitably, the alliance might usurp the spice trade of the region's Muslim merchants.

To the north, the Venetian known to King Henry as John Caboto had already departed on his second voyage for Henry, sailing that May with five ships and a year's worth of provisions to the enormous landmass he'd reconnoitered the previous year (Newfoundland).* The goal was to possess the Indies up north and then course its coastline south, claiming the land Cristóbal had yet to disembark upon, including territory west of Española and the Cipangu (Japan) told of by Marco Polo (AD 1254–1324). The vision was to establish a colony by which London became a more important mart for spices than Alexandria.

◻   ◻   ◻

Rounding up the cattle on São Tiago was slow business, and Cristóbal soon concluded the risks of his men falling ill outweighed prolonging the effort. Addressing Isabel and Fernando in his journal, he again beseeched the Holy Trinity to guide serving Him and pleasing them and all of Christendom. On July 4, he gave the order to cross the Ocean Sea, setting the initial tack southwest to pass the equator, whereupon the ships would veer west to reach the Indies south of Dominica.†

One morning, as the fleet coursed slowly in light breezes, Cristóbal summoned his two enslaved, teenage Indian interpreters to inform them what tasks they'd perform when the southern landmass was found. He'd regularly abducted and enslaved Indian youths to serve as interpreters or guides while he explored and conquered—a practice perfected by Portugal's Prince Henrique (AD 1394–1460) during the exploration of Guinea—and, in his view, the interpreters' duties were nearly as critical as those of his captains.‡ The interpreters remained naked according to their custom, permitting their

---

* *Columbus and Caonabó*, chapter XII, discusses Caboto's first voyage.
† On this voyage, Cristóbal's estimate of his latitude and that of Caribbean and African places usually was a few degrees south of actual.
‡ Prince Henrique being "Henry the Navigator."

conversation and rapport with local peoples encountered, and helped peacefully find sites for fresh water, determine the ships' location and next routes, and trade for food and gold. The youths' most delicate task was apprising locals that their land had become Fernando and Isabel's. They were threatened with beatings for desertion and awarded with treats and occasional affection to establish a master-slave bond that delivered reliable information and servitude.

The two teenagers had been born in Taíno villages near Isabela on Española, and following their conscription, trained in Spanish by Cristóbal's once favorite interpreter, known after his baptism as Diego Colón, whom they'd replaced. Both had translated when Cristóbal and Bartolomé imposed tribute on caciques in conquered chiefdoms and during the hostile conversations between Cristóbal and Caonabó while the latter was imprisoned at Isabela for a year (1495–1496). They'd been hauled to Spain at the conclusion of the second voyage, baptized there, and given their Christian names Pedro and Cristóbal (1496).[*]

"Will we find Indians, Caribes, or other peoples when we make landfall?" Cristóbal asked, the teenagers kneeling before him in the captain's quarters.

"I think many Caribes," Pedro responded, understanding that *Indian* meant *Taíno*. "Like on Guadalupe. Maybe others, also," he added, contemplating lore he'd picked up as a boy in Haiti and while on Guadalupe, which his voyage to Spain had used as a way station for two weeks. "Some may carry spears tipped with guanín," he speculated, aware that Haitians obtained guanín from overseas trade.

"Will you be able to talk to them?"

"Admiral, we no know," the Taíno Cristóbal replied.

"When we meet people, you must assure them with words or signs that we come in peace, as friends," Cristóbal instructed. "Promise that we wish to trade for gold and gems and intend no harm to anyone."

The youths nodded in trepidation, having understood from Diego Colón that he'd suffered that duty during Admiral's first two voyages.

---

[*] Readers of *Columbus and Caonabó* may recall that Pedro and Cristóbal were first given the fictitious birth names Ukuti and Wasu.

Greeting Caribes and unknown peoples could be dangerous, even deadly—especially when deceiving them.

"When I possess their land, praise King Fernando and Queen Isabel as the greatest sovereigns in the world," Cristóbal commanded. "Assure them that Fernando and Isabel will protect them from their enemies. Vouch that they'll be taught Christ's faith as the path to eternal salvation, as you have been."

"Yes, Admiral," the Taíno Cristóbal replied obediently, bitterly recalling that his and Pedro's hometown villages lay abandoned and deserted. Their entire families and other residents had died of the pestilence and hunger that accompanied the pale men and their Christ-spirit.

"When we return to your homeland, you'll help me finish establishing tribute throughout the island." Cristóbal had watched many of his guides and interpreters grow ill and die, a depletion of resources no less critical than the depletion of ammunition. "Do you feel ill?" he asked.

They shook their heads. Cristóbal kindly offered them biscuits and honey before dismissing them. "Stay healthy. You'll soon arrive home princes among your people, just like your tutor Diego is."

▢　▢　▢

Within days of departing São Tiago, the ships entered the wide expanse of thick weeds Cristóbal had encountered on his prior westward crossings, but the winds he'd expected grew feeble.* To his chagrin, on July 13 they died entirely, becalming the ships in the blazing equatorial sun.† The decks were too scalding to touch, the holds steamed like cauldrons, and he feared the ships would catch fire and sailors expire. The next day, he sighted the polestar with his quadrant and judged that the ships lay seven degrees north.

Nightfall provided some relief, and clouds and rainfall provided a partial rescue over the next week. But the daytime heat brought a sense of doom, conjuring descent into Satan's inferno. Wine and water barrels began to snap their hoops and burst, wheat scorched, and meat and cheese putrefied. The crews whispered that they'd burn

---

* The Sargasso Sea.
† The ships had entered the "doldrums," the belt of calm and variable winds lying below the southern limit of the northern permanent trade winds.

alive with the ships, and after a week of surging anxiety, they cursed openly. Cristóbal beseeched the Holy Trinity to preserve at least the barrels, so they'd have enough drink to survive and make landfall. On prior crossings, he'd observed the temperature grow cooler and the sea calmer after passing 100 leagues west of the Azores' longitude (W 28 degrees), so he resolved to sail due west to that more temperate zone as quickly as possible when wind returned.

On July 22, the Lord answered, abating the woes He'd inflicted with fair southeasterly winds.* Cristóbal urgently veered his fleet west, postponing the exploration and hoping to reach the Caribe islands he knew lay there. Within days, terns and frigate birds flew by, an albatross roosted on a mast, and Cristóbal and the crews took guarded solace that land and its fresh water were off the bow.

Yet, by dawn's first twilight on July 31, landfall remained elusive, and curses burst to cries. The water and wine barrels were drawn to the last cask on each ship, and the mariner's nightmare of thirsting to death while surrounded by water gripped all. Cristóbal diverted the ships due north, desperate to find Dominica.

At midday, the Lord spoke again. High in the flagship's crows' nest, a sailor bellowed that mountain tops lay distant to port off the bow. The crews wept and danced.

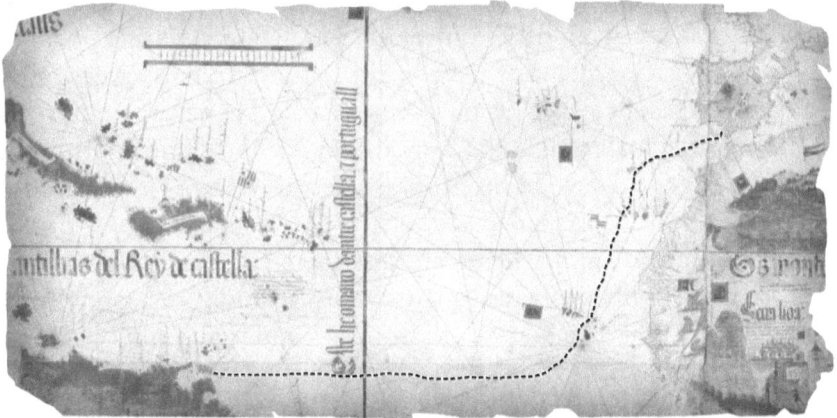

Portion of Cantino World Map of 1502, marked for route from Spain to landfall.

---

* The ships had entered the southern permanent trade winds.

Trembling with gratitude, Cristóbal coursed the fleet northwest, and as the landfall emerged distinctly, he recognized three mountains in a group. The Holy Trinity had revealed Itself! Cristóbal fell to his knees, giving infinite thanks for the miracle, and named the island Trinidad.

Cacique Diego Colón, born Bakako,
near Guaricano and Fort Concepción, Magua

Before morning's twilight, nineteen-year-old Cacique Diego Colón woke abruptly in his hammock, his temples pulsing hotly. His nightmare had revisited dangers past and portended torments imminent.

Months before, Roldán had browbeaten him to supply cazabi to the famished rebels before their departure from Magua for Xaraguá, granting him protection in the sovereigns' name if Bartolomé ever sought to punish him for such assistance. Weeks before, Bartolomé and soldiers had stomped into his village, unaware of that assistance, but demanding that he divulge the whereabouts of his brother-in-law Guarionex, scorning his denial of any clue and threatening a whipping for his duplicity. Just the day before, commander Ballester had summoned him to Fort Concepción to take responsibility for men arriving wounded from battle in Ciguayo, warning that if he'd obstructed payment of tribute by abetting Roldán's treason or Guarionex's disobedience his punishment would be severe. In days to come, the pale man ultimately responsible for uprooting and utterly transforming the course of his life was likely to return—undoubtedly to twist his destiny further.

Diego sat dangling his feet, horrified by the slave's work that loomed in his struggle to survive by straddling two civilizations. As twilight glimmered, he stood—slender and nimble—and slipped quietly from his caney, respectful to not wake his wife Ariana or their young son Diego, intending to seek counsel from the spirits and the dead before meeting Ballester. As customary for Taíno men, his black hair was cut short above the ears, with a few strands untouched that fell down his back and flickered as he walked.

His small village was silent but for the buzz of crickets, and he ambled by the bohíos where his naborias and the pale men under his care slept. Admiral could be thanked and cursed for all of it! Admiral and Guarionex had struck a treaty, and to cement it, agreed that he and one of Guarionex's sisters marry (1495). The wedding to Ariana had conferred upon him her naborias, who tended his crops and other wants. Admiral later had awarded him the village and farmland as his own chiefdom, rendering the villagers his subjects. Admiral had tasked him to serve as emissary to and spy upon Guarionex, to assist Ballester in collecting Guarionex's tribute, and to tend pale men too ill to remain at the fort (1495–1496). He'd had no choice in any of that—other than refusal and harsh punishment.

Diego trod a worn path uphill through his yuca field, and as Magua's great temperate valley emerged from darkness, he halted before a narrow gulley washed in a bluff bordering the crop. That spring, he'd buried Yutowa there, the truest comrade of his life, a fellow Lucayan also born on Guanahaní (San Salvador). Together, they'd served Admiral from his very first arrival, when he'd enslaved them on the same fateful day (1492). Between the two of them, they'd witnessed Admiral's entire conquest, translating his deceptions and lies to Haiti's supreme caciques (1492–1495), traveling to serve as conquest exhibits in his homeland across the ocean (1493), interrogating Haitian caciques captured on battlefields, and assisting enslavements of the conquered peoples (1495). Yutowa had even translated the ruse that sealed Caonabó's capture (1495). Diego had succumbed to baptism and received his Christian name before Isabel and Fernando in Barcelona when but thirteen years old (1493), a fate Yutowa fortuitously had escaped, having been too ill to travel there.

Diego knelt at his comrade's grave and intimately paid his respects. They'd made different choices, and a vision of the sucking remora fish haunted him. Enslaved, strung to a cord by a fisherman, the remora was dispatched below to latch upon prey, hauled back to deliver it, and then recast time and again into the sea to do the same, surviving rather than being eaten itself. Yutowa had taken his own life rather than continue that duty. While pained and ashamed, Diego had grown to manhood resigned to persevere by remaining strung to the cord. Although he'd never warmed to the Christ-spirit or his baptism, he'd come to think and speak as Diego, only rarely as Bakako, the true name his parents had chosen. He was grateful that Yutowa hadn't condemned his submission and even blessed it as essential for protecting his wife and child.

Diego shut his eyes, disquieted by the tasks and quandaries then looming, silently beseeching Yúcahu's omniscience and Yutowa's ancestral wisdom, praying for compassionate guidance. The first task was the least troubling, likely to be imposed on him at that morning's meeting with Ballester. He'd be told to care for the pale men wounded while hunting Guarionex and enslaving Ciguayans.

Is that wrong to do? Diego pondered, humiliated by assisting the pale men in hostilities.

Moments passed, and he sensed that neither Yúcahu nor Yutowa objected. Like the remora, he'd have no choice. Refusal would result in punishment, perhaps even of his wife and son.

A breeze rippled through the yuca crop, reminding Diego that nothing was static. His temples flushed again with both fear and guilt. The rebels favored Roldán over Admiral, as did most Haitian caciques, who'd lost hope of driving the pale men away. If Admiral fell to the rebellion, Roldán would be the fisherman holding the cord and the power to punish him.

Shall I abandon Admiral to serve Roldán? he brooded—as many pale men on Española did often. His affection and admiration for Admiral welled side by side with hatred and contempt.

Admiral had treated him kindly in daily life, favoring him like a son, albeit enslaved. Admiral had saved his life countless times in storms at sea when no other person could have. Admiral showed Taíno caciques the deference due their stature, while other pale men treated all Taínos as if naborias or slaves. Through countless hardships, they'd forged a singular bond both acknowledged, and Admiral had promised to protect him. Without Admiral, he'd be but a Guanahanían fisherman, not a Haitian cacique.

As the sun's rim pierced the horizon, Diego perceived Yúcahu's guidance. He owed no obligation to any pale man. They habitually broke their word, Admiral no exception. Admiral had ordered slaughters and enslavements and felt gratitude for no one, even those assisting him, pale men included.

Bakako, a vision of Yutowa scoffed, *Admiral will betray you shamelessly, so betray him likewise.*

Diego shivered, recalling Yutowa's contempt for the name Diego. But he wasn't cowed and mused that Yutowa was insufficiently shrewd. Admiral rarely gave up and, uncannily, always rebounded. Their special bond might wither and fray, but Admiral would never forget it. Whether loyalty was due or not, betrayal of Admiral was unsafe and foolish unless his defeat was beyond doubt.

As clouds drifted overhead, Diego confronted his gravest qualm. Guarionex likely would be captured, and he'd be ordered by Admiral or Bartolomé to interpret as they extracted from Guarionex whatever they demanded in punishment. His role could be to pronounce the punishment of execution.

Shall I participate in my brother-in-law's punishment? Diego beseeched, bracing for condemnation.

Diego had lived with Guarionex as long as with Admiral, and his bond with the conquered chieftain had grown just as close and tortured. As interpreter, he'd witnessed his brother-in-law's painful interactions with Admiral, Bartolomé, and their behique, the friar Ramón Pané. The naive, deferential attempts to fashion coexistence with them. The devastating submission to tribute. The mortifying defeat of an uprising. The submission to study Christianity with Fray Pané, only to reject it. Through it all, Guarionex had watched over him as a dutiful brother-in-law, despite his service as Admiral's emissary and spy.

As the clouds parted, Yúcahu replied that Guarionex was the most august Taíno living, unmatched in wisdom of the Taíno people's ideals and spirits. A man so honorable deserved no punishment, no less by a people so evil. Yutowa scorned the pale men's belief that their Christ-spirit excused all evil done in his name or faithfully confessed to him. Those who did evil had no recourse to a spirit's absolution—on death or otherwise. Both warned that those who participated in Guarionex's punishment would put their own souls in everlasting jeopardy. Diego despaired, doubting his courage to disobey.

Bathed in sunshine, he grimly rose, bid his comrade goodbye, and returned to his village. Ariana met him at the caney, young Diego on her hip, and they shared cazabi and pineapple juice. He informed her that he would leave for Fort Concepción and return with more pale men to tend, which disgusted her.

"You must abandon them to die," she blurted. "They deserve worse for hunting my brother."

Cacique Diego Colón.

"We shall care for them," he replied. "That's the price of our son's well-being and our own."

"We can barely care for ourselves and our people," she retorted.

Diego watched the pale invalids stepping out of their bohíos, commanding his naborias to fetch water and cazabi. Some suffered fevers, others emaciation from hunger, vomiting, or diarrhea, and many pained from *scabs* (syphilis).* Many of his subjects were departing, the men to hunt fowl and the women to mulch the yuca fields. Ariana was right. The additional pale men would aggravate everyone's hunger. The village's population had shrunk to less than

---

* The fevers, vomiting, and diarrhea likely were caused by influenza, swine flu, typhus, and/ or bacterial dysentery.

half its former number, and villagers continued to die of famine and diseases brought by the pale men and their Christ-spirit. Admiral had cared nothing for Haiti's dead and dying—other than the loss of their tribute.

"You must ask of my brother's fate," Ariana urged.

"I won't. The pale men suspect we know his whereabouts, and they'd surmise I was spying on his behalf." Diego caressed his son's cheek and headed south for the forty-minute trek through the valley and Guarionex's town, Guaricano, to the fort.

Guaricano was a ghost of its former self. Its population had once exceeded that of many of the towns he'd seen in Spain, but most residents had perished or fled to the mountains. He ambled across Guarionex's great ballcourt—where he'd interpreted the chieftain's submission to tribute—now deserted except for scavengers scouring for food. Some scrounged through Guarionex's abandoned caney. In the distance, hordes of vultures prowled among decayed corpses strewn along the town's river. Diego's incredulity matched his horror. Haiti's food production had once been so abundant that no one hungered.

He came to the site of Fray Pané's church, where he'd translated Pané's lessons to Guarionex. It too was abandoned. Bartolomé had burned villagers at the stake for defiling its cemís of the Christ-spirit, and Guarionex had murdered villagers who'd been baptized within in retaliation for their disloyalty to his uprising.

Diego crossed the river to arrive at the ruins of the first Fort Concepción, which Manicoatex had burned to the ground.* For a moment, he paused on the very ground where he'd translated Manicoatex's submission to tribute as Admiral beheaded caciques and warriors whom Manicoatex had led into battle. Slaughter lingered everywhere.

Further south, he approached the hills and peak beneath which the great battle had been fought, Admiral's men prevailing (1495).† Countless skeletons still littered the fields, the once verdant farmland now an oblivion.

Finally, at the base of the hills, Diego arrived at the rebuilt Fort Concepción, which had a gushing spring. He'd visited there many

---

* The river is the Río Verde, its indigenous name unknown.
† Now known as the battle of Santo Cerro, depicted on the cover and in chapter VII of *Columbus and Caonabó*.

times, including to interpret when Guarionex delivered tribute. The fort's commander now served as his direct supervisor in implementing Admiral's conquest. The sentries recognized him and bid him enter the compound, a few fortified wooden houses protected by trenches and a stone and earthen wall. Cautiously, he strode across the foreground, where—as two Taíno caciques burned at the stake—he'd translated Guarionex's surrender to Bartolomé upon failure of the uprising.

Commander Miguel Ballester, an elderly Catalan loyal to Admiral, came to greet him. "Diego, how goes it? Is your wife ready to tell us where Guarionex hides?"

II

ENSLAVEMENTS, TREATIES, SETTLEMENTS

ANACAONA AND ROLDÁN, SQUATTERS' HAVEN GROWS,
Xaraguá, Summer 1498

After Behecchio acquiesced that they could remain in Xaraguá, Roldán and his gang brusquely but bloodlessly imposed themselves on the chiefdom's daily life, and the Spaniards' and Xaraguáns' fear of assassination and carnage subsided. In June, emboldened, the gang warily ventured from the two bohíos in Behecchio's hometown to scatter into neighboring villages that they conceived—with Roldán's blessing—as their own, demanding that the village caciques provide food, bohíos, and villagers to service their wants. The gang remained vigilant against reprisal, squatting in groups, brandishing weapons as a warning, and sometimes moving from village to village in search of gold, better food, or more beautiful women. For himself, Roldán chose a village with fertile gardens a half hour on horseback from Behecchio's caney, a buffer permitting vigilance against attack and privacy for his men's assembly.

Behecchio and Anacaona apprised the village caciques that they no longer owed the guamiquina tribute and remained the rulers of their villages, their rank and prerogatives unaltered. But they were expected to peacefully accommodate the pale squatters and allow the squatters to use their common subjects and naborias as laborers and servants. The caciques were grateful that bloodshed, tribute, and their own servitude had been avoided, and they and many of their subjects grimly perceived that the squatters' use of their naborias was a novel adaptation of an established practice. For ages prior to the pale men's arrival, Haiti's caciques had traded the labor of naborias in borderland or disputed areas.

But all Xaraguáns feared the peace would simmer with abuse and the arrangement would inevitably erode the village caciques' authority, perhaps even Behecchio and Anacaona's own. Behecchio and Anacaona assured them they shared those fears and directed the caciques to inform them of transgressions.

As traditional, Behecchio had married wives from villages throughout Xaraguá to solidify his command of the chiefdom—more than thirty of them, mostly daughters, sisters, or cousins of village caciques—bonding the caciques' vassalage to him. To implement his rule, he regularly summoned the caciques to meet in council at his residence, and Anacaona often attended as well. By July, almost all seventy squatters possessed Xaraguán concubines, and the councils focused keenly on that and the squatters' conduct. The information shared jarred all.

One day, rather than attending a council, Anacaona summoned to her garden a few of the caciques' wives visiting with their husbands—all acquaintances of hers—seeking their perspective while their husbands reported to Behecchio. The women sat on *duhos* (ceremonial or chief's seats), befitting members of caciqual families.

"Who are the squatters' concubines?" she inquired pointedly, indicating the discussion was just as serious as Behecchio's.

"My husband and some caciques have relented to the squatters' want for attractive women and teenagers, sometimes sisters or cousins, fearing bloodshed if possession were denied," a prominent wife grimly replied. "The squatters don't deserve such gestures, and my husband is deeply ashamed." Sex prior to marriage wasn't taboo for Taíno women, and for ages, caciques sometimes had offered an esteemed visitor a pretty, unmarried woman for the night, sometimes a daughter or sister. A woman's virginity wasn't prized or expected before marriage, and although expected to be faithful to one husband after marriage, unmarried women so presented traditionally suffered no stigma precluding subsequent marriage. "Nevertheless, bloodshed has been avoided."

"The squatters in my village force their naborias to lie with them," the youngest wife warned, her voice cracking with revulsion. "Squatters often demand caciques or husbands provide several women, threatening retaliation if refused. Some demand girls."

"A few of our women have snuggled into the squatters' arms, just as they would with an esteemed visiting cacique," the eldest recounted. "They're taken by the squatters' power and hope concubinage will bring stature and fortune. They try to adopt to the pale man's ways, washing the clothing he wears and cooking meals as he directs."

"Occasionally, some concubinage is no different than with our own men," one pregnant observed. "The pale men can woo or be smitten, just as our own. For lust or loneliness or simply want of a cook."

"The pale men swagger as if they rank superior to our husbands!" the prominent wife declared bluntly, barely shying from an accusation, drawing Anacaona's gaze.

"I assure you, we haven't anointed them caciques," she responded, hiding her remorse. "Behecchio and I already know of these abuses." She turned slowly to face each wife, in sympathy and to forestall outbursts. "We've warned their leader to discipline his men, and we'll continue to warn him."

The wives remained sullen, unconvinced.

"Do the squatters show our women any affection, or is it merely lust and domination?" Anacaona probed, seeking deeper insight into the enemy. She didn't invite discussion of how the women felt.

"I've heard that some pale men can be affectionate," the pregnant wife responded. "My impression is that a few nurture long-term bonds."

"The pale men assume they're entitled to domination," the eldest wife answered. "Not just by manhood, but by virtue of their spirits and traditions—and obviously their weapons. Undoubtedly, they're already married in their homeland. Women expecting husbands will be deserted one day."

"When the squatters leave, we'll all be delighted," Anacaona rejoined. Again, she circled her gaze to each woman. "Do you foresee marriages?"

The wives shrugged, disgusted and doubtful yet uncertain.

"Beware of marriages, particularly to your daughters and sisters," Anacaona warned. "Marriage may afford shelter from the squatters' bludgeon. To some women, it may seem an advancement. But marriage of women of caciqual families—such as ourselves—elevates the pale man to the family's lineage and erodes our caciques' authority. The squatters may lust for that elevation, just as much as to mount us."

"So, they mimic our men in this regard," the eldest wife gibed.

"I once resolved never to wed again," Anacaona confessed, stroking her nagua. She'd never met a man Caonabó's equal. "Who knows if I'll ever change my mind. But I'll never marry and share my rank with a pale man."

The wives nodded.

"What else have you observed about the concubinage?"

"The Christ-spirit is important to the pale men," the prominent wife replied, the others concurring. "In addition to cooking the squatters' meals and washing their clothing, some women imitate that worship."

"We must always put our own spirits and traditions first," Anacaona counseled. "Remember Guabonito. We must follow in her footsteps, and our role may be as fundamental as hers." Guabonito, the Taínos' ancestral heroine, had nurtured their ancestral hero, Guayahona, from sickness to health so he might assume the leadership of their people. "We must ensure our spirits and traditions endure, despite the squatters' wish or their example."

After dismissing the women, Anacaona sat alone, her thoughts turning to Behecchio's suggestion that her own teenage daughter spy on Roldán. Higueymota had learned to draw men's want, and to discard them in the morning, but she was young to surmount the vulgarity the pale men showed Taíno women, no less smite and deceive their leader. Regardless, Higueymota was hardly as defenseless as the teenage girls just discussed. Her protectors—Xaraguá's supreme cacique and Anacaona herself—could extract her from abuse, if Roldán even dared such. Anacaona brooded somberly that her own flirtation with Roldán would signal an equivalence entirely inappropriate.

❏ ❏ ❏

Captains Carvajal, Colombo, and Arana adeptly executed Cristóbal's sailing instructions across the Ocean Sea and through the
Indies' eastern islands, but they missed the mark at Española. Strong
current and wind on the island's southern coast drove them west, and
they substantially overshot the new settlement at Santo Domingo.
In late July, belatedly recognizing their error, they anchored more
than 50-leagues' sail west, on Xaraguá's southern coast (near modern
Jacmel, Haiti). Roldán quickly learned of the three ships' arrival, and
fearing Cristóbal finally had returned, he gathered Múxica, Escobar,
and a substantial contingent of well-armed rebels and hiked to the
anchorage for the confrontation they'd dreaded for over a year. Carvajal dispatched a launch to bring him and several others aboard.

On deck, they embraced—Roldán anxiously, Carvajal heartily—
as if renewing the friendship they'd struck before, while serving Cristóbal on Española.

"The Admiral returns!" Carvajal beamed. "We've shipped in
advance, bearing the wine and meat you've hungered!" He scanned
the reactions of Roldán and his lieutenants, surmising an odd wari-
ness as well as joy. "We realize we're far downwind of your new
township. Where are we, and why are you here?"

"The Indians call this Xaraguá," Roldán responded, struggling to
maintain cheer. "Brother Bartolomé dispatched us here to secure provisions and pacify the natives." He glanced at Múxica and Escobar.
"We delight that you've come! When will the Admiral arrive?"

"Within weeks! He explores for the southern shores the Indians
speak of, searching for more gold." Carvajal eyed Roldán's men
again, curious that their torsos weren't as lean or haggard as he'd
envisioned. "You all must be thirsty. Let's drink!" He bid the ship's
boatswain break out the wine.

Celebration consumed the next two days, both aboard and
ashore, and Carvajal and Roldán briefed each other as to what had
transpired—or ought to have transpired—in Spain and Española
during the past two years. The voyagers and rebels feasted and
chummed, the former eager to understand life on Española, the latter

to learn of Andalusia and their hometowns. The rebels' accounts soon grew inconsistent, then implausible, and finally untenable. No, they weren't collecting gold tribute from the savages. No, they hadn't lived in the new township at Santo Domingo. No, they weren't eager for the Admiral's return, and they hated Bartolomé. They'd fled Bartolomé, seeking a better life, all while loyal to the king and queen by serving Roldán, the island's duly appointed magistrate.

On the third day, Roldán conceded the bare truths to Carvajal and succinctly pled the justifications for his actions.

"Cease this rebellion before the Admiral returns!" Carvajal admonished compassionately. "The king and queen support him, despite his faults. Submit to Bartolomé now, and I'll recommend to the Admiral that this recklessness be forgotten and clemency be granted all, without word reaching the king and queen."

"Understand that I've faithfully executed the king and queen's rule," Roldán retorted, fearing Carvajal hadn't warmed to his arguments. "It's Bartolomé's despotism that has failed the sovereigns. The Admiral owes me and my men that clemency."

Carvajal was speechless, shocked by Roldán's insistence that he possessed royal authority.

"Alonso, join me and my men," Roldán pushed on. "Together, we can implement the king and queen's rule dutifully—without the Genoese. We also may enrich ourselves with estates and servants."

Carvajal shuddered. Española's enormous distance from Spain, its wilderness and conquerable savages, and the absence of the sovereigns' soldiers and jailers had emboldened a self-importance and righteousness that wouldn't have germinated in Spain.

"You deceive yourself, Francisco. Neither king nor queen has heard of you, much less authorized you to rule this island. They've chosen and reaffirmed Colón as its governor—even after entertaining all the criticisms against him. You have no authority to promise your men land or villages. Homesteads are for Colón to award, pursuant to authorities the king and queen granted him alone. The sovereigns expect tribute from the Indians, just as Spaniards pay taxes. If the king learns you've undone it, you'll be imprisoned."

For days, the discussions went nowhere. Roldán pressed to recruit voyagers to augment the rebels' strength and perceived the ongoing commingling and rapport between voyagers and rebels favored that.

"You must stay with us," a rebel counseled a voyager, the son of an acquaintance in Seville. "Colón offers but wages for hard work and hunger, and—if you kiss his hand—he'll dangle a homestead. Roldán will give you an entire village tomorrow, plus all its savages to farm and cook for you."

"Roldán's a Spaniard of common blood, just as you and me," a second rebel told a peasant farmer from Extremadura. "He understands that you have little to boast of in Spain. He, too, has suffered the scorn of idle gentlemen and indolent heirs of dead knights. Here, he'll make you a lord of heathens. Colón's a travesty, a Genoese weaver masquerading as Spanish nobility, and he offers only that you continue to toil as a lowborn."

"Colón's justice is cruel," many rebels exhorted. "Here, freedom and liberty abound."

Carvajal, Colombo, and Arana soon realized that Roldán wasn't moved by Carvajal's cajoling. They resolved that Colombo would march overland to Santo Domingo with the salaried voyagers, while Arana sailed the ships there and Carvajal remained behind to force Roldán to his senses. When the ships were ready, Colombo led voyagers ashore to begin the trek east. But Roldán stood at the shoreline, beckoning silently.

Those disembarking knew the Admiral and Bartolomé largely through reputation alone, and knowing it dreadful, they'd enlisted anyway. For many, the rebels' criticisms of the brothers were insufficient cause to abandon the journey they'd chosen or the admiral their sovereigns had anointed. Yet, they'd all come for fortunes and contentment, and the rebels had drawn a vision of opportunity in Xaraguá that overwhelmed their bitter experience of its absence in Spain. Slowly, forty of those disembarking deserted to stand with Roldán.

Colombo angrily retreated to the ships with a few men still loyal, whereupon the ships sailed. Roldán exulted, his gang having grown by half to nearly one hundred fifteen strong.

◻   ◻   ◻

Behecchio and Anacaona sat in their ballcourt soberly awaiting Roldán at sunset, his approach announced by naborias that now served him. Caciques' reports from the coast were ominous—the pale men's presence in Xaraguá was burgeoning. Brother and sister had envisioned supporting a small minority against a growing contingent of the guamiquina's men, rather than the minority quickly multiplying.

"Roldán comes to claim victory over the guamiquina and demand haven for his new followers," Behecchio grittily surmised. "I shall admonish him to curtail his people's transgressions. You and your daughter must gird to coo and pry. Assure our friendship. Entice his confidence to spy his intentions."

Roldán arrived at dusk on horseback, followed by other rebel leaders and his indentured manservant on foot. Naborias ported their weapons and provisions.

"I come victorious," he announced. "I've enlisted many more men to protect you from the guamiquina." As the manservant translated, he stared into Behecchio's black eyes. "You doubted that I possessed the power to defend you, but my word is proven."

"What do you request of me now?" Behecchio inquired, shrugging.

"These new recruits require villages, bohíos, gardens, and naborias. Where best should I locate them?"

"Your men's conduct displeases me," Behecchio replied gruffly. "You must address that before asking permission for more men to live in my chiefdom."

Roldán's swell momentarily wasted. Homage remained due to ensure the fragile facade of harmony and peace.

"Your displeasure sorrows me," he replied, as if courteously. "What conduct do you speak of?" Certain of the criticism, he assured, "I've warned my men that a woman's nakedness isn't an invitation and that maids are for cooking, not mounting."

"All my villagers are my subjects," Behecchio retorted. "Including your men's naborias, who have spouses, children, and their own bohíos. Your men may not harm, prey, or lust upon any of them."

"I understand, Your Highness," Roldán blustered. "I promise my men will do better."

"Your promises have been false! Now warn them sincerely—with punishment," Behecchio barked, intent on wrenching improvement.

"In your homeland, don't you punish those who demand or steal another's wife or daughter?" He gazed away, not expecting an answer. "In my chiefdom, throughout my island, we do. I expect you to chastise wrongdoers severely, hereafter." He bitterly refrained from threatening to exact punishment himself, fearing the hostility that would trigger.

"Of course, Your Highness." Roldán nodded vigorously, likewise fearful of triggering hostility, yet silently scorning the absence of that threat. His own men's loyalty would disintegrate if he ever punished them on behalf of an Indian. Their freedom and liberty were conceived free of such justice.

Behecchio rose abruptly and left rudely, without addressing Roldán's request or a parting salutation, leaving him for Anacaona. She scrutinized the wrinkle and twitch of his eyebrows and fingers, discerning both anguish and trepidation but not remorse. She affected a pleasant smile.

"Your new followers may remain," she said. "Be sure they behave."

Roldán bowed to excuse himself, tired of truckling to Indians. But Anacaona tossed her head, flitting her long black hair from her breasts. "Don't leave," she coaxed. "As I recall, you enjoy poetry."

He nodded mutely.

"Would you like to see my garden? It's where I hide alone to compose areítos."

Roldán's aggravation melted, replaced with wary intrigue. "I would enjoy that, Your Highness." He shifted, uncertain what was expected of his manservant.

"We don't need others. Your Taíno is marvelous," she fawned, taking his hand. "Come, I will teach you of Haiti's flowers and trees."

As the sun set, Anacaona ambled with Roldán through the magnolias at the garden's entrance. She raised her arm to point to their pink blossoms, placing her other hand on his shoulder, summoning his gaze up while her breasts tempted it down. "They thrive throughout the island. The charm of their petals complements their sturdy limbs. Do you understand the spirits' revelation?"

"My Anacaona, tell me."

"Beauty and strength go hand in hand, pleasing and advancing each other."

She led on toward the riverbank, where the lilies floated sub-limely on the water's surface, resisting the current's downstream tug. She spoke softly, drawing his eyes to her lips. "Do you understand the meaning of the lilies in the stream?"

Roldán struggled. "Everyone seeks water," he managed.

She laughed gayly, only hinting derision. "They remind us that harmony can reign in the midst of opposition." She softly squeezed his hand. "So long as the opposition is gently balanced."

Their shoulders and hips lightly grazed as they entered a narrow path. To the left, stately orchids beckoned with intricate and delicate blossoms. To the right, cacti menaced with bristling needles. "Do you understand what this trail tells us?" she asked coyly.

"Not as well as you, my Anacaona," he replied graciously, content to admit she possessed wisdom he lacked.

"It's the simplest guidance," she replied. "All may live in har-mony, from the graceful to the vicious, so long as they respect each other's land."

Anacaona brought him to two duhos set among the bayahibes, and they sat face-to-face, close upon each other, his back nearly brushing a bush's pink petals, he unaware of the needles beneath. She beckoned with a grin, commanding him to lead, silent as to the bayahibes' revelation. Twilight's darkening shade ushered in a pri-vacy that conjured intimacy.

Roldán beheld the whole of Anacaona's eyes, breasts, and the nagua veiling her womb. "My Anacaona, perhaps we can enjoy each other in harmony and union," he proposed. "You're the most beau-tiful woman I've ever beheld." Uncertain of her sincerity and wary of deception, yet taken by want, believing she invited, and consumed with ambition, he reached forward to grasp her hands and kiss her.

But Anacaona gently pushed him backwards toward the needles.

"That's what your enemy Bartolomé told me as we sat here a year ago," she whispered, observing him recoil. As he startled, she sat upright, her smile withdrawn but her gaze still pleasant. "We are now friends, Francisco. The better your men treat my people, the better friends we can become." She relished him frustrated, duped, confused, and enraged—far less degradation than he deserved—and she hoped he'd recoil further to be spiked.

"You brought Bartolomé Colón to this garden!" Roldán stammered, his heart pounding, infuriated by a vision of Anacaona inviting Bartolomé's mount. "To what end?" he demanded, irate he'd been manipulated by a heathen queen.

"To deliver the same message, among other things," Anacaona replied honestly.

Bayahibe bush.

Roldán stared away, seeking to regain composure and take control of the conversation, as befit a conqueror and a man. He exhaled gruffly, folded his arms, leaned forward from the unseen needles, and peered into her eyes, convinced his manipulations could outdo hers.

"My Anacaona, you bid me here, and I remain eager to stay. Should you wish, I'd be delighted to embrace you as my lover. That would enrapture and benefit us both." He took her hands forcefully.

"Perhaps someday we could rule together." He'd mulled that dream for weeks. "We could rule both peoples, mine and yours." He resisted identifying a kingdom or time or even predicting that he'd replace the guamiquina.

"Francisco, Behecchio rules Xaraguá. Pale men never will." She withdrew her hands, having never trusted for an instant that a pale man—whether husband or lover—would willingly share rule with a Taíno woman. "As for us, you are not my equal," she pronounced plainly, reveling as his jaw gaped and shoulders slumped. But her eyes moistened, and she dangled the bait.

"But, if you prove your respect for my people, perhaps my daughter would take a more intimate interest in you."

ISABEL AND FERNANDO, SUCCESSION IN ARAGÓN,
Zaragoza, May–August 1498

Isabel, Fernando, and their court departed Toledo on May 17 for Zaragoza, the ancestral seat of Aragón's royalty, to obtain recognition of Princess Isabel as Fernando's heir to that kingdom's throne. Queen and princess traveled in carriages, all concerned for the princess's unborn child. Kings Fernando and Manoel rode steeds decorated with their banners and colors, accompanied by honor guards of Aragonese and Portuguese knights. A procession of carriages, wagons, horses, mules, and donkeys lumbered in train, bearing a thousand courtiers, diplomats, administrators, servants, friends, and supplicants, as well as the royal wardrobes and jewelry and the entire entourage's luggage. Most expected celebrations and the succession to be approved. Like Castile's, Aragón's commerce and well-being had advanced handily during the decades of Isabel and Fernando's joint rule, and Princess Isabel's succession would unite the kingdoms' rule in a single monarch for the first time.

But as they rode, Isabel and Fernando were circumspect, wary lest their public remarks and countenances suggest that they took the approval of Aragón's nobility for granted. These noblemen had long denied succession to daughters, fearing a husband would overpower the daughter to favor his factions, or even worse, that a foreign husband would absorb their small kingdom into his own and encroach on their entitlements.

The court arrived in Zaragoza on June 2, and fiestas and homage buoyed the next two weeks. Manoel did his utmost to project a friendly, nonaggressive stance, aware of lurking suspicions and jealousies. Portugal's dukes and counts were likewise distrustful of foreign husbands.

By mid-month, Aragón's assembly convened, and according to custom, their beloved king opened the session in their chambers, with his queen, daughter, and son-in-law seated in the front row. Fernando proposed the princess's succession courteously, and the princess and Manoel bowed deeply when assuring they'd respect the nobility's rights. The church affirmed its approval—with the blessings of both the Archbishop of Toledo, Cisneros, and the Archbishop of Zaragoza, Alonso of Aragón, the kingdom's daily administrator and Fernando's illegitimate son (b. ca. 1470). The debate opened.

"Your Highness, my utmost wish is to serve you," a duke pronounced, bowing to Fernando. "But your illustrious father's will does not permit this. Your heir must be male." Fernando's father, King Juan I, had dictated that after Fernando, the crown would pass to his sons or, in their absence, to the sons of his daughters, reflecting the view that women—even those of his own line—were too weak to rule.

"My liege, no one can doubt my father's wisdom," Fernando replied. "But I suspect, as he watches over us, he sees different circumstances than at his death. Aragón has risen with the Castilian union to rank as a formidable power, and his lineage through me is best suited to ensure such union and strength persevere, whether through a king or queen. Were he here today, Father would support Princess Isabel's succession."

"Your Highness, I welcome King Manoel's friendship," a knight proffered. "But the prohibition on succession by women is also a matter of our law, as you may remember." Decades earlier, Juan and Fernando had advanced that precept to Castilian noblemen unsuccessfully, plotting to claim that Fernando, as the closest living male heir to a previous Castilian king, was entitled to be anointed Castile's king in his own right—irrespective of marriage to Isabel—and as king by blood to dominate her as queen.

"My eminence, I have always upheld our laws," Fernando responded. "But there have been exceptions to the general rule, permitting queens in centuries past," he declared. The precedents were true but undistinguished.

Not all were opposed. "My brethren, our kingdom will revert to the sidelines unless jointly ruled with Castile," a nobleman proclaimed.

"None of the French, Flemish, or English will fear us," another added. "We must let the king interpret the law as he wisely judges."

To Isabel and Fernando's dismay, opposition had a fierce, bumptious core, and the dispute dragged on for days. Eventually, Isabel tired of sophistry and grew cross and then enraged. The noblemen's intransigence was pretentious. She ruled a more powerful kingdom. She possessed more power than their king.

"It would be better to reduce your kingdom by arms at once, rather than endure more of this insolence," she exclaimed to the assembly, brandishing Castile's and her might, scorning men's hubris. She'd proven a woman could rule. Protesting that to men was a waste of time.

The room grew hush, all peering about and shifting in their seats, wondering whether any present were bold or brash enough to respond. Fernando let the awkward moment linger, pleased that more pressure had been applied.

"Your Highness, we are your loyal subjects," a nobleman assured his queen, breaking the silence and signaling he and his brethren weren't cowed. "We must be excused if we move cautiously in a matter so difficult to justify by precedent."

⌧ ⌧ ⌧

As the debate stumbled, Isabel and Fernando occasionally excused themselves to conduct other business. While the Indies conquest waited for Cristóbal's reports, their Granadan conquest—which hadn't demanded close attention for years—now required calculation and machination. The influx of Castilian Christians settling in the city of Granada had swelled beyond the space available, testing the sovereigns' scruple to honor the promises they'd made to the city's conquered Mohammedan residents.

The siege of the illustrious city had been the Reconquista's final confrontation, and Isabel and Fernando had pressed a truce to preserve the city's wealth, economy, and magnificent Alhambra fortress while compelling the residents to submit to vassalage as Mudejar. To that end, they'd agreed to surrender capitulations that encouraged the residents to emigrate to other kingdoms but guaranteed those choosing to remain the freedoms to practice Islam and bear arms, with mosques protected from conversion and homes from confiscation (1491).* A substantial majority of Mohammedans working in the city had chosen to remain on those terms. The most prominent had since been offered substantial sums to publicly convert and, upon conversion, been welcomed at court.

The transition to Christian rule had been largely peaceful, and the conquered had continued to participate in the city's daily administration, including as a minority on the city of Granada's ruling council. Isabel and Fernando had appointed an experienced diplomat, Count Íñigo Lópes de Tendilla, as the territory's governor, and their confessor, Hernando de Talavera, as its archbishop (1492). Both men maintained a respectful approach toward the Mudejar to avoid strife and rebellion. From a converso family, Talavera esteemed the volitional essence of conversion, believing it took time and persuasion for men to shed their customs and religion to adopt a new one. At his insistence, Isabel had promised that Mudejar converting would be exempt from the Inquisition, which functioned to root out and punish converts secretly practicing a former religion, for forty years.

Nevertheless, since the surrender, resentment of inferior status had simmered among the Mudejar, and hostility of the Christian settlers toward the Mudejar had risen steadily as the streets they shared grew ever more crowded. Recently, Mudejar had protested taxes imposed disproportionately, and Christian settlers had imposed segregation of public baths and other functions in the neighborhoods they wished to call their own (1497). The settlers now demanded not only segregation but appropriation of land and homes to satisfy the continuing influx of Christians.

Isabel and Fernando recognized that demand as a clear-cut

---

* *Encounters Unforeseen*, chapter VI, discusses the surrender and capitulations.

violation of their most fundamental promises, respected over the seven years since surrender. They also accepted that the Mudejar had rights as inferior vassals and benefitted their kingdom, which profited by the Mudejars' industry and disproportionate payment of taxes. But the Mudejar could never impede their Christian settlers' or Christianity's advancement. As they'd intended, the territory's former Mohammedan leadership had emigrated. After seven years of co-optation, the Mudejar had no ruler left to demand observance of the capitulations.

On June 27, with Isabel and Fernando's silent approval and support, the city's governing council adopted an ordinance to remove Mudejar residents from their city homes and segregate Christian and Mudejar residents. Mudejar who hadn't resided in the city when it surrendered had to depart, and those working outside the city had to sell their city homes to Christians and relocate to where they worked or the city's Albaicín neighborhood, which was reserved for Mohammedans. The city would be kept for Christian settlers, except for the Albaicín and a small morería, where a limited number of merchants most critical to daily life might remain, serving the Christian settlers.

◻ ◻ ◻

By July, the sovereigns and Aragón's nobility tired of bickering and struck a compromise to defer recognition until Princess Isabel delivered. If a boy, recognition of him would readily proceed.

The postponement came none too soon. Isabel was bedridden with high fevers, and her physicians feared the worst, bleeding her twice. Prayers and masses were held for her in Zaragoza, and as word passed, throughout Aragón and Castile. But she remained undaunted. The Lord hadn't yet called her. As she fought to recover, Princess Isabel sat at her bedside and the two confided, childbirth expected within weeks.

"God helps those who help themselves, my child," Isabel preached. "Eat more, fatten up. Your baby eats too."

The princess had heard it before and simply nodded.

"You must pray and persevere, resolutely," Isabel lectured. "I did it five times. It took over twelve hours to deliver you, and my suffering was rewarded." She gently caressed her daughter's cheek.

"Mother, I don't welcome death. I merely sense it approaching." Death always loomed at childbirth. The princess sought to change the subject, not far astray, but to intimacies rarely discussed. "How did you feel the instant the midwives told you I was a girl?"

"The agony of labor dwarfs the disappointment. Every princess— including yourself—must pray for a boy. But if the Lord delivers a girl, when the pain subsides and you first cradle her to your nipple, you care little what men think."

"What did Father feel when he first learned?"

"He was relieved I survived so he could take Castile's throne with me," Isabel reflected wryly, mustering a wan chuckle. "Obviously, he was frustrated you weren't a prince, but he expected I'd deliver him more children." She held her daughter's hands tightly. "Manoel will be no different, boy or girl. Your survival assures him at least the crown of Castile, and he'll continue to cherish you, even if you bear a girl."

"But then who'll succeed Father?"

"We'll surmount that hurdle if the Lord so challenges us." Isabel winced. "Perhaps your father can force the impudent to kneel at your feet. More likely, be prepared to conceive again promptly."

Isabel grew silent, fitfully entertaining her firstborn's premonition and shuddering to contemplate the possibility that neither princess nor child would survive. Cheerful news had arrived that Princess Juana also was pregnant, childbirth due before year's end, but otherwise reports from Philippe's Burgundian court were alarming. He had booted most of Juana's staff back to Castile, emasculating her independence. Rumor had it he coveted most everything French, particularly their women, and that he'd wrapped Juana around his finger, snaring her adoration yet tormenting her with infidelity. Juana rarely wrote home, and it was unclear whether she promoted Castile and Aragón's interests or had been dragged into serving those of Flanders and Austria. The absence of even an occasional missive from daughter to mother—be it about pregnancy, daily life, or merely a pleasant whim or tiding—manifest a more personal estrangement.

"It falls to you to bear our dynasty," Isabel rasped to her firstborn, cringing at the thought of that falling to Juana. "That includes ruling these Aragonese."

◻ ◻ ◻

Late on August 23, Princess Isabel confessed, took communion, and went into labor, surrounded by her mother, midwives, and witnesses. After a night of agony, at noon the next day, the princess delivered a prince, and queen and princess delighted at his first cries. The kings were advised that the prince heir to the three Hispanic kingdoms had been born.

But Princess Isabel continued to bleed, hemorrhaging, and Isabel took her in her arms, beseeching the Lord to give her strength and bless her survival. Physicians hovered frantically, and the kings were notified that all was not well. Isabel felt the princess's strength and consciousness ebb and held more tightly, fearing the Lord might take her as He'd taken Juan. She begged Him not to. Fernando and Manoel were admitted to the birthing room. When the princess's breath grew faint, Isabel desperately promised her that, if death came, she would care for the prince as if her own son. When the princess gasped for breath, she prayed for her soul. Within the hour, Princess Isabel died.

Isabel wept wretchedly. Parents lost children daily, often at far younger ages, and she duly praised the Lord for the blessing of the life the princess had been granted. She beseeched Him not to take another child.

Fernando and Manoel were crushed. Fernando sent everyone away, and with only Manoel, the midwives, and the infant present, he wept together with Isabel, also holding his daughter's lifeless body. Manoel cried for his wife and cradled his son. Archbishop Cisneros entered briefly but had no explanation of the Lord's design.

That evening, Fernando emerged to instruct what happened next. The baby appeared slight, perhaps infirm, but all measures would be taken to ensure he survived to assume his three crowns in decades to come. Isabel retired to her own chambers in a stupor of grief and renewed fever, where she would remain for the next month, other than as ceremony demanded. Mourning commenced throughout the Hispanic Peninsula.

Bartolomé, Mayobanex, Guarionex, Enslavements and Imprisonments,
Summer 1498

In June, a few Spanish and native scouts were reconnoitering the high-land trail that led toward Mayobanex's hometown when they discovered the severed heads and cadavers of the Maguan and Ciguayan messengers. Enraged by the spurn, Bartolomé resolved to spare neither Mayobanex from capture nor Ciguayo from punishment as he hunted Guarionex.

Over the next week, his ninety Spaniards and native allies trekked inland to Mayobanex's hometown, burnt it to the ground, and took hundreds more Ciguayans captive. Mayobanex fled the invaders, accompanied by family, loyalists, and warriors, and Guarionex and family fled both the invaders and Ciguayans bent on handing him over. Ciguayo's mountainous rainforest provided countless caves, ravines, and inaccessible pinnacles for hiding.

Bartolomé's arduous hunt for the two chieftains tormented all over the ensuing month. His men wearied of tramping daily up and down thickly forested, insect-infested mountain trails, often in mist, and sleeping in commandeered bohíos, incessantly vigilant for attack and increasingly doubtful of the invasion's wisdom. Wherever they searched, Ciguayans were indentured to hunt, cook, port, and otherwise meet their individual wants. All Ciguayans feared reprisals and mass enslavement. Convinced resistance was futile, Mayobanex's vassal caciques dispatched search parties to apprehend Guarionex.

Guarionex and his family eluded both Spaniards and Ciguayans, surviving on roots and bark in unfarmed, unpopulated hinterlands. His slender frame drew gaunt, but his resolve didn't waver. Mayobanex and family retreated to a remote mountain crevice. He recognized his vassals no longer respected his decision to go to war and that many were deserting him. But he remained undaunted in his opposition to betraying Guarionex and succumbing to conquest.

Bartolomé grew anxious to retain his men's loyalty and avoid another rebellion. As June waned, he entertained their grievances and excused sixty from service in Ciguayo, permitting them to return to the homes they'd fashioned or envisioned in Fort Concepción or Santo Domingo and assuring that Ciguayan slaves soon would toil on everyone's behalf. He induced thirty to persist in the hunt, so assuring them and promising grand estates when Cristóbal returned. His men expected these assurances—their loyalty and hardship certainly merited as much Indian land and labor as Roldán's rebels had achieved. All perceived Indian land and enslavement as the natural fruits of conquest due them—like the estates, farms, and vineyards of infidel appropriated by Christian settlers during the Reconquista. Bartolomé was relieved, as he had no gold to reward them.

His command reduced, Bartolomé resorted to torture and trickery rather than attack, and scores of Ciguayans native to Mayobanex's hometown and elsewhere were brutalized to betray their chieftain's whereabouts. Two naborias eventually broke, revealing the crevice. At night, naked and smeared with the charcoal and black dye worn by Ciguayan warriors, Bartolomé and a dozen Spaniards trailed the two naborias to the site. Before dawn, they captured Mayobanex, a wife, and children, and Mayobanex was thrust at sword point to kneel at Bartolomé's feet.

"You are my prisoner, and you'll be delivered to the guamiquina for justice," Bartolomé brusquely admonished. He waited for translation, now provided by Cristóbal Rodríguez—nicknamed "La Lengua" ("the tongue") for his command of Indian speech—an Andalusian sailor, thereby more trustworthy than indentured Indian interpreters. "I wished to leave you and your subjects alone, but you have forsaken that. Tell me where Guarionex hides, and the guamiquina will consider that when he punishes you."

"I don't know where he hides," Mayobanex responded. "But I wouldn't tell you if I did."

Bartolomé's men kicked Mayobanex viciously.

"You should reconsider," Bartolomé retorted, hoping the pain and bruises would undercut the intransigence. He moderated his tone to bargain. "If you tell me, I shall spare your wife and children. If you don't, I'll enslave them, just as I've done with hundreds of your people."

"I will never answer to you or pale men," Mayobanex scorned, hiding his pain. He'd already weighed his honor, friendship with Guarionex, love for his family and people, and the fate of his soul.

Mayobanex was chained and his wife and children bound with rope. Exhausted from hunting Guarionex, Bartolomé let it be known that he might be willing to exchange imprisoned Ciguayans for him. In July, he and his soldiers marched Mayobanex, his family, and hundreds of Ciguayan captives over the coastal mountains to Fort Concepción. Mayobanex was jailed in a cell at the base of a blockhouse and his family and other captives corralled in pens in a clearing nearby.

Forced march of Indian slaves in Peru. Taken from Pieter van der Aa, 1706. The John Carter Brown Library, portion of rec. no. 08984-98.

Within days, one of Mayobanex's principal vassal caciques arrived at the fort with an entourage of nitaínos, intent on arranging an exchange. Bartolomé and Ballester met them, with La Lengua as translator.

"I come in peace, sorrowful for the recent war," the cacique declared. "If you release Mayobanex and those you imprison, my brethren Ciguayan caciques and I will submit to you and your caciques." He stared plainly into Bartolomé's eyes. "One of your captives is my wife, a cousin to Mayobanex. Others are her naborias and friends."

"Will you lead me to Guarionex?"

"I cannot. I don't know where he hides."

"The guamiquina will decide Mayobanex's fate. What do you offer me for your wife and her servants?"

"I will direct thousands of naborias to plant crops for your men," the cacique responded. "Your men will leave my villages and territory alone, and I will betray Guarionex if I discover his whereabouts. We have no gold."

Bartolomé accepted the offer, pleased to have secured peace and an additional food source for Cristóbal's loyalists, satisfied Ciguayo hadn't gold worth its conquest. Other Ciguayan caciques soon appeared at the fort, seeking release of their loved ones and subjects, as well as Mayobanex's wife and children, on similar terms. Bartolomé obliged. A cacique soon revealed a cavern where Guarionex then hid, and Bartolome's soldiers captured the chieftain there and hauled him and his family back to Fort Concepción.

Bartolomé summoned Cacique Diego to act as interpreter for Guarionex's chastisement, hoping Diego would assist in convincing Guarionex to reinstitute tribute payments of Magua's gold.

"Warn your brother-in-law that he'll be executed if gold tribute isn't restored," Bartolomé ordered. "All his subjects must understand the consequence of shirking it."

"I can threaten him so," Diego replied gingerly. "But he understands you didn't chase him for three months simply to kill him." He refrained from explaining that Guarionex no longer feared death, lest it be interpreted as a recommendation for murder. Nor did he protest that Maguans hadn't much gold left to give. Fishermen didn't expect impudence from their remoras. He suggested simply that practical, although doubting Guarionex's subjects would obey him. "I could ask him to plant and deliver cazabi, mahisi, and other crops, like you've agreed with the Ciguayans but in far greater quantity. More food would benefit both his subjects and your men."

Bartolomé's cheeks flushed with anger. "Warn as I command! Fear will drive your brother-in-law and his subjects to collect Magua's gold, and together we shall instill it. Also warn him that his wives and children will be enslaved."

For the second time within years, Guarionex was brought in chains to grovel at Bartolomé's feet. The men eyed each other with loathing, both cognizant that Bartolomé was a conqueror in need of assistance and Guarionex a conquered with no choice but to comply or be punished.

"How are you, Bakako?" Guarionex asked in Taíno, disdaining Bartolomé, Ballester, and La Lengua's presence. "How are my sister and nephew?"

Diego trembled, wary that a fisherman would distrust a remora befriending its prey. "We survive," he replied wanly.

Bartolomé had anticipated familial intercourse and showed no offense, hopeful it would thaw resistance.

"You've betrayed the king and queen, the Admiral, and—as you well know—me," he charged. "You merit death and your wives' enslavement, and I'll so counsel the Admiral when he returns. But if you collect Magua's gold, you can all be spared." He glared at Guarionex. "We do seek to live in harmony with your people, and you could still remain their ruler."

"I prefer execution to extorting tribute from my people," Guarionex retorted.

Bartolomé was impassive, resolved that he'd have to degrade the chieftain before threatening him again.

"So be it. Say goodbye to your wives and children. They'll tend my fort's gardens, cook my men's food, wash our clothes, and sweep our homes until you relent. You'll rot in prison. Tell a guard to inform me if you change your mind and wish to honor the promise for which I spared your life. Your king and queen await the gold tribute of their subjects."

Soldiers led Guarionex to the pens where—together with the remaining Ciguayans—his wives and children were held, and they tearfully parted. At the blockhouse, Diego promised to bring him cazabi when Ballester permitted. The soldiers chained him to the ground within the cell, side by side with Mayobanex, the dank, lowly space barely fitting them both. Guarionex was repulsed by the stench of piss and excrement and unnerved by the sight of Mayobanex's undressed bruises, still swollen. Worse, he rued his tormented flight to Ciguayo and return to incarceration in Magua. Incarceration without the flight would have spared others the horrors inflicted.

"I'm disgraced," he shamefully pleaded to his friend. "You've lost your chiefdom, wives, and subjects, simply on my behalf."

"But our souls remain unconquered."

CRISTÓBAL, PARIA, TERRESTRIAL PARADISE,
August 1–30, 1498

On the evening of July 31, Cristóbal's fleet arrived in bright moonlight off the southeastern tip of his Trinidad, which some of its native peoples called Cairiani. Villagers at the tip fled inland, terrified by the windblown stalk of alien hulks prowling their shoreline. With strong wind at his back and current pushing below, he directed the ships to jog cautiously west along the island's southern coast during the night, searching for a natural harbor with a stream. Successive villages were roused in alarm, and their residents joined the flight inland.

Unknown to Cristóbal, Cairiani was populated by a half-dozen tribes. Those along the southern coast were Arawaks, who shared an ancestry with the peoples of Haiti, Boriquén, Cuba, and Yamaye (Jamaica). Those on the northern were Carinepagoto, a Kalina (Mainland Caribe) tribe cousin to the Kalinago (Island Caribes) living on Caloucaera (Guadeloupe), Ouitoucoubouli (Dominica), and neighboring islands to the north. Like the peoples of Europe, Asia, and Africa, they lived in both peace and war among themselves and their mainland neighbors, often enslaved each other, and despite their differences, regularly traded food and goods among themselves. Both Arawak and Kalina tribes flourished on the mainland south of Cairiani, in the fertile alluvial plain of the great Yuyaparí River (the Orinoco, Venezuela). Kalina tribes predominated on the mainland extending west (Paria Peninsula, Venezuela). Languages and religions varied, and farther west along the mainland, ritual included human sacrifice.

At dawn's twilight, Cristóbal anchored the ships offshore a stream and village just deserted and dispatched crewmen ashore to replenish the ships' water (near Erin Point, Trinidad). He typically slept little while on the open sea, only rarely when sailing unknown coastal waters, never forgetting the *Santa María*'s midnight foundering on shoals during the first voyage. The exploration's first sleepless night had begun a strain on his eyes, but with the water restored, he burned to determine what he'd discovered. Where was he?

He was crestfallen that the village huts resembled those on Española—rather than Cathay's gold-roofed temples. But the huts' construction and cultivated farms indicated a civilization more refined than Española's, perhaps auguring that a greater civilization soon would appear. Gazing south, he spied another landmass on the horizon, and believing it an island, he named it Isla Sancta (Holy Isle).* He resumed coursing the ships west along Trinidad's coast, and by the next day, veered north at Trinidad's southwestern tip, riding a powerful tidal current through a strait between it and Isla Sancta, coming to anchor in the placid waters at the tip's lee (Icacos Point, Trinidad).

A large canoe bearing twenty-five islanders approached, and Cristóbal's sailors invited them aboard by clacking the brass pots they intended as gifts and dancing to a fife and tabor tune. The canoeists perceived a war dance and responded with a hail of arrows. The interpreters Pedro and Cristóbal couldn't understand the canoeists' tongue, and a return hail was dispatched over the canoeists' heads. But after cajoling, a friendly exchange of pots and other gifts was achieved. Another disappointment—the canoeists didn't appear oriental and their ruler obviously wasn't Cathay's Grand Khan. Another encouragement—they bore shields and wore some clothing, cotton scarfs like the Mudejar in Spain and loincloths, more advancements over Española's peoples.

Cristóbal remained at the anchorage for two nights, letting his men recuperate ashore. Disappointment again—the locals wouldn't meet, precluding discerning location from them. But the strait's fierce current and the moderate climate and temperature were intriguing clues. The mornings were cold, reaffirming his past observation that the earth's climate grew more temperate after passing 100 leagues west of the Azores, regardless of the equatorial latitude. The locals' skin color wasn't black like Guineans, who scorched under a blazing sun at the same latitude.

Before dawn on August 4, Cristóbal ordered the crews to weigh anchor for departure north toward another landmass punctuating the moonlit horizon, believing it also an island and naming it Isla de Gracia (Isle of Grace). Horrifically, at that moment, a great roar

---

* Actually Point Bombeador, Venezuela.

rumbled from the strait and an enormous white-capped wave hurdled through it toward the ships, which rose to great height as the wave came upon them. But at impact, the wave crested beneath them rather than crashing upon them. Cristóbal named the strait Boca de la Sierpe (Serpent's Mouth) for its peril. In his journal, he confided to Isabel and Fernando that God had been pleased to spare the ships. Yet the natural causes of the Boca's wave and current bewildered him.

By evening, the fleet anchored at Isla de Gracia,* whose latitude Cristóbal estimated at seven degrees north—the same latitude at which the torrid heat had tormented the ships after departing São Tiago. Regardless, the climate remained temperate. Astonishingly, another great strait with a furious current lay east, between the island and Trinidad. The cascade of Isla de Gracia's headlands west in the moonlight was serene, and Cristóbal resolved to take possession of the territory for Isabel and Fernando.

In the morning, he anchored a few leagues west offshore a substantial village, keen to conduct the formal possession ceremony before native witnesses.† Disappointment yet again—the villagers fled, leaving no witnesses for the ceremony, and he sailed on. The mystery of location mounted—the seawater grew fresher the farther west they coursed, soon resembling the brackish water of the Guadalquivir.

On August 6, his eyes bloodshot and vision impaired by lack of sleep, Cristóbal anchored the ships before a large village on Isla de Gracia where, finally, the locals didn't flee.‡ The interpreters Pedro and Cristóbal still couldn't converse with them, but a seaman brusquely dunked some canoeists to force a get-together. After gift-giving, word spread that the pale visitors came to trade in peace, and many villagers clambered aboard the ships. They called their land Paria.

Local witnesses abounding, Cristóbal commanded that Isla de Gracia be possessed for the sovereigns, and given his infirmity, he reluctantly dispatched Pedro de Terreros ashore to conduct the ceremony in his stead. Terreros duly recited in the villagers' presence that their lands were Fernando and Isabel's unless they objected. None

---

* Actually off Macuro, Paria Peninsula, Venezuela.
† Actually near Ensenada Yacua, Venezuela.
‡ Actually Güiria, Venezuela.

objected—not understanding a word or perceiving the ceremony as their conquest. In virgin camaraderie, Spanish truck was then traded for native guanín and cotton cloth, with Spanish wine and local brews enjoyed by all.

On August 8, just before heading west, Cristóbal took advantage of that camaraderie and ordered the abduction of six unsuspecting canoeists to serve as captive guides through the neighboring islands. The fleet soon anchored at another large village, and at last, fortune was found. The women wore pearl bracelets, the men necklaces and collars bearing guanín leaf and mirrors. Their hand signals intimated that the pearls came from oyster beds on Isla de Gracia's northern coast and that gold abounded to the west. Cristóbal bartered generously for the pearls, amassing nearly one hundred seventy, keen to deliver them to the sovereigns.

Two days later, he coursed his ships still farther west, searching for Isla de Gracia's western tip and the passage to the pearl beds on its northern shore and on to Española. Landmasses dotted the horizon to the south and west, indicating potential passage there, but not to the north, and in the evening, the fleet anchored off Isla de Gracia for yet another night.* Sounding leads indicated the sea had shallowed. The seawater had sweetened even further, and rainfall was frequent. The mystery of location darkened—was he sailing into an inlet's dead end? If so, he was improvidently risking further spoilage of the provisions meant for Española and delaying the voyagers' deployment in Española's gold mining.

Cristóbal dispatched the *Correo* and Captain Mateos to search for the elusive passage, and Mateos returned to report finding simply a gulf with four apparent river openings discharging a tremendous flow of fresh water.† There was no passage north. Cristóbal resisted the information, doubting so much water could flow from rivers, suspecting the openings were simply additional straits between islands. But he fleetingly recalled the words of Genesis—*a river went out of Eden to water the garden and then parted into four heads.*

On August 11, Cristóbal reluctantly determined the safest course was to backtrack rather than advance. Bartolomé could be dispatched later to locate and harvest the pearls and gold. He worried that Isabel and Fernando would disapprove of delaying that harvest, and in his

---

* Actually west of Point Alcatráz, Venezuela.
† Actually the four northwestern rivers in the Orinoco's delta.

journal, he reminded them that he'd already won them vast lands that are *an other world*. In moonlight, the ships sailed back east toward the northern strait they'd visited a week earlier, arriving the next evening.

At dawn on August 13, he and the other captains and their pilots evaluated the furious torrent of currents clashing in the strait, as large tidal bores rose and crashed on crags and shoals lurking within. The roar of the surf thundered about them, and visions of the great wave at the Boca de la Sierpe haunted them. Cristóbal named the strait the Boca del Drago (Dragon's Mouth).* He intuited that he might have been traversing a great enclosed gulf into which an enormous river gushed, and that the turbulence was the victory of the river water's outflow against the sea's inward opposition.

The crews grimly said their last prayers. By mid-morning, lacking wind but with the freshwater current dominating, the ships entered the strait, where they were buffeted and swirled to the brink of disaster. But fresh water and the Lord were pleased to deliver them without a scratch. All erupted to sing His praises, relishing their survival and looking forward to telling of their sail through the dragon's mouth.

Cristóbal veered the fleet west, intending to confirm that Isla de Gracia was an island and perhaps briefly chance on the pearl beds before turning northwest to Española. The wind and current west were formidable, the ships' pace brisk. Yet by the evening of August 14, the island's coastline still extended far west into the distance. There was no strait connecting to the gulf he'd departed.

With the ships safely at anchor† and his eyes inflamed and sight wavering, Cristóbal retired early to his cabin and sat alone in can-dlelight. His journal was spread before him on the bed stand, and a chest beneath his bunk held his maps and texts of the prophets, ancients, and learned men he'd once cited to prove the distance from Spain west to the Indies was short. While exhausted, he was consumed.

Isla de Gracia wasn't an island!

The explosive discharge of fresh water through the Dragon's Mouth, and the enormity of the expanse of fresh water within the gulf it constrained,‡ could only be explained by the presence of a massive

---

* Today called the Boca de la Serpiente and Bocas del Dragón.
† Offshore Morro de Chacopata, Venezuela.
‡ The Gulf of Paria.

river or rivers, the likes of which could be supported only by an enormous landmass. The conclusion was astonishing, altering mankind's understanding of the globe earth, begging explanation of how such landmass and its peoples had factored in mankind's history since Creation.

Cristóbal was enthralled. It was the conclusion he'd suspected and sought, and nearly as triumphant a discovery as the route to the Indies across the Ocean Sea. He'd sensed it for nearly a week but had been reluctant to claim it prematurely, shying from an assertion so fundamental and reigning his vanity. Awed, Cristóbal now penned it in his journal. *I have come to believe that this is a mighty continent which was hitherto unknown.*

He also expressed that the conclusion was supported by Esdras's teachings that six parts of the globe were land and only one water— foretelling that the other world he was traversing was full of land, not sea—and because Indians and Caribes previously had so told him.

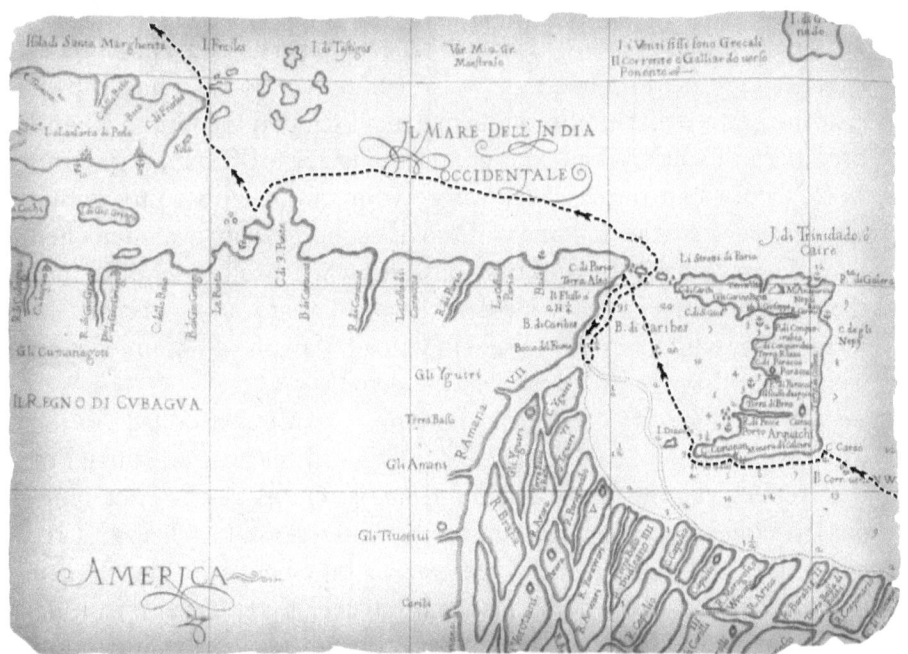

Portion of Sir Robert Dudley's map of the coast of Guiana showing the mouth of the Orinoco, Gulf of Paria, and Trinidad, 1661. The John Carter Brown Library, portion of rec. no. 08109-1. Marked for route through the Gulf of Paria.

◻ ◻ ◻

The next day, the ships weighed anchor and bore northwest toward Española's eastern tip, as Cristóbal expected the sea's current would push them further west toward New Isabela. Portside, three islands flanked the ships while departing Paria, and he named the largest Margarita—the word for *pearl* in Latin, marking where Bartolomé would return, and in memory of Prince Juan's widow.* But he didn't linger even briefly to reconnoiter the pearl beds. His premonition of Española's disorder, the supplies' spoilage, and his deteriorating eyesight now compelled ending the exploration. Unsatisfied, he also churned to better understand, justify, and articulate his momentous conclusion.

The ships plowed smartly, borne by strong wind and current north, and with the trajectory set, he again secluded in his cabin, pondering. How was a mighty continent consistent with the geographic theory upon which he'd based his career and learned precedent, and most fundamentally, the scriptures, which revealed all knowledge?

The continent readily fit within his geographic theory. For almost two decades, he'd argued that the Venetian Marco Polo had shown that the eastern extremities of terra firma included the Grand Khan's provinces of Cathay and Mangi and the island of Cipangu (Japan). Marco Polo had returned to Venice from the Khan's court sailing west by sea, so the landmass discovered necessarily was detached from terra firma, allowing that passage while itself extending into the southern hemisphere. He'd maintained that Cuba was part of terra firma, while everyone else—Indian and Spaniard—claimed it an island, but that disagreement was incidental.

As Margarita fell from the horizon, Cristóbal brooded on the four rivers Mateos had reported sighting and his hasty dismissal of that report, despite the words of Genesis. Genesis—the root Holy explanation of the world and universe—was irrefutably clear. At Creation, the Lord had planted the tree of knowledge in the Garden of Eden and watered the garden with a river that parted into four. Christians and others had sought for centuries to find the Terrestrial Paradise, and his chest of maps and learned authorities contained

---

* Margarita's indigenous name was Paraguachoa.

descriptions of it and theories of its location that he'd already read. As the day grew long, he opened the chest and immersed himself in reconsidering them.

The French cosmographer Cardinal Pierre d'Ailly (AD 1350–1420) had devoted chapters of his *Ymagio Mundi* (*Description of the World*, ca. 1410) to describing the world's great rivers and, central to that discussion, analyzed the identity and location of the four rivers flowing from the single river in the Terrestrial Paradise. The cardinal's theory, consistent with that of Bishop Isadore of Seville (ca. AD 560–636) and church doctrine, was that the river of Paradise was in the orient, separated by a large distance from the inhabited world. Paradise's ground was upon a mountain, high enough to have been untouched by the great flood survived only by Noah, and its airs were temperate. The four rivers flowing therefrom were none other than the Nile, the Ganges, the Euphrates, and the Tigris, which emerged on the earth in their respective locations, the water emanating underground from Paradise.

The popular writer John Mandeville had included in his *Travels* (first circulating 1356–1366) essentially the same information as the cardinal, albeit presented more engagingly. The water sank into the ground in the Terrestrial Paradise and ran many a mile underground to rise in distant lands. No living man, including mariners, could enter Paradise without the grace of God because of wild beasts, unpassable hills, dark places, strong currents, and noise so great communication was impossible. Those who'd so attempted had died.

At dusk, Cristóbal emerged from his cabin to preside over the watch the entire night and directed the ships to jog slowly, with most sails limp or furled. Yet his thoughts still raced, and the immensity of the starlit heavens and the ocean about him suggested revelation was at hand. What explained the moderation in climate and temperature, and the paling of skin color, that he'd observed at common latitudes crossing the sea westward? Was the temperateness of the mighty continent that of the Terrestrial Paradise? Had his ships risen with the globe to Paradise's height while crossing the sea?

When dawn emerged on August 16, he ordered full sail restored and returned below, exhausted yet frenzied. To his recollection, Aristotle, Ptolemy, Pliny (ca. AD 24–79), and the cardinal all held that the earth was round. Even the gossipy Mandeville hadn't deviated from that view. Yet none of them had visited the other world he was exploring or known of the differences in climate, temperature, and skin color. While the globe certainly was round in the hemisphere they knew, there was no reason it had to be round in this other world. Wouldn't the earth rise to the height of the Terrestrial Paradise, wherever it lay?

Sleepless, drained, yet enraptured by his speculations, Cristóbal resumed watch on deck that evening, and as he did regularly, estimated his compass needle's divergence from the polestar's true north, believing the nocturnal variance in that divergence was caused by the polestar's rotation in a small circle above the earth's pole. He'd been stunned that the variance he'd measured from dusk to dawn the previous night had been almost twice normal. Couldn't that variance be caused by the globe rising toward the Terrestrial Paradise, lifting the ships to be nearer the polestar? Wasn't the ships' rapid daylight progress to Española consistent with descent from a height?

Soon after dawn on August 17, Cristóbal descended to his cabin, wasted yet still animated, at the moment of revelation. His journal spread before him, he took stock. The continent had been an inescapable deduction and told of by Indians, subject to reconnoitering. The presence of the Terrestrial Paradise was conjectural. He hadn't seen it, and perhaps no man could. His theory that the earth wasn't entirely round bucked Ptolemy and all others, and he bitterly recalled the scorn heaped on him when his arguments contravened Ptolemy. Boldly, but shying from the last conclusion, he penned that in the continent discovered *there is the Terrestrial Paradise.*

□   □   □

Birds soon flocked the skies. Española was sighted in the moonlight on August 19, reaffirming the pilots' reverence for their Admiral's renowned seamanship. In the six weeks since they'd left the Cape Verde Islands, he'd dead reckoned—with compass, quadrant, and the heavens—a course traversing unexplored regions of the Ocean Sea, crisscrossed back and forth among unknown southern islands and landmasses in strong currents, then veered north to approach the southern coast of an island whose northern coast he'd departed for

Spain two years before. The Admiral's sense of location on the globe earth was extraordinary.

Cristóbal judged himself more harshly in the morning, when the ships anchored off Española. He recognized small islets he'd sighted on his return from exploring Cuba and was displeased that he'd underestimated the westward push of the current, as the anchorage lay 30 leagues downwind of New Isabela. Impatient, he dispatched the interpreter Pedro ashore to carry a note overland informing Bartolomé he'd made landfall at the islet he'd named Beata and to await his arrival.

During the day, when Indians visited the ships, his impatience turned to alarm. One of them bore a crossbow, its cord, bolt, and rack complete, with arrows in a sling. That evening, he was haunted by a vision of Caonabó's scornful refusal to submit to the sovereigns' rule. Contemplating the bow's once Christian bearer, in his journal he beseeched the Lord that nobody had died. As he lay to sleep, apprehension for Española drove his cosmographical theories from consciousness.

Unknown to him, Bartolomé was already sailing a caravel west, searching for three ships that reportedly had strayed. To his surprise, on August 21, the brothers united aboard the *Santa María de Guia* off Beata. They embraced blissfully. Cristóbal whispered that his sons remained in good health at court, and Bartolomé assured him that brother Diego so remained on Española. To those assembled on deck, Cristóbal triumphantly proclaimed that Isabel and Fernando continued to rule and had confirmed his authorities. He returned as their admiral, governor, and viceroy to settle Española on their behalf. Bartolomé heartily led a boisterous applause.

But both brothers recognized that a reckoning loomed. Cristóbal was startled by Bartolomé's soiled, tattered clothing and the crestfallen dart of his eyes, and Bartolomé was alarmed that Cristóbal could barely see, ambled stiffly, and struggled to stay alert, his fresher attire failing to mask his frailty. Cristóbal braced to learn which of his nightmares had borne true. He quickly secluded Bartolomé in the captain's quarters, both trembling to discuss the news of almost two years. Bartolomé's bluster faded abruptly, his face revealing humiliation.

"There's chaos," he blurted, his eyes tearing as he recounted the rebellion, the release of caciques from tribute, and Guarionex's incarceration. "I've failed you."

Cristóbal's cheeks flushed and his frame quaked with outrage. He'd expected dissent, factions, and decay among Spaniards, but not outright rebellion. He'd anticipated shirking and paltry delivery of gold tribute from Indians, but not outright abandonment.

"Who led this rebellion?" he cried.

"Your own supplicant, Francisco Roldán!" Seething, Bartolomé recounted Roldán's incitement of the rebellion, the futile settlement parleys, the gang's haven in Xaraguá, and the suborning of Carvajal's crews. Cristóbal listened contemptuously, wincing often, his fury tinged with sorrow at his brother's undoing.

"I've compiled an indictment against him," Bartolomé exhorted. "I recommend his beheading."

Cristóbal stared at the sea through a window, brooding darkly. He met adversity whenever he came ashore, and he rebuked himself for leaving his younger brother on the most treacherous shore for two years.

"You've done your utmost and suffered an inexcusable failure of support," he consoled, suppressing his own rage, tenderly caressing Bartolomé's shoulders. "The greatest travesty in this business is serving the sovereigns while their own subjects deceive and disobey them."

"Their greatest deception is that they claim I'm the disobedient one!" Bartolomé rasped.

"You did right in trying to settle with Roldán," Cristóbal soothed, unnerved by his brother's animosity, pondering whether there was another side to the story. "Now tell me of Guarionex."

"The savage renounced tribute on his own," Bartolomé vented. He reviewed Guarionex's desertion of Magua, the failure of gold tribute, the war with Mayobanex, and the capture and enslavement of Ciguayans and Guarionex's family. Guarionex's disloyalty affronted Cristóbal, but his anger was tempered by pride in his brother's mettle and bravery.

"I felt entitled to behead both chieftains," Bartolomé advised. "But I reserved that decision for you, as well."

"Did you punish the other caciques who've disavowed tribute?" Cristóbal pressed, keen to make an intimidating example of them.

"I didn't have sufficient men to do so. Tribute's renunciation has been pervasive," Bartolomé replied. "Those punishments are due, also for you to decide."

"What of the enslaved Ciguayans?" Cristóbal inquired, contemplating uses for those remaining.

"We've tasked them to build men's homes, hauls things about, and wash and cook. Some still survive in adequate condition, available to continue that or as you direct."

The brothers spoke long into the night. Bartolomé assured that the streambeds of the upper Jaina River and tributaries abounded with gold, but Carvajal's failure to arrive had precluded dispatching miners. Cristóbal related his discovery of the pearl beds and Terrestrial Paradise and promised to send Bartolomé to reconnoiter and exploit the territory within the month, which he suspected might also facilitate settling with Roldán. They discussed the construction of the new settlement by the Ozama River, which had progressed according to plan, and Cristóbal criticized Bartolomé for naming it Santo Domingo.

"It must be renamed New Isabela, as I promised the sovereigns," he chided.

"I think the name is sticking," Bartolomé replied steadfastly. "Many here have terrible memories of Old Isabela, and some believe it's haunted. I suspect that those who've starved here—certainly myself—care little to honor those who failed to resupply us."

Cristóbal clutched Bartolomé's head and laid it on his shoulder.

"My brother, calm yourself, as we have much to fix. We deserve riches, and I assure you we will fix in a manner that enriches us at last."

◻ ◻ ◻

In the morning, Cristóbal's fleet departed for Santo Domingo, fighting the prevailing easterly headwinds and current. He'd fallen asleep dreading that the survival of his enterprise depended on placating Roldán, quashing the rebellion, and restoring tribute, all before dispatching ships and reports back to the sovereigns. Yet he rose confidently, optimistic that the sovereigns' renewed support of his command, his presence, and his higher authority would cow Roldán and the rebels to the submission they'd denied Bartolomé and the Indians to resume honoring the tribute pledges they'd made directly to him.

These challenges could be addressed only ashore, and, relinquishing the ships' captaincy to Bartolomé, Cristóbal utilized the interlude at sea to compose his first letter to Isabel and Fernando reporting on the voyage. He intended that it summarize the triumphs won prior to arrival on Española and his final geographic conclusions. Reports of Española's crises would be held for later letters—hopefully after their cure. For over a week, he lay nights in his berth rather than standing watch, and his exhaustion was relieved. But his passions weren't, and his moods seesawed between bitterness, distrust, and premonitions of demise in one moment and confidence, righteousness, and premonitions of ascendancy the next. When he wrote, he envisioned himself in direct conversation with his queen and king.

The letter opened grandly—now his signature—hailing the Holy Trinity for moving both them and him to pursue their enterprise of the Indies, whose discovery Isaiah had prophesied. His first two voyages had proclaimed His name to innumerable peoples, including Española's, who would pay them tribute. Yet it then laced harangues of his sufferings, their counselors' short-sightedness, and the model patience displayed by other kings—regardless that the sovereigns themselves had devoted weeks to considering his proposals, generously reaffirmed his authorities, and might then expect simply a straightforward report. He'd endured years waiting for their approvals, defamed by critics and maligned by enemies. Great princes—such as Solomon and Alexander—needed time to augment their fame. The perseverant Portuguese had sacrificed gold and men before realizing success and even promoted the Faith regardless of temporal return.

Upon turning to business, the letter reported what had transpired following his departure from Spain through the exploration of the land of Gracia, highlighting the discovery of gold and pearls, excusing the exploration's curtailment, and marking the key evidence of temperature, climate, skin color, and the great river. He reviewed the established wisdom that the globe was spherical and the Terrestrial Paradise in the east and rendered his conclusions.

The hemisphere he was exploring *is as the half of a very round pear, which has a raised stalk, or like a woman's nipple on a round ball.* The Terrestrial Paradise *is at the summit where the stalk of the pear is and there is a gradual ascent to it.* If the great river wasn't from the Terrestrial Paradise, it originated *from an infinite land, lying to the south.*

Perhaps overwhelmed, Cristóbal omitted to expressly state a conclusion more mundane and obvious to a mariner yet dearly sought by his sovereigns—that the unknown lands he'd visited were theirs under the Tordesillas treaty. Closing emphatically, he swiped at Fonseca—albeit unnamed—for earning more than expended on the Indies, and he promised to dispatch Bartolomé promptly to explore what in his heart he believed was the Terrestrial Paradise.

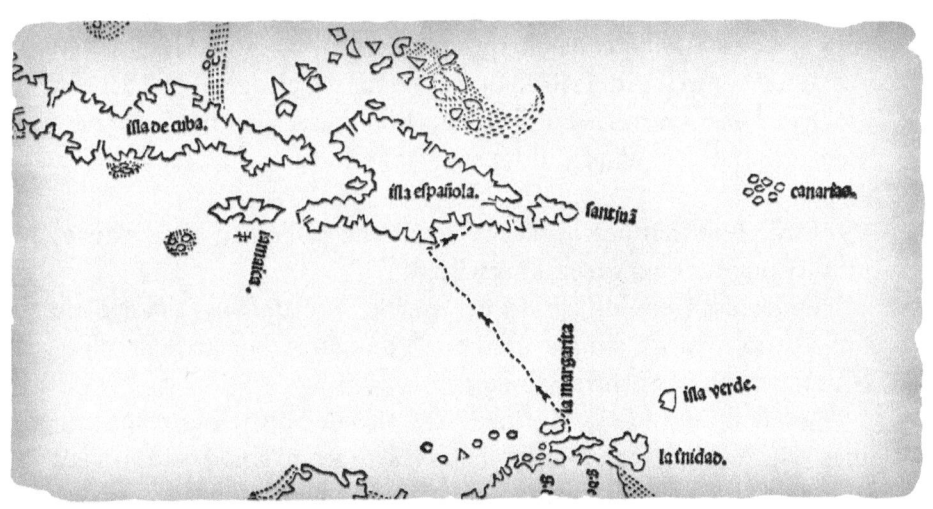

Portion of Peter Martyr d'Anghera's map of the Caribbean, 1511.
The John Carter Brown Library, portion of file 0232-1. Marked for
route from Margarita to Santo Domingo.

CRISTÓBAL AND ROLDÁN, AWARDS FOR THOSE DEPARTING,
August 31–October 18, 1498

Caciques residing on the coast had alerted Behecchio of the guamiquina's return, and at sunset, while Cristóbal sailed to Santo Domingo, Anacaona led Higueymota by the hand to her garden. They sat on duhos by the stream, gazing at the lilies.

Before speaking, Anacaona bittersweetly recalled being summoned as a young teenager, no more mature than Higueymota, to her uncle's caney and told that she would marry Caonabó to affirm alliance between Xaraguá and Caonabó's Maguana.* As it happened, the husband selected for her had been everything a girl could desire— regal, powerful, wise, and virile. Sadly, her daughter's wish for such a husband could no longer be fulfilled. The supreme Haitian caciques surviving weren't worthy of Higueymota's hand. Feigning affection for a crude intruder was vile and perilous.

"Your uncle expects the guamiquina will seek to reimpose tribute on us and perhaps inflict harsher punishment," Anacaona related. "We must understand whether Roldán will honor his pledge to protect us."

"Everyone knows you brought him here, Mother," Higueymota responded. "What did he say?" She lowered her eyes. "What happened?"

"I told him that he wasn't my equal and disdained his advances. But I let on you might feel otherwise."

Higueymota couldn't hide her startle. She quickly gleaned the conversation wasn't simply mother to daughter, but at Behecchio's request on behalf of their people.

"What should I feel, Mother?" she asked, caustic but respectful. Since the dancing ceremony, she'd shied from conversation with Roldán during chance encounters, gazing away deafly, snubbing his ogles and flattery. "What do you and Uncle want me to do?"

"Simply toy with him, smite his want, warm him to converse freely with you. Tease that you'll consent to his advances one day." Anacaona studied her daughter's reaction. Like herself, since

---

* *Encounters Unforeseen*, chapters I and III, discuss caciqual succession and Anacaona's marriage to Caonabó.

childhood Higueymota had always dreamed of a purpose and stature beyond marriage. "Without kindling suspicion, find out where he intends to go, whom he'll meet, what he plans."

"That won't be difficult," Higueymota scowled. "He fawns and leers at me, calling me his 'Indian princess.' When he clutches me, do you expect me to relent?" Higueymota shook her head. "Don't let Uncle wed me to him!"

"There's no cause for intimacy now," Anacaona assured. "You'll never be married to him, I promise." Anacaona drew her daughter's eyes to her own. "My child, you have the mettle for this. But never lose conviction of your rank and dignity, which are ennobled, not soiled, by serving our people. Remember, he is beneath you. You are neither his nor the pale men's 'Indian princess' but the proud bearer of Xaraguá's caciqual lineage and civilization. The day may come when spying on him requires intimacy, and you must be prepared both to stomach that and to poison him to death."

⊡   ⊡   ⊡

On August 31, in tow to their launches, Admiral Cristóbal Colón's ships floated upstream through the mouth and lower bay of the Ozama River to a bluff on its eastern bank where Santo Domingo had been founded, anchoring in a small cove beyond. He was moved that the settlement's first church, a wooden structure, beckoned prominently on the bluff. Bartolomé pointed to the family's forti- fied residence, set northeast to the church to overlook the cove, and explained that a royal warehouse lay inland to the church's south- east. Dungeons were to be constructed at the bluff's foot. Cristóbal spied Indian lookouts on the western bank, and Bartolomé related that the friendly *cacica* (Spanish for a woman cacique) who ruled the villages west of the river had agreed to supply cazabi, chicha, and other provisions in return for kindly treatment.

As he disembarked, Cristóbal was overcome with gratitude, as friends and loyalists jubilantly mobbed him, led by his younger brother Diego (b. ca. 1466), who'd presided at the settlement while Bartolomé warred and collected tribute. The two hugged dearly. The gentleman Pedro Fernández Coronel, whom he'd appointed cap- tain general of the two supply ships dispatched in February, bowed.

Cristóbal studied Coronel's expression for clues about the settlement's fate, trusting the man's judgment and loyalty as much as Carvajal's. "We must speak soon, my Admiral," Coronel advised plainly, without more.

The crowd, though enthusiastic, was smaller than Cristóbal had envisioned, even after discounting the absence of Roldán's rebels. He surmised that a portion of his command was either suffering from scabs, prejudiced against his Genoese heritage, or merely too disgruntled to honor him. But he maintained the optimistic demeanor of a governor. Those present were healthy and adequately nourished, undoubtedly having adapted to Indian food. With the welcomers trailing behind, brothers Diego and Bartolomé deferentially led him up a narrow path to the church, where he briefly knelt to honor the Holy Trinity for the safe passage from Spain, having lost neither ship nor man.

When he rose, Bartolomé introduced and praised two trusted officers, veterans of the past four years who'd directed the settlement's build-out—Miguel Díaz, of a respected Aragonese lineage, and Francisco de Garay, one of the crown notaries. Like Isabela, Santo Domingo had been laid out in the tradition of a Spanish town, with a central plaza set beyond the church and bordered by the fort and other crown buildings. The settlers' wood shacks emanated from there according to social rank. Díaz and Garay assured Cristóbal that the church soon would be rebuilt in stone and consecrated with the bell furnished by the queen five years before for Isabela's church. They proudly escorted him around the plaza, showed him the works in progress, and recommended the outskirts where the commoners arriving might live. A corral held some surviving Ciguayan slaves, who could be tasked to build shacks for the new arrivals.

Cristóbal was pleased and generously complimented Díaz and Garay for their accomplishment. But he was disquieted by the degree Christians and Indians commingled within the town. Some Spaniards appeared to have two or three Indian servants, and Indian women abounded among them, cooking meals before the shacks and undoubtedly residing there. Many were pregnant, some tending toddlers.

Cristóbal disputed the lack of an outer town wall and ditches to protect against Indian attack, but Bartolomé assured that the local

Indians didn't pose danger. He and the cacica had agreed their peoples should peacefully coexist, and bolstering that, Díaz and she cohabited occasionally. Embarrassed, Díaz related that he and others referred to her as Cacica Catalina, and that Catalina and her people could be trusted as friends, although he didn't mention that she carried his unborn child. Cristóbal hid his surprise.

At the tour's finale, Bartolomé and Diego escorted Cristóbal into the family's fortified compound, sentinel to the ships' anchorage on one side and bordering the plaza on the other. Like Cristóbal's former compound at Isabela, it was surrounded by its own defensive wall, guarding entrance from any hostile Indians, Spanish rebels, pirates, or simply thieves. The residence had ample space for servants, guards, weapons, and safeguarding gold, including a governor's room built for him. The walled area was much larger than at Isabela, encompassing a grassy patch for meetings, a garden, corrals for pigs and horses, and a chicken coop.

Cristóbal cringed as he opened the crate that stored the gold amassed for the crown during the past two years. Incredulous, he scanned a slip of parchment Bartolomé had scrawled with Roldán's indictment, strewn with invective. Yet undaunted, he took possession, directing that his chests of wardrobe and learned precedents, maps, and the book compiling his entitlements be brought from the flagship. The cache of Paria's pearls was easily stored with the gold.

At dawn the next day, he and Coronel met alone on the bluff overlooking the Ozama, observing Indian canoeists departing to fish.

"In your own words, what's happened here?" Cristobal asked, seeking an unvarnished account.

"Roldán and his men are guilty of treason, plain and simple, and they deserve the severest punishment," Coronel replied authoritatively. He'd previously served as chief constable of the second voyage and of Española (1493), and Cristóbal had promoted him to serve as a member of Española's ruling council during the Cuban exploration (1494). "While Bartolomé is extremely harsh, he did nothing to them that excuses a rebellion."

Cristóbal nodded, appreciating both the conclusion and the issue. "Why has Bartolomé failed to arrest and punish them?"

"Many of those not rebelling saw no reason to help Bartolomé punish those who did. They suspected the king and queen had given up on Española and doubted you'd return." Coronel frowned. "Some have perceived Roldán of equal rank to Bartolomé. Others have loathed assisting a foreigner, or at least Bartolomé, in confronting fellow Spaniards. The mood is foul. The men haven't been paid or found gold."

"Most of the ships must be sent back to Fonseca by month's end," Cristóbal related, "and they must berth at least two hundred veterans so the head count here is reduced to five hundred." His tone darkened. "I must also transmit reports of Española's progress. How can this rebellion be undone and the Indians' tribute restored before then?"

"Roldán demanded forgiveness and amnesty in return for obedience, but he never trusted Bartolomé's offer," Coronel observed. "The well is forever poisoned between those two. But rumor has it that he's sent notes to friends here intimating he would accept an offer from you."

"Pardon is too much," Cristóbal exhorted, appalled by the thought of excusing treason and certain the sovereigns would condemn such weakness. "I must investigate the rebellion myself—as if neutral between Roldán and Bartolomé—and dispatch the traitors home with a report for the king and queen's judgment."

"My Admiral, the traitors dread hanging in Spain. You must give them your unequivocal pardon," Coronel counseled. "I suspect few, if any, will sail without that, and many may not trust it."

Cristóbal scowled and stomped, entirely unreceptive to that advice.

"Caciques promised me tribute, and those reneging must dread harsh punishment!" he barked. "Which one most deserves to be made an example?"

"The Xaraguán caciques, but we don't have the wherewithal to punish them," Coronel responded. "Caciques in the Vega Real (Royal Plain) gave Roldán support earlier this year," he suggested, referring to Magua's great fertile valley. Yet he equivocated. "From their perspective, caciques may have believed Roldán was entitled to undo tribute."

Cristóbal glowered. He might be forced to consider absolving a Christian of treason, but he needn't excuse Indians for following that Christian's lead.

"Denying king and queen their tribute in conspiracy with rebels is a far cry from an inability to pay. It's grounds for enslavement!" he pronounced, disregarding Isabel's wishes.

He abruptly dismissed Coronel and sought solitude in the church. The rebellion had to be crushed at once or the sovereigns might replace him for incompetence. The unfilled gold crate would fail their expectations for Española's riches and inflame his critics, Paria's pearls notwithstanding. Even allowing for tribute's undoing, the crate had failed his own guarded premonitions. A slave trade was essential for Española's progress, and Isabel and Fernando at last would have to grasp and bless that.

◻   ◻   ◻

Within days, Carvajal, Terreros, and Colombo's ships finally reached Santo Domingo, and they reported to an incredulous Cristóbal and Coronel how Roldán had suborned freshly arrived voyagers.

"Roldán promises an easy life with servants and women, rather than the work and sacrifice of Christian enterprise," Colombo related. "Those weak and of little faith succumbed."

"I must lure or force every rebel to depart for Spain, ridding the island of all of them," Cristóbal declared after his anger subsided, now envisioning that as the best course of action. "How can that be accomplished?"

"Their hearts are torn," Carvajal replied. "They want to return to Spain free from prosecution, but they also relish lingering here in leisure and debauchery. Roldán believes he holds the winning hand, betting that you won't dispatch ships home without settling with him lest the king and queen perceive chaos. You must grant Roldán an unequivocal pardon, or he and most of his men will choose to remain debauching. I promised you'd reach out to him."

Carvajal gazed to Coronel, who nodded agreement.

"We can't overpower them?" Cristóbal pleaded.

Colombo shook his head, and the others followed.

"Pardon is unacceptable, a travesty of justice." Cristóbal glared at Carvajal and Coronel. "But I'm willing to make a grand gesture to convince them to quit the island. The men here have pined and whined to return home for years, especially the rebels. Hundreds can now be granted that wish." He eyed his lieutenants' faces, discerning doubt.

"I'll offer everyone free passage home, without pardon, and I'll entice them by giving them slaves to take home, awarded for their service and suffering here, be they loyal or rebel." His lieutenants' faces evinced consternation. "If enough rebels accept, the rebellion withers and justice remains the sovereigns' prerogative, as it should be. The slaves will be gathered from a cacique reneging tribute, warning all others."

"My Admiral, I fear any solution without pardon will fail," Carvajal counseled, Coronel concurring.

Cristóbal was silent for a time. Carvajal might be correct, but justice would be forsaken. He shook his head.

On September 12, Cristóbal publicly announced in Santo Domingo that any Christian who wished to go to Spain could sail on the ships departing at month's end, and that no one would be held on Española against their will. Each man returning home would be permitted to take a slave or two. He dispatched Bartolomé to Magua to gather fresh slaves for the hundreds of rebels and those loyal who'd undoubtedly clamor to sail, as well as the ships' crews. He also commenced gathering testimony about the rebellion to relay to the sovereigns.

Slaves rounded up. Taken from Theodore de Bry, 1595.
The John Carter Brown Library, portion of rec. no. 34724-5.

⬜ ⬜ ⬜

Cacique Diego fearfully entered the command headquarters at Fort Concepción and sat before Bartolomé and Ballester. Like most Taínos, he bathed daily, and the griminess and odor of his masters, who bathed infrequently, reminded him that brutality lurked.

"The Admiral will visit here within weeks and sends his love," Bartolomé announced coldly. "Before then, we require information."

Diego trembled, suspecting Guarionex's final punishment loomed.

"The Maguan caciques have evaded tribute, following your brother-in-law's example," Bartolomé charged. "Which of them is most guilty of aiding Roldán with food and servants?"

"Who abetted Roldán when he besieged this fort?" Ballester barked. "Whose womenfolk did he drag to Xaraguá? If he were to return, whom would he choose to overlord?"

Diego's thoughts churned, answers apparent, but their consequences to him and his family uncertain. Harm undoubtedly would befall anyone he identified, and they might seek vengeance. "You come to punish them?" he asked, biding time to think.

"To enslave them," Bartolomé replied.

"Roldán's men spent months along the trail northwest to Isabela, nearer the Yaque," Diego indicated, judging that Taínos in his own village were unlikely to have relatives or other ties there. "Some of the caciques there assisted him."

"Give us a name!" Ballester blustered.

Diego shrugged, his conscience pricking, his will to survive pricking harder. "I'm not sure."

Bartolomé raised a fist. "Try harder to remember. When the Admiral arrives, he'll judge the favors you've afforded Roldán—past and present."

Diego succumbed, averting his eyes in shame. "I've heard the cacique nearest the Yaque has fled to the mountains, fearful of Admiral's return."

Cristóbal's orders were fulfilled. During the next week, Bartolomé, horsemen, and foot soldiers surrounded the villages in the cacique's territory and announced that, as punishment for failure of tribute, the residents had the singular choice of submitting to slavery or their imminent massacre. Forlornly, the villagers—extended families of grandparents, parents, and children—submitted and were bound and towed on the trail to Santo Domingo. Mortified, Diego witnessed more than a thousand trudge past.

In Santo Domingo, eight hundred were chained in the holds of five caravels being provisioned to sail for Spain, the remainder imprisoned in Santo Domingo's slave corrals, together with the last of the Ciguayans. Each settler departing would be awarded at least one slave, some more, and two hundred were reserved for the ships' owners and captains. Many could be expected to die on the crossing, and the sailors might profit from any excess surviving. Cristóbal inspected the slaves, satisfied justice had been done and determined to convince his sovereigns that slavery would make their conquest profitable.

□   □   □

The public proclamation of free passage home, with a slave or two in tow, fell on deaf ears and roused anger among the rebels. Nearly a month had passed since the Admiral's return, and they'd yet to receive an overture of pardon from him.

Roldán fumed that Colón hadn't even dispatched him a personal note, much less a request to meet. His men argued daily over the demands they'd make and how pardon negotiations should proceed. One evening, he called an assembly to obtain his men's authorization to parley.

"Colón insults our station and ignores our grievances, dissembling strength," he declared. "But we shall call his bluff. I will ride with lieutenants to Bonao to initiate pardon discussions." Bonao was the inland fort closest to Santo Domingo.

"No one may receive a pardon unless all receive one," a second-voyage veteran admonished. "No one may sail home unless all so wishing sail." Murmurs reverberated that those who cut others from a deal would have their throats cut.

"Enslavement of the Maguans who harbored us is an outrage," another cried. "We released them from tribute, and they bowed to serve us. Colón can't steal them."

"Those Indians remain our maids and butlers, not his!" a third bellowed to a crescendo of cheers. "They're ours to claim whenever we wish."

"We promised to defend them from Colón," a fourth exclaimed, only to find himself ignored.

"I'll never trust his pardon," a third-voyage recruit protested. "We who've only just arrived can't depart so quickly. Colón will take his revenge on us after the ships sail."

"You swine are deserting us!" another new arrival shouted at Roldán. "You entreated us to join you and the savages merely weeks ago and now you quit, deserting us among them. You're not authorized to negotiate anything on my behalf." Threats curdled that new arrivals would testify to the veterans' treason and that the veterans ought to have their throats cut.

As the moon crested, Roldán uneasily concluded the fracas by consenting that a large group would accompany him to Bonao, representative of their disparate interests.

⊡   ⊡   ⊡

Word of the Maguan enslavements flew like the wind from village to village across Haiti, and just as the guamiquina intended, caciques and their subjects who'd reneged on tribute dreaded receiving the same punishment. Behecchio and Anacaona were shocked that the bondage exceeded that previously inflicted, which had been in response to resistance, not simply failure to pay homage. Anacaona also learned that concubines whispered that the squatters' leadership planned to confront the guamiquina or rejoin him.

Alarmed, Behecchio and Anacaona summoned Roldán to remind him of his promise. Roldán rode to the ballcourt, tethered his mount to a tree, and ambled out to bow before them and their nitaíno interpreter.

"What's Your Highnesses' pleasure?" he posed cockily, as if he didn't know.

"You must prepare to defend us," Behecchio demanded. "The guamiquina's enslavements revolt us. Don't expect to survive if you intend to permit that here."

"Your Highnesses, I'm as outraged by the enslavements as you are," Roldán professed. "I've never espoused such cruelty between our peoples, and I can assure you we will defend you from it."

"Your men must spill their own blood to do so," Behecchio pressed.

"It won't come to that, Your Highness," Roldán answered blithely, eluding an affirmation. "The guamiquina will never attempt to enter Xaraguá. He knows he cannot prevail over me. You'll suffer neither tribute nor punishment."

"We hear you and others soon depart to parley with him." Glaring meanly, Behecchio spread his arms. "To what end?"

Roldán hesitated, aware his followers' servants and concubines were neither content nor loyal, pondering whether the Indian king and queen had notice of his true intent. "Your Highnesses, we seek to defend ourselves, yourselves, and our mutual presence here."

"Will those you take to meet the guamiquina return here?" Anacaona asked. "Or will some desert to him?"

"My Anacaona, my men's love for me and Xaraguá shall hold steadfast, just as my love for you."

Behecchio gave up. He upbraided Roldán that mistreatment of villagers had grown worse. Roldán swore it would improve. Anacaona promised a festive ceremony celebrating independence from the guamiquina—if the parley achieved that. With another bow, Roldán tersely bid them farewell, departing for his village.

But he was surprised and delighted to discover Higueymota studying his mount, stroking its forehead. For the first time, she smiled at him gayly.

"Where are you going?" she asked.

"Home to my village, my Indian princess. Would you like to come?" he answered in the Taíno he'd learned. "My caney is grand."

She smirked and shook her head in coy refusal. "When will you return?"

"Soon, I hope. But first I'll meet the guamiquina, to protect you."

"I was sad to hear you might depart for your homeland," she replied softly, studying his lips and eyes for the slightest flicker or twitch. "Perhaps you could teach me to ride when you return." He grinned and nodded, but no flirtation followed.

◻ ◻ ◻

In early September, across the Ocean Sea, grandparents Isabel and Fernando witnessed the baptism of Princess Isabel's son Miguel in a church chapel dedicated to Saint Miguel, who'd thrown Satan from Heaven. The grandparents were appointed the child's guardians, and later that month, Aragón's noblemen confirmed Miguel as Fernando's lawful heir, pledging to obey the boy at maturity. But the tragedy of the princess's death hadn't inhibited the nobility's cautions and jealousies, and their recognition was provisional, to be undone if Fernando thereafter had a lawful son by a later wife.

Manoel saw that Isabel was best fit to raise his child, and he didn't oppose the grandparents' guardianship. No longer a prince of Castile, never one of Aragón, he sadly departed for Portugal to prepare his countrymen to recognize Miguel as his kingdom's heir.

By the end of September, Isabel's fevers had subsided, and while only half herself, she resolutely assumed Miguel's daily care, just as she'd cared for Princess Isabel, Prince Juan, and her other three children. In mid-October, she, Fernando, and daughters María and Catalina departed with the court for Ocaña, where Castile's noblemen would be summoned to swear Miguel's recognition. All wore mourning black, including the horses, mules, and donkeys.

Fernando and Isabel rode side by side, he on his steed, she in a carriage with Miguel cradled in her lap, husband and wife united in rule and grief, stupefied that defeat now arrived more often than triumph. The union of the entire peninsula rested on one very delicate heartbeat. Each understood that the nobility of the other's kingdom offered homage and respect but not trust or love. Spain remained but a word.

◻ ◻ ◻

By September 24, Cristóbal somberly acknowledged that his proclamation wouldn't rid him of Roldán's rebellion. Three hundred of Española's four hundred nominally loyal veterans clamored to berth on the five ships—but not one of the one hundred–plus rebels. He prayed often at the church, and from the bluff, he monitored the provisioning of the five ships, as well as three caravels being equipped for Bartolomé's exploration of Paria. The eight hundred slaves aboard starved for water and food beyond that provisioned and gasped for air in the stifling heat below deck. As the month waned, death by thirst and suffocation struck and accelerated, and corpses were unloaded to be thrown into the sea daily.

Cristóbal despaired that Roldán held the better hand, and on learning that rebel leaders had amassed in Bonao, he dispatched Ballester to meet them and offer a pardon, good treatment, and a promise to forget their errors in letters to the sovereigns. But Ballester's reception was acrid. Roldán refused to negotiate with him, demanding to parley with the gentleman Carvajal instead, and sent him back to Santo Domingo with a message for Cristóbal.

"Advise the Admiral that he must release to us all the slaves he's holding," Roldán dictated. "Those slaves are ours, under our authority and protection, and the Admiral has no claim to enslave them."

Cristóbal refused to entertain that demand. But he dispatched Carvajal back with Ballester, the urgency of the ships' passage mounting as the head count of the slave cargo diminished.

"All of us have come to Española to serve God, Isabel, and Fernando," Carvajal proclaimed to the rebel leadership, attempting grand magnanimity. "Our differences pale against this service, which unites us gloriously. The Admiral offers to pardon all, both those boarding the ships and those remaining. Come kiss his hand in Santo Domingo, and all will be forgiven and forgotten before he reports to the king and queen. The ships are stowed, their sails set to unfurl to bear you home. But they cannot be delayed further."

"What of our slaves?" Roldán barked, affronted his demand was ignored.

"The Indians are the Admiral's captives, to be awarded as he alone sees fit," Carvajal responded firmly. "They'll be hauled to Spain, awarded only to those returning home, including yourselves. If you depart, you may share in them. You can sell them in Spain or keep them for your households."

The rebels quarreled among themselves, most desperate that the window for returning home was closing. Sensing his hand fully played, Roldán vouched that he was convinced the Admiral's pardon could be trusted at last. He, Múxica, and Escobar would ride to kiss Colón's hand on everyone's behalf.

Unity in that trust blossomed in the afternoon, and distrust thereof reemerged by the evening. Colón hadn't even granted safe-conduct to parley. On October 16, as Roldán, Múxica, and Escobar mounted their horses to ride to Santo Domingo, their own gang restrained them, insisting a kiss was hardly sufficient. Colón's pardon had to be in a writing that expressly applied to all.

As rebel harangued rebel, Ballester wearily scrawled a note to Cristóbal, warning that he'd be endangered by failing to agree to whatever they next demanded, as most other men on the island—particularly the common born—couldn't be mustered in his support and would stand for Roldán. But no such demand was delivered, as Roldán's gang couldn't trust themselves.

On October 17, with an agreement on pardon tortuously elu-sive, Roldán, Múxica, and Escobar wrote to Cristóbal that the rebels would no longer serve him and renouncing their salaries. There were now to be two independent Spanish governments on the island, mutually hostile.

◻   ◻   ◻

By mid-October, death hourly depleted the ships' slave cargo, and waiting for the parley's outcome, Cristóbal had concluded he couldn't delay dispatch further. He'd feared the negotiations might fail—just as he'd feared that tacks might fail their mark countless times in storms at sea—and he steeled himself to compose a report to Isabel and Fernando revealing the situation. Like a storm, the rebel-lion wasn't spent, and setting the next tack was the only course.

Cristóbal wrote that Roldán and the traitors had rebelled against his authority, plundering violently, taking Indian men's wives and daughters, and perpetrating other crimes. They now mistreated the entire western part of the island. He'd attempted—and was still attempting—to settle with Roldán, even taking evidence of the rebels' grievances for the sovereigns' review, and his goal remained a peaceful resolution. To that end, he implored that the sovereigns send churchmen—who were needed more to restore the settlers' faith than

convert Indians—and a justice to impose order. But if peaceful resolution failed, he would have to seek to destroy the rebels. More men
were necessary to restore order and settle Paria.

Cristóbal assured Isabel and Fernando that Española was
already straightening out and proposed that exportation of Indian
slaves and brazilwood be the cornerstone of its financing. Four
thousand slaves could be exported annually, yielding twenty million maravedís, as well as four thousand quintals of brazilwood,
yielding another twenty million, dwarfing the related expenses of
six million maravedís.* Settlers could be given slaves to labor for a
year or two, reducing or eliminating the salaries the crown otherwise owed them, and the slaves could then be transported for sale in
Castile, the profit inuring to the settlers. The Indians enslaved would
stop dying at high rates on the ocean transport, decreased mortality
having been achieved over time with Guinean and Canarian slave
shipments, improving revenues.

Before dawn on October 18, Cristóbal boarded the *Santa María
de Guia* and entrusted cousin Colombo—now captain general of the
return fleet—with his letters, including his announcement of the Terrestrial Paradise, his voyage journal, a map depicting Paria's exploration, samples of brazilwood, and the light crate with pearls and gold,
all to be delivered directly to the sovereigns. Rebels' letters home had
trickled aboard as well, some charging that the Genoese brothers had
unjustly whipped and hung Spaniards.

Cristóbal briefly bid goodbye and thanked those of the three
hundred Spaniards who'd served him truly for years. He understood their dreams of gold hadn't been realized and that life had
been harsh. He hoped the slaves provided partial compensation for
that suffering.

As the crews weighed anchor, Cristóbal ascended to the church
to watch the ships drift down the Ozama and to pray, desperate
for divine guidance and support. Over the past week, most settlers
remaining at his command, particularly seamen who'd served on
prior voyages and the gentlemen, had vouched willingness to assist
in arresting Roldán. But many of them were infirm, timid, or shifty.
Cristóbal beseeched the Holy Trinity to vanquish Satan from the

---

* One quintal represented one hundred pounds.

rebels' side, humbled himself to reach out to his enemy, and prayed for his enemy's entrapment.

As the sun rose, the five ships entered the sea, crammed—far beyond typical or prudent—with Spaniards and Taínos, homeward and slavery bound.

Settlement, More Awards,
October 19–November 1498

My dear friend, Cristóbal wrote the next night, composing his first letter to Roldán. You were the first nonkindred person I sought on my return, having held you in *total confidence.* I was surprised when you didn't come to account to me, as normal and honorable, a *safe-conduct being unnecessary.* I delayed departure of the ships for eighteen days so you and your followers could return to Spain, and *I would have detained them longer except the Indian slaves aboard were very costly and dying.* I've always praised your services to the king and queen, but now the ships will bear opposite tidings. *Consider what can be done and let me know.*

Roldán grimaced when he read it. It contained no offer. It fawned. Colón had plotted Caonabó's abduction during a parley. Roldán refused to meet without the safe-conduct.

Entrapment failed, Cristóbal wanly granted one, conceding there had been differences between Roldán and Bartolomé. He needed to hear Roldán's view to settle the matter in a manner that served their highnesses.

By October's end, Roldán and his lieutenants, including Múxica, Escobar, and Pedro de Riquelme, traveled to meet Cristóbal, Carvajal, and Ballester in Santo Domingo's nascent central plaza, accompanied by a contingent of rebels porting muskets and crossbows. Cristóbal's loyalists lined the plaza, similarly armed. Bartolomé wasn't invited.

Cristóbal stood formally to receive the rebels' entrance, as if they visited as supplicants in a governor's audience. His silk camise and gem-studded jerkin heralded his nobility and the authority granted by the king and queen. A few of Roldán's followers trembled as they approached, the falsity of their sovereign loyalty self-evident, the treachery of their treason transparent. Cristóbal neither offered his hand to be kissed nor expected it. Instead, he simply beckoned Roldán to come before him.

Roldán hadn't the attire to match. But he comported himself as the royal magistrate, and his demeanor compensated, a haughty gait and brazen smirk proclaiming the superior strength of his following. Most of his men weren't cowed and ambled pugnaciously at his side, hailing their friends among Cristóbal's loyalists, reminding that all there were Spaniards save one. Some boasted of having taken a better course, inviting camaraderie and subornation. Yet the wood and stone buildings under construction about them evoked memories of family and Spain, and they all wished to reclaim the right to live there.

Benches were brought forward, and the leaders sat face-to-face, Cristóbal and Roldán head-on, other loyalists circling behind. Cristóbal studied Roldán's sunburnt, windblown face and judged that five years upon Española had crusted his skin and soul as much as they had Bartolomé's.

"Tell me your grievances and wishes," he bid.

"My Admiral, the time for listing grievances and wishes has passed," Roldán replied curtly. "Most Spaniards living here—whether with me or you—have found life under your brother's rule intolerable. We shall now propose the terms of reconciliation." Roldán studied Cristóbal's bloodshot eyes and bloated calves and relished that his physical decline underscored his authority's demise. "But I will oblige and briefly recount Bartolomé's transgressions."

Cristóbal listened patiently as Roldán succinctly stated his accusations. While physically unharmed, Roldán had been unlawfully stripped of his office. Without authority, Bartolomé had unlawfully and cruelly punished Spaniards, unjustly favored those who supported him with both provisions and access to mine gold, and mismanaged the settlement, including the Indians. Ignoring the ships just departed, Roldán demanded passage to Spain for himself and most of his men on ones newly equipped.

"I'm prepared to provision two more caravels for your men's departure," Cristóbal proposed bittersweetly, keen to rid the islands of all rebels yet pained to delay Paria's exploration. "Your men must depart promptly and refrain from enticing others to your side."

"Closure is due on what has transpired," Roldán countered. "You must decree that my men and I have faithfully served the king and queen and admit that our disobedience to your brother was justified. We demand your confirmation that we're entitled to wages for the entire duration of the disobedience. You must grant my men embarking slaves, commensurate with the grants made to your men just departed."

"Other than slaves, these demands are preposterous," Cristóbal responded, just as gruffly. "I'm willing to grant an amnesty, but only subject to Their Highnesses' review of the evidence. It's their prerogative to decide whether you deserve wages while disobedient."

While civil, the parley at Santo Domingo ended quickly without concord, and Roldán and his lieutenants returned to Bonao to discuss Cristóbal's perspective with their followers.

⊡   ⊡   ⊡

In Xaraguá, scouts reported to Behecchio and Anacaona about the five ships' departure and the pale men's gatherings in Bonao and Santo Domingo. Undoubtedly, none of the Maguans abducted would ever return to relate the horror of their fate. Nothing could be gleaned from the gatherings except that the guamiquina and Roldán had parted opponents but not ceased parleying.

Yet there was surprising information. While not a single squatter had departed Xaraguá, the ships had removed hundreds of other pale men from Haiti—more men than all those who'd arrived on ships that year. On his return, the quamiquina had reduced the pale men's presence in Haiti rather than enlarging it.

"I surmise good," Behecchio observed. "The guamiquina's command shrinks, perhaps also his ambitions. Roldán's strength surges in comparison. The two remain enemies, so Roldán needs our haven and has reason to defend us."

"I don't share that optimism," Anacaona rejoined softly. "Roldán promised the Maguan caciques he'd defend them, just as he promised us. No longer needing them, he abandoned them to slavery. The guamiquina perseveres, and Roldán and his lieutenants still linger to talk to him."

"I see that," Behecchio conceded. "But we've always recognized that Roldán might make peace with the guamiquina and forsake us. That hasn't happened yet, and the guamiquina has fewer soldiers to invade Xaraguá."

"Behecchio, there is much we don't understand," Anacaona warned. "The concubines whisper that the squatters may yet depart for their homeland. We'll then revert to confronting the guamiquina alone. Higueymota reports that Roldán doesn't woo as if he'll be here for long."

Grimly, brother and sister stared into each other's eyes, vexed they hadn't learned enough, resigned to wait impotently for the pale men's next move.

◻ ◻ ◻

In Bonao, the rebels were entirely unsympathetic to Roldan's depiction of Cristóbal's perspective, and they united upon delivering Cristóbal a rehash and embellishment of bald demands. In Santo Domingo, Cristóbal furiously rejected them. He'd never recite that he or Bartolomé had done wrong or that the rebels' disobedience had been justified.

But on November 10, he grittily dispatched Carvajal to Fort Concepción to nail a proclamation of amnesty on its door. Those presenting themselves could return to the Catholic Monarchs' service as if nothing had happened and obtain free passage home with an order approving payment of past wages. Those failing to present would be prosecuted.

In rude reply, the rebels mocked Cristóbal's retreat and the proclamation. It was Cristóbal who needed a pardon, from them. Tempers on both sides flared. Nevertheless, Carvajal and Roldán negotiated on, arguing over amnesty, wages, and slaves, and Roldán sought consensus among his gang. All expected a slave award—Cristóbal had so agreed already—yet a heartfelt angst rose during one of their endless assemblies.

"I must bring my mate home," a younger rebel declared. "She bears my child, and I plan to marry her in my church. She must be given passage, along with the slaves to which I'm entitled."

"My woman also must sail, in addition to the slaves due me," an older rebel demanded. "She shall come as a servant, as I'm already married."

Roldán mused what condemnation awaited these men and their concubines in Spain. But he doubted Cristóbal would oppose such requests—subject to the ships' capacity—so long as the men departed.

"We shall demand that," he agreed. Many applauded, glad their lust or affection might be accommodated.

"I have children with my mate, and I want to take them too," a third rebel announced. Many others seconded the request.

"We shall insist on that, too, and Colón should accommodate," Roldán assured, although his concern for the clergy's censure rose. To his surprise, opposition came from within.

"I object! I'm not taking the wenches I've mounted or the bastards born," another rebel exclaimed. "There's not enough room on two caravels for everyone's frolics, and I'm not giving up slaves so others' wenches and bastards can berth." Cheers rose from those similarly inclined and jealous.

"We shall demand that slave awards not suffer from these personal dispensations," Roldán responded uneasily, uncertain how so many passengers could be crammed aboard.

"The pardon must also proclaim that my children are freemen, not slaves," the third rebel insisted.

There was silence, some perceiving that the issue loomed beyond both Roldán and Cristóbal's ken and authority, lying likely within the church's or the sovereigns' control, or perhaps dictated by some law or precept. But there was applause, and none objected.

"We shall demand that too," Roldán replied.

Within a week, with Cristóbal's desperate approval, Carvajal and Roldán compiled an agreement setting forth the rebels' and Cristóbal's promises, to be executed first by Roldán at Fort Concepción and, within days, by Cristóbal in Santo Domingo. Roldán signed on November 16, agreeing not to suborn more rebels and that he and his company would embark for Castile within fifty days of the Admiral's signature, so long as the slave distribution was duly berthed aboard the ships. Cristóbal signed on November 21, promising he'd deliver two properly manned and provisioned ships to the port of Xaraguá, the innermost bay of Haiti's western gulf, since many rebels now lived nearby and—as Behecchio maintained his coastal residence there—Indian food and labor for provisioning the ships would be plentiful (Bay of Port-au-Prince, Port-au-Prince). He would also prepare a letter to the sovereigns attesting to Roldan's followers' good service and authorize payment of wages up to the date of sailing. Rebels choosing not to return to Spain would be given safe-conduct to collect their wages. Those concubines who were pregnant or had birthed children could be berthed in place of slaves. Children could accompany and would be free.

After executing the agreement, Cristóbal sat alone at the church for hours, trembling that his enemies at court would scorn his weakness for the concessions he'd tolerated and poison the sovereigns' favor. He recalled the trials other prophets and messengers had suffered in the Lord's service, conceiving that his own struggle to persuade the court of the Indies' glory was no less than Moses's to convince Israel's children of the Promised Land. But he was resolute that, despite the humiliating terms, the rebellion's elimination did allow tribute's reinstatement and gold mining's expansion, thereby opening the path to Española's viability.

The next morning, he ordered Bartolomé to refit two of the caravels set for Paria's exploration for the rebels' ocean crossing, optimistic that, in fifty days, he'd no longer have to contend with Roldán or rebellion.

⊡   ⊡   ⊡

Across the ocean, Isabel and Fernando arrived in Ocaña on November 19, their court having lumbered slowly from Zaragoza. They'd rested often en route, sometimes in small towns, mindful of Isabel's illness and baby Miguel's frailty. As always, wherever they stopped, messengers from throughout their kingdoms arrived to keep them informed, and the news during October and November was mostly good.

In Castile, Archbishop Cisneros had successfully concluded a synod adopting reforms of the clergy, dear to Isabel's heart. Priests were to live in their parishes, banish their concubines, celebrate Mass and teach children on Sundays without fail, keep baptismal records, and note those failing to confess on Easter. From Burgundy, Isabel and Fernando's ambassador reported that Juana had given birth to her first child, a girl named Leonor, and mother and babe were healthy. Yet by November's end, to Isabel's distress, Juana hadn't taken the time to send a private tiding.

There was no news from the Indies, and Isabel and Fernando wondered what new territory their admiral had possessed, if any. They also yearned guardedly for confirmation that he'd succeeded in reinvigorating Española according to their wishes and commenced shipping the gold mined and rendered in tribute.

□   □   □

Following execution of the settlement agreement, the rebels departed Fort Concepción for Xaraguá.

As he rode through fertile valleys, Roldán delighted that he'd outwitted the Genoese brothers and, within months, would dine at home in Spain with his wife and daughter. Coursing mountains, he plotted the riches he'd loot from Indians during his last weeks on Española, the final plunder of his five-year adventure. Traversing desert, he schemed how best to translate his rank as chief magistrate of Española into an appointment in a Castilian ministry, raising his station to that of a gentleman.

Yet, as he entered Xaraguá, it struck him that the countryside he passed was every bit as beautiful as Spain. On arriving at the village he ruled, he was gratified Indians cowed in fear and that his pretty concubines stood obedient to prepare him meals and lie before him. He recognized his gang of Spaniards in Xaraguá was more numerous than any unit of men he might command in Spain and that a liaison with Higueymota could make him king of far more. The daydream of advancement in Spain was as much a delusion now as when he'd enlisted.

He resolved he wouldn't trust Colón to honor the agreement until he saw the ships anchored in Xaraguá's port. The peace and tolerance of Xaraguáns had to be preserved at least through that moment—and indefinitely if Colón reneged or rebels chose to remain. Rather than resting in his village, he rode on to inform Behecchio and Anacaona of what could transpire, seeking a safe transition for both departure and continued squatting. When he arrived at the ballcourt, he awaited their audience and bowed when they entered, as if deferentially.

"Your Highnesses, I come to report that I and others may depart for our homeland within weeks," he declared, eyeing whether Behecchio revealed joy or fear as a nitaíno translated.

"Is departure your wish or the guamiquina's demand?" Behecchio asked coldly, revealing only surprise and contempt for the pale man's habitual duplicity. "Have you defended us? Has the guamiquina assured that Xaraguá will remain untouched and free from tribute, whether you depart or not?"

"I have told him tribute no longer is due here," Roldán replied plainly, ignoring a full response.

"Has he assured that he won't enslave Xaraguáns?" Anacaona demanded.

"My Anacaona, as you know, I've always opposed enslavements."

Displeased by the evasions, Behecchio folded his arms on his chest and Anacaona grimaced, awaiting more information.

"Your Highnesses, I've enjoyed your friendship immensely," Roldán puffed on. "Some of us may remain." All three understood insufficient squatter head count invited assassination. "In fact, many of us may remain, myself included."

"Our relationship hasn't flourished as we hoped," Behecchio declared, pondering carefully. Roldán's command, grit, and hunger for authority were core to the squatters' break from the quamiquina, and the gambit for their alliance against the guamiquina likely would fail if Roldán himself departed—rendering pointless the harboring of any squatters thereafter. "If you depart, take all of your men."

"Francisco, when will you decide for yourself?" Anacaona pressed, both pining for the riddance of every squatter and fearful for the loss of their alliance.

"Soon, my Anacaona. The guamiquina will provide two vessels, arriving shortly in the bay where you maintain your coastal residence."

"What will happen to the women who live with your men?"

"Some may wish to depart with their men to Spain."

⊡   ⊡   ⊡

Behecchio summoned a council of his principal vassal caciques to review the unremitting stagger of the pale men's invasion, and

Anacaona reinvited wives to her garden. The news that squatters would depart brought hope and relief despite the threat of a hostile guamiquina. A crescendo of plunder had commenced, as pale men stomped in bands from village to village to loot gold jewelry, tear gold pieces from venerated face masks, and seize amulets, feather crowns, and other trophies.

"What of the concubines?" Anacaona asked the wives.

"There's fright and chaos in my village," the prominent wife reported. "One cries that she'll be dragged off by her man, as if an amulet or feather crown. Another fears being abandoned. My daughters have fled to the mountains lest they be abducted."

"The women marked to depart are terrified," the youngest explained. "They dread being friendless in a strange land, forever losing their families here."

"Even those who want to please the pale men are distraught," the eldest related. "They fear abandonment in the pale men's homeland when the men's desire wanes or the children are grown."

"What of the children?"

"Some pale men see themselves in their offspring and will take them," the prominent wife surmised. "Others don't and will discard mother and child."

"Have most pale men chosen to depart?" Anacaona pushed.

The wives shrugged.

"Many haven't said, perhaps trickery, perhaps undecided," the eldest wife responded. "But if most depart, it may be safe to eliminate the few remaining."

CONFIDENCE LOST, ISABEL AND FERNANDO'S COURT,
December 1498–March 1499

In early December, a cold fog shrouded the five ships as they anchored in Cádiz's harbor. The joy and excitement of the three hundred Spaniards aboard pierced the gloom, and they disembarked jubilantly to return to their families and homes, mostly in Andalusia and Extremadura. The fog befitted the fate of the mere three hundred Taínos surviving, as they vanished into it as slave property, divvied among masters and bound for either the masters' homes or sale in slave markets. With minor exception, their existence thereafter would be ignored in history recorded. They desperately prayed they'd elude the pale men's diseases that—together with hunger, crowding, and suffocation—had stricken in two months the five hundred others, whose corpses had been dumped overboard. Briefly, the roadways and ferries from Cádiz north to Sanlúcar de Barrameda and Seville and west to Huelva and Palos bulged with the masters' and slaves' migration, which would trickle farther into Spain.

Masters conferred Christian names on their slaves, mostly following family traditions, sometimes for king or queen. There were multiple Juanicos, Catalinas, Marías, and Isabels. Cristóbal had made specific grants of promising, healthy captives to long-serving officers and others he trusted. Among them, Pedro de Las Casas, brother to the gentleman captain of the second-voyage foot soldiers, had received a sturdy boy, whom he'd named Juanico. On arriving home in Seville, Pedro awarded Juanico to his fourteen-year-old son, Bartolomé.

Cousin Colombo sped on horseback to deliver Cristóbal's letters, journal, map, chest of gold and pearls, and samples of brazilwood directly to Isabel and Fernando in Ocaña. The four other ship captains promptly reported to Fonseca in Seville. Almost as quickly, rebels' letters and copied fragments of Cristóbal's circulated surreptitiously to his critics, some reaching Fonseca. A knowledgeable account of the pearls reverberated among the Sevillian merchants who'd provisioned the third voyage. Returning Spaniards broke the news in their own words to their wives and mistresses, church congregations, plaza and barroom chums, and other acquaintances, who relayed it on as they'd heard it or liked to tell it. Collective impressions gathered momentum like a wind-blown dust swirl.

Rebellion had ruined the Indies! The Admiral's cruelties and greed had finally brought him to his knees. King and queen would discover his foreign plots and turn against him. Yet treasures in virgin lands still beckoned—pearls, gold, and more savages fit for servitude.

In Seville, Bishop Fonseca was both shocked and vindicated. He'd never expected a rebellion, as opposed to occasional disobedience, or such clear-cut proof that Cristóbal was unfit to govern.

The settlement's ruin now loomed, not just chronic disappointment. Regardless, the Indies' potential had burgeoned, perhaps with a mighty continent to conquer, irrespective of whether Cathay was nearby. He churned impatient to review Cristóbal's reports, which undoubtedly trumpeted a bright outlook. His discussions with Isabel and Fernando would be agitated, if not tortured. He'd honored their support of their admiral for six years. But support was no longer due or in their kingdoms' interest.

In Ocaña, when Cristóbal's correspondence arrived, Isabel had retired to her bedchamber in the mansion of a long-standing courtier.* Her illness now surged and abated recurrently. Fernando digested the material and briefed her at bedside, alone but for Miguel and nursemaids. King and queen were incredulous.

"Española is chaos!" he stammered. "The Admiral reports a rebellion—not of Indians, but our own men! He's tried to quell it peacefully, but he seeks a judge to assist him and more soldiers to repress it." He simmered, and Isabel's jaw clenched. "The rebel's leader is the man he himself appointed as the island's chief magistrate."

"Has there been bloodshed?" she whispered, slowly sitting.

"Apparently not. But his letters are rambling, sometimes incoherent, relentlessly denouncing Fonseca and his subordinates, often intemperate." Fernando recalled reports that Cristóbal had slugged Briviesca. "His stature and command have withered. Many on Española no longer fear or respect him."

"Those there have always been unjust, carping, and jealous, without inspiration or faith," Isabel scorned, her voice gathering strength. "We must fulfill his requests so the guilty are punished." Her frame trembled as she searched for the positive, hoping for better news. "What of the exploration, Española's gold, and the Indians' tribute and conversion?"

"He casts the exploration as a triumph, claiming to have discovered an infinite southern mainland and islands with pearls. But what's true, what's boast?" He shuddered. "Much may be delusion. He claims to have found the Terrestrial Paradise and discovered the earth isn't a globe, but pear-shaped."

---

* Gutierre de Cárdenas.

Isabel brooded. Her admiral's self-importance and faith increasingly clouded his perceptions, a failure common to princes that she sometimes monitored within herself.

"The gold remitted is paltry!" Fernando decried. "The mines have failed his promises, the Indians' tribute lost in the rebellion." He gazed away from Isabel, reluctant but resigned to dash her dearest aspirations. "The Admiral fails to report on the conversions accomplished. My queen, he ignores our instructions—he writes of establishing a slave trade of four thousand souls annually, and the ships returning bore hundreds of them."

Isabel seethed. She tolerated failure of performance, not disobedience.

⊡ ⊡ ⊡

Isabel and Fernando labored to arrange the pomp and homage for Miguel's recognition, and in January, she'd recovered enough to host the ceremony. They shared Cristóbal's communications with Fonseca, which sharpened the bishop's contempt for the chaos. When the celebrations concluded, the three met beyond earshot of subjects and court chroniclers.

"Tell me of the Indians abducted here," Isabel demanded. "On what basis were they enslaved?"

"Your Highness, I believe most failed to pay the tribute due yourselves," Fonseca replied calmly.

"That's not a basis for enslavement," she retorted. "We directed light punishment only. Unless the theologians decide otherwise, warful resistance is the only justification. You must gather these Indians back from slavery."

"Your Highness, I would, were they the crown's possessions to gather," Fonseca responded, ignoring her reference to the spectral council. "But the Indians apparently aren't the crown's. The Admiral awarded them as slaves to the men returning home and the ships' captains and crews."

"What power does my admiral have to give anyone my vassals?" Isabel shouted. "These Indians were seized in the crown's name, and they must be freed in the crown's name, to be sold on our behalf only if and when it's determined lawful."

"Slaves taken in our conquest become our possession, just like gold," Fernando interjected brusquely, incensed at having to remind his minister of that. "Not the property of our Spanish vassals. Decisions awarding even proper slaves as compensation are ours alone."

"Your Highnesses, I will do as you decree, but I fear the consequences," Fonseca warned, gazing plaintively to Fernando. "You can expect an outcry. The men returning believe they've been duly compensated, for both their sufferings and the back wages we haven't paid."

Isabel and Fernando fumed and scowled for some moments, and Fonseca sought to placate them and justify the enslavements. He reminded that they'd provisionally allowed past slave shipments, pending the church's blessing or manumission on condemnation. He cautioned that Castilian families would be incensed if the men they'd sent to the Indies were stripped of their booty and household labor. He counseled that financing future voyages depended on pleasing the financiers, merchants, and sailors. They'd already embraced conquest funded by slave trading of heathen Canarians and Africans and expected the same in the Indies.

Fernando acknowledged the expectations of the men returning and the financiers. He raised a hand, staring into Isabel's eyes.

"Perhaps it's best we continue to await the theologians' decision on Indian slavery. If they determine enslavement to be unlawful, these Indians will then be manumitted, and the sailors, merchants, and financiers will have to understand." He frowned. "My queen, as always, it should remain the church's decision, not ours."

Isabel's fury was slow to subside, but she capitulated.

"We shall put aside discussion of the Admiral's reprimand for usurping my authority," she remarked sullenly. "My bishop, what should we do to bring order and profitability to the Indies conquest?"

"Our Admiral is faltering, and Española is nearly lost," Fernando rasped, his vexation unbridled.

"You must replace the Admiral with new leadership," Fonseca stated plainly, relieved to squarely express his abiding concern. "He's failed his promises of gold and a shortcut to Cathay. His projections of profitability are delusional—if not fabrications, given the experience of five years. Whether fair or not, most Spaniards in Española despise him, perceiving him an unjust tyrant. The result is that Your Highnesses cannot effectively implement your rule through him. With respect to slavery, he ignores everything you say." Fonseca exhaled heavily, his judgment unambiguous. "You could wait upon an investigation of his conduct and performance before deciding, but I think we know enough to remove him now. The losses you incur in the Indies mount daily, and your resources to counter European adversaries are diminished."

A frigid silence lingered, neither sovereign warming to Fonseca's advice, both steadfast in maintaining their course through adversity. His counsel ignored the Admiral's exceptional ability to navigate to unknown lands. It smacked of outright betrayal of the one who'd singularly conceived and brought them the Indies conquest. The innuendo at court that the Admiral had turned traitor for foreign princes was a malicious lie.

Fonseca read their hearts and minds.

"Your Highnesses, your capitulations grant the Admiral an interest in all mainlands and islands he and his heirs discover, and the territory he's found now dwarfs that contemplated six years ago. When you struck those agreements, none of us thought he'd find much of anything, and many thought he'd vanish over the horizon never to be heard of again." He glanced into Isabel's eyes, seeking to appeal to her destiny. "It's your fame and legacy to exploit glorious conquests overseas, just as the Reconquista at home. The Admiral is not a governor capable of that exploitation in Española alone, much less the landmass just discovered. He is simply a mariner, fit for exploration and discovery."

"As for my legacy, I've never wilted upon disappointment," Isabel responded, albeit in a softer tone, cognizant that her bishop's analysis was sincere. "I acknowledge your criticisms of the Admiral, but the next step is to help him, not remove him. We must send him the judge and soldiers he requests and encourage a stern but bloodless resolution to this rebellion. We must investigate both his and the rebels' conduct. But with each voyage, he's brought us more unknown lands to conquer. It'd be utterly foolish to demote and alienate him."

"King Henry races west for territory to possess, and our son Manoel races east," Fernando noted warily, contemplating a middle ground. "We must seize what we can, expeditiously. My bishop, are there others fit to race and claim Paria for us?" He hesitated, exhaling. "The queen is correct. We must help the Admiral bring Española to order. But if he fails to do so, who's fit to replace him as governor?"

"Many are capable of exploring and possessing the southern coastline," Fonseca replied. He'd already shared his impressions of Paria's potential with three tested Indies veterans—Alonso de Hojeda, Juan de la Cosa, and Pero Alonso Niño—and all three had boasted eagerly of their ability to rake the pearl beds and possess territory beyond. "As for replacing the Admiral, I must give it thought," he admitted, keen for the opportunity to do so.

"Give us your advice and recommendations for both," Fernando instructed.

Isabel nodded wanly.

◻   ◻   ◻

One morning, the sovereigns summoned Cisneros to discuss the Indies, which surprised him, as they typically hadn't sought his counsel regarding overseas conquest. While he and Cristóbal knew one another, they lacked cause to interact at court, and he hadn't ventured to intrude on the sovereigns' and Cristóbal's close bond. But he hadn't been shy in proclaiming that the greatest glory of the Indies lay in the Indians' conversion.

"My confessor, do you have views on the constant criticisms of the Admiral?" Isabel asked.

"Your Highness, he appears to care more for slaves than conversions," Cisneros responded firmly, a view long simmering. "Few Indian souls have been saved."

"What should be done?"

"Your Highness, I would dispatch missionaries to evaluate the causes of this failure." Cisneros was respectful but not afraid to thrust his office forward. "The language barrier is an insufficient reason, as baptism is an acceptance of devotion to Christ rather than a test of doctrinal knowledge. I suspect there's a lack of resolve among many of your Christian subjects, not only the Admiral. They worship gold and temporal pleasures more than the Lord."

"Would you replace the Admiral?" Fernando probed.

Cisneros shrugged, stepping back, uncertain what Isabel wished. "The governor of the Indies must be committed to baptizing Indians, that glory inuring to yourselves."

◻   ◻   ◻

Paria's pearls flamed the ambitions and calculations of Andalusian merchants and sailors. Word of the Terrestrial Paradise and the earth's pear-shaped rise failed to whet the curiosity of most Spaniards. Nevertheless, the latter topics did intrigue the court's geographers, cosmographers, and devoutly religious, and it roused them that the centuries-old search for Eden might come to a glorious conclusion. Isabel was curious and felt duty bound to review the claimed discoveries, their momentousness outweighing her doubt. One day, she called an assembly of a learned and pious group to discuss the matter. Attendance overflowed, including the court's presiding Italian humanist, Pedro Mártir de Anglería, and Cristóbal's sons, Diego and Fernando, present as Isabel's pages and standing in the background.

"Your Highness, all of Aristotle, Ptolemy, Pliny, and Saint Augustine hold the earth to be round," a cosmographer pronounced. "The Admiral's observations regarding temperature and climate beg other explanations, rather than revisions to this fundamental truth."

"I'm not so sure," a geographer disagreed. "No one has ever understood the earth to be perfectly round. Mountains rise above, valleys descend below, and Aristotle himself believed the seas' currents north to south are explained by the waters north being of higher elevation. The Admiral's pear-shaped theory is not unreasonable."

"It is fantastical," a mathematician scorned. "But the location of the Terrestrial Paradise is a separate issue. The scriptures indicate Eden lies on a mountain, and the Admiral's claim that he's found it bears scrutiny. He's correct that most learned men believe Eden to be in the east, where he most certainly is."

"Eden lies on a mountain, not a woman's nipple," a churchman observed wryly.

The room erupted in laughter, and even Isabel had a good chuckle. When the merriment subsided, she turned to Mártir, who was lettered and learned in the ancients' wisdom and had generously lauded Cristóbal's past discoveries.

"Pedro, what's your opinion?"

"I confess not to understand the reasons for the Admiral's conjectures, either as to the earth's shape or the Terrestrial Paradise," he advised. "To me, they seem fabulous."

Diego and Fernando listened gingerly, gleaning that their father's latest geographical conclusions would be ignored. Fernando resolved not even to mention them when trumpeting his father's praises.

⊡   ⊡   ⊡

As February waned, the rebellion demanded a response from the sovereigns, lest they appear weak or resigned to Española's failure, and Cristóbal's fitness to serve grated on, the subject of unremitting quarrel. His critics at court echoed and amplified the complaints of the newly returned Spaniards and appealed to the sovereigns' closest ministers to replace him. In early March, the court relocated to Madrid's alcazar, set defensively within city walls at a plateau's edge, and Isabel and Fernando wearied of the dissension. As cold wind swirled through the city, they summoned Fonseca to the alcazar's throne room to hear his definitive recommendations.

"Your Highnesses, I propose that you promptly license other explorers to claim all remaining territory to be possessed for your kingdoms in the Indies, beginning with Paria," he stated. "The Sevillian merchants are eager to underwrite such explorations at their own expense, and I could dispatch half a dozen capable fleets within the year. Ships captained by Alonso de Hojeda, Juan de la Cosa, and Pero Alonso Niño—all known to you—could sail within two months." Fonseca had recommended Hojeda for Cristóbal's second voyage, and he'd served as Cristóbal's trusted lieutenant on Española for three years, his responsibilities including the most dangerous confrontations with Indians. La Cosa and Niño were seamen whom Cristóbal had enlisted to master and pilot ships on both the first and second voyages.

Isabel and Fernando had already warmed to the idea, and they glanced at each other, confirming their mutual approval, pleased by the caliber of the initial explorers.

"Send us Hojeda, Niño, and others you wish to license, so we may interview them," Isabel ordered. "You may license those we approve to explore and possess in our name. But you must carefully honor the Admiral's entitlements."

"The licensing must lawfully skirt our promises to him," Fernando clarified. "His entitlements extend to his discoveries but not beyond, and while we can dispatch others on voyages to his discoveries, he has the right to participate in them." Cristóbal's capitulations entitled him to underwrite an eighth portion of any ships so dispatched, and he'd objected to the licensing of others when the sovereigns proposed such three years earlier.* "Proceed with haste beyond his discoveries. Kings Manoel and Henry advance, and the Admiral himself intends to discover more of Paria. The crown's participation should be a fifth of what the licensees net."

Fonseca nodded dutifully, concealing his glee that further exploration of the Indies now fell within his singular authority. He'd thumb his nose if Cristóbal demanded involvement or participation. Queen, king, and kingdom might finally profit from the conquest. He frowned and spread his arms, raising the tougher issue of Española.

"Although you resist, the more I learn, the more I urge replacing the Admiral as Española's governor. I propose that his successor be none other than the esteemed Francisco de Bobadilla, intimate to your court."

Fonseca scrutinized the sovereigns' reactions, certain his nomination for governor would satisfy their vision of a strong-willed, devout, and lawful soldier and gentleman. Francisco de Bobadilla was a knighted commander in a military order that protected Christian towns in Granada from Mudejar attack and a combat veteran and administrator of the Reconquista esteemed for bravery. He'd served as a chamberlain to the sovereigns for years and was brother to Isabel's closest woman confidant, Beatriz de Bobadilla. Although occasionally intemperate and severe, he was respected for honesty, faith, and chastity, and he wasn't tainted as a Fonseca cohort.

"We are prepared to consider removing the Admiral as governor," Isabel grudgingly conceded. She glanced at Fernando, who nodded his satisfaction. "We're also pleased with this recommendation and

---

* *Columbus and Caonabó*, chapter XII, discusses the argument.

will discuss it with Commander Bobadilla." She stared into Fonseca's eyes. "But, without more information, we are not yet convinced removal is the right course. Were we to become so, our promises to the Admiral will have to be respected."

"Your Highnesses, governors may be removed from appointments for failure of their command, normally following crown investigation," Fonseca replied. "In my view, regardless of the wording, the Admiral's capitulations conferring his governorship reserved your power to remove him for failure of duty. You may wish the cover of an investigation to make that determination, but I believe his failure of duty is transparent."

"We share that view," Fernando confirmed.

"But we don't step there yet," Isabel pronounced, raising her voice. "Much depends on the Admiral's ability to quell the rebellion. It also matters whether Admiral himself has committed wrongs." She raised her chin, reverting to the sternness she'd cultivated for decades. "Regardless of the Admiral's shortcomings and fate, our subjects must understand we don't change horses in fear of rebellions. We crush them."

Fonseca nodded dutifully, sublimating his disappointment that Cristóbal still managed a hold on Española, albeit with a grasp eroding.

"The king and I shall obtain Bobadilla's willingness to serve in Española and discuss the potential scope of his service and authority," Isabel directed, signaling that exercise was beyond Fonseca's authority and concluding the audience.

Within days, Bobadilla agreed to serve, if authorized. Fonseca departed with Cristóbal's map of Paria, eager to share it with the proposed explorers and invite them to thumb their noses to Cristóbal, as well.

III

LIFE IN HAITI (QUISQUEYA) AND ESPAÑOLA

SANTO DOMINGO,
December 1498–January 1499

The November settlement with Roldán required that the two ships be delivered to Xaraguá's port by mid-January, and artisans commenced refitting the *Niña* and its sister caravel *India* for the rebels' crossing to Spain.* Cristóbal turned to reestablishing his leadership and household staffs on Española. Bartolomé vouched for those proven loyal, discouraging those untested and vetoing those untrusted. Cristóbal also sought to shore the satisfaction of the town's rank-and-file settlers—the predominance of the men he still commanded—and gave instructions for Santo Domingo's operation as the conquest's port of entry and administrative headquarters.

Miguel Díaz and Francisco de Garay, Santo Domingo's founders, were promoted, Díaz to warden of the town's fort, Garay to presiding notary. Ballester, the trusted veteran of the interior, retained his wardenship of Fort Concepción, the post most important for overseeing gold's collection from Indians once tribute was restored. Coronel assumed Roldán's position of chief magistrate, with power to imprison and punish. Carvajal was given similar power and dispatched overland

---

* Designed as the *Niña*, the *India* was the first caravel constructed in the Americas, as discussed in *Columbus and Caonabó*, chapter IX.

with the more perilous assignment of monitoring the rebels' preparations for departure and ensuring compliance.

Pedro de Terreros was promoted from steward and captain to
master of Cristóbal's household, responsible for maintaining the family's fortified compound. The help therein included Cristóbal's long-
standing chambermaid, María Fernández, a veteran of the second
voyage and one of Española's few Spanish women, and his faithful
Guinean manservant, Juan Portugués, a sailor of the first voyage
who'd returned to Española on the two supply ships dispatched in
February. Cristóbal had enlisted a personal chaplain on the voyage
just completed, Pedro Ortiz, a newcomer to the Indies, and Ortiz
resided in the compound to take confession and observe canonical
hours whenever Cristóbal wished.

Cristóbal was impressed with the town's food supply and the
arrangements Bartolomé had bludgeoned to ensure it. A local
cacique residing to the east, Agüeybana, had agreed to furnish naborias to plant and harvest eighty thousand yuca mounds close to the
town, and his naborias occasionally hauled stone and wood to assist
building construction.* Across the Ozama, Cacique Catalina's subjects often shared the fish and fowl they caught. In return, Bartolomé
had promised the two chieftains that their people could continue to
live in their villages unmolested and free from intrusion. For Agüeybana, it was a bargain to be left alone, not friendship. For Catalina,
it was the recourse for survival, and she cemented it with the union
with Díaz.

In some respects, life in Santo Domingo now resembled that of
an undistinguished, rustic town in Spain, pleasing Cristóbal. Most
Spanish gentlemen had berthed on the five ships just departed,
leaving artisans, laborers, farmers, soldiers, and sailors. For two
years, with their salaries unpaid and the settlement inadequately
resupplied, these commoners had scrounged and improvised to survive by bartering among themselves their services, possessions, and—
on the sly—gold pieces occasionally obtained from Indians, which
were rightfully the sovereigns' property. The tailor sewed shirts for
the carpenter in return for a roof, the cobbler stitched boots for a
farmer's basket of cucumbers and garlic, and the blacksmith shoed

---

* Not the same person as Boriquén's famous cacique of the same name.

a commander's horse to secure the horse's occasional labor. At Cristóbal's instruction, Bartolomé had encouraged such initiative and perhaps honesty in gold mining by awarding salaried laborers mining for gold with the gold they found exceeding a quota. A bordello supported a Spanish woman or two, including the Castilian lady who ran it with her husband. Sailors sometimes frequented it, as did Coronel, Carvajal, and Bartolomé.

But, as Cristóbal had observed upon arrival, Santo Domingo differed fundamentally from Spanish and Christian towns. Spaniards were well outnumbered by naked Indians—whether concubines, servants, slaves, or simply Agüeybana's or Catalina's naborias delivering food baskets or assisting in construction. Cohabitation of Spanish men and Indian women was pervasive, and the cry of infants and patter of youngsters emanated from many shacks. The women worshipped heathen idols and served meals including both Spanish and Indian foods, such as pork and chicken side by side with cazabi and *boniata* (sweet potato). Some Spanish men had adopted a few Indian ways, such as inhaling the smoke of rolled *tabaco* (tobacco) leaves to dispel hunger or pain, resting in *hamacas* (hammocks), and eating with their women and children before firepits. Cristóbal was disquieted that his men's cohabitation with Indian women—be it by force, fear, or allure—had led them to a life neither properly Spanish nor Christian. The unions were sinful—Christians living with heathens, the unions outside marriage, the children illegitimate.

Like in Spanish towns, the small church overlooking the Ozama was a focal point of town life. But the settlers' worship had a different focus than that of congregations in Spain. The Indians hadn't always been friendly and couldn't be trusted to be so. Settlers prayed daily for survival, conquest, and the destruction of unfriendly Indians and their hostile spirits, including Satan, who lurked at their side. Few settlers shared Cristóbal's vexation for their sins, and most hoped churchmen wouldn't condemn their unions and children with Indian women. Some grew anxious that marriage to their women and baptism of the children would be permitted.

Slaves had been awarded to the three hundred loyalists who'd departed, and slaves were now promised to over a hundred rebels in settlement of treason. Cristóbal understood that those who'd stalwartly remained to serve him on Española expected to be treated at least as well. He'd already proposed to the sovereigns awarding settlers slaves which they could use or sell in lieu of salary. Cristóbal didn't issue a proclamation applicable to all rank and file, but he occasionally saw fit to bolster a man's loyalty or alleviate his poverty by granting slaves in lieu of wages unpaid.

Soon, enterprising settlers organized a new mercantile site off Santo Domingo's central plaza, near the corral for captured Indians— an auction block for slave sales, resembling those in Seville and other Spanish cities.

⊡   ⊡   ⊡

Although preoccupied with Española's administration and Roldán's departure, Cristóbal found time to review the progress of the sovereigns' missionary effort. The dozen churchmen brought to Española on the second voyage had dwindled to a handful, owing to desertions, departures, and the absence of new recruits. When he'd departed for Spain in 1496, the missionaries hadn't achieved a single baptism on the island. One Sunday, Cristóbal summoned the young friar he'd then trusted with sustaining the neglected effort to share communion at the church and recount what had been accomplished since.

A Hieronymite from Catalonia, Ramón Pané had begun his service on Española preaching in a village along the Yaque, and at the commencement of Caonabó's war, Cristóbal had relocated him to Guaricano to convert Guarionex to Christianity, hoping Indians throughout the island would follow that example (1494–1495). Cristóbal had also instructed him to study and write a report about the Indians' religious beliefs, rites, and idolatries. Lacking formal education, Pané had accomplished that largely through conversations with Guarionex.

After the congregation departed, the two men and Chaplain Ortiz sat gazing over the Ozama. Pané bore a satchel containing his study, sheaves of parchment bound in cord.

"Tell me what you taught Guarionex and of the Indians' willingness to learn," Cristóbal directed. He'd instructed the missionaries to teach the core truths and catechisms, believing that a heathen's conversion required basic doctrinal understanding, consistent with church doctrine. "Did Guarionex accept the faith before rebelling?"

"I taught him for almost two years," Pané responded, "including the Pater Noster, Ave María, and Creed (the Lord's Prayer, Hail Mary, and Apostles' Creed), just as you instructed. He learned them by heart and prayed daily. But then he grew angry, reproached by other caciques who said we Christians are wicked, taking lands by force, and he denied Christ and conspired to kill our men." Pané shrugged. "He never accepted the faith."

"Was it the reproach that led him astray?"

"Somewhat, but he retreated from the faith largely of his own accord," Pané replied, recalling his acrimonious parting from Guarionex and the chieftain's blasphemous scorn that Christ was brother to Satan. "He wouldn't forsake his false idols."

"How is it to teach others?"

"Some listen and then laugh at the catechisms. With them, there is a need for force and punishment. Others are inclined to believe easily, simply on teaching them there's a God who made all things and created the heaven and the earth. The language barrier is a great hurdle, and thousands could be baptized if I traveled about the island with La Lengua." Pané beamed and opened his palms, but Cristóbal shook his head.

"My friar, heed that baptism is my prerogative, and I won't approve it lightly." After the sovereigns' papal nuncio deserted Española (1494), Cristóbal had assumed sole authority to approve baptisms. "Knowing acceptance of Christian truth is essential, as is acceptance of our customs and clothing. Before baptism, we must be sure the individual is truly Christian and won't rebel. If force has been necessary, or the instruction simply a sermon, I won't approve." Baptism compromised the potential for enslavement.

"I understand, my Admiral," Pané responded, obedient yet profoundly disappointed. The Admiral had approved Pané's baptism of an Indian family living by the Yaque, but the Admiral's insistence on a strict volitional threshold for conversion had proven—after five years of labor—utterly unrealistic to widely achieve.[*]

---

[*] *Columbus and Caonabó*, chapters VI and XI, discuss the teaching and baptism of Gautí-cabanu and his family.

Pané quivered. He'd received pleas from settlers to lower or entirely excuse that threshold for their concubines, and he desired the Admiral's specific guidance and blessing thereof.

"My Admiral, some in today's congregation wish to marry the Indian women with whom they live in sin," he confided. "The church favors baptizing women to permit marriage and cure the sin. May I oblige our men, accordingly? Their women are with child but have yet to master the catechisms."

Cristóbal pondered, acknowledging both Pané's argument and the reality that such women posed no risk of resistance. Yet the sovereigns hadn't given guidance on intermarriage between their Christian subjects and naked heathens, and the baptism of these women would constrain his ability to enslave them if later appropriate. In any case, his men likely had coerced most of their women, rendering their marriages impure.

"The threshold for baptism for these women is no different than for others," he replied. "They must understand the faith and adopt our customs."

Pané and Ortiz were shocked. The wishes of Spaniards were being denied, not just the salvation of Indian souls. Pané's conscience pushed him on. "My Admiral, what of the infants? I'll be asked to baptize them when born, regardless of denying marriages."

"My Admiral, the men loyal to you expect at least that," Ortiz interjected cautiously. "The church regularly baptizes infants, their innocence of doctrine as blessed as their innocence of sin. The son doesn't bear the father's guilt. You mustn't cross your men in this regard."

Cristóbal reflected, but not for long. He had no leeway to forsake loyalists, and he conceded that infants could be baptized.

"What have you found regarding the Indians' worship and rites?" he inquired, tired of the audience.

"Here is my final report," Pané advised, handing over the parchment. "May it redound to His benefit and service."

As Pané recounted a few of the idols, Cristóbal gazed across the Ozama to the Indian sentries on duty for Cacique Catalina, brooding on what he'd promised the sovereigns. The Indians were timid and would submit easily. They believed in the soul's immortality and judgment on death, so they'd flock to convert. So far, neither promise had proven true.

XARAGUÁ,
January–Early March 1499

The *Niña* and *India* timely departed Santo Domingo to anchor in Xaraguá's port by mid-January, but they failed to arrive. A storm engulfed and mangled them, and they harbored impaired on the southern coastline only 20 leagues west of Santo Domingo, the *Niña*'s damage requiring a major overhaul. Cristóbal grimly dispatched artisans to make repairs.

In Xaraguá, the rebels' final looting spree abated when word arrived of the caravels' wreckage. Every rebel knew Cristóbal hadn't intended such, and most initially expected the ships would be duly repaired so they could sail home, with the negotiated promises otherwise honored. Carvajal repeatedly so assured Roldán and all who'd listen. But the delay afforded time for changes of heart.

Many rebels sobered to recognize that the gold jewelry and trophies they'd amassed wouldn't transform their rank in Spain to that of idle gentlemen or even buy a plot of farmland. Their experiences on Española and the spears and feather headdresses they'd pillaged would captivate barrooms and grandchildren but otherwise were valueless. Those married now fully reckoned the rupture with wives if they brought concubines and children home. Those unmarried grew apprehensive of answering to relatives why they'd chosen a heathen as mate rather than a Christian. The overarching treasure they'd all found in Xaraguá couldn't be transported. In multiple ways, their lives there were better than their lives in Spain.

Their lives in Xaraguá also were better than those of their compatriots in Santo Domingo. Roldán's purported land grants were large estates, including both villages and farmland, and Cristóbal hadn't begun to award his loyalists the modest homesteads envisioned by the sovereigns' order. While Roldán shied from formal slave awards, his land grants assumed the indentured labor of the resident Indians. Daily life had assumed a rhythm of rebel dominance over fearful villagers with the customs of both commingled—pleasantly for the rebels, particularly in the bohíos they shared with their concubines and children. The concubines had learned to blend pork and Spanish onions in the Taínos' traditional "pepper pot" of yuca and peppers—not quite a Spanish feast, but not far short. The rebels had assumed the prerogatives of caciques and were often ported by naborias on litters—not quite the equivalent of a nobleman on a horse, but more regal. Hunters hunted and fishermen fished for them, as if they were gentlemen.

Roldán took the pulse of his men frequently and sensed a growing ambivalence toward departure, even in his own heart. Squatters contemplated becoming settlers. Allegations soon surged that Colón had intentionally violated the November agreement and now sought everyone's prosecution in Spain. The agreement was void, no longer requiring either return to Spain or submission to Colón!

Carvajal apprised Cristóbal of the discontent and cajoled Roldán to compel his men to prepare for departure. Anxious, Cristóbal dedicated more workers to the caravels' restoration, but mending ships on Española's unpossessed coastline would take longer than in a Spanish port, no matter how urgently he pressed. He desperately considered dispatching Bartolomé to Xaraguá to offer Behecchio and Anacaona favorable treatment if they assisted in expelling Roldán's gang onto the ships when repaired, but a resort to violence seemed premature and success uncertain. Then unable to do more to ensure Roldán's departure, Cristóbal turned to restore gold tribute in the interior chiefdoms he thought possessed gold, and on February 20, he departed Santo Domingo to compel caciques throughout Magua to resume rendering it.

Xaraguá's village caciques and most of their subjects also pined for the ships' arrival. Concubines and their relatives alone prayed that maybe they wouldn't be dragged away after all. Many Xaraguáns daydreamed that every squatter would depart and the guamiquina thereafter would leave Xaraguá alone.

Behecchio and Anacaona listened shrewdly and pessimistically to all sources and believed their subjects' daydream fanciful. When the enemy sorted itself out, they'd be stuck dealing with either Roldán or the guamiquina, and they anguished not knowing which enemy they should strive to placate. Weeks passed, and word of the guamiquina's march to compel gold tribute and the interminable uncertainty of Roldán's departure tested their patience.

"We must force Roldán to reveal his and the guamiquina's intentions," Behecchio declared to Anacaona one evening, that patience lost. "I shall threaten to betray him. You must dangle Bartolomé's affections. Again, bid your daughter inveigle his secrets."

◻ ◻ ◻

Summoned, Roldán rode to the ballcourt, tethered his horse to a tree, and as many times before, stood before Behecchio, Anacaona, and their interpreter. But he no longer bowed.

"When are the vessels coming to take you home?" Behecchio grilled straight away, without the courtesy of a salutation, recognizing the insult. "We understand the guamiquina marches to reestablish tribute. We trust you've warned him not to march here."

"Your Highnesses, nothing has changed since we last spoke," Roldán blustered. "The guamiquina still promises ships will arrive in your port shortly. Some of us may leave. Some may not." Not caring a whit what happened if he departed, he smiled and lied more directly than before. "The guamiquina promises he won't impose tribute on you should I choose to leave."

"Why should I rely on your word?" Behecchio replied. "I could extract that promise from Bartolomé directly—in return for throwing you and your gang onto the vessels."

"Why shouldn't I entice my friend Bartolomé here?" Anacaona challenged. "He delights in my company. He and I might amicably resolve our differences—and your fate."

"Your Highnesses, Bartolomé's involvement serves no purpose." Roldán was alarmed by the mention of his enemy but scornful of the threat. The chieftain's spears and arrows remained no match for swords, crossbows, and muskets, and Colón wouldn't be so foolhardy to ask his followers to fight other Spaniards. "The guamiquina rides north, not here. Whether I remain or depart, you won't suffer tribute."

"Why do you refuse to volunteer your own plans?" Behecchio barked.

"I've never misled you," Roldán responded contemptuously, brandishing his upper hand. "I simply haven't decided."

Behecchio spat and walked away. Roldán sighed in relief. The heathen king couldn't spur him to stay, depart, or even decide.

"Your Highness, worry not," he puffed to Anacaona. "I hold your interests to my bosom."

"Francisco, are you happier here than in your homeland?" she asked softly, as if she cared, peering into his eyes, inviting him to stay longer. She caught a flicker, more than a blink.

"I love your kingdom, Your Highness," he replied, suppressing his startle at the question. "But I love and miss my homeland, too."

"Your Fernando and Isabel must miss you, as well," she responded soothingly, catching a dart of his eyes. "It must be dreadful awaiting these vessels' repair." She gleaned a slight blush in the pale man's cheek. But the pale man knew not to be drawn further.

"Your Highness, I take my leave. You'll know my decision when made." He waved goodbye.

Roldán again found Higueymota caressing his mount's forehead, which was suspicious, premeditated rather than earnest. But it delighted nonetheless, as did her pretty face, breasts, and pubic hair. His domination of heathens could deflect any subterfuge. What could she tease from him?

"My Indian princess!" he exclaimed. "Are you game to ride?" he asked in broken Taíno, patting the horse's back.

Higueymota smiled and barely nodded. "Is it dangerous?" She mustered her courage, the pale man's lust to woo now unbridled.

"Not if you hold me tightly." He hopped, looped a leg over the horse to land seated on its back, and extended his hand down. Higueymota giggled as he yanked her up, and she likewise straddled a leg across the beast's back. She was astonished at the height she found herself and that the beast barely noticed, its hide smooth and warm.

"Put your arms about me, so you don't fall," the pale man instructed, pulling her hands to his waist while gently nudging the beast with his heel. It began to walk, as if one with the pale man and even herself, directed by the pale man through a rope tethered to its snout, its gait curious and intriguing.

They rode for some moments, and Higueymota grew comfortable. She let her hands fall onto the pale man's thighs and pressed her nipples and womb against his back.

"Francisco, do you have 'horses' in your homeland?" she asked gayly.

"Many. I have a herd of them," he boasted, although he hadn't one.

"You must miss them," she replied. "When you depart, will you take this 'horse' with you?"

"No, she's too big for the ship," he explained. "But the guamiquina has already agreed that I'm to be paid for her if I depart."

"So, you've decided to leave us," she whispered softly. She waited for a response, shifting the grasp of her hands slightly inward, toward the pale man's crotch, sensing his anticipation. But he didn't answer. She mused that all men were similar and that flirting with an enemy should be no different than with a friend, irrespective of skin color and custom as well, and she tested him to bare his potency. "Or does the guamiquina force you to leave?"

"I'm in command, my princess. The guamiquina can't force me to do anything. I may choose to remain, so long as the guamiquina accepts my demands."

When they arrived at his village, Roldán helped Higueymota dismount. Villagers were astonished by her presence and congregated around her. She smiled regally to all and studied the women cooking in the firepit before the pale man's commandeered caney, evaluating which were his concubines.

"My princess, come join me inside," the pale man invited with a leer, making his intent transparent. "Or perhaps you'd prefer that we walk alone in the forest."

"I don't play so easily," she responded gently, touching his shoulder, as if tenderly. "Tell me when you've decided to go or stay." She glanced at naborias nearby, clapped her hands, and bid for a litter. "I shall arrange my own way home."

Later, when the naborias lowered the litter from their shoulders, Higueymota stepped off to stand before Behecchio and Anacaona in the ballcourt. She glanced to her mother, shaking her head to mark she hadn't slept with the pale man.

"What did you learn?" Anacaona asked.

"I'm not sure. But I suspect he first argued with the guamiquina so he might depart. He now envisions arguing so he may remain."

"Well done, my child."

FORT CONCEPCIÓN AND ISABELA,
February 20–May 21, 1499

As Roldán's gang prevaricated, Cristóbal and Bartolomé rode along the trail that curled northwest from Santo Domingo to Isabela, well-worn by the settlers' migration in the other direction three years prior, with a troop of foot soldiers and artisans trudging behind. En route, Bartolomé and a contingent camped at Bonao to build a larger outpost in anticipation of gold mining nearby, planning thereafter to march west to reimpose gold tribute in Maguana. As February waned, Cristóbal continued to Fort Concepción with the remaining men to reimpose it throughout Magua and mountains to the south, intending to use Cacique Diego Colón as interpreter in parleys with caciques.

At the fort, Ballester toured Cristóbal about the small com-pound—several wooden buildings on an acre south of Guaricano protected by defensive ditches and walls. Cristóbal had chosen the site—a strategic bluff beneath a hillside peak dominating the fer-tile surrounding valley. He'd been enchanted by its temperate airs and gushing spring. The shacks and bohíos home to the garrison, a battle-tested band of Cristóbal's most loyal Spaniards, lay scattered outside the defenses, and a church was under construction nearby. The garrison had repelled attacks and outlasted sieges by Manicoatex, other caciques, and Roldán's rebels. Like those in Santo Domingo, many lived intimately with Indian women and had fathered children with them. Ballester introduced Cristóbal to each man, and he warmed to their heartfelt appreciation of his visit. He sensed he'd attained inland a safety and security not possible by the sea in Santo Domingo.

At dusk, Cristóbal summoned Diego to dine at a table set by the gushing spring. Three years had passed since they'd last met, and as the young man approached, Cristóbal reflected on Ballester's warning that Diego hadn't been entirely trustworthy, shielding his brother-in-law Guarionex and succoring Roldán. Diego trembled, fearful Admiral had been so told and that he'd fallen from Admiral's grace.

But when they stood face-to-face, Cristóbal was overcome with affection and gratitude. Diego was unequalled, the person with whom he'd shared most intimately the exploration and conquest of the Indies—for the longest period, the harshest deprivations, and the deadliest perils—and for whom he'd once felt a paternal tenderness. Doubt vanished, and he beckoned a heartfelt embrace. Diego's fear and hatred melted to vestiges of love and admiration, and he hugged in return, acknowledging to himself that Admiral truly was the father of what he'd become. Both recognized their unique bond.

They briefly reacquainted, Cristóbal examining Diego's trim frame and cleanliness and inquiring of his son, Diego studying Cristóbal's bloodshot eyes and bloated calves, wondering what ailed him. Cristóbal was pleased that his former guide and interpreter appeared fit for service. Diego was astonished that Admiral had aged so much in only three years.

"I've returned to complete the island's conquest, and you shall return to my side occasionally," Cristóbal instructed, eyeing Diego's reaction. "Francisco Roldán will depart the island within weeks, taking his entire gang of criminals. I trust that pleases you."

"It does, greatly," Diego replied, summoning as best he could the bravado with which pale men lied. "Roldán robbed my supply of cazabi," he professed, recasting his fearful acquiescence to Roldán's prior coercion.

Cristóbal surmised that Diego would be dependable regardless of any previous remission, his loyalty born of both fear and love, albeit not as true as that of a natural son. He bid the youth sit, and indentured villagers served a Spanish meal.

"Española's caciques will quickly understand their folly for colluding with Roldán," Cristóbal declared. "Bartolomé shall restore gold tribute from Maguana's caciques, and we shall compel it from Manicoatex and others here. We'll force your brother-in-law to assist."

Diego nodded, speechless, reminded of Admiral's mercilessness. Admiral well understood that famine, disease, and death had ravaged the chiefdoms he'd subjugated, devastating the inhabitants' capacity to pay tribute. But Admiral was neither shamed nor regretful.

"What measure of gold can we order them to collect every season?" Cristóbal asked, admitting no excuse to alter his conquest's design.

The European concept of tribute, shown in Mexico. Taken from Theodore de Bry, 1598. The John Carter Brown Library, rec. no. 0683-6.

Diego hesitated, afraid to reply honestly. Remoras didn't anger fishermen by reporting there were no fish to catch. But it was in Admiral's interest—as well as that of Haiti's peoples—that Admiral at least account for, if not pity, their exhausted capacity. Diego spoke carefully.

"Admiral, the island's caciques have little gold jewelry left to collect. Roldán has already confiscated it. Many of their subjects have perished, so far fewer can hunt for new pieces. Manicoatex's people have suffered the worst, and while the streams in his mountains bear gold, he no longer has enough healthy subjects to search for it. As for Guarionex, he no longer leads his people."

Admiral's face contorted with displeasure, and Diego retreated hastily. Remoras that refused to hunt were eaten.

"But I will help as you direct," he exclaimed. He searched for that attainable. "Adelantado's arrangements—whereby caciques supply food for peace—are accepted and honored."

"The sovereigns and I expect gold!" Cristóbal retorted, fighting to contain his fury, his suspicion surging. Fort Concepción's purpose was to amass the interior's gold, both mined and delivered in tribute, and to eclipse the fame of Manoel's Mina. If the Indians refused to deliver gold, why not force them to dig it?

Diego knew not to respond and waited. Cristóbal gazed north, where vultures circled overhead, low in the darkening sky, undoubtedly spying Indian corpses farther upstream. He grimaced curtly.

"My Diego, I provide special protection to you and your subjects in recognition of my love and your service. You aren't responsible as a cacique for delivering gold. But your service—and my love—requires holding other caciques so responsible." Albeit unique, their bond was that of master and slave.

⊡ ⊡ ⊡

Before dawn the next morning, Diego returned to the fort to warn Guarionex. Ballester had permitted Diego to supply the chieftain food after his incarceration, and with the sentries' approval, he approached the blockhouse cell where Guarionex and Mayobanex were chained, bearing a basket of cazabi and a gourd of pineapple juice. The two chieftains lay side by side in the dirt, flies swarming the cell. Guarionex acknowledged his arrival, but Mayobanex slept fitfully on, quite ill. His bruises had festered purple, his lengthy hair was compacted with dirt, and his black skin dyes were soiled to dusty gray.

"The guamiquina says he'll force you to assist in reimposing gold tribute."

"I shall scorn him," Guarionex replied. "Do you come as Cacique Colón or brother-in-law Bakako?"

"I come to forewarn you, so that you may consider how to dissuade him," Diego replied, ignoring the pique. But he was insulted, and while he'd intended to visit longer, he left the basket and the blockhouse, regardless that Guarionex bid him remain. He sat in the compound, awaiting Admiral's call, his thoughts stifled by a vision of Yutowa and his hatred of straddling two civilizations. After sunrise, Guarionex was brought to kneel before Admiral, and he rose to stand at Admiral's side to translate.

Cristóbal studied Guarionex's grimy, emaciated frame, contemplating how to bend his will. Guarionex stared defiantly, surprised that his enemy appeared defeated, as well. He turned to Diego and murmured, "Hello, my friend, Bakako."

"My lord, I never intended to behold you thus," Cristóbal observed solemnly and sincerely. "Let us find a new beginning and return to the arrangements we once agreed. I offer to forgive you and reinstate your kingdom in return for tribute as before."

"My guamiquina, I offered to plant you a garden across the island, studied your Christ-spirit, and invoked our brotherhood— but that friendship didn't satisfy you," Guarionex responded. "My people have suffered and perished, and they've rejected my rule. But even if they accepted me again, I'd die before assisting you. Your soul has a terrible destiny. I'll not share it."

Diego translated verbatim as best he could, averting his eyes from both men.

"We need not be friends or brothers, my lord," Cristóbal responded. "If you assist me, you will be released, no matter our mutual hatred. If you deny me, you will remain bound, to be hauled to Spain to answer to our Queen Isabel and King Fernando."

"Then I shall remain bound until my soul is called by my spirits, whether here or in your homeland." Guarionex spat toward the wooden cross in the compound's foreground. "My spirits don't for-give evil deeds simply so they might be worshipped."

Cristóbal shrugged disdainfully. "You are free to change your mind, and I hope you do. Your death accomplishes nothing." He motioned for the guards to haul Guarionex back to his cell and bid Ballester summon Manicoatex.

▫ ▫ ▫

Prior to Cristóbal's invasion, Manicoatex had ruled a small chiefdom nestled along the Yaque's headwaters in the moun-tainous region the Taínos called the *Cibao* (rocky, mountainous region). His brother, Caonabó, had installed him there, as the area buffered Caonabó's Maguana from Guarionex's Magua. Fol-lowing Cristóbal's invasion, Manicoatex had fought valiantly in Caonabó's war, eventually leading the greatest battle against the invaders with bravery and acumen. When writing the sovereigns,

Cristóbal had lauded him as a great warrior, on par with a Castilian or French general.

But Manicoatex had been captured and suffered successive repressions and humiliations. He'd been compelled to collect tribute in both his chiefdom and his brother's. He'd relinquished a son to Cristóbal as hostage to discourage further resistance, and after Roldán's rebellion, another son to Roldán to ensure loyalty to the rebels. Cristóbal had taken the first son to Spain with Caonabó, never to return.

Still, Manicoatex's surviving subjects hadn't forgotten his valor. He possessed a will to survive and outlast the pale men, perceiving their conquest unorganized, infirm, and unable to sustain itself permanently. He understood better than anyone the futility of engaging them in open warfare, and he knew he'd never outlast the guamiquina if chained and left to deteriorate like Guarionex and Mayobanex. Like Behecchio and his sister-in-law Anacaona, he'd chosen to retain his chiefdom, warriors, wives, and naborias, unwilling to relinquish hope that he might rise again if the guamiquina's conquest ultimately withered.

Manicoatex entered the pale men's fort hoisted on his litter by a dozen warriors, a dozen more honorifically trailing behind, and was lowered to dismount before Cristóbal, Ballester, and Cacique Diego, all of whom he knew and despised. He studied the murderer of his son, brother, and peoples and nodded. He had come to talk.

Cristóbal acknowledged the gesture, and to the extent capable, began with an apology. "Your son grew ill and died in Spain. There was nothing I could do to help."

As Diego translated, the two men glared at each other, neither willing to express or admit more reaction.

"I've come to reimpose tribute," Cristóbal announced. "You will be forgiven for following Roldán, who will depart the island within weeks. Our prior arrangements now govern."

"Those arrangements no longer work," Manicoatex retorted. "Your conquest has wrought famine and disease, decimating my people. I no longer have subjects to gather gold."

"Your subjects suffer famine by their own design, shirking their crops to inflict hunger and defeat on my men," Cristóbal replied gruffly. He'd expressed that explanation of the Indians' crop failure and famine to the sovereigns many times. "Order your people to plant their crops for their own good, and they'll recover to collect the tribute you owe Fernando and Isabel."

Manicoatex grunted derisively. "Believe what you will, but I can't promise to deliver any measure of gold over any period. I can only promise to deliver whatever gold my surviving subjects find. Your men must leave my territory alone."

"I will hold you to that promise," Cristóbal barked, as if imperiously. But he grimly sensed the bark impotent, as the decimation of the Cibao's population was beyond debate and the failure of its gold tribute more than foreseeable. His sovereigns' continued favor was the unknown.

☐ ☐ ☐

Ballester dispatched messengers summoning other caciques to parley at the fort, and Cristóbal cajoled each who came to deliver whatever gold he could muster. Some protested they possessed no gold, others agreed they'd try, a few fled to the hills to feign absence, and all feared enslavement. Cristóbal assured he'd honor their rank and privileges. Some sought cordial relations, including Maguatiquex, who'd studied Christianity with Pané, and Macís, whose warriors were renowned, and a cacique Ballester's men called the "Doctor," who lived along the Yaque. Platitudes acknowledging that the guamiquina sought gold and professing friendship abounded, but firm commitments were rare. Diego doubted Admiral was fooled and feared what he'd do when the gold disappointed him.

In mid-March, Cristóbal, Diego, and soldiers departed for Isabela, and Cristóbal beheld the utter wreckage of the proud inland chiefdoms he'd conquered five years before. Diego led him and his mount through the ghost town of Guaricano, the battlefield where Manicoatex had been defeated, and into the countryside toward the Yaque, passing thousands of unburied skeletons, deserted and overgrown farmland, and famished orphans and others destitute scouring for roots to eat. A day later, they visited the tiny garrison of soldiers at Fort Santiago, overlooking the Yaque, who'd made peaceful arrangements with local caciques to provide food but hadn't collected any gold—at least not for the king's account. Cristóbal's praise and encouragement cheered them, and he met with local caciques to reinstitute tribute, receiving the same cordial platitudes, guaranteeing nothing.

The entourage continued west along the Yaque, passing through the floodplain villages where men of the second voyage had committed the first widespread atrocities to Indians. Once home to thousands, the scant few surviving were embittered, hateful, and terrified by his return. Within days, the entourage surmounted a pass through the northern mountains and began the descent toward the coast and Isabela, the villages en route utterly depopulated.*

Diego himself grew embittered and hateful when they trekked through the village where he'd met, romanced, and fathered a child with the truest love of his life, Niana, the daughter of a cacique who'd supplied Isabela with food in return for peace. He'd protected her and her family from brutality, but she and the infant had perished from the pale men's diseases, as had nearly every villager living nearby Isabela.

When they arrived at Isabela, Cristóbal flushed with proud memories. It, too, was a ghost town, but its establishment as the conquest's headquarters on the second voyage had been a triumph over adversity. He'd built it on a defensible promontory by the sea—the first Spanish town in Española, thousands of miles from Spain—the site divinely blessed by a fulsome river, ample anchorage, a stone quarry, and beaches for offloading cargo and building ships. The Lord had guided him to it.

Diego recollected that the pale men he cared for frequently sniped that the town was haunted by the specters of Spanish gentlemen who'd met painful deaths chasing Admiral's gold, only to find it a lie. Others disparaged that the river was too far from the town, the cove was unprotected from northerly and westerly storms, and the site's humidity was unhealthy and caused provisions to rot.

Diego tailed Admiral to the church, where he prayed briefly, surrounded by the gravestones of men of the second voyage. Then they ambled a stone's throw to Admiral's residence, where Admiral asked to be left alone.

---

* Cristóbal named the pass Puerto de los Hidalgos (Pass of the Gentlemen) during the second voyage, which remains its name today.

Cristóbal chafed. The site he'd built had been abandoned, maligned by critics, and left to waste as a forgotten ruin, regardless of the monumental effort he'd devoted to its establishment. Diego recoiled. Nothing in the journey there had so moved Admiral.

◻   ◻   ◻

In late March, Cristóbal received word that the *India* was repaired, and he directed Pedro de Arana and Francisco de Garay to sail it to Xaraguá's port. In early April, when the *Niña* at last was ready, he dispatched Carvajal to sail it there and prepared letters imploring Roldán and Múxica to observe the November agreement for their own good.

When Carvajal arrived, Roldán publicly proclaimed that both caravels were unfit and the rebels had been released from the agreement. He and his entire gang refused to depart on them, intending instead to petition the sovereigns for redress.

On April 25, after Garay attested the ships were fit for the ocean crossing, Carvajal dispatched them back to Santo Domingo. Understanding that most rebels wished to live in Xaraguá indefinitely, he nevertheless remained there to convince Roldán otherwise. Roldán vacillated occasionally. One day in May, when the two huddled in secret, Roldán agreed to meet Cristóbal privately in Santo Domingo to commit to return to Spain. Carvajal wrote Cristóbal so advising, optimistic of eventual success. By then, Cristóbal and his entourage had returned to Fort Concepción, resigned that there were no Indians surviving near Isabela upon whom tribute might be imposed.

◻   ◻   ◻

On receipt of Carvajal's advice, on May 21, Cristóbal sat at the table by Fort Concepción's spring, enchanted by the countryside surrounding the fort, but brooding. Whatever tribute he'd receive likely would fail to satisfy his sovereigns. Carvajal's optimism likely was misplaced—Roldán simply always lied. All other efforts failing, enlisting the Indians' assistance in forcefully expelling the rebels loomed necessary. Dejected but undaunted, Cristóbal commenced writing two letters.

The first was to Ballester, instructing that an estate be set aside for Cristóbal's eldest son Diego in an area near the fort bounded by the site of a monastery to be built and streams abutting villages subject to Manicoatex's rule. It would serve as his heirs' sanctuary from enemies.

The second was a letter to Isabel and Fernando urging the sovereigns to arrest rebels returning home for canceling tribute, hoarding gold, and so alienating the Indians they'd kill settlers remaining. The Indians were industrious, although they'd been depopulated warring against him, and he'd had more difficulty with the Christians. His enemies had said he was worse than a Moor, led by conversos intent on ruining the enterprise.

Cristóbal planned to dispatch the letter to the sovereigns secretly on the same ships eventually transporting Roldán, and he hoped he'd written Roldán's epitaph. But Isabel and Fernando were then writing his.

IV

REPLACEMENT AUTHORIZED, EXPANDING HORIZONS

As spring passed, criticisms of Isabel's admiral rose to a crescendo, her bishop's recommendations grew in prescience, and no news arrived from Española to comfort her that Cristóbal had ended a rebellion of which he was innocent. His own words corroborated the charges that his outlook and process were uncontrolled. His grandiose heralding of profits and baptisms was hollow. His open disobedience to her direction that Indians be vassals rather than slaves was shocking. Their patience for dissension and disappointment spent, she and Fernando sadly turned to appointing his replacement—Francisco Bobadilla, knight commander of the Order of Calatrava.

The knight was of their generation, slightly older, and he'd witnessed how they'd overcome adversity during the Reconquista. In early May, after formulating such, they summoned him to receive his authority and mission, the three seated alone in the audience room of Madrid's alcazar.

"Francisco, your assignment in Española requires tact and command," Isabel advised. "You will have two titles. When you first arrive, you shall act as our judicial investigator. When the time is right, you shall make public that you are also our temporary governor, taking the oath before our subjects to observe our laws and receiving for yourself their obedience. Proceed moderately, and if possible, delay the second step in deference to the Admiral."

"As investigator, you must find those who rebelled against our rule, determine the causes, and punish the guilty," Fernando explained. "As governor, you shall replace our Admiral in all respects, taking control of the forts, appointing administrators as you deem necessary, and resolving disputes. You have the power to expel from the island those you wish removed. Take a few soldiers to assist."

"Your Highnesses, how long must I serve?" Bobadilla asked, honored to have been promoted for the assignment yet disappointed it had fallen to him, as he hadn't volunteered for it. Conquering and plundering the infidel at home had thundered glorious. Punishing Spaniards and jousting with Cristóbal among impoverished heathens far distant rang base.

"You must restore the settlement to order and report the crimes and injustices you find," Isabel directed. "When that is done, we'll arrange a permanent successor."

"Your Highnesses, what of the Admiral himself?" Bobadilla pressed. "Do I investigate him?" He puckered his lips, seeking an unvarnished response. "If so, do I find wrongdoing?" A vision of the Genoese flickered through his thoughts, and he muffled his disdain. While they'd known of each other, they'd never been acquainted. He'd always found Cristóbal's boasts insincere and the title Admiral undeserved.

"We look forward to your honest judgments on the Admiral's conduct, which must be shared with us alone," Isabel replied. "Your appointment as temporary governor does not depend on finding wrongdoing on his part. You must right Española from chaos."

Bobadilla hesitated, brooding on his sovereigns' sincerity rather than Cristóbal's. They'd dispatched an investigator three years before to report on their admiral, only to summarily discard the investigator and his report and embrace the Admiral upon his return from Española.* Bobadilla trembled, wary that soldiers sometimes were dispatched to certain death. Was he the sovereigns' sword of justice

---

* Juan Aguado, as depicted in *Columbus and Caonabó*, chapter VIII.

or but a messenger to be shot when the dirty work was done? There was no turning back.

"What if the Admiral resists me?" he asked, recalling Cristóbal's frequent, intemperate criticisms of Fonseca and other crown officials and the innuendo regarding his cruelties.

"That's quite possible," Fernando acknowledged, foreseeing Cristóbal's rage. "Our orders will command everyone in Española— including him—to obey you and turn over the forts and munitions. None will doubt that disobedience by the Admiral to you is disobedience to us."

"Should I send him home?"

Isabel and Fernando glanced uneasily at each other.

"We wish the Admiral neither harm nor unnecessary disgrace," Isabel observed. "While you shall assume his title as governor, at this time we see no merit in stripping him of his title as Admiral. That may preserve his loyalty and soften the blow to him."

"You may send him home if you judge that necessary to restore order or in furtherance of our justice," Fernando replied.

◻   ◻   ◻

While the sovereigns arranged Cristóbal's demotion in Española, Bishop Fonseca returned to Seville to authorize new voyages to the Indies to claim that yet undiscovered entirely without him. There were many qualified applicants. Pero Alonso Niño and Juan de la Cosa had sailed on Cristóbal's first and second voyages, and Vicente Yáñez Pinzón had captained the *Niña* on the first. The Guerra family, leading Sevillian shipowners, had provisioned the third. Dozens of other Andalusian merchants regularly trafficked to and from the Canaries. But Fonseca favored awarding the first license to his protégé for years, who possessed credentials, competence, brazen ambition, and ruthlessness exceeding the others.

Not yet thirty years old, Alonso de Hojeda (b. ca. 1470) had captained a ship on the second voyage and risen to become Cristóbal's most valued lieutenant on Española other than Bartolomé. Cristóbal had chosen him to lead the first inland exploration, command the first inland fort, daringly abduct Caonabó in the chieftain's own village, and lead troops in reprisals and battle against Indians, enslaving the defeated (1494–1495). Short, lean, nimble, and unmarried, he hailed from a Castilian family of minor nobility, and his youth had been strewn with quarrels and scrapes in which he'd always drawn first blood.

Fonseca summoned the would-be conquistador to his office in Seville's great cathedral and spread Cristóbal's map of Paria on a table.

"If I award you a voyage, who will finance it?" Fonseca asked, drilling into the sole credential Hojeda hadn't established.

"The Duke of Medinaceli will clamor to participate," Hojeda boasted, referring to a former patron in Puerto de Santa María. "I'll recruit Niño as a captain, and he'll bring other backers," he puffed. "He can sell the Guerras. I'll bind four ships easily."

"Commit four and you may sail as captain general," Fonseca promised. He pointed to the map. "The terms of your license will prohibit you from sailing to islands or mainland belonging to King Manoel or within 50 leagues of lands Colón has discovered."

"My bishop, Colón's pearls whet everyone's thirst!" Hojeda decried. "They cannot be denied."

"They will be denied, in the license," Fonseca curtly retorted, bridling his protégé's quick temper. "The king and queen shall respect Colón's interests in territory he's found for them." But he gazed out his window and softened his tone. He'd once given his protégé a small image of the Virgin Mary, whose protection the protégé trusted alongside his own. "Obviously, a trove of pearls will delight them wherever found, and while Colón still has their ear, it deafens. The map is hardly so precise."

Hojeda quickly embraced the steer and nodded. Colón's demise invigorated rather than sobered him, regardless of Colón's prior supportive promotions.

"Are there restrictions on the riches I'm entitled to seize?" he inquired.

"None, except don't take brazilwood in quantity." Fonseca would defer the wood's exploitation to later voyages. "Their Majesties expect pearls. Obviously, gold and gems are a priority. Trophies such as animals and birds are of interest. Even monsters, if they be found."

"What of slaves?" Hojeda barked, irritated Fonseca had ignored the plain focus of his question.

"Slaves aren't the treasure the queen wants," Fonseca warned. Still, a vision of financiers coursed through his thoughts. "But I'll consider what I can allow."

⊡   ⊡   ⊡

Hojeda left the audience keen to arrange the financing and partnerships for his fleet. His renowned knavery neither comforted nor cowed the financiers, and Pero Alonso Niño was no innocent. To Hojeda's chagrin, the negotiations didn't go smoothly.

Financiers he approached would underwrite three ships, but they had no appetite for giving him carte blanche as captain general of two of them. Instead, two of the ships would sail semiautonomously, directed by their own captains when they reached Paria and plundering their own treasures, subject to Hojeda's overriding generalship merely when crossing the Ocean Sea. Only one ship would bear his own booty.

Hojeda also couldn't strike a deal with Niño on their respective authorities and participations. While Niño (b. ca. 1468) had loyally served Cristóbal as a pilot, even transporting slaves from Española to Spain (1496), he shared Hojeda's enthusiasm for ransacking Cristóbal's pearl beds. But he concluded that Hojeda eventually would ransack him, too, and he quit, taking the Guerra brothers' financing for the fourth ship with him, resolved to obtain a separate license.

Despite procuring only three ships, Hojeda was undaunted, and invoking the Virgin, he began enlisting crews and provisions for four. Recruitment wasn't difficult, as his reputation lured those enticed by adventure and plunder. He was assisted by a younger accomplice and admirer, the smooth-talking *Don* Fernando de Guevara, born of a noble family titled by the crown and owning estates in Murcia, who echoed that riches and romp awaited in the Indies. The handsome Guevara already had been to Española and back, looted the savages' gold, frolicked with its women, and so infuriated Cristóbal for shirking work and this behavior that Cristóbal had punished him (1494–1496).

Hojeda and Niño competed for the crewmen best suited for sailing directly to Cristóbal's pearl beds. Hojeda enlisted one of the pilots who'd served Cristóbal on the voyage to Paria and returned to Spain, Niño two of them. La Cosa, esteemed for his seamanship and acquainted with both men, chose to sail with Hojeda, perceiving him a better gamble. Hojeda's financiers had a say in recruitment for the two ships under their control, and they enrolled a Florentine expert in gems also versed in ship finance, one Amerigo Vespucci.

Middle-aged, Vespucci was eager for the berth, as he'd yet to find fame or fortune in past careers as a fixer, financier, and slave trader. Born (ca. 1454) into a well-connected family of modest means, he'd once carved a niche for himself in Florence managing his extended family's meager businesses and the household affairs and incidental pursuits of the powerful Medici family, trading gems as an agent, collecting debts, and arranging his patriarchs' dalliances with concubines and others. He'd eventually sought to better himself in Seville by assisting Cristóbal's Sevillian financier for the first and second voyages, and he'd briefly risen to visibility in the Sevillian merchant community as the liquidator of the financier's estate upon the financier's untimely death before the third voyage (1495).[*] Unfortunately, he hadn't leveraged that visibility to independently establish himself as a merchant or financier. He hadn't experience navigating or sailing a ship anywhere, no less hand-to-hand combat with natives. But the deceased financier had been Seville's leading slave trader, and Vespucci had mastered that trade. Like other financiers, he perceived trading slaves no different than trading gems.

Hojeda was practiced in royal audiences, and when it came time to briefly present his plan to Isabel and Fernando, he impressed them with his notable reliability for performing the grittiest assignments on Española.

⊡ ⊡ ⊡

Fonseca issued Hojeda a license by mid-May and informed his protégé that Cristóbal's days were numbered, the king and queen's favor lost. Fonseca also provided cover for enslaving those who ought to be slaves, whether black, brown, or otherwise, permitting enslavement of those reportedly impeding Paria's possession. Fonseca separately licensed Niño, as well.

Always restless, Alonso seethed. Not only did he lack a second ship for his own booty, but in trials, the one he possessed had proven

---

[*] The financier was Juanoto Berardi. For the story, see *Columbus and Caonabó*, chapter VIII.

to be a mediocre sailor. Niño would beat him to Cristóbal's pearls! In darkness on the night of May 18, Alonso directed the crews on his three ships to weigh anchor and pirate a better caravel floating nearby while departing Puerto de Santa María's harbor, swapping the mediocre ship for it. By dawn, he was racing with three ships for Margarita first, determined to arrange the elusive fourth ship en route.

On May 21—the very day Cristóbal wrote them urging Roldán's punishment—Isabel and Fernando issued three proclamations stripping him of his authority in Española, designed to be recited publicly on the island after Bobadilla arrived. The first pronounced that, on the Admiral's report, a magistrate in Española had risen in rebellion and committed crimes, and they'd commissioned Bobadilla as judicial investigator to arrest the guilty and dispense stern justice. The second was addressed to every man in the Indies, ordering all to receive Bobadilla as the island's judge-governor and obey his governorship, which encompassed authority to execute justice, appoint and replace officers, and expel any he wished from the island. The last informed Cristóbal and everyone else that Bobadilla was the Indies' temporary governor and ordered all crown property—including forts and munitions, ships and buildings, provisions and livestock—be handed over to him or his officers.

Envisioning Cristóbal's affront and disbelief, Isabel and Fernando soon also prepared an intimate private note addressed to him as their Admiral of the Ocean Sea. *We have sent Commander Bobadilla to speak to you of some things on our behalf. We ask you to give him faith and belief and put those things into practice.*

Unbeknownst to Isabel and Fernando, while Hojeda coursed south flying the flag of the Castilian crown, two ships limped north along the African coast flying that of the Portuguese crown, having rounded the Cape of Good Hope in March en route to Lisbon from Calicut. King Manoel was about to triumph.

Anacaona, Behecchio, and Bartolomé, Counterplotting and Courtship,
June 1499

On June 7, Cristóbal lost hope that Roldán would depart of his own accord and dispatched Bartolomé, La Lengua, and a few soldiers to

Xaraguá to convince Behecchio and Anacaona to betray the rebels and assist in their expulsion from the island. Chaplain Ortiz accompanied, and if that failed, would reside indefinitely in Xaraguá to attempt reforming the rebels to orderly Christian conduct.

As they entered Xaraguá, Bartolomé and soldiers trekked vigilantly, spying for rebels' settlements and alert for rebel opposition. Bartolomé expected no resistance from Xaraguáns, and the tranquil countryside's bountifulness and teeming populace whetted his memory of Behecchio's civility and dominance, its beauty of Anacaona. Scouts quickly informed Behecchio of the incursion, and while fearful, he dispatched warriors to conspicuously escort the intruders to his inland village, assuring Bartolomé safe-conduct and warning Roldán that his haven wasn't assured.

"Does Bartolomé march to punish or befriend us?" Behecchio mused anxiously, seeking Anacaona's advice. "If he seeks that we betray Roldán, should we make good our threat to do so?" He quashed his emotions to reason soberly before changing alliances. "The guamiquina and Bartolomé's deceptions and crimes on Haiti have been far worse than Roldán's."

"Little would give me more pleasure than betraying both Roldán and Bartolomé," Anacaona replied. "Roldán may depart and betray us, anyway. Yet I suspect he wishes to remain, perhaps to betray us, but perhaps not. Let's listen before we abandon him."

Brother and sister each grimaced. Roldán's intentions remained undivulged.

When the intruders arrived at the ballcourt, Behecchio spread his arms, grandly beckoning Bartolomé to embrace, and Anacaona waved gayly, as if joyful that he'd returned to her. Bartolomé heartily joined the embrace, and when Behecchio released him, gazed directly into Anacaona's eyes, grinning to confirm he'd longed for her too.

"Your Highnesses, I've come to express my brother's sorrow for the conduct of the lowborn men who foul your lands, contrary to his orders," Bartolomé announced, then pausing for La Lengua's careful translation. "You broke our previous arrangements, but I offer to reinstate them just as they were, with love and without penalty. Cazabi and cotton, not gold, for peace. You shall remain your people's rulers. We come to arrange the exile of these lowborn from the island, hopefully with your assistance."

Brother and sister hid their relief. Bartolomé had come in weakness, not to punish.

"Their departure would delight us, as their conduct has been deplorable," Behecchio replied slowly, his mind racing to decide a response. Roldán apparently did intend to remain—over the guamiquina's objection, no less—and the pale men remained in quarreling factions! Behecchio glanced at Anacaona, who folded her arms on her chest, confirming her view that harboring Roldán should remain their strategy.

"But Roldán and his men don't war on Haiti, as you did in Ciguayo," Behecchio continued, now curtly. "They don't incarcerate supreme caciques, as you've done to Guarionex and Mayobanex. Nor do they enslave Haiti's peoples and abduct them to your homeland—a destiny you've inflicted on multitudes." He raised his fist, determined to dissuade Bartolomé from ever attempting that in Xaraguá. "Why should I believe your offer after these transgressions?"

"We've fought and enslaved only those resisting us," Bartolomé replied. "Many caciques now see the wisdom of our friendship and have agreed to arrangements for food and peace, including Mayobanex's own vassals in Ciguayo and Agüeybana by the Ozama."

"I rule my people right now," Behecchio pronounced sternly, "not Roldán nor your Fernando and Isabel, and my chiefdom has peace without tribute." Placing trust in the guamiquina was only the last resort. "If Roldán ever departs, our friendship might extend as you suggest."

"Your Highness, the guamiquina dispatched ships here to rid the island of these men, which is in your interest as well as ours," Bartolomé pressed. "The guamiquina can provide ships again, and you could brandish your spears and arrows to advise Roldán he's no longer welcome here."

"My Bartolomé, we do not fight your peoples' battles."

Bartolomé was crestfallen. He held no advantage, and his enemy Roldán continued to outmaneuver him. Threatening Behecchio would be hollow.

"Your Highnesses, I hope you change your mind, and we must continue to discuss," he conceded. With a flourish, he introduced Ortiz. "With your permission, the guamiquina has dispatched a churchman to live with you. Fray Ortiz is the guamiquina's own chaplain, versed in the true faith. He shall seek to reform the conduct of those here and convince them to leave."

"I shall receive him," Behecchio agreed. "But don't depart hastily. We invite you to remain some nights in recognition of the peace already between us." He stroked one of the shark's teeth strung on his necklace. "While I no longer pay you tribute, I continue to honor my promise not to oppose your peoples' conquest of Haiti outside Xaraguá. I trust the guamiquina will continue to honor your promise never to invade Xaraguá or enslave my people."

Startled by the chieftain's deftness, Bartolomé merely nodded. Promises to Indians were broken when expedient.

That evening, Anacaona hosted a ceremony, as loud as she could remember, delighted that Roldán would fear his haven lost. Behecchio relished the noise, musing that Bartolomé's and Roldán's cohorts would come to blows and destroy each other. As the moon rose, Anacaona led Bartolomé by the hand to her garden. They sat alone on duhos intimately facing each other, his back to a bayahibe bush, just as they had two years earlier.

"My Anacaona, you told me in this very garden that love would follow friendship, when proven," Bartolomé reminded in broken Taíno, gently yet imperiously. "Must I prove more?" he asked. Believing wooing invited, he reached to grasp her hands.

"My heart is eager," Anacaona replied, accepting his hands courteously. "But there is more to prove, my Bartolomé." She drew him closer. "Tell me, are the peoples you've conquered on the island happier than my subjects who host Roldán?"

"Certainly, I assure you they are. The guamiquina conquers with love, not the terror Roldán inflicts," Bartolomé droned, as if honestly, the mantra well practiced. "The peoples who accept the guamiquina become my king and queen's vassals."

"Do they even know of your Isabel and Fernando, much less appreciate such vassalage?"

"They will learn and appreciate someday." He shifted to kiss her.

"Do they worship your Christ-spirit?" She drew back.

"They'll be taught, some day." He lustfully pulled her closer.

"Do they consider you and the guamiquina their rightful rulers?"

Bartolomé released his tug, startled by her line of questions, frustrated they weren't prelude to intimacy, and wary of where they led. He withdrew toward the bayahibe, delighting Anacaona as he was pricked and cried out.

"Bartolomé, you must be careful," she exclaimed, as if caring. "Needles hide beneath the flowers."

"We are their rulers!" Bartolomé stammered, lurching forward, dismissive of the sting.

Fleetingly, Anacaona brooded on the pale man's cursory retorts, which confirmed the essence of what she already knew. After six years, the guamiquina's conquest hadn't captured the soul of Haiti's surviving peoples any more than Roldán's squatting had in her Xaraguá. Virtually none of the island's peoples perceived themselves vassals of the guamiquina's caciques or worshipped the Christ-spirit. They simply were conquered peoples. None perceived the pale men deserved obedience, although all feared disobedience.

"Bartolomé, do you and the guamiquina care if my people love you?" she challenged, raising her voice, pleased that the pale man squirmed to concoct a reply.

"No, we demand that they fear and respect us," he countered, unwilling to be baited by a heathen queen. But his desire had been roused beyond restraining. "My love, what more must I prove?"

"When I brought Francisco here, I told him that the better he treated my people, the better friends he and I could become." She relished that the pale man's face contorted with jealousy. "But my Bartolomé, I pine to love you before him. Simply prove to me that the guamiquina will spare Xaraguá's people from invasion and enslavement." She kissed the pale man's forehead and stood, marking the liaison over.

POSSESSION OF PARIA, NIÑO, HOJEDA, GUEVARA, AND VESPUCCI,
June–August 1499

Isabel and Fernando's decision to license explorers to possess the southern landmass began to bear fruit that summer, although Isabel would have been angered by much that transpired in her name.

By early June, two weeks after Hojeda's departure, Pero Alonso

Niño and a Guerra brother sailed from Palos in one caravel, also racing—in disregard of her and Fernando's instructions—for the island Cristóbal had named Margarita. Niño won the race, with better navigation and fewer diversions. He accurately replicated his mentor's route from the Cape Verdes to landfall on Trinidad, then west along Paria's coastline, arriving at Margarita by July.

He'd also learned in Cristóbal's service how best to encounter unknown peoples peacefully, and with one exception, he avoided conflict. At Trinidad, there was an exchange of arrows and cannon shots with a fleet of Carinepagoto canoes hauling a cargo of Arawak slaves, during which the crew seized and hauled a slaver and slave on deck. While his mentor and queen used violence to conquer, Niño let his crew unbind the slave and amuse themselves with violence, cheering the slave on as he butchered the slaver to death. At Margarita and the neighboring island Cubagua, Niño victoriously traded for buckets of pearls. When he'd exhausted the locals' supply, he sailed south to the mainland and harbored there for some weeks, trading for more pearls (near Cumana, Venezuela) and claiming the area for the sovereigns.

Pearl trading. Taken from Pieter van der Aa, 1707. The John Carter Brown
Library, rec. no. 08984-9.

Hojeda's passage to Margarita was slowed by detours to secure and provision his fourth ship—the second to haul his own booty. After leaving Spain, he diverted to Cape Aguer in Africa (Morocco) to pirate an Andalusian caravel trading with the infidel, forcing the crew from the ship and installing his own. Accomplice Don Guevara became the caravel's captain, in recognition of nobility and loyalty, if not ability. Days later, Hojeda detoured to raid the barns of Beatriz de Bobadilla's daughter on the Canary Island of Lanzarote, looting rigging, anchors, and supplies. Hojeda's ocean crossing was efficient but, to his chagrin, the landfall was considerably southeast of Trinidad (perhaps Cape Orange, at the border of Guiana and Brazil). He immediately sped northwest toward Margarita with two ships, but the financiers' ships parted from him to explore independently southeast.

When Hojeda at last stepped ashore on Margarita, few pearls remained for barter, and his insistent snarl dissuaded many locals from trading at all. Impatient, he sailed west along Paria's coast, hunting for fresh pearl beds and overtaking—without sighting— Niño, beginning the exploration beyond Cristóbal's discoveries.

As the financiers' ships explored the southeast coast, to Vespucci's astonishment, they reconnoitered an enormous river mouth whose monumental discharge permitted them to replenish their fresh water when twenty miles offshore (the Amazon, Brazil). The crews traded peacefully with local inhabitants but were disappointed by the lack of pearls and gold. When the current turned adverse, the captains reversed course and sailed to rejoin Hojeda, reuniting with him along Paria's coast considerably beyond Margarita (perhaps Cape Codera, Venezuela), and the fleet of four continued westward.

Hojeda had never appreciated Isabel's instructions and Cristóbal's efforts to peacefully interact with locals encountered, and here and there, his habitual pugnaciousness triggered skirmishes rather than barter (including at Cape Codera and Chichiviriche). One hundred and fifty villagers were slaughtered in one battle, with one Spaniard killed and over twenty wounded. The experienced merchants on the financiers' ships sometimes induced peaceful trade, including for cotton. In early August, the fleet anchored near a peninsula (Paraguaná, Venezuela) where the locals lived in houses built on stilts over water, resembling Venice in Italy, and someone gave it a name that would stick, *Venezuela* ("Little Venice").

In late August, some 200 leagues west of Trinidad, the crews abducted local women and girls to mount as they sailed along the coastline of an island or mainland the locals called Coquibacoa (Gulf of Maracaibo and Guajira Peninsula, Venezuela). Don Guevara delighted in a few of them. Hojeda rewarded himself with the prettiest girl, not only for the exploration but to bring home to Spain. He would grow covetous of her and name her Isabel.

Sex slaves aside, Hojeda and his crews chafed that Paria hadn't rewarded pearls, gold, and gems in the quantity they'd sought. With his two ships leaking and their provisions almost spent, he veered them toward Española, intending to seek their repair, fresh supplies, and finally plunder the booty of his dreams, although his license didn't extend there, and he'd promised Isabel and Fernando to avoid it. The financiers' ships lingered, trading longer on the coastline before rejoining him in Española for their own repair.

V

REPARTIMIENTO

REPARTIMIENTO'S INCEPTION,
June–October 1499

Cristóbal remained at Fort Concepción through June. His despair surged when Bartolomé returned from Xaraguá to report the mission there had failed, and he sensed his grip on Española's settlers was deteriorating rather than firming. The impotence to force Roldán even to parley, much less quit the island, was stultifying.

In turn, while Cristóbal couldn't dislodge them from Española, Roldán and his lieutenants grimly acknowledged to themselves that the notion of seeking redress directly from the sovereigns was bluster and likely would fail and trigger punishment. Isabel and Fernando would never authorize two factions on the island, and any notion they'd choose Roldán over Colón was chimeric. For rebels to remain on Española, the rebellion had to be settled on terms that protected them on Española, which the existing settlement agreement failed to address.

In July, Cristóbal departed for Santo Domingo, alarmed that even his most loyal men there were tiring of his command and resolved to initiate discussions with Roldán on whatever terms necessary. Curses that the rebels had better lives and opportunities swelled. Whispers abounded that those in Santo Domingo should desert to establish their own haven with the Indians in eastern Española.

Not all was dark. Then unbeknownst to Cristóbal, a few Spaniards had grown impatient panning the western tributaries of the upper Jaina River and taken their Indian servants to scour the creeks and streamlets on its eastern bank. Rain often brought the dirt to life, and when the clouds parted, panning in sunshine consistently revealed specks and even nuggets of gold in quantity. Inured to meager returns, the miners were cautious to herald victory. But they informed Bartolomé, and he dispatched a few more sentries to a bunker he'd built by the Jaina as a headquarters for safeguarding gold and denying unlicensed persons access to the area.

When alerted of the find, Cristóbal's optimism for Española guardedly recovered. The portents both dire and bright, he often sought rejuvenation in Santo Domingo's church, praying that the newfound gold would decisively purge his loyalists' doubts.

Rumor, if not the Lord, came to his aid. Word of "New Mines" soon reverberated in Santo Domingo and filtered to the inland forts and Xaraguá. Many scorned and most shrugged, all embittered by prior false promises and reports. The New Mines were no more "mines" than the Old Mines found years prior to the north—riverbeds typically of barren yield. But most hoped against hope that the rumors were true and dreamed how to secure a share. Rebels in Xaraguá were quick to charge that the Colóns would hoard whatever found, yet those still intent on returning to Spain had second thoughts.

On August 3, Cristóbal's officers provided Roldán a written safe-conduct to parley in Santo Domingo. When he failed to come, Cristóbal bitterly forsook rank and appearance, and with the officers, sailed west on two ships to anchor in a bay off mountainous, neutral territory east of Xaraguá (Bahía de Ocoa, offshore Azua, Dominican Republic). Roldán and his rebels commandeered a nearby village, and in late August, he and his lieutenants came aboard Cristóbal's ship to talk.

The two leaders eyed each other starkly, neither feigning respect, Cristóbal grim that he would agree to injustices, Roldán invigorated that he'd come to a triumphant fork. Their mutual hatred glowed as transparently as the sunshine, and without shaking hands, they commenced discussions across a table on the main deck.

"My Admiral, I've come to resolve our differences, provided my men ashore approve what we agree," Roldán pronounced.

"So have I. We sit on a ship that will bear you and your men to Spain," Cristóbal replied. "I'm prepared to honor our previous understanding, including slaves for those who leave."

"You broke our understanding, and it no longer suffices," Roldán declared. "These ships must carry those of my men wishing to return to Spain on the terms previously agreed. But perhaps only fifteen so desire. We must agree additional terms for the majority who've chosen to remain."

"Most of your band wishes to remain?" Cristóbal stammered, incredulous and devastated.

"Yes, and they will agree to return to your service, respecting your leadership," Roldán replied, studying the grimace curling Cristóbal's lips and the bewilderment his stare betrayed. "In return for that loyalty, you must grant them estates of land of their choosing and vouchers for all past wages. You must also proclaim that all allegations against them have been but the false testimony of evil men."

"What of yourself?" Cristóbal blurted.

"My Admiral, I shall remain, and I, too, shall submit to your authority," Roldán promised, steeling his gaze into Cristóbal's eyes. "You must appoint me Española's perpetual chief magistrate, your second-in-command, and no other person may hold that rank." Uncertain of Cristóbal's reaction, Roldán drew breathless. All understood he was unwilling merely to be Bartolomé's equal. Perhaps it was less obvious that he hungered to rule if Cristóbal were recalled or dismissed.

Cristóbal brooded, gazing at the sea, and those assembled had the courtesy to remain silent. He'd improvised countless times over the last two decades, trusting in the Lord to reveal solutions, and the proposal—while outlandish—would end the rebellion, at least so far as he could report to the sovereigns. The traitor's fealty undoubtedly would be hollow, but it would permit the enterprise to progress at last. Promises to rebels could be ignored when advantage returned, just as promises to Indians.

"You pledge to obey my command as admiral, governor, and viceroy?" Cristóbal asked, breaking the silence, staring into Roldán's eyes. "You'll dutifully help me restore the tribute you dissolved?"

"My Admiral, I shall obey you in all your authorities, and I shall cause my men to do so," Roldán vouched. "But we must discuss how to please the king and queen. The Indians are best fit for farming and laboring, not searching for gold to pay you. It would be better to use them to mine the gold you've already found."

"What lands do your men desire?" Cristóbal probed, delving further, noting the evasion and avoiding a response. "The king and queen envision that I repartir homesteads with commitments to work the land for four years."

"My men have already settled in Indian villages, commanding the village caciques to direct their subjects to work the land and build our estates. The *repartimientos* (lands granted) you award my men will be for the Indian land they already inhabit and then more, as they reasonably demand," Roldán dictated. "Those not returning to Spain intend to remain here indefinitely."

Cristóbal again grew silent, recollecting Isabel and Fernando's expectations. They'd intended land grants to reflect a settler's status, service to the crown, and the quality of his person and lifestyle—not to compromise the unlawful demands of unchristian, licentious rebels, including those once criminals in Spain. But the rebels had already awarded themselves the land, and his own loyalists expected the equivalent—regardless of merit. He gazed back to the sea, which he'd mastered, then ashore to Española, which he hadn't, and last to the sky, where the Lord judged.

"What repartimiento do you yourself request?" He reasoned that his discretion extended to whatever was necessary to cure the rebellion.

"The lands of Behecchio that I've already taken, as well as others we agree upon," Roldán replied. "Behecchio shall direct his subjects living throughout Xaraguá to do my bidding."

⊡　⊡　⊡

Cristóbal soon relented to Roldán's new demands and confirmed the other terms set a year prior. Consensus among the rebels for concluding the rebellion coalesced by early September, and Cristóbal, Roldán, and their lieutenants promptly departed together on the two ships to publicly announce the understandings in Santo Domingo.

Behecchio and Anacaona had scrutinized the pale men's parley offshore and departure for Santo Domingo through scouts alone, without a spy to listen. But they'd gleaned the gist of the outcome well enough, and their confidence, which had risen only months earlier, now faded. Roldán and the guamiquina had somehow resolved their differences. Concubines whispered that most squatters would stay, likely including Roldán. While Roldán hadn't so admitted, all signs ominously portended that he would, in league with the guamiquina.

Dreadfully, mere days later, two vessels of pale men anchored on the southern coast within Xaraguá's bay of Yaquimo (Jacmel, Haiti), west of the site of the parley. Fearing the guamiquina's invasion, Behecchio ordered his most powerful vassal cacique of that coastline to meet the intruders and find out all he could. Haniguyabá, an august elderly man, trekked to the anchorage, and after a cordial encounter, immediately dispatched a runner relaying that the vessels' leader was none other than the notorious warrior who'd abducted Caonabó and led the great battle defeating Manicoatex, Alonso de Hojeda. The pale man claimed he came in peace, promising to depart soon and that he sought only a quarter shipload of cazabi and to cut timber.

Anacaona shuddered bitterly. The tragedies of Caonabó's abduction and Manicoatex's defeat, both intimate to her and collective, had been cornerstone to the success of the pale man's conquest. Hojeda's return augured the guamiquina's conquest would resume brutally and envelop Xaraguá. Utterly dismissive of Hojeda's promises, Behecchio and Anacaona nevertheless bid Haniguyabá honor Hojeda's requests for the moment and directed him to invite Hojeda to his village while the cazabi was baked in order to pry for more information. They also furnished Haniguyabá a nitaíno to better translate conversations and a few women who'd bitterly assimilated some of the pale men's tongue to eavesdrop.

Cristóbal and Roldán then entered Santo Domingo, unaware of Hojeda's arrival. Cristóbal assured his loyalists they'd be rewarded commensurately with the rebels, including repartimientos, and on September 28, the formal agreement ending the rebellion was publicly proclaimed. Roldán was to prepare a memorandum itemizing the repartimientos of Indian lands to be awarded each former rebel while Cristóbal provisioned the two ships. But the alarming news of Hojeda's arrival came the same day, interrupting these preparations.

Astonished, Cristóbal publicly presumed that his former lieutenant had sailed astray while bringing fresh supplies to Santo Domingo. Privately, his gloom resurged, as he dreaded the sovereigns had lost patience and authorized Hojeda's return to reorder Española. Roldán knew Hojeda from prior service on Española, and he foresaw knavery as inevitable, jeopardizing his reign over Xaraguá. Their interests at last truly aligned, Cristóbal ordered Roldán to sail before sunset with two dozen men to confront Hojeda in Xaraguá and take action as appropriate.

◻   ◻   ◻

Hojeda accepted Haniguyabá's invitation, and he brought only his sex slave, Isabel, and a handful of armed men to the cacique's village, leaving Don Guevara in command of the ships and brazilwood cutting. At dawn on September 30, Roldán and his squad of two dozen snuck to surround the village.

Hojeda woke to the realization that he was outmanned. Undaunted, he strutted to meet his old acquaintance, as if amiably, and invited him to sit at the firepit before Haniguyabá's caney while Indian women prepared them a meal.

"Francisco, I anchor here only to repair and provision my ships and cut brazilwood before returning to Spain," Hojeda professed. "I've explored Paria for the king and queen."

"You're welcome to refit and resupply," Roldán replied skeptically, yet thrilled to glean that the sovereigns were no longer tied to Cristóbal. "Has your voyage been licensed by the king?"

"I'll show you the license, which is aboard ship."

"By what fortune did you attain it? The Admiral knows nothing of this."

"The queen is on her deathbed, and when she passes, Colón will no longer have a protector. Bishop Fonseca favors me, and I'll claim the southern mainland for the sovereigns."

Roldán shifted warily, startled, tantalized that his dream of controlling Española without Cristóbal was attainable. He treaded cautiously, seeking camaraderie prior to inveigling. He asked who'd served as crew on Paria's exploration and what treasures had been found. Hojeda answered boastfully that Don Guevara and La Cosa had sailed as his lieutenants. The mainland's coastline stretched over 600 leagues, and they'd constantly battled ferocious savages, limiting the pearls and other booty taken. Roldán complimented Isabel's beauty, and Hojeda remarked that he was teaching her Spanish and of the Virgin so she might be baptized when he took her home. They chatted about Guevara, who was cousin to Roldán's own lieutenant Múxica, and Roldán inquired whether the sovereigns had chastised the nobleman after he returned from Española to escape Cristóbal's punishments. Hojeda answered that the sovereigns now rarely cared what Cristóbal thought and more rarely punished nobility.

"Do the sovereigns still trust Colón to lead Española?" Roldán ventured at last, gazing at the women cooking.

"No, his days are numbered. The lack of gold disappoints them." Hojeda paused and raised his eyebrows, calculating that the camaraderie belied a brazen ambition no less burning than his own. "The chaos also disappoints. They understand that you've rebelled, disregarding Colón's commands and calling this Xaraguá your own."

Roldán blushed momentarily, one rogue catching another. But he answered firmly. "Colón and I have since reconciled, and I am here on his behalf as the island's chief magistrate, his second-in-command."

"Do your men really wish to reconcile with him?" Hojeda probed, sensing ambition unfulfilled. "Española's veterans constantly harangue at court that he hasn't paid anybody. Francisco, you and I know that he and Bartolomé will siphon Española's gold for themselves and their cabal."

"My men's wages soon shall be paid, and I'll install them to watch the gold."

"Good for you, my friend. Perhaps one day you'll rule Española, and I Paria."

"Alonso, after your ships are refitted and provisioned, present your license to the Admiral in Santo Domingo, so he understands your authority. Then sail home." Roldán judged Hojeda was satisfied with his new entitlement and eager to return to Spain to boast about Paria.

"I've always intended to submit and report to the Admiral before departing," Hojeda lied graciously.

The next morning, Roldán escorted Hojeda and his band to the ships, reviewed the license, and instructed soldiers to watch over the rogue until the ships sailed for Santo Domingo.

Alone, he departed north for his village, intending to finally admit to Behecchio and Anacaona that he'd reside in Xaraguá indefinitely and to advise them of most of his escalating expectations. But full disclosure would have to wait until soldiers stood beside him.

◻ ◻ ◻

Haniguyabá was astonished how witless the two pale men perceived Taínos, assuming the women cooking for them understood nothing. While Roldán rode north, he dispatched a faster runner relaying his view that Roldán was serving the guamiquina and Hojeda wasn't, as well as mentioning Hojeda's prediction of the guamiquina's demise. He caveated that his views were uncertain, and the language barrier wasn't the only impediment. The two pale men likely dissembled to each other, as eager to share fortune as vultures prey.

"What should we believe?" Behecchio asked Anacaona the next day as they awaited Roldán in the ballcourt. His tone was dark, his gaze wide-eyed.

"It's clear enough that Roldán now serves the guamiquina," she replied softly, careful to avoid a recriminating tone. She recalled Hojeda pledging friendship moments before abducting her husband. "Nothing Hojeda says can be trusted. We've heard of the guamiquina's demise before, only to find it a lie."

"The question remains whether Roldán will do the guamiquina's bidding in our chiefdom," Behecchio posed, desperate for a hopeful path. "Perhaps their understanding contemplates otherwise."

Anacaona sorrowed and suppressed disdain. Her brother's denial couldn't hide or undo the stark erosion looming in his authority and their people's independence. Roldán had become the guamiquina's lieutenant.

Roldán soon sauntered cockily into the ballcourt, his signature entrance, pleased that Behecchio and Anacaona waited to attend him.

"Your Highnesses, I bring you news at last. Most of my men and I have decided to live with you, perhaps forever. We love you, your friendship, and your people. I trust this delights you, as we shall continue to teach your people much."

"We expect more than love," Behecchio responded curtly, having already understood that news. "How will you continue to protect us from the guamiquina?"

"The guamiquina and I have resolved our differences, whereby I shall continue to control my people's presence and conduct in Xaraguá," Roldán declared, believing it so.

"I trust that I shall not pay him tribute."

"Your Highness, you shall not pay gold," Roldán puffed. "The arrangements you and I have struck among our peoples work and shall continue." To himself, he mused that gold tribute was dead, regardless of Cristóbal's illusions. "But I now may bid you dispatch cazabi and cotton to Santo Domingo from time to time, when the guamiquina so requests."

"We once were willing to do that for the guamiquina—in return for being left entirely alone." Behecchio bitterly shook his head.

"You violate your promise to us, Francisco," Anacaona declared more softly. "Xaraguá is to be separate, spared whatever your people do elsewhere on the island."

Roldán had anticipated this moment, and he'd rehearsed his words.

"Your Highnesses, I have always served Fernando and Isabel, and my presence on the island—including in your Xaraguá—is and always has been on their behalf, regardless of past disagreements with the guamiquina. My friendship and that of my men is now proven, and you must recognize that I will allow you to remain rulers of Xaraguá's people, provided your subjects serve me in the manner I request. My men and I will reside in your villages as before, as subjects of Fernando and Isabel. The guamiquina, his brother, and their followers will not settle here."

Roldán halted at the precipice, recognizing further honesty might trigger violence. But to himself, he trumpeted victory. *Your lands shall be ours—repartimientos awarded in the queen's name—and your people's role is to work them for us. Your own role is to obey me.*

There was silence, brother and sister wretchedly acknowledging that Roldán had advanced from seeking haven as a squatter to asserting joint dominion or more as a permanent settler. They anguished that there would be practical changes in daily life and dreaded descent toward utter subjugation. But no other friend was available.

Roldán broke the silence, interpreting the lack of a response as the acquiescence of a conquered people. "Your Highnesses, Higueymota and I have come to enjoy each other's company. We might now cement our people's friendship by celebrating that bond. I would be honored were Higueymota to live with me in my village. We might even marry."

Anacaona had already rehearsed a response. She'd never consider him and pale men as more than squatters.

"Such a relationship requires Matunherí Behecchio's approval, regardless of your wishes," she replied. "You have yet to prove to us the love for our people you profess."

Repartimientos Awarded,
October–November 1499

In early October, fifteen former rebels left their bohíos and villages in Xaraguá to assemble with Roldán and travel to Santo Domingo, where they would board the two ships provisioned by Cristóbal to return to Spain. Some brought their concubines and children, others neither. Local caciques and villagers rejoiced at their departure. The concubines and children mostly trembled or wept, whether departing or deserted.

Although proclaimed only days before, Roldán and Cristóbal each began to undermine the settlement. Roldán wrote a letter justifying his actions and indicting the three Colón brothers for betraying Isabel and Fernando. Cristóbal wrote to Isabel and Fernando, proving why the settlement was void and Roldán should be prosecuted. Roldán had no access to the sovereigns, but two Burgundian friars intending to berth on the ships—the Franciscans Juan Leudelle and Juan de Tisín—had volunteered to deliver his charges to Archbishop Cisneros. They'd assisted Pané in the first baptisms on Española, and while never joining Roldán's rebellion, they'd come to deplore Cristóbal's administration of Española and the meager missionary effort and hoped the archbishop would convince the sovereigns to recast at least the latter.

Magnificent Lord—Roldán addressed Cisneros in his letter—Bartolomé had inflicted severities and wrongs against the settlers, usurped his own command, threatened to behead him, and left him to fight alone many battles with Indians resisting conquest. He and his men had fled to Xaraguá to escape this wrath and find food. When Carvajal's ships arrived, he'd harbored the men who arrived when they feared submitting to Bartolomé's rule, *taking them in so they wouldn't cause trouble and the Indians wouldn't kill them.* When the Admiral set off the five ships, he'd been forced *to give him a number of slaves* for dispatch to Spain. Even the baptized Indian Diego Colón had favored him over Bartolomé, for which the Admiral had enslaved the Indian.

Cristóbal's proof of the settlement's nullity consisted of nine roughly hewn lawyers' arguments. He'd signed it under duress, the rebels had signed in violation of their oaths to the sovereigns, the royal accountants' signatures were lacking, and so on. Beyond this proof, Cristóbal bared his plight and weakness as plaintively as he ever had. He was *now very broken, leading the worst life of any man in the world,* and he bid the sovereigns dispatch his natural son, Diego Colón, so he could *rest a little and Their Highnesses be better served.* Again, he requested a lettered person to serve as justice in Española, given the disobedience of the settlers.

When Roldán and the departing rebels arrived at Santo Domingo, Cristóbal duly complied with the settlement, awarding each between one and three slaves, as well as slaves to compensate the captains and crews. Some slaves were merely children, and stripping them from their parents triggered even more heart wrenching than the family separations had in Xaraguá. Roldán entrusted his letter to Leudelle and Tisín, and Cristóbal trusted his to Ballester, who would return to Spain to defend Cristóbal and impugn Roldán before the sovereigns.

At Hojeda's request, Roldán also brought Don Guevara to Santo Domingo, purportedly to herald that Hojeda would soon present himself. Instead, Don Guevara slunk about Santo Domingo—unattended by either Roldán or Cristóbal—drumming about the odiousness of Cristóbal's rule, identifying those who hated him most, and scouting out where the munitions were stored.

Cristóbal mulled returning to Spain to indict Roldán himself but decided it was essential to stay on Española. The repartimientos to be awarded to Roldán's loyalists and his own would critically affect the balance of power between them. He dispatched the two ships to Spain in mid-October, and Roldán rode back to Xaraguá to confer with his remaining one hundred and two loyalists and prepare the memorandum enumerating the repartimientos they demanded.

◻ ◻ ◻

Most of the one hundred and two told Roldán they wished to remain in the Xaraguán villages they'd already commandeered, the village caciques well intimidated. The more prominent squatters, including Roldán himself, also sought additional repartimientos elsewhere, particularly near Bonao and the so-heralded New Mines. All perceived the grant received would include that which made the land valuable, the labor of the resident Indians, who would farm it and build the grantee's estate thereon.

During the last two weeks of October, Cristóbal and Roldán met in Santo Domingo to discuss the memorandum and conclude the bald negotiation to allocate Indian land envisioned by their settlement. The settlers' status in Spain was considered, service to the crown and quality of person or lifestyle wasn't, and loyalty—to Cristóbal or Roldán, rather than king and queen—was central. Treatment of, and acceptance by, the resident Indians were irrelevant.

"In Xaraguá, the bounds of the initial repartimientos shall be the same as those of the land farmed by the cacique now cowed," Roldán pronounced. "Each of my men already rules that cacique and can dictate the labor of the Indians living there. My men also deserve additional repartimientos, both in Xaraguá—where the entire kingdom shall be ours—and elsewhere, as I wish to allocate them. My gentlemen shall receive additional lands planted with thousands of yuca mounds, those common bred fewer mounds."

"The framework is acceptable." Cristóbal nodded, having anticipated as much. "But I won't permit all your men remaining in Xaraguá." The risk former rebels would congregate to foment another rebellion had to be reduced. "Your principal lieutenants must spread throughout the island, without repartimientos in Xaraguá."

"I alone shall control Xaraguá and Behecchio, and you may never grant your men awards there," Roldán countered. "Your chaplain Ortiz may not remain." But compromise was possible, given the wishes of his men. "A third of my men would be satisfied with lands elsewhere. Some would be content to live in Bonao, others in Cahay, north of Xaraguá, and a few near Forts Esperanza or Santiago or in the Vega Real."

"What lands do you wish, in addition to those in Xaraguá?" Cristóbal inquired, satisfied with that dispersion.

"The lands of Ababruco, the cacique living south of Isabela, as well as those of the caciques living along the Yaque near the ruins of Fort Magdalena."*

By early November, Cristóbal and Roldán agreed the repartimientos of Indian lands to Roldán's loyalists. Cristóbal and the notary Garay issued the individual settler grants, referencing the caciques' lands or yuca mounds awarded and conferring the labor of the resident Indians.

Soon, Cristóbal and Garay held audiences with all those seeking commensurate repartimientos who hadn't joined the rebellion. Cristóbal readily granted them, keen to maintain goodwill and retain territory in loyal hands. Many of those who applied had never possessed a plot or servants of their own in Spain, and dreams of an estate with slaves were transparent. Often, when a cacique's lands were large, Cristóbal encouraged two or three settlers of common heritage to join in partnership. Applicants presented themselves for days.

⊡ ⊡ ⊡

One morning, seated in his compound's courtyard, Cristóbal held an audience with a carpenter. Garay assisted, apprising him of the applicant's contributions and loyalty, and he recalled speaking to the man years before at Isabela. The carpenter was a swarthy Andalusian, his skin crusted and burnt from the sun, his clothing worn and torn. Cristóbal admired his apparent work ethic and mused that Spanish gentlemen shared none of it.

---

* *Columbus and Caonabó*, chapter VI, discusses Fort Magdalena's establishment.

"Carlos has assisted building Santo Domingo's church, fort, and storehouse," Garay related, putting the applicant at ease. "Previously, he built at Isabela for two years."

"My Admiral, I also defended your brother Diego when Roldán sacked Isabela," Carlos blustered, unaccustomed to audiences. "While traitors and others have departed, I've chosen to remain to finish building the settlement for you and the queen."

Cristóbal nodded to show appreciation and mused that many spoke falsely. Undoubtedly, Carlos hadn't crossed an ocean to continue building houses. He'd enlisted to find gold, and while unsatisfied, he still dreamed a pot of it might fall his way. Yet he now came for a repartimiento, perhaps committed to remain indefinitely on Española, envisioning that as a rise from the ignobility his destiny in Spain. Cristóbal had founded his enterprise on such dreams, and he replied smoothly, probing the applicant's ability and commitment.

"Building an estate is more than building a home. Can you farm animals and produce?"

"My Admiral, I had a cow, pigs, and vegetable garden in Spain. I know farming," Carlos puffed. "I can command the Indians to farm, as well. I use a few in my work now."

Cristóbal doubted the applicant knew much of farming but was satisfied he perceived what needed to be done and how to proceed.

"Do you have family here?" Cristóbal gazed away to avoid triggering embarrassment.

"Yes, my Admiral." Carlos understood what Cristóbal asked. "I have two children."

Cristóbal nodded, satisfied the applicant had other ties keeping him on the island. He shied from asking whether the applicant also had a family in Spain.

"Do you attend church and confess often?" Cristóbal didn't remember seeing the applicant in church.

"I do, and I can do better, my Admiral."

"Where would you like your plot, and how long will you commit to remain?"

"I desire the plot that best serves you and the king and queen, and I'll live there at least four years," Carlos knowingly and emphatically proclaimed. "I'd like one where the earth is fertile, and the Indians are peaceful and industrious."

"Which do you prefer—near Santo Domingo or Concepción?"

"As you wish, my Admiral." Carlos bowed his head in homage, sensing he stood at the precipice of becoming a landowner and gentleman.

Cristóbal recognized the deep want, rooted in a life of undistinguished toil, and struck for it.

"We've achieved peace and tranquility on Española, but they remain fragile," he observed. "Should dissent and treason ever rear their heads again, do you commit to serve me fully and faithfully?"

Garay extended his arm, a small cross set in the palm of his hand, bidding the applicant place his own hand upon it.

"That will be my honor, as I've already proven. My Admiral, I so commit."

Cristobal delighted the applicant, awarding a small plot near Concepción. The sovereigns' criteria of status, service to crown, and quality of person satisfied, Garay dutifully recorded the repartimiento in a ledger.

⬚　⬚　⬚

Pursuant to Cristóbal's awards, Indian lands surrounding Santo Domingo and Fort Concepción and in much of the Vega Real soon were commandeered by individual settlers, just as in Xaraguá.

Roldán returned to Xaraguá to inform his men of their repartimientos and to inform Behecchio and Anacaona of the final arrogation of their new relationship. This time, he rode into the chieftain's village not alone, but with a dozen armed settlers, and bid the Indians present to summon Behecchio and Anacaona to the ballcourt.

"Your Highnesses, I come with news that I expect you'll appreciate. A third of my men shall depart this kingdom to assume lands elsewhere. Some seventy shall remain."

Behecchio and Anacaona understood that the squatters' harquebuses and crossbows portended inimical news. Behecchio folded his arms, fortifying himself.

"Francisco, will you remain with us?" Anacaona asked.

"Your Highness, I shall, and I shall continue to fulfill my promise to protect this kingdom from the guamiquina. The lands of my departing men shall be assumed only by my men remaining. The guamiquina has agreed his men will never settle in Xaraguá." He folded his arms, mirroring Behecchio, and glared at the chieftain.

"I shall continue to honor you as the natural king of this kingdom, provided you accept my greater authority throughout. I expect you to obey whatever I command. When I ask that naborias port cazabi to Santo Domingo to feed the guamiquina's men, you must so order. Your people's lands now are my men's, theirs to control, subject to my rule. My men shall continue to respect your vassal caciques—so long as the caciques obey them."

Behecchio stood rigidly, denying the expression of any reaction, and Anacaona gazed at the ground, unable to witness her brother's humiliation and crushed by her own. Behecchio chose silence, rather than hollow threats, evasive sophistries, or false submission. Yet he remained defiant, committed to persevere for vengeance, whether futile or not.

"May your command always be in my people's interest," Anacaona responded, similarly resolute, recalling the bayahibe's bristle. "Remember who hosts you, bears your children, and feeds you."

VI

MORE REBELLIONS, SPAIN
AND ESPAÑOLA

SURRENDER TERMS OBLITERATED,
Granada, Autumn 1499–January 1500

Portion of city of Granada in the sixteenth century. Civitates Orbis Terrarum.

On July 2, 1499, Isabel gazed from her carriage across the city of Granada's lowland plain to the hill adorned by the Alhambra and recalled the glorious procession by which she and Fernando entered the citadel as conquerors after the Mohammedans' final surrender.

For the first time since 1492, they now approached it as entrenched rulers. According to her wishes, their court's long train was still dressed in mourning black.

Although mourning and ill, Isabel remained driven to implement her vision of Christian rule. She and Fernando came to review the progress of the city and kingdom's integration into their realms, particularly the Christianization of the city's daily life and the Mudejars' conversion. Over the last year, they'd adopted more measures to those ends, advantaging their Christian settlers and toughening life on those not converting. A new tax, readily avoidable by conversion, had been imposed on Granadan Mudejar in celebration of Prince Miguel's birth. The 1491 surrender capitulations had freed Mohammedan slaves who'd fled to the city from throughout their kingdoms, yet they'd issued an interpretation that Mohammedan slaves who'd so fled after the surrender could be captured and reclaimed, pleasing all their Christian subjects. Granada's Christian settlers had come to expect the favoritism would unfold further, and some cried that the Mudejar should be expelled from Spain just as the Jews had been, regardless of the surrender capitulations.

Isabel and Fernando entered the Alhambra to the welcome of Governor Tendilla and the acclaim of the city's leadership, both Christian and Mudejar. To the Mudejar, they heralded themselves as beneficent protectors from the settlers' base cries, just as they'd once avowed themselves to Spain's Jewish leadership. They halted briefly to pray at the Alhambra's great church—until 1492 its great mosque—and Isabel took confession from Archbishop Talavera, her confessor and adviser for over a third of her life, from ascension to the throne through the Reconquista's completion. She welled with comfort to kneel before him, recalling he'd humbly but firmly instructed her to so kneel the first time he took her confession.* His ascetic virtue, intellectual and compassionate outlook, and constant communion with Christ had once influenced how she worshipped, reasoned, and ruled and her aspirations. As Granada's archbishop, he'd set about training pastors to preach among the Mudejar and establish new churches both among them and the city's Christian settlers.

---

* *Encounters Unforeseen*, chapter III, depicts the first confession.

The sovereigns took up residence in the Alhambra's royal palace, and for a few days, recuperated in the tranquil beauty of its stately gardens and pools. Occasionally, they strolled through the ramparts of the military defenses to admire the pope's silver cross, which had been raised at the time of surrender on the Alhambra's tallest tower. It reminded that the surrender—along with their expulsion of the Jews and support of the pope against his enemies—had earned them the pope's award of their peerless title, the Catholic Monarchs.*

Yet, over the next weeks, Isabel and Fernando grew upset that the city itself looked and sounded little different than when conquered seven years before. Streets remained crowded with turbaned men and veiled women, mosques still overflowed with infidel reciting the Koran, and while criers no longer wailed the call to prayer from minarets, horns did so instead, from dawn to sunset. Their vision of Christian ascendancy and homogeneity peacefully shuttering out a dwindling Mohammedan presence wasn't being realized. Talavera's persuasive approach to conversions—translations of the catechisms into Arabic, missionaries teaching in Arabic, Arabic instruments played in churches—had failed to produce the substantial conversions necessary to bring that ascendancy. Worse, of the few Mudejar who had converted, a small number—the so-called *elches*—had then changed their minds and reverted to Mohammedanism, a heresy fit for the Inquisition's persecution.

Isabel chafed, considering the want of Christianization a failure of both policy and her sacred duty, tarnishing her and Fernando's renown as the most valiant bearers of Christ's sword. Fernando also smarted, although he drew comfort that the peace among Christians and Mudejar had retained the latter's productivity and wealth to tax and extort. Both sovereigns deplored that the elches' heresy remained protected by the surrender capitulations' guaranties of freedom to practice Mohammedanism and from forced conversion, as well as their promise to Talavera to spare such converts from the Inquisition for forty years.

As July waned, the sovereigns' self-esteem and pride in preeminence were also punctured by a letter from King Manoel borne by a Portuguese courtier. One of Vasco da Gama's captains had returned

---

* *Columbus and Caonabó*, chapter XI, discusses the award.

to Lisbon, having reached India and neighboring kingdoms, including splendid cities and the spice and gem trade that extended from there to Mecca, Cairo, and around the world.* Manoel's title as king of Portugal and lord of Guinea soon would include lord of Ethiopia, Arabia, Persia, and India.

Isabel and Fernando projected optimism that Hojeda and others sailing west would conquer more territory and trading wealth than Manoel's route east ever could. Before releasing the courtier, they hastily summoned their court's cosmographers and geographers to analyze da Gama's discoveries. While admittedly unclear, it seemed that the lands discovered—being a shorter sail west from the Hispanic peninsula—likely fell within the part of the world Pope Alexander had awarded to Castile. Nevertheless, Isabel and Fernando assured the courtier that they rejoiced the Faith would spread and grow in the most remote parts of the world and that Manoel had found it before other Christian princes, given their great love for him and hope that good things came his way.

⬚   ⬚   ⬚

The sovereigns had always accepted the church's doctrine that a conversion was duly voluntary regardless of compulsions short of death, and based on that doctrine, they had offered the Jews the choice of conversion or exodus and established the persecutorial method of the Inquisition directed against conversos.

After dismissing the Portuguese courtier, Isabel and Fernando devoted October to speeding conversions without triggering Mudejar unrest. They met in audience with Christian and Mudejar leaders and prominent Mudejar converts, entertaining grievances and pleas. They retreated from recent encroachments, declaring that runaway Mohammedan slaves would be considered free and that the crown would compensate former slaveholders. They probed Talavera's capacity and willingness to pursue conversions more forcefully. But they soon tired of the audiences, mercies, and Talavera's moderation and recalled that, in past years, the choice of conversion or exodus and the tortures of the Inquisition had consistently achieved baptisms and reformed heretics.

---

* Nicolau Coelho arrived at Lisbon on July 10, Manoel's letter was dated July 12, and da Gama would arrive at Lisbon in September.

One evening, secluded in a rose garden, Isabel and Fernando weighed what to do in Granada and Talavera's leadership, much as they'd debated months earlier regarding the Indies and Cristóbal's leadership.

"The paucity of conversions is deplorable, the elches' regression detestable, and both signal abandonment of our resolve," Isabel pronounced piously and shrewdly, concerned for both her salvation and legacy. "The choice of denying Christ must be made starker, as we did with both Jews and conversos."

"Tendilla and Talavera have maintained order, and our treasury and Christian subjects have profited thereby," Fernando observed. "We mustn't take the Mudejar's submission for granted. We've vanquished them, but we've made promises we can't break without jeopardizing order. I have no wish to ride into battle again."

"I have no wish for that either," Isabel exhorted. They sat in silence for some moments. She grasped that it fell to her to lead on the Christianization of their Granadan subjects.

"At minimum, we must demonstrate we won't tolerate the elches, and we must set the Inquisition upon them," she declared. "The other Mudejar should appreciate we otherwise honor our promises to them." She paused, more disturbed by the betrayal of her former confessor. "Talavera must understand our promise to him has been superseded by his failure."

"The elches are few and isolated, a minority of the minority of converts. Perhaps most Mudejar wouldn't care what we do to them." Fernando nodded, indicating his comfort with taking the risk. "But our archbishop hasn't the will to set the Inquisition upon them." Talavera had served as his confessor, as well.

"His will is strong, but his method and outlook fail." Isabel scowled. "His tolerance of Mudejar customs is perceived as license to retain them. His heart has never embraced the Inquisition." She peered into Fernando's eyes, knowing he'd disagree. "We must bring Cisneros here and grant him the Inquisition's authority."

"He's fanatical." Fernando shook his head vigorously. "He cares little for anything but faith and the afterlife. He belittles peace and prosperity on earth."

"His authority would extend to the elches alone, leaving Talavera's authority otherwise intact. His vigor and righteousness may cow others to convert. His example may firm Talavera's resolve to be tougher."

They argued over Cisneros, but Fernando soon acquiesced, accustomed to Isabel's headstrong insistence regarding policies of faith in Castile and Granada. That evening, they invited Archbishop Talavera to discuss their joint decision regarding the Inquisition's introduction into Granada.

"My confessor, we once promised you that the Inquisition wouldn't operate here during your tenure," Isabel acknowledged. "But the king and I grow older, and there are tasks I must complete for Him before He judges me, paving the way for Christ's return." She brought her palms to her chest, as if prelude to prayer. "For my part in His design, I must accelerate redelivering the elches to His fold."

Talavera nodded to indicate his obedience. He knew he'd failed her expectations and that they'd never seen eye to eye on the use of the Inquisition and compulsion.

"Christ's sword must be unleashed on them," Isabel explained. "Archbishop Cisneros has the temperament for leading the Inquisition here to that end."

▫   ▫   ▫

Cisneros arrived in Granada by early November, took residence and offices in a small palace in the city near the Albaicín, and began preaching to prominent elches and other Mudejar. His sermons were severe but not unique, contrasting everlasting salvation and damnation following Christ's second coming. Like Talavera and the sovereigns, he offered his audiences monetary rewards, perquisites, and honors for converting.

He then began to assert his inquisitorial authority over prominent elches, threatening incarceration, property confiscation, and torture, and when those failed to produce reaffirmations of Christ, he incarcerated indefinitely, confiscated, and tortured. Soon, his inquisitorial threats extended beyond the elches to their loved ones, and he turned to baptizing elches' children without their consent. Within a month, he'd baptized about a hundred elches or their children in ceremonies held at his palace. Isabel purchased robes for the converted Christians, marking her support of his methods.

When December approached, Isabel and Fernando left with their court to winter in Seville, instructing Tendilla to supervise Cisneros. Beyond the sovereigns' eye, Cisneros soon exceeded his mandate, threatening prominent Mudejar who'd never converted with coercions, not just elches. Throughout Mohammedan Granada, alarm and loathing surged that Isabel and Fernando were on the precipice of violating the freedom from forced conversion they'd promised all. By December 18, Cisneros had baptized three hundred more Mudejar, predominantly but not entirely elches, and passions simmered dangerously.

That day, when his officers entered the Albaicín to arrest an elche for interrogation, the fear and hatred boiled into a riot that engulfed the entire neighborhood and those nearby. One of the officers was killed, and the rioters barricaded the Albaicín from entry. Over the next days, Tendilla led troops from the Alhambra and sought to restore order, displaying but not employing force. Bearing a cross, Talavera walked among the rioters promising a pardon to all except the officer's murderers if peace and order were restored. Peace and order weren't Cisneros's concern, and falsely in the king's name, he offered the rioters the choice of conversion or death. Terrified, almost three hundred more elches and other Mudejar converted, and many thousands began to flee the city.

On December 21, when Castilian reinforcements arrived from neighboring Andalusian towns, Tendilla and Talavera finally restored peace, and rioters surrendered their arms. By then, Isabel and Fernando had learned of the riot.

☒   ☒   ☒

After arriving in Seville on December 10, the sovereigns had sought to focus again on the Indies. They'd met with Fonseca, who'd just dispatched two expeditions to explore the coastline southeast of Trinidad, led separately by Vincente Yáñez Pinzón and Diego de Lepe. Hojeda and Niño still hadn't returned, and with Fonseca's attention directed to the other expeditions, ships hadn't been provisioned for Bobadilla's departure. While unspoken, the sovereigns still hoped for news that Cristóbal had resolved the rebellion in Española before they set in motion his removal.

Isabel and Fernando hadn't been informed of Cisneros's unauthorized zealotry, and the abrupt news of riots enraged them, particularly at their own ministers. Fernando angrily dispatched a handwritten letter to Tendilla criticizing the failure to supervise Cisneros, Cisneros himself, and the coercions used. Only the officer's murderers should be punished. He chided Isabel that they hadn't labored ten years to conquer and subdue the infidel only to trust a fanatic to jeopardize all that.

But the sovereigns soon received reports that the riot had been quelled and peace restored. The Mudejar were fleeing en masse from the city to the countryside, and baptisms were accelerating. Isabel grew pleased and expectant, Fernando placated. She counseled patience, without chiding him. Terror didn't invalidate conversion.

Together, they dispatched another letter, to both Tendilla and Cisneros, marveling at how they'd been kept uninformed and demanding ongoing contemporaneous reports. Yet they now commended how the peace had been restored. In conversion—they observed—one makes all the fruit one can make.

After Christmas, they dispatched noblemen to Granada to instruct Tendilla to offer a general pardon to all Mudejar who converted, other than the murderers, with punishment for nonconverts found guilty of the unrest. Justice would be harsher than Talavera's pardon-for-peace, kinder than Cisneros's conversion-or-death. They also ordered Cisneros to cease his persecutorial activities.

News from Española then arrived. The two ships bearing the fifteen homecoming rebels, their slaves, and Cristóbal's unhinged reports—but without any gold for the crown—had anchored at Cádiz around Christmas. Although its rebellion had been settled, Española was a travesty of its promise, and compared to Manoel's triumphs of Mina and Calicut, it was a disgrace.

Isabel was furious and ranted again that the Admiral continued to disobey her. Her Admiral had no authority to enslave her Indian vassals.

Beyond fury, more gravely, Isabel's conscience could bear it no further, and her patience with the festering issue of Indian enslavement and her own five-year equivocation finally broke. She and Fernando had manumitted Canarians wrongfully enslaved, and they would do the same for the Indians. Angrily, she pronounced her own intent—irrespective of the wishes of the merchant community, the deliberations of any commission or clerics then considering the matter, and the views of Bishop Fonseca. All who'd brought to Spain Indian slaves granted by the Admiral had to send them back on the first ships sailing. Under pain of death.

⊡　⊡　⊡

Yet there was no time for the Indies. On New Year's Day, peace and order graced the city of Granada, but Isabel and Fernando feared unrest might resume there and spread elsewhere, particularly in provinces to which the city's Mudejar had fled. Cisneros's conversions weren't true enough to trust returning the weapons the converts had surrendered. But the newly converted needed protection from both Mudejar and Christian attack, so the sovereigns ordered soldiers deployed to police the city. They also warned Castilian townships to protect their Mudejar populations from Christian retribution.

As for Cisneros, steeled by the sovereigns' offer of conversion or punishment, he resumed baptizing en masse the Mudejar who remained in the city. He recorded some two hundred baptisms on January 10, over three thousand on January 11, almost five hundred on January 12, and three hundred on January 13. Atop the Albaicín, he christened its centuries-venerated mosque the Church of San Salvador. He resolved to direct the burning of thousands of Korans and other Mohammedan religious books. On January 16, he boasted that no non-Christians remained in the entire city and all its mosques were now churches.

That afternoon, Isabel and Fernando sat alone, shaded by the orange trees of the grand gardens of Seville's alcazar, criticizing each other and themselves, as the bond of respect they'd forged for three decades allowed.

"Your fanatic is a fool," he chided. "He believes these conversions are meaningful."

Anacaona.

"My husband, the Lord knows what they are and sees progress," she retorted. "Since faith hadn't rooted, the sword was necessary to open the infidels' hearts. Time will show that opening is irreversible. The converts' children and grandchildren will become true believers."

"All say I'm the unclean one," he observed wryly.

"I appreciate that. Have faith. The Lord sees both our contributions. He rewards those who brandish His sword, so long as struck with devotion."

Both were unfulfilled, brooding silently over the trials they'd suffered during the past two years. It would come as no surprise that Mudejar who'd fled the city were plotting more.

Isabel. Juan de Flandes, ca. 1500–1504.

HOJEDA'S REBELLION,
Haiti (Quisqueya), November–December 1499

As October waned, Haniguyabá warned Behecchio and Anacaona that fevers and grotesque red skin blisters—footprints of the pale men's presence elsewhere—had beset some of his villagers, wholly debilitating a few of the oldest and youngest.[*] He'd sequestered the sickest to be cared for in secluded bohíos and lean-tos, and at least one appeared close to death. Anacaona shuddered, having witnessed the decimation of Maguana's population from such illnesses, and she scanned her household and subjects for symptoms, exhorting Yúcahu that Xaraguá be spared. Behecchio requested frequent reports of afflictions.

---

[*] Perhaps typhus borne by lice carried by Hojeda's crews or the ships' rats.

Days later, Haniguyabá related that Hojeda and his two vessels had departed west along Xaraguá's southern peninsula, rather than east to submit to the guamiquina, and scouts soon tracked the ships' ominous course back east along the peninsula to harbor in Xaraguá's port, offshore Behecchio's coastal residence (Port-au-Prince). Roldán was away, apparently marching the island to instill his authority in territory awarded his loyalists elsewhere, and the squatters at the port appeared to welcome the newcomers.

When alerted, Anacaona was at her inland residence, teaching girls of the caciqual family to perform areítos. She exhaled deeply, purging a pang of hatred and weariness, determined to investigate herself whether this fresh intrusion—by her husband's abductor, no less—posed new dangers that required a reaction. Behecchio would do exactly that, but she sensed his pride hadn't fully recovered from Roldán's debasements and that he'd come to trust her foresights and judgments on par with his own, a confidence she embraced, doubtless of her ability to lead. But she was respectful to not graze her brother's self-esteem further. She excused her pupils and entered his caney to learn the scouts' full report.

"The squatters hailed Hojeda when he came ashore," Behecchio related. "He struts among them as a hero, brash and impudent as before, and he ignores his obligation to present himself to me. I shall summon him to learn his intent."

"My brother, we can learn his intent better from the squatters' concubines," she responded, bitterly recalling her husband's fate for heeding the pale man.

Within a day, Behecchio and Anacaona departed for his coastal residence, summoned the local caciques and their wives, and heard their reports of Hojeda's boasts, as intimated by concubines or otherwise overheard. Isabel and Fernando had anointed him to seize control! He'd lead squatters to storm Santo Domingo and overthrow the guamiquina. He'd demote Roldán, too, and rule all of Haiti. Truth and falsehood were difficult to parse, but one aspect was startlingly transparent—many squatters had soured on Roldán and favored Hojeda.

"We must stay the course you've set and outlast them all," Anacaona counseled Behecchio that evening. "Befriending Hojeda is prudent in case he never leaves. But his plots against the guamiquina and Roldán are too uncertain to assist. Allying with him would infuriate them."

"You wouldn't join him in hurling both the guamiquina and Roldán to the sea? We might then hurl him too."

"No. Summon him courteously, without reprimand for his impudence," she decided. "We shall host but not ally with him."

⊡   ⊡   ⊡

Hojeda then was haranguing a crowd of former rebels to follow him and his crews to Santo Domingo to demand the Admiral pay their back wages with the gold the Admiral had wrongfully hoarded. Bishop Fonseca had appointed him to do that, and if denied, they'd throw Colón off the island, dead or alive, and loot the gold!

But to Hojeda's chagrin, while many veterans rallied to his side, many didn't, either cowards or simply spent of rebellion. He was delighted to receive Behecchio's invitation to parley. An alliance of his crews, veterans, and Indian confederates might overpower everyone else, and he might commandeer Española for himself.

With an elegant bow, he presented himself to Behecchio and Anacaona in the ballcourt overlooking the bay and his caravels, and he instantly recollected having met her five years before. Her scant attire, fine jewelry, and uncommon beauty had cast an enduring memory. He also recalled kidnapping her Caonabó and was cocksure there'd be no revenge. His sailors and the Virgin stood ready to massacre any naked heathen attack. No apology was due her or Behecchio, as conquerors and Christians owed none.

"Your Highnesses, I present myself to express my gratitude for your and your subjects' hospitality," Hojeda swaggered, waiting for Behecchio's nitaíno to translate. "I bring tidings and love from Queen Isabel and King Fernando."

As Behecchio expressed welcome, Anacaona studied Hojeda's eyes dart from her brother to herself, and she was certain he recognized her. His cemí of the Christ-spirit's mother cast omens of disease, war, and doom. His brazen confidence that they wouldn't slay him was spiteful, his naked pride in her husband's abduction contemptuous.

"How long do you wish to stay with us?" she inquired, assuming control of the parley.

"Isabel and Fernando have ordered me to right their settlement here," Hojeda professed. "Admiral Colón has mistreated their men, as well as you and the island's peoples." He hesitated, pondering the heathen king and queen's relationship with Roldán. "I'm to take command of their settlement, even if the Admiral or others resist."

"I'm startled," Anacaona pronounced sternly, withholding her customary warmth. The insinuation that he'd treat her people better was insipid. "We've understood Francisco and the guamiquina now see eye to eye and that all your people stand with the guamiquina. Does Francisco know you will replace him?"

"Your Highness, Isabel and Fernando have entrusted me to bear their authority. Francisco will come to recognize that."

"When will this succession occur?" Anacaona probed, the tenor of her voice imparting a chieftain's challenge.

"As soon as I muster a squad of men to accompany me," Hojeda replied, ever invigorated by unfriendliness. "Force may be necessary to remove the guamiquina. The men living with you may enlist their servants, and I may invite the Ciguayo to join us. I now so invite you."

"We wish you safety and good health, Alonso," she lied, judging him to be a lieutenant, never a ruler. "But Xaraguáns don't join disputes among your people. My brother remains Xaraguá's supreme ruler, and we expect to be left alone—no matter who rules your people elsewhere."

Hojeda bowed, as if to acknowledge her expectation.

"You may stay with us until you depart to meet the guamiquina." She withheld a smile. "Until then, is there any assistance we may offer?"

"You're gracious, Your Highness. My ships need further repair."

That evening, Anacaona arranged an areíto, as though commemorating friendship with the pale man. Odiously, seated at his side, she promised him naborias to haul and hoist timber for his vessels as his men directed. Through his boasting, she was both astonished and disgusted to learn of the sex slave Isabel. No Xaraguán nitaíno was so demented to name a captive Caribe Anacaona. The supreme cacique Isabel and her husband ruled through lieutenants openly bestial to women.

In days following, Hojeda's entreaties to veterans to join his crew's march upon Santo Domingo grew abrasive and urgent and the turmoil among the veterans intense. The confusion spiraled when Hojeda's two vessels were joined by the two directed by his financiers, with more pale men spilling into the coastal village, their ships also requiring assistance in repairs.

One evening, Hojeda summoned his crews and those veterans who would obey him to slay those who wouldn't, and for the first time since the invasion of 1493, Spaniards drew blood of Spaniards on Española, dozens wounded, some mortally.

Behecchio gloated. Anacaona shared his delight but despaired that new evils loomed. The pale men laid their corpses in the earth and set crosses of the Christ-spirit on top, swelling the spirit's presence in Xaraguá. The newest intruders—bearing their own cemís of the Christ-spirit—brought other captive women, and they wandered ashore entreating and cajoling for more. As countless times before, Anacaona invoked Yúcahu to guard her subjects' health and safety.

Behecchio soon summoned her to confide that he felt ill, although he would hide it publicly. She wept that it be not so.

❏   ❏   ❏

Roldán was furious when he learned of the bloodshed, and with Cristóbal's urging, he sped to Xaraguá's port to expel Hojeda from the island. He investigated the plot to depose Cristóbal, dead or alive, and dispatched a messenger with Chaplain Ortiz to Santo Domingo to warn him.

On Christmas, as the Indians last enslaved disembarked in Cádiz, Cristóbal worshipped with his loyalists in Santo Domingo's church—although he sat apart, greeted no one, sang not a single hymn, and barely followed the service. Most presumed he'd immersed himself in beseeching the Holy Trinity. That was accurate, but no one could imagine how tortured the dialogue. Another rebellion! More violent than the last. A yearlong struggle to settle treason undone in weeks.

Cristóbal had plummeted from cautious optimism into an abyss of paranoid despair and fear. His very life was now in jeopardy—not merely the worst of any man alive. All remaining support was crumbling. The sovereigns had deserted him for rogues, regardless of the vast territory he'd single-handedly delivered them. Their ungrateful subjects still despised him, regardless of the riches he'd bestowed on them. The Indians still resisted, regardless of his peaceful outreach. As the congregation celebrated Holy Communion, he envisioned Isabel and Fernando seated beside him, partaking with him, and he shut his eyes to address them.

Neither the Greeks nor Romans expanded their empires with such slight cost as the Indies expanded Spain, he cried, imploring their appreciation for what he'd brought them. *So many souls will be saved! Your triumph shall be spoken of as a marvel among all Christians.*

When the service ended, Chaplain Ortiz and others came to sit beside him, offering companionship. But he declined, choosing solitude and his communion with the sovereigns, and Ortiz and the congregation departed. Perceiving himself utterly abandoned and friendless, he walked to the embankment and gazed across the Ozama to Cacique Catalina's sentries.

Do not judge me as a governor sent to a city or two under settled government, he pleaded to Isabel and Fernando, bitter that they'd woefully underestimated the Indies' obstacles and hardships. *Judge me as a captain who has long borne arms, never laying them down for an hour, who went from Spain to the Indies to conquer a people warlike and numerous and, by the will of God, brought them under your dominion—whereby Spain, which was called poor, is now most rich.*

He gazed north to the cove, where a caravel lay anchored, and trembled whether to flee to it. The signs were unmistakable! Hojeda had massed a bloodthirsty mob to murder him. Don Guevara had plotted the ambush in Santo Domingo. The Ciguayo hungered to join in revenge. Did Isabel and Fernando care whether he survived? Shuddering uncontrollably, he stared behind to Santo Domingo's central plaza, exhorting the sovereigns to understand their own men were his greatest enemies.

I am a poor hated foreigner, untruthfully criticized for my settlements, treatment of people, and much else. I beg you command Fonseca to favor my enterprise rather than obstruct it.

Abruptly, Cristóbal swooned, falling to his knees, bolted by the recognition that the Lord had always watched over him at sea. He'd spoken with Him there intimately many times, including at the edge of death. He was overwhelmed by a vision of the horrific maelstrom of his first voyage's homeward crossing. The Lord had brought the *Niña* nigh to doom, his triumph never to be known, and then reprieved it, his fame then everlasting.

His life again at the precipice, Cristóbal rose, staggered down to the cove, clambered into a launch, and feverishly rowed to board the caravel, seeking His presence, call, and protection once more. Astonished, the ship's sentry helped him climb aboard, and when he requested solitude, led him to a chair on the stern deck. He remained there in tormented prayer, recrimination, fear, and self-pity the entire day, waiting on the Lord.

As night descended and darkness enveloped the Ozama, he gazed to starry heavens and declared the root cause for all Española's failures to the Lord and the sovereigns.

Satan lurks behind the disappointments and rebellions, setting himself to obstruct this great enterprise with his entire might.

Exhausted, Cristóbal crumpled on the deck and was blessed with a few hours of sleep. As dawn broke, his energy and resolve reemerged, as well, and he heard the Lord's reply.

I shall disperse your enemies, grant your wishes, and restore your sinner's trust in the world.

MOHAMMEDAN UPRISING,
Granada, January–March 1500

"You mustn't lead the first charge any longer," Isabel bid Fernando as he mounted his steed to leave Seville.

"You must bring your confessor back home to Castile," he retorted.

In late January, Fernando assumed command of the army gathering in the plain of the city of Granada. By then, most of the city's remaining Mohammedan population had submitted to baptism, nigh fifty thousand souls. But the Mudejar fleeing the city had regrouped in remote villages of the Sierra mountains to the east and south. Hoping Mohammedans in Africa would send aid, they'd proclaimed that the sovereigns had breached and thereby undone the 1491 surrender terms, and they'd appointed a new emir of Granada as their rightful ruler to defend their faith and people. In turn, Isabel and Fernando had pronounced that the riots breached the surrender terms and constituted a rebellion, and they'd issued an order calling all Andalusian men between the ages of fifteen and seventy-five to military service.

Before attacking, Fernando announced that he'd pardon all Mudejar who surrendered their weapons, reaffirmed obedience to Isabel and himself, and adopted Christianity. Almost none sought that pardon, and for two months, Christians and Mohammedans fought furiously in mountain villages and ravines and at the crown forts that Mohammedans briefly seized. Isabel participated in decisions daily, receiving and dispatching messengers on horseback.

Thousands of Mohammedans with the fortune of being captured rather than slain were enslaved, many to be sold in Seville at the same auction market as Canarians and some Indians were sold. A portion were hauled to the sovereigns' court to serve in their household and those of their courtiers. In one town reconquered, Fernando baptized the surviving residents en masse and then executed them, a warning that his patience and mercy were spent. In early March, after subduing a region central to the rebellion, he so baptized residents and imposed a crushing ransom for their lives, confiscating their entire wealth.

Fernando soon returned to the Alhambra and then Seville, entrusting his troops to crush what unrest remained. Isabel stripped Cisneros of all remaining authority in Granada and recalled him to Seville. They awarded the recent converts the protection of the Castilian justice system and eliminated Mudejar-based taxes, but they withheld the right to bear arms.

HIGUEYMOTA'S ENGAGEMENT,
Xaraguá, February–April 1500

Cristóbal recovered his wits by News Year's Day and summoned and confronted Don Guevara. The two men despised each other. Cristóbal was infuriated by the perpetual favor the sovereigns bestowed on noblemen openly disloyal to him, particularly on one so young, brazen, and indolent. Guevara was scornful of the sovereigns' grant of a Castilian coat of arms to a failing Genoese weaver and embittered by the punishments the weaver had inflicted on him years earlier for shirking labor unbefitting a nobleman.

Each bridled his passion. Cristóbal recognized that Guevara hadn't participated in Roldán's rebellion and surmised the sovereigns wouldn't punish those loyal to Hojeda. Rather than jailing him, Cristóbal simply directed that he rendezvous with Hojeda in Xaraguá and depart when Hojeda was booted from the island. Cristóbal also lent him a horse to speed his journey, as if respectful of his stature. Without alternative, Guevara submitted and dutifully rode there, chagrined. He'd sailed for gold in Paria and left with empty pockets. He'd conspired to usurp Española and failed. He'd had adventures to boast of, but so far, had attained neither riches nor glories sufficient to embellish the Guevara coat of arms.

Worse, when he arrived in Xaraguá by mid-February, he found himself stranded. Roldán and lieutenants had expelled Hojeda from the island—Spanish weapons having drawn more Spanish blood—and Hojeda's four ships had sailed for Spain.

Without recourse again, Guevara gingerly presented himself to Roldán. The two were acquainted but unfriendly—Roldán bitter for Guevara's plotting with Hojeda, Guevara dismissive of Roldán as baseborn. Nevertheless, Roldán acknowledged Guevara's superior lineage, favor with the sovereigns, and kinship with Múxica, and recognizing his isolation, simply bid him live where he wished, without restraint, until Cristóbal advised otherwise. Guevara promised to encamp with Múxica, who'd been awarded a repartimiento in Cahay, within Xaraguá on the northern shore of the western gulf.

More schooled than Hojeda, Guevara also rode one morning to present himself to Behecchio as Xaraguá's natural king, cognizant that courtesy due and expectant that Behecchio would reciprocate the homage with comforts appropriate for a foreign prince.

"Your Highnesses, I come to praise you and request the honor of entering your kingdom," he articulated with a dignified swell, kneeling before Behecchio and Anacaona in the ballcourt of their inland village. "I am Don Fernando de Guevara, and I serve as Queen Isabel and King Fernando's noblest emissary in your Haiti." He eyed the heathen rulers' reaction while their nitaíno translated. "Your renown and friendship delight my queen and king, and I bring you their love."

Behecchio and Anacaona were startled by the pomp and struck that the youthful pale man's demeanor was demonstrably more noble than that of others they'd met, including Bartolomé, Roldán, and Hojeda. His hands were smooth, clothing well kept, and gold jewelry fine and fulsome, signaling others labored for him. His speech was self-assured but without swagger, as if certain his claims were true. Recognizing the island by their name for it was deferential.

"Tell me more of yourself and what brings you here," Behecchio requested skeptically.

"Your Highness, I've resided on your island for some years, arriving with the guamiquina six years ago. But he and I didn't see eye to eye, and regretfully, I returned to Spain for a time," he related, as if lamenting. Pivoting to Anacaona, he lowered his voice. "I berthed on the ships transporting your husband, and I am deeply sorrowed by your loss." He scrutinized the heathen king and queen to glean whether he'd favorably moved them. They were stunned by the commiseration, but their sentiments otherwise remained impenetrable.

"Isabel is displeased with the guamiquina, and she dispatched Alonso de Hojeda and myself to replace him," Guevara explained. "But that has been thwarted wickedly, and Hojeda has retreated to Spain without me. Your friend Francisco Roldán has approved that I may reside with my kinsman Adrian de Múxica in Cahay to the north." He smiled affably, as if unrattled by adversity. "I'm simply passing through your village on my way there."

Anacaona peered at Behecchio, surmising his curiosity as whetted as her own.

"Don Fernando, it's our pleasure to receive you in Xaraguá as Isabel and Fernando's noblest emissary," she proclaimed, marking her authority to the pale man. "Tell me how you came to that appointment. What's your relationship to the guamiquina?"

"Your Highness, I come from an illustrious family that has served Isabel and Fernando for decades. As their devoted courtier, I've stood at their side at the most pivotal moments, including the births, marriages, and acclamations of their children and, tragically, the recent burials of two of them." Guevara grimaced, as if personally sorrowed. "They requested my service here, then choosing an older man to lead their people's settlement. But that choice—the guamiquina—now angers them, as he lacks the eminence to rule providently and mistreats both your people and mine." He raised his chin and folded his arms, well-aware the heathen king and queen feared Colón. "The guamiquina despises me for being nobler and a successor, and I despise him for his misdeeds."

"If you are enemy to the guamiquina, how is it you are friend to Roldán?" Anacaona probed distrustfully, ignoring the intimation of better treatment.

Guevara hesitated, searching for the most pleasing answer. "Francisco and I are colleagues, having served the guamiquina together for years. Francisco now does the guamiquina's bidding, denying the guamiquina's demotion." He shrugged and smiled assuredly again. "While he labors dutifully, Francisco lacks the lineage to represent my queen as she is accustomed. It's unfortunate he prevailed over Hojeda."

"Where were you when the two fought?"

"I was in Santo Domingo, bidding the guamiquina to step aside. He would not."

"Don Fernando, you're welcome to remain in Xaraguá. Stay with us a few days before you pass on to live with your kinsman." Anacaona pointed to a bohío for his use. "Tonight, share a meal and areítos with us."

              □   □   □

At sunset, led by Guanahattabenecheuá, women and girls of the caciqual family performed dances celebrating the fertility of Xaraguá's peoples and lands. Anacaona found Guevara's etiquette refined. Through an interpreter, he commended the honor of the performance, and as it unfolded, the grace of the dancers, without lusting for them. As the meal was served, he courteously summoned naborías for water to cleanse his hands.

"That was extraordinary!" Guevara puffed. "My knowledge of your language is deficient, and I failed to understand most, but Xaraguá is blessed."

"Your appreciation warms me," Behecchio responded perfuncto-rily. "How long do you intend to stay in Cahay?"

"Your Highness, perhaps indefinitely," Guevara replied. "I prom-ised my queen to cure that wrong here, no matter how long it took."

"Tell me of your cacique Isabel," Anacaona inquired, scrutinizing the intimacy the pale man had vaunted. "How does she find amuse-ment and pleasures?"

"Your Highness, she is much older than yourself, nearing the end of her glorious rule," Guevara explained. "She gave birth to a son and four daughters and watched the son waste away of disease. She held the eldest daughter in her arms while dying on the birth of a grandchild. She also has given birth to a kingdom as great as any. Tragically, Isabel now frets that she has no successor capable to maintain it when she passes." Guevara studied Anacaona, surmising he'd satisfied her doubts. "Isabel has no pleasures and amusements other than our god, Christ the Lord."

Anacaona chafed. Such losses were inconsequential compared to her people's catastrophe. Yet she was intrigued that her conqueror suffered a mother's pain.

"Did she ever dance and compose areítos?" she asked.

"Her renown was born riding into battle with her soldiers, her command as feared as any man's. But I saw her dance, when younger."

"Does she favor her vassals' brutishness?" she pressed, testing the pale man's perception of his own people, surprised a pale woman would be a warrior, like Caribe women.

"Of course not. That is why she sent me here."

After an interlude of more amiable conversation, Anacaona brought the feast to conclusion. "My daughter Higueymota shall perform the final areíto. It honors Yúcahu for the blessing of every being's survival."

Higueymota led other unmarried, fully naked teenage girls in a pantomime of Xaraguá's living things—people, fish, fowl, trees, flowers, yuca, and so on—as they nourished, stalked, and fed on each other daily. "Each yields what it can and takes only what it needs, so that all endure forever," she sang.

Anacaona saw that Guevara could no longer conceal arousal, be it lust or ambition. Sixteen-year-old Higueymota's twists and

incantations beckoned him. When the dance ended, Anacaona introduced the two. "Don Fernando travels to live in Cahay while he
waits for orders from his cacique Isabel."

"Your dance was magnificent, your charm as beguiling as your
mother's," Guevara complimented. "One day, you will make a
great queen to a great prince." For years, he'd dreamed of claiming
a daughter to attain overlordship of a village—no less an entire
chiefdom! Roldán undoubtedly had craved her. Guevara gracefully
turned from daughter to mother and delicately took his turn to probe.

"You must have arranged her marriage years ago. Isabel chose
her daughters' marriages when they were but children."

"I haven't yet decided my niece's marriage," Behecchio interjected, as if unfulfilled, rising to leave.

Guevara sensed an absence of attachment or support for Roldán.
Even the savages understood the rebel as lowbred. That night, he
couldn't sleep, machinating over the tantalizing fortuity he'd walked
into.

▣   ▣   ▣

As the stars appeared and Guevara plotted, Anacaona anguished
alone in her garden, contemplating Xaraguá's fate. Roldán had
promised that the guamiquina's men would never squat in Xaraguá,
which he claimed to rule, albeit within the guamiquina's greater conquest. But Roldán no longer feared or disparaged the guamiquina.
He even fought for the guamiquina! His own need to honor this
promise had faded, perhaps to no need at all, and he often was absent
from Xaraguá, squatting elsewhere. It loomed inevitable that he'd
break the promise—as he had all others—and that the guamiquina's
men would come to live in and plunder Xaraguá. Roldán had begun
dispatching Xaraguán cazabi to the guamiquina's men in Santo
Domingo, but those men could just as well squat in Xaraguá to eat it.

Anacaona knelt before the bayahibes, grimly beseeching revelation of any solution to prevent that assimilation short of war. While
she resisted so admitting, the possibility at hand was the obvious,
the traditional, and the one she'd criticized for years—marriage or
union of a woman of caciqual rank with a pale man, who might
serve as Xaraguá's protector when Roldán no longer cared to.

Roldán lieutenants remaining in Xaraguá still hated the quamiquina, yet none had the mettle or command to become that protector. But could this Don Guevara be recruited as such—to defend against both the guamiquina and Roldán? He had no power, but what if the union brought him power?

Trembling, Anacaona confessed that the dance just concluded had confirmed who was best suited for such a vile duty. No revelation could be starker—the pale man had already been enticed! Higueymota's union with him would place him subordinate to Behecchio's and her own rank and sway, and they could protect her and empower him as no other cacique could. She'd promised Higueymota that she'd never be married to Roldán. But fate had darkened since, and Guevara was of noble stature. Anguished, Anacaona brought the idea to her husband and spirit.

Caonabó was horrified that his daughter would be so desecrated. Warriors must draw pale men's blood instead, whatever the result. Yúcahu condemned the idea. Inviting conquerors to share caciqual blood was the worst of all assimilations, as she herself had warned.

Anacaona responded bitterly. To her husband—that a war would be lost and warriors and villagers massacred and enslaved. To her spirit—that He'd blessed marriages between the rulers of opposing chiefdoms to resolve disputes since time immemorial, and this was no different, albeit more fateful. She begged both to reveal other alternatives. They didn't.

With the moon high, she entered the inner sanctum of Behecchio's caney and found him supine by the fire circle. He coughed hoarsely for some moments, too exhausted to sit or maintain the facade of wellness before his sister. His soul plainly suffered more severely, as the humiliation of his submission to Roldán's brusque command was now widely understood. He glanced into her eyes, inviting her lead.

"All pale men lie," she began, acknowledging it was naive to rely on their words. "But this Guevara truly hates the guamiquina. He's a usurper, just as Hojeda. I suspect he would have fought with Hojeda against Roldán had he been present." She raised her forefinger. "I also suspect he's truly a nitaíno in his homeland, not just a warrior or seafarer. Neither Bartolomé nor Roldán have this Guevara's noble comportment, regardless that they command men and he doesn't."

"Guevara has hatred and nobility," Behecchio concurred. "But what use are they? He commands no one."

"My brother, our options vanish. Roldán can't be trusted to prevent the guamiquina's conquest from enveloping Xaraguá." She hesitated, afraid to overstep a line not yet crossed, but bent on talking it through. "Were we to award this Guevara my daughter, it would empower him as my son-in-law, and he'd be beholden to us, reliant on our rule and power for his own. He might then be inspired to keep us separate from the guamiquina's rule, just as Roldán once was."

"He might not act as a loyal son-in-law," Behecchio rasped wanly. "He might betray us for his own advantage, just as Roldán did, submitting to the guamiquina in return for rank. His isolation is impotence. He hasn't any followers bearing deadly weapons, and Roldán and the guamiquina could easily slay him."

"All that is true," Anacaona admitted. "Such a union would mock Roldán and Bartolomé, perhaps triggering more hatred and bloodshed among the pale men or toward us. This Guevara might cowardly recant the union or be executed." She shrugged. "But he is young, and he might outlast the guamiquina and Roldán if our squatters come to obey him as their natural, noble-born leader."

She let her brother digest the idea, and they gazed at the embers dying in the fire circle, silently pondering Xaragua's survival. He soon nodded, and she resumed.

"As you've said, we must be nimble. If Guevara became a coward or corpse after such a union, Higueymota could return to my side. I ask not for your approval, but your understanding that I consider the idea further."

"You'd expel Roldán from Xaraguá?"

"That's beyond our reach. But if Guevara amassed followers among our squatters, we might eventually exhort him to do so." She grew somber, awaiting Behecchio's reaction.

"I respect your willingness to entertain this degradation," he concluded. "Our people would now recognize the union as expedient for their protection. You may both consider and proceed with it, as you see fit."

⊡ ⊡ ⊡

Over the next days, Anacaona occasionally hosted the pale man for meals and refreshments and observed his comportment, with both Xaraguáns and squatters. Guevara perceived her scrutiny and sought to fulfill the credentials he imagined a heathen queen would seek in approving a strategic marriage—other than all the credentials he lacked, such as a crown, a kingdom, a treasury, and soldiers. His flaunted his fine clothing, horse, and sword, as if the envy and aspiration of every Spaniard and Indian. He flourished grandiosely when conversing with squatters, as if he held rank and authority over them in their homeland, and they accepted his company. He expected the service of both nitaínos and naborias and treated them kindly when served. He flirted only with Higueymota, never leering at others, making his intention transparent, and he was respectful never to touch her. Higueymota recognized his nobility and refinement.

Anacaona listened politely as he proclaimed on and on that he and Hojeda had been Isabel's appointed successors to the guamiquina, with authority to reform the treatment of her people. That bluster disgusted her, as did his Christianity. Regardless, one evening she retired to her caney's inner sanctum to decide, her heart pounding, breath short, and conscience embattled.

All pale men were unworthy for her daughter, this Guevara no exception. But Xaraguá's survival now rested on its squatters' hostility to the guamiquina, and Guevara was the only choice left to lead that. Under her direction, her daughter's union with him might raise and mold him to that end. Caonabó would never forgive her. Many might charge she favored the union merely to safeguard her own rule.

Anacaona realized she'd come to exercise her brother's authority and that doing so often would be odious. Relief from the pale man's conquest might never come, but hopelessness was inexcusable. A vision of a bayahibe flickered before her, and she trembled that she no longer was so passive.

As moonlight flickered though the caney's thatch, she ambled to hover over Higueymota's hamaca. Higueymota woke startled but instantly understood that her mother's midnight visit involved the pale man.

"Uncle asks that I lie with him?" she whispered.

"I ask that," Anacaona replied. "He may be of use as my daughter's lover." She caressed her. "He is of acceptable nobility and may also be useful as my son-in-law."

"In the final verse, do I love or poison him?"

⊡   ⊡   ⊡

Anacaona hosted Don Guevara at breakfast the next morning, and Higueymota gayly asked if she might ride his horse. Guevara chivalrously replied that it would be an honor to escort the princess anywhere Anacaona and Behecchio approved. That afternoon, the two sat as friends by a secluded brook, and Higueymota sang and danced an areíto for him, neither concerned by their inability to comprehend much of each other's speech. By dusk, they were laughing intimately at the seaside, where Higueymota took him to swim. By nightfall, they shared a bohío in a small Xaraguán village nearby, and as if lovers, consummated their union.

Guevara fell asleep, smitten by his Indian's beauty, exhilarated by his ascending fortune and visions of ruling countless heathens. As he snored, Higueymota brooded that it wasn't unlike sleeping with a Taíno man, although the pale man was heavier and bristled with more hair. She shed tears for some moments, tormented that she'd never lead the life she'd expected, and then silently cried uncontrollably. But she understood her duty, as well as her father's and mother's legacies, and she resolved to tell her mother she remained prepared to do as bid.

The following evening, after the couple had returned to his village, Behecchio summoned Guevara to the ballcourt, Higueymota standing at Anacaona's side.

"You wish my niece's companionship?" he asked.

"I love her passionately, Your Highness," Guevara gushed, bowing. "There's nothing on earth I desire more. She's as exquisite as any princess in my homeland. Union with her and admittance into your household would be as glorious as any honor I know."

"Do you wish marriage?" Anacaona inquired, peering into his eyes.

"With all my heart and soul!" Guevara exclaimed, clasping his hands to his breast.

"You must pledge to recognize and honor me as Xaraguá's ruler and as your uncle," Behecchio pronounced. "You must defend me, my family, and my chiefdom from the guamiquina. Xaraguá must remain free from his men's incursion."

"Your Highness, all that suits me," Guevara prattled, not concerned with the substance, accustomed to doing whatever he wished no matter what he promised, particularly with common Spaniards and naked heathens. "The guamiquina mustn't rule anywhere."

"My daughter and grandchildren must live in Xaraguá, always," Anacaona pronounced. "They may not be taken elsewhere."

Guevara resoundingly concurred again. He'd never take her or them anywhere if the union failed his expectations. He'd just ditch them and depart.

European kisses hand of Native American woman. By Madame Marie-Anne du Boccage, 1756. The John Carter Brown Library, portion of rec. no. 3350-3.

⊡   ⊡   ⊡

Preparations for the wedding commenced, but lacking a command, Don Guevara proved no match for Roldán, whose loyalists with repartimientos nearby urgently alerted him to the whirlwind courtship and wedding that would demote him. Roldán rode hellbent to Behecchio's village to apprehend Guevara and thwart it. They met outside Anacaona's caney—Roldán the jilted cuckhold, Guevara the despoiling rake—but it was their overlordship at stake that frenzied them.

"You gravely wrong me!" Roldán bellowed. "This princess is mine! Retreat to Cahay, remain there, and never visit her again. You remain disgraced with the Admiral and now me."

"Francisco, the princess and I are lovers already, and we are to be married," Guevara retorted calmly, lifting his chin as if frowning at a butler. "We are both of noble blood and meant for each other. I shall remain here to wed, and you must find another more suited to you." He puckered his lips. "You don't have the lineage for this princess."

Roldán's eyes bulged as if to burst and his neck flushed crimson, the umbrage borne since youth brought to boil. No one would disdain him in his kingdom, much less an unworthy don.

"Depart or I will place you in irons, pursuant to the Admiral's authority," he exhorted, summoning henchmen.

Thwarted and powerless, Guevara barely bid Anacaona and Higueymota goodbye before he was escorted from the village.

But within a day, he was sheltered by cousin Múxica in Cahay, and after reviewing all that had transpired, the two reckoned that a fiefdom of Xaraguá lay just a hair's breadth beyond the family's grasp. Múxica's three years as a rebellion ringleader and key lieutenant didn't bar him from stabbing Roldán in the back. They had fought the Colóns together, but not for each other. Roldán had no place denying nobility's entitlements. After a week of scheming, Múxica supplied Guevara with five cohorts for holding Roldán at bay and hustling a wedding ceremony.

Under starlight, Guevara snuck back to Behecchio's village and assured Anacaona he'd consummate the marriage the next day. He lay cockily with his fiancée until dawn, when he and the cohorts struck, surrounding Roldán's village and caney to disarm and muzzle him.

"Face the truth—none that followed you are friends!" he shouted at Roldán, trusting that the Spaniards living nearby would rally behind nobility. "Colón still schemes to cut off your head. My wedding shall proceed."

Still, the outcome was the same. Roldán's loyalists nearby far outnumbered Guevara's five and, in turn, soon surrounded them. Quickly, save Guevara, all participating grasped his threat of force a dupe's hollow foolery.

"I will tear out your eyes or slay you if you stand in my way," Guevara wailed vainly at Roldán, affronted that in Española his rank held no sway among his countrymen.

"I exile you to Cahay," Roldán declared, bitterly sparing him imprisonment owing to the favor the sovereigns showered noblemen. "You may petition the Admiral for a review of your grievances. I assure you he won't approve the marriage you seek." He ordered his men to escort Guevara to Cahay.

▢ ▢ ▢

After the confrontation, Anacaona anguished, disappointed yet not without hope that Guevara might persist in pursuing the marriage. Behecchio shrugged, chagrined the gambit had foundered, as he'd feared. But they both delighted in the insult dealt Roldán, and they appreciated the gambit had wedged further hatred among the squatters, which might blossom into more bloodshed eroding their presence. Higueymota collapsed, bewildered by what her future held, tears streaming gratefully.

Gold Mining,
January–May 1500

Cristóbal had departed Santo Domingo for Concepción on horseback after New Year's Day, riding the trail northwest across the mountains to the Jaina River's headwaters and through Bonao. Premonitions of his lynching and the sovereigns' abandonment continued to harrow him, but there was also cause for optimism. The unvarnished truth was that the creeks and washes east of the Jaina abounded with gold. The sovereigns had known of the rebellion for over a year, yet he'd received no correspondence from them—odd if they intended to reprimand him for it. Like the sovereigns, he was blissfully unaware that King Manoel planned to award da Gama with the title Admiral of India.

Cristóbal intended to reside much of the new year in Concepción, overseeing the mines' development and planning his heirs' estate there. En route, he met Bartolomé at the bunker near the Jaina, and accompanied by the family's Genoese factor, Rafael Cattaneo, they rode east to review progress at the New Mines. Bartolomé had brought order to the collection process, with Spanish laborers and their indentured Indian servants scouring streambeds for nuggets and dust, then depositing the yield with sentries for safekeeping. The laborers and sentries were encamped in bohíos commandeered from local Indians, who cowered and cooked meals. The incentives for hard work and honesty had been realigned, with the miners entitled beyond their salaries to almost two-thirds of the gold produced, leaving a third for the king and the tithe for himself.

At midday, as Spaniards and Indians scooped and panned before them in shallow water under a blazing sun, the three men knelt briefly at a creek's embankment to observe Sext and beseech the Lord to deliver the New Mines' riches promptly. Collection was urgent, both to preserve the sovereigns' favor and in case they withdrew it. The family remained poor, despite two decades of struggle. Smarting from the yoke of gritty assignments, Bartolomé was hard-heartedly driven to amass the riches due Cristóbal before enemies usurped or undid them.

Cristóbal thirsted likewise. But he also envisioned the gold fields as heralding more. They affirmed Española was King Solomon's Ophir from which gold had been hauled from Asia, yet another proof he'd sailed as the Lord's servant to the Indies.

As governor, Cristóbal had directed most settlers to build Española's settlements, including now their repartimientos, and he'd authorized only those enlisted as miners and a few other laborers to mine full time. But many settlers now demanded fulsome access, and some were keen to redeploy the Indians that would otherwise farm their repartimientos to mine the New Mines on their behalf. As they rose from worship, Cristóbal and Bartolomé debated how to allocate access and bring more manpower to bear.

"Why trust those who rebelled against the king to collect his gold?" Bartolomé scoffed pointedly, staring vindictively into Cristóbal's eyes. "Why share any riches with them?"

"We must appear evenhanded," Cristóbal bristled, determined to avoid renewed rebellion at any cost. Withholding access from former rebels would redouble their tirades that he hoarded for loyalists and foreign princes. "Brace yourself to watch over some you fought. Bid cousin Giovanni reside here to prohibit access to the worst of them."

Cristóbal contemplated the several Indians digging before him, perceiving their labor for miners as a natural extension of the settlers' pervasive practice of indenturing Indians as household servants. Although once unsettled by it, he now understood that practice as the very essence of his settlements' daily subsistence and progress in Española's build-out. Other than gold, the Indians themselves were the wealth of the island, available to work as both men and beasts of burden.

But he'd always conceived tribute as simply payments of gold the Indians possessed or gathered on their own, rather than produced through forced or slave labor in mines he controlled. That had been the express understanding when he'd first imposed tribute on Guarionex and other chieftains subjugated (1495–1496). That also was Isabel and Fernando's conception of tribute, as he'd warranted to them and their courtiers for years. They'd embraced it in their instructions.

"Do the Indians mine well enough?" Cristóbal asked, bitter that chieftains had reneged on tribute despite being spared forced labor.

"As well as the Spaniards," Bartolomé responded. "Now that we've found the gold, we could utilize them just as well. It'd be far easier to intimidate them from pilfering, and they don't even covet gold. We could put herds of them to work."

Cristóbal and Bartolomé discussed the logistics of housing and feeding more laborers at the New Mines. But Cristóbal still hesitated to utilize more Indians, clinging to the hope that the tribute system the sovereigns understood and approved would yield sufficient gold. He directed only that all gold collected be stored at Concepción, the securest site for guarding it from former rebels or passersby like Hojeda, and that more crosses be erected to mark the Lord's presence. As the afternoon waned, he and Cattaneo departed northwest.

⊡   ⊡   ⊡

In Concepción, Cristóbal met with men of the fort's garrison and inspected the build-out of repartimientos awarded in Magua and the settlement's common areas, which pleased him. Tribute's collection unnerved him, confirming his worst fears. At dusk, he summoned Cacique Diego Colón to dine alone at the gushing spring.

"Have Magua's caciques accepted that I've awarded their lands to Christians?" Cristóbal probed. "Do any plot resistance?"

"Admiral, many feel betrayed," Diego responded plainly. "You promised they'd retain their lands if they paid tribute, and they abhor the notion that they're now the squatters. But some don't perceive much difference, lamenting that you'd already conquered their lands and your parsing it among your subjects was to be expected." The Maguans' vigor and capacity to rebel had been crushed beyond restoration. "I've heard no rumors of resistance, even with respect to Manicoatex. The 'Doctor,' Maguatiquex, Macís, and others you met remain pacified."

"The tribute delivered is unacceptable," Cristóbal reproached. "Which caciques have contributed, which have shirked?"

"All have tried their best, including Manicoatex," Diego reported, aware that most had contributed nothing.

"Has your brother-in-law reconsidered his intransigence?"

"Admiral, I haven't asked him, but I expect he'd still prefer death to paying tribute."

Cristóbal gazed away for a long interlude, engulfed by defeat. Tribute hadn't produced the gold he'd promised everyone, and it wouldn't, no matter how sternly he pushed it. An avalanche of criticism would cascade when the failure became known. Fonseca would finally convince the sovereigns to abandon him. He'd seen the crisis coming for a long time, and he now had to accept it.

As the sun set, with the soul of a mariner, he bridled his despair and fortified his resolve. For decades at sea, he'd suffered fierce headwinds forcing abandonment of courses dearly held and resort to those achievable. Unmistakably, this was such a headwind, imperiling his very survival. Only a surge in gold production could stanch the criticisms looming—at least among the courtiers, who cared nothing of its source and little of the sovereigns' conception of Indian vassalage.

"You once told me of these peoples' gold hunt," he observed, breaking the silence. "Don't most of the island's men have experience digging gold in rivers?" Haitian men engaged in an annual month-long homage where they scoured for gold in streambeds, delivering it to their caciques in honor of Taíno spirits.

Diego froze. He'd translated Admiral's promise to the island's caciques countless times. If they paid tribute, their people wouldn't be enslaved.

"Admiral, the gold homage is sacred," he indicated. "Gold is hunted and delivered, but the homage to one's cacique and spirits is the essence, the amount delivered less important. Men fast and remain celibate for weeks prior to the hunt, but they have no remorse if little is found."

"Aren't they practiced in digging it?"

Diego shrugged and nodded, too ashamed to say yes.

Cristóbal understood. "Our hunt for gold has a sacred purpose as well. It's but a means to an end, reclaiming Jerusalem, by which time all your people shall have been baptized."

Diego brooded whether Admiral sought that end sincerely or would merely use it as an excuse to betray his past promises. He was shocked that tribute would be succeeded by oppression far worse.

▫ ▫ ▫

Cristóbal soon approved utilizing Indians in the New Mines, and by February he returned to Santo Domingo for some weeks to implement the arrangements. While not publicly conceding tribute's abandonment, he began granting settler requests to mine with the forced labor of bands of Indians drawn from villages within their repartimientos. These Indians hadn't resisted conquest, and the sovereigns' instructions didn't permit their enslavement. So their toil in the Jaina and tributary streambeds had to be fashioned, or at least articulated, as something less than slavery—work for a limited period of months for the singular purpose of mining in vassalage to the sovereigns, absent other duties of personal servitude.

Grants purportedly were withheld from settlers who failed to confess and take communion—a test of faith, not loyalty—but Cristóbal's supporters readily prevailed over former rebels in grants awarded. He encouraged settlers to form partnerships to organize their Spanish overseers and the Indian laborers, so those with managerial expertise—such as Díaz and Garay—pooled Spanish overseers to direct greater numbers of Indians in both farming and gold mining.

Taínos panning for gold. Oviedo's *Historia General*.

In March, upon receiving word of Hojeda's expulsion, Cristóbal established an inquiry into Hojeda's crimes. The testimony of two eyewitnesses—one expelled from Hojeda's fleet, the other whom Cristóbal promised an appointment—not only proved the pirating and abuse of natives for which Hojeda was already known, but other misdeeds certain to offend the sovereigns. Hojeda had sold gunpowder to the infidel in Africa, traded a lance to Haniguyabá, and damaged the peaceful relationship Cristóbal had established with Paria's natives, injuring the sovereigns' imperial and mercantile expectations.

⊡   ⊡   ⊡

Meanwhile, in Fort Concepción's blockhouse, Mayobanex was expiring. Blistering reddish welts cloaked his entire body, presaging death was but days away.

Cacique Diego received word from Guarionex to fetch cazabi, pineapple juice, and cohoba and brought them to the fort one evening. Mayobanex lay prostrate on the cell's floor, Guarionex at his side. Guarionex offered the gourd of juice to his lips, and Mayobanex sipped meekly and mustered the energy to prop himself upon his elbows.

"What can you report of the guamiquina?" he whispered, alert and interested in intelligence to the end.

"We haven't heard his voice for weeks," Guarionex observed.

"He's away, perhaps a moon or two, but he'll return," Diego related. "He's pleased his subjects obey him and no longer quarrel. He awards them the lands and villagers he's conquered. Every pale man in the conquered chiefdoms now has a cacique in his service."

"In Ciguayo?" Mayobanex rasped, his breath labored.

"No, your vassals have kept the pale men out. Perhaps the pale men don't wish to farm in the mountains or be distant from the gold they've found."

"How have my subjects reacted?" Guarionex probed.

"My brother, all recognize the guamiquina's conquest is permanent," Diego related. "Each pale man now builds his own home to remain forever. The guamiquina's will border Guaricano. None have the strength to protest."

"Not even Manicoatex or Behecchio?" Guarionex pleaded.

"I suspect Manicoatex quietly endures humiliation while praying for a moment to uprise," Diego responded. "I understand Behecchio and others who live side by side with the pale men recognize they've been double-crossed." He searched for something encouraging to relate. "But they still hope to survive."

"Harmony with invaders is an illusion," Mayobanex replied softly, as he lay prone again, his strength ebbing.

"Bakako, are my people now slaves to the pale men awarded their lands?" Guarionex asked.

"Yes. They are forced to farm and build for their masters. Some are marched to the Jaina to dig for gold. Cooks and household servants now are bound to their masters permanently, through death."

⛶   ⛶   ⛶

By May, Cristóbal returned to Concepción, relishing that the gold collected for the sovereigns and himself had surged dramatically. Cattaneo estimated the value of Cristóbal's share at two to three million maravedís—a fortune finally sufficient to make the Admiral a nobleman in fact rather than name only. Cristóbal didn't tap the collection to pay salaries, continuing to award slaves instead when payments were demanded or necessary.

The gold rejuvenated his bravado, and one day he sat by the fort's spring composing an optimistic report to Isabel and Fernando. He had ordered *the Indians to be joined together in large towns to be converted to Christianity and serve Their Highnesses like their Castilian vassals.* Without injury or unwarranted force, and with moderate effort, they'd now provide sixty million maravedís in annual revenue. The wealth would exceed fifty million maravedís by 1503. Tribute wasn't mentioned.

In the blockhouse cell some yards away, Guarionex helped Mayobanex inhale cohoba to comfort his transition to the afterlife. They embraced as brothers a last time, and before hallucinating, Mayobanex whispered the final words of the last supreme cacique of the Ciguayo.

"Do not sorrow for me or second-guess what we did. Our souls remain unvanquished. One day, you may reason with the caciques Isabel and Fernando rather than the guamiquina. Of all our people, you are the best suited for that."

VII

ISABEL'S CONQUEST AND
DYNASTY REORDERED

BOBADILLA'S DISPATCH, MANUMISSIONS AND ENSLAVEMENTS,
Seville, March–June 1500

As spring dawned in Seville, with the Mohammedan uprising suppressed, Isabel and Fernando at last turned to dispatching Commander Bobadilla and reordering Española, their remiss in so doing and faded expectations for the island transparent. They authorized him to sail with merely two caravels and fifty passengers, half salaried settlers committed to remain on the island for a year, most of the remainder these settlers' household servants. Fonseca, now risen to Bishop of Córdoba, set about procuring the ships and crews in Palos, commissioning the *Señora de la Antigua* to be captained by one of his uncle's servants, Alonso de Vallejo, and the *Gorda* by Andrés Martin de la Gorda, a mariner long acquainted with Cristóbal who'd sailed on the second voyage.

Better news had arrived from Paria. By March, one of the bishop's newly licensed voyagers had returned, and the pearls and other treasures he'd amassed augured that the great landmass could be brought to profit expeditiously, with limited expenditure compared to Española. Pero Alonso Niño's cargo included one hundred fifty pounds of pearls, a chest of guanín, and some cords of brazilwood—a great haul for a single ship. Niño and others had been caught and briefly incarcerated for secreting some of the pearls for themselves, also auguring that tighter crown oversight of cargos was essential.

The consequence of further delay in their Indies conquest also loomed darker. Emissaries and spies reported that King Manoel was boldly advancing to consolidate mercantile dominion of his Indies, dispatching a fleet of thirteen ships berthing twelve hundred men to Calicut—rivaling the triumphant fleet of Cristóbal's second voyage and dwarfing Bobadilla's. The nobleman Pedro Alvares Cabral (b. 1467) commanded, and passengers included bedecked minor nobility and gentlemen to flatter the Indies' rulers and merchants and bring them to Christianity.

Isabel still smarted from her admiral's disobedience, openly scorning on multiple occasions that Cristóbal had no authority to award her vassals as slaves. She'd also come to rue that her vision of a benign conquest benefiting primitive peoples often had been perverted by base oppressions inflicted by many of her subjects. While she'd precluded Cisneros from working on Granadan issues, one spring day, she and Fernando summoned him to contribute to Española's reordering.

"Assemble friars to accompany Bobadilla," Isabel instructed. "Bid them propose how best to evangelize the Indians. We conquer for Christian vassals, not slaves."

"Request their assessment of the Admiral," Fernando directed, seeking a source of information more reliable than Cristóbal's loyalists and enemies.

"Your Highnesses, I embrace these duties," Cisneros responded, gratified to be entrusted anew, aware from Roldán's letter that a dispassionate review of both Cristóbal and those in rebellion was long overdue. "I also shall direct the friars to baptize all those they can." His eyes beamed without remorse for his recent conduct. Mass baptism was a great sword in the struggle with Satan.

Isabel nodded approval but frowned.

"My archbishop, our concerns go beyond baptism. It's now regularly brought to our attention that the Indians have been mistreated from the beginning. Their women have borne countless sins, including concubinage against their will and outright rape." She raised her voice. "The Indians must be treated as all seeking Christ deserve to be treated. Advise us how best to improve the Christian conduct of our Spanish vassals."

"My religious shall examine that," Cisneros affirmed. He paused, as if deferentially, before engaging an issue precariously both temporal and spiritual.

"Your Highnesses, if the Admiral's enslavements have been improper, mustn't they be undone? As you know, there is precedent for that." Financing the Canarian conquests had come to rely on selling resisters into slavery, but Alonso de Lugo had been required to manumit Canarians he'd double-crossed by enslaving after they'd agreed to peacefully submit (1497–1498).

"We've begun to consider that," Isabel responded, dismissing him.

░   ░   ░

As Isabel's conscience simmered, Fonseca's explorers who hadn't returned were adding more fuel to the fire. Hojeda's fleet was then slave raiding some two hundred thirty Indians in the Lucayan islands (the Bahamas) north of Española. Vicente Yáñez Pinzón had disembarked on the landmass southeast of Paria, surmising it King Manoel's territory on the Indian coast near the Ganges, and sighted an enormous river (the Amazon). His crews had engaged in brutal skirmishes with locals, taking slaves. Diego de Lepe, exploring the same coastline, was also taking slaves.

░   ░   ░

From the time she'd sought her throne, Isabel's triumphs as the Lord's servant had occasionally necessitated her own deceptions, broken promises, and treacheries, or those of men she directed. She took solace that most of these transgressions were responses to those initiated by her enemies, and that other transgressions of those she commanded were unauthorized and never intended by her, or even direct disobedience to her contrary instructions, for which her soul wasn't truly impugned. The Indies' conquest certainly had involved unauthorized, unintended, and disobedient transgressions—many horrid—for which she bore remorse as sovereign but perceived no direct guilt for which she ought to atone.

But what of the Admiral's enslavements? she beseeched Christ, kneeling before the altarpiece in the alcazar's private chapel. *How can I still retreat behind theologians and lawyers?* Six years had elapsed since their counsel had been interposed, and hundreds of enslaved Indians had now resided in Castile for almost two years.

That evening, she and Fernando dined alone, unpleasantly and beyond the ken of court chroniclers.

"We must free the Indian slaves Colón has awarded his men," she declared heatedly. "They weren't in rebellion. He had no cause to enslave them and no authority to award them to others for any purpose, much less as wages in place of the gold he's failed to produce or as bribes to the treasonous." She paused regally, folding her arms, reflecting more broadly on her sovereignty. "Española shall grow as an extension of Castile, without overlords intervening between ourselves and our vassals."

"You speak righteously," Fernando observed coolly. "I agree, yet we must be deft, sticking to decisions and articulations that preserve the merchants' and financiers' appetite. They struggle to find reward. We also should be mindful of the settlers' hardships. Like soldiers, their loot and trample of the conquered is inevitable, no matter how righteously condemned."

"We first must emulate Christ," Isabel responded coldly. Her husband's counsel grated, both amoral and patronizing. "Our policy will be sound, recognizing that others inevitably fall short."

"A narrow, enforceable order is preferable to disobeyed platitudes or insuperable restrictions," he countered. "We cannot burden Bobadilla with disaffecting the rank and file the moment he arrives."

After further thrash and accord, as March waned, Isabel and Fernando instructed their household courtier, Pedro de Torres, to locate and sequester all enslaved Indians brought into Spain on the Admiral's last two shipments and deliver them to Bobadilla for return to freedom in Española.

Isabel insisted that Torres's search be exhaustive. Yet of the near one thousand Indian slaves he sought, he succeeded in sequestering twenty-six, thirteen men and boys and thirteen women and girls. Five of the women and girls died of disease while sequestered, including a María, an Isabel, a Juana, and a Catalina. Of the thousand, an overwhelming number had already died, and some surviving could never be found.

By conclusion of the effort, the twenty-one remaining for delivery to Bobadilla included a few Juanicos, among them Bartolomé de Las Casas's, two more Catalinas, and another María, with the rest bearing other common Spanish names, including an Alfonso, Diego, Johan, and Matheo. Most had toiled in Andalusia. Some of the masters who relinquished them had returned from Española with them. Others were subsequent purchasers.

※　※　※

As the Indians were sequestered, Archbishop Cisneros enlisted six clerics to sail, led by the master of his own household, the Franciscan Fray Francisco Ruiz, who would be accompanied by two other aides, the Franciscans Juan de Trasierra and Juan de Robles. The Franciscans Leudelle and Tisín—who'd delivered Roldán's letter—volunteered, still burning to baptize Indians, as did a Benedictine chaplain, Alonso del Viso. Cisneros directed them to convert Indians and deliver a written report of their observations and recommendations, including on how to establish Española's church.

By mid-June, Isabel and Fernando prepared to return to Granada, having supplemented and finalized Bobadilla's instructions for Española. They'd ordered him to pay settlers' long unpaid salaries from crown property on the island. They'd proclaimed that henceforth the island's officers and administrators would all be Spanish, not foreign born.

Bishop Fonseca took Bobadilla aside to impress that his greatest service would be to restore order among the queen's Spanish vassals and haul Colón, his brothers, and other Genoese home, preferably in chains.

Isabel met with the clerics, who kissed her hand, and Torres, who displayed the Indians he'd found. She asked Ruiz to report to her what was truly going on in the Indies. Angry and determined, she'd arrived at the moment to impose her will.

On June 20, the eve of their departure for Granada, she and

Fernando issued a sparse royal decree to Torres ordering that all Indians he'd sequestered who'd been brought from the Indies and sold in Seville and Andalusia on the Admiral's command were to be freed, instructing him to deliver them before a witness to Bobadilla for return to the Indies. Isabel's conscience spoke sternly— the decree warned Torres to comply, foreseeing him accosted with bribes, threats, and other impediments. Her conscience also spoke entirely alone—the decree didn't invoke or even mention theologians or lawyers, after six years of purportedly waiting on them. Baldly, her will was the authority, not the church. Yet her conscience and will were bridled—the decree expressed no principle freeing other Indians enslaved, either in Española or by persons beyond the Admiral's command.

Miracle of the Loaves and Fishes, with Isabel seated to Christ's right.
Juan de Flandes, ca. 1502.

Bobadilla clearly understood that future enslavement of Española's Indians was limited to resisters and to not award Indians as slaves to compensate settlers. Yet he wasn't forced to free slaves already held by Española's settlers. The decree's application to returning settlers who'd retained slaves and never sold them was assumed, and crown reimbursement for the manumission wasn't mentioned—although that issue would be addressed later.

The next day, Isabel and Fernando departed for Granada, abruptly leaving Cisneros to mind the manumitted and Fonseca to deal with the merchants and financiers, the decree then barely noted by court chroniclers.

Cisneros instructed Fray Ruiz to accompany and safeguard the manumitted Indians to Española. On June 23, Torres delivered twenty of the twenty-one sequestered to Frays Leudelle and Tisín on behalf of Bobadilla, with Bobadilla and Briviesca as witnesses. One of them, a twelve-year-old girl, indicated that she wished to remain in Seville as a free person, and she was released to a Sevillian for his care—or perhaps vice versa. Leudelle and Tisín traveled with the Indians by barge down the Guadalquivir and boarded the *Antigua* and *Gorda* in Sanlúcar, where an additional Indian was brought aboard. One of the Juanicos—not Las Casas's—succumbed en route, leaving only nineteen.

Fonseca's discussion of Isabel's new approach with the merchants and financiers was complicated by news that Hojeda had disembarked in Cádiz in mid-June with two hundred surviving enslaved Indians and brazilwood. There had been some bluff and carp between Fonseca and Hojeda and an awkward, murky recounting with Isabel and Fernando—particularly since the territory slave-raided was considered unworthy of conquest and outside Hojeda's license. But the decree of June 20 did not apply, and the two hundred were promptly sold in Cádiz's slave market. Perhaps their resistance, or their not being the sovereigns' vassals in a conquered land, had justified their enslavement.

Bishop Fonseca was pleased by the net financial result. The crown's share of that sale would more than offset the cost of the twenty-six manumissions.

⊡   ⊡   ⊡

Commander Bobadilla sailed by month's end. Captain Gorda knew the route, affording the commander time to reflect on the task before him. He'd been dispatched by his sovereigns to replace an imposing, controversial admiral of foreign birth on a distant island where four hundred Spaniards of unknown loyalty and persuasion already held their own court among untrustworthy savages. While fifty green-horn settlers and their butlers and maids might stand at his side, his principal armaments were the parchments that the sovereigns had signed. He dutifully prayed to the Lord for a safe passage, fervently beseeched His protection on arrival, and resolved that entreating the loyalty of the four hundred was a high priority.

Southern Landmass, Vespucci, La Cosa, and Cabral,
April–July 1500

Amerigo Vespucci was now out of work and in need of a new career or, at least, a commission to tide him over. To that end, on July 18, Amerigo dispatched a letter describing his voyage— the one that had departed Spain at night on May 18, 1499—to the Florentine Medici patriarch he'd once served, relating that, at the sovereigns' commission, he'd departed with two caravels to make discoveries in the western regions. The letter omitted mentioning Hojeda or any other ships, voyage officer, or finan-cier anywhere, even by indirect reference, and it credentialed Amerigo for multiple career paths. While privately addressed, he scattered copies among merchants and courtiers.

According to the letter, Amerigo had set the voyage's course and secured the provisions—the mark of a merchant captain. He'd explored and navigated celestially with Ptolemy and Dante in mind, utilizing instruments and astronomical tables, observing the polar star vanish from the sky and longing to be the discov-erer of the southern polar star—all befitting a mariner, discov-erer, or cosmographer. He'd thoughtfully observed the exotic peoples and cultures encountered and fought—as if possessing the intellect and urbanity of a Pedro Mártir to serve at a court. The geography was Cristóbal's—continental land bounded by the eastern part of Asia, the ships approaching the Kattigara that constituted the southeasternmost point of terra firma known to Ptolemy (Indonesia, southern Vietnam, or China). The trees' beauty suggested entrance into the Terrestrial Paradise. Words chosen occasionally echoed Cristóbal's own—the air was fresher and more temperate in the regions explored, the peoples naked as they were born. Amerigo did remind that the Admiral had been Española's discoverer.

An experienced slave trader, Amerigo also perfunctorily reported taking the two hundred thirty Indian souls by force and the survivors' sale in Cádiz. The voyage profit—slaves, gold, pearls, and brazilwood offset by expenses, ship damages, and the sovereigns' fifth—was but five hundred ducats. Perhaps a slip of the pen, he implied that his take of that was 1/55, certainly less than the lion's share due a merchant captain. But he was optimistic. Vessels were being fitted for him so that he might again go forth to make discoveries.

An expedition to the southern landmass was in fact authorized that July—unfortunately for Amerigo, without him. Fonseca licensed the Sevillian merchant captain Rodrigo de Bastidas to extend coastal exploration west of Hojeda's Coquibacoa with two ships. La Cosa would serve as a pilot, and enlistees among the crew would include a struggling, unknown third son of a minor nobleman of rustic Extremadura, Vasco Núñez de Balboa (b. ca. 1475).

Bastidas's financing and provisioning arrangements would delay departure for months, leaving La Cosa time to draw a world map depicting the enormous western coastlines he then knew explored by his sovereigns and Kings Manoel and Henry VII. He disregarded his mentor Cristóbal's discredited claim that Cuba was part of the Indies mainland. But he placed an image of Saint Christopher—who carried Christ across a river—at the coastlines' unexplored western extremity, neither impugning nor embracing Cristóbal's assertion that he could sail west of Cuba to return to Europe, as Marco Polo had, along the Indies' southern shores.

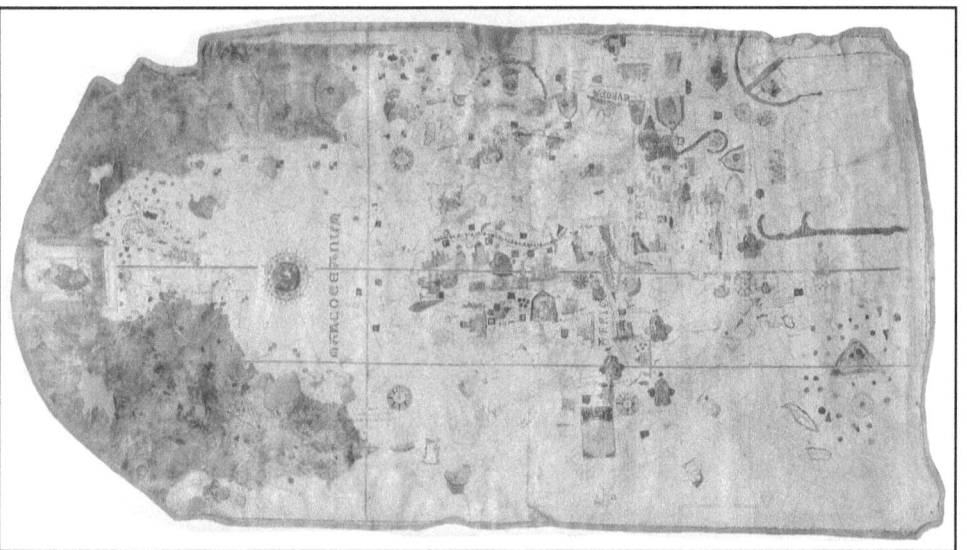

Juan de la Cosa's World Map, 1500.

Earlier that spring, while extending Vasco da Gama's dramatic ocean loop westward to attain the Cape of Good Hope, Pedro Alvares Cabral's expedition had found and disembarked upon the great landmass south of Pinzón's landfall. He'd briefly explored, traded peacefully with the local Tupí-Guaraní peoples, and—to civilize them—deposited two condemned bandits brought for that purpose. Prior to sailing east for the Cape, Cabral dispatched a ship home with letters describing the territory found. Manoel judged the sites and hosts to offer little commercial value but thanked the Lord for the discovery. The shores were very convenient and necessary for the voyage to India.

PLOTS AND DESTINIES FRUSTRATED, HAITI (QUISQUEYA) AND SPAIN,
June–August 1500

Anacaona studied her daughter's composure as they conferred hastily at midday, secluded beneath the magnolias of her garden, the sun's heat baking.

"Cahay's cacique suspects Don Fernando still intends to marry you," she related. "Múxica's naborias say he talks of murdering Roldán to that end." She shrugged in doubt. "Uncle is hopeful—at least for the murder."

"You still favor the wedding?" Higueymota asked with trepidation.

"I wish there were no pale men." Anacaona nodded grimly, despairing her daughter's marriage choices. "But Don Fernando is both the noblest and weakest among them, a dimwitted nitaíno, perhaps useful to protect our people and preserve our families' rule—including your own, one day."

"Mother, I received word from him this morning through a pale man," Higueymota revealed. "He coos he loves me and assures I'll be his 'queen.'" She scowled. "He assumes I haven't the mettle to discern his motive."

"Use that arrogance to your advantage. If you wed him, he may not recognize when you lead him about."

◻︎　◻︎　◻︎

While mother and daughter conferred, Guevara machinated in Cahay with Múxica, plotting the marriage and to rule Xaraguá over Roldán's dead body until Colón's replacement arrived on the island—and hopefully even longer. But the cousins' Spanish neighbors disdained their pretensions and further rebellion, and Múxica's slaves despised his overlordship. Roldán learned of their plotting almost as quickly as Anacaona and Behecchio.

In mid-June, Roldán arrested Guevara and seven accomplices for treason, although Múxica eluded seizure. Roldán wrote Cristóbal, requesting that he judge the matter impartially, given Roldán and Guevara's enmity and Guevara's nobility. Cristóbal assumed the responsibility and directed that Guevara and the accomplices be delivered to Bartolomé for transfer to the prison in Santo Domingo. Pending transfer, the prisoners remained chained in a holding pit in Xaraguá for a month.

Anacaona visited the pit a few times to hail Guevara as if a son-in-law, in case fortune changed. Dutifully, Higueymota occasionally snuck by under cover of moonlight to wave to him, as if wishing him free and hopeful for their union, relieved it wouldn't happen but unsettled he would die. Behecchio came once to smirk at the accomplices, relishing them dead.

One evening, Anacaona cradled Higueymota's head in her lap as they lingered before the fire circle in her caney. She caressed her daughter's face and sensed a fleshiness not apparent before. Quivering, Higueymota drew her mother's hand to her womb.

"Mother, I believe I'm with child," she whispered bittersweetly, unsure if it was good or bad, pleased to have a babe to nurture, anxious there might be no father to love it, and vexed that the father was of an enemy people.

Anacaona fought to contain her reactions—shock that her plan had taken a new course, anger that the pale man's defilement now touched her own daughter, and remorse for having sanctioned the pale man's mount. She softly covered Higueymota's eyes with her hand to conceal her own angst and filled the moment whispering intimate questions—how do you know, for how long, and how do you feel? As her daughter responded, she exhorted Attabeira, *Why nurture the pale man's seed without promise or advantage in return?* But she was well-aware of the answer. Bald one-sidedness transpired all the time with men of all origins.

She steeled her resolve to never surrender to the guamiquina and quashed all recriminations. Perhaps her daughter's relationship with the father or the child itself might someday provide an advantage. There was no turning back, second-guessing, or placing doubt or shame on Higueymota. Anacaona took her hand from Higueymota's eyes and sought to reassure that the child would be accepted like any other, regardless of what happened thereafter.

"We shall love your child," she comforted, envisioning her grandchild. "The man has done sowing, and you no longer need him."

□　□　□

In the Alhambra, Isabel sat in the shade of a palace courtyard with her grandson on her lap, dabbing his forehead with cold spring water, anguished that the heat radiating from his body wasn't abating. She'd watched her son Juan's body waste to death and was nigh certain Miguel soon would join him. The child wasn't even two years old.

She and Fernando had seen Miguel's death looming for months, and earlier that year, they'd interpreted the birth of their daughter Juana's second child, a boy christened Charles, as a loathsome portent thereof. Denying Juana—now their oldest surviving child and possessed of male offspring—the throne would be radically perilous, and fearing Juana's succession on Miguel's death, they'd buttressed other alliances meant to counter French aggression. The kinship with Manoel uniting the Hispanic Peninsula had been reaffirmed with the betrothal of their younger daughter, María, to him. Following that marriage, their youngest, Catalina, would depart for England to meet her betrothed, Prince Arthur, King Henry VII's son, wedging France between opponents north and south.

At sunset, awaiting Fernando, Isabel handed her grandson to a nurse and ambled to a courtyard rail to gaze over her greatest conquest—the magnificent fortress about her, the Albaicín on the hillside opposite, teeming with converted, conquered peoples, and the great fertile valley below. She prayed, acknowledging that the Lord also dealt defeat.

I accept your punishments, just as your blessings, she vouched to Christ, contemplating His entrance into Jerusalem and the deaths of Juan, Isabel, and Miguel.

I shall fulfill your design through death, she promised, envisioning the thorns thrust upon His brow.

I, too, await the joy of sitting at your feet, she exhorted, contemplating His final judgment.

As darkness descended, Fernando joined her at the rail to address the inevitable, his voice betraying a mortality not regal. Both perceived that fortune no longer favored them.

Christ's Entry into Jerusalem. Juan de Flandes, ca. 1497–1498.
Gallery of the Royal Collections, National Heritage,
inventory no. 10002024.

"After the Lord calls him, we must promptly summon Juana and Philippe to take their oaths," he noted wanly, vexed that Philippe was too untrustworthy to merit a court's recognition.

"We must remind Juana that she and her children are Spanish," Isabel bemoaned, anguished that her bond with her daughter had ruptured.

"We must speed María and Catalina's marriages," Fernando chafed.

"Juana, the children, and Philippe must live with us, honoring our family and lineage," Isabel pleaded, pining to mend the rupture.

As stars appeared, Isabel took her grandson from the nurse and lifted him to her face to love, bless, and kiss him.

"He shall be reunited with his mother, his uncle, and the Lord," she whispered, gushing tears.

◻ ◻ ◻

Miguel died in Isabel's arms on July 20. Mourning commenced. A letter was promptly dispatched to Juana and Philippe summoning them to Castile for recognition as heir to the throne and consort. Manoel grieved for his son, as did many who'd envisioned the Hispanic Peninsula as ascendant.

Isabel and Fernando continued to engage ministers and render decisions as before. They held audiences with Granada's newly converted *Moriscos*, whom Isabel instructed to dress as Christians, donating clothing.* They pardoned Moriscos for crimes committed as part of the uprising and reappointed those prominent to positions held in the kingdom's ministries before the uprising. Harsh treatment was made even harsher for those few Mudejar in the city who hadn't converted. In August, culminating their review of Granada's Christianization, they dispatched churchmen to conduct a broad program to mass baptize the unconverted throughout the kingdom outside the city.

But all this was done joylessly, as if they'd been thrown among thorns. Their tranquility of spirit was a facade transparent to everyone.

◻ ◻ ◻

Proud of his minor nobility, Adrian de Múxica had come to Española to find gold, master naked heathens, and raise his stature, coveting a grander nobility. In Española, he'd grown infuriated when instructed to labor by Genoese weavers and then enraged when lowborn Spaniards prevented cousin Don Guevara—true nobility—from marrying to overlord the heathens. The last straw was Don Guevara's incarceration by the weavers and lowborn.

Incensed, Múxica harangued former rebels to join him to liberate Guevara, slay both Roldán and Colón, loot the gold at Concepción, and assume reign of the entire island, at least until the king and queen said otherwise. Two dozen cheered or truly conspired in one or more

---

* *Morisco* refers to a Mohammedan vassal who has converted to Christianity.

of those plots. As before, there were no secrets among former rebels or their slaves, and when Roldán learned of the machinations, he immediately wrote Cristóbal requesting direction what to do.

Cristóbal's confidence had continued to surge—gold was amassing, and settlers were working, not agitating—and the news sent him into a rage. The triumph he'd finally achieved by delivering on Española's promises was imperiled. Disobedience and treason lurked perpetually—encircling, taunting, and torturing him—even after he'd overcome the worst challenges. He furiously ordered Roldán and Bartolomé to lead armed squads to capture Múxica and conspirators and deliver them to Concepción or Santo Domingo.

Guilt was written on their foreheads! Torture could extract confessions to their crimes, trials were unnecessary, and executions could proceed with his approval. Rebellion now merited death. The squads should include chaplains to administer final confession.

Former cohorts soon revealed Múxica's general whereabouts, and the slaves he'd overlorded were keen to pinpoint where he slept. By August 8, he and two others were captured in the dark of night, manacled, and dragged to grovel at Cristóbal's feet at Fort Concepción. Chaplain Ortiz attended at Cristóbal's side, and a crowd encircled them.

"I proudly confess to seeking the end of your governorship," Múxica declared to Cristóbal, sparing himself torture to extract that admission. "I've served my king and queen with the fullest devotion. You are the traitor to their rule." Searching for delay, he pronounced, "Trial shall so prove."

"Your guilt has already been established," Cristóbal retorted brusquely, ignoring the insolence.

"The sovereigns and the Lord condemn your ruthless justice," Múxica exhorted, as if he'd previously cared about judicial process. "I request that my son be brought here, so I may impart final blessings," he improvised, invoking a child born by a concubine, grasping for a postponement affording a window for escape.

"There is neither time nor excuse for mercy!" Cristóbal bellowed, his eyes bulging with blood and venom. "But you may confess your sins to the Almighty." He pointed to hangmen bearing a noose and Ortiz.

"I refuse. I haven't sinned before Him!" Múxica shouted back, flailing for yet another cause for interruption.

The crowd was cowed by the confrontation's intensity and Cristóbal's unbridled rage, an animus far beneath viceregal comportment.

"My Admiral, perhaps this man is in no condition to properly confess," Ortiz gingerly cautioned, gazing upon Cristóbal instead of Múxica. "Perhaps we should imprison him and revisit his fate another day."

"Take his confession or just absolve him," Cristóbal commanded Ortiz. "Throw him from atop the fort," he barked at the hangmen.

The hangmen brought Múxica before Ortiz, letting the two whisper briefly, and then hauled him atop the fort's highest wall, the noose tight about his neck. As they shoved him, Múxica cursed the traitors and dogs below. After he expired, the two others were tortured, then hanged.

◻ ◻ ◻

Anacaona sat with Behecchio as he lay before the fire circle in his inner sanctum.

"Both your friends came today, Bartolomé and Roldán," he noted wryly. "They demand that I assist them in capturing those loyal to Múxica and Don Guevara." He frowned. "The guamiquina is executing all so loyal." He stared into her eyes. "Don Guevara's turn approaches."

Anacaona bit her lip, knowing Behecchio would pivot to acquiesce to what Bartolomé and Roldán demanded. It was the correct decision, given Guevara's demise.

"My brother, Guevara's death would bring no grief."

"Don't be hard on yourself. Guevara won't protect us from the guamiquina. But your plan bears fruit, as the pale men's commotion over him blossoms into their murders of themselves."

"Higueymota bears Guevara's child," Anacaona related, sorrowed by a vision of Higueymota's puffed cheeks. "The child might yet be of use. So might Guevara, if he yet survives."

"Bless Higueymota for her sacrifice," Behecchio reflected, not surprised. "I look forward to offering the child a name. But at this moment, we are friend again to Don Guevara's enemies." He stared vindictively at the embers in the fire circle. "It shall give me great pleasure to deliver squatters to the guamiquina for execution."

☐ ☐ ☐

By mid-August, Bartolomé had rounded up sixteen alleged conspirators hiding in Xaraguá, eleven delivered by Behecchio's warriors, five by Roldán's squad, their flight marking them guilty of some conspiracy. They were shackled and imprisoned in a gully. Most were tortured for confessions or evidence against others, and Bartolomé determined that a dozen merited execution then and there, subject to Cristóbal's approval. More former rebels—allegedly conspirators—were seized and thrown into Santo Domingo's jail beside Guevara and his accomplices, including Roldán's lieutenant Riquelme.

Cristóbal eventually bridled the rage that had overcome him, supplanting it with a steeled conviction that public hangings of the condemned—particularly Guevara and Riquelme—would finally cow Española's Christians from contemplating another rebellion. At his direction, four imprisoned in Santo Domingo were hanged at scaffolds erected on opposing bluffs overlooking the Ozama.

By August 23, a corpse still dangled on each bluff, five of the jailed men awaited execution, including Guevara and Riquelme, and Bartolomé awaited approval to execute the dozen in Xaraguá.

Taínos throughout the island were astonished when they learned what was transpiring. The pale men's corpses barely merited notice, as countless Taínos had perished over the last few years, their bodies decaying unburied throughout the island. What horrified was how virulently the invaders' barbarity extended to themselves.

VIII
CRISTÓBAL'S DEMISE

BOBADILLA AND CRISTÓBAL,
August 23–September 14, 1500

At seven a.m. on August 23, Captain Gorda brought Commander Bobadilla's fleet of two caravels offshore the Ozama at Santo Domingo, fired a cannon shot, and directed that the ships jog into the seaward wind until the outgoing tide and wind abated. Cheers erupted throughout the town, as all envisioned replenishment of the settlement's Spanish wine and beef and letters from family. Brother Diego—maintaining the family compound alone—dispatched Indian canoeists bearing La Lengua and others to learn who'd arrived and welcome them.

Aboard the *Gorda*, Bobadilla studied the canoe, naked Indians, and wizened Spaniards approaching—which matched his expectations—and readied himself for the unfolding revelation of his authority as the sovereigns had dictated. He walked to the rail with Gorda when the canoe glided below and identified himself as the king and queen's judicial investigator.

"Are the Admiral and his brothers present?" he asked, peering down. "Has the Admiral crushed the rebellion?"

"The Admiral is in Concepción, Bartolomé in Xaraguá to the west. His brother Diego is resident." La Lengua groped for what to reveal. "My commander, the Admiral has long settled the principal rebellion, but lesser mutinies have surfaced, and the Admiral has just apprehended the guilty."

"How many have just mutinied, how many apprehended?" Bobadilla probed.

"Over two dozen, and all have been caught, with order fully restored. Seven have been hanged already. Five await execution here and a dozen in Xaraguá."

"We shall anchor upstream shortly," Bobadilla indicated. "I bring fresh supplies, more settlers, and news from home." He surmised he'd made sufficient impression to disquiet those ashore without triggering plotting. He stepped back from the rail to conclude the audience, grimly envisioning a task of subduing a territory in perpetual rebellion.

La Lengua hastily returned to report to Diego, and Santo Domingo's cheers abruptly mummed. The heartbeats of Roldán's former rebels pounded and skipped, and those who'd implemented Cristóbal's most partisan decisions drew short of breath. Most whispered that an investigation would reveal the injustices suffered under Cristóbal's rule. All hungered for their salaries to be paid.

Captain Gorda directed the caravels up the Ozama at midday. Bobadilla's trepidation surged when he floated beneath the corpses strung on opposing banks, triggering a premonition he'd entered the gates of hell. The fifty newcomers gasped, doubting their decision to enlist. The nineteen Taínos barely noticed, enthralled to be home. When the ships anchored in the cove beyond the church, Bobadilla chose to remain onboard and receive those who wished to pay homage. He hoped to gather more information before debarking into the inferno, and he signaled his independence from the Colóns, slighting brother Diego by not extending him an invitation to come aboard.

Some came to bow, fawn, and vouch for their unwavering loyalty to the sovereigns, and Bobadilla listened sympathetically and invited information about the rebellions and the Admiral's governance. As

the afternoon passed, his astonishment at the unremitting chaos and
Cristóbal's infirm command of the past years swelled, as did the
callers' impression that the investigation would extend to include the
deprivations they'd suffered.

Diego shied from calling, and he dispatched a horseman to
warn Cristóbal that a newly arrived courtier discourteously claimed
authority as the sovereigns' judicial investigator of the rebellion and
invited settlers to air grievances. That evening, as Bobadilla lay to
sleep in his berth, he scorned that Española had descended to a lawlessness his king and queen would deplore. Rebellion in a king's settlement was the fault of the commander as well as the rebels.

In the morning, Bobadilla came ashore with his royal scribe, officers, and newcomers and was met by Diego at the church, where they
and veteran settlers celebrated Mass. The scribe then read aloud the
sovereigns' proclamation appointing Bobadilla judicial investigator
and directing the Admiral and everyone else in the Indies to respect
his authority. Bobadilla turned to face Diego.

"I command you to turn over all prisoners awaiting execution
and the indictments charging them," he ordered. "As investigator, I
shall determine and dispense justice."

"I cannot," Diego responded gingerly. "As governor, the Admiral
has higher authority than you as judicial investigator, and he hasn't
empowered me to do that. Provide me a copy of the sovereigns' order,
and I shall deliver it to the Admiral."

"Since you have no power, I will not give you a copy," Bobadilla
retorted, angered to be disobeyed. But he refrained from ordering
Diego to instruct Cristóbal and Bartolomé to present themselves
for investigation, calculating that their absence afforded unexpected
advantage in his assuming the settlement's control. The resistance to
sovereign authority was clear-cut, albeit through a brother, and he
brooded whether resort to the sovereigns' proclamation of his governorship would be necessary sooner than they'd instructed.

The two men parted icily. Diego retired impotent to the family
compound and dispatched another horseman to Cristóbal. Bobadilla
and his officers and newcomers lingered at the church and central
plaza, inspecting, touring, and sharing stories of Spain and Española
with veterans who chose to mix. The veterans were guarded when

addressing Bobadilla, but his officers and newcomers gleaned useful information, which also matched his expectations. Expressions of admiration or support for Cristóbal were few and muted. Resentment that neither Cristóbal nor the king had paid their salaries was pervasive and thundering. Complaints that Cristóbal denied their participation in gold mining were frequent and loud.

But the veterans chumming were Santo Domingo's rank and file, and none of Cristóbal's lieutenants came in friendship, their aloofness ominously as apparent as Diego's. That evening, Bobadilla retired aboard the *Gorda*, too anxious to sleep soundly, suspecting Cristóbal would seek to undercut his authority and judging he had to preempt that boldly.

After dawn on August 25, Bobadilla again came ashore with officers and newcomers to share Mass with Diego and veteran settlers, and at its conclusion, he directed all to gather on the promontory before the church. The veterans hushed as the royal scribe loudly read the sovereigns' proclamation appointing him judge-governor, with authority to execute justice, appoint and replace officers, and expel anyone from the island. The veterans trembled as he swore to faithfully execute those duties and bid them—and all others in the Indies—to affirm their obedience to him. Premonitions of a reckoning of the tumult of the last few years were finally fulfilled, and every veteran feared for his own future, anguishing whether to align with Bobadilla or Cristóbal. Bobadilla stared at Diego and restated his demand that the prisoners and indictments be turned over.

"I understand you speak for the king, but I cannot comply," Diego replied, now boldly, openly inviting the assembly's loyalty to Cristóbal. "The Admiral's higher office affords him the right to cause others to ignore yours."

"Your disobedience is now witnessed by all," Bobadilla retorted, shaking his head and folding his arms viceregally, concealing angst and fear. Sensing the assembly vexed and bewildered over whom to obey, he turned to the scribe and bid him render the two remaining sovereign proclamations. The veterans gasped as the scribe recited that Bobadilla was the temporary governor of all the Indies and that all crown property was to be handed over to his control. They blushed as the scribe read that Bobadilla was to pay everyone's salaries.

"In addition to your salaries, I shall issue franchises to mine Española's gold to those of you who obey my command, for twenty years no less," Bobadilla proclaimed. "Instead of merely two-thirds of that mined, you may retain all but one-eleventh reserved for the king," he trumpeted, promising an unprecedented whittling of the sovereigns' share, a complete elimination of Cristóbal's tithe.

Most of the assembled cheered, although Cristóbal's servants and closest lieutenants remained mute. Bobadilla again faced Diego.

"Release the prisoners and their indictments!"

"I refuse."

With his arsenal of public proclamations discharged, his store of inducements largely bared, Bobadilla dismissed the assembly. He and his entourage strode to the fort to demand that Miguel Díaz, then guarding it, release the prisoners, which Díaz refused. Patient, Bobadilla then lingered in the central plaza through the day, and many veterans came to swear the obedience he'd sought. At dusk, he led a large crowd—both veterans and newcomers—to the fort, and Díaz again refused the prisoners' release. But Bobadilla and the crowd stormed in, breaking the lock on the fort's door, and with it, the fading specter of Cristóbal's rule of Española. Don Guevara, Riquelme, and the three others awaiting execution were released from its dungeon to the royal scribe's custody.

The next morning, indictments nonexistent, the five and all other prisoners were set free. Over the next days, Bobadilla wrote Roldán and other former rebels, demanding their submission and participation in the inquiry he would commence. But he chose not to dispatch a similar demand to Cristóbal, nor even a kinder overture or personal note, unilaterally assuming control in Cristóbal's absence, regardless of the insult and breach of custom. He interrogated Díaz to ascertain that the king's gold held in Santo Domingo was stored in chests in the fortified compound, and he seized the chests and commandeered the compound as his royal residence. He dispatched the royal scribe inland to recite the sovereigns' four proclamations to settlers there.

Bobadilla then began his full inquiry, intending to take many depositions, both of Cristóbal's officers, servants, and other loyalists and those who'd been in rebellion. But he remained anxious that his command would hold. Cristóbal's reaction and response remained unknown, and as countless courtiers could attest, he rarely wilted from a fight.

◻ ◻ ◻

By August, Cattaneo had assessed Cristóbal's share of the gold amassed at four million maravedís. On August 25, unaware of Bobadilla's arrival, Cristóbal pined for the tranquility that would permit that fortune to multiply, and he longed for his son Diego's and a subordinate justice's arrival, who would lighten the yoke of governing the many Spaniards who wished him ill.

He was seated alone at Fort Concepción's spring beholding a rising sun when brother Diego's first horseman brought the news. Ships had arrived without son Diego, but bearing a Commander Bobadilla, purportedly the sovereigns' judicial investigator of the rebellion, yet unfriendly and moved by settler grievances. Cristóbal leapt in disbelief and anger, envisioning Bobadilla as yet another interloper. Another Hojeda! Perhaps licensed for something, but surely not to investigate himself or foment settler dissatisfaction.

Over the next three days, horsemen arrived bearing the more sinister information, and Cristóbal swooned, as wretchedly as Christmas past aboard the caravel. The interloper had concocted the sovereigns' retraction of his authority! To destroy him. Without investigation. Buying the mob's vengeance with salaries and gold franchises. Releasing his worst enemies.

Cristóbal dismissed the last horseman and trembled by the spring long into the night. Visions of death looming at sea on the first voyage, offshore Cuba on the second, and at the Boca de la Sierpe cascaded through his thoughts, and he begged the Lord reveal why He hadn't taken him those times, sparing unremitting torture thereafter. He brooded bitterly that he'd never shared the triumphs of building Santo Domingo, discovering pearls off Paria, and exploiting the New Mines with his sovereigns face-to-face or received the credit due.

At dawn, haggard, Cristóbal rose, and as countless times before, furiously resolved not to be undone. Bobadilla had to be outmaneuvered—just as Hojeda and Aguado before. He summoned his faithful Pedro de Terreros and Cacique Diego Colón, as well as Francisco Velázquez, Ballester's replacement as the fort's captain.

"Bobadilla is an impostor, just like Hojeda was," he cried. "He's fabricated an authority the king and queen never awarded. Satan has dispatched him."

Terreros and Cacique Diego—acquainted since Cristóbal's first voyage—glanced to each other warily, pondering if their master was mistaken, lying, or hallucinating.

"Just as Hojeda, we must expel him from the island," Cristóbal exhorted. "Squadrons of both settlers and Indians must storm Santo Domingo and throw him onto the ships that bore him."

"Gather Concepción's settlers for that duty," he barked at Velázquez. "Ride to Xaraguá and direct Bartolomé do the same there," he barked at Terreros. "Those enlisting will be specially compensated. Promise I'll award them the repartimientos previously granted Múxica and the others to be executed."

Velázquez and Terreros nodded dutifully. Terreros rued that a more effective inducement would be to satisfy unpaid salaries with the gold amassed, although Cristóbal wouldn't countenance that. Cristóbal turned to Cacique Diego.

"Inform caciques throughout the Vega Real that they must supply me warriors for this duty. Warn them this Bobadilla is another Hojeda, scheming to plunder and enslave them. Convince your brother-in-law to support me. I shall remember and favor those who assist."

Diego's mind raced for a plausible response. The notion that caciques would rescue Admiral for fear another pale man would be worse was ludicrous. Such a two-faced warning was repugnant and outrageous.

"Admiral, I shall try hard," he lied.

Over the next week, Velázquez and Diego went to work in and beyond Concepción and found virtually no support. Some settlers longed for a competent governor, others' patience with Cristóbal and Bartolomé was spent, and all angered that Cristóbal wouldn't pay their salaries when Bobadilla would. The cacique "Doctor" refused to participate in the plan, Guarionex scorned it, and Diego didn't bother entreating Manicoatex. Macís offered one hundred warriors, enticed by the opportunity of plundering some pale men.

In Xaraguá, Terreros met briefly with Bartolomé to deliver Cristóbal's instructions and a personal note written in encrypted Ligurian, and Bartolomé vigorously tried to enlist both settlers and Indians. But Xaraguá's settlers had hated him and Cristóbal for years, and even offers to commute sentences failed to persuade them. Haniguyabá and other local caciques would have nothing to do with it, and Bartolomé knew it pointless to contact Behecchio and Anacaona.

◻ ◻ ◻

Behecchio and Anacaona learned of Bartolomé's efforts from Haniguyabá. They also heard from concubines and scouts of the new pale man claiming—like Roldán and Hojeda before—to be the true representative of Fernando and Isabel, rather than the guamiquina. One evening, as Behecchio lay supine before his caney's fire circle, they discussed the ever-bizarre pale men's invasion, including the new claimant's release of Don Guevara from prison.

"The guamiquina appears imperiled," Behecchio observed. "But we've thought that before." He grimaced. "Don Guevara is in no apparent rush to return here to marry your daughter."

"The concubines report their squatters fear the new claimant," Anacaona replied. "Guevara must perceive he's lost the opportunity to become a Xaraguán ruler." She resolved to tell Higueymota that night. "I suspect he'll never return—not even to behold his child."

◻ ◻ ◻

Cristóbal cringed when Velázquez and Cacique Diego reported that virtually none of Concepción's settlers or neighboring Indians supported resisting Bobadilla. He staggered when Terreros returned from Xaraguá to report no better results there. He fell to his knees when a horseman, dispatched by brother Diego, informed him that Roldán and his loyalists had submitted to Bobadilla's governorship.

Raging that Bobadilla hadn't contacted him, machinating how to maneuver their confrontation, he departed for Bonao and dispatched a letter inviting Bobadilla to parley there—a compromise between Concepción and Santo Domingo. In Bonao, he read Isabel and Fernando's orders borne by the scribe, and his fury warped his interpretation.

"Instruct every officer and settler that Commander Bobadilla possesses merely the authority to investigate the rebellions," he harangued Terreros. "Bobadilla can be obeyed to that extent alone. I retain overriding authority as governor." Anguishing in limbo, he dispatched another letter to Bobadilla explaining that conclusion.

⊞   ⊞   ⊞

Bobadilla didn't reply to either of Cristóbal's letters.

By the first week of September, Cristóbal's isolation was transparent, and Bobadilla dispatched Fray Trasierra to deliver him Isabel and Fernando's intimate note to put into action what Bobadilla said.

Cristóbal knew to submit as soon as he read it, and after discussing that with Trasierra, on September 14, he forlornly departed Bonao for Santo Domingo. Bobadilla was alerted and incarcerated brother Diego in the fort's dungeon to prevent the brothers from conspiring.

SUBMISSION AND INVESTIGATION,
Santo Domingo, September 15–October 12, 1500

On the morning of September 15, Cristóbal and two dozen servants, officers, and other loyalists entered Santo Domingo, escorted by Fray Trasierra. The entire settlement was hush, stupefied at what would follow. Cristóbal wished to worship briefly at the church, and Trasierra obliged. The sovereigns occasionally investigated and replaced their commanders, both in Spain and the Canaries, and Cristóbal knew of that process and to acquiesce therein. But he beseeched the Lord that the seeds of its reversal be planted, burning that such an ignominious proceeding had never been inflicted on a servant who'd borne such triumphs.

Bobadilla met him as he left the church, halted him rudely without the courtesy of a handshake, and stared into his eyes inimically, menacing contempt for his Genoese heritage, as though as detestable as an infidel's, and mocking his nobility as admiral, as though unmerited and hollow. Cristóbal didn't concede the victory, averting his eyes and gazing beyond to the Ozama, as if the knight were a plebe, unworthy to stand beside him on the promontory. But he couldn't contain his bitterness and despair and began to quiver.

Bobadilla relished the pain inflicted, gloating that a Spanish knight who'd bought loyalty had outwitted a foreign-born admiral who'd alienated nearly everyone. His dominance asserted, he ordered Cristóbal to accompany him to the governor's chamber in the fortified compound, together with the royal scribe. Upon entering, he peremptorily assumed Cristóbal's former chair, directing Cristóbal to the seat of a supplicant. Aghast, Cristóbal studied Bobadilla's possessions and papers intermingled with his own, including his life's work—his learned treatises and maps, his journals, and the compilation of his entitlements. He trembled uncontrollably.

Bobadilla arrests Columbus. Taken from Theodore de Bry, 1594.
The John Carter Brown Library, rec. no. 09887-12.

Bobadilla grudgingly softened his demeanor and tone to calm his witness and predecessor, hoping that both incriminating and useful information would be secured. He reported that Cristóbal's sons were well at court, and servants offered water and sweets. When Cristóbal calmed somewhat, Bobadilla turned to the lawlessness most readily apparent and provable.

"What were Don Guevara and Riquelme's crimes?" he asked. "Should I prosecute them? Do you have indictments for them and the others?"

"They were in rebellion against the king and queen, but there are no indictments. There wasn't time—the island would have been lost, and possibly my life," Cristóbal responded. "So, you may release them, pending your own investigation of their treason," he allowed, as if concerned with judicial process, bitterly aware that Guevara, Riquelme, and the others already had been freed. "I would have taken indictments of those executed to Spain," he professed, as if recognizing that Múxica, at least, was due that.

"What of your brother's prisoners?" the scribe interrogated. "Does he have indictments?"

"I will write Bartolomé to release them," Cristóbal conceded ruefully. "You may investigate them, as well."

"Order Bartolomé to submit before me here, promptly," Bobadilla instructed, keen on quashing further resistance.

The knight questioned the admiral regarding the island's day-to-day operation—where settlers were dispersed, the function of each fort, and the rule of the Indians. When Cristóbal tired, Bobadilla released him in the company of guards to find lodging elsewhere. Two days later, the questioning resumed with the goal of marshaling Española's crown property.

"You must turn over all the king's gold wherever stored—here, Concepción, with your brother, and anywhere else—and you must swear you've delivered it all," Bobadilla commanded.

"I must first use that gold to pay the salaries of three hundred and thirty settlers," Cristóbal responded curtly, his wits and mettle partially restored. "I won't turn the remainder over until that's done."

"The king's gold must be surrendered now!" Bobadilla barked, denying Cristóbal that latitude and largess. "As governor, I shall satisfy those settlers' salaries."

Cristóbal angered, and while recognizing his impotence, sought to impart reciprocal condemnation.

"You've gravely erred in awarding franchises that so diminish the sovereigns' share of the gold," he lectured. "The settlers' share I've set is sufficient inducement and yields much more for the king. You will regret your folly."

Bobadilla eyed Cristóbal contemptuously, dismissive of the lecture, hostile to undoing inducements underlying his command, and wary that Cristóbal no longer trembled. He concluded the audience, contemplating never gracing Cristóbal with another.

Cristóbal duly dispatched orders to Concepción and Bartolomé that the king's gold be surrendered to the royal treasurer who'd arrived with Bobadilla. On September 23, Bartolomé submitted in Santo Domingo, and both Cristóbal and he swore to the amount of the king's gold in their separate control and that they'd delivered it all.

With that gold accounted, Bobadilla abruptly incarcerated both Cristóbal and Bartolomé in the fort's dungeon beside Diego.

⊡   ⊡   ⊡

Cristóbal's Genoese factor Cattaneo had been entrusted to separately safeguard Cristóbal's own share of Española's gold, and after seizing that gold also, Bobadilla directed it be used to pay the unpaid salaries of the remaining men for whom Cristóbal was financially responsible. Quickly, the knight came to view all the admiral's property—pearls, jewels, furniture, mementos, livestock, and even the learned treatises, maps, and journals—as property of Española's governor, just like property he'd expropriated from Mohammedans during the Reconquista.

Bobadilla understood his mandate as judicial investigator was to bring those who'd rebelled against Cristóbal to justice, and he summoned Roldán, who—with Cristóbal incarcerated—was the most powerful veteran settler and official on the island.

"Recount your rebellion," Bobadilla demanded.

"My commander, I'm pleased to," Roldán replied, smoothly exuding confidence. "But I must note at the outset that I never rebelled against the king and queen. I merely disobeyed the Admiral's misrule. The Admiral and I settled the matter of my disobedience to him and recorded our agreement in a writing executed by the Admiral, as governor. I, and those loyal to me, have obeyed him ever since." He folded his arms across his chest, as countless times before. "It would grieve and displease me were your investigation to revive issues already so legally and competently resolved."

Bobadilla folded his arms similarly, not to appear cowed, his mind racing. The sovereigns' order didn't contemplate such exoneration, yet the argument bore the tenor of a sly magistrate.

"You must tell me what happened," he reiterated curtly.

Roldán did so, much in the vein of his letter to Cisneros, blending a string of lies with enough grains of truth to be credible to some. In conclusion, he again challenged his interrogator.

"Whether you credit my account or not, you yourself have witnessed the Genoese's disobedience to our sovereigns and yourself—enlisting Indians against their rule, no less," he blustered. "For that alone, you did well to incarcerate him, and he deserves greater punishments for his earlier conduct." He gazed into Bobadilla's eyes. "I am key to this settlement's well-being, and I have already sworn obedience to you."

"I'm authorized to investigate your conduct and incarcerate you too," Bobadilla retorted coldly, doubting much of Roldán's yarn, disgusted that the commoner was as untrustworthy a knave as any he'd met. "Tell me of Múxica and Guevara's treason, and your role in imprisoning them."

"Those two and their gang mutinied against both the Admiral and myself," Roldán responded, fearing he'd overestimated his vantage. "It was the Admiral who directed punishment without trial."

The knight dismissed the rebel and brooded. His sovereigns' eyes and oversight were far distant, their orders perhaps grown stale, the facts and circumstances murky, and as governor, his discretion in interpreting their orders fulsome. His governorship certainly empowered him to apply justice to Cristóbal for acts he witnessed personally. According to Fonseca, the sovereigns' first imperative was restoring order on Cristóbal's removal, and upsetting former rebels jeopardized that and the command and comforts he'd assumed. What's more, his previous disdain for Cristóbal had mounted to hatred.

Bobadilla angrily resolved that his investigation would focus on Cristóbal's misconduct, rather than past rebellions against him, and wouldn't trigger findings that led to punishment of former rebels. He'd ignore the sovereigns' order to investigate Roldán's rebellion, and the supersession of Roldán's magisterial authority would be sufficient penalty.

◻   ◻   ◻

Accordingly, the principal charges to be investigated were whether Cristóbal had opposed Bobadilla's authority, impeded the Indians' baptisms to enslave them, or unjustly and cruelly punished Spaniards.

Testimony was compelled from a small number of Cristóbal's officers and servants, former rebels, and some less partisan. Witnesses loyal to Cristóbal included Terreros, Salcedo, La Lengua, and Ortiz, and former rebels included Diego de Escobar and two prisoners whom Bobadilla had just released, Juan Vallés and Rodrigo Montoya. Those less openly aligned included Fray Ramón Pané. All testified knowing Cristóbal was to be expelled from Española, thereby rendered powerless to control their futures or take vengeance, barring an improbable resurrection of his fortune. All knew Bobadilla now determined their fates, including payment of their salaries.

The witnesses nigh unanimously—including Terreros—testified that Cristóbal had resisted Bobadilla's authority by attempting to organize Spaniards and Indians to expel him from the island or, at least, undo his command. His awards to so enlist Spaniards included farms and mares for Salcedo and Concepción's captain Velázquez, two horses for Francisco de Garay, and parts of Manicoatex's chiefdom for others. Cacique Macís had pledged a thousand warriors and been whipped for proffering only a hundred.

Witnesses didn't doubt the sincerity of Cristóbal's faith, and the testimony whether he'd deliberately refused to approve baptisms of Indians so they could be enslaved was mixed. Some witnesses answered the question yes, some no, and many didn't respond clearly, indicating simply that he refused most requests for conversion, insisting converts possess doctrinal knowledge, and sought tribute more than conversion. Pané bitterly lamented that he could have baptized a hundred thousand souls if Cristóbal had lent him La Lengua to translate. La Lengua testified that Cristóbal had sent him to induce Indians who'd fled tribute to return home, only to seize and award them as slaves in lieu of salaries or for shipment to Spain. One witness testified that Cristóbal declared that all Indians were his, the women available for his and the king's sale. Another reported that Cristóbal believed the Indians wouldn't become Christians unless hauled to Spain. A few bitterly related that Cristóbal denied the baptism of concubines, precluding marriages.

The most virulent testimony recorded regarded the third charge, Cristóbal's injustices to Spaniards. Escobar and many others recounted an accumulation of punishments since 1493—beheadings, mutilations, and whippings—as unduly and cruelly inflicted, including for trivial infractions. Chaplain Ortiz and Cristóbal's lieutenants Rodrigo Pérez and Lope Muñoz described the treatment doled to the Spanish noblemen, Don Guevara and Múxica, and Riquelme's torture. Testimony justifying the appropriateness of Cristóbal's justice and punishments of Spaniards—particularly those who'd shirked manual labor—wasn't sought and only sparsely volunteered.

Testimony regarding Cristóbal's harsh treatment of Indians wasn't of focus—either not constituting a crime, unworthy of punishment, or so pervasive that Cristóbal hardly could be singled out.

◻ ◻ ◻

Upon arrival in August, Fray Francisco Ruiz had fulfilled his master Archbishop Cisnero's instructions by delivering the manumitted Taínos ashore in Santo Domingo. Contemporary chroniclers gave little more notice to that event than they'd given the manumissions months earlier, and with minor exception, the manumitted vanished into their homeland and history. Ruiz and his five churchmen didn't record assisting the manumitted in repatriation.

As Bobadilla sparred with Cristóbal, the churchmen were gripped instead with introducing Cisneros's sword of mass baptism to Española—the soul's afterlife perhaps of more concern than the body's state on earth. Although Fray Ruiz fell seriously ill, he led his churchmen in gathering and baptizing crowds of Indians living in and about Santo Domingo, as well as subjects of Catalina, Agüeybana, and other caciques farther distant. Fray Leudelle estimated that more than two thousand converted within weeks, Fray Robles more than three thousand.

◻ ◻ ◻

Crammed in the dungeon with his brothers, Cristóbal forlornly listened as his legacy and reputation were trampled. Taunts and catcalls filtered through the cell's doorway mocking his fall from nobility, deriding his heritage, scorning his governorship, and threatening vengeance for his unfulfilled promises and uneven justice. He recognized the voices of many he'd favored, even some who'd been his servants only weeks before. He understood the charges Bobadilla was investigating and ignoring, and he loathed that the treasonous would go free while he was jailed. Even death loomed, either by the mob's lynching or Bobadilla's justice. Bobadilla never visited the dungeon to talk or offer courtesies sometimes afforded fallen courtiers. Cristóbal's trembling resumed, accompanied by a resurgence of painful leg cramps.

By October, Bobadilla directed the removal of Cristóbal and his brothers to the *Gorda* and *Antigua*. He instructed Captain Vallejo to prevent their escape by shackling them and to deliver them to Fonseca for the sovereigns' consideration. When Vallejo arrived at the dungeon, Cristóbal feared the moment of death had arrived, but the captain assured him otherwise, and Cristóbal's former cook—trusted as one of the few who wouldn't mistreat him—imposed the shackles. But jeers and threats accosted him as he was escorted down to the harbor and launch, and Cristóbal desperately envisioned Christ's march up to Golgotha.

On October 12, the caravels were set to sail—the eighth anniversary of Cristóbal's first landfall in the Indies. He and his brothers were secured onboard, and Bobadilla's investigation report had been completed and entrusted to Vallejo. The ink had barely dried on letters and a memorandum the friars had written to Cisneros, borne by Ruiz himself, who was too ill to remain in Española.

These letters trumpeted the baptisms the friars had achieved and observed that the Indians didn't object and appeared to desire it. Their memorandum recommended that the sovereigns dispatch many missionaries to accelerate conversion and teach doctrine and that tithes be established in Española to fund its church's growth under the auspices of a sovereign appointee. They asked for guidance regarding the marriage of settlers and Indians, noting the concubinage and children born thereby.

As for Cristóbal, Fray Leudelle's letter indicated that he had resisted Bobadilla's authority with Indians and loyalists. Fray Trasierra compared his rule to Pharaoh's. The memorandum recommended that the Admiral, his family, and any Genoese never be allowed to return to the island or they'd destroy it and no Christian or churchman would remain. It didn't express whether Cristóbal had denied baptisms to enslave Indians, but it warned that the Genoese would take the island's riches for foreign kings.

Beyond their writings, Fray Ruiz and the churchmen perceived mistreatment of the queen's Indian vassals, and—unlike Bobadilla's investigation—their concern extended beyond Cristóbal's conduct to that of the Spanish settlers. The churchmen were most disturbed by their brethren's treatment of their many concubines. They didn't question the repartimientos awarded or the attendant forced labor, perceiving those appropriate—as the Indians would be brought from a state of nature to Christianity and civilization. But they were troubled that the Indian labor was uncompensated—as if they were slaves, not vassals. Some of those baptized had been slaves.

ANACAONA AND BEHECCHIO, GUAMIQUINA'S DEPARTURE

Caciques throughout the island had scorned the guamiquina's appeal for warriors, and rumors that he and Bartolomé had been imprisoned and would be executed or hauled away brought astonishment and raucous jubilation.

Behecchio and Anacaona shared their delight publicly, yet in private their apprehension for Xaraguá's course mounted. Behecchio's stupor and cough had worsened precipitously—symptoms of the diseases that accompanied the pale men and the Christ-spirit—and he could no longer conceal frailty and decline from his subjects. A glimmer of hope remained. The high fevers and red blisters that had marked death's imminence for multitudes hadn't onset, and some Taínos—including Anacaona herself—had recovered from illness in their absence.* Nevertheless, they understood death was drawing near.

Upon learning of the guamiquina's transfer to a vessel, Behecchio summoned Anacaona to sit yards distant from him while he lay beside his ballcourt. Naborias maintained their seclusion, marking the moment's gravity. She was sobered by her brother's suffering and fleetingly recalled Caonabó instructing her what to do if he failed to return.

"It shall fall to you to deal with this Bobadilla and whatever he plots," Behecchio said, struggling to raise his voice. "Informants report many pale men appear to be departing Haiti, not just

---

* Perhaps influenza or typhus.

the guamiquina and Bartolomé. Perhaps more men than Bobadilla brought, reducing their presence on the island yet again."

Anacaona shuddered, saddened but relieved by his alertness. A lifetime shared with her brother was concluding.

"When I inherited Xaraguá, we knew you might succeed me someday, and that time arrives. Our vassal caciques will acclaim your ascension. What I pass to you is fallen from what I received, our strategy for survival now unknown."

"You've preserved our rule and spared Xaraguá from the guamiquina, even outlasting him," she replied. "I once questioned some of your decisions, but no chieftain has done better. When the time comes, I shall seek to outlast this Bobadilla in the same way."

"Your husband and I should've massacred the guamiquina and his men when they were defenseless, just after he came ashore at his Isabela," Behecchio reproached. "I could have slain Bartolomé's gang when he first visited us, as well as Roldán's. My soul's path may be dark and dreadful."

Anacaona had heard similar recriminations countless times before—from Caonabó, Behecchio himself, and other caciques—and she chose not to debate them now, deeming such hindsight fruitless and degrading. The truth was more nuanced. Whether good-heartedness, naiveté, or foolishness, it had taken time to grasp the pale men's intent, squandering advantage.

"You've done no evil, my brother. Your subjects have been led and served better than those trampled by war and enslavements. Your soul shall reunite pleasurably with our ancestors."

Behecchio grunted and struggled to lift himself, leaning forward and bracing himself with his elbows. His gaze imperious, Anacaona understood he would impart his most important counsel.

"Most of our subjects now assume that the pale men's weapons empower them to maintain their conquest indefinitely. But as cacique, it shall fall to you to scrutinize their weaknesses vigilantly—their anarchy, their mistreatment not only of us but of themselves, and most importantly, their declining numbers. Never forget that our accommodations to them are for the singular purpose of outlasting them. Uprising may be achievable one day, if their numbers decline so much that their weapons become surmountable." He stared, drawing her eyes to his. "Xaraguá's cacique must harbor hope for that day, and if it comes, make the fateful decision to war."

"I pray for that day, and I accept that responsibility," Anacaona assured. Yet she quivered as she spoke, recognizing that her ability to war didn't match his. She'd always left military judgments to him. Her role in their rule had been to counsel solutions other than war, not to plot it and certainly not to fight it. She was silent momentarily, digesting the responsibility.

"Who then should be the general?" she asked, acknowledging what would be necessary.

"Guaorocuyá," Behecchio responded, referring to their most accomplished nephew, pleased his sister's thoughts had been and remained remarkably in unison with his own. "As I depart, I shun counseling war, executions, or poisonings. It will fall to you to decide if and when, and I pray you possess the wisdom neither your husband nor I showed."

Anacaona nodded, recognizing Guaorocuyá—youthful, charismatic, and proven in leading warriors—as the best choice.

Behecchio's head slumped forward, his agenda nearly fulfilled. They'd both been disturbed by reports that the pale men's behiques had demanded that villagers living near Santo Domingo worship their Christ-spirit.

"What if Bobadilla dispatches behiques to corrupt our subjects?" he rasped.

"That would discomfort me," Anacaona ruminated aloud. "But I might acquiesce in some minor compromise. Other than the concubines, our people do not heed their behiques." According to informants, subjects of caciques Catalina and Agüeybana had insincerely obliged the behiques' demands, feigning worship rather than triggering friction by objecting. Many had grown more convinced that the conquerors' spirit was evil.

Anacaona and Behecchio discussed the transition of power until dusk, when she rose to depart. She shed tears as they said goodbye without embracing but strode away confidently. Two decades as wife and sister to supreme caciques had already molded her into one.

Entering her garden, she pondered whether she'd underestimated the Christ-spirit's potency. Every day, his presence was welcomed in the bohíos shared by concubines and their squatters—at dawn, at dusk, and when meals were shared. The concubines themselves invoked him, whether from fear, duty, or mere acquiescence. It was he that would smite Behecchio, as no pale man dared do so.

At sunset, she beseeched Yúcahu to guide her through the transition approaching and fortify her to war if uprising beckoned. As darkness came, her thoughts returned to her brother's suffering, and she despaired whether the time had come to pray for mercy to his assassin.

CRISTÓBAL, ISABEL AND FERNANDO, VOYAGE HOME AND AUDIENCE,
October 13–December 17, 1500

On October 13, the *Gorda* and *Antigua* drifted down the Ozama to commence the crossing to Spain, with Cristóbal and brother Diego aboard the former and Bartolomé separated onto the latter. Vallejo and Gorda offered to remove their shackles when the ships entered the ocean, escape no longer possible. Cristóbal insisted on retaining them, bitterly resolved to publicly brandish them at court as proof of the injustice, ingratitude, and malevolence to which he perceived himself subjected. He'd been chained in the sovereigns' name, and the chains would remain until the sovereigns themselves removed them.

In addition to Fray Ruiz, the passengers included Cristóbal's officers Terreros, Carvajal, and Coronel, household servants Salcedo and Juan Portugués, and kinsmen Giovanni Colombo and Pedro de Arana, all fleeing Bobadilla's rule. Bobadilla had encouraged as much, keen to remove them from the island. Cristóbal had directed Cattaneo to remain behind to monitor Bobadilla's squandering of his gold and other property, envisioning their recovery when he appealed to the sovereigns. Others departing—either previously loyal to Cristóbal or Roldán—simply feared Bobadilla's cold-heartedness might turn on them, a risk greater than the lure of the new gold finds. Don Guevara berthed, vexed to be without a protector, cognizant that he'd do better in the Indies as Hojeda's accomplice than he could for himself. Higueymota lingered in his memory as merely another failed scheme.

As the ships bore northeast, Cristóbal composed three writings in defense of his rule and rebutting Bobadilla's charges—a memorandum to the council of courtiers that could be expected to review Bobadilla's investigation report, a letter addressed to the queen's household confidant Juana de la Torre, who'd long been his friend and supporter, and the third a mere paragraph intended directly for the queen and king.* Copies were made of the letter to Juana so she'd pass them about court. The paragraph—an addendum to a never-dispatched letter he'd written earlier to the sovereigns—informed that Commander Bobadilla had sent him back a prisoner in chains, swearing he didn't know why.

True to form, the memorandum and letter cast the spiritual and sinister contexts boldly, harping on his rants of the past three years. As Isaiah and Saint John had prophesied, he'd voyaged to *a new heaven and new earth* and found the sovereigns pearls and gold, wrestling obstacles just as St. Peter and the Apostles had. The case against him was *trumped-up malice*, based on the false testimony of rebels trying to overthrow him, orchestrated by a predisposed courtier corruptly seeking the governorship through testimony bought by awarding away the king's gold.

As to the investigation's first charge, Cristóbal spun that he'd never knowingly resisted sovereign authority. When informed of Bobadilla's arrival, he'd believed another interloper like Hojeda had come to usurp the island, but he'd reconsidered when the sovereigns' friar explained their orders. He'd then tried to convince Bobadilla to rescind the awards squandering the sovereigns' gold, asserting Bobadilla had no authority to grant them, possessing only limited power subordinate to his own. He'd even written Bobadilla a welcoming note—rudely unanswered—assuring that he would immediately hand over the government.

He ignored the second charge—denying Indians baptism to enslave them instead—surmising the issue of little concern to most courtiers, perhaps of import only to the queen, and implying it moot from the perspective of Christianity. He'd reduced to *obedience more land than is contained in Africa and Europe*, whereby the Holy Church would flourish greatly.

---

* The council likely was the Council of Seville. Juana de la Torre was Prince Juan's former nurse.

As for injustices to Spaniards, Cristóbal pleaded his case with respect to nobility alone, the base concern of king, queen, and courtiers. Múxica and Don Guevara had revolted, and while he'd resolved *not to touch a hair of anyone's head*, Múxica's ingratitude precluded mercy. He would have rendered the same death sentence to his own brother. Roldán had arrested and punished Don Guevara without his order.

The ships' crossing was efficient, and within four weeks, they attained the latitude of the Spanish Peninsula, the ink on Cristóbal's parchments largely dry. Like most experienced mariners, Vallejo and Gorda venerated Cristóbal's seamanship and treated him respectfully, and his opponents and enemies aboard restrained their glee.

The ocean also rejuvenated him, as it always did, regardless of imprisonment. The pound and woosh of the surf about the *Gorda* reminded that he remained the Admiral, both in crest and the eyes of seamen. Fear and humiliation receded to resolution, driven by the catharsis of letter writing and trust that the Lord ultimately favored him. Instead of the friar's costume donned before, he plotted disembarking adorned in the chains and thereby launching a new campaign. He'd been excoriated unjustly by an unfit successor and was entitled to recover all that had been lost—his governorship, gold, papers, and noble honor.

The ships anchored in Cádiz on November 20. Bearing the friars' letters, Ruiz departed to report to the sovereigns in Granada before traveling north to Cisneros. Vallejo conveyed Bobadilla's investigation report and Cristóbal's memorandum to Fonseca and the courtiers' council in Seville for review before subsequent relay to the sovereigns. Faster than both Ruiz and that relay, Gorda arranged for a horseman to speed delivery to the sovereigns of Cristóbal's letter to Juana and the paragraph addendum.

Cristóbal, Bartolomé, and Diego were escorted in chains down the gangplanks into the custody of the town's chief magistrate. The spectacle stunned the mariners beholding, and word soon reverberated through Andalusia's ports and Seville that the Admiral's treatment was too rough and ungrateful for one who'd conquered the ocean and discovered so much, regardless of his faults.

▢   ▢   ▢

Isabel lay ill, slumbering in her bed in the Alhambra palace, when her husband brought the news that Cristóbal had returned inauspiciously to Cádiz. Fernando angrily waved letters they and Juana had received, and his wide-eyed glare proclaimed an uncharacteristic weariness and revulsion. She dismissed her chambermaids. The moment—the last week of November—found them tired from the press of attention elsewhere, ill-disposed to focus on more upsetting news from the Indies.

Of dynastic concern, Juana and Philippe hadn't even responded to—no less fulfilled—the summons to present themselves for recognition as heirs to Spain's crowns, as if Philippe mocked his marriage and kingdom's alliance to Spain and would embrace France's King Louis XII instead. Of domestic concern, Granadan Mohammedans again had uprisen in mountainous territory west of the capital city, and she and Fernando had organized troops to crush them.

"Española remains in shambles!" Fernando exclaimed furiously when they were alone, explaining that Bobadilla had sent Colón home chained as a criminal, with Colón protesting incoherently.

"We commanded only his removal!" Isabel gasped, laboring to sit at the bedside. "Has he been harmed?"

"Not enough to silence him! He's already sought the ear of the entire court."

"Many will perceive us as uncharitable. We must release him promptly and review the charges later."

"My queen, we know better than to credit his word. A few more days should bring more information, and we can release him then, if satisfied."

By the first week of December, Fray Ruiz arrived at the Alhambra. Isabel and Fernando were surprised that he'd returned so soon and relieved he bore some good news. Gold had been discovered in abundance at last, and Española's Indians were mining it dutifully. Three thousand souls had been baptized. But the fresh perspective Isabel had sought was damning. Cristóbal's rule had been a disaster for both Christianity and Española, and his exile from the island should be permanent. He'd rarely approved baptisms, enslavement was his norm, and the Indian population had suffered an extraordinary decline. The sovereigns' Christian subjects needed reform, too, their treatment of the Indian women filthy and unchristian.

Isabel and Fernando were shocked by the allegation that Cristóbal had marshaled both Spaniards and Indians to rise against Bobadilla. She was sorrowed by the Indians' extraordinary demise. They recalled the pope's award of the title Catholic Monarchs and his instruction to bring the Indians to Christianity, and they grimly brooded that the travesty transpiring in Española tarnished not only Cristóbal but their own legacy. They received further information from Fonseca regarding the substance of Bobadilla's investigation, and when alone again, they concluded their deliberations.

"Our decision to replace the Admiral is confirmed," Isabel pronounced. "He lacks the wherewithal to govern. His disobedience is chronic, and his letters irrefutably demonstrate he's no longer capable of even perceiving his shortcomings." She scowled, palled by Cristóbal's incessant self-anointments to the perch of the scripture's truest Christ-bearers. She winced, as well, regretting having demoted one who'd brought her so much. "For bringing us the Indies, he deserves restoration of his liberty, property, and the ongoing financial entitlements for the discoveries he's made. We owe him that, but nothing more."

"What we owe him now depends on his past conduct and obedience," Fernando countered. "We consider first our acclaim and our conquest's health, rather than his."

"Airing these charges would prolong his suffering unnecessarily," Isabel observed sadly. "Our renown would also suffer."

"My queen, there's no cause to make public whatever Bobadilla has prepared, although I shall parse it when received," Fernando declared. "We should avoid a trial or proceeding revealing the details. I suggest we magnanimously call the matter closed. We shall be rid of both him and the unsavory record."

⊡ ⊡ ⊡

The sovereigns dispatched orders that Cristóbal and his brothers be freed and a letter to Cristóbal summoning them to court, including two thousand ducats to cover travel and living expenses. Cristóbal received the letter in the second week of December in Seville, where he'd been relocated. After refusing the chains' removal yet again, he and his brothers left for Granada. On December 17, the three were ushered into the ambassadors' greeting chamber of the Alhambra palace. King, queen, and Cristóbal's sons awaited in the throne room with a multitude of courtiers.

Cristóbal had calculated a spectacle conveying an unparalleled martyrdom of injustice inflicted despite exemplary service. But as he entered the throne room, he came undone, the theater abruptly collapsing into true torment. As friend and foe parted to let him pass, his recurring agony of being utterly deserted and surrounded by only foes revisited, and he burst into uncontrollable tears. He spied Isabel beckoning from her throne and was shocked how she'd aged and grown sickly, and his despair deepened, doubting she'd still protect him. He trembled that Fernando appeared just as he remembered, casting a forbidding indomitability.

The shackles' clank pierced all, even those who knew them staged. Isabel beheld Cristóbal's approach, his face torn by exposure and angst, the shackles a reminder of the ceaseless impediments and insults Fonseca and other ministers had dealt him for years. She welled with grief and despair that a faith so strong and true and abilities so extraordinary were coupled with a personality so headstrong, contentious, bombastic, and despised. The clamor about him never ceased! Fernando was jarred that Cristóbal's commanding presence had wilted beyond recognition, proving he'd suffered far more than most others in the crown's service. His exhaustion resembled that of soldiers who'd fought bitterly in battles woefully lost, who were due honor and respect even if misguided or witless—certainly not the affront of chains.

When he reached them, Cristóbal fell to his knees sobbing and quivering, speechless. Isabel touched his forehead, inviting him to kiss her hand, which he did, as well as Fernando's.

"My Admiral, rise," she bid. "Tell us what has happened. Rest assured the king and I never intended any harm to befall you." Gazing about the crowd, she pronounced angrily, "We never intended or instructed that you be chained."

"It causes us great grief to see you so treated," Fernando proclaimed. "Recount the harms and injustices you have suffered."

Cristóbal slowly stood and rambled first to the constant rebellions, his rage unbridled.

"Those guilty shall be punished," Isabel declared.

He drifted to Bobadilla's confiscations, his rage unabated.

"Your gold, possessions, and entitlements will be restored," Fernando promised.

He turned to Bobadilla's charges. Tears gushing anew, he denied them vehemently. But he recognized that many wouldn't agree and pleaded innocence.

"Your Highnesses, while I've committed errors, I never intended to do you ill."

Isabel and Fernando glanced to each other. Each believed that was true, if nothing else.

"My Admiral, you are pardoned for any misdeed charged by anyone, and you retain our favor as our Admiral," Isabel announced for all to understand and obey. "Stay with me a moment, as I wish to hear more," she directed, concluding the public audience and dismissing everyone else.

Cristóbal fell to his knees again, overcome with relief that he'd survived so far, a vision of the Lord saving him at sea flickering at the edge of consciousness. As Fernando and the crowd exited, Isabel bid him sit beside her, and after the shackles were removed, both understood a final question remained.

"Your Highness, I must return to Española to right its course—as its governor."

Anticipating his renewed collapse, Isabel began to cry also. Yet, despite her failing health and affection for the man who'd brought her the Indies, she would continue to rule as she always had, with a clear vision and steeled hand, doing what she perceived needed to be done for the benefit of her kingdoms.

"Cristóbal, you remain my Admiral, but not governor. We shall dispatch someone to Española to retrieve your property. You're forever welcome here at court."

⊡　⊡　⊡

As the new year dawned, courtiers speculated what Bobadilla's investigation had found. Gonzalo Fernández de Oviedo (b. 1478), since childhood one of Prince Juan's household companions and witness to Cristóbal's entire career at court, suspected the truth would never come out. While Cristóbal had gotten out of hand, his services were so notable that it wasn't consonant with royal gratitude to maltreat him, his reform preferable instead.[*] Pedro Mártir, typically Cristóbal's supporter, got wind that Cristóbal and Bartolomé had resisted Bobadilla's authority and prudently chose to suspend writing favorably of Cristóbal lest that offend the sovereigns.[†] Andrés Bernáldez, compiling information to write a glowing history of the Catholic Monarchs' reign and once Cristóbal's admirer, also stepped back from chronicling him.[‡]

Their advance of two thousand ducats was soon spent, and while they understood Cristóbal would remain penniless until his gold was retrieved from Española, Isabel and Fernando didn't replenish it.

---

[*] Oviedo would chronicle the Indies extensively, his seminal work being *Historia General y Natural de Las Indias.*

[†] Mártir was then chronicling the Indies extensively, his principal work being *De Orbe Novo.*

[‡] Bernáldez's work was *Historia de los Reyes Católicos D. Fernando y Doña Isabel.*

IX

ANACAONA'S ASCENSION, OTHER TRANSITIONS

Bobadilla's Governorship,
October 1500–1501

Santo Domingo had stilled as the *Gorda* and *Antigua* vanished from view, the exile of the Indies' founding conqueror hardly believable, the brusque imposition of his successor's rule a rude reckoning. Roldán and his lieutenants exhaled gratefully, having escaped prosecution, judging the successor worthy of support for that reason alone. Cristóbal's followers inhaled skeptically, deploring the absence of that prosecution, having expected their long-standing loyalty merited favor over rebels, yet placated Roldán's magisterial authority was superseded. All hoped Bobadilla's rule would enrich them by at last establishing the order appropriate for a Castilian province.

Commander Bobadilla had a righteous, Christian vision of how to institute that order and prosperity consistent with the sovereigns' instructions. Domination of the conquered, non-Christian population was fundamental thereto—just as it had been during the Reconquista—and the queen's direction that the Indians be treated kindly and not enslaved had to be applied practically without triggering settler dissatisfaction or jeopardizing that domination. In the days following Cristóbal's exile, he studied how best to proceed and readily embraced

Cristóbal's awards of repartimientos as key to farming's advancement. He also relished that the reduction of the royal gold share had brought settlers clamoring to mine. As all settlers, he recognized that Indian labor was essential to farming and could be to mining, as well.

When prepared to recast Española, he summoned an assembly of a dozen settlers representative of past factions, intending to announce his and the sovereigns' expectations and dangle his largesse. They sat before him in the grassy patch of the governor's compound, Cristóbal's prior supporters led by Díaz and Garay from Santo Domingo, the former rebels by Roldán and Escobar, who then resided in the Vega Real and at Concepción, respectively.

"For the time being, we must rely on the arrangements whereby caciques living elsewhere supply food in return for peace," Bobadilla observed. "But soon, settlers' repartimientos should fill and improve the land to produce all the food we need, and every law-abiding settler should possess and improve a repartimiento. I'll grant plots to those without them, including the newcomers I brought with me. I'll grant additional plots to those most capable of improving them."

All concurred, although apprehensive that new awards might diminish or surpass their own. All understood that *law-abiding* meant abiding Bobadilla.

"All law-abiding are also entitled to mine, and I shall award mining licenses to those who haven't received them," he added.

Roldán and Escobar were heartened, envisioning the zeal of their followers who'd been barred from mining. Díaz and Garay were miffed, their advantage shorn. All gleaned that their prior disagreements no longer distinguished them. Only Bobadilla's favor or disfavor mattered, and he might favor newcomers over veterans who displeased him.

"All may task Indians living on their repartimientos in mining as well as farming," Bobadilla declared to applause, confirming Cristóbal's past approval of the practice.

But the knight then rose and peered at each man, drawing their close attention.

"Our queen forbids the Indians' enslavement. They are her vassals and freemen, just as laborers in Spain."

The assembled glared back, bewildered and apprehensive.

"What freedom does she intend they have?" Díaz asked. "How would you have us treat them?"

"The Indians are free to serve you according to their ability," Bobadilla responded. "As they live on your repartimientos, you may use their labor. Her highness recognizes that the Indians' service is appropriate to their station. But they shall retain their own homes and possessions. There will be no more slave raiding, enslavement of peaceful Indians, or awards of Indians as salary."

"My commander, we didn't come here to labor like peasants for the queen's enrichment and the Lord's glory," a settler bristled. "We came expecting to compel Indians to labor toward those ends and our own enrichment—and that labor was promised."

"Why would anyone suffer Española's deprivations if denied that labor?" a second settler interjected.

"You need to acquaint yourself with these savages," a third railed. "They're not due the same human dignities as Christians."

"There are only two dozen horses on the island," a fourth cried. "But there's an endless supply of Indians to do a horse's work, and they should have no more freedom than a horse."

The knight folded his arms, concealing his trepidation and irritation, realizing that these views were widely held and sympathetic to them. Yet he was angered to be crossed.

"Rest assured you may continue to utilize the Indians' labor," he answered, seeking to satisfy his duty to the queen without upsetting the settlers. "But they are her vassals, and they shall serve you as if laborers in Spain—treated as men despite their inferiority. However, as they reside on your land, you don't owe them salaries."

"Do you ask us to free the slaves Colón awarded us?" Roldán shook his head in disbelief, and the entire assembly shifted anxiously.

Bobadilla's heart thumped, and he was thankful the sovereigns hadn't so ordered.

"That's not required," he responded. "Those enslaved for resisting the sovereigns' conquest remain rightfully enslaved," he observed, not contesting whether those enslaved had resisted. "Resisters may always be enslaved hereafter."

Discussion rambled on for some moments, until everyone understood that the existing relationships between conqueror and conquered on the island could continue unaffected and serve as the basis for Española's build-out. The refinement in relationships was conceptual—to satisfy the queen—but without practical impediment in the use of Indian labor.

"I encourage two things," Bobadilla lectured on, seeking to advance the settlers' repartimientos and domination of the Indians. "First, your repartimientos should flourish when you firmly befriend and command the cacique of the land you master. He need not labor so long as he honors you as his master."

All understood, and someone observed that caciques might be addressed as *dons*.

"Second, the king and queen permit marriages with Indian women if it isn't forced on them. Marry well, claiming the cacique's daughter or sister—so you come to rule your repartimiento by kinship as well as fear."

Roldán lowered his brow, shielding a blush of humiliation, his blunders in attempting such a union long gossiped. Díaz lifted his chin, glowing with vindication, the wisdom of his union finally recognized by royal authority but for the sin condemned by churchmen.

Bobadilla concluded the discussion with a wink to snuff any lingering resentment of his authority.

"Take advantage of everything you ask for, because you don't know how long this will last."

▣   ▣   ▣

By the beginning of 1501, most of Española's settlers, individually or in partnership, had conscripted Indians residing in their repartimientos to dig, pan, and port in the Jaina and its tributaries, typically in bands of fifteen or more supervised by a settler. Díaz and Garay's workforce topped forty. Within two months, twelve hundred pounds of gold were mined—almost all inuring to the settlers—and settlers considered Española's prospects surging.*

The settlers cared little whether the Indians they utilized were overworked or adequately housed and fed. Unlike horses, those sick and dying could easily be replaced without cost.

---

* This pound was eight ounces, not sixteen.

Collage of Taínos panning for gold, created from engraving from Oviedo's
Historia General previously shown.

As 1501 progressed, the trickle of Indians so perishing rose
to droves and then to a substantial minority of those mining, and
mining labor came to rival the pale men's diseases as the harbinger of
Taíno death. The knight shrugged—as if such deaths were a natural
conclusion of the Indians' service as the queen's vassals.

To the relief of Taínos in chiefdoms never invaded, Bobadilla
didn't seek to extend conquest throughout the island. He was content
that the burst of gold production would reward the king and queen
sufficiently during his temporary duty.

Bobadilla also shied from confrontation with the former rebels in
Xaraguá, leaving them alone to govern themselves, not dispatching
fresh settlers to lead them other than missionaries, and permitting
them to participate in gold mining. To Anacaona and Behecchio's
relief, the squatters' presence in Xaraguá remained static, and their
natural rule wasn't challenged. But assimilation into the pale men's
conquest darkly crept on.

ANACAONA'S ASCENSION
(Early 1501)

After red hives burst over his limbs, naborias ported Behecchio upon a ceremonial litter to a secluded bohío in the foothills north of his inland village, close by the burial ground of his and Anacaona's ancestors. Of his thirty-some wives, his first wife and Guanahattabenecheuá chose to accompany him, committed to attend him through life and the afterlife beyond. When he could barely speak, Guanahattabenecheuá summoned Anacaona, who arrived just after dawn. An elder behique invited her to sit on a duho outside the bohío, whereupon Behecchio was borne on the litter to lie in the warming sunshine, some yards from her.

"What do the scouts report?" he asked faintly, roused by the scent of fresh dew, perceiving the earth welcoming his return.

Anacaona had steeled herself for their final meeting, determined to share their last moments and the formal transfer of caciqual authority intimately and optimistically, unencumbered by ceremony, decision-making, or grief. Her ascension to supreme authority had been expected for so long, her exercise of power so regular already, and the threat of Xaraguá's demise so enveloping, that her youthful fancy and ambition for anointment had faded, supplanted by a grim acceptance that it fell to her to prevent such demise. She grew misty-eyed, struck by how her brother dismissed death, insisting to be informed through the end, though the scouts now reported the news to her.

"The new guamiquina is difficult to decipher," she related. "He hasn't sent squatters or emissaries here, nor elsewhere apparently. But naborias throughout the island have been enslaved and marched to the Jaina to dig for gold. While distant, some squatters have demanded that our caciques provide them a dozen or two naborias for that purpose."

"What have you instructed?" Behecchio rasped.

"I've told our caciques to honor these demands. More naborias are enslaved than before, yet the number is minor." She gazed to the ground, mortified by her answer. "Uprising remains improvident."

Behecchio exhaled and shut his eyes. With extreme effort, he nodded.

"The only other news is that a pale behique seeks to live among us," Anacaona continued. "He seeks to attend the squatters and teach our subjects of the Christ-spirit. I told him he may befriend squatters and their concubines but that our people otherwise will ignore and avoid him. He asked to teach me, and I refused." Anacaona bit her lip. "Perhaps someday he might serve a role in restraining the squatters' abuses."

Behecchio was still, this last issue beyond his watch, his life force ebbed. "It's time," he murmured.

The behique came to kneel at Behecchio's side, gently raised his head, and removed the necklace bearing the guanín medallion that adorned his chest. It depicted two rainbows—one rising above a flat earth, the other descending below—proclaiming the bearer's caciqual authority and responsibility to influence the spirits for the benefit of his subjects and bridge spiritual and temporal life. The behique humbly approached Anacaona, who rose to receive it and rule Xaraguá alone.

As the medallion slipped to her chest, she felt neither joy nor accomplishment but the crush of duty. For caciques immemorial, that duty had been to advance their subjects' lives and worship. That remained true for her, but the overriding duty was to outlast and prevail over the conquerors. As Behecchio's breath tapered away, she inhaled deeply, sensed the medallion rise on her chest, and exhorted Yúcahu to guide her to do that.

◻ ◻ ◻

Hundreds of caciques attended Behecchio's funeral, virtually all the Xaraguán subordinate caciques and many from Haiti's unconquered chiefdoms. A few pale men, their concubines, and the friar, a Franciscan, chose to attend, believing it appropriate—sincerely or expediently—to demonstrate their respect for the ruler who'd harbored them. All attendees paid homage to Anacaona, the caciques vouching their loyalty to her, the pale men bowing insincerely.

Gazing at the crowd, Anacaona sorrowed for its sparsity compared to that typical of a supreme cacique's funeral before the pale men's invasion. Yet it was fulsome enough to retain the semblance of majesty. She'd presided at Caonabó's memorial service surrounded merely by starved, forlorn survivors of Maguana's pillage and demise—a travesty of the honor due, the grievers' confidence in their way of life trampled. In contrast, Xaraguá remained intact, and Xaraguáns mostly retained their self-esteem.

She listened as a youthful Guaorocuyá honored his uncle's legacy and the elder Haniguyabá praised her as successor. Proud of her womanhood, she stepped forward to rule.

"Ages ago, after emerging from the caves nearby, all men lived in peace, guided by Yúcahu, Attabeira, and our other spirits and heroes," she declared, raising her arm to point northeast. "The Taíno people flourished, superior to those unimportant, and the cradle of Xaraguá rose to become the pinnacle of man's civilization." She scanned faces in the crowd, seeking confirmation that she'd girded her people's pride, determined that they understood the pale men's society was inferior.

"That peace has been shattered by those unimportant," she condemned. "Today, we honor the ruler who has done the utmost to preserve our civilization. Behecchio's leadership in times of conflict and pain will forever hold a preeminent place in our hearts and memories."

Anacaona pointed to Behecchio's corpse, swathed in cloth, and bid his nitaínos lower it into the burial chamber—a pit cleanly lined with wood and thatch, resembling a bohío—and to seat it upon a duho within.

"This burial ground has been the final stepping-stone to the afterlife for Xaraguá's greatest caciques," she proclaimed. "My brother, while your body leaves us, may your soul ever lead us."

She turned to gaze upon the bodies of Behecchio's first wife and Guanahattabenecheuá, also wrapped in cloth, both women heavily sedated with cohoba.

"My sisters-in-law, you may accompany your husband," Anacaona pronounced, bidding the nitaínos to lay them on duhos beside Behecchio in the pit.

The Taínos in the crowd esteemed the two wives' ultimate loyalty, including Behecchio's thirty wives who'd chosen otherwise. The pale men squirmed, some envisioning Satan stalking. Their concubines foreswore ever choosing to so honor their masters. Anacaona invited the thirty other wives a last opportunity to join their husband.

"This is savage and unchristian!" the friar shouted, rushing forward, waving his arms wildly. "Release these two and take no more of them. Christ forbids murder. The king and queen prohibit this."

The attending caciques loathed that the murderers' behique decried murder and invoked the murderers' spirit. The pale men, disquieted but fearing retaliation, believed it wiser to let the savages be savages, and a few stepped forward to muzzle the friar.

Angered by the interruption, Anacaona nevertheless remained aloof, content that the pale men had resolved it, and signaled for the nitaínos to complete the burial. Behecchio's most venerated cemís were set beside him, together with offerings of cazabi and fruit, and a thatched shield—like a bohío's roof—was placed above the three bodies.

"My brother, may our spirits carry your soul to live in bliss in the valley of our ancestors," Anacaona declared, whereupon dirt was cast over the shield, burying the three.

As the underground bohío and pit vanished, Anacaona grasped the medallion on her chest, and it reminded her of all it had witnessed while worn by Behecchio. Fleetingly, dark visions flashed through her thoughts—of the first guamiquina's invasion of Haiti, the failed battles to expel it, and Behecchio's and her own humiliating submissions to Roldán. But she quashed the visions, lest her subjects see despair in her, and sought comfort that Behecchio's body had been freed of these ignominies. A premonition of her own death came to her, and she beseeched Yúcahu that when that time came, there'd be no pale men left in Xaraguá to attend her funeral.

◻ ◻ ◻

Soon after the ceremony, Higueymota felt contractions and alerted her mother. Anacaona embraced her and beseeched Attabeira for a speedy labor and safe childbirth. Accompanied by their dearest womenfolk, mother and daughter ambled slowly to a secluded grove along the streambank to sit on duhos by a tree with a limb low enough to grasp and hang on to while squatting below. When labor came in full, Higueymota stood, grasped the limb, and sagged—her legs widely spread, her feet providing some support. As the pain mounted, Anacaona prayed more fervently while serenely encouraging that all was well.

All mankind's primal urges for creation and survival were satisfied. Within hours, Higueymota gave birth to a girl. As the baby emerged, the womenfolk cradled her and severed the cord uniting mother and child. Higueymota—exhausted and wan—lay back on her duho to recover, and Anacaona—relieved—took the babe into the stream and gently washed the blood and sinew from her, praising Attabeira that both daughter and granddaughter were healthy. The babe was paler than others, a bewitching combination of the seed planted and the womb that nurtured it.

Anacaona churned with crossed emotions and visions. A woman's pride and joy in becoming a grandmother. A cacique's satisfaction with the birth of a marriageable heir. Trepidation for the child's future and her treatment by pale men. Consternation that the father didn't care for his child. Guilt for having bid her daughter to suffer the union. Love for the baby—as deep as for any.

When stable, Higueymota bathed in the stream, then was hoisted onto a litter and borne to Anacaona's caney, cradling the infant in her arms. According to Taíno custom, over the next weeks, caciques throughout Xaraguá came to pay their respects and suggest names for the child. Most proposed Xaraguán names. A few suggested some Maguanan variations in recognition of the child's venerated grandfather. None of the caciques, Anacaona, nor Higueymota thought to honor the departed father with a name typical of the conquerors.

One day, the friar visited to pay his respects and offered to baptize the mother and child.

"Your Highness, Christ welcomes your daughter and granddaughter into His fold, regardless of your reluctance," he declared to Anacaona. He turned to Higueymota. "If you and your child accept Christ, you both will be reborn as Christians, entitled to His protection and your souls' eternal salvation. That rebirth and transformation may be marked by assuming new Christian names."

"What would you name my child?" Higueymota asked dismissively.

"There are many Spanish names for girls," the friar responded. "Perhaps Mencia would please you."

"What would you name my daughter?" Anacaona interjected angrily.

"Perhaps Ana de Guevara, recognizing the father and yourself," the friar suggested.

"I have no interest in the Christ-spirit, either for myself or my child," Higueymota replied curtly.

Anacaona scowled. The notion of her daughter or granddaughter named in the image of conquerors was unthinkable in the absence of a marriage providing protection. She waved her hand to dismiss the friar.

"You may always change your minds," he said.

Cristóbal Discarded, Book of Prophesies,
January–June 1501

After his audience with the sovereigns, Cristóbal found lodging in the Franciscan monastery Isabel had established within the Alhambra following its surrender. He enjoyed occasional visits from his sons, who continued to serve as Isabel's pages. But he soon understood that Isabel and Fernando, though gracious in random encounters, wished to spend little time with him—perhaps none at all.

Events often precluded doing so anyway. Mudejar in the mountains nearby Ronda had terrorized Christian settlers, then resisted troops dispatched to restore order, the skirmishes mounting to considerable bloodshed on both sides. In reprisal, Mudejar men and teenage boys sometimes were executed en masse and women and children refusing conversion enslaved. But even that failed to bring the region to obedience. Isabel mustered troops and supplies, and by late March, Fernando rode to oversee the fighting and ensure that this latest rebellion was crushed.

Isabel—serious, artful, and compassionate in one stroke—did entrust Cristóbal with an assignment to keep him busy, requesting that he prepare a memorandum on how she and Fernando could lead Christians to retake Jerusalem from the infidel. Every Christian monarch had a duty to that, and the one who succeeded would attain unsurpassable glory. She and Fernando had already dispatched fleets to repel encroachments of the Turks toward the Italian Peninsula. Cristóbal had always implored her to spend the Indies' gold for that purpose, and he was convinced men could sail west past Española to the Arabian seas. Was the idea to surround Jerusalem and assault the infidels from both east and west? Thankfully, reviewing that issue with him could be divorced from discussing the Indies.

Cristóbal received the assignment ecstatically, like a drowning man thrown a rope, and he calculated exactly the opposite. The project was the lifeline to rekindling the sovereigns' attention, confidence, and love, prelude to full restoration of his gold, governorship, and legacy! It also was the stage to announce a new revelation he'd embraced.

The revelation had been inchoate when it first came to him, while aboard the caravel midstream in the Ozama, then murkily discernible during his incarceration awaiting lynching, and finally transparent only when brooding upon Isaiah and Saint John's Apocalypse while composing the letter to Juana at sea. He'd fully understood it upon parsing the scriptures and learned precedents when solitary in the monastery. According to John, the world corrupted by Satan would end when Christ returned to earth at Jerusalem, whereupon the souls of Christians would be blessed to remain at His side in a new heaven and new earth through eternity. Cristóbal wasn't just the messenger Isaiah had prophesied to evangelize peoples across the sea. His service as that messenger, that evangelization, and the recapture of Jerusalem from the infidel were all inextricably linked, essential precursors to Christ's second coming and the salvation of humankind.

Rejuvenated, Cristóbal conceived of compiling all the scriptural passages and cosmographical analyses prophesizing Jerusalem's reconquest within that divine eschatology into a treatise for presentation to the sovereigns. It would captivate them—a discovery commensurate with that of the Indies! The effort would take time and require learned assistance. As the initial step, he'd draft the memorandum requested, presenting a summary of the revelation as the answer Isabel sought. Amassing the supporting, venerated proof would follow.

Alone in dim candlelight in his rude cell, Cristóbal captioned the memorandum his *plan for the restitution of the holy temple* and devoted the initial paragraphs to introducing his role in the revelation. The Lord had endowed him with great talent for seamanship, opened his mind to sailing to the Indies, and, through the Old and New Testament scriptures, insisted that he sail his miraculous voyage to encourage him and others to retake the temple. While he might be criticized as an unlearned sailor, Saint Matthew recognized that the Lord *kept many things secret from the wise and revealed them to the innocent.*

Approaching the issue at hand, Cristóbal explained that everything said by Christ and written by the prophets must be fulfilled and that both the Old and New Testament prophets pronounced the world would end with Christ's second coming. Saint Augustine predicted that end in the seventh millennium after Creation, and Castile's King Alfonso the Wise (AD 1221–1284) calculated that there were close to 5,344 years between Creation or Adam and Christ's coming. By this count—adding 1,500 completed years and 1 uncompleted year since Christ's birth to 5,344 years and subtracting that sum from 7,000—the end was due in 155 years. The Calabrian abbot Joachim of Fiore (ca. AD 1135–1202) predicted that the retaker of the holy temple would come from Spain. The preaching of the gospel in so many lands was a sign of the acceleration of the Lord's activities toward the end. Cristóbal was unequivocal with respect to Jerusalem's taking, assuring Isabel and Fernando that if they had faith, they would certainly have victory. Logistics of the assault weren't addressed.

Using the draft memorandum as an outline, Cristóbal began scouring and recording the proof of saints, sages, prophets, and cosmographers supporting his revelation. Passages from Isaiah, Augustine, Fiore, and Cardinal d'Ailly obviously were to be included, but the authorities to be cited would range far and wide, assisted by an extremely broad interpretation of relevance to the revelation. Lofty eminences would include Isidore, Seneca, and Nicholas of Lyra. Older scriptural wisdom would be drawn from the Psalms, Jeremiah, Ezekiel, Zechariah, and the Chronicles. The four New Testament gospel writers would be represented, and among them, perhaps Matthew most directly made the point dearest to him. *And this gospel of the kingdom will be preached throughout the world in witness to all the people; and then the end will come.*

Cristóbal bid his son Fernando, who possessed an aptitude for reading and study, to help review the scriptures for proof, as well as the Carthusian friar Gaspar Gorricio de Novara (d. AD 1515), an Italian who then resided in Seville's Monastery of Santa María de las Cuevas. After their criticisms of his governance, Cristóbal distrusted further reliance on Franciscan counsel. He'd befriended Gorricio prior to the third voyage, and Gorricio had sheltered him in Seville while awaiting the sovereigns' audience, offering not only confession but flattering homage and practical advice in dealing with royalty and courtiers.

Months passed without meaningful discussion with the sovereigns, and Cristóbal's mood swung as wildly as before. Days of isolation and despair regularly alternated with days of resolution and hope.

When optimism prevailed, Cristóbal's revelation, memorandum, and compilation of prophecies receded in his thoughts, and his Genoese merchant's acumen ascended. He convinced Genoese financiers in Seville to fund voyages he was entitled to underwrite and whatever future voyage the sovereigns ultimately granted him. He whittled the financiers' largess to fund his living expenses until he sailed. Gorricio was entrusted with a copy of the documents defining his privileges and financial entitlements. A lawyer was hired to argue he was due an additional third of everything acquired and to be acquired in the Indies—beyond the tenth already understood. He grasped that restoration of his governorship would require the proposal of a credible, improved plan for governance.

May 24 was a day of mixed despair and hope. Cristóbal wrote Gorricio that the Indies were always relegated to the background at the sovereigns' court but—with Princess Catalina finally departed for England—something would be done at last. He was partly prescient.

A few more enslaved Indians he'd awarded to pay salaries had been located, and on May 28, they were manumitted and indemnification payments were distributed to the masters of Indians theretofore manumitted. In early June, the sovereigns awarded Hojeda a second license to explore, with a fleet of up to ten ships, the governorship of Coquibacoa, and a plot of land on Española.

Impugned and spurned, Cristóbal grimly recognized the Indies enterprise was proceeding without him and that neither emotional nor religious appeals to king and queen would restore him to their graces. On a day of clarity, calculation, and ignominy, he reviewed the draft memorandum and compilation of authorities assembled and concluded the argument, proof, or both were not yet sufficiently convincing for delivery to the sovereigns.

ISABEL, CATALINA, AND JUANA,
Summer 1501

For Isabel, May 20 was particularly heart-wrenching, and bothering over Cristóbal wasn't even an afterthought. Daughter María had left to live with her husband King Manoel last September, and ever since, Isabel had stalled daughter Catalina's departure for Prince Arthur in England, recoiling from losing her youngest. But Henry VII's patience had worn thin, excuses run out. Catalina would depart the Alhambra the next day, leaving the nest bare, and there'd be no child for conversation and intimacy.

As the sun set, Catalina entered Isabel's chamber to closet and commune alone for the last time, the two gravely aware they'd likely never see each other again. Isabel welled with pride for her daughter's beauty, intellect, and enlightenment, savoring the reddish-gold hair, blue eyes, and virgin coquetry. They hugged dearly.

"They say your husband is handsome and firm, a good tiding for your bedroom," Isabel teased, amused at contemplating the fourteen-year-old husband mounting her fifteen-year-old. "You must snare Arthur's want first, then his love and partnership."

Catalina nodded without blushing, having heard this talk for years. She'd been destined for England for over a decade, the nuptials solemnized and concluded indissolubly by proxy multiple times, and she now regularly was introduced as the Princess of Wales. She and Arthur had exchanged love letters in Latin, their common language, and she'd begun to study French and English to better flirt with him.

"Your mother-in-law counsels the English water is undrinkable and to drink the wine instead," Isabel bantered on, desiring that their final moments be light. "At least do so on your wedding night. It'll help you ignore the notaries peeking while you and Arthur mate."

Catalina did blush, her mother rarely so forward.

"He writes me as 'his most entirely beloved spouse,'" she observed, seasoned that chivalric promises were hollow. "It's utterly rote. I've dutifully written him much the same." She hesitated and puckered her lips somberly, tears welling. She appreciated the cheer, but this was the moment for her most intimate fears.

Isabel sobered and hugged more tightly, beckoning her daughter's most guarded concerns. She was satisfied that she'd prepared all her daughters for life in a husband's foreign court—tutoring in the classics, musical instruments, and other feminine cultivations, warning that they'd be relegated subordinate to their husband's ministers, estranged by barriers of language and custom, and scorned if they failed to produce a son. She also felt blessed to have born her youngest, albeit bittersweetly—unlike her other children, Catalina amply manifested the keen wit, judgment, and willpower expected of her and Fernando's blood and lineage.

"If the Lord takes Arthur prematurely, may I return to your side?" Catalina asked, gazing into Isabel's eyes. Visions of Princess Isabel's ghastly arrival from Portugal—within months of her first marriage—coursed through both mother and daughter's thoughts.

"It may be your duty to marry the next English prince heir to its crown," Isabel answered firmly and honestly. "Your dowry is substantial, and Henry will be loath to forsake it.* Even if he would, we will always need an ally to threaten the French. So does he, and he pines for our friendship and trade."

"What if Arthur parades unfaithful, like Philippe?" Catalina probed softly, both understanding to whom she also was referring.

"You know the answer. Bear it, but demand his tarts be barred from court," Isabel replied unequivocally. "Your children with him

---

*A hundred thousand gold ducats to be paid on the wedding date, fifty thousand six months thereafter, and fifty thousand worth of jewels and fine cutlery held by Catalina until the first anniversary.

will be his heirs, regardless of others he may seed." She frowned, embittered by decades of Fernando's bedroom infidelity and pained by reports of Philippe's transgressions and Juana's unhappiness. "Never contemplate straying yourself. Fidelity to an unfaithful husband is degrading, but infidelity to him jeopardizes your children's succession and perhaps even your crown."

Catalina recognized her mother's wound and pressed no further, turning from degradation to betrayal.

"What if my father-in-law or husband plot alliances against us?" she posed, upset by the recurring news that Juana struggled with that predicament.

"Get word to us," Isabel blurted, exasperated by Juana's failure to write. "You must always attend your husband, as his love is foundation to your well-being as princess and queen. Privately argue our kingdoms' interest with him. Avoid opposing him or his father in public, but stand apart, not at their side." Isabel lowered her voice. "My child, there's no one answer—use your judgment. Your father and I trust you, and we know you'd never forsake us willingly."

Tears shedding, Catalina turned to her toughest and saddest questions.

"Mother, if the Lord were to take you, whom shall I answer to?" she whispered hoarsely, confounded by the uncertainties of Juana's succession and rule. "May I return home to attend your mourning?"

"My child, the Lord signals He will take me sooner rather than later," Isabel pronounced, knowing Catalina so understood. She broached no ambiguity. "Juana will assume our crowns, and you and María will remain in allegiance to her and her heirs." She bit her lip, regretting having wed Juana to Philippe and doubting Juana's ability to rule. "But you must write your father first and often. He— not she—can tell you what to do. As for me, mourn from afar. Your aim hereafter is to bear a son who rules the English."

Isabel anguished as Catalina cried on her shoulder. Her youngest child was the most fit of the five to rule Spain.

⊡ ⊡ ⊡

The next day, following majestic celebrations in the Alhambra attended by much of Spain's nobility, Isabel and Fernando grandly bid Catalina farewell. She would travel to Spain's northern coast, and from there, sail for England. Her escort was an archbishop, two bishops, a guard of knights, and five dozen attendants entrusted with the dowry, as well as the staff of courtiers and household servants who would serve her permanently as Princess of Wales.

Catalina. Michel Sittow,   Juana. Juan de Flandes, ca. 1500.
sixteenth century.

During the next weeks, Isabel and Fernando turned charily to succession, Philippe and Juana's presentment in Spain for recognition as heirs still unfulfilled—and cloaked in a morass of unremitting deceptions. After Miguel's death last summer, Philippe had schemed to arrange the marriage of their son Charles—the sovereigns' remaining grandson—to the French King Louis XII's toddler Claude! Adding insult, last November he'd merely dispatched to Spain an interim proxy, his counselor and confidant the Archbishop of Besançon, who'd had the gall to ask Isabel and Fernando for their approval of that marriage.* Eating crow, Isabel and Fernando had feted and plied the archbishop for three months, reminding that the

---

* The archbishop was François de Busleyden.

purpose of Juana and Philippe's union was to align Spain, Burgundy, and his father Maximillian's Holy Roman Empire against France. Incredibly, the archbishop had hemmed and hawed—a small principality nestled beside France required France's friendship.

Eventually, flatteries, gratuities, and the dangle of a Castilian appointment had warmed the archbishop. The news that Juana was expecting a third child had warmed all, and Isabel and Fernando had received assurance the couple would come to them when Juana could travel safely—after childbirth that July. But as July approached, Isabel and Fernando doubted and turned to the man they then considered their most competent minister.

"You shall drop the Indies for the moment and bring Juana and her husband here to take their oaths," Isabel commanded Bishop Fonseca. "Responsibility for the voyages under license will be assumed by Commander Cervantes." Gonzalo Gómez de Cervantes then served as chief magistrate of Jerez de la Frontera, just north of Cádiz.

"A smooth succession—to a queen whose husband loves and favors Spain—takes precedence over claiming Indian territory," Fernando pronounced. "Our ambassador warns that Philippe plots traveling first to kiss Louis's hand. Prevent that. Prepare a fleet to transport Juana and Philippe directly to Spain by sea."

"Take Juana into confidence and report to us how she fares," Isabel ordered. "Is she now properly maintained?" Philippe had curtailed Juana's financial support after the birth of their daughter, restoring it when she finally produced a son. "Is she still of sound mind?"

"Is she being forced to abandon support of our kingdoms?" Fernando fumed.

"When Juana, Philippe, and the grandchildren arrive, we must take every step to ensure they feel welcome and loved so they remain here," Isabel entreated, although she knew a command couldn't make it so.

Bishop Fonseca understood and accepted the assignment. He briefly reviewed the status of all the voyages newly licensed or at sea and then left for Seville to reorder the Indies' command and hire ten vessels to sail to Flanders. The new responsibility couldn't be more difficult than dealing with Colón.

That evening, as she prayed before sleep, Isabel fondly recalled the auburn hair, slim figure, and bewitching perceptivity of her third child. While a girl, Juana had possessed all Catalina's beauty, intellect, and enlightenment, yet little of the wherewithal, judgment, and constancy. A dark moodiness had waxed within. As mother, Isabel beseeched the Lord to relieve her child's marital tortures, rid the turmoil that boiled within, and convince the child to return to live at her side through her last years, content as the girl once had been.

As monarch, Isabel also earnestly but doubtfully beseeched the Lord that one day her daughters would reign concurrently as queens of Spain, Portugal, England, Burgundy, and the Holy Roman Empire.

Southern Landmass, Xaraguá,
Summer 1501

Isabel, Fernando, Fonseca, and his stand-in, Cervantes, now envisioned appointing governors to possess and settle much of the territory explored along the southern landmass, intent on precluding prior claims by Henry VII or other princes. Hojeda's award of Coquibacoa's governorship covered a western portion of the explored territory. Vicente Yáñez Pinzón would be awarded governorship of a portion southeast of Trinidad through wherever Manoel's claim began. For the moment, the coastline between the two—now heralded as the *Pearl Coast*—would be reserved for merchant traders, such as Seville's Guerra brothers, without a governor.

Isabel had grimly acquiesced when—within days of her manumission of Cristóbal's enslaved Indians—Fonseca had sold the surviving two hundred enslaved by Hojeda. She'd chafed soon thereafter when Pinzón and Diego de Lepe returned from the southern coastline bearing and then selling more enslaved Indians. She trusted Cervantes no more than Fonseca to respect her wish that her Indian vassals not be enslaved, and she insisted that new licenses prohibit enslavement outright, except as she and Fernando specifically approved, including the license struck for Hojeda's second voyage.

Three voyages previously dispatched remained afloat, and when they returned, Isabel would scrutinize their cargos closely.

In early June, the first of them returned from exploring southeast of Trinidad, bearing Indians seized well beyond Castile's claim, within Manoel's territory.* Isabel warily didn't prohibit their sale as slaves—the explorers' license arguably permitted resisters' enslavement, and in any case, these Indians likely weren't her subjects. Son-in-law Manoel and his predecessors had slave traded in Africa for decades, and Manoel wasn't concerned that Indians be treated better than black-skinned Africans. The Tordesillas treaty applied pole to pole, and Manoel had dispatched his nobleman Gaspar Corte Real to claim what was his on the northern landmass previously reconnoitered by John Caboto (Newfoundland), and Corte Real then and there was enslaving some fifty Indians.†

Hojeda was delighted with his new license and governorship, despite the prohibition on enslavement. He'd never bother seeking specific approval for enslaving anyone—he'd simply claim that those he'd enslaved had attacked first. He set about procuring and financing a fleet of ten. His young Isabel hadn't perished of diseases in Spain, and she would help rule the Coquibacoans. Don Fernando de Guevara had returned to his side and would captain a ship. Hojeda's license permitted him to cut brazilwood in Española or elsewhere, and the sovereigns had promised to grant Guevara such a license insofar as Guevara hadn't received appropriate compensation for the wood he'd previously cut on Española. So, there'd be an excuse to return to Xaraguá if they wished, and if advantageous, Guevara might revisit his Indian princess.

◻   ◻   ◻

In mid-July, Don Guevara bowed deeply before his queen as she sat on her throne in the Alhambra, primed to regale her with a chivalric tale or two of his exploits on the Pearl Coast, Coquibacoa, and Española in furtherance of securing his license to cut brazilwood.

---

* The voyage of Luis Guerra and Alonso Vélez de Mendoza, licensed June 5, 1500, the Indians being Tupís.
† The Indians were Beothuks.

"Your Highness, your Indies are a marvel, islands and coastlines of tremendous riches and beauty," he puffed. "I look forward to bringing you some of the finest brazilwood ever cut."

"My liege, of all the Indies you've seen, where is civilization most advanced?" Isabel probed of the young nobleman, seeking yet another perspective on her possessions.

"It is undoubtedly the kingdom of Xaraguá, on Española's western side," Guevara declared. "Their farming is the most sophisticated, and as ourselves, they love poetry and art—albeit primitive. I dined with its King Behecchio and his sister Anacaona, who shares his rule. He's Española's most powerful king, and she's renowned for her beauty and wisdom."

"Tell me of her," Isabel bid, already having heard of Anacaona and a few other Indian queens.

"She is remarkable and majestic, without peer among her people. I spent hours conversing with her. She sees the wisdom of your conquest and allows our people to live in peace among hers and to teach them the faith and their improvement." Guevara hesitated. A recollection of mounting Higueymota flickered through his thoughts, and he chose not to mention her. "I informed Anacaona that you reign as Christendom's greatest queen, and she is supremely honored to be your vassal," he assured, spinning on.

"Does Behecchio or she have a son to inherit this kingdom?" Isabel mused joylessly.

"I'm not sure," Guevara replied, as if innocently, the memory of failing to become Anacaona's son-in-law yet rankling.

"Do our men living in this kingdom treat the womenfolk Christianly?"

Don Guevara understood Isabel wouldn't be content with a chivalric response.

"Your Highness, I cannot lie," he replied, as if gravely. "Our lowborn treat them shabbily."

On July 24, Isabel and Fernando issued Don Guevara the license he sought to cut brazilwood on Española or elsewhere.

⊡ ⊡ ⊡

The two licensed voyages remaining afloat struggled over the summer. Cristóbal Guerra—previously a partner on Pero Alonso

Niño's voyage—was disheartened that the pearl beds of the Pearl Coast weren't as teeming as ballyhooed, and he contemplated slave raiding. Rodrigo de Bastidas and Juan de la Cosa had sailed beyond Coquibacoa to reconnoiter lands the Indians called Citurma, Caramari, and Urabá (the northern coast of Colombia, east to west, and north into Panama), triumphantly trading for seventy-five pounds of gold, and where their intrusion was unwelcome, abducting slaves. The aggregate value of their cargo was estimated at five million maravedís.* But their two ships were sieving, riddled with shipworms. They abandoned trading to seek repairs on Española and barely made landfall at the tip of its southwestern peninsula before the ships crumbled and sank.

The Indians ashore weren't hostile, and Bastidas traded trinkets for food, his provisions depleted and crews famished. He'd never visited Española, and he perceived the land was neither conquered nor pacified—like Urabá and the other territory he'd explored. La Cosa had resided on Española and was startled to share that perception. Spaniards, Spanish custom, and Christianity hadn't reached this part of the island, and its savages appeared submissive, perhaps in dread conquest now loomed.

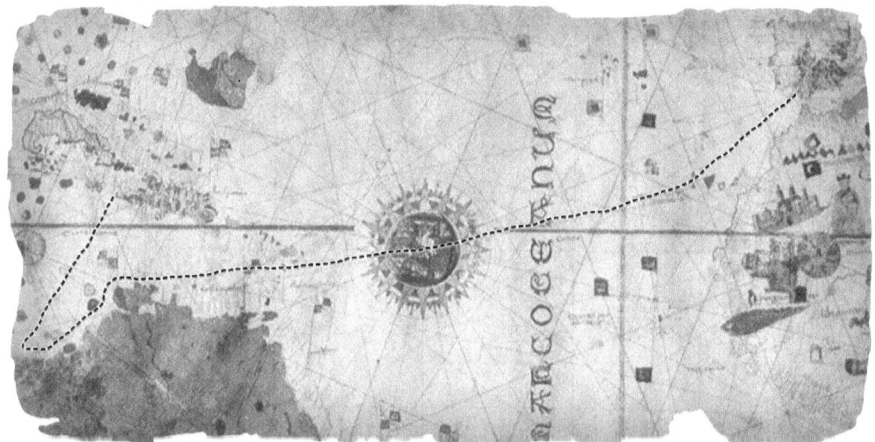

Portion of Juan de la Cosa's World Map, 1500, marked for Rodrigo Bastidas's and La Cosa's 1501 voyage.

---

* The slaves were perhaps Urabá or Cenú peoples.

▣   ▣   ▣

Anacaona was frightened when runners from caciques on the peninsula warned that two vessels bearing some sixty-five pale men had intruded the extremity of Xaraguá, and she regretted having been lulled into optimism that her chiefdom would be spared from ruin.

With the new guamiquina preoccupied elsewhere—and the first guamiquina, Roldán, and Don Guevara gone—Xaraguán daily life had regained a semblance of its traditional order. The seventy squatters had even receded from her daily concern. They'd settled into domestic routines with their concubines and naborias, and their number had remained unchanged for well over a year, minor and diffused among the thousands of her subjects. That multitude, and the scores of subordinate caciques through whom she ruled, still lived much as before—tending crops, fishing the sea, and worshipping their spirits. Reports of harsh servitude—particularly of those dragooned to pan for gold, never to return—and abuse of women continued to surface regularly to her shame and revulsion. But the great majority of her subjects had yet escaped those fates, at least until now.

Anacaona rushed word to Haniguyabá to investigate. Perhaps the new guamiquina had invaded to compel submission. Perhaps another upstart like Hojeda had come to overthrow him. Whatever the intruders' intention, preventing them from remaining in Xaraguá was urgent. Haniguyabá promptly spied on the intruders' encampment, spoke with the local caciques fearfully trading with them, and returned to sit before Anacaona in her inland caney's inner sanctum.

"I found neither an invasion nor more squatters," Haniguyabá reported. "These intruders say they've arrived from the southern shores to reach Santo Domingo so they may return to their homeland. Their vessels have sunk, and they ask to be led overland there and supplied with naborias to haul the gold and other goods they've brought. Our naborias would share the load, as the intruders have enslaved captives from those shores who'd port, as well."

"What of their weapons?" Anacaona probed.

"They're well armed," Haniguyabá replied. "We've tried to trade cazabi for the weapons, but they've resisted."

"Who are the captives? Do they include women?" Anacaona recalled Hojeda's Isabel.

"Their tongue is unintelligible, and they call their homeland Urabá. There are many women and girls among them."

Anacaona winced, pondering Xaraguá's interest.

"Escort all the pale men and slaves to Santo Domingo," she ordered. "Don't permit any to remain in Xaraguá. Prevent them from mixing with the squatters, lest they collude."

"What if the slaves seek our sanctuary or to flee?"

"They aren't my subjects, so they aren't our concern. Don't assist their escape."

Haniguyabá returned to the tip of the peninsula and committed caciques to oversee the lengthy escort of the intruders, their goods, and slaves to Santo Domingo along the southern coastline. Before departing on the trek, cognizant of his responsibility to the crown's empire, Bastidas burned or buried weapons too large to port, thereby precluding the Indians' possession.

Weeks later, when Bastidas and his crews and slaves arrived, Bobadilla assumed he was an interloper like Hojeda and charged him with entering Española to trade for gold and food in violation of his license, selling weapons to the Indians, and killing many of them. He was imprisoned indefinitely in Santo Domingo's fort for later trial in Spain.

When apprised, Anacaona sighed with relief that her chiefdom's fragile, contaminated coexistence hadn't been further debased. Yet she grimly recognized that she'd pass her life fearing she'd be told of an incursion that came to conquer.

ISABEL AND FERNANDO, GRAND DESIGNS,
July–September 2, 1501

As summer passed, Isabel and Fernando barely noticed the Alhambra's sublime pooled terraces, exquisite gardens, and splendid views, laboring warily and anxiously through conundrums, setbacks, and disappointments.

Their need, avail, and respect for the decade-old surrender capitulations eviscerated, Isabel invited Archbishop Cisneros to return to the city of Granada. On July 20, she and Fernando issued a decree outright prohibiting Mohammedans from living in the kingdom of Granada—on pain of death and confiscation of estates—thereby requiring the exodus or conversion of the last unconverted Mudejar. The decree mirrored the sovereigns' decade-old edicts expelling the Jews from Castile and Aragón, warning that the continued presence of those who clung to their prior faith endangered the newly converted. Terror quickly spread to Mudejar living in Castile and Aragón, who feared that their expulsion loomed imminent, as well.

They received good tidings from Flanders. Juana had birthed her third child, a girl christened Isabel! Juana, Philippe, and grandchildren—Leonor, Charles, and Isabel—could now safely travel to Spain. But their cheer turned to frustration when they learned that Philippe refused to board the fleet Fonseca had harbored in Flanders, announcing instead that he and Juana would travel overland to France first, residing some months at Louis's court before coming to Spain. Charles, heir to Spain's crowns, and the girls would remain in Flanders, rather than getting to know them and absorbing their Spanish heritage! Charles's marriage to Louis's Claude had been agreed at last, and Philippe and Louis would discuss the alliance of Burgundy with France.

Enviously, they digested a letter from son-in-law Manoel proudly reporting that his nobleman Cabral had returned from his kingdom's second voyage to the Indies—meaning the Indies where gentiles, Muslim merchants, and countless other wealthy peoples with grand fleets traded gold, spice, and other treasures in great ports. A third voyage was already sailing there.*

Nevertheless, despite their domestic concerns and Manoel's letter, for the first time in years, Isabel and Fernando were gratefully startled to find in their own Indies a potential and imperative that momentarily beckoned attention more than other endeavors. The landmasses and islands reconnoitered—by themselves in the southern seas, by others in the northern—were both enormous and many months' shorter sailing distance than Manoel's Indies, and they held a commanding lead over other princes to claim the southern. Even Manoel's own report intimated that his Indies weren't the ideal

---

* A fleet of four vessels led by João da Nova.

he boasted. Cabral had fought with competing Muslim traders in Calicut and slain some of the hosting raja's own people, destroying mercantile relations there, although friendly trading kingdoms had been located elsewhere. Almost half Cabral's fleet and many men had perished in storms or the hostilities, and informants whispered that some in Manoel's court opposed further voyages as a drain on resources.

Auspiciously, Española's gold was confirmed at last—by Cristóbal's critics, no less—and countless merchants and subjects clamored to dig it. Settler enlistment would surge, necessitating allotment rather than incentive. Cristóbal's failure and removal as governor had been sordid, and Bobadilla's temporary service marred by improvident execution, including unduly catering to Española's corrupt old-guard settlers. What else could explain his dereliction of reducing the royal gold share? But they were now free to reorder Española without Cristóbal's bombast, whine, and craze.

In July, Isabel and Fernando set about doing that, organizing an ambitious resettlement of the island, envisioning a grand fleet with twice the ships and head count of Cristóbal's second voyage, dwarfing the meager enrollments of his third voyage and Bobadilla's interim mission. They would jettison the limitation on Española's settler head count. New orders would regulate the conduct of Spaniards and their treatment and use of the Indians, and the island would become the hub of new Spanish territories on the southern landmass. The resettlement would assure that the old-guard settlers—both those installed by Cristóbal and those who'd rebelled against him—could be cast aside.

Despite Bobadilla's shortcomings, Isabel and Fernando envisioned that his successor as Española's governor would possess much the same credentials and outlook—those of a foot soldier of Christ dedicated to protecting Christian settlements. Isabel desired a courtier more undaunted in Christianizing her Spanish vassals, as well as the Indians. Fernando sought one craftier and shrewder, better capable of disguising severity and punishment with viceregal charity. Both required a selection with proven obedience in implementing their instructions and the noble heritage that would draw the respect of all Spaniards, both those in Española and crown officials in Spain. While they consulted Fonseca and Cisneros, on their own they chose a courtier they'd known well for decades, one of the handful of men of their generation whom they'd entrusted to educate Prince Juan to be king.

Fray Nicolás de Ovando, born in Extremadura (b. ca. 1451) and a commander of the Order of Alcántara, had risen to become a knight-friar of the order and taken its Cistercian vows of poverty, chastity, and warring against Christ's enemies. His mother had served as a chambermaid to Isabel's mother, his father had fought for Isabel during the war over her succession, and his order had fought on the front lines during the Reconquista. Some lauded that his lineage descended from a bastard son of King Alfonso IX. His acclaimed faith, bravery, humility, and competence had sealed his appointment to Prince Juan's inner circle. Some faulted him, whispering that a capacity for scheming, vengeance, and cruelty in Christ's name lurked beneath.

One afternoon, Isabel and Fernando summoned Ovando to their throne room to discuss his appointment. Like Bobadilla, he hadn't sought or desired the assignment, believing other career opportunities more favorable, or at least far less risky. But Isabel and Fernando had prevailed.

"My commander, Española's gold augers reversal of its fortune, and your appointment as governor of it and the Indies is a great advancement for you, as well," Isabel puffed. She studied Ovando's modest build, reddish-brown beard, and plain attire, practical for a mounted, armed soldier of God. "You will spearhead both the Lord's acceptance in the Indies and Castile's realization of its wealth. We hope you will remain on Española indefinitely, but you must commit to serve at least two years."

"Your Highnesses, service to Christ and yourselves is my greatest honor," Ovando dutifully replied.

"Hojeda and Pinzón shall establish their own governorships on the southern coastline and islands. But their territory is limited, and they won't interfere with you," Fernando explained. "Your authority will extend over the coastline wherever we don't make such arrangements." He held Ovando's eyes. "We also won't allow Admiral Colón to return to Española or interfere with you."

"You must promptly set the gold mining in order," Isabel pronounced. "But your greater mission is to build Española as if it were an extension of Castile in every respect. Just as you tutored Juan, you must tutor our Spanish subjects in their Christian conduct, which is miserably lacking. You must reform their treatment of the Indians and bring our Indian vassals into our service, so they labor productively on Christian terms."

"I'll require ample men to accomplish this," Ovando replied. "All reports indicate that the Spaniards on the island are unchristian, forever stabbing each other in the back, fornicating as libertines with the Indian women, rarely worshipping the Lord. Some say Satan reigns. I'll need carrots in my pockets to reward obedience, as well as daggers to compel it."

"You shall have all the men and authorities—and carrots and daggers—necessary," Fernando promised. "Your command of mining licenses, land grants, and the terms of Indian service will empower you to buttress your lieutenants and dispossess troublemakers. Your supporters will far outnumber those already there." He puckered his lips. "But it won't be easy, as you recognize. You must reverse the reduction in our share of the gold—which we never authorized. Undoubtedly, many will rant while being so disentitled or otherwise reformed."

"Shall that reduction be retroactive or only prospective?" Ovando inquired.

"Retroactive!" the sovereigns bristled in unison.

"How should I treat Commander Bobadilla?"

"Our beloved commander has well pleased us and may return home on the very ships transporting you," Isabel proclaimed, not caring if Ovando believed her. "He's to be treated kindly and with dignity."

"As customary, you must investigate his conduct and report to us," Fernando instructed. "But whatever you find, don't punish him on Española. Apparently, he never investigated those who rebelled against Colón, and you must now investigate them. That inquiry alone should instill fear in the unruliest."

"What of Admiral Colón?" Ovando asked, glancing back and forth between Isabel and Fernando, vexed by Cristóbal's perpetual success in resuscitating himself.

"The Admiral remains our Admiral of the Ocean Sea, and all his property and entitlements must be faithfully accounted and remitted here to him," Isabel replied. "We shall consult him carefully while we draw your orders, particularly as to his entitlements, but he will have no authority over you."

"His title and authorities hereafter are but words," Fernando assured. "We may have some future use for him, but that won't be of concern to you."

□ □ □

As the review of Española's reordering accelerated, Isabel sadly invited Cristóbal to an audience. He'd written her a rambling, courtly missive that warned the Indies enterprise was being lost, reiterated his plea for retaking Jerusalem, vouching it sincere, and pledged his fullest dedication to either endeavor if only authorized.

To his satisfaction, she reconfirmed he remained her Admiral of the Indies and that his gold and entitlements would be restored, promising he'd be able to appoint an agent to monitor the restoration. To his chagrin, she noted that he wouldn't be allowed to return to Española to do that himself. She soothed his pride by requesting his written views on reordering Española's gold production and resettling it with new recruits. She dashed his dreams by confiding that another would be selected as governor.

"My Admiral, you may underwrite an eighth of the next governor's voyage to Española, as your entitlements allow," she consoled, watching his jaws drop, shoulders slump, and tears well.

"What of my own next voyage?" Cristóbal implored, his voice cracking. "If not Española, why not the southern landmass, the Terrestrial Paradise, or Jerusalem?"

Isabel shook her head firmly.

"As the prophets foretell, I could sail beyond Cuba to locate the passage to Marco Polo's Cipangu and the shortcut to Calicut," he persisted. "We've intended that since the moment I first knelt at your feet."

Isabel dismissed him.

CACIQUE DIEGO AND GUARIONEX,
Concepción

Enveloped in moonlight and the buzz of crickets, Cacique Diego knelt before the narrow gulley bordering his yuca crop and the grave of his departed comrade Yutowa. They hadn't communed in months, and Diego was heartened to relate that his life had taken a turn for the better. Ariana was bearing another child. His yuca crop was producing abundantly. Then he confided what had transpired as a remora.

I no longer tend sick pale men, he gratefully mused, liberated from the shame of caring for conquerors so they could resume conquest. *Those healthy have departed for their repartimientos. The incurable have died.* Shutting his eyes, Diego waited patiently for Yutowa's reaction, comforted that the crickets' enduring buzz resonated with Yutowa's enduring friendship. Yutowa's specter soon flickered through his thoughts and congratulated him.

I never betrayed Admiral, Diego confessed. *But I no longer serve him. His own people did him in.*

Bakako—Yutowa rejoined—*rejoice in Admiral's demise. But to which pale man shall you answer now?*

Diego shrugged, uncertain that he would answer to any of them. None of Concepción's pale men had sought his skills or services, not even the fort's commander, Velázquez. None had requested that his naborias farm their repartimientos or scour for the Jaina's gold, although Manicoatex and other caciques were forced to provide naborias for those tasks. The new guamiquina hadn't ordered him to submit or even contacted him. Perhaps Admiral's ghost still watched over him. While Yutowa derided the name *Diego Colón*, the relationship it marked still exempted him from serving other pale men and the harsh treatment they dealt other Taínos.

Perhaps I'm no longer a remora, Diego yearned.

Perhaps the pale men don't need a remora today, Yutowa scoffed.

Thunder rumbled nearby, and Diego felt the graze of a breeze strengthening.

I never assisted Guarionex's execution, and he still survives, Diego vouched. *I shall bring him nourishment and companionship tomorrow.*

Guarionex is more kin to you than Admiral ever was, Yúcahu scolded. *Reject the false name the Christ-spirit calls you.*

Diego rose, weary of self-criticism. The pale men's conquest still dictated his fate, unpredictably. He had to stick to the course he'd chosen, despite his comrade's entreaties. His son, young Diego, already spoke both Taíno and Spanish. He bid Yutowa good night and departed.

Clouds shrouded the moon, and as rain came, he quickened his pace, arriving at his caney just before a deluge. As little Diego slept, he and Ariana listened to a torrent careen off their palm-thatched roof, content with the security of their solitary haven, pleased that pale men no longer lived on his land. Ariana had prepared cazabi and gourds of juice for him to bring Guarionex the next day.

"I'll ask Velázquez what the new guamiquina intends for your brother," he promised.

"Convince Guarionex to relent and parrot what the pale men wish to hear, so he may be freed," Ariana said. "What could he possibly do to them now? He has neither land nor subjects to command. He must accept that he's been conquered, just as us all."

"He's never been a parrot."

At dawn, Diego left for Fort Concepción, ambling through Magua's great valley, which burst verdant and lush from the rainfall. Streambanks once littered with corpses now were overgrown with reeds, as if virgin and forever untouched by men, the skeletons sunken in mud. Guaricano—deserted following Guarionex's demise—had resumed a new life, now parsed into the repartimientos of a few Spanish soldiers and artisans who overlorded the surviving Maguans. A blacksmith had commandeered Guarionex's caney. The great battleground where Manicoatex had fought was divvied into repartimientos as well, the site of Haiti's peoples' greatest resistance forgotten as if it never happened.

Diego raised his satchel of cazabi above his head as he approached the fort's compound, signaling he came to feed Guarionex, and the sentries let him pass to the blockhouse. He sat at the cell's doorway, and when roused from stupor, Guarionex was pleased to see him and eat.

"Tell me Admiral's expression when they threw him into prison," Guarionex bid, relishing an account, eagerly yet infirmly struggling to sit, transcending the squalor about him.

"Velázquez told me he feared execution," Diego replied. Guarionex's wan grin relaxed into wonder, the pale men's cruelty to their own always astonishing.

"Tell me of the new guamiquina. How do my fellow caciques deal with him?"

"This Bobadilla continues Admiral's conquest. He's bent on collecting as much gold as possible," Diego related. "The pale men compel the caciques whose lands they've usurped to supply ever more subjects to dig for it. Most every Maguan's lands—including your own—are now overlorded by pale men." He shied from mentioning the Spaniard usurping the caney. "But Bobadilla hasn't conquered more territory, at least so far. Mayobanex's vassal caciques continue to supply the pale men food in return for being left alone."

"With Behecchio gone, how fares Anacaona?" Guarionex asked, having learned from his captors of Behecchio's death.

"By all accounts, she rules just as he did. Bobadilla has left Xaraguá alone. The pale men she harbors have usurped more of her subjects' land and enslaved naborias, just as here. But her chiefdom survives."

They sat in silence. Guarionex no longer engaged in self-recrimination or second-guessing his decisions. Four years of incarceration had spent his appetite for shame and hindsight. Instead, he'd steeled himself to die with a purpose. Father Cacibaquel had received a prophecy of Taíno extinction, which remained to be undone and vanquished.

"Why does Bobadilla still hold me here?" he pondered aloud.

"I suspect nothing has changed," Diego responded. "You must submit to Fernando and Isabel's rule, either to Bobadilla here or to them in Spain. If here, I cannot see why he'd fear granting your release. I can ask him."

"Don't. I don't desire release here. I must appeal directly to their Fernando and Isabel. That remains the only route to our peoples' survival."

Diego studied the undaunted resolve on Guarionex's face, belied by his meager, wasted frame, and nodded gravely. He rose to depart.

"Pass my best wishes to my sister and nephew," Guarionex bid.

Diego spied Velázquez approaching, and the two spoke. To Diego's surprise, Velázquez had been thinking much the same.

"There's no longer need for the chieftain's incarceration," Velázquez indicated. "He could be restored as cacique if he recognizes the sovereigns' rule and that of the settlers who own his former lands and home."

"Don't take that risk. He'd rebel again," Diego replied. "The only solution is to haul him to grovel at Fernando and Isabel's feet."

X

VISIONS, ISABEL'S ESPAÑOLA
AND ANACAONA'S XARAGUÁ

KNIGHT COMMANDER OVANDO'S ORDERS,
September 3–December 1501

As August passed, Isabel and Fernando labored with ministers to frame the instructions they'd hand Ovando for the reordering of Española's conquest and the delivery of its gold home to Spain. Isabel's insistence on the Christian treatment of their Indian subjects and Fernando's determination to restore order among their Spanish subjects branded the effort. With Christ's example in mind, Isabel's resolution hardened. Her conscience could no longer tolerate her Spanish subjects' lust for Indian slaves and coerced concubines.

Commencing September 3, she and Fernando issued a series of proclamations and orders to appoint Ovando governor and supreme justice of the islands and mainland of the Indies, other than Hojeda's and Pinzón's territories, and designed to fundamentally recast the relationship among Española's settlers and Indians and displace the old guard of settlers. On October 2, many of these orders were publicly proclaimed.

Henceforth, the Indians were to be well treated as the sovereigns' good subjects, and Ovando was to ensure that by punishing those who harmed them and restoring everything seized from them, including wives. The Indians were freemen owing vassalage to the crown. Enslavement of nonresisters, vassalage to and forced labor for settlers ancillary to repartimientos of lands, and usurpation of homes were prohibited. Thereafter, the sovereigns' Spanish subjects would live in existing and newly founded townships rather than scattered in their repartimientos about the island, although they could retain their own huts at the repartimientos. The Indians would be required to work in mining and other tasks in the sovereigns' service, but as freemen they were to receive salaries Ovando deemed just. As Isabel and Fernando's Spanish subjects owed taxes, their Indian subjects would owe tribute that Ovando negotiated with the ruling caciques, payable from the salaries Indians received from mining and farming. The pope had promised Isabel and Fernando the tithes to be paid the church throughout the Indies, and Ovando was to impose those on everyone, Spaniard and Indian.

Española's veteran settlers were to be substantially thinned or purged from the island. Ovando was instructed to dismiss existing settlers on the crown payroll from service, prohibited from paying them salaries any longer, and authorized to recover salaries Bobadilla had paid to undeserving rebels. Bobadilla's reduction of the royal gold share below one-third was retroactively rescinded, with veterans required to pay up the amounts they'd over-retained. Ovando's authority to investigate Roldán and his henchmen included the power to expel them, and he was directed to expel those settlers not native to Spain. Only true Spaniards could settle in the sovereigns' Indies thereafter, and Mohammedans, Jews, and other heretics would be prohibited from traveling there, thereby preventing impediments to the Indians' conversion. Slaves couldn't be imported except for African or other slaves born and baptized in Spain and appropriately accustomed to servitude, thereby excluding slaves who might foment Indian rebellion.

Prospectively, the royal gold share would rise to one-half. Fray Trasierra would enlist churchmen and missionaries to attend both the conduct of Spaniards and the conversion of Indians. In addition to Ovando's main fleet, a separate fleet under command of Luis de Arriaga would sail bearing two hundred Spanish families—wives and children included—to seed four new Christian townships on the island. Arriaga was a veteran of Española, having commanded the first fort attacked by the Indians (1495).

One morning, seated on their thrones in the Alhambra, Isabel and Fernando summoned Ovando to discuss their expectations for a productive society of Española's Spaniards and Indians. They'd authorized the recruitment of a hundred crown officials and lieutenants to assist him in bludgeoning the changes envisioned. Ovando bowed courteously, anticipating the queen's pent frustration would boil, and determined to discern what she and the king truly expected without challenging it.

"The Indians must be converted to our Catholic faith forthwith. Years have been squandered!" Isabel admonished, adamant that her conquerors at last realize her dearest vision. "The greatest benefit we can give them is their souls' salvation. Take care the priests teach with love and provide all necessary support."

"Your Highness, I shall," Ovando affirmed. "What should I do if the Indians resist their instruction?" He recalled the blood freshly drawn in Granada.

"Don't use force," she commanded. "The Indians are innocent, unlike infidel or Jews. Push them benignly."

"How should I address the sinful concubinage with Indian women? Do I promote marriages with chieftains' daughters?"

"Indian women mustn't be forced into marriage relationships, much less concubinage," Isabel upbraided. "Existing relationships against their will must be undone. Quash our men's abuses." She slowed, calming herself. "Our Spanish and Indian subjects may marry freely in the church," she pronounced, contemplating an Indian woman's baptism prior thereto. "These unions shall integrate the Indians into our Christian and Spanish civilization and cure the concubinage."

"Do I have authority to undo repartimientos the Admiral has awarded settlers?"

"Certainly," Isabel and Fernando declared in unison. "You should undo those grants you deem failed the proper exercise of his authority," Fernando indicated, affirming wide discretion.

"Our Spanish and Indian subjects must live in peace, friendship, and harmony," Fernando continued, the recent bloodshed flickering through his thoughts, as well. "Order that our weaponry cannot be sold to Indians. Confiscate weapons possessed by Indians in satisfaction of their tribute. If Spaniards or Indians rebel, make war on them."

"May I receive gifts from Indians to acknowledge friendship, rather than refusing them, which may appear unfriendly?" Accepting homage from the conquered had been part of establishing peaceful relationships during the Reconquista.

"Of course, but in moderation, so it is understood as gratuitous, not as a payment for peace," Isabel counseled.

"What force should I use to subjugate portions of the island not conquered?" Envisioning battles of the Reconquista, Ovando brooded that peaceful conquest was an illusion.

Isabel and Fernando each wondered what the other might answer. Their orders to Cristóbal at the commencement of Española's conquest had also left that question unanswered.

"Only force you deem necessary," Fernando directed.

"We wish the Indians' peaceful assimilation wherever possible," Isabel added. "Lead them to embrace our civilization as superior to theirs."

▣   ▣   ▣

After the announcement of Ovando's appointment, Cristóbal spent much of early September sulking alone, mulling his isolation and book of prophecies, the sovereigns' glaring disappointment with his legacy in Española transparent to all. He took little solace that some of his recommendations were replicated or mirrored in Ovando's orders. But by mid-September, the sovereigns summoned him to settle arrangements with respect to his property and entitlements, and he dispatched the draft book to Fray Gorricio in Seville, requesting the friar improve it while he focused on other activities.

Isabel and Fernando had concluded that the vast territories Cristóbal had claimed for Spain had earned his entitlements and excused his failures and transgressions. By late September, the three agreed Ovando would be responsible for compelling Bobadilla to account for and hand over Cristóbal's property. Carvajal would represent Cristóbal in Española thereafter, monitoring the properties' return and Cristóbal's ongoing receipt of his interest in profits derived from Española and other territories he'd discovered and ships he chose to underwrite. Brothers Bartolomé and Diego would be restored, as well.

Isabel and Fernando also were keen that the arrangements fully terminate Cristóbal's active service in the Indies. His eagerness to underwrite ships of Ovando's fleet augured acceptance of a purely commercial involvement thereafter. A normal, rational man of his and their maturity would graciously accept, or at least stomach, retirement as an acclaimed merchant admiral soon to be wealthy. Regardless, Cristóbal still whined.

"What of my next voyage?" Cristóbal implored as their negotiations wound down, unrelenting in his aspiration to resume his prophesied destiny.

Isabel and Fernando exchanged beleaguered glances.

"I promised to bear your standards to the shores of Cathay," Cristóbal droned on, the Genoese merchant rising within. "None of those you license have my knowledge of the earth's geography or my mariner's acumen. Most are my former pupils, poorly imitating what I taught them. They all rely on my charts." He spread his arms, beckoning. "Award me four ships and I'll sail past Cuba to Cathay and Manoel's Calicut in weeks, rather than the months he wastes at sea."

"You still believe you can do that?" Fernando asked doubtfully, peeved to be drawn in. Some mariners now speculated that the great southern coastline would link to the northern, preventing passage.

"I am certain," Cristóbal declared, the Christ servant resurging. "All of Esdras, Isaiah, and Saint John tell us so."

Isabel and Fernando dismissed him, curtly indicating they would reflect on that, fulsomely praising the service he'd completed. Then they peered to each other, shaking their heads in disgust, utterly worn of dealing with him. Yet Spain still had an interest in a voyage achieving Manoel's Indies, and while vexed, they didn't doubt he was their best explorer. Isabel's remorse for discharging him still lingered.

"Other than Niño's pearls, Colón's proteges haven't brought us much yet," Fernando admitted. "We would profit if this voyage were successful."

"He remains the best suited for what he proposes," Isabel observed. "Perhaps we encourage him to put the arrangements in train at our expense, leaving our review, approval, and instructions to follow Ovando's departure, when time permits."

"Ovando must be installed as the Indies' governor first," Fernando insisted.

⊡   ⊡   ⊡

As October dawned, the court prepared to relocate to Seville for the winter and reside in Ecija for a few weeks en route. Prior to departing the Alhambra, Isabel and Fernando issued an edict applicable throughout Granada—long sought by confessor Cisneros—requiring that all Korans and other Mohammedan religious tracts be burned so they'd no longer corrupt the newly converted. They also asked Cristóbal to prepare a memorandum detailing what he'd require for a voyage past Cuba. His response was prompt—a fleet of four caravels berthing one hundred fifty men provisioned for two years. Without approving it, they bid Castile's treasurer analyze and prepare to so requisition.

In November, great news arrived from England. Violent ocean storms had delayed Catalina's departure from Spain, but she'd disembarked to tumultuous acclaim and married Arthur. Dismal reports arrived from Paris. Juana languished surrounded by French tarts as Philippe schemed with Louis.

Isabel and Fernando confidently continued to issue writs and orders defining Ovando's mission and instructing Cervantes and others to enlist the voyagers, hire the vessels, and dispatch the mission promptly. On November 16, Pope Alexander rendered his bull approving the collection and use of tithes from the Indies natives and settlers to erect churches and cast down damned sects so the Highest might be worshipped. Supplementing prior orders, they set the gold tribute payable by Indians at one-half, equal to the royal gold share assessed on Spaniards.

But Isabel's vision that she'd reform the Indies conquest was assaulted when she learned that Cristóbal Guerra had returned from his voyage to the Pearl Coast and was selling a cargo of slaves abducted there in Seville—a direct violation of his license. Guerra had brought home but few pearls and retained an Indian girl at his side. On December 2, Isabel furiously dispatched a letter directing

Cervantes to manumit those enslaved and return the sales proceeds to the buyers. The Indians so rescued and yet unsold were to be transferred to Ovando for repatriation in their homeland at Guerra's expense. Guerra and his accomplices were to be jailed without bail under heavy guard while prosecution proceeded.

SUPREME CACIQUE ANACAONA

Concern among Anacaona's vassal caciques mounted as more naborias dragooned for mining never returned and the squatters whom they served dragooned yet more—even beyond replenishment. Weeks after Behecchio's funeral, she summoned over a hundred caciques to council, hoping to air and resolve their anger.

On the day chosen, she sat awaiting them at the center of the great ballcourt that now was hers. Most caciques entered borne on litters, some accompanied by nitaínos, warriors, or wives, a few with behiques. All submitted dutifully before her, and she requested their honest voices. Squatters were neither invited nor welcome. When the ballcourt was full, she rose to address them without any prefatory ceremony or areíto.

"Nothing has changed since my brother's death," she declared. "Like you, I long for the day Xaraguá is free of pale men." She scanned the crowd seeking supportive nods but was accosted with skeptical grimaces from those whose masters mined gold. "Like you, I deplore this newest wickedness. But we must remain patient. Despite the first guamiquina's departure, the enemy's vulnerability hasn't ripened to permit its defeat."

"Matunherí, this new oppression goes beyond enslavement," a cacique exclaimed. "Over a third of my naborias tasked to dig die from exhaustion and hunger. My squatter considers them expendable, as if firewood."

"In truth, my naborias digging for gold are being murdered," another cacique exhorted. "Dozens so far, undoubtedly many more soon. I've lost them to hunt and fish, and unless that stops, hunger will afflict my village."

"This will affect all Xaraguáns, including those now spared the demands to mine," a third warned. "Hundreds of Xaraguáns have died so far, thousands in other chiefdoms, countless more to follow. When the pale men kill all those they master, they'll come for others. As a people, we cannot merely watch and obey."

Anacaona bowed to indicate sympathy with their thoughts and pain. But visions of Caonabó chained and dying, Guarionex and Mayobanex imprisoned, and their subjects enslaved coursed through her thoughts, reminding her what was at stake.

"My subjects, I understand squatters are killing our people while forcing them to dig for gold. The issue is whether we suffer reprisals by refusing to provide them naborias, or more drastically, bloodshed by uprising." Again, she gazed about the crowd, discerning loathing and despair. "At present, I see that those refusing to provide naborias will be whipped until they relent. I see uprising as resulting in vastly more enslavements, as well as the bloodshed of our women and children, not just warriors. But these are matters of judgment, and those who disagree should speak."

The assembly was hush as the more militant gathered their wits.

"Matunherí, I urge war on the pale men now, as this new oppression amounts to a war on us," an elder cacique argued.

"We are without direction, as though afloat at sea praying for the gale to abate," another exclaimed. "The gale may never abate, so we have no choice but to rise up now."

"The squatters are diffuse, leaderless, and ignored by their new guamiquina," a third cried. "What more must we await before slaying them?"

Anacaona turned to stare at the last crier and raised her fists.

"I must make the critical judgment that we can surmount the enemy's strength and resolve to conquer us," she declared resoundingly, her frame shaking uncharacteristically. "That depends on their number on the island, not just the squatters here, and on the stamina of their caciques in their homeland. We cannot fool ourselves that we could simply massacre those here."

Hush returned, and Anacaona sensed the men doubted her resolve to initiate war and suffer bloodshed. Behecchio wouldn't have been so doubted, and that rankled her.

"I shall not shrink from ordering the pale men's massacre if I believe our liberation is achievable!" she pronounced angrily. "Remember that I labored side by side with Caonabó to summon the alliance that confronted them. By design, the pale men have since come to perceive me as a peacemaker, perhaps even a friend, and that lulls them into complacency." *Like you, they don't perceive a woman as a warrior*, she simmered to herself.

She calmed and waited for other caciques to speak, but none did, and the silence confirmed that she'd commanded their obedience. "Come to me whenever you believe the moment has arrived for our liberation, and I will listen," she promised. "Guaorocuyá stands ready to lead you into battle if I so order."

Naborias served pineapple juice, and the shuffle and refreshment dispelled the tension.

"Is there more we should discuss of the squatters?" she inquired. "What of the treatment of our womenfolk? Where has their Christ-spirit intruded?"

"The abuses continue as before," a cacique related. "There are now some marriages, many coerced."

"Nearly all the concubines now worship the Christ-spirit, or pretend to," a second observed. "Some even help their masters teach the spirit to their children."

"That's unfortunate," Anacaona replied. "The Christ-spirit assists the pale men's conquest. Women such as me with children or grandchildren of pale men mustn't shy from so warning the children. Always teach that our spirits alone will defend us."

⊡   ⊡   ⊡

Despite condemnation of the Christ-spirit, Anacaona recognized that his presence in the squatters' bohíos had come to root unassailably, and she understood Behecchio's death to be a starkly intimate monition that honoring and appeasing the spirit could be prudent. Since time immemorial, her people had honored and sought the forbearance of many destructive spirits, albeit spirits of their own traditions rather than those of Caribes or other enemy peoples. Guabancex, the spirit of hurikáns. Her heralds Guataubá and Coatrísquie, who brought wind, rain, and floods. Maquetaurie Guayaba and Opiyel-guobirán, lord and guardian of the dead. The Christ-spirit's mercy might be as beneficial as theirs.

Guarionex had found worship of the Christ-spirit intolerable. But she now felt compelled to investigate herself, to uncover any benefit such homage might bring, however improbable and notwithstanding the awkwardness of appearing duplicitous in condemning it. The behique had continued to pester her to study his spirits, and she hadn't dismissed asking him to prevent squatter misconduct.

One *Sunday*—as the squatters called it—Anacaona bid naborias port her to a nearby village where the behique, squatters, and concubines gathered in their thatched *church*—as they'd named a bohío. She released the litter-bearers at a distance and stalked alone and unheralded to hover in the shade of trees, observing the worshippers assemble, as she'd once spied on Behecchio's first greeting of Roldán.

Pale men were sauntering into the clearing, hailing their *friar* and each other, most accompanied by their concubines and children. The crowd about the behique grew fulsome, but not all local pale men came. Nor did a single villager other than the concubines and their children. The concubines, and even some of the children, were fully or partly wrapped in clothing, unabashedly in the pale men's custom. Within moments, the behique led them all into the bohío.

Anacaona heard chanting and treaded softly to stand unobtrusively in the bohío's doorway. The behique was shocked and gratified. The squatters were vexed that their homage would be sought. The concubines trembled that their Christ worship would be condemned. Forthrightly, Anacaona smiled and spread her arms in friendship, intending to put all at ease.

"My friends and subjects, I have come to listen and learn," she pronounced. Addressing the behique, she bid, "Proceed with your incantations, just as you would without me. You may teach me later."

Anacaona listened as the behique and congregation murmured in unison, all in the pale man's tongue, and she understood enough to glean that they attributed all earth and sky to be the Christ-spirit's chiefdom and asked him for their daily cazabi. She doubted the concubines sincerely believed the falsehood. Yet she admitted to herself that—notwithstanding their alien chant and clothing—the women had progressed from the forlornness apparent in years past. They possessed purpose and place, at least to mother their children and tolerate life with their masters to that end. Perhaps it no longer mattered to them whether cazabi was provided by Yúcahu or the Christ-spirit.

The squatters murmured the falsehood doubtlessly, as arrogant as ever, dedicated to their Christ-spirit's dominance. But Anacaona was startled by the warmth they held for their women and children, barely evident in years past. Perhaps the *Sunday* ritual was meant as an interlude when conquest and submission were momentarily forgotten. The children—like any children—paid no heed to the behique's teaching, and she wondered who they imagined themselves to be and who they would become. She shuddered that her granddaughter would ever disgrace herself by wearing clothing.

"Christ taught us which of His commandments are the most important," the behique instructed, presiding in front of the assembly beside a cemí of the Christ-spirit dying on the cross. He waited for a Xaraguán manservant to translate for the concubines' benefit. "The first is that you shall love the Lord with all your heart, soul, and mind."

Anacaona winced. The precept was but a veiled requirement to desert all other spirits.

"The second is related," the behique expounded. "Love your neighbor as yourself."

Anacaona trembled. The hypocrisy was astonishing, undoubtedly designed to mislead those conquered to embrace their conquerors.

The behique lectured for some time, calling for chants and areítos, then bid two of the older boys to assist in *Holy Mass*, passing cazabi and a gourd of juice among the congregation.

"As Christ's followers, we commemorate His sacrifice upon the cross to atone our sins," he pronounced. "We now share Christ's flesh and blood."

Anacaona smiled wanly as one of the boys offered her a piece of cazabi and juice, courteously declining, studying the others partaking. The ritual's spectral barbarism was unnerving, auguring she'd never fully comprehend the pale men's outlook. They abhorred the Caribes, and they regularly accused her people of being Caribes, yet their incantations embraced the abhorrent.

The behique concluded the ceremony with an areíto, and after the congregation departed, Anacaona and he sat in the pale men's chairs outside the bohío, the Xaraguán manservant kneeling in between.

"Your Highness, what did you think?" he beamed pleasantly.

"The areítos were beautiful, the tranquility pleasant, the community promising," she replied. "But I seek to understand how the Christ-spirit may benefit my people if I venerate him. Tell me."

"Your soul will achieve eternal salvation, as will the souls of your subjects who worship Him," the behique replied earnestly.

"I beseech my spirits for their alliance on earth, before death," Anacaona explained. "I ask Yúcahu to make our crops grow throughout the year, Attabeira to bless our women's fertility every single day, and Guabancex to direct hurikáns to rage elsewhere during the season of hurikáns. May I so beseech the Christ-spirit, before my death?"

"Of course."

"May I ask him to guide your people to return our land?" she posed softly, emphasizing she sought knowledge rather than confrontation. "Would he see that return as just?"

The behique squirmed, speechless.

"If not, may I ask him to halt the enslavement of our naborias? He must see that as cruel."

"Your Highness, our peoples have much to offer each other, according to their ability," the behique responded. "My people share knowledge of the soul's salvation and a better civilization on earth. Yours share labor, improving and integrating themselves. Christ is content with our joint society."

"So, you doubt he'll hear these pleas?"

"He sees all, knows all, and loves all. Do not question His design, simply trust Him, and eternal salvation shall be yours."

"Instead of Christ, may I ask you to convince your people to treat my people kindlier?" Anacaona challenged, raising her voice. "We are neighbors, are we not? I trust you and your people love my people as yourselves."

"Your Highness, I and we do, as Christ has commanded," the behique blustered, countenancing no retreat. "My love for your people has brought me here to teach them. My people's love, albeit imperfect, will advance them."

Anacaona stood, loathing that the deceits of the Christ-spirit made him unworthy of any chiefdom at all. His preacher of love was no better than the others—certainly not a potential protector. She scowled. "I shall not come again."

Grand Colonizing Fleet Sails, Cristóbal's Exploratory Fleet Authorized,
December 1501–March 1502

In early December, Isabel and Fernando issued orders spurring Cervantes, Ovando, and Arriaga to hasten preparations, expressing displeasure with the delay, keen that their grand colonizing fleet depart before year's end.

Isabel bluntly reminded Cervantes that Guerra's manumitted Indian slaves were to be returned to the territories where they'd been seized and warned that voyagers be stopped from enslaving them en route to Española or after arrival there. The Indians were corralled near the Guadalquivir's embankments, together with a few more of Cristóbal's manumitted slaves who'd been located. Many of them were sick, and Cervantes was reluctant to board them, fearing they'd infect those healthy. When he asked what to do, Isabel sadly directed that all the Indians be berthed so they'd understand her intent and those surviving would understand what happened to the rest.

By mid-December, the sovereigns arrived with their court in Seville, and Fernando paraded by horseback inside the royal shipyards and along the Guadalquivir's embankments, where most of the fleet was being fitted and provisioned, to inspect, criticize, and demand haste of Ovando and Arriaga face-to-face. Ovando handily had enlisted recruits and crews for the primary mission—all thirsting for a quick haul of gold, repartimientos if they merited and remained permanently, and Indian servants, be they "freemen" or lawful slaves. Despite offering free passage, Arriaga had struggled to entice merely seventy-three families to settle townships with repartimientos guaranteed after five years of residence. While enlistment was complete, when the new year arrived departure remained weeks distant. Many of the thirty-two ships were not yet fit or provisioned and not all the twenty-five hundred crew and passengers had gathered.

Isabel and Fernando took comfort in January when Bishop Fonseca's favorite, Alonso de Hojeda, sailed in four caravels from Cádiz to assume governorship of Coquibacoa and police the southern landmass's far shores from incursions by King Henry's explorers. Don Guevara captained one. Hojeda's young Isabel was tasked to serve as interpreter.

Throughout January, ships of the grand fleet departed one by one when ready down the Guadalquivir to the sea at Sanlúcar de Barrameda, joining others provisioning and boarding passengers there, the complete assemblage to consist of five large naos and twenty-seven caravels. The crown financed many, but most sailed for the owners' accounts.

Voyage administrators, captains, and crews—almost five hundred enlistees—brimmed with Indies' veterans once Cristóbal's lieutenants. The fleet's captain general, Antonio de Torres, had sailed as the crown's senior official on Cristóbal's second voyage and thereafter crossed the ocean back and forth, resupplying Española and hauling Cristóbal's first slave shipments to Spain. The fleet's overseer, Diego Márquez, had served as an overseer on the second voyage. Pero Alonso Niño would sail as the fleet's second pilot, his experience essential, though his incarceration for pilfering the sovereigns' pearls precluded first rank. Captains included those who'd once served Cristóbal as officers or seaman, and crews included brothers, sons, and cousins of those who'd so served. Ovando and Torres would berth on the flagship, the *Santa María de Antigua*. Most of the other ships bore names of saints—including *Santas Ana*, *Catalina*, *Clara*, and *María*—or their masters.

The great majority of Ovando's passengers were commoners native to Andalusia, Extremadura, or elsewhere in Castile—farmers, artisans, miners, unskilled laborers, and a handful of doctors and apothecaries—all venturing unsalaried and bearing their own passage or in the employ of gentlemen also berthing or remaining in Spain. The one hundred crown officers and knights were accompanied by over fifty foot soldiers, almost sixty horses, and dozens of household servants, including a few baptized Guinean slaves. High nobility included Juan Ponce de Leon, who'd fought in the Reconquista, sailed on Cristóbal's second voyage, and since served as Fernando's page, and Cristóbal de Cuéllar, Isabel's cupbearer and once accountant for Prince Juan's household, now acting as the crown's accountant on Española.* Knights and squires included Juan de Esquivel, a Sevillian who'd sailed on the second voyage and since served in crushing the Granadan uprisings, and Diego de Nicuesa, a servant in the royal household.† Three men had been selected to establish and warden new inland forts, including a young Salamacan, Rodrigo de Alburquerque.‡ The life force of Arriaga's seventy-three families were the seventy-three wives, together with their husbands, children, and servants numbering over two hundred. Ovando's passengers also included a handful of wives and maids.

A few manumitted Guinean slaves were enrolled as Castilian freemen. Carvajal would sail as Cristóbal's factor, with three servants. Pedro de Salcedo, long Cristóbal's page, berthed with crown licenses to sell ham and cut brazilwood on Española and permission to sell wine to passengers.

At Isabel and Fernando's order, quarters on the fleet were reserved for twenty-five religious, spearheaded by seventeen Franciscans sailing for the crown under the leadership of Fray Alonso del Espinar, the guardian of a small Galician monastery. Under Espinar's supervision, the Franciscans had assembled the sacramental accoutrements for establishing Española's church, including eight sets of altarpieces, chalices, candlesticks, and bells, a wardrobe of garments, a small store of missals, and one complete bible. They'd also collected the instruments, medicines, and potions necessary to found the island's first Christian infirmary. Berths were awarded to other clerics who brought servants to mine gold for their parishes. Pursuant to the sovereigns' order, most churchmen and accoutrements would sail in a single caravel, the *Santa María de la Rabida*, captained by Andrés Martin de la Gorda. Espinar's instructions were to establish new churches in Santo Domingo, Concepción, Xaraguá, and the four townships to be built.

---

* Juan Ponce de Leon would later conquer and govern Boriquén (Puerto Rico) and explore Florida. Cristóbal de Cuéllar would participate in the conquest of Cuba.
† Diego de Nicuesa would later explore and become governor of the Central American coastline the Spanish called Veragua.
‡ Rodrigo de Alburquerque would conduct the census and redistribution of Indian labor referred to as the Repartimiento de Alburquerque of 1514.

Almost a hundred Sevillians enlisted, among them Pedro de Las Casas and his son Bartolomé. Since returning from Española in 1498, Pedro's financial fortunes had declined, and he and Bartolomé hoped to turn that around. Then seventeen, Bartolomé had been educated in Christian doctrine and Latin at a cathedral school, served in one of the militias raised to repress the Mohammedan uprisings, and received tonsure prelude to becoming a Dominican priest. He was qualified to both master and evangelize Indians, as well as massacre them.

One unknown from Medellín, perhaps Extremadura's most unruly den of cutthroats, would miss taking his berth on the armada, having injured himself—some said—while climbing to a woman's window and then taken fever. Hernán Cortéz—eighteen (b. ca. 1484), perceived as talkative by many, haughty and quarrelsome by some, affable and modest by others—had studied grammar in preparation for studying law, a calling his cleverness and scheming favored. But he'd vexed his parents by not pursuing that, finding school theory a bore, and considered enlisting instead either with Ovando, who knew of him, or as a soldier in Fernando's war contesting the French for control of the Italian peninsula. Perhaps the Indies' gold beckoned more strongly. When the grand fleet departed, he would reconsider serving in Italy but soon land a job as a notary.*

⊡　⊡　⊡

The prior October, when the court departed Granada for Ecija, Cristóbal had traveled instead directly to Seville to oversee arrangements implementing his one-eighth participation in ships of Ovando's fleet, still lacking the sovereigns' approval for his own voyage. He'd taken lodging with Fray Gorricio in the Monastery of Santa María de las Cuevas, conveniently set on an embankment of the Guadalquivir only a short distance upstream from the grand fleet's provisioning, although Seville's main river bridge spanned the river in between, precluding—as if a portent—seafaring ships to anchor before him.†

---

* *Columbus and Caonabó*, chapters V and VI, discuss the Italian war.
† The bridge was at the site of the present Puente de Isabel II.

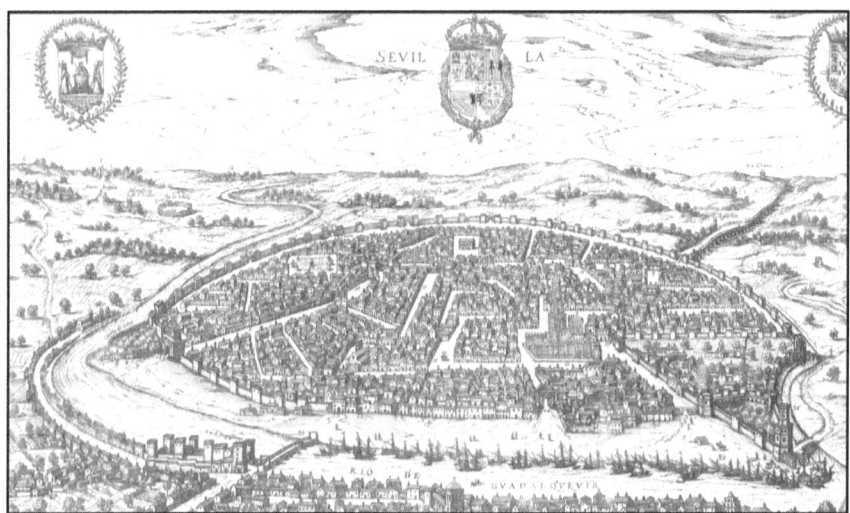

Portion of map of Seville in sixteenth century, with the Monastery of Santa María
de Las Cuevas located on the western embankment to the far left.
Civitates Orbis Terrarum, 1588.

In January, Cristóbal and his Sevillian-based Genoese financiers occasionally huddled in the city center and on the downstream embankments to finalize the particulars of his participation
with shipowners and crown officials.* But Cristóbal's presence was
mostly despised there, particularly by bitter or ungrateful veterans
of Española, and more acridly by two crown officials directly supervising the fleet's provisioning. The overseer, Diego Márquez, would
never forget that Cristóbal had imprisoned him on the second voyage
for flouting orders. The sovereigns' accountant Briviesca—still in
charge of voyage expenditures—would never forgive being slugged
on the wharf at the commencement of the third.

Accordingly, Cristóbal spent most of January shunned, in limbo,
impotently gazing from the monastery's embankment at the small
riverboats coursing before it, mere skiffs and barges, despairing how
far he'd fallen and been discarded. The isolation was occasionally
tempered by brother Bartolomé's companionship, and when the
court arrived in mid-December, visits by sons Diego and Fernando.

---

* The Genoese financiers were Francisco Cataño, Francisco Doria, Gaspar Espindola, and
Francisco de Riberol.

One day, Cristóbal and Bartolomé's inviolable bond was tested by a rare disagreement. They sat at dusk on the monastery's embankment gazing south over the river's sandbanks to the bridge and the tips of tall masts rising beyond, contemplating the horde of newcomers and former underlings massing there to exploit the conquest they'd established.

"The king and queen will approve my next voyage, and you must accompany me," Cristóbal advised. "We'll sail in the Holy Trinity's name, and He shall bless the voyage as our highest glory. The route will course the coasts known to King Solomon's mariners, Marco Polo, and now the Portuguese. We'll land there in weeks rather than half a year."

"You've never needed me to explore the sea," Bartolomé responded curtly, eager to retire or at least rest, worn from duty on Española as Cristóbal's henchman. His lifelong comfort would be amply satisfied by his draw upon Cristóbal's accumulated gold, soon to be shipped from Española, and recurring participations in gold mined for years thereafter. His exhausted older brother's refusal to rest was galling. "You'll find the pilots and mates to obey your orders, just like with your other voyages."

"I'm older and weaker than before, Bartolomeo. I need you now, even at sea. Crews are fickle, and peoples encountered often hostile."

"Sailors afloat continue to venerate you. Savages have never pursued you offshore."

"I expect more than exploration! Ovando shall blunder and fall from the king and queen's favor, just like Bobadilla." Cristóbal glared into his younger brother's eyes, beseeching comprehension. "Then the sovereigns will turn to me to resume Española's rule, and I'll desperately need you."

Bartolomé exhaled deeply, exasperated by Cristóbal's limitless obstinacy, be it to defend his geographic theory, promote his prophetic destiny, or reclaim the sovereigns' favor. Decisive proof of their lasting disfavor floated and clamored beyond the bridge.

"Cristoforo, you'll need me here when you're at sea," Bartolomé reasoned, resigned that debating illusions would be fruitless. "Carvajal may dispatch the gold, but Briviesca will pocket it. Preventing that is my best use."

"Our financiers will thwart that, more keenly than you ever could," Cristóbal countered. "It's their pockets too. They have no love for the Spanish, and they won't be bought."

"You should sail with young Fernando. He's old enough for adventure and hardship. If you're reappointed to rule Española, I'll join you there then."

"Fernando will sail. With us! That'll lighten your duty."

At sunset, Cristóbal and Bartolomé were joined by Diego and Fernando, who'd been released from the queen's service for the night. They brought bread, ham, and cheese from the queen's kitchen, which the four shared.

"Any word on the queen's approval of our next voyage?" Cristóbal asked.

Both sons shook their heads.

Convinced that approval imminent, tiring of living a pariah's existence until Ovando departed, Cristóbal traveled to Granada and back, retrieving belongings left there. He filled time by composing a courtly letter to the sovereigns on the mariner's art and the craft of judging winds and weather at sea. In passing, he noted a caution he'd heeded his entire career. *Seamen desire money and to return home but risk everything without waiting to see if the weather is certain.*

⊡   ⊡   ⊡

As January waned, Princess Juana and Prince Philippe finally crossed the French border into Spain, and the court's vim, vigor, and vexation pivoted to succession and traveling to greet them in Toledo. On February 2, irritated to still focus on the Indies, Isabel and Fernando angrily instructed Ovando to depart immediately with whatever ships were ready. He complied, with twenty-nine of the ships raising anchor and sailing on February 13. Arriaga finally followed a week later with three ships bearing the seventy-three families, and the sovereigns—thoroughly disgusted—licensed another Indies veteran to organize a new fleet to bear fifty additional families to Española.* The grand fleet barely escaped the sovereigns' full wrath, as they then received word that Vasco da Gama had departed Lisbon on February 10 with the principal squadron of a fleet of twenty ships, returning to

---

* The veteran was Alonso Vélez de Mendoza, who'd sailed south of Trinidad in 1501 and would sail with the families in 1503.

Manoel's Indies to wrest its commerce—forcibly, if necessary—from Mohammedan traders.

Long awaited, on February 20 the sovereigns issued the order expelling those Mohammedans who didn't convert from Castile, and the court thereafter departed for Toledo on a route through Extremadura. Isabel pined for a week of rejuvenation at the renowned Monastery of Santa María de Guadalupe, where she'd worshipped some dozen times since childhood, contemplating it might be her final visit.

Abruptly, as the court wended north through the mountains, the Lord ominously reminded her and Fernando that failure continued to be their fortune. Word arrived of an enormous storm engulfing the grand fleet, the wreckage washing Spain's southern coast. For a week, they dreaded that the entire fleet and their labor of months—the redesign of the Indies' governance, the noble appointments and commands, and the thousands of recruits, provisions, and other expenditures—had all sunk. But news gradually trickled in that only one ship had floundered. Ovando and the leadership survived, and the fleet's provisions would be restored on Gran Canaria and Gomera. At least this time, the Lord had reprieved them.

◱ ◲ ◳

Cristóbal chose to accompany the court as it rode north, pining for Isabel's notice, his next voyage still not approved.

One day, rather than intruding on the sovereigns' preoccupation with succession, he wrote to Pope Alexander instead, professing that he had intended to visit His Sanctity after first returning from the Indies. But he'd been called into service by the sovereigns repeatedly thereafter—on a second voyage *to discover and conquer all there was* and a third to find vast southern lands, *believing that in that region is the Earthly Paradise*. Unfortunately, he still couldn't visit, as he'd been called for a fourth—to augment His Sanctity's and Christianity's honor and glory. He pleaded for the pope's assistance and command in recruiting six religious to accompany him and declared his endeavors' profits would be used to reclaim Jerusalem. He lamented that *Satan has upset all this*, and—skirting criticism of Isabel and Fernando—baldly suggested that his ejection from

Española's governorship was a matter to be discussed directly rather than by letter.

Finally, as February waned and the court rested in tiny Cantillana, Isabel asked him to succinctly brief the proposed route of his voyage and any final requests beyond those itemized in his prior memorandum.

Cristóbal replied, ecstatic. He'd sail west past Paria and Coquibacoa to locate the strait that led to the Indian seas. He wanted permission to harbor on and utilize Española as a way station, a letter of introduction to Vasco da Gama, and authority to enlist Arabic interpreters. He also wished his privileges reconfirmed and son Fernando released from duty as her page to accompany the voyage.

On March 14, while in tiny Valencia de las Torres, Isabel and Fernando issued a reply and order approving a voyage to discover and possess islands and mainland in the Indies region belonging to them, rather than Manoel, and the requested letter of introduction. They outright prohibited him from visiting Española on the outbound voyage, permitting only a resupply there if necessary on his return, and outright prohibited him from enslaving anybody. They assured that they'd been sorely grieved by his imprisonment. They also equivocated—they couldn't decide the issue of his hereditary entitlements while traveling—and they blustered—they were more eager than before to preserve those entitlements in full.

But they never intended to reinstall him as the governor of the Indies. The next morning, to their great relief, they bid him farewell, graciously commending him. He tearfully kissed their hands and departed south for Seville, eager and apparently satisfied.

XI

INVASION RENEWED

HIGUANAMÁ AND COTUBANAMÁ, COHOBA CEREMONY
(March 1502)

Supreme cacique Higuanamá had ruled her unconquered chiefdom of Higüey at Haiti's eastern tip for some years. Her powerful vassal caciques included Cotubanamá, who lead Higüey's warriors when necessary, and the widow of Cayacoa, who'd fought with Caonabó against the first guamiquina.

With Higuanamá and Cotubanamá's approval, Cotubanamá's village caciques living on Adamanay—an island offshore Higüey's southeastern coast—had agreed to supply food to pale men from Santo Domingo in return for peaceful coexistence and being left alone by the second guamiquina. For a year, caravels had anchored in the protected strait between the coastline and Adamanay to load cazabi baked from the island's plentiful yuca farms. Cristóbal had named the island La Bella Saones, or simply Saona, when he harbored in the strait for over a week to shelter from a hurikán while returning from his Cuban exploration.[*]

In March, an Adamanay cacique was supervising his subjects as they ported baskets of cazabi to the canoes that would ferry them to a caravel anchored yards offshore. A few Spaniards, armed with

---

[*] The island is so named today. For depiction of Cristóbal's visit there and renaming of the island, see *Columbus and Caonabó*, chapter V.

swords and an attack dog, lounged on the island's beach overseeing the work. The dog repeatedly growled at the cacique, who carried a stick. The Spaniard handling the dog mused aloud about what would happen if it were prompted to attack, and with a chuckle, another Spaniard so prompted, cockily daring the handler's strength to restrain it. The dog lunged to attack, overpowered its handler, and tore into the cacique's stomach, tearing his guts out. The cacique collapsed in agony, bleeding to death, and pandemonium erupted. The cacique's subjects scattered, fearing worse would follow, decrying the peace's breach and the Spaniards' sadism. The Spaniards, outnumbered, unprepared for battle, and frightened, fled in their launch to the caravel and hastily sailed for Santo Domingo. Remarkably, no other blood was shed.

Dogs attack Native Americans, Panama. Taken from Pieter van der Aa, 1707. The John Carter Brown Library, portion of rec. no. 08984-29.

When alerted, Higuanamá and Cotubanamá were outraged and stopped their vassals from supplying cazabi to the pale men, vowing to take vengeance. They knew better than to attack Santo Domingo and plotted that Cotubanamá would inflict punishment on those Spaniards next visiting Higüey.

Cotubanamá summoned his lieutenants and nitaínos to a cohoba ceremony, exhorting that vengeance be harsh. None disagreed. The attack had been wanton, not accidental. The pale men had breached their word, and justice demanded retaliation. Word of Cotubanamá's intent passed from village to village along Haiti's southern coast.

When the caravel returned to Santo Domingo, the crew attributed the shortfall in cazabi hauled to the Indians' intransigence. Higüey's Indians had grown unruly and rebellious.

GRAND INVASION ARRIVES,
April–May 1502

One mid-April day, Anacaona sat in her garden, minding her daughter and granddaughter as the toddler was taught to walk. A nitaíno entered to whisper that scouts reported hordes of pale men arriving at Santo Domingo. Cheer fading to anxiety, she excused Higueymota and her granddaughter and bid the scouts brief her.

The more she heard, the more her dread rose. Sixteen vessels had newly anchored in the Ozama, crowding its waters, and more than a thousand pale men and almost sixty horses had streamed ashore. Hundreds of the invaders were brightly attired in the custom of pale nitaínos. Scores were armed soldiers, dozens robed behiques.

Ominously, pale women tending pale children were among them, undoubtedly the men's families. A faction of caciques had once dismissed Caonabó's calls to war as unnecessary, asserting that the pale men wouldn't remain on Haiti for long because they hadn't brought their own women. The invaders' intent to conquer Haiti now extended to populating it with their own blood.

Anacaona instructed Guaorocuyá and Haniguyabá to learn all they could about the guamiquina's intent for these reinforcements, and they began seeking information from Agüeybana, Catalina, and other caciques serving the pale men at Santo Domingo. But before that was accomplished, another sixteen vessels anchored in the Ozama, cramming its waters beyond capacity, and a thousand more pale men, women, and children disembarked. Anacaona's dread surged.

◻ ◻ ◻

The tempest had scattered the grand fleet throughout the Canary Islands and onto the African coast, sinking a caravel with one hundred twenty lives lost and dashing overboard the provisions stored above deck on most other ships. But Ovando had marshalled the thirty-one surviving ships on Gomera, reprovisioned them, and even purchased a replacement caravel. With a month lost, he'd departed the Canaries with the swifter ships in March, arriving at Santo Domingo on April 14, and Torres had followed with the slower, arriving on May 1.

Anacaona and her lieutenants weren't the only ones astonished and anxious when the first ships anchored in the Ozama. So was every Spaniard on the island. As the royal launch brought Ovando ashore, those once loyal to Cristóbal—such as Díaz and Garay—trembled that they'd be treated unfairly by whomever the sovereigns had newly authorized. Roldán and his followers writhed that they'd finally be hauled to Spain to answer for their crimes. Even those who'd skirted the two factions' hostilities cringed, alarmed that the repartimientos, servants, and slaves they'd amassed might be real-lotted or confiscated in favor of newcomers. Commander Bobadilla instantly warmed that the fleet bore his replacement—the sovereigns honoring their word—yet he brooded whether the sovereigns would deem he'd fulfilled their expectations.

As Ovando stepped onto the Ozama's embankment, he and Bobadilla hailed each other cordially, and surrounded by the town's leading settlers, the two conversed amicably, having known each other at court. Dutifully pious, they knelt together at the church's altar to praise the Lord for the passage. Dutifully loyal, Bobadilla stood at Ovando's side in Santo Domingo's plaza as Ovando circumspectly proclaimed the grand public purpose of his arrival with thousands of settlers. Queen Isabel and King Fernando's Española, the jewel of their Indies, would now grow and thrive. Their Spanish settlers would better themselves and the realm, and the Indians would be peacefully welcomed to the faith and Spanish custom.

Later that day, bluntly and coldly, Ovando met alone with Bobadilla in the governor's residence, which both understood now was Ovando's.

"As customary, I must investigate and report on your performance," Ovando pronounced. "My secretaries will review your written commands and take testimony from those pleased with your governance, as well as those critical. Sit. I have some questions."

"I assume this is a formality," Bobadilla replied. The taller of the two, he lifted his chin and puckered his lips before taking a supplicant's chair.

"Why did you reduce the king's share of the gold?" Ovando asked, stroking his beard. "The king and queen are furious."

"So that Española's gold finally is mined," Bobadilla retorted. He wouldn't be demeaned by another commander, of whatever order. "In the short period of my governance, more gold has been mined than during six years of Colón's rule. The ships bearing me home will carry much for the sovereigns, even at their reduced participation, far more than all they've previously received. I shall be happy to explain that to the king myself, who shall understand."

"You will accompany more gold home than you expect," Ovando countered tartly. "By the king's order, your reduction in the crown's share is rescinded retroactively. I shall collect the portion you squandered before the ships depart."

Bobadilla squirmed.

"Did you investigate Roldán and those who followed him? I understand they roam free, possessed of lands awarded them through duress."

"I didn't come here with hundreds at my side, as you have," Bobadilla pushed back. "I found Colón guilty of disloyalty to the crown, not merely incompetence, and flagrant abuse of judicial process, directed particularly against those he alleged had rebelled. I saw no justice—and certainly no advantage for this realm's advancement—in prosecuting Spaniards loyal to the sovereigns who disobeyed a foreigner himself guilty of treason."

"One man's treason does not excuse another's." Ovando observed that Bobadilla didn't contest that the rebels' repartimientos had been wrongfully obtained. "Moreover, the king and queen were rankled that you sent Colón home in chains. They'd expected that of rebels, not of their Admiral."

Bobadilla held his visage undecipherable, yet he cringed inside. The nightmare he'd often dreaded—that Colón would prevail to crush him at court—loomed real. Reluctantly exposing his angst, he asked, "Colón survives the report I sent the king and queen?"

"He does. It's your report that has disappeared." Ovando stared into Bobadilla's eyes. "He remains the queen's admiral, and she'll award him with yet another voyage. She and the king were displeased that you squandered his gold and belongings, and you are now responsible for restoring every bit of them. You must answer to his agent, the jackal Carvajal."

Bobadilla gazed away bitterly, recognizing defeat. After a moment, hoping for mercy, he softly rejoined, "What more can I do to please you, my governor?"

"I will tell you what I need. So long as you comply, I will uphold and protect your honor. The king and queen desire that you return home with dignity and their commendation—no matter how they feel."

▣ ▣ ▣

That evening, Ovando retired to sleep in the bed just Bobadilla's and once the Admiral's, dozing only occasionally, his thoughts churning over the method and timing for introducing Española's new order. He would devote his first few days on Española to apprising himself of its daily functioning before deciding, meeting with veterans whose support mattered and observing their use of Indian servants and slaves and their relationships with concubines.

Díaz and Garay clearly held prominent status and the respect of many settlers. When Ovando summoned them, they recounted that the town received its food supply from both repartimientos and Indian chiefdoms elsewhere, all of it farmed by Indian labor. They lauded the use of Indians to mine gold and displayed an enormous nugget—the size of a loaf of bread—that one of Díaz's Indian servants recently had found. When they discussed concubinage, Ovando was skeptical of Díaz's sinful relationship and two children with Cacica Catalina. But he grasped its dimension in conquest—without analogue in the Reconquista—and grudgingly accepted as undoable that nearly all veterans kept Indian concubines and had children with them. The newcomers inevitably would want to, as well, given the lack of Spanish women.

Among others he met, Ovando was particularly impressed by a middle-aged Castilian gentleman who cold heartedly related how Indian labor was most thoroughly exploited. Diego Velásquez de Cuéllar (b. ca. 1464) had sailed on Cristóbal's second voyage and since quietly amassed perhaps the largest repartimiento, stash of gold, and workforce of Indians of any settler living nearby Santo Domingo.*

While Ovando studied, Santo Domingo celebrated, veterans and newcomers delighting in camaraderie if not unity. Thirsty old-timers gulped wine fresh from Spain, warming as newcomers related news of relatives at home and the king and queen. Newcomers beamed as old-timers ballyhooed the fortunes of gold to be made and the Indian women's beauty. The old-timers hungered for clothing, ammunition, household goods, and utensils, the newcomers for Indian labor. A feverish barter commenced, although there weren't nearly enough Indian servants or lawful slaves to fill demand. Still, the newcomers, including Bartolomé de Las Casas, were encouraged by what they heard. The Indians to the east were ready to uprise, affording an excuse to war against them and take many lawful slaves. The short-fall soon would be cured.

Within days of disembarkation, the celebrations petered out. As in past years, a high proportion of the newcomers grew ill from drinking the local water and sampling the local food. Barely off the ships, hundreds soon languished, and the scourge and its severity accelerated ominously.

Whether ill or not, many newcomers were unwilling to wait for Ovando's and Arriaga's decisions regarding the founding of new townships and awards of land plots. Gold had been their only real motivation for braving Española. After spending a few nights in Santo Domingo without shelter, hundreds began streaming toward the Jaina in search of it, like ants returning to an anthill. Ovando acquiesced. Disciplining the men's basest urges would be difficult and contentious, and in any case, Santo Domingo's housing and food

---

* This Velásquez would tangle years later with Hernán Cortés.

supply were insufficient. Old-timers facilitated the newcomers at a price, bartering Indian labor in return for partnership participations or even use of a horse.

Notwithstanding his deliberateness in planning, Ovando didn't bother to fulfill the queen's command by designating a ship to return Guerra's manumitted slaves to their homeland. These freemen had disembarked fearful of all the pale men—newcomer and old-timer—as well as the island's olive men of unknown tongues. The pale men's barter soon enveloped them, and they quickly regressed to servitude on Española, perhaps never having expected otherwise.

◻   ◻   ◻

One afternoon, when set to introduce Española's new order, Ovando invited Díaz, Garay, and Diego Velásquez to the governor's residence, having identified them as settlers whose support mattered and who possessed a squire or crown official's sophistication sufficient for understanding Isabel and Fernando's aspirations and orders. Díaz's lineage included reputed Aragonese public servants, and as the crown's notary, Garay had witnessed most of the repartimientos of land and Indians awarded on Española. Velásquez—a cousin to Española's new crown accountant—hailed from a distinguished Castilian lineage whose members had long served Isabel's family and himself had fought in the Reconquista. All three had stood loyally for Cristóbal, yet they all had deftly wended the internecine sparring when Roldán usurped authority and Bobadilla assumed it.

"Our king and queen have ordered changes to our men's conduct on Española, applicable to both newcomers and old-timers," Ovando announced. "As Commander Bobadilla instructed you, the Indians are the sovereigns' vassals, to be treated as freemen just as laborers in Spain. Repartimientos will not operate to award their labor. Landowners farming and mining must now pay the Indians salaries for their work, and tribute will be collected from those payments as if taxes for the sovereigns." He stared into the eyes of the settlement's establishment. "How sternly or graciously do you recommend I implement these orders, and how shall I expect your assistance?"

Affording the three a moment to reflect, Ovando bid his butler serve a round of Andalusian wine, himself abstaining.

"So, are we to understand that the king and queen wish us to free the Indians from service, hire them back with a salary, pay them with gold, and then collect half the gold to pay the king and queen?" Díaz asked plainly, shrugging. "How shall we proceed if the Indians refuse to be hired back?"

"All Española's hard labor—the building, farming, and mining—is done by the Indians," Garay lectured. "They fearfully bear that now. But many, if not most, will flee to the mountains if they believe they have a choice." He peered back into Ovando's eyes. "When they flee, who will build your settlers' homes and townships? Who will farm their gardens?"

"Be aware that some among them will perceive this freedom as an invitation to rebel," Velásquez warned.

"Do you protest the king and queen's orders?" Ovando replied. "Infidel conquered during the Reconquista now work for wages as the sovereigns' vassals—and, as I may attest, they do so obediently and cowed. Can you not forge Española on the same terms?" He gripped the sword at his hip, marking his upper hand, his adoration of the militant supremacy of Christian civilization readily apparent. But he allowed the three more time to think.

"We could try," Díaz conceded reluctantly. "But the more seamless the transition, the better. The less the Indians appreciate that they might have the choice not to work for us, the better."

"The king and queen don't want the Indians to shirk laboring for you, much less flee," Ovando clarified. "They desire and expect the Indians to improve this realm, just as laborers improve Castile. But the Indians must be treated as vassals, like laborers free in their persons and fairly compensated."

"I suggest you proceed slowly, implementing this plan only partially to preview the consequences," Garay cautioned. "Roldán and his henchmen never deserved the repartimientos they extorted from Colón, the service of the Indians living thereon, or the slaves awarded them." He looked to Díaz and Velásquez, inviting their support. "My governor, you might initiate the king and queen's policy by freeing the Indians laboring for Roldán and his cohorts."

"You also might revoke those traitors' repartimientos entirely." Velásquez chuckled affably. "You could redistribute their lands to the knights and gentlemen whom you've brought to serve you, ensuring their love." He stroked his plump belly with one hand, his reddish beard and locks with the other. "I'm sure the Indians living there will continue to work for the new owners—just as the Granadan infidel work for the Christians who replaced their slain masters." Díaz and Garay nodded their agreement. Ovando revealed no reaction, having expected that settlers of one stripe would backstab those of another. Velásquez continued, emboldened.

"We've understood from Commander Bobadilla that enslavement of Indians was prohibited generally, but that those captured in war could remain in servitude," he observed, his words spoken softly and smoothly, as if in confidence to a new friend. "Must Indians taken in war now be freed?"

"No, that is not the sovereigns' intent," Ovando responded. "But the king and queen won't be deceived. The queen grew furious with Colón's enslavements, and she won't tolerate falsehoods. She knows the Indians now working the mines and farms didn't war against us."

"We three have never wished to deceive the queen," Velásquez replied. "But be cautioned that the Indians aren't always friendly. As Commander Bobadilla can confirm, the Indians at the eastern tip now foment rebellion, and you will need to crush that." He smiled and shrugged. "Slaves might then be taken, not only for your knights and gentlemen but for all the others you've brought."

Circumspectly, Ovando didn't respond. He bid his butler serve another round of wine, signaling he'd progress to another topic.

"Are there Indians caciques whom I might elevate to the rank of gentlemen to lead their people into our fold and custom?" he posed. "Have any prominent among them embraced the faith?"

"The Admiral attempted that and failed, and many of the most powerful caciques warred against us," Díaz responded. "The most prominent surviving—the cacique Guarionex—remains incarcerated at Concepción, having foresworn submission to the sovereigns countless times. The many who've submitted do so from fear and to survive in peace, but not to share society." He reflected momentarily on his Catalina, who hadn't forsaken her Indian ways and perspective regardless of the closest intimacy. "This is conquest, not community."

"Bless the friars for their perseverance, but few caciques have embraced Christianity, and I know of none wishing to serve as

Christ's disciple," Garay observed. "Our men's mates have no choice but to worship Him. The rest of the Indians prefer their idols. Those baptized en masse don't attend church."

"That must change!" Ovando bristled. "But what of Colón's interpreter, whom the queen baptized Diego Colón? Might he be elevated to lead as an example and disciple?"

"He is still assisting us," Díaz indicated. "He's clever and can provide useful information and sometimes insight. But he's Lucayan and holds no stature among the island's peoples. The island's Indians view him as a traitor."

The conversation, and a traditional dinner of Castilian beef, wore on past sunset.

"Which of our countrymen rules the land the Indians call Xaraguá?" Ovando asked as the meal concluded.

"The Spaniards there have no leader, and none of them pay heed to us here," Díaz replied.

"The Indian cacica Anacaona is Xaraguá's only ruler," Garay responded, recalling when he'd sailed to Xaraguá's port. "She is a friend, so long as left alone."

"She once was set to give her daughter's hand to one of our dons," Velásquez observed. "Do not underestimate her cunning."

"Xaraguá must be integrated into my control, starting with the Spaniards," Ovando pronounced.

All three agreed emphatically. On that harmonious note, Ovando dismissed them, without revealing policy decisions or affection. He would reserve his judgments on whom to purge until the grand fleet was set to sail home.

In the morning, he dispatched horsemen to summon Roldán to submit in Santo Domingo and to transfer Guarionex to Santo Domingo's jail in the company of the Indian Diego Colón.

⊡ ⊡ ⊡

In the following weeks, the newcomers mining at the Jaina found their dreams largely unfulfilled. Digging themselves, and even supervising conscripted Indians, was arduous. Straining in the streambeds aggravated the illnesses brought on by the local food and water, and that food couldn't adequately support the hundreds digging anyway. Many of those who'd rushed in from Santo Domingo began to stagger back. Death accelerated, and within a month of disembarkation, hundreds of hungry newcomers perished from fevers and dehydration.

◻ ◻ ◻

After coming ashore, Fray Espinar had met with the few veteran churchmen in Santo Domingo and decided initially to divide his Franciscan missionaries into four groups, pending the founding of new townships. He instructed a handful of friars to establish the island's first Franciscan monastery and a small hospital in Santo Domingo under his leadership. A second group was dispatched to establish a second monastery in Concepción, and friars were assigned to Bonao and Santiago. Two stalwart friars began the trek west though Indian country to Xaraguá, intent on establishing a third monastery, their altarpiece and accouterments born by a donkey.

Implementing Cisneros's command, the Franciscans regularly baptized the villagers they encountered en masse, unconcerned by the language barrier.

◻ ◻ ◻

At sunset, Guaorocuyá and Haniguyabá reported to Anacaona, all seated in the inner sanctum of her caney as naborias fanned a small flame.

"Matunherí, there is yet a new guamiquina," Haniguyabá advised, pausing as Anacaona registered surprise.

"What of the first guamiquina, his brother Bartolomé, and Don Guevara?" she asked.

"There's no sign of them."

"What did you learn of the newcomer?" She repressed her remorse for having offered Higueymota's hand to a failure.

"Nothing," Guaorocuyá replied. "We do know that Roldán has departed Magua to meet him in Santo Domingo. Horsemen visit the pale men's inland forts, summoning others. We have no information why."

"What are the new intruders doing? How many march for Xaraguá?"

"Hundreds have gone to gather gold at the Jaina," Guaorocuyá indicated. "But most still linger in Santo Domingo. Many could come here."

"At present, the only pale men approaching Xaraguá are two behiques," Haniguyabá comforted. "The pale men's keenest interest remains the Jaina's gold."

Anacaona sighed heavily. The intelligence was far more favorable than it might have been.

"Dispatch a few warriors to watch over these behiques," she commanded Haniguyabá. "None of my subjects will draw the newest guamiquina's ire by harming them. I shall welcome them, as if graciously."

"Many of the arriving pale men are stricken with disease," Guaorocuyá related. "Some have died."

"Most of the sick languish at Santo Domingo, some at the Jaina," Haniguyabá explained. "But those still healthy don't tend those ill, apparently content to let them die. It's inexplicable from a military perspective, not to mention cruel."

Anacaona's heart thumped, and while resisting optimism, under her breath she exhorted Yúcahu to spare none the pestilence.

"I have information too," she pronounced. "The concubines fear that their masters shall be called to Santo Domingo, just like Roldán. We will benefit if they leave us, so make certain our subjects don't take revenge on them either."

"Cacique Higuanamá reports the pale men have violated her truce with them and that her general shall inflict vengeance," she added. "If that occurs, we pray for her victory. But we shall not join her in battle. War was improvident before. It's impossible now."

Caciques Guarionex and Diego Colón, Summoned to Santo Domingo
(May 1502)

Cacique Diego somberly beheld a horseman approaching and instructed Ariana to take young Diego and their newborn son into the caney. Without dismounting, the rider pronounced that Diego and Guarionex would depart for Santo Domingo the next morning to submit to the new guamiquina Ovando.

"You must obey," Ariana implored after the horseman left. "Remind the newest guamiquina of your service. Convince my brother to relent."

Diego nodded wanly, fearing that Ovando might view his service for Admiral as vice rather than laurel. He reflected that pale men punished more than they rewarded and writhed that his final acts for Admiral would be judged harshly. That night, Yutowa's warning that he'd forever serve as a remora echoed in nightmares.

At dawn, he grimly hugged the children and a tearful Ariana, then hiked to meet the horseman at the gates of Fort Concepción. Guarionex—filthy and emaciated, his ribs protruding from his sunken chest—had been unshackled, lifted from his cell, lain on a litter, and fed. Diego was startled by the singular mercy, and after expressing gratitude to the horseman, he knelt at his brother-in-law's side.

"The newest guamiquina seeks that I become a traitor," Guarionex wryly rasped. "Yúcahu hears my plea."

"Open your eyes wide to your fallen world," Diego implored, astonished by the vitality beneath the frailty. "Prepare to resuscitate yourself to lead what remains of your people."

The horseman ordered naborias to hoist the litter, and they began the trek southeast through the great valley, Diego trudging on foot behind. Villagers they encountered along the path occasionally recognized their once supreme cacique and that he'd been freed at last. Some shouted praise, others prayed for his recovery, and many despaired that his demise had sealed their own.

They rested the night at Bonao and traversed the hills at the Jaina's headwaters the next morning. Diego was astounded to see scores of pale men prone and wasting on streambed embankments. Scores more forlornly stumbled toward Santo Domingo, devastated to have found little or no gold before falling too ill to mine. Corpses littered the area, both pale men and starved Taínos who'd succumbed, exhausted, while panning.

Diego had resided at Isabela but never seen Santo Domingo, and Guarionex had never seen either. When they arrived on the third day,

Diego marveled at the sight of the grand fleet dominating the Ozama's terminal bays, and Guarionex shuddered with dread as he com-
prehended the spread, potency, and permanence of the pale men's
settlement. The horseman deposited them with sentries outside the
guamiquina's fortified residence, and Diego mused that Admiral
must have anguished while being stripped of it.

Commander Ovando soon summoned the two Indians to the
courtyard inside, Guarionex still litter-borne, and bid his butler graciously serve them olives, almonds, and dried oranges from Spain, del-
icacies infrequently shared. He'd grown accustomed to the Indians'
nakedness, and while intending to reform it, he studiously avoided
denigrating that of the two before him, just as he'd refrained from
demeaning the customs of Granadan infidel he met in audience. Guarionex's resilience impressed him more than the emaciation, as men
everywhere regularly died during extended imprisonment. The young
interpreter's maturation to manhood kindled a memory of when he'd
witnessed the youth's baptism in Spain, along with five other Indians
brought to Barcelona after Cristóbal's first voyage. One of the five
had been held to live permanently under his and others' tutelage in
Prince Juan's household.*

Guarionex silently scorned the display of civility, remembering
that Admiral's graciousness was belied by treacheries and enslavements. Diego reflected that the new guamiquina comported himself
with stature and nobility, just like Admiral, superior in courtesy to
other pale men.

"I have come on behalf of King Fernando and Queen Isabel to
institute a more benign rule of this their kingdom and your people,"
Ovando declared. "We don't intend to enslave those loyal to us. I
offer to reinstate you as a cacique and restore your rank, property,
and subjects." He gazed into Guarionex's eyes as Diego interpreted.

"But first, you must accept obedience to the rule of Fernando
and Isabel and myself. Thereafter, as vassals of the king and queen,
your life, and the lives of your subjects, will improve. Your subjects
will attend you and labor for the settlers who own the land, receiving

---

* *Encounters Unforeseen*, chapters IX, X, and XIII, and *Columbus and Caonabó*, chapter IV,
relate the life of this Taíno.

wages for the work, and paying such portion thereof as you and I agree as tribute to the king and queen, setting an example for all." Diego shuddered when translating, the proposal's bare ignominy hateful.

"Guamiquina, I have heard countless promises of friendship, ever diminishing in scope, increasingly odious," Guarionex responded faintly but firmly. He stared back into Ovando's eyes. "Worse, these promises have always been lies, and yours is no exception. I would prefer to die in your jail rather than deceive my subjects into trusting your word."

Diego quivered again, but he translated word for word, unsure of Ovando's expectations or reaction. Ovando folded his arms upon his chest.

"I understand that your home has been taken, as do my king and queen, who sorrow therefore," he replied, pondering whether love or fear would break the chieftain. "On your liberation, I shall return it and provide gifts of clothing, jewels, and such metal cookery as you desire. You will have your own friar to welcome you to the faith so you achieve eternal salvation. You shall have access to me if you or your family or subjects are ever mistreated."

"I have heard all this before," Guarionex replied coldly. "Bribes do not move me. Most of my family and subjects have perished during your conquest. I've already studied and rejected your false religion. I shall achieve eternal salvation by opposing you." He paused before hatching his final gambit. "Your predecessor threatened to dispatch me to your Fernando and Isabel, certain they would persuade me. That is your only recourse, save burying me in your jail."

Ovando churned at the insult to Christ but remained expressionless, hardened to both the battlefield and peacetime hatred of conquered peoples. He'd underestimated the Indians' intellect. Yet he'd felt no sorrow for the infidel, and unlike the queen, none for these naked savages. Colón should have executed this chieftain years ago, leniency for troublemakers bearing no benefit. Hauling the chieftain to Spain served no purpose in conquest. It merely excused him from rendering a punishment that might draw the queen's ire.

"Your intransigence harms your people and yourself," he retorted. "You shall be imprisoned until ships sail to transport you to the king and queen. But my offer stands, and you may accept it if you have a change of heart before then."

Ovando summarily bid sentries haul Guarionex to the fort's prison, then pivoted to Diego.

"The cacique will now languish in the same dungeon that held the Admiral, your protector," he declared softly. He paused, watching the interpreter tremble. "My Diego, you wouldn't remember, but I attended your baptism years ago. I was then a liege to Prince Juan, who honored one of your friends by having him remain as a gentleman at court."

Diego was incredulous and speechless.

"Your friend—and the prince—attained eternal salvation some years thereafter," Ovando noted. "Have you faithfully worshipped Christ since?"

"Yes," Diego lied, struggling for composure.

"Tell me, Diego, why does this cacique still resist our rule? He and his subjects have been conquered, irreversibly. His lands belong to the queen forever. My society is superior to his, and the king and queen offer him and his subjects peaceful admission into it while allowing them to retain their ancestral homes."

"He knows he has lost, but he doesn't see that superiority," Diego replied honestly. "He shuns that admission."

"What of you, Diego? Do you wish that admission and to lead others into it?"

Diego cringed with alarm, hatred of pale men, and self-contempt, loathing for the countless time that a remora's survival achieved merely perpetual torment.

"I've always dutifully served the king and queen's conquest," he mustered.

"The king and queen want peace, not war," Ovando responded, ignoring the failure to respond. "They want your people unmolested and unharmed, content with being their subjects. They want your people to know Christ's love."

Diego scrutinized the pale man's comportment when he chose those words, brooding darkly whether he truly shared his sovereigns' desires or couldn't bear to express their sentiments as his own. His eyes twinkled with cunning, his courtesies were sweet but smacked of insincerity, and his Christ-spirit undoubtedly stood ready with a sword.

"We shall get to know each other, Diego," Ovando declared, certain of Diego's worth at his side, yet doubting loyalty. "I command you to serve me here in Santo Domingo. You may relocate your family here, and you shall remain cacique of your village in the interior, as well."

XII

PRAYERS AND PUNISHMENTS

ISABEL AND CRISTÓBAL,
April–May 1502

On the evening of April 5, Isabel knelt in torchlight before a bare cross in one of the humble, sparse chapels tucked within the cavernous Monastery of Santa María de Guadalupe, where she and Fernando would pass a week en route to Toledo. In the following month, she'd preside at the third succession ceremony transferring her Castilian crown to a child. As a young mother, she'd brightly imagined but one.

The grandeur of the enveloping monastery, the treasure of its venerated Virgin icon, and the majesty of the surrounding mountains comforted her, as they always had. Christ and the Virgin remained content with her devotion and heard her prayers. Memories of decades of worshipping in the monastery cascaded through her thoughts, and she gratefully recognized that its Virgin had shepherded her through darkness many times.

At thirteen, when just a woman, she'd knelt beneath Her beside her half brother, King Enrique IV, as he plotted her marriage to Portugal's king. At twenty-four, she'd worshipped beneath the monastery's great altarpiece together with the husband she herself had chosen. At twenty-six, after interring Enrique's body in the monastery, she'd prayed beneath Her alone, having seized the crown on his death.* She and Fernando had revisited the monastery several times, notably when summoning their nobility to fulfill the Reconquista. At forty-one, she and Fernando had returned triumphantly to thank the Lord for that fulfillment and the Christianization of their kingdoms.

But this evening, at fifty, Isabel couldn't deceive herself with optimism, and the warm memories faded to bald reckonings. Her vigor and strength to follow the Lord's path to victory had declined decidedly. Illness was now the norm, wellness only occasional, and her prayers increasingly extended to matters beyond her influence. She had possessed the power of the Inquisition to reform the worship of thousands, but she couldn't remake Juana with the wisdom and guile to lead her husband to obey. She'd expelled thousands from her realms, but she couldn't ensure that any of her daughters would flourish in foreign kingdoms. She'd conquered and Christianized the infidel at home, but she struggled to compel her subjects across the ocean to Christianly conquer and convert heathen Indians.

Isabel prayed that she and Juana would reconcile and commune, renewing love and lessons on ruling. Death invited union with Christ and rest at His side, together with the souls of Princess Isabel and Princes Juan and Miguel. Death also loomed foreboding, yet only because her work on earth was incomplete. She pledged to herself to finish what she could until her last breath.

▫ ▫ ▫

The next day, April 6, Cristóbal floated his newly requisitioned fleet of four crown-funded caravels a few miles down the Guadalquivir from Seville and beached them on the alluvial sandbanks near Pueblo Viejo (La Puebla del Río), where Bartolomé would supervise the hulls' caulking. During the past weeks, he'd also contemplated death, dispatching documents and instructions to safeguard his legacy and pass on matters of heart and conscience not covered in his will. The Lord had watched over him through fierce tempests, burning calms, and the unworldly Bocas de la Sierpe and del Drago,

---

* *Encounters Unforeseen*, chapter III, depicts the 1477 visit.

but His beneficence was never assured on the ocean—particularly in the unknown, such as beyond Paria and Coquibacoa.

As his legacy's foundation, Cristóbal had added records to the book compiling his financial and other entitlements—now called his *Book of Privileges*—and distributed copies to Fray Gorricio and Nicolò Oderico, Genoa's ambassador to Isabel and Fernando's court. The prior compilation—seized by Bobadilla in Santo Domingo—was to be recovered and entrusted to son Diego. To Oderico, who'd departed for Genoa, he'd penned a brief explanatory letter, opening with a lamentation regarding his loneliness in Spain with Oderico gone, and recording that Isabel and Fernando had promised to fulfill his entitlements. *Their Majesties promise to give me everything that belongs to me.*

Cristóbal had also written the directors of Genoa's prominent Bank of St. George, opening by expressing affection for his homeland. *Although my body walks here, my heart remains there.* He'd honed the swipes at the sovereigns sown in his letter to the pope, noting that the achievements of his enterprise *would shine even more if the shadow of the government did not obscure them.* Son Diego would help the bank with a tenth of his yearly income to reduce Genoa's tax on its citizens' consumption of wheat and wine.

Grasping that the sovereigns would remain the only source of his legacy, he'd privately dispatched a memorandum to Diego with intimate biddings on Diego's conduct at their court and uses of the inheritance. *Serve the king and queen and their children with much love.* Serve the Lord by donating a tenth of the income to the poor. *For her love of me,* look after your brother Fernando's mother Beatriz as your own, distributing her ten thousand maravedís annually, and distribute the same to your aunt Violante. Convince the sovereigns to award your uncle Diego an ecclesiastic appointment.

On April 22, Cristóbal and son Fernando joined Bartolomé to float the caulked caravels downstream and sail them to Cádiz for provisioning. Bartolomé continued to assist, having finally agreed to serve on the voyage. His brotherly love and veneration had surmounted his doubt of the riches and renown to be achieved by the voyage. He'd also foreseen stumbling, ignored and unheeded, if not at Cristóbal's side.

"If we attain Calicut, do we continue round the globe or return east?" Bartolomé asked, daunted by the enormity of attempting the globe's circumvention.

"East!" Cristóbal responded jealously, having wheedled the right to call at Española on the return voyage. "The route is far shorter, as I've proved." He ruminated on the temperate air and gushing spring at Fort Concepción, where his heirs' estate was already plotted. It might be suitable for his own burial. "We may then ascertain whether Ovando remits our lawful share of the gold. We may find proof he misrules."

⊡ ⊡ ⊡

The sovereigns' court arrived in Toledo on April 22, Isabel's fifty-first birthday, and she retired to bed, ill and exhausted. But she and the entire court had closely scrutinized the reports of Juana and Philippe's celebratory ride south through Spain, and she and Fernando had grown guardedly optimistic. Their nobility had extended courtesies and homage in the most grandiloquent Spanish tradition—and Philippe had basked in it. The hospitality had extended to the couple's considerable entourage, as well—two hundred Flemish courtiers, knights, and servants who influenced Philippe's heart and policy—their seduction also being essential.

From Burgos to Madrid—through Valladolid, Medina del Campo, and Segovia—the couple had been greeted by the cities' ranking nobility and prelates beneath a gold brocade canopy heralding Spanish royal authority, then feted with fiestas, bullfights, jousts, hunting forays, and other amusements. They'd been celebrated for a month in Madrid, and Philippe had been served a taste of the Catholic Monarchs' Christian ascendance. Over the Easter holidays, he and Juana sponsored baptisms of Mudejar renouncing their prior faith as a condition to remain in their homeland.

As they approached Toledo, Philippe suffered a bout of measles, and the couple rested in tiny Olias while he recuperated. Unfurling parental love and devotion, Fernando rode urgently with his doctors to Philippe's side, leaving Isabel behind only because she was too infirm to travel. When he arrived, Juana bounded to embrace him, their warmth genuine but tinged with a daughter's resentment of manipulation and a father's despair of control lost.

After Philippe recovered, on May 7, Fernando grandly escorted him and Juana beneath the golden canopy and through Toledo's ancient town gate to tumultuous applause. Isabel and Juana soon tearfully reunited. Their love was heartfelt yet seared with a daughter's resentment of sermon and inability to emulate and a mother's judgment and inability to understand. At Isabel's direction, Archbishop Cisneros conducted Mass for the entire family, and Philippe received another dose of the Catholic Monarchs' temporal and spiritual supremacy.

The effort to wean Philippe from his French attachments was jarred by news arriving from England that Catalina's Arthur had died, and the opulent, gay costumes of successional ceremonies and fiestas were doffed for the black robes of mourning. A requiem Mass was dutifully convened, delaying the succession ceremony. In the interlude, Isabel and Fernando considered Catalina's return to Castile or remarriage to Arthur's younger brother Henry—while Philippe plotted Henry's marriage to his sister Margarite, Prince Juan's widow.

Whispers and moans mounted among Castile's nobility. Philippe's recognition as king consort was improvident, his Flemish knights were knaves. Philippe's courtiers continued to promote King Louis's embrace over Isabel and Fernando's, and Philippe's knights—like Philippe himself—itched and rutted, chafing that Castilian hospitality was long on devotion and short on debauchery.

On May 22, Isabel and Fernando summoned Castile's court to Toledo's great cathedral to recognize Juana as heir to Castile's crown, just like her older brother and sister before, and Philippe as heir king consort. Long overdue, it was finally done, and celebrations would dutifully proceed in the subsequent weeks. That evening, Isabel and Fernando spoke alone.

"We must continue to endear him, snaring his ambition for our crown and presiding among us," Fernando mused aloud.

"I possess neither the wish nor the will to entertain him as would most please him." Isabel grimaced.

"That is secondary. He simply must grasp that our crown holds a greater power for him than the French king's mere alliance."

"We will never make him Spanish."

⊡ ⊡ ⊡

By this time, Cristóbal had provisioned his four ships and sailed with one hundred forty recruits to Gran Canaria.

Like Cristóbal's *Niña*, all four caravels were small and nimble, each bearing fifty to seventy tuns, suited for coastal exploration but large enough to circumvent the globe. Cristóbal and son Fernando berthed on the flagship, nicknamed *La Capitana* and captained by Diego Tristán, a Sevillian leather merchant who'd served faithfully on the second voyage and in Española. Bartolomé presided on the *Santiago de Palos*, which was nominally captained by the crown-nominated Francisco de Porras and berthed his brother Diego de Porras, the crown's accountant and voyage provisioner. Francisco had sailed on Pero Alonso Niño's exploration, and the brothers' sister was mistress to Castile's treasurer. The steadfast Pedro de Terreros served as captain of the *Gallega*, and the *Vizcaína* was commanded by the Genoese merchant nobleman Bartolomeo Fieschi, who hailed from a family that had long provided patronage in Genoa to Cristóbal's late father Domenico.

Cristóbal and Diego de Porras each had enlisted crewmen, a third of whom were teenagers, just as son Fernando, permitting a lower payroll than typical, perhaps attracting those keener for adventure and more pliable during adversity. Most hailed from the small Andalusian ports where sailors still respected Cristóbal's seaside command, although at least seven were Genoese and one Milanese—the sovereigns' prohibition on foreigner settlers either having been waived or considered inapplicable. The Italians' loyalty to Cristóbal could be expected to offset the loyalty of those recruited by the Porrases. Ever committed to Cristóbal, Pedro Fernández Coronel berthed on the *Capitana*. There were a handful of soldiers and a physician. The Franciscan Fray Alexander was the sole cleric willing to sail. Tristán brought his Guinean slave, Diego.

After sundown on May 25, the caravels departed from Gran Canaria southwest across the ocean toward Dominica, where all assumed they'd veer east to traverse Paria's coast.

While ecstatic to be at sea, Cristóbal brooded that any true mariner departing the Canaries to sail beyond Coquibacoa would plan to use Santo Domingo as a way station. A decade earlier, he'd refused to risk his life crossing the Ocean Sea until Isabel and Fernando agreed that he'd rule what he discovered—and he now couldn't even call there.

Ovando, Cacique Diego, Guarionex, and Anacaona,
May–June 27, 1502

"I understand you've prospered on the repartimientos you exacted from Colón," Ovando asserted coldly, as Roldán bowed before him in the courtyard of the governor's residence. "Seat yourself, as we discuss the king and queen's continuing inquiry into your conduct."

"My commander, your predecessor already concluded that inquiry and judged that I have always served the king and queen faithfully," Roldán declared brazenly. "Moreover, the churchmen concluded that this island's riches would have been siphoned to the Genoese if I hadn't opposed Colón's misrule."

"The king and queen weren't satisfied with Commander Bobadilla's inquiry," Ovando replied. "At their order, I shall complete the review of your rebellion against Colón, taking testimony from witnesses to your actions and those of your lieutenants. My findings will be forwarded to the sovereigns, who alone will pass judgment on you."

"Then I shall defend my loyalty and trust in their wisdom."

"I'm also directly empowered to revoke repartimientos I determine were improperly awarded," Ovando pronounced. "The king and queen intended grants only to honorable men of stature with proven service to the crown, not lowborn troublemakers." He relished watching Roldán fight to restrain a crimson blush. "I shall scrutinize every grant you and your followers extorted."

"My commander, be aware that the repartimientos Colón's henchmen received were bribes for their loyalty to him, rather than for their stature or service to the crown." Roldán relished as the newcomer flinched. "Some men followed me, others followed Colón. A man's worthiness in Española hasn't mirrored whether he was born a gentleman in Spain. Those worthy here have become Española's gentlemen, with ranks of Indian butlers and maids." He raised a finger. "Evaluate the material improvements made by those receiving grants. My followers and I have aggrandized this province for the queen as much as anyone."

Ovando sat back in his chair, unable to muster a response, somberly recognizing both Roldán's viewpoint and why Bobadilla hadn't touched him. His warning rendered, he pivoted to seek information.

"Do you control the men residing among the Indians in Xaraguá? Do I need your participation to implement my orders there?"

Roldán scanned Ovando's demeanor, reckoning whether an affirmation would credential a lieutenancy or confess treason.

"After Colón and I settled our differences, I served him by hunting rebels against him who'd settled in Xaraguá," he articulated cautiously. "I no longer reside in my repartimiento there, but those living there would heed my authority were I your lieutenant there."

"Do you command Cacica Anacaona?"

"Certainly," Roldán swaggered.

"Remain in Santo Domingo during my investigation and summon the principal men who have been your followers. I see no need for you or them to be shackled so long as you cooperate."

◫   ◫   ◫

As June dawned, the sailors began to mend the grand fleet and stow fresh water and cazabi, anticipating that by month's end some two dozen ships would leave for Spain under Torres's command.

As June progressed, Ovando duly completed his inquiry into Bobadilla's conduct and delivered a sealed report to Torres for the sovereigns' eyes only. Bobadilla lingered in temporary quarters, free from physical threat yet the butt of derision as settlers surrendered their rescinded share of Española's gold to the crown's treasurer. With Ovando's imprimatur, Carvajal possessed four thousand pesos of gold, worth 1.8 million maravedís, in Cristóbal's name—an allocation Cristóbal would dispute—as well as the chests containing private papers, maps, and learned precedents. Bastidas was released from prison, as Ovando was content to transmit him to Spain for the sovereigns' judgment, and his voyage's booty of gold and captives from the southern coastline was provisionally restored. Arriaga's plan to settle the seventy-three Castilian families in new townships went nowhere, as the husbands and sons joined those hunting for gold rather than seeking plots to homestead and farm.

Death now ravaged the newcomers, who succumbed by the scores daily, approaching a thousand lost. Santo Domingo was overwhelmed by invalids vomiting, excreting, fevering, and languishing incapacitated. They'd returned from the streambeds poorer than before, the cost of their equipment and items swapped with old-timers dwarfing the riches dug. The churchmen could barely bury the corpses. Newcomers also hungered as the grand fleet's haul of biscuits and dried meats and Santo Domingo's native food stores dwindled. Those suffering with families were nursed, but most expiring met death alone and discarded, a lust for gold their only bond to others.

As news of the calamity spread, Taínos throughout Haiti rejoiced—Anacaona in the west, Higuanamá in the east, the Ciguayo to the north, and beneath her breath, even Cacica Catalina at Santo Domingo. Vengeance was sweet, and hope flickered that the pale men would abandon their conquest.

That thought never entered Ovando's consciousness, and as the date for the fleet's departure approached, he made his first decisions public. Roldán and most of the former rebel leadership would be exiled to Spain—as prisoners but unchained—their Indians freed and repartimientos revoked. Another sealed report set forth his findings regarding the rebellion, leaving it to the sovereigns to determine additional punishment.

Roldán and others knew better than to protest. They secreted what gold they could on their persons and said goodbye to their concubines and children, sometimes heart-wrenchingly, sometimes not. Former rebels not exiled who lived outside Xaraguá trembled to proffer homage to Ovando. For the moment, he simply ignored exiling or otherwise punishing the seventy residing in Xaraguá.

After collecting the rescinded gold share, Ovando feared challenging other old-timers further. He also brooded on Díaz, Garay, and Velásquez's warning that Indians would flee upon understanding they were freemen, abandoning farming and mining and thereby exacerbating the mounting hunger and despair.

His obedience to Isabel and Fernando surmounted much of his alarm, but only barely. He proclaimed that, by their order, Indian servants were to be paid fairly for their labor as freemen and tribute would be reimposed on caciques to collect a portion of those payments. But informing the Indians of this freedom wasn't required, and he recoiled from any pronouncement undoing repartimientos of those not exiled.

While deploring concubinage as sinful, he shied from undoing it or promoting marriages, decreeing only that marriage required his approval. Marriage would augment the Spanish husband's claim to the wife's lands and naborias, and he intended to deny it to those whose repartimientos he determined to revoke. More fundamental Christianization of the settlement would have to wait for the abatement of the crisis of sickness and hunger.

□   □   □

Cacique Diego squatted outside the protective wall of the governor's residence, beholding the daily clamor of Santo Domingo's plaza while awaiting Ovando's call. He reminisced that he'd so attended Admiral years before, aboard the first *Santa María*, then the *Niña*, and finally outside Admiral's residence at Isabela. So much hadn't changed since then. So much had.

Most pale men had sickened and hungered within the first weeks of Isabela's settlement, many soon dying, unable or unwilling to digest Taíno food—just as now. Despite that crisis, Admiral had dispatched men from Isabela into the interior to find gold—just as newcomers now rushed of their own volition. The pale men had learned little in conquest, and gold always debased brotherhood.

But Admiral and Isabela's veterans had understood they'd come to conquer a people and an island and that conquest required parley or war with the island's reigning supreme caciques. Whether parleying with Guacanagarí or Guarionex or warring on Caonabó or Mayobanex, Admiral and others had importuned, deceived, and come to blows with an appreciation that the supreme caciques were adversaries who had to be outwitted and outmaneuvered. But now, those arriving perceived they'd come to populate an island already theirs and that the Indians were merely the resident labor force, just like horses and mules in Spain. They used the word *savage* less, *dog* more.

Cacique Diego had overheard his new master speak of Isabel and

Fernando's orders, including to show kindness to the Indians and the precept that they were to work as freemen. But as he watched newcomers trading shirts and pots for Indian servants, he doubted his master's sincerity and brooded that his life as a remora would continue to skirt damnation. While unaware of their new freedom, Taínos living in villages that supported Santo Domingo or mining had begun to flee to the mountains, fearing that the influx of newcomers and the peril of mining would devastate their lives further. He trembled to consider how Ovando would respond and what he'd be tasked to do.

◻   ◻   ◻

Cacique Diego was permitted to bring Guarionex water and cazabi, and for brief interludes, the news from outside. Guarionex was shocked and delighted. The prior occupant of his dungeon had been the first guamiquina! Newcomers were perishing at an astonishing rate. Taínos were resisting oppression, hiding in the mountains. Ships were ready to bear him to Fernando and Isabel.

He ruminated on Yúcahu's prophecy of Taíno extinction and pondered what he'd argue to Fernando and Isabel to undo it. What could he say to them that he hadn't already said to their first guamiquina? After ten years, did they sincerely believe the Christ-spirit blessed their conquest? They'd already replaced their guamiquina twice. Their subjects had fought among themselves and died of disease en masse. Unless they relented, their own souls would follow a dark and dreadful path.

Forlornly, he envisioned that the pale caciques would possess as harsh a character and outlook as their guamiquinas and lieutenants, albeit perhaps within a frame of greater sophistication and wisdom. Words alone would hardly shatter their aspirations or resolve, and before he met them, more proof of their conquest's futility was essential. For the countless time, he knelt in the darkness of a prison to beseech Yúcahu to undo the prophecy, vengeful that Admiral's soul now overheard and invigorated that Yúcahu had recast disease and hunger upon the enemy.

Spare no pale man death, he exhorted. *Starve their wives and children. Destroy their settlements, scatter their gold, and convince*

Fernando and Isabel of their conquest's demise.

◻ ◻ ◻

In mid-June, Cristóbal's fleet of four made landfall at the island south of Dominica (Martinique), having traversed the ocean in twenty-one days, the shortest of his four westward crossings. The *Santiago*, Bartolomé's and the Porrases' ship, had proven itself a poorer sailor and drag on the others, heeling excessively to take water over the rail when the sails swelled. The caravels remained at anchor for three days while their fresh water was replenished.

On the eve of departure, Cristóbal chafed whether to do as he'd promised—course southwest directly to Paria and then past Coquibacoa—or that prohibited—detour significantly northwest to Santo Domingo first. He hadn't repaired the *Santiago* or swapped it for another ship at Gran Canaria, where mariners often addressed fleet defects. But even the Porrases recognized the problem, and the caravel's deficiencies now served as justification for calling at Santo Domingo, despite the sovereigns' prohibition.

Whether others would perceive the excuse as true or trumped-up, Cristóbal pined to confirm that Carvajal was collecting his rightful share of gold and to discover what could be reported of Ovando's failures on the island rightfully his. On June 18, he coursed his fleet north to pass Dominica en route to Santo Domingo. The triumphant demonstration of his geographical theory could wait on the restoration of his rightful station.

◻ ◻ ◻

Anacaona sat in her ballcourt, receiving reconnaissance from scouts and informants regarding the pale men's activities at Santo Domingo, preparing to meet the two behiques who'd just arrived from there.

The information was startling. Many vessels were preparing to depart. Rumor had it that Roldán would be exiled and hauled away! She'd outlasted not only the first guamiquina and Bartolomé, but Xaraguá's greatest defiler. A thousand pale men had now perished at Santo Domingo, and still none more than the two behiques approached Xaraguá. The strategy of separation still held.

But she wouldn't deceive herself. Concubines had related that their masters intended to remain in Xaraguá. The enemy's presence in Santo Domingo and Xaraguá yet maintained their conquest unassailable.

Anacaona courteously summoned the two behiques to present themselves in the ballcourt and informed them that she consented to their presence so long as they respectfully observed her chiefdom's customs. They displayed the idolatries they'd brought to solemnize their incantations to the Christ-spirit and revealed that they planned to establish a *monastery* for worship and a *school* to teach children of caciqual families. She told them that a monastery and school wouldn't violate Xaraguán custom but bid they teach therein only squatters and their families. No one else respected the Christ-spirit. She laughed at them when they proposed mass baptisms.

⊞ ⊞ ⊞

As June waned, the ships of the grand fleet departing awaited only embarkation of their passengers.

Ovando was delighted with the principal cargo stowed with Captain General Torres on the *Santa María de Antigua*—chests bearing a hundred thousand pesos of gold for the sovereigns, worth forty-five million maravedís, as well as the bread loaf–sized nugget. That yield far exceeded all the gold previously remitted from the Indies since the beginning of conquest. Torres relished the thought of placing the chests at Fernando and Isabel's feet and witnessing their joy and relief that their tremendous investment and wait had been gloriously rewarded. Another hundred thousand pesos would be stashed in the pockets of those departing.

One of the smaller caravels, the *Aguja*, separately bore Cristóbal's four thousand pesos under Carvajal's watch.

On June 27, unknown, unexpected, and unwelcome to Ovando and Isabel and Fernando, Cristóbal's four ships skirted Boriquén's coastline, approaching the passage to the eastern tip of Española.

HURIKÁN,
June 28–July 2, 1502

As dawn broke on June 28, fishermen counseled Cotubanamá to examine the sea and sky, and he accompanied them to their beach in the sound sheltered by the island of Adamanay at Haiti's south-eastern coastline. The easterly winds were mild and customary, and nothing suggested a storm that day. But the clouds in the eastern sky—the origin of hurikáns—glowed red and orange, and the water's surface was unctuous, resisting the jaggy ripple occasioned by breezes. Dolphins and other fish jumped perhaps more than usual. Cotubanamá thanked his subjects and bid them alert him promptly if the wind strengthened or veered to northerly. Warning his people of a hurikán was premature, but he'd reevaluate that decision often during the day.

Miles to the south, Cristóbal's fleet coursed past Española's eastern tip and the island he'd named Saona, and he grew similarly concerned about a hurikán. He'd experienced three before, the first when circumventing Española on return from his Cuban exploration, when he'd sheltered in the sound protected by Saona for over a week. At that time, he'd sighted a huge unknown fish at the sea's surface and fiery purple clouds to the east, and Diego—not yet a cacique— had explained that a hurikán lurked nearby. He'd since witnessed hurikáns destroy caravels anchored at Isabela twice. The clouds' tint and formation and fish flying now were ominously similar. Perhaps a trick of the mind, his legs pinched mildly as he strode about the deck, eerily prelude to pains he'd experienced during great storms.[*]

Caciques along Haiti's coasts consulted the sky, sea, and spirits regularly during the day. Cotubanamá judged that the tide had risen higher on the shore than normal, and he warned Higuanamá that he suspected a hurikán at sea. She beseeched Guabancex to spare Higüey—typically the first chiefdom of the island raged upon— and turn Her fury elsewhere. On the northern coast, which some-times bore the fiercest northerly cyclonic winds, Ciguayan caciques implored Guabancex's herald Guataubá to exhaust his gale and rain before landfall. On the southern, Agüeybana suspended his naborias'

---

[*] Perhaps arthritis, aggravated by low barometric pressure.

portage of cazabi to Santo Domingo so his chiefdom would accumulate a reserve, and Haniguyabá dispatched a runner to Anacaona to warn that homage to Guabancex was provident. Anacaona implored Her to spare her people and smite pale men.

As dawn broke on June 29, Haiti's caciques still weren't certain a hurikán would strike, but all recognized that preparing for one was urgent. So did Cristóbal. The eastern clouds glowed darker crimson and even black, waves pushed higher on beaches, and while the weather remained rainless and temperate on land and at sea, mild squalls frequently swirled across the ocean's surface. In Higüey, Cotubanamá ordered his subjects to yank their canoes and fishing gear inland, and Higuanamá directed nitaínos to gather cazabi and other food for a week. She also initiated a chain of smoke signals warning those inland across the island. In Magua's great valley, Manicoatex spotted signals and relayed on his own. He urged Guabancex's assistant Coatrísquie to forebear the flooding of rivers and ordered his subjects to relocate to bohíos on ground above the floodplains of the Yaque and Camú. On the northern shore, Ciguayan caciques bid villagers congregate in bohíos unendangered by falling trees and mountain mudslides, and along the southern, Agüeybana, Catalina, and Haniguyabá directed their villagers to flee inland for the shelter of hills and mountains. In Xaraguá, Anacaona commanded her subjects, including the concubines, to seek haven in caves or their villages' sturdiest bohíos.

Cacique Diego had relocated Ariana and their children to a bohío in Catalina's village across the Ozama from the governor's compound, and when he awoke with them there that morning, he instructed Ariana to take the children to the riverbank at dusk. As a remora, he remained on call and risked reprimand by deserting his duty to lead them to safety inland. He assured her they'd all shelter within the compound's stone wall that evening.

As he left for the compound, Diego mused that the remora wasn't duty bound to warn a foolish fisherman of looming doom. Liberation might follow the fool's demise. He disdained warning his new master, and while anxious for his family's safety, he relished—for the first time in years—that deep within he remained *Bakako*.

As the sun rose, Ovando, Torres, and the fleet's captains and pilots observed balmy weather, and Ovando directed the crews and passengers—over seven hundred persons—to commence embarkation onto the two dozen ships for departure the next morning. Passengers included crown officers responsible for the fleet, Commander Bobadilla, Roldán and his exiled rebels, and Cristóbal's factors, as well as some quitting Española, old-timers wary of Ovando and newcomers jarred by failure in mining and wracked by fever and diarrhea. Bobadilla and Roldán were ferried to board the *Santa María de Antigua* to sail under Torres's custody. Pero Alonso Niño would serve as the flagship's experienced pilot, its chests of gold just as vital—at least to Isabel and Fernando—as the lives of those sailing. Carvajal, safeguarding Cristóbal's gold, would be joined aboard the *Aguja* by Bastidas and his pilot La Cosa, who required a ship to return from the expedition they'd begun two years earlier, together with their former crew and slaves from the southern landmass.

At midday, Ovando ordered Guarionex's transfer from the fort's dungeon to Torres's custody aboard the flagship, and with the chieftain's arms braced on their shoulders, Cacique Diego and a guard hoisted him to the ferrying launch at the Ozama.

"I fear you depart into a hurikán," Bakako told him, confident the guard understood none of his words. "The pale men fail to see it. They risk not only their lives but yours, as well as the gold they've amassed."

Guarionex was startled, nearly losing his grip, and Bakako and the guard clutched him to prevent his collapse.

"That is excellent," he whispered. "Don't tell them. Let Guabancex inflict vengeance long overdue."

The two men embraced at the Ozama, understanding it was for the last time.

"Take care of your family, Bakako," Guarionex whispered. "I shall beseech Guabancex to rage more horribly than ever before."

⊡   ⊡   ⊡

Late that afternoon, Cristóbal's fleet hove to off Santo Domingo, and he dispatched Terreros ashore to request Ovando's permission to harbor in the Ozama to replace one of his ships and shelter for eight days to ride out an imminent great storm.

"Your presence here violates the king and queen's express orders!" Ovando stammered to Terreros when they met outside the church. "Your fleet is 100 leagues off course." He welled with distrust for Cristóbal's infamous exaggerations and deceptions. "The weather suggests no storm." He folded his arms menacingly, furious that Cristóbal likely intended to disrupt his nascent command of Española, stirring dissatisfaction and even rebellion.

"My governor, crown officers aboard the Admiral's fleet can attest that their own caravel should be replaced," Terreros replied. "You needn't take the Admiral's word alone. As for the weather, these Indies experience tremendous storms that the Indians call hurikáns. I've beheld them thrice serving the Admiral. The conditions are ordinary before they hit, horrific after. You tempt the devil by disregarding the Admiral's judgment."

"Don't dare deceive me," Ovando retorted. "Plenty of experienced mariners serve me, including none other than Pero Alonso Niño and Juan de la Cosa. They board my fleet to return to Spain and will depart tomorrow, carrying the Admiral's gold. No one has warned of a dangerous storm. Tell the Admiral permission to harbor on Española violates his orders and is denied."

That evening, Cristóbal and Terreros huddled aboard *La Capitana*. Cristóbal chaffed at the denial of permission to swap out the *Santiago*. The rejection of his mariner's plea for shelter from a storm—no less on the very island and port he'd discovered and built for the sovereigns—brought him to a jealous rage. But his anger was short-lived. During the night, the customary easterly wind petered and died, supplanted by a northern breeze. By morning twilight on June 30, the breeze had strengthened to a brisk northeasterly wind.

By dawn, Cristóbal—and all Haiti's caciques—had no doubt a hurikán was bearing directly upon them. Cristóbal hurriedly dispatched Terreros ashore to warn Ovando to delay his fleet's departure until the storm passed and to advise that, despite his denial of permission, Cristóbal's ships would shelter at the nearest natural harbor to the west.

At the church, Terreros again warned Ovando—with Torres and a group of mariners circled about them—that the Admiral predicted a hurikán soon would strike. He beseeched Ovando to keep his fleet anchored and well battened down in the Ozama and to secure the town's buildings. Ovando and the captains and pilots remained unconvinced, including Niño and La Cosa, marveling instead that the weather and sailing conditions were ideal and shouldn't go to waste. The northeasterly offshore wind permitted skirting Española's coast east in one tack, rather than bucking the prevailing headwinds for days, as typical. Some laughed, mocking the Admiral as a visionary or prophet. Niño and La Cosa chuckled politely yet silently ruminated that mocking the Admiral's seamanship was dimwitted.

◻   ◻   ◻

As the sun rose and Taínos everywhere scrambled for shelter, Torres commanded his fleet to weigh anchor and depart for Spain. The two dozen ships soon were strung in a line smartly coursing the coastline eastward. All aboard—save Guarionex and the slaves from the southern landmass—perfunctorily sang a hymn to the Virgin for safe passage. Cristóbal promptly took his four ships a few miles west to anchor in the mouth of the Jaina, which provided some protection from northerly and westerly winds, and he led his crews in fervent worship to both the Lord and Virgin.

Chained on deck to a bulwark of the *Santa María de Antigua*, Guarionex relished observing the clouds and winds and the arrogance of the men who'd abused and enslaved his people for almost a decade. Torres and Niño, who'd hauled his subjects to servitude in Spain, now cheerfully hauled the gold the guamiquina had always demanded. Roldán, whose lieutenant had raped one of his wives, sauntered smugly about the deck unchained, pockets bulging with the gold panned by deceased Taíno slaves. The second guamiquina's pockets were stuffed similarly. Guarionex exhorted Guabancex, Guataubá, and Coatrísquie to strike and Yúcahu and Attabeira to grant no mercy. *Sink every ship afloat, destroy every building in Santo Domingo and Concepción, and drown or crush every pale man!*

At the governor's residence, Bakako squatted at his usual station for some hours, awaiting tasks. He had a choice to whom he'd worship, and he took no chances, pleading to each of Guabancex, Yúcahu, and the Christ-spirit to spare him and his family. When the sky darkened before sunset and the northeasterly wind heightened to a gale, he stole away to commandeer one of the launches beached at the Ozama and ferried a trembling Ariana and their boys across. As the first rain came, Bakako implored the compound's sentries to permit him to shelter his family within, and with a storm no longer in doubt, the sentries admitted them inside the protective wall. After sunset, Bakako snuck about the compound's storeroom, gathering cazabi sufficient for his family for a week.

During the night, the hurikán swept onto Haiti and Española, hurtling across Higüey's eastern coast to engulf and devastate the entire island. Torrential rains flooded villages and plazas. Ferocious winds uprooted trees and shattered Taíno bohíos and Spanish shacks, including in Santo Domingo and Concepción. Debris hurtled danger- ously, mortally threatening those whose shelters were swamped or destroyed. Along the coasts, enormous waves tore viciously, and the sea breached inland, ruining farms. In the interior, the Yaque, Camú, and other rivers flooded their embankments, destroying cropland in the fertile valleys. The fury and darkness pierced every Taíno and Spaniard's heart that death was at hand, and no one felt the dread of death's precipice more than those at sea.

When the maelstrom hit, Torres's fleet had rounded north off- shore Espanola's eastern tip, now taking the cyclonic winds and driving rains over starboard, which propelled the fleet toward its shatter on the craggy coastline. Towering waves crashed on the ship's decks, drenching the crews flailing in darkness, flooding the holds, and hurtling the stowage and passengers to and fro. Captains feared the hulls would rupture, pilots desperately fought to tack into the storm to avoid ruin ashore, and sailors clung to masts and bulwarks lest they be thrown overboard. Many were, rendering the ships even more helpless.

Aboard the flagship, Torres grimly rued he'd known Cristóbal to be both a liar and the greatest mariner living and that he'd erred gravely by ignoring the latter. Delay in the fleet's departure of just a day to test Cristóbal's sincerity and mariner's know-how could have diverted the disaster looming. Commander Bobadilla despaired that he'd never wanted to serve in Española, hadn't pleased his sover- eigns, and might never arrive to tell them why Cristóbal's incarcera- tion had been necessary and just. Roldán gritted his teeth, incensed that Cristóbal might now be revenged. Guarionex, furiously washed and whipped by the waves, wind, and rain while chained on deck, rejoiced that his prayers were being met and beseeched Guabancex to rage even more harshly.

Aboard both the flagship and the *Aguja*, Torres, Niño, Carvajal, and La Cosa each wretchedly reproached himself for failing to seek a harbor when the rain first began. La Cosa had sailed with Cristóbal on the Cuban exploration and anchored with him in the sound at Saona to wait out the hurikán then blowing. In the darkness, he turned the *Aguja* about to backtrack there, running with sea pounding the hull portside and astern while the cyclonic gale veered southerly, hurtling spray across the bow and into his face. Niño hadn't participated in the Cuban exploration or visited the sound, but he'd seen enough tempests and heard enough of hurikáns to admit Cristóbal's prescience. He, too, brought his ship about, seeking the sound he understood existed.

Torres and Carvajal both beseeched the Lord's mercy—Torres that He spare the flagship, so the sovereigns received their gold, Carvajal that the *Aguja* be spared, so Cristóbal received his. Niño and La Cosa brooded that they'd sailed about the Indies side by side with Cristóbal for years, yet his understanding of the Indies' waters and weather uncannily exceeded their own.

Aboard his fleet to the west, Cristóbal and his crews prayed the anchors of their ships would hold them close by the Jaina's mouth. Wind and current began to drag the ships apart, and Cristóbal despaired for the lives of his son and brother.

Santo Domingo and Cacique Catalina's village were razed to the ground during the night as the hurikán's eye approached. Only the stone portions of the governor's compound and a few stone homes survived. Ovando and his lieutenants hunkered in the residence in darkness, overwhelmed by the storm's severity, worshipping the Lord and Virgin as they never had. Like his queen, Ovando perceived that human strife was embedded within the encompassing struggle between the Lord and Satan, and he dreaded that Satan had come to punish him and his mission. The deadly storm undoubtedly would further decimate his command, already halved by disease and hunger. All the sovereigns' gold might sink to the bottom of the sea. Most everything already built in Española would be destroyed, forcing him to start afresh from nothing.

Bakako, Ariana, and the children clutched each other inside a doorway of the residence, grateful for their admission inside. Bakako prayed desperately for the structure to hold intact. But he envisioned Guarionex beseeching quite the opposite and bittersweetly mused that his own death would end the remora's duty.

On July 1, dawn broke darkly and late, as the hurikán raged on. At the Jaina's mouth, the *Santiago*'s anchor chain snapped and the caravel was driven to sea, losing the shoreline's lee to be engulfed in the storm's full rage. Bartolomé fought to regain the lee by sailing into the wind, but the imperfect ship could barely stay afloat, no less advance. While *La Capitana*'s anchor chain held, those of the other two ships soon also broke, and Cristóbal watched them swept out of sight into the fury, trembling he'd lost them too.

Torres's fleet was scattered across a broad swath of ocean as the cyclonic gale, now southerly, thrust swells north in conflict with those marching east. He and the fleet's captains scanned a full circle to sight other ships in vain, each despairing that all the others had foundered. Many ships had or would that day, hulls rupturing at sea or dashed upon Española's eastern shore. Many captains and pilots attempted retreat—as the flagship and the *Aguja*—although many were unaware of the haven of Saona's sound or missed it.

The *Aguja*, piloted by La Cosa, did attain the sound's safety. Carvajal collapsed with relief that he might yet fulfill his mandate to deliver his master's gold. Bastidas rejoiced he might yet complete his voyage. The slaves from the southern landmass simply wondered what horror came next.

The conflagration of waves surging north and marching east massed pyramidical tops towering over troughs sucked deeply below, pushing the *Santa María de la Antigua* to pinnacles from which it precipitously plummeted to be overwhelmed by enormous walls of water surging over it. Torres and Niño fought to maintain their stations, clenching their jaws as the ship's sails, rigging, and masts were torn away. Sailors disappeared overboard, and the hull groaned even louder than the gale. All aboard knew they were doomed and said their last prayers. As the hull rose to astounding height, Niño forlornly recognized that the sound would never be reached. As the hull crashed, it shattered, and the ocean claimed everyone aboard and all the sovereigns' gold.

As he gasped his last breath, Antonio de Torres's final memory was of Isabel and Fernando complimenting his loyal service and entrusting him with great endeavors. While he would miss his family and royal ennoblements dearly, death was preferable to returning without the gold. As the sea washed over him, Pero Alonso Niño's last visions were of his wife and children, the glory of kneeling at the king and queen's feet when they anointed him to explore, the pearls and slaves he'd reaped, and as he sucked water into his lungs, Cristóbal lecturing him not to sail until the weather was certain.

Commander Francisco de Bobadilla met his drowning as the Christian knight he was, accepting that duty for the sovereigns always risked death. His last thought was that Satan had won a battle, his last wish that Satan would take Cristóbal, as well.

Francisco Roldán clutched the gold in his pockets and knew that the weight mercifully would send him to the bottom quickly. He held his breath to the end, as a train of visions cascaded before his eyes—his Spanish wife and daughter, his command of highborn and lowborn countrymen in Española, his rule of a kingdom of savages, and most pleasantly, Higueymota's supple body. As he sank, his final vision was darker—Anacaona mocking that Higueymota would never be his.

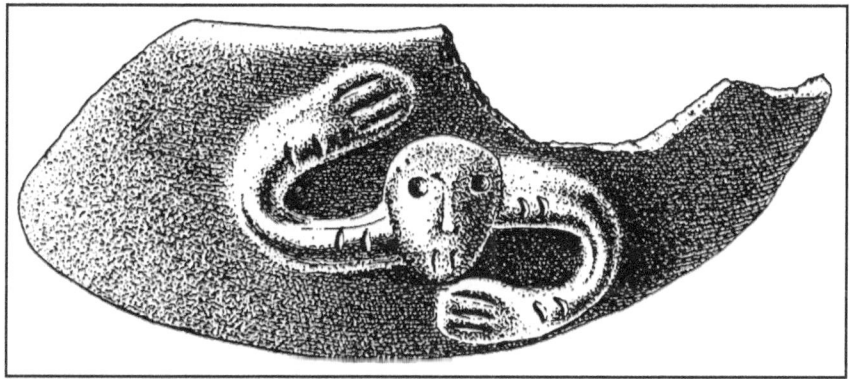

Guabancex.

When the hull collapsed, supreme cacique Guarionex was already nigh dead, having suffered exposure to the sea, wind, and rain for almost two days. Yet he, too, knew that he'd taken his last breath. His last invocation was simply to thank Guabancex and Yúcahu for hearing the voices of all Taíno peoples—living and dead—and to exhort Guabancex to continue to rage until the prophecy of extinction was undone.

⊡   ⊡   ⊡

On July 2, the sun rose over a tranquil sea and a serene Haiti and Española. Of Torres's fleet, eight ships, including the *Aguja*, had survived intact enough to proceed to Spain after mending that summer and autumn, the remainder having sunk at sea or shattered ashore. Five hundred men had drowned. All four of Cristóbal's fleet—and all his crews—survived, and as he'd instructed prior to the hurikán, they rendezvoused the next day in a small natural harbor further west on Española's southern coast (Puerto Viejo de Azua). But only the Lord and Guabancex then knew all that, and it would be weeks, months, or even years before those surviving the hurikán knew the fate of the others who'd suffered it.

In Santo Domingo, Commander Ovando—unaware of what had transpired elsewhere—surveyed the death and destruction, strutting through the ruins of the town with lieutenants and Cacique Diego. The old-timers and Indians had known the best places to shelter, so death had visited newcomers disproportionately. When they arrived at the ruins of the small church, Ovando gazed across the river.

"Where did all the Indians flee to?" he asked Diego.

"Mountains and hillsides, ravines and caves."

"Perhaps we shall rebuild there, on the ruins of their village," Ovando observed, folding his arms across his chest.

Diego trembled as he contemplated the man he now served. The only other man he'd known with such undaunted resolve in the face of disaster and doom was Admiral.

Isabel and Anacaona,
Early July 1502

By early July, Toledo's celebrations had concluded, and Isabel and Fernando prepared to travel to Zaragoza to obtain the Aragonese nobility's recognition of Juana's succession later that month. Good news had arrived from Lisbon—María had safely given birth to her firstborn, a boy poignantly named Juan. But Isabel's health had deteriorated again, forcing her to bed, where the doctors bled her to remove impurities apparently plaguing her. The effort to wean Philippe from his French attachments and enjoy a Spanish heritage was souring.

One morning, Fernando sat alone with Isabel at her bedside as they decided that Isabel would recuperate in Toledo while he, Juana, and Philippe traveled to Zaragoza without her.

"You must write me how it goes," she bid her husband. "Perhaps the Lord spares me another debate on the ability of a woman to rule." She smiled. "Perhaps He relieves me of the duty of beholding Philippe trumpeted yet again."

"My beloved, rest," Fernando replied. "What comforts would you enjoy?"

"Have a few of my altar paintings set before me. Perhaps later today, when I'm stronger, I shall pray in the church we built."

Fernando left her, and a dozen or so of the religious panels were arrayed about the bedside, including depictions of Christ teaching in the desert, entering Jerusalem, and serenely converting the Samarian. Isabel was pleased, and her thoughts drifted back and forth between Christ's reign on earth and her rule of her kingdoms. She was comforted that she'd warred and conquered righteously in His name throughout her life. The depictions also reminded that He'd converted followers with love, and she fleetingly recalled that she still hoped to do so in the Indies—at least with those Indians who peacefully accepted her conquest and a lesser station within superior Christian Spanish civilization.

That evening, she rose feebly but determined to worship alone in the church of San Juan de los Reyes. She declined the participation of a confessor and even Fernando's companionship. Attendants helped her from her bed to a carriage, then to the first pew before the altarpiece.

Penitently, she mused that, for her entire adult life, she had confessed to the Lord her guarded secrets and bouts of conscience mostly through two churchmen, Archbishops Talavera and Cisneros. The

seizure of the throne before rival claimants, including her own husband. The cold-hearted breaking of friendships, promises, and alliances when circumstances changed. The excesses of men under her
command that might have been restrained, particularly in the Indies.

But she hadn't resumed her once intimate relationship with Archbishop Talavera when in Granada, and while Archbishop Cisneros
remained her confessor publicly, she'd dismissed him from her side
after the Koran burnings, permitting him to return to his palace and
cell in Álcala de Henares until the succession ceremony. She still
admired him. But she no longer considered any prelate's guidance or
blessing necessary for her decisions on how Christ wished her kingdoms ruled.

She reflected on Cisneros's admonishment, rendered during confession in that same pew five years before. *All means devoutly taken
to bring souls to Christ are blessed and absolved.*

Deep within, at the boundary of consciousness, Isabel brooded
whether her conquest of the Indies was so devoutly taken and worthy
of such absolution.

▣   ▣   ▣

When the hurikán departed west, Anacaona devoted a week to
healing her subjects who'd lost loved ones and inspecting the damage.
She was borne on a litter through Xaraguá's great plain, over the
southern mountains to Haniguyabá's chiefdom, west along a portion
of the coastal peninsula, and then back along the shore lining the
great gulf, where she was taken by canoe to the large island within.
She conducted solemn funerals for those who'd drowned in floods or
been crushed by debris, cheered villagers to rebuild their bohíos, and
led village councils allocating cazabi and other food while damaged
crops were restored. Everywhere she went, her subjects rejoiced that
Guabancex had dealt a blow to the pale men—regardless of the blow
to themselves. Everywhere, they adored and adulated her as their
supreme cacique—now a year after her brother's death and a decade
since the enemy's invasion.

On return to her inland village, she summoned Guaorocuyá and
Haniguyabá to her garden to report what they'd learned of the enemy's fate.

"Their homes and forts in Santo Domingo and Concepción have been destroyed, but most men ashore have survived," Guaorocuyá reported. "Incredibly, many departed on their vessels directly into the hurikán, and hundreds perished at sea. Corpses and the vessels' wreckage have washed onto Higüey's beaches."

"Four vessels were blown west and harbor offshore, east of us," Haniguyabá added. "They appear not to pose a threat, seemingly intent on departing after repair. Scouts monitor them."

"How many pale men remain in Santo Domingo? Did Guabancex spare the new guamiquina?"

"More than a thousand survive in Santo Domingo, still far exceeding the number in prior years," Guaorocuyá warned. "The new guamiquina struts unharmed."

After dismissing them, Anacaona strolled in the garden alone. She was humbled by Guabancex's extraordinary power, which vastly exceeded that of men, olive or pale. But Guabancex hadn't fulfilled all her prayers, and perils and evils still loomed. The pale men's presence remained committed and invulnerable.

She halted before the bayahibes and gazed respectfully at their delicate flowers and vicious needles. The day for violence might come, at the newest quamiquina's hand or her own. She prayed it would be hers.

PARTICIPANTS AND TAÍNO SPIRITS

(AS OF 1498 UNLESS OTHERWISE INDICATED)
(ALL HISTORIC PERSONS UNLESS OTHERWISE INDICATED)

TAÍNOS

Supreme Taíno caciques and family members:

Anacaona, of Xaraguá's caciqual family, younger sister of Behecchio, widow of Caonabó

    Higueymota, daughter

Behecchio, supreme cacique of Xaraguá

Caonabó, deceased supreme cacique of Maguana

Guaorocuyá, Behecchio's nephew

Guacanagarí, deceased supreme cacique of Marien

Guanahattabenecheuá, one of Behecchio's wives

Guarionex, supreme cacique of Magua

Higuanamá, supreme cacique of Higüey

Manicoatex, cacique in northern Cibao, younger brother of Caonabó, successor ruler of Maguana

Mayobanex, supreme cacique of Ciguayo

Other Taíno leaders:

Agüeybana, cacique of coastal territory east of Santo Domingo

Cacibaquel, deceased supreme cacique of Magua, Guarionex's father

Catalina, cacique of village on west side of Ozama River opposite Santo Domingo (Taíno name unknown)

Cotubanamá, vassal cacique and general for Higuanamá, residing in Higüey

Haniguyabá, vassal cacique to Behecchio and Anacaona, residing on Xaraguá's southern coastline

Maguatiquex, cacique in Magua

Macís, cacique in Magua

"Doctor," cacique in Magua (Taíno name unknown)

Taínos enslaved to serve Cristóbal Colón directly and family (all historic persons, with fictitious birth names as indicated):

Cacique Diego Colón, Guanahanían, enslaved October 14, 1492, baptized in 1493 in Spain, fictitious birth name Bakako

Ariana, younger sister of Guarionex, fictitious birth name, married in 1495 to Cacique Diego Colón

Diego, son

Cristóbal, Haitian, born in a village near Isabela, enslaved in 1494, baptized in 1496 in Spain

Pedro, Haitian, born in a village near Isabela, enslaved in 1494, baptized in 1496 in Spain

Yutowa, deceased Guanahanían, enslaved October 14, 1492

EUROPEANS

Spanish royal family:

Queen Isabel I of Castile, queen of Aragón

King Fernando II of Aragón, king of Castile

Isabel, daughter, married to Portugal's King Manoel

Miguel, son

Prince Juan, son, deceased

Juana, daughter, married to Archduke Philippe of Austria and Burgundy

Leonor, daughter

Charles, son, b. 1500

Isabel, daughter, b. 1501

María, daughter

Catalina, daughter

Cristóbal Colón and family:
Admiral Cristóbal Colón (Cristoforo Colombo in Ligurian), referred to by Taínos as the guamiquina (the "leader" of his people)

Diego, Cristóbal's first son, born of his deceased Portuguese wife, Filipa Moniz Perestrelo

Fernando, Cristóbal's second son, born of the Andalusian mistress he discarded, Beatriz Enríquez de Arana

Bartolomé Colón, Cristóbal's oldest surviving younger brother, appointed Adelantado (frontier governor) in Cristóbal's absence from Española

Diego Colón, Cristóbal's youngest brother

Principal ministers and administrators for Queen Isabel and King Fernando, in Spain:
Ximénez de Cisneros, confessor to Isabel, Archbishop of Toledo

Hernando de Talavera, Archbishop of Granada

Alonso of Aragón, Archbishop of Zaragoza, King Fernando's illegitimate son

Juan Rodríguez de Fonseca, Bishop of Badajoz

Íñigo Lópes de Tendilla, governor of Granada

Gonzalo Gómez de Cervantes, interim replacement for Fonseca in 1501

Jimeno Briviesca, royal accountant for Indies

Diego Márquez, royal overseer for Indies treasury functions

Crown courtiers or appointees serving in Indies:
Antonio de Torres, crown's senior courtier on Cristóbal's second voyage (1493) and for various resupply fleets thereafter

Juan Aguado, dispatched in 1495 to investigate Cristóbal Colón

Francisco de Bobadilla, a knight Commander of the Order of Calatrava, temporary Indies governor installed in 1500

Fray Nicolás de Ovando, a Commander of the Order of Alcántara, Indies governor installed in 1502

Cristóbal Colón's Officers and Settlers in Española loyal to him or not in rebellion:

Pedro de Arana, third voyage fleet captain and brother of Cristóbal's former lover Beatriz Enríquez de Arana

Miguel Ballester, Fort Concepción's commander

Carlos, a fictitious carpenter

Alonso Sánchez de Carvajal, third voyage fleet captain

Rafael Cattaneo, Cristóbal's Genoese factor

Giovanni Antonio Colombo, third voyage fleet captain and Cristóbal's first cousin

Pedro Fernández Coronel, captain general of supply ships dispatched in February 1498

Diego Velásquez de Cuéllar, nobleman, participated in Cristóbal's second voyage and settled in Española thereafter

Miguel Díaz, founder of Santo Domingo

María Fernández, Cristóbal's chambermaid

Francisco de Garay, crown notary and founder of Santo Domingo

Hernan Peréz Mateos, third voyage fleet captain

Pedro Ortiz, Cristóbal's chaplain

Juan Portugués, Cristóbal's Guinean manservant

Cristóbal Rodríguez, nicknamed "La Lengua" (the "tongue")

Pedro de Salcedo, Cristóbal's page

Pedro de Terreros, third voyage fleet captain

Francisco Velázquez, Fort Concepción's captain, successor to Ballester after 1499

Settlers in Española in rebellion against Cristóbal Colón:

Francisco Roldán, leader of rebellion

Adrian de Múxica, minor nobleman, cousin to Don Fernando de Guevara

Diego de Escobar

Pedro de Riquelme

Churchmen in Española:

Ramón Pané, Hieronymite, arriving on Cristóbal's second voyage (1493)

Juan Leudelle, Franciscan, arriving first on Cristóbal's second voyage, returning with Bobadilla (1500)

Juan de Tisín, Franciscan, arriving first on Cristóbal's second voyage, returning with Bobadilla

Francisco Ruiz, Franciscan and master of Archbishop Cisneros's household, arriving with Bobadilla

Juan de Robles, Franciscan, arriving with Bobadilla

Juan de Trasierra, Franciscan, arriving with Bobadilla

Alonso del Viso, Benedictine, arriving with Bobadilla

Alonso del Espinar, Franciscan, arriving with Ovando (1502)

Voyagers licensed by Bishop Fonseca and sailing with those licensed (commencing 1499):

Alonso de Hojeda (1499)

    Don Fernando de Guevara, nobleman

    Juan de la Cosa

    Amerigo Vespucci

Pero Alonso Niño and Cristóbal Guerra (1499)

Vicente Yáñez Pinzón (1499)

Diego de Lepe (1499)

Luis Guerra and Alonso Vélez de Mendoza (1500)

Cristóbal Guerra (1500)

Rodrigo de Bastidas (1501)

    Juan de la Cosa

Alonso de Hojeda (1502)

    Don Fernando de Guevara, nobleman

Captains sailing with Francisco de Bobadilla in 1500:

Alonso de Vallejo

Andrés Martin de la Gorda

Voyagers sailing with Nicolás de Ovando in 1502:

Luis de Arriaga, also participated in Cristóbal's second voyage

Cristóbal de Cuéllar, nobleman, royal accountant

Juan de Esquivel

Pedro de Las Casas, also participated in Cristóbal's second voyage

Bartolomé de Las Casas, son

Juan Ponce de Leon, nobleman, also participated in Cristóbal's second voyage

Diego de Nicuesa

Officers on Cristóbal's fourth voyage:

Bartolomeo Fieschi, Genoese nobleman, captain

Diego de Porras, crown accountant

Francisco de Porras, captain

Diego Tristán, captain

Others in Queen Isabel's court or associated with her reign or Cristóbal Colón:

Pedro Mártir de Anglería, Italian humanist in Isabel's court

Andrés Bernáldez, curate of Los Palacios (near Seville)

Beatriz de Bobadilla, engaged to Alonso de Lugo, a former lover of Cristóbal Colón

Beatriz de Bobadilla, Queen Isabel's confidant, sister to Francisco de Bobadilla

Alonso de Lugo, Canarian conquistador

Gaspar Gorricio de Novara, Carthusian friar assisting Cristóbal

Nicolò Oderico, Genoa's ambassador to Queen Isabel's court

Gonzalo Fernández de Oviedo, courtier in Prince Juan's household

Juana de la Torre, Queen Isabel's household confidant

Pedro de Torres, entrusted by Queen Isabel to gather Indians to be manumitted

Papacy:

Pope Alexander VI, the Aragonese Rodrigo Borja

Portuguese royal family:
  King Manoel I

Austrian royal family:
  Maximillian of Austria, leader of Holy Roman Empire
    Philippe, son, Archduke of Austria and Burgundy
    Margarite, daughter, widow of Prince Juan

Other European royalty:
  King Henry VII of England
    Arthur, son
  King Louis XII of France
    Claude, daughter

Portuguese and English explorers:
  John Caboto, Italian explorer for King Henry
  Vasco da Gama, Portuguese explorer for King Manoel
  Pedro Alvares Cabral, Portuguese nobleman sailing for King Manoel
  Gaspar Corte Real, Portuguese explorer of northern landmass for King Manoel

TAÍNO SPIRITS AND ANCESTRAL PERSONS

Yúcahu, the spirit of yuca and male fertility, also being master of the sea, fatherless, and the most important spirit in daily life

Attabeira, Yúcahu's mother and the provider of water for crops and other nourishment

Guabancex, the female spirit of hurricanes and destruction

  Coatrísquie, Guabancex's male assistant who floods land

  Guataubá, Guabancex's male herald who orders wind and rain

Guabonito, ancestral heroine who is rescued from the sea by Guahayona and cures him

Guahayona, ancestral hero who leads Taíno women from the Cacibajagua (Cave of Jagua)

Maquetaurie Guayaba, lord of the dead

Opiyelguobirán, guardian of the dead

Yaya, the supreme spirit

GLOSSARY

TAÍNO WORDS

Consistent with *Encounters Unforeseen* (2017) and *Columbus and Caonabó* (2021), Taíno words are presented herein as shown in the left column below, with their Spanish spelling based upon Julian Granberry and Gary Vescelius's *Languages of the Pre-Columbian Antilles*, William F. Keegan and Lisabeth A. Carlson's *Talking Taíno: Caribbean Natural History from a Native Perspective,* and other sources.

Indigenous Taíno scholars have undertaken projects to revive Taíno language and compile dictionaries with word spellings and definitions consistent with linguistically related languages, recently including Jorge Baracutay Estevez and Jessie Hurani Marrero's *Hiwatahia: Hekexi Taino Language Dictionary* (2nd ed., 2023) and Roberto Múkaro Agueibaná Borrero and Erica Mercado Moore's *Gu'ahia Taíno: We Speak Taíno, A Classic Taíno Dictionary and Grammar Guide*, vol. 1 (2023). Alternative spellings (but not alternative definitions) for the words used herein according to these works are shown in italics below (H for *Hiwatahia*; G for *Gu'ahia*).

areíto	song, dance (H&G, *areíto*)
batey	ball game, ballcourt, or ceremonial plaza (H, *batey*; G, *batei*)
behique	shaman (i.e., a priest and doctor) (H&G, *behike*)
bohío	house, home (H&G, *bohio*)
boniata	sweet potato (H, *batata*; G, *batáta*)
cacique	chief (H, *kaxikwa*; G, *kasike*)
caney	a chieftain's home (H, *kaney*; G, *kanei*)

cazabi	cassava, a toasted bread made from yucca (H, *kasabi*; G, *kasabe*)
cemí	spirit or object that represents spirit, typically of stone, wood, or cotton (H, *semi*; G, *semí*)
chicha	corn beer (H, *xixa*; G, *chicha*)
cohoba	narcotic powder used in communication with spirits, or the communication ceremony itself (H&G, *kohoba*)
duho	ceremonial or chief's seat (H&G, *duho*)
guamiquina	a people's leader (G, *guamikení*)
guanín	a composition of gold, copper, and silver, with reddish hue (H, *wanin*; G, *guanín*)
hurikán	hurricane (H, *hurakan*; G, *hurakán*)
hutia	cat-sized rodent (H, *hutiya*; G, *hutia*)
mahisi	corn (H&G, *maisi*)
matunherí	supreme lord (H, *matunheri*; G, *matúneri*)
naboria	servant, the servant class (H&G, *naboria*)
nagua	married woman's loincloth (H, *nawa*; G, *nagua*)
nitaíno	nobleman, lord (G, *nitaino*)
tabaco	tobacco (H&G, *kohiba*)
taíno	noble or good person (H, *taino*; G, *taíno*)
yuca	yucca, manioc (H, *yuka*; G, *iuka*)

SPANISH WORDS

adelantado	frontier governor
alcazar	fortress, castle, or palace
cacica	a female chief
conversos	Christians who have converted from Judaism
harquebus	musket
Mudejar	Muslims living in a Christian kingdom, practicing Islam while vassal to a Christian sovereign
Morería	neighborhood where Mudejar live
Moriscos	Mudejar who have converted to Christianity
elches	Moriscos who have reconverted from Christianity to Islam
repartir/repartimiento	to grant and distribute a plot of land/the land so granted

HAITI/QUISQUEYA/ESPAÑOLA NAMES AND PLACES

Taíno names:

Adamanay	Saona Island

Bohío	a name for the island of the Dominican Republic and Haiti, typically used by Lucayans (including Bakako and Yutowa) and used by Cristóbal in his journal of the first voyage (in reliance on Bakako and Yutowa) until he renamed it La Isla Española
Camú	Camú River, Dominican Republic
Cibao	rocky, mountainous region in central Dominican Republic
Ciguayo	Mayobanex's chiefdom, northern Dominican Republic
Guacca	Lake Trou Caïman, Haiti
Guaricano	Guarionex's hometown in Magua, central Dominican Republic
Hagueygabon	Lake Enriquillo, Dominican Republic
Haiti	*Ayiti* phonetically, a name for the island of the Dominican Republic and Haiti
Higüey	Higuanamá's chiefdom, eastern Dominican Republic
Jaina	Jaina River, Dominican Republic
Magua	Guarionex's chiefdom, central Dominican Republic
Maguana	Caonabó's chiefdom, southwestern Dominican Republic
Marien	Guacanagarí's chiefdom, northern Haiti and Dominican Republic
Ozama	Ozama River, Dominican Republic
Quisqueya	a name for the island of the Dominican Republic and Haiti
Xaraguá	Behecchio's chiefdom, southwestern Haiti and Dominican Republic
Yabanea Toeya	Catalina Island
Yainagua	Lake Étang Saumâtre, Haiti
Yaque	Yaque del Norte River, Dominican Republic
Yaquimo	Bay of Jacmel, Haiti
Yasica	Yásica River, Dominican Republic

Spanish names:

Beata	islet off southwestern coast of Dominican Republic
Bonao	fort and settlement established in 1496, named for cacique of region
Concepción	fort and settlement established in Guarionex's

	Magua in 1495
Esperanza	fort built along Yaque River in 1495-6 to replace Fort Magdalena
Magdalena	fort built along Yaque River south of Isabela, destroyed by Caonabó's alliance in 1495
Santiago	fort and settlement built along Yaque River in 1495-6
Isabela	Cristóbal's first settlement and headquarters on Española, established in 1494 on northern coast, abandoned prior to 1498
La Isla Española	the Spanish Island, a name for the island of the Dominican Republic and Haiti
La Vega Real	the Royal Plain, Dominican Republic, largely Guarionex's Magua
Santo Domingo	town and headquarters established in 1496 to replace Isabela, on southern coast

CARIBBEAN AND SOUTH AMERICAN
NAMES AND PLACES

Indigenous names:

Ayay	St. Croix
Boriquén	Puerto Rico
Caloucaera	Basse-Terre, Guadalupe (the Spanish spelling for the now French Guadeloupe)
Caramari	northcentral coast of Colombia
Cairiani	Trinidad
Citurma	northeastern coast of Columbia
Coquibacoa	Coastlines of Gulf of Venezuela, Venezuela
Cuba	Cuba
Cubagua	Cubagua Island, Venezuela
Cumana	coastline surrounding Cumana, Venezuela
Curiana	coastline approx. between Barcelona and Caracas, Venezuela
Guanahaní	San Salvador
Lucayans	island people, from the Bahamas or Turks and Caicos
Ouitoucoubouli	Dominica
Paraguachoa	Margarita Island, Venezuela
Paraguaná	Paraguaná Peninsula, Venezuela
Paria	Paria Peninsula, Venezuela
Urabá	Gulf of Uraba, Colombia

Yamaye	Jamaica
Yaramaqui	Antigua
Yuyaparí	Orinoco River, Venezuela

Spanish names:

Boca del Drago	Dragon's Mouth, strait between northern Trinidad and Venezuela's Paria Peninsula
Boca de la Sierpe	Serpent's Mouth, strait between southern Trinidad and Venezuela's Orinoco delta
Little Venice	On or about Paraguaná Peninsula, Venezuela
Pearl Coast	coast of Venezuela, approx. from Margarita Island to Cabo Cadera, Venezuela

SOURCES

The principal primary (P) and secondary (S) sources considered are listed in the bibliography and then by applicable story (whether supportive or at variance with the story), including for primary sources, the chapter, section, paragraph, or date considered. Stories occasionally quote or paraphrase words from the primary sources so identified (or, infrequently, secondary sources), without quotation marks to preserve the novel style. Translations from Spanish to English incorporate my own judgments and sometimes are my own.

The Sources sections for *Encounters Unforeseen: 1492 Retold* and *Columbus and Caonabó: 1493–1498 Retold* include citations relating to events and thoughts in periods prior to 1498 described in detail in those books but merely summarized in this book, and such citations are not repeated herein.

BIBLIOGRAPHY OF PRINCIPAL SOURCES

Primary Sources:

P: Aguirre, Isabel. Edition and transcription. *La Pesquisa del Comendador Francisco de Bobadilla*. (Second part of Consuelo Varela, *La caída de Cristóbal Colón: El Juicio de Bobadilla*.) Madrid: Marcial Pons Historia, 2006 ("Bobadilla Investigation Testimony").

P: d'Anghera, Peter Martyr. *De Orbe Novo: The Eight Decades of Peter Martyr d'Anghera*. Translated by Francis Augustus MacNutt. New York: Burt Franklin, 1912 (together with the "Raccolta De Orbe Novo" noted below, "Martyr").

P: de Anglería, Pedro Mártir. *Epistolario*. Translated (into Spanish) by José López de Toro. Vol. 9, *Documentos inéditos para la historia de España*. Madrid: Imprenta Góngora, 1953 (together with the "Raccolta Epistolario" noted below, "Martyr Epistolario").

P: Anghiera, Peter Martyr of. *The Discovery of the New World in the Writings of Peter Martyr of Anghiera*. Edited by Ernesto Lunardi, Elisa Magioncalda, and Rosanna Mazzacane, with introduction by Lunardi ("Lunardi"). Translated by Felix Azzola, revised by Luciano F. Farina. Vol. 2, *Nuova Raccolta Colombiana*. Rome: Istituto Poligrafico e Zecca Dello Stato, 1992. Contains English translations of portions of Martyr's *Epistolario* ("Raccolta Epistolario") and *De Orbe Novo* ("Raccolta De Orbe Novo").

P: Benzoni, Girolamo. *History of the New World: Shewing His Travels in America, from AD 1541 to 1556: with some Particulars of the Island of Canary*. Translated and edited by W. H. Smyth, 1857. Reprint, Cambridge: Cambridge University Press, 2009 ("Benzoni").

P: Bergenroth, G.A., ed. *Calendar of Letters, Despatches, and State Papers, relating to the Negotiations between England and Spain*. Vol. 1. London: Longman Green, 1862 ("Bergenroth").

P: Bernáldez, Andrés. *Historia de los Reyes Católicos D. Fernando y Doña Isabel*. Seville: D. José María Geofrin, 1870. 2 vols. (together with "Raccolta Bernáldez" noted below, "Bernáldez").

P: *The Diario of Christopher Columbus's First Voyage to America, 1492–1493*. Translated by Oliver Dunn and James E. Kelley, Jr. Norman: University of Oklahoma Press, 1989 (the "D&K Journal").

P: *The Journal of Christopher Columbus (During His First Voyage, 1492–93) and Documents Relating the Voyages of John Cabot and Gaspar Corte Real*. Translated by Clements R. Markham, 1893. Reprint, Cambridge: Cambridge University Press, 2010 (together with the D&K Journal, "First Voyage Journal").

P: *Christopher Columbus: Accounts and Letters of the Second, Third and Fourth Voyages, Part 1*. Edited by Paolo Emilio Taviani, Consuelo Varela, Juan Gil, and Marina Conti, translated by Marc A. Beckwith and Luciano F. Farina. Vol. 6, *Nuova Raccolta Colombiana*. Rome: Istituto Poligrafico e Zecca Dello Stato, 1994. Section 2 of *Part 1* includes the "Libro Copiador"—copies of lost letters purportedly written by Columbus discovered in 1985—in Spanish and English (together with the Spanish versions in the "CDDD" noted below, the "Libro Copiador"). Section 1 of *Part 1* includes other Columbus writings related to the second, third, and fourth voyages previously known ("Raccolta Letters"). *Part 2* of this *Nuova Raccolta Colombiana* volume, identically titled, presents an explanatory analysis of the letters (the "Raccolta Letters Notes").

P: Columbus, Ferdinand. *The Life of the Admiral Christopher Columbus.* Translated and annotated by Benjamin Keen. New Brunswick, NJ: Rutgers University Press, 1959 ("Ferdinand Columbus").

P: Cristóbal Colón. *Textos y documentos completes.* Edition by Consuelo Varela. *Nuevas cartas.* Edition by Juan Gil. 2nd ed. Madrid: Alianza Universidad, 2003 ("Varela Gil Textos").

P: D'Ailly, Pierre. *Ymago Mundi y otras opúsculos.* Prepared by Antonio Ramírez de Verger, revised by Juan Fernández Valverde y Francisco Socas. *Biblioteca de Colón, Vol. 2.* Madrid: Alianza Editorial, 1992 ("D'Ailly").

P: Davenport, Frances Gardiner. *European Treaties Bearing on the History of the United States and its Dependencies to 1648.* Translated by William Bollan. Washington, DC: Carnegie Institution of Washington, 1917 ("Davenport").

P: Díaz del Castillo, Bernal. *The Discovery and Conquest of Mexico.* Translated by A. P. Maudslay. 2nd ed. Cambridge, MA: Da Capo Press, 2003 ("Bernal Díaz").

P: Dotson, John, ed. and trans. *Christopher Columbus and His Family: The Genoese and Ligurian Documents.* Vol. 4, *Repertorium Columbianum.* Turnhout, Belgium: Brepols Publishers, 1998 ("Dotson").

P: Duquesa de Berwick y de Alba. *Autógrafos de Cristóbal Colón y Papeles de América.* Madrid: Librería de D. Mariano Murillo, 1892 ("Duke d'Alba"). Includes the Pesquisa contra Alonso de Hojeda sobre su primer viaje á las Indias ("Hojeda Pesquisa").

P: Fernández-Armesto, Felipe. *Columbus on Himself.* Indianapolis: Hackett, 2010 ("Fernández-Armesto *Himself*"). Contains translations of Columbus's writings, as a primary source, and analysis thereof, as a secondary source.

P: Formisano, Luciano, ed. Translated by David Jacobson. *Letters from a New World: Amerigo Vespucci's Discovery of America.* New York: Marsilio, 1992 ("Vespucci Letters").

P: Gil, Juan and Consuelo Varela, ed. *Cartas de particulares a Colón y relaciones coetáneas.* Madrid: Alianza Editorial, 1984 ("Gil Varela Cartas"). Includes the letters and memorial from the friars Luedelle, de Robles, and de Trasierra to Cisneros, October 1500 ("Friars' Letters to Cisneros").

P: Jane, Cecil, trans. and ed. *The Four Voyages of Columbus: A History in Eight Documents, Including Five by Christopher Columbus, in the Original Spanish, with English Translations.* 2 vols. New York: Dover, 1988 ("Jane"). Contains Columbus's letter to sovereigns regarding the third voyage, dispatched October 18, 1498 ("Third Voyage Letter"), Columbus's letter to Juana de la Torre, end of 1500 ("Letter to Juana"), Columbus's letter to sovereigns regarding the fourth voyage ("Fourth Voyage Letter"), and Diego Mendez's testament, June 19, 1536 ("Mendez Testament").

P: Las Casas, Bartolomé de. *A Short Account of the Destruction of the Indies.* Edited and translated by Nigel Griffin. London: Penguin, 1992 ("Las Casas Short Account").

P: Las Casas, Bartolomé de. *Apologetica historia de las Indias.* 3 vols. Edition by Vidal Abril Castelló, Jesús A. Barreda, Berta Ares Quieja, and Miguel J. Abril Stoffels. Vols. 6, 7, 8, *Fray Bartolomé de Las Casas: Obras Completas.* Madrid: Alianza Editorial, 1992 ("Las Casas Apologetica").

P: Las Casas, Bartolomé de. *Historia de las Indias.* 3 vols. With prologue, notes, and chronology by André Saint-Lu. Caracas, Venezuela: Biblioteca Ayacucho, 1956 ("Las Casas Historia"). This is the entire work in Spanish.

P: Las Casas, Bartolomé de. *History of the Indies.* Edited and translated by Andrée M. Collard. New York, Harper Torchbooks, 1971 ("Collard Translation"). Translates into English portions of *Historia de las Indias*, including post-Columbus.

P: *Las Casas on Columbus: Background and the Second and Fourth Voyages.* Edited and translated by Nigel Griffin. Vol. 7, *Repertorium Columbianum.* Turnhout, Belgium: Brepols Publishers, 1999 ("Las Casas Repertorium—2nd, 4th Voyages"). Translates into English portions of *Historia de las Indias* relating to Columbus.

P: *Las Casas on Columbus: The Third Voyage.* Edited by Geoffrey Symcox, textual edit by Jesús Carrillo, translated by Michael Hammer and Blair Sullivan. Vol. 11, *Repertorium Columbianum.* Turnhout, Belgium: Brepols Publishers, 2001 ("Las Casas Repertorium"). Translates into English portions of *Historia de las Indias* relating to Columbus.

P: López de Gómara, Francisco. *Cortés: The Life of the Conqueror by His Secretary.* Edited and translated by Lesley Byrd Simpson. Berkeley: University of California Press, 1964 ("Gómara").

P: Moseley, C. W. R. D., trans. *The Travels of Sir John Mandeville.* London: Penguin, 2005 ("Mandeville").

P: Morison, Samuel Eliot, ed. and trans. *Journals and Other Documents on the Life and Voyages of Christopher Columbus.* New York: Heritage, 1963 ("Morison Documents"). Contains Bartolomé de las Casas's abstract of Columbus's journal of the third voyage, May 30–August 31, 1498 ("Third Voyage Journal"); Royal Mandate Ordering Restitution of Columbus's Property, September 21, 1501 ("Order of Restitution"); sovereigns' reply to Columbus, instructions for fourth voyage, and letter of introduction to da

Gama, March 14, 1502 ("Fourth Voyage Instructions"); Diego de Porras's Roster and Payroll for Fourth Voyage ("Fourth Voyage Roster").

P: Nader, Helen, ed. and trans. *The Book of Privileges Issued to Christopher Columbus by King Fernando and Queen Isabel 1492–1502.* Philologist Luciano Formisano. Vol. 2, *Repertorium Columbianum.* Eugene, OR: Wipf & Stock, 1996 ("Nader").

P: Navarrete, Martín Fernández de. *Colección de los Viages y Descubrimientos que Hicieron por Mar Los Españoles Desde Fines del Siglo XV.* Vols. 1–5. Buenos Aires: Editorial Guarania, 1945 ("Navarrete").

P: Oviedo, Gonzalo Fernández de. *Historia General y Natural de Las Indias.* Edition by Juan Pérez de Tudela Bueso. Madrid: Biblioteca de Autores Espanoles, 1959 ("Oviedo").

P: *Oviedo on Columbus.* Edited by Jesús Carrillo, translated by Diane Avalle-Arce. Vol. 9, *Repertorium Columbianum.* Turnhout, Belgium: Brepols Publishers, 2000 ("Oviedo Repertorium"). Translates into English portions of *Historia General y Natural de las Indias* relating to Columbus.

P: Pané, Ramón. *An Account of the Antiquities of the Indians.* New edition by José Juan Arrom, translated by Susan C. Griswold. Durham, NC: Duke University Press, 1999 ("Pané" and, as to Arrom's introduction and footnotes, "Arrom *Pané*").

P: Parry, John H. and Robert G. Keith. *New Iberian World: A Documentary History of the Discovery and Settlement of Latin America to the Early 17th Century.* Vol. 2. New York: Times Books, 1984 ("Parry & Keith"). Contains doc. 18:7, sovereigns' instructions to Juan Aguado, April 1495 ("Aguado Instructions"); doc. 19:2, Francisco Roldán's letter of October 10, 1499, to Cisneros ("Roldán Letter"); doc. 19:6, sovereigns' decree ordering the release of Indian slaves, June 20, 1500 ("Manumission Order").

P: Pérez de Tudela, Juan (director), Carlos Seco Serrano, Ramón Ezquerra Abadía and Emilio López Oto. *Colección documental del descubrimiento (1470–1506).* 3 vols. Spain: Real Academia de la Historia, Consejo Superior de Investigaciones Científicas, Fundación MAPFRE América, 1994 ("CDDD").

P: Phillips, Jr., William D., ed. and trans. *Testimonies from the Columbian Lawsuits.* Philologist Mark D. Johnston, translated by Anne Marie Wolf. Vol. 8, *Repertorium Columbianum.* Turnhout, Belgium: Brepols Publishers, 2000 (the "Pleitos," i.e., the "lawsuits").

P: Reyes Ruiz, Manuel, ed. *Testamento de la Reina Isabel la Católica: Testamento del Rey Fernando el Católico.* Granada: Capilla Real de Granada, 2004 ("Testamentos").

P: Rodriguez Valencia, Vicente. *Isabel La Católica en la Opinión de Españoles y Extranjeros*. 3 vols. Valladolid: Instituto "Isabel La Católica" de Historia Eclesiástica, 1970 ("Rodriguez Valencia").

P: Rumeu de Armas, Antonio. *Libro Copiador de Cristóbal Colón Correspondencia Inédita con Los Reyes Católicos Sobre Los Viajes a América.* Vol. 1. Madrid: Testimonio Compañia Editorial, 1989. This is Rumeu de Armas's analysis of the Libro Copiador. Vol. 2 contains his transcription of the letters.

P: Rusconi, Roberto, hist. and text. ed. *The Book of Prophecies Edited by Christopher Columbus*. Blair Sullivan, trans. Vol. 3, *Repertorium Columbianum*. Eugene, OR: Wipf & Stock, 1997 ("Book of Prophecies"). "Rusconi" refers to his historical analysis. The Book of Prophecies consists of i) Columbus's letter to Fray Gaspar Gorricio, dated September 13, 1501, ii) Gorricio's response to Columbus, dated March 23, 1502, iii) a memorial from Columbus to the sovereigns regarding restitution of Jerusalem's holy temple to the holy Church Militant, c. late 1500/early 1501 ("Prophecies Memorial"), and iv) a collection of scriptural, philosophical, cosmographical, and other ancient and then modern authorities.

P: Santa Cruz, Alonso de. *Crónica de los Reyes Católicos*. Vol. 1. Edition and study by Juan de Mata Carriazo. Seville: Escuela de Estudios Hispano-Americanos de Sevilla, 1951 ("Santa Cruz").

P: Symcox, Geoffrey ed. *Italian Reports on America 1493–1522: Letters, Dispatches and Papal Bulls*. Vol. 10, *Repertorium Columbainum*. Additional editing and translation by Giovanna Rabitti and Peter D. Diehl. Turnhout, Belgium: Brepols Publishers, 2001 ("Symcox *Italian Texts*").

P: Symcox, Geoffrey, ed., Luciano Formisano, Theodore J. Cachey, Jr., and John C. McLucas, eds. and trans. *Italian Reports on America 1493–1522: Accounts by Contemporary Observers*. Vol. 12, *Repertorium Columbianum*. Turnhout, Belgium: Brepols Publishers, 2002 ("Italian Reports Repertorium").

P: Thacher, John Boyd. *Christopher Columbus: His Life, His Works, His Remains*. 3 vols. New York: G. P. Putnam's Sons, 1903–4. English translation of Majorat or Entail of His Estates and Titles by Christopher Columbus, February 22, 1498 ("Columbus's Majorat").

P: Triolo, Gioacchino and Luciano F. Farina, trans. *Christopher Columbus's Discoveries in the Testimonials of Diego Alvarez Chanca and Andrés Bernáldez*. Vol. 5, *Nuova Raccolta Colombiana*. Rome: Istituto Poligrafico e Zecca Dello Stato, 1992 ("Raccolta Bernáldez"). Contains English translation of portions of Bernáldez's *Historia de los Reyes Católicos D. Fernando y Doña Isabel*.

P: Zurita, Jerónimo. *Historia del Rey Don Hernando el Católico: de las Empresas y Ligas de Italia*. 6 vols. Edition by Angel Canellas López. Zaragoza, Spain: Diputación General de Aragón, 1989 ("Zurita").

Secondary Sources:

S: Abulafia, David. *The Discovery of Mankind: Atlantic Encounters in the Age of Columbus*. New Haven: Yale University Press, 2008 ("Abulafia").

S: Alchon, Suzanne Austin. *A Pest in the Land: New World Epidemics in a Global Perspective*. Albuquerque: University of New Mexico Press, 2003 ("Alchon").

S: Altman, Ida. *Life and Society in the Early Spanish Caribbean: The Greater Antilles 1493–1550*. Baton Rouge: Louisiana State University Press, 2021 ("Altman").

S: Altman, Ida. "Marriage, Family, and Ethnicity in the Early Spanish Caribbean," The William & Mary Quarterly, vol. 70, No. 2 (April 2013), pp. 225–250 ("Altman *Marriage*").

S: Altman, Ida and David Wheat, eds. *The Spanish Caribbean & the Atlantic World in the Long Sixteenth Century*. Lincoln: University of Nebraska Press, 2019 ("Altman/Wheat").

S: Álvarez Álvarez, Arturo. "Guadalupe, devoción predilecta de la Reina Católica." *Historia* 27, no. 334, pp. 35–66 (February 2004) ("Álvarez").

S: Angel Ortega, P. *La Rábida: Historia Documental Crítica*. 3 vols. Seville: Impr y Editorial de San Antonio, 1880 ("Ortega").

S: Aram, Bethany. *Juana the Mad: Sovereignty & Dynasty in Renaissance Europe*. Baltimore: The John Hopkins University Press, 2005 ("Aram").

S: Arrom, José Juan. *Mitología y artes prehispánicas de las Antillas*. 2nd ed. Coyoacán, Mexico: Siglo Veintiuno Editores, 1989 ("Arrom *Mitología*").

S: Ballesteros Beretta, Antonio. *Cristóbal Colón y el Descubrimiento de América*. 1st ed. Vols. 4, 5. *Historia de América y de los Pueblos Americanos*. Barcelona: Salvat Editores, 1945 ("Ballesteros").

S: Barreiro, José. "A Note on Tainos: Whither Progress?" In "View from the Shore: American Indian Perspectives on the Quincentenary," edited by José Barreiro, Columbus Quincentenary Edition, *Northeast Indian Quarterly*. Vol. 7, no. 3, Fall 1990, pp. 4–22.

S: Bello León, Juan Manuel. "Las milicias andaluzas en la sublevación mudéjar de 1500 y 1501," Historia, Instituciones y Documentos, no. 37 (2010), pp. 9–61 ("Bello León").

S: Bakewell, Peter, with Jacqueline Holler. *A History of Latin America to 1825*. 3rd ed. United Kingdom: Wiley-Blackwell, 2010 ("Bakewell").

S: Boomert, Arie. *The Indigenous Peoples of Trinidad and Tobago: From the First Settlers Until Today*. Leiden: Sidestone Press, 2016 ("Boomert").

S: Borrero, Roberto Múkaro Agueibaná and Erica Mercado Moore. *Gu'ahia Taíno: We Speak Taíno, A Classic Taíno Dictionary and Grammar Guide*, vol. 1. New York: United Confederation of Taíno People (2023).

S: Boxer, C. R. *The Portuguese Seaborne Empire, 1415–1825*. Middlesex, UK: Penguin, 1969 ("Boxer").

S: Canedo, Lino Gómez. *Evangelización y Conquista: Experiencia Franciscana en Hispanoamérica*. Mexico: Editorial Porrúa, 1988 ("Canedo").

S: Carroll, Warren H. *Isabel of Spain: The Catholic Queen*. Front Royal, VA: Christendom Press, 1991 ("Carroll").

S: Cervantes, Fernando. *Conquistadores: A New History*. Great Britain: Allen Lane, 2020 ("Cervantes *Conquistadores*").

S: Cervantes, Fernando. *The Devil in the New World: The Impact of Diabolism in New Spain*. New Haven: Yale University Press, 1994 ("Cervantes *Devil*").

S: Cook, Noble David. *Born to Die: Disease and New World Conquest, 1492–1650*. Cambridge: Cambridge University Press, 1998 ("Cook *Disease*").

S: Cook, Sherburne F. and Woodrow Borah. *Essays in Population History: Mexico and the Caribbean*. Vol. 1. Berkeley: University of California Press, 1971. Chap. 6, "The Aboriginal Population of Hispaniola."

S: Cook, Noble David and W. George Lovell. *"Secret Judgments of God": Old World Disease in Colonial Spanish America*. Norman, OK: University of Oklahoma Press, 1992 ("Cook *Judgments*").

S: Crosby Jr., Alfred W. *Ecological Imperialism: The Biological Expansion of Europe, 900–1900*. 2nd ed. Cambridge: Cambridge University Press, 2015 ("Crosby *Ecological*").

S: Crosby Jr., Alfred W. *The Columbian Exchange: Biological and Cultural Consequences of 1492*. 30th anniv. ed. Westport, CT: Praeger Publishers, 2003 ("Crosby *Exchange*").

S: Crowley, Roger. *Conquerors: How Portugal Forged the First Global Empire*. New York: Random House, 2015 ("Crowley").

S: Curet, L. Antonio, and Mark W. Hauser, eds. *Islands at the Crossroads: Migration, Seafaring, and Interaction in the Caribbean*. Tuscaloosa:

University of Alabama Press, 2011 ("Curet").

S: Danticat, Edwidge. *Anacaona: Golden Flower*. New York: Scholastic, 2005. A historical novel.

S: Deagan, Kathleen and José María Cruxent. *Columbus's Outpost among the Taínos: Spain and America at La Isabela, 1493–1498*. New Haven: Yale University Press, 2002 ("Deagan *Isabela*").

S: Deive, Carlos Esteban. *La Española y la Esclavitud del Indio*. Santo Domingo: Fundación García Arévalo, 1995 ("Deive").

S: Denevan, William M., ed. *The Native Population of the Americas in 1492*. 2nd ed. Madison: University of Wisconsin Press, 1992. Chap. 2, Ángel Rosenblat, "The Population of Hispaniola at the Time of Columbus."

S: Downey, Kirstin. *Isabella: The Warrior Queen*. New York: Nan. A. Talese/Doubleday, 2014 ("Downey").

S: Dussel, Enrique. Translated and revised by Alan Neely. *A History of the Church in Latin America: Colonialism to Liberation (1492–1979)*. Grand Rapids, MI: William S. Eerdman, 1981 ("Dussel").

S: Edwards, John. *Ferdinand and Isabella: Profiles in Power*. Harlow, UK: Pearson Education, 2005 ("Edwards").

S: Errasti, Mariano. *America Franciscana: I. Evangelizadores e Indigenistas Franciscanos del siglo XVI*. Santiago, Chile: CEFEPAL, 1986 ("Errasti").

S: Estevez, Jorge Baracutay and Jessie Hurani Marrero. *Hiwatahia: Hekexi Taino Language Dictionary*. 2nd ed. United States: Higuayagua Taino of the Caribbean, 2019.

S: Fernández-Armesto, Felipe. *Amerigo: The Man Who Gave His Name to America*. New York: Random House, 2008 ("Fernández-Armesto *Amerigo*").

S: Fernández-Armesto, Felipe. *Columbus*. London: Gerald Duckworth, 1996 ("Fernández-Armesto *Columbus*").

S: Fernández-Armesto, Felipe. *Columbus and the Conquest of the Impossible*. London: Phoenix, 2000 ("Fernández-Armesto *Conquest*").

S: Fernández-Armesto, Felipe. *Ferdinand and Isabella*. New York: Dorsett, 1975 ("Fernández-Armesto *Ferdinand Isabella*").

S: Floyd, Troy S. *The Columbus Dynasty in the Caribbean 1492–1526*. Albuquerque: University of New Mexico Press, 1973 ("Floyd").

S: Forbes, Jack D. *The American Discovery of Europe*. Urbana: University of Illinois Press, 2007 ("Forbes *American Discovery*").

S: Forbes, Jack D. *Africans and Native Americans: The Language of Race and the Evolution of Red-Black Peoples*. 2nd ed. Urbana & Chicago: University of Illinois Press, 1993 ("Forbes *Africans/Native Americans*").

S: Forte, Maximilian C, ed. *Indigenous Resurgence in the Contemporary Caribbean: Amerindian Survival and Revival*. Chap 3. Lynne Guitar, Pedro Ferbel-Azcarate, Jorge Estevez, *Ocama-Daca Taíno (Hear Me, I Am Taíno): Taíno Survival on Hispaniola, Focusing on the Dominican Republic*. New York: Peter Lang, 2006 ("Ocama-Daca Taíno").

S: Friede, Juan and Benjamin Keen, eds. *Bartolomé de Las Casas in History: Toward an Understanding of the Man and His Work*. DeKalb: Northern Illinois University Press, 1971 ("Friede/Keen").

S: Galván, Manuel de Jesús. *Enriquillo: Leyenda Histórica Dominicana*. Ed. de Pedro Henríquez Ureña. Santo Domingo: Ediciones Cielonaranja, 2018 ("Galván"). A historical novel.

S: García Oro, José. *El Cardenal Cisneros: Vida y empresas*. Vol. 1. Madrid: Biblioteca de Autores Cristianos, 1992 ("García Oro").

S: Gibson, Carrie. *Empire's Crossroads: A History of the Caribbean from Columbus to the Present Day*. New York: Atlantic Monthly Press, 2014 ("Gibson").

S: Gil, Juan. *Columbiana: Estudios sobre Cristóbal Colón 1984–2006*. Santo Domingo: Academia Dominicana de la Historia, 2007 ("Gil").

S: Gould, Alicia B. *Nueva Lista Documentada de los Tripulantes de Colón en 1492*. Madrid: Real Academia de la Historia, 1984 ("Gould").

S: Granberry, Julian and Gary S. Vescelius. *Languages of the Pre-Columbian Antilles*. Tuscaloosa: University of Alabama Press, 2004.

S: Granberry, Julian. *The Americas That Might Have Been: Native American Social Systems Through Time*. Tuscaloosa: University of Alabama Press, 2005 ("Granberry *Americas*").

S: Green, Toby. *The Rise of the Trans-Atlantic Slave Trade in Western Africa, 1300–1589*. New York: Cambridge University Press, 2012 ("Green").

S: Greenlee, William Brooks. *The Voyages of Pedro Álvares Cabral to Brazil and India*. London: Hakluyt Society, 1938 ("Hakluyt Cabral").

S: Griffiths, Nicholas. *Sacred Dialogues: Christianity and Native Religions in the Colonial Americas 1492–1700*. Lulu, 2017.

S: Guitar, Lynne. "Cultural Genesis: Relationships among Indians, Africans, and Spaniards in rural Hispaniola, first half of the sixteenth century. PhD diss., Vanderbilt University, Nashville, TN. UMI Microform no. 9915091 ("Guitar").

S: Hanke, Lewis. *The Spanish Struggle for Justice in the Conquest of America*. Philadelphia: University of Pennsylvania Press, 1949 ("Hanke").

S: Harvey, L.P. *Islamic Spain, 1250 to 1500*. Chicago: University of Chicago Press, 1990 ("Harvey").

S: Herrera, Antonio de. *Historia General de los hechos de los Castellano en las Islas y Tierrafirme del Mar Océano*. With notes by Angel de Altolaguirre y Deuvale. Madrid: La Academia de la Historia, 1934 ("Herrera").

S: Hillgarth, J. N. *The Spanish Kingdoms, 1250–1516*. Vol. 2. Oxford: Clarendon Press, 1978 ("Hillgarth").

S: Inchaustegui Cabral, J. Marino. *Francisco de Bobadilla: Tres homónimos, y un enigma colombino descifrado*. Madrid: Ediciones Cultura Hispanica, 1964 ("Inchaustegui Cabral").

S: Ishikawa, Chiyo. *The Retablo de Isabel la Católica: by Juan de Flandes and Michel Sittow*. Turnhout, Belgium: Brepols Publishers, 2004 ("Ishikawa").

S: Keegan, William F. *Taíno Indian Myth and Practice: The Arrival of the Stranger King*. Gainesville: University of Florida Press, 2007 ("Keegan *Myth*").

S: Keegan, William F., and Lisabeth A. Carlson. *Talking Taíno: Caribbean Natural History from a Native Perspective*. Tuscaloosa: University of Alabama Press, 2008.

S: Kellogg, Susan. *Weaving the Past: A History of Latin America's Indigenous Women from the Prehispanic Period to the Present*. New York: Oxford University Press, 2005 ("Kellogg").

S: Kulstad-González, Pauline M. *Hispaniola–Hell or Home? Decolonizing Grand Narratives about Intercultural Interactions at Concepción de la Vega (1494–1564)*. Leiden: Sidestone Press, 2020 ("Kulstad").

S: Ladero Quesada, Miguel Ángel. *Granada Después de la Conquista; Repobladores y Mudéjares*. 2nd ed. Granada: Diputación Provincial de Granada, 1993 ("Ladero Quesada").

S: Lamb, Ursula. *Frey Nicolas de Ovando: Gobernador de las Indias (1501–1509)*. Madrid: Consejo Superior de Investigaciones Científicas, Instituto Gonzalo Fernández de Oviedo, 1956 ("Lamb").

S: Leguina, Enrique de. *Juan de la Cosa: Estudio Biográfico*. Madrid: Librería de M. Murillo, 1877 ("Leguina").

S: Liss, Peggy K. *Isabel the Queen: Life and Times*. Rev. ed. Philadelphia: University of Pennsylvania Press, 2004 ("Liss").

S: López Alvarez, Ana María, Santiago Palomero Plaza and Luisa Menéndez Robles. *Guía del Museo Sefardí*. Spain: Ministerio de Cultura, 2023 ("Museo Sefardi").

S: Lovén, Sven. 1935. *Origins of the Tainan Culture, West Indies*. Preface by L. Antonio Curet. Tuscaloosa: University of Alabama Press, 2010 ("Lovén").

S: Lyell, James Patrick Ronaldson. *Cardinal Ximenes, Statesman, Ecclesiastic, Soldier and Man of Letters, with an Account of the Complutensian Polyglot Bible*. London: Coptic House, 1917 ("Lyell").

S: Manzano Manzano, Juan, and Ana María Manzano Fernández-Heredia. *Los Pinzones y el Descubrimiento de América*. Vol. I. Madrid: Ediciones de Cultura Hispanica, 1988 ("Manzano").

S: Márquez, Luis Arranz. *Repartimientos y Encomiendas en las Isla Española (El Repartimiento de Alburquerque de 1514)*. Santo Domingo: Ediciones Fundación García Arévalo, 1991 ("Márquez").

S: Menéndez Pidal, Ramón. *Historia de España. Vol. 17, La España de los Reyes Católicos, vol. 2*. 4th ed., by Suárez Fernández, Luis and Manuel Fernández Alvarez. Madrid: Espasa-Calpe, 1990 ("Menéndez Pidal").

S: Miller, Townsend. *The Castles and the Crown: Spain 1451–1555*. New York: Coward-McCann, 1963 ("Miller").

S: Mira Caballos, Esteban. *Conquista y destrucción de Las Indias (1492–1573)*. Sarrión, ES: Muñoz Moya Editores, 2009 ("Mira Caballos *Conquista*").

S: Mira Caballos, Esteban. *El Descubrimiento de Europa: indígenas y mestizos en el viejo mundo*. Barcelona: Editorial Planeta, 2023 ("Mira Caballos *Indígenas*").

S: Mira Caballos, Esteban. *La Española, epicentro del Caribe en el siglos XVI*. Santo Domingo: Academia Dominicana de la Historia, 2010 ("Mira Caballos *Española*").

S: Mira Caballos, Esteban. *La Gran Armada Colonizadora de Nicolás de Ovando, 1501–1502*. Santo Domingo: Academia Dominicana de la Historia, 2014 ("Mira Caballos *Armada*").

S: Mira Caballos, Esteban. *Nicolás de Ovando: y los orígenes del Sistema colonial español 1502–1509*. Santo Domingo: Patronato de la Ciudad Colonial de Santo Domingo, 2000. ("Mira Caballos *Ovando*").

S: Mörner, Magnus. *Race Mixture in the History of Latin America*. Boston: Little Brown, 1967 ("Mörner").

S: Moya Pons, Frank. *Después de Colón: Trabajo, Sociedad y política en la economía del oro*. Madrid: Alianza Editorial, 1987 ("Pons *Colón*").

S: Moya Pons, Frank. *Historia Colonial de Santo Domingo*. 2nd ed. Barcelona: Universidad Católica Madre y Maestra, 1976 ("Pons *Historia*").

S: Moya Pons, Frank. *La Española en el siglo XVI, 1493–1520*. 3rd ed. Santiago, Dominican Republic: Universidad Católica Madre y Maestra, 1978 ("Pons *Española*").

S: Moya Pons, Frank. *The Dominican Republic: A National History*. New Rochelle, NY: Hispaniola Books, 1995 ("Pons *Dominican Republic*").

S: Morison, Samuel Eliot. *Admiral of the Ocean Sea: A Life of Christopher Columbus*. Boston: Little Brown, 1942 ("Morison *Admiral*").

S: Morison, Samuel Eliot. *The European Discovery of America: The Northern Voyages, AD 500–1600*. Oxford: Oxford University Press, 1971 ("Morison *Northern*").

S: Morison, Samuel Eliot. *The European Discovery of America: The Southern Voyages, AD 1492–1616*. Oxford: Oxford University Press, 1974 ("Morison *Southern*").

S: Ochoa, Margarita R. and Sara Vicuña Guengerich, eds. *Cacicas: The Indigenous Women Leaders of Spanish America, 1492–1825*. Norman, OK: University of Oklahoma Press, 2021 ("Ochoa/Guengerich").

S: Oliver, José R. *Caciques and Cemí Idols: The Web Spun by Taíno Rulers Between Hispaniola and Puerto Rico*. Tuscaloosa: University of Alabama Press, 2009 ("Oliver").

S: Oliver, José R., Colin McEwan, and Anna Casas Gilberga, eds. *El Caribe precolombino: Fray Ramón Pané y el universo taíno*. Spain: Ministerio de Cultura, Museu Barbier-Mueller d'Art Precolombí, Fundación Caixa Galicia, 2008. Includes Consuelo Varela and Juan Gil, chap. "La Española a la llegada de Ramón Pané" ("Varela Gil *Pané*"); and José R. Oliver, chap. "Tiempos difíciles: Fray Ramón Pané en la Española, 1494–1498" ("Oliver *Pané*").

S: Pagden, Anthony. *The Fall of Natural Man: The American Indian and the Origins of Comparative Ethnology*. Cambridge: Cambridge University Press, 1982 ("Padgen").

S: Pennock, Caroline Dodds. *On Savage Shores: How Indigenous Americans Discovered Europe*. New York: Alfred A. Knopf, 2023 ("Pennock").

S: Pérez, Joseph. *Cisneros, el cardenal de España*. 3rd ed. Barcelona: Penguin Random House Grupo Editorial, 2015 ("Pérez").

S: Perez Montas, Eugenio. *República Dominicana: Monumentos Históricos y Arqueológicos*. Mexico: Instituto Panamericano de Geografía e Historia, 1984 ("Perez Montas").

S: Phillips, Jr., William D., and Carla Rahn Phillips. *The Worlds of Christopher Columbus*. Cambridge: Cambridge University Press, 1992 ("Phillips").

S: Prescott, William H. *History of the Reign of Ferdinand and Isabella*. Vols. 1, 2. New York: J. B. Millar, 1885 ("Prescott").

S: Priego, Joaquin. *Cultura Taína: Prehistoria de Quisqueya*. 2d ed. Santo Domingo: Dominicana, 1971 ("Priego").

S: Reséndez, Andrés. *The Other Slavery: The Uncovered Story of Indian Enslavement in America*. Boston: Houghton Mifflin Harcourt, 2016 ("Reséndez").

S: Restall, Matthew. *Seven Myths of the Spanish Conquest*. Oxford: Oxford University Press, 2003 ("Restall *Myths*").

S: Restall, Matthew. *When Montezuma Met Cortés: The True Story of the Meeting that Changed History*. HarperCollins Publishers, 2018 ("Restall *Meeting*").

S: Robiou Lamarche, Sebastián. Translated by Grace M. Robiou Ramírez de Arellano. *Tainos and Caribes: The Aboriginal Cultures of the Antilles*. San Juan: Editorial Punto y Coma, 2019 ("Lamarche").

S: Rouse, Irving. *The Tainos: Rise and Decline of the People Who Greeted Columbus*. New Haven: Yale University Press, 1992 ("Rouse").

S: Rubin, Nancy. *Isabella of Castile: The First Renaissance Queen*. Lincoln, NE: ASJA Press, 2004 ("Rubin").

S: Rumeu de Armas, Antonio. *La Conquista de Tenerife: 1494–1496*. Madrid: Aula de Cultura de Tenerife, 1975 ("Rumeu de Armas *Tenerife*").

S: Rumeu de Armas, Antonio. *La Política Indigenista de Isabel La Católica*. Valladolid, Spain: Instituto "Isabel La Católica" de Historia Eclesiástica, 1969 ("Rumeu de Armas *Indigenista*").

S: Saco, J. A. Cond. and rev., A. Garzón del Camino. *Historia de la Esclavitud: Desde los tiempos más remotos hasta nuestros días*. Buenos Aires: Editorial Andina, 1965 ("Saco").

S: Scheker Ortíz, Luis, ed. *Santo Domingo and its Colonial Monuments*. 2nd ed. Santo Domingo: Ediciones Pasado, 2000 ("Scheker Ortíz").

S: Smith, Merril D., ed. *Sex and Sexuality in Early America*. New York: New York University Press, 1998. Chap. 1, "Sexual Violence in the Conquest of the Americas" ("Smith/Wood").

S: Socolow, Susan Migden. *The Women of Colonial Latin America*. 2nd ed. New York: Cambridge University Press, 2015 ("Socolow").

S: Stone, Erin W. *Captives of Conquest: Slavery in the Early Modern Spanish Caribbean*. Philadelphia: University of Pennsylvania Press, 2021 ("Stone").

S: Vilar Sánchez, Juan Antonio. *1492–1502: Una Década Fraudulenta;*

Historia del Reino Cristiano de Granada desde su fundación hasta la muerte de la Reina Isabel la Católica. Granada: Editorial Alhulia, 2004 ("Vilar Sánchez").

S: Santos-Granero, Fernando. *Vital Enemies: Slavery, Predation, and the Amerindian Political Economy of Life.* Austin: University of Texas Press, 2009 ("Santos-Granero").

S: Sauer, Carl Ortwin. *The Early Spanish Main.* London: Cambridge University Press, 1966 ("Sauer").

S: Settipane, Guy A., MD, ed. *Columbus and the New World: Medical Implications.* Providence, RI: OceanSide Publications, 1995 ("Settipane").

S: Stevens-Arroyo, Antonio M. *Cave of the Jagua: The Mythological World of the Taínos.* Scranton, PA: University of Scranton Press, 2006 ("Stevens-Arroyo").

S: Steward, Julian Haynes and Louis C. Faron. *Native Peoples of South America.* New York: McGraw-Hill, 1959 ("Steward/Faron").

S: Subrahmanyam, Sanjay. *The Career and Legend of Vasco da Gama.* Cambridge: Cambridge University Press, 1997 ("Subrahmanyam").

S: Sued Badillo, Jalil, ed. *General History of the Caribbean.* Vol. 1, Autochthonous Societies. Malaysia: UNESCO Publishing/Macmillan, 2003 ("Sued Badillo *History*").

S: Sued Badillo, Jalil. *La mujer indígena y su sociedad.* 6th ed. Río Piedras, Puerto Rico: Editorial Cultural, 2010 ("Sued Badillo *Mujer*").

S: Tarsicio de Azcona. *Isabel La Católica: Estudio crítico de su vida y su reinado.* 3rd ed. Madrid: Biblioteca de Autores Christianos, 1993 ("Tarsicio").

S: Thomas, Hugh. *Conquest: Montezuma, Cortés, and the Fall of Old Mexico.* New York: Random House, 2003 ("Thomas *Conquest*").

S: Thomas, Hugh. *Rivers of Gold: The Rise of the Spanish Empire, from Columbus to Magellan.* New York: Random House, 2003 ("Thomas *Rivers*").

S: Tolentino, Hugo. *Raza e historia en Santo Domingo: los origines del prejuicio racial en América.* Santo Domingo: Editora de la Universidad Autónoma de Santo Domingo, 1974 ("Tolentino").

S: Tremlett, Giles. *Isabella of Castile: Europe's First Great Queen.* Dublin: Bloomsbury Publishing, 2017 ("Tremlett").

S: Pérez de Tudela, Juan. *Las armadas de Indias, y los orígenes de la política de la colonización.* Madrid: Instituto Gonzalo Fernández de Oviedo, 1956 ("Tudela").

S: Universidad de Santa María de la Rábida, ed. *Andalucia y América en el siglo XVI*. Seville: Escuela de Estudios Hispano-Americanos de Sevilla, 1983 ("Universidad Rábida").

S: Varela, Consuelo. *Cristóbal Colón y la Construcción de un Mundo Nuevo, Estudios, 1983–2008*. Santo Domingo: Archivo General de la Nación, 2010 ("Varela *Estudios*").

S: Varela, Consuelo. *La caída de Cristóbal Colón: El Juicio de Bobadilla*. Madrid: Marcial Pons Historia, 2006. Part 1 is Varela's history, "Varela *Caída*"; Part 2 is Isabel Aguirre's Bobadilla Investigation Testimony (see primary sources).

S: Vega, Bernardo. *Los Cacicazgos de la Hispaniola*. Santo Domingo, Dominican Republic: Museo del Hombre Dominican, 1987 ("Vega").

S: Vigneras, Louis-André. *The Discovery of South America and the Andalusian Voyages*. Chicago: University of Chicago Press, 1976 ("Vigneras").

S: Watts, David. *The West Indies: Patterns of Development, Culture, and Environmental Change since 1492*. Cambridge: Cambridge University Press, 1987 ("Watts").

S: Williamson, J. A. *The Cabot Voyages and Bristol Discovery under Henry VII*. Published for the Hakluyt Society. Cambridge: Cambridge University Press, 1962 ("Williamson").

S: Wilson, Samuel M. *Hispaniola: Caribbean Chiefdoms in the Age of Columbus*. Tuscaloosa: University of Alabama Press, 1990 ("Wilson").

S: Zamora, Margarita. *Reading Columbus*. Berkeley: University of California Press, 1993 ("Zamora").

Throughout the novel, Isabella and Ferdinand's whereabouts track the study by Antonio Rumeu de Armas, and Columbus's whereabouts in Spain generally track the study by Jesús Varela Marcos and M. Montserrat León Guerrero:

Rumeu de Armas, Antonio. *Itinerario de los reyes católicos: 1474–1516*. Madrid: Biblioteca Reyes Católicos, 1974.

Marcos, Jesús Varela and M. Montserrat León Guerrero. *El Itinerario de Cristóbal Colón (1451–1506)*. Valladolid: Diputación de Valladolid, et al., 2003.

The volumes of the *Repertorium Columbianum* prepared and/or published by the UCLA Center for Medieval and Renaissance Studies and Brepols Publishers n.v. include English translations of writings of Las Casas, Oviedo, and others relating to Taíno as well as European participants in events;

accordingly, I am especially grateful to both the UCLA Center for Medieval and Renaissance Studies and Brepols Publishers n.v. for undertaking the endeavor to make and publish the English translations in the first place.

This book is a novel for which I bear full responsibility, and no person, institution, or publisher has participated in or bears any responsibility for how I have used their work herein.

CHAP I: THE GUAMIQUINA RETURNS

Anacaona, Xaraguá, Haiti (Quisqueya), Spring 1498

P, prev. cit.: Ferdinand Columbus, chaps. 74–77. Las Casas Apologetica, chaps. 5, 197. Las Casas Historia, vol. 1, chaps. 113, 114, 117–120 (chaps. 117–119 transl. in Parry & Keith). Las Casas Short Account, "The Kingdoms of Hispaniola". Las Casas Repertorium, chap. 147. Las Casas Repertorium—2nd, 4th Voyages, sec. 5.4. Martyr, decade 1, bks. 3, 5, 7. Oviedo Repertorium, sec. 3.16. Pané, preface, chaps. 1–4, 5, 23. Parry & Keith, Roldán Letter.

S, prev. cit.: Abulafia; Arrom *Mitología*; Ballesteros; Deagan; Fernández-Armesto *Columbus*; Floyd; Gil; Herrera; Keegan *Myth*; Inchaustegui Cabral; Kulstad; Tudela; Pons *Española*; Sauer; Stevens-Arroyo; Sued Badillo *Mujer*; Thomas *Rivers*; Tolentino; Varela *Caída*; Varela Gil *Pané*; Wilson.

No primary source relates the meetings between Behecchio, Anacaona, and Roldán depicted. Primary sources do discuss Roldán's agreements with Manicoatex and other chieftains generally, which I have used as guides for the story's conversations. *Columbus and Caonabó* describes the agreements that Columbus and/or Bartolomé imposed on supreme caciques prior to 1498, and my speculation of that agreed to by Behecchio is based in part on Wilson's analysis of Las Casas.

Columbus and Caonabó also depicts the failure prior to 1498 of the Christian missionary effort on Española to achieve more than a few Christian baptisms among the island's peoples and caciques, who—including Guarionex, Caonabó, and Anacaona—then were satisfied with their religion and spirits and distrustful of the conquerors'. For me, this satisfaction and distrust are sufficient to explain the failure, although secondary sources often attribute it to the language barrier, the small number of missionaries, and Columbus's opposition to baptism. See Chap. X, "Supreme Cacique Anacaona," below for further discussion of Anacaona's later reaction to Christianity.

As portrayed in *Encounters Unforeseen* and *Columbus and Caonabó*, both Taínos and Europeans then understood that a healthy person might contract disease from contact with a sick person, but neither understood that disease might also be contracted from contact with a healthy person from a population separated by millennia bearing latent disease strains. *Columbus and Caonabó* depicts prior to 1498: (i) Spanish settlers' beliefs that their illnesses and other misfortunes (including hurricanes) were the result of Taíno spirits or spirit worship, including ascribing Taíno spirits as being in league with Satan, and that Christ or the Virgin Mary protected them from disease and caused epidemics afflicting Taínos; and (ii) my corollary speculation that Taínos held parallel beliefs, i.e., Anacaona and other caciques feared that Christ, sometimes present through Spaniards' erection of crosses, assisted their conquerors in their conquest, including by inflicting epidemic diseases even where conquerors weren't regularly present. For discussion of universal beliefs in the divine causation of disease, see Alchon. For discussion of beliefs later in the conquests of Mesoamerica, see Cervantes *Devil*.

The historical record contains sparse biographical information regarding Roldán in Spain, although the identities of his wife and daughter, as claimants to his property, are known. Modern historians disagree whether Columbus willingly appointed him as Española's chief magistrate or he sailed with a crown assurance that he would be so appointed.

Isabel, Toledo, Castile, April 29–May 1498

P, prev. cit.: Bernáldez, chap. 154. Davenport, Romanus Ponifex (January 8, 1455), Inter Caetera (March 13, 1456), Inter Caetera (May 4, 1493). Ferdinand Columbus, chap. 65. Las Casas Repertorium—2nd, 4th Voyages, secs. 6.1, 6.2. Martyr Epistolario, docs. 105, 108 (letters describing Cisneros, April 5 and May 29, 1492), 182 (letter re: Juan's death, October 19, 1497), 183 (letter re: sovereigns' grief, October 30, 1497), 187 (letter awaiting Margarite's child, December 1, 1947), 194, 192 (letters re: Princess Isabel's recognition). Nader, sovereigns' license to settle or trade in the Indies, April 10, 1495; sovereigns' authorities to take 330, and to increase to 500, colonists, each April 23, 1497; sovereigns' writ for payment of wages, April 23, 1497; sovereigns' instructions re: Indies colonization, April 23, 1497; sovereigns' instructions re: colonists and supplies, June 15, 1497; sovereigns' grant of authority to apportion land, July 22, 1497; sovereigns' pardon of criminals, dated June 22, 1497; sovereigns' order for banishments, June 22, 1497. Oviedo Repertorium, 3.17, 3.18. Santa Cruz, chaps. 36, 40. Zurita, bk. 3, chaps. 6, 9, 18, 20.

S, prev. cit.: Angel Ortega; Aram; Ballesteros; Carroll; Fernández-Armesto *Ferdinand Isabella*; Friede/Keen; Gil; Ishikawa; Liss; Lyell; Miller; Morison *Admiral*; Museo Sefardi; Nader; Pérez; Prescott; Rumeu de Armas *Indigenista*; Rubin; Sauer; Socolow; Thomas *Rivers*; Tudela.

I have relied as to third voyage enrollment largely on Gil's analysis. For discussion of the miners' share of gold mined, see Chap. VI, "Twilight, Concepción, January–May 1500," below.

Mayobanex, Guarionex, and Bartolomé, War in Ciguayo, May 1498

P, prev. cit.: Benzoni, bk. 1. Ferdinand Columbus, chap. 76. Las Casas Historia, vol. 1, chaps. 120, 121. Martyr, decade 1, bks. 5, 7. Pané, chap. 25.

S, prev. cit.: Deagan; Floyd; Herrera; Rouse; Sauer; Varela Caída; Vega; Wilson.

Martyr explains Guarionex's departure from Magua as a decision to enlist Ciguayans in war against the Spanish, indicating raids were launched by an alliance, while Las Casas describes it as a flight for refuge. As depicted in this and a subsequent story, I've reasoned that Bartolomé's principal motive in the lengthy effort to capture Guarionex while avoiding war with the Ciguayans was to restore tribute's collection in Magua, not prevent raids, and that Guarionex's motives for traveling to Ciguayo included undermining that collection and escaping his responsibility therefor.

Primary sources do not indicate the precise location of Mayobanex's hometown village, but I've followed Vega and others in assuming it lay inland on the Yásica River and, by deduction from distances expressed in the primary sources, speculated that the first battle took place close to that river's mouth at the sea.

Cristóbal and Holy Trinity, Ocean Sea, May 30–July 31, 1498

P, prev. cit.: Bernáldez, chap. 131. CDDD, doc. 338 (monastery's notice for baptism of Cristóbal and Pedro, July 20, 1496). Columbus's Majorat. Davenport, Treaty between Spain and Portugal concluded at Tordesillas (June 7, 1494). Dotson, doc. 145, October 11, 1496 (agreement of Giovanni Colombo and brothers). Ferdinand Columbus, chaps. 66–68. Jane, Third Voyage Letter, Letter to Juana. Las Casas Historia, vol. 1, chap. 73. Las Casas Repertorium, chaps 131, 132, 138, 140, 150, 162. Las Casas Repertorium—2nd, 4th Voyages, secs. 3.1, 5.4, 6.1, 6.2, 7.1 Martyr, decade 1, bk. 6. Morison Documents, Third Voyage Journal. Nader, Santa Fe capitulations, April 17, 1492; Granada capitulations, April 30, 1492; sovereigns' confirmations of privileges, April 23, 1497; sovereigns' order re: Columbus's financial share, June 12, 1497. Libro Copiador, Libro Copiador, letter 5 (October 15, 1495). Oviedo Repertorium, 3.17. Pleitos doc. 23.1, testimony of Hernan Pérez Mateos. Book of Prophecies, Prophecies Memorial. Varela Gil Textos, Columbus's letters to Gaspar Gorricio, May 12 and 28, 1498. Williamson, Letters patent granted John Caboto, March 5, 1496 and February 3, 1498; Letter of Raimondo de Soncino to Duke of Milan, December 12, 1497; Letter of Pedro Ayala to Spanish Sovereigns, July 25, 1498. Zurita, bk. 3, chap. 21.

P: Isaiah, 11: 11; 41: 9, 11; 42: 4, 10; 60: 4, 7, 9.

P: Meyers, Jacob M., trans. *I & II Esdras*. Garden City: Doubleday, 1974. Bk. 2, chap. 6, paras. 42–52.

S, prev. cit.: Abulafia; Ballesteros; Boxer; Cervantes *Conquistadores*; Crowley; Curet; Fernández-Armesto *Columbus, Conquest*; Floyd; Forbes *American Discovery*; Gil; Green; Morison *Admiral, Northern Voyages, Southern Voyages*; Raccolta Letter Notes; Subrahmanyam; Thomas *Rivers, Slave Trade*; Varela *Estudios*: Williamson.

During Columbus's lifetime, Isabella's court chroniclers and others who knew and wrote of him said that he was Genoese, from Genoa or its environs, and when they discussed his faith, that he was a devout Catholic. In the centuries since his death, many have challenged that origin and, to a lesser extent, that faith. According to a recent announcement on Spanish TV, a new unpublished genetic study of Columbus's and his relatives' remains concludes that Columbus was born in Western Europe, likely in Spain, and had Jewish ancestry and may have been Jewish. I address Columbus's origin, ancestry, and faith separately.

In my view, and that of most historians, overwhelming documentary evidence unambiguously establishes that Columbus was born in Genoa or its environs in 1451—as I've depicted in (and cited in the Sources sections of) *Encounters Unforeseen, Columbus and Caonabó*, and this book. Ligurian notarial documents record various activities and real estate ownership of Columbus's ancestors in Genoa commencing in the 1430s. Columbus's own statements express his Genoese origin or pride therein (including testimony in a lawsuit in 1479; his testament in 1498; his letter to Genoa's Bank of St. George in 1502). Writings of his friends (such as Michele de Cuneo) and critics (including the friars later depicted herein) so indicate. After the first voyage, he placed relatives and acquaintances who came from Genoa or its environs on his fleets, and he often relied on financing from Genoese or other Italian sources. I believe the genetic study is consistent with the documentary evidence so long as its conclusion is limited to Western Europe.

As for ancestry, I believe it plausible that Columbus had Jewish ancestors, and some historians, including the Italian Paolo Emilio Taviani, confirm this possibility. As discussed in *Encounters Unforeseen*'s Sources section, the Spanish historian Salvador de Madariaga argued, *inter alia*, that Columbus was born in Genoa into a Spanish–Jewish family that had emigrated from Catalonia to Genoa during the repressions of the 1390s, and while a sincere and devout Catholic, he was influenced by Jewish faith and loyal to that heritage as a descendant of conversos. The argument is compatible with both the Ligurian notarial records and the genetic study. An emigration of Jewish ancestors to Genoa, whether in the 1390s, before then, or up to forty years later to the 1430s, leaves at least two decades, if not six or more, for the lineage's conversion to Catholicism before Columbus's birth. Madariaga suggests that conversion most likely occurred at the time of emigration.

In my view, consistent with Jewish ancestry, Columbus's writings reveal familiarity with the Old Testament (as well as the New Testament) and do not evidence the cultural anti-Jewishness prevalent in many of the era's primary sources. As discussed in *Encounters Unforeseen*'s Sources section, he was comfortable in relationships with conversos (for example, Luis de Santángel) and accepted that a converso could become a true Christian, although he wasn't above criticizing his enemies as conversos as depicted in Chap. III, "Fort Concepción and Isabela, February 20–May 21, 1499," below.

As for Columbus's faith, *Encounters Unforeseen, Columbus and Caonabó*, and this book relate (and cite) some of his numerous writings over the decade commencing in 1492 that consistently and ceaselessly indicate a devout Catholicism. While it can be argued that a portion of these writings were calculated and dissembling, some were heartfelt and urgent, expressed alone at the precipice of death at sea or at the hands of enemies. When threatened or desperate, or simply when circumstances didn't involve seeking favor or creating an impression, Columbus prayed to Christ the Lord, the Holy Trinity, or the Virgin Mary—often multiple times a day. Assuming that his ancestors were Jewish, I believe the lineage's conversion would have occurred well before his birth and that he never perceived himself as Jewish.

For more discussion of Madariaga's theories, see *Encounters Unforeseen*'s Sources section or his book itself, first published in 1940: *Christopher Columbus: Being the Life of The Very Magnificent Lord Don Cristóbal Colón* (New York: Christopher Columbus Publishing, 1978). For a summary of the debates about Columbus's origins and faith, see Taviani's book, *Christopher Columbus: The Grand Design*, translated by William Weaver (London: Orbis, 1985), and John Noble Wilford's *The Mysterious History of Columbus: An Exploration of the Man, the Myth, the Legacy* (New York: Alfred A. Knopf, 1991). See also Simon Wiesenthal, *Sails of Hope: The Secret Mission of Christopher Columbus*, translated by Richard and Clara Winston (New York: Christopher Columbus Publishing, 1979); and Carlos Esteban Deive, *Heterodoxia e Inquisicion en Santo Domingo 1492–1822* (Santo Domingo: Taller, 1983).

Cacique Diego Colón, born Bakako, near Guaricano and Fort Concepción, Magua

P, prev. cit.: Ferdinand Columbus, chap. 75. Las Casas Repertorium—2nd,

4th Voyages, secs. 5.4, 10.1. Libro Copiador, letter 5 (October 15, 1495). Martyr, decade 1, bks. 3, 4. Parry & Keith, Roldán Letter.

S, prev. cit.: Cook *Disease*; Herrera; Kulstad; Mira Caballos *Española*, *Indígenas*; Ocama-Daca Taíno; Perez Montas; Watts; Wilson.

Ferdinand Columbus mentions Diego's village, but its location is unknown. I speculate that it lay north of Fort Concepción and Guaricano on the route to Isabela, given that its key initial function was to serve as a hospital for men at the fort or those relocating from Isabela.

Rumeu de Armas's transcription of Columbus's letter of October 15, 1495 (contained in his analysis of the Libro Copiador listed under primary sources above), identifies Diego's wife as "Cora." The transcriptions presented in the Nuova Raccolta Colombiana and Varela Gil Textos (which I have favored) do not contain a name transcription, and Ariana is my fictitious name for her.

CHAP II: ENSLAVEMENTS, TREATIES, SETTLEMENTS

Anacaona and Roldán, Squatters' Haven Grows, Xaraguá, Summer 1498
P, prev. cit.: Benzoni, bk. 1. Ferdinand Columbus, chaps. 75, 78. Las Casas Historia, vol.1, chaps. 118, 119 (transl. in Parry & Keith). Las Casas Repertorium, chap. 147, 154. Martyr, decade 1, bks. 5, 7. Oviedo Repertorium, sec. 3.16. Pané, chap. 6. Parry & Keith, Roldán Letter.

S, prev. cit.: Altman; Deagan; Fernández-Armesto *Columbus*; Floyd; Gil; Granberry *Americas*; Guitar; Herrera; Kellogg; Kulstad; Márquez; Tudela; Morison *Admiral*; Mörner; Pons *Española*, *Historia*; Sauer; Smith/Wood; Socolow; Stevens-Arroyo; Sued Badillo *Mujer*; Thomas *Rivers*; Tolentino; Varela *Caída*; Wilson.

Primary sources provide scant information regarding Roldán's initial settlements in Xaraguá and the inception of concubinage depicted and no information regarding discussions among Behecchio and Anacaona or between them and Roldán; my speculations are extrapolations from what is known about the settlements and concubinage in 1499 and thereafter. Ferdinand Columbus, Las Casas, and Martyr—sometimes criticizing Roldán to defend Columbus—portray the conduct of Roldán's men to Taínos as relentlessly brutal, deceitful, and prurient. Some historians believe these criticisms are excessive, and I have speculated less brutality in the initial stages of settlement in recognition of Roldán's needs at the time for a haven and to convince Behecchio and Anacaona to provide it peacefully.

Primary and/or secondary sources relate that the following occurred during the Spanish conquest of Haiti (Quisqueya), as depicted in this book:

Spanish men sometimes forced Taíno women into concubinage or marriage or raped them; Taíno women sometimes reluctantly or voluntarily entered into such concubinage or marriages to attain insulation for themselves or their families from brutal treatment; and Spanish men sought concubinage or marriage with Taíno women of caciqual families to attain or have access to caciqual authority, land, or naborias.

Stories herein also reflect my corollary beliefs, based on the totality of the historic facts presented in this book, that: sophisticated Taíno caciques—including Anacaona and the other woman caciques (cacicas) specifically named herein—understood as well as their conquerors that marriage would confer the conquerors with conjugal and caciqual advantage and evaluated this detriment against the protections that marriage would provide; and Anacaona and possibly other cacicas deliberately avoided their own marriages to Spaniards, having the status, practical power, and material wherewithal to refuse. Kellogg affirms that Anacaona so avoided marriage, and Socolow so affirms with respect to some indigenous women later elsewhere subject to the Spanish conquest. As depicted in *Encounters Unforeseen*, at the time of conquest the island's supreme caciques knowingly used marriage to establish alliances, similarly to European princes, maintaining control of their chiefdoms through marriage of relatives to subordinate caciques, with Anacaona and Caonabó's marriage representing the use of marriage to ally separate chiefdoms.

For discussion of the debate about whether there were cacicas in the Caribbean prior to 1492, see Chap. IX, "Anacaona's Ascension (Early 1501)," below.

Isabel and Fernando, Succession in Aragón, Zaragoza, May–August 1498

P, prev. cit.: Bernáldez, chap. 154. Harvey, pp. 315–321, partial translation of 1491 surrender capitulations. Martyr Epistolario, docs. 194, 197, 199 (June 22, September 1, and October 4, 1998). Santa Cruz, chap. 40. Zurita, bk. 3, chaps. 20, 24, 30.

S, prev. cit.: Carroll; Edwards; Fernández-Armesto *Ferdinand Isabella*; Harvey; Ladero Quesada; Liss; Menéndez Pidal; Miller; Prescott; Rubin; Tarsicio; Vilar Sánchez.

Bartolomé, Mayobanex, Guarionex, Enslavements and Imprisonments, Summer 1498

P, prev. cit.: Benzoni, bk. 1. Las Casas Apologetica, chap. 120. Las Casas Historia, vol. 1, chaps. 120, 121. Las Casas Repertorium, chap. 150. Martyr, decade 1, bk. 7.

S, prev. cit.: Deagan; Floyd; Herrera; Rouse; Sauer; Stone; Varela *Caída*; Vega; Wilson.

Historians generally agree that Bartolomé treated the Ciguayan captives and Guarionex's family as slaves taken in a just war, but there is disagreement as to the fate of those he didn't release. Some believe these slaves were the cargo shipped to Spain depicted in the next story. Following Las Casas, I believe the slaves shipped to Spain were Maguans later enslaved, or at least predominantly so. I speculate that the unreleased Ciguayan slaves and Guarionex's family were promptly used after capture for work on Española.

Cristóbal, Paria, Terrestrial Paradise, August 1–30, 1498

P, prev. cit.: Benzoni, bk.1. Bernáldez, chap. 131. D'Ailly, chaps. 1, 55, 56. Ferdinand Columbus, chaps. 68–73. Jane, Third Voyage Letter. Las Casas Repertorium, chaps. 132–148, 156. Mandeville, chaps. 20, 33. Martyr, decade 1, bk. 6. Morison Documents, Third Voyage Journal; Toscanelli Letters, June 25, 1474, and undated. Libro Copiador, letter 6 (another version of the Third Voyage Letter); Oviedo Repertorium, secs. 3.17, 3.35. Pleitos docs. 1.4, 1.8, 1.12, 14.6, testimonies of Andrés del Corral, Hernando Pacheco, Bartolomé Colón, Pedro de Ledesma. Santa Cruz, chap. 50.

P: Genesis, 2: 9–14.

S, prev. cit.: Boomert; Cervantes *Conquistadores*; Davidson; Fernández-Armesto *Columbus*, *Conquest*, *Himself*; Morison *Admiral*; Raccolta Letter Notes; Sanders; Santos-Granero; Steward/Faron; Sued Badillo *History*; Thomas *Rivers*; Zamora.

I have generally followed Morison's analysis of events at sea, which in turn follows his translation of Las Casas's abstract of Columbus's third voyage journal and Las Casas's own history.

Columbus's letter expressing his cosmographic conclusions was dispatched to Spain on October 18, 1498, and historians debate its reasoning, interpretation, and when it was composed—whether seriatim during the voyage, when Columbus arrived on Española and traveled to Santo Domingo (August 21–31), or over the longer period ending October 17. As presented in the text, my speculation is that it was written at sea from August 22 to 31; the letter organizes facts underlying the conclusions, suggesting it wasn't written seriatim, and he knew that he'd have other business to attend to upon disembarking in Santo Domingo.

Ligurian notarial records indicate Domenico Colombo, Columbus's father, died sometime between 1494 and 1500.

Cristóbal and Roldán, Awards for Those Departing, August 31–October 18, 1498

P, prev. cit.: Benzoni, bk. 1. Ferdinand Columbus, chap. 79. Las Casas Historia, vol. 1, chaps. 150, 154, 155, 169. Las Casas Repertorium, chaps. 149–156, 176. Martyr, decade 1, bk. 7. Oviedo Repertorium, sec. 3.18. Parry & Keith, Roldán Letter.

S, prev. cit.: Ballesteros; Cervantes *Conquistadores*; Deagan; Fernández-Armesto *Columbus, Himself*; Floyd; Guitar; Morison *Admiral*; Philips; Sauer; Scheker Ortíz; Stone; Thomas *Rivers*; Universidad Rábida; Vigneras.

Sources for Miguel's baptism, guardianship, and recognition as heir are included in "Isabel and Fernando, Succession in Aragón, Zaragoza, May–August 1498" above.

Historians differ about whether the slaves shipped were the Ciguayan "war captives" or Maguans later enslaved for shirking tribute; whether Roldán and/or Columbus plotted armed seizures of each other; and whether the slaves were awarded entirely to settlers returning to Spain, shipowners, and crew or reserved partly for the crown. I have largely followed Las Casas, including that the slaves were at least predominantly the Maguans; Roldán's letter describes Columbus as forcing the rebels to hand over these slaves, from which I speculate the slaves were selected among the Maguan chiefdoms Roldán had released from tribute.

Las Casas confirms a close relationship between Higueymota and Roldán as hereafter depicted, and European secondary sources often cast the relationship as sexual, with Roldán as initiating, abusing, and/or wooing; it's my speculation that none of Behecchio, Anacaona, or Higueymota were simply reactive in that relationship.

Settlement, More Awards, October 19–November 1498

P, prev. cit.: Benzoni, bk. 1. Ferdinand Columbus, chaps. 80–82. Fernández-Armesto *Himself*, letter to Franciso Roldán, October 20, 1498. Las Casas Repertorium, chaps. 152–157. Martyr, decade 1, bk. 7. Parry & Keith, Roldán Letter. Zurita, bk. 3, chap. 32.

S, prev. cit.: Abulafia; Aram; Ballesteros; Carroll; Deagan; Fernández-Armesto *Columbus, Himself*; Floyd; Morison *Admiral*; Philips; Pérez; Rubin; Tarsicio; Thomas *Rivers*.

Confidence Lost, Isabel and Fernando's Court, December 1498–March 1499

P, prev. cit.: Benzoni, bk. 1. CDDD doc. 444 (list of Indians to be repatriated, April 1500). Ferdinand Columbus, chap. 85. Italian Reports Repertorium, letter of Simone dal Verde, January 2, 1499 (reporting Indians arriving Cádiz). Las Casas Historia, vol. 1, chap. 176. Las Casas Repertorium, chaps. 140–142, 161, 176, 177. Las Casas Repertorium—2nd, 4th Voyages, sec. 8.0. Martyr, decade 1, bks. 6, 7. Oviedo Repertorium, sec. 3.19. Santa Cruz, cap. 43. Zurita, bk. 3, chap. 33.

S, prev. cit.: Ballesteros; Davidson; Fernández-Armesto *Conquest, Ferdinand Isabella*; Floyd; Friede/Keen; Gil; Inchaustegui Cabral; Lamb; Mira Caballos *Conquista, Española*; Morison *Admiral, Southern Voyages*; Philips; Pons Colón, *Española, Historia*; Raccolta Letter Notes; Rubin; Sauer; Thomas *Rivers*; Varela *Caída*; Vigneras.

Las Casas reports that Isabella's famous remark that Columbus hadn't the power to give away her vassals was made multiple times, but he's unclear whether the remark was first made with respect to the slave shipment described in this story or the one in October 1499 later depicted; most historians have interpreted the former (as I have), some the latter.

CHAP III: LIFE IN HAITI (QUISQUEYA) AND ESPAÑOLA

Santo Domingo, December 1498–January 1499

P, prev. cit.: Bobadilla Investigation Testimony. Bernáldez, chap. 131. Ferdinand Columbus, chaps. 82–84. Las Casas Historia, vol. 1, chap. 119. Las Casas Repertorium, chaps. 154, 155, 157. Las Casas Repertorium—2nd, 4th Voyages, sec. 5.4. Martyr, decade 1, bk. 7. Pané, chaps. 25, 26. Parry & Keith, Roldán Letter. Oviedo Repertorium, sec. 3.12.

S, prev. cit.: Altman; Arrom; Ballesteros; Deagan; Fernández-Armesto *Conquest*, *Himself*; Floyd; Gil; Guitar; Mörner; Ocama-Daca Taíno; Pons *Colón*, *Dominican Republic*, *Española*; Sauer; Sued Badillo *History*; Thomas *Rivers*; Varela *Caída*.

The primary and secondary sources differ regarding the order of events depicted in Chap. III; although Ferdinand Columbus's ordering is internally inconsistent, I have largely followed his order, being the primary source most focused on chronology.

During the period of this novel, the word *mestizo* was not yet used to refer to a person of mixed European and Amerindian descent, and, as suggested in the text, many Spanish fathers simply considered such children "Spanish," albeit illegitimate. Historians disagree whether the sovereigns and/or the church had indicated a policy toward intermarriage of Spaniards and Amerindians at the time of this story, with some asserting a policy of permission and some prohibition. The record is clear that the sovereigns previously had sanctioned intermarriage of Spaniards and Canarians, but I suspect—if there was a policy in Europe—Columbus and the men in Española were uninformed or uncertain of it.

In my view, Columbus's writings don't explain his aversion to such marriages. Historians disagree on the explanation (e.g., the church's prohibition on marriage with non-Christians, the absence or uncertainty of sovereign approval, or as discussed below, his general desire to enslave rather than baptize), although most shy from attributing a racial motivation. The story is my speculation, reflecting the Bobadilla Investigation Testimony that Columbus did permit baptisms of infants more freely than of their mothers.

Historians have debated whether Columbus deliberately withheld approval of Indians' baptisms so he could enslave them, and the Bobadilla Investigation Testimony includes testimony directly relevant to the issue. See Chap. VIII, "Submission and Investigation, Santo Domingo, September 15–October 12, 1500," below. Las Casas unambiguously asserts that Columbus hoped Indians would fail to pay tribute and/or rebel so that he would be justified in enslaving them (chap. 150) but withholds judgment on the baptism charge when discussing the investigation, noting it was sacrilege to baptize the uninstructed (chap. 179).

Cacique Catalina's indigenous name is unknown. Secondary sources sometimes assume that, after 1492, Taínos with Christian names had been baptized; I speculate instead that Spaniards regularly gave Taíno concubines, servants, and others subjugated Spanish names, regardless of baptism. I'm unaware of a primary source indicating that Catalina was baptized.

Oviedo relates that Catalina liked Diaz and invited him to live at the Ozama, to which Las Casas scoffs, relating that woman chieftains didn't voluntarily invite their conquerors to live with them. Following Las Casas, the story depicts nonromantic motivations for both Diaz and Catalina in their extended relationship.

Xaraguá, January–Early March 1499

P, prev. cit.: Ferdinand Columbus, chaps. 82–84. Las Casas Historia, vol. 1, chap. 169. Las Casas Repertorium, chaps. 154, 157. Martyr, decade 1, bk. 7. Parry & Keith, Roldán Letter.

S, prev. cit.: Abulafia; Floyd; Guitar; Keegan *Talking Taíno*; Ocama-Daca Taíno; Pons *Colón, Española*; Sauer; Varela *Caída*.

Las Casas suggests Roldán took Higueymota as a concubine for whom he felt a lover's jealousy, and some secondary sources so conclude. The story reflects my speculation that—from both persons' perspectives—their relationship had nothing to do with love.

Fort Concepción and Isabela, February 20–May 21, 1499

P, prev. cit.: Bobadilla Investigation Testimony. Bernáldez, chap. 131. Ferdinand Columbus, chaps. 76, 82–84. Fernández-Armesto *Himself*, Fragment of an Account of Roldán's Rebellion, addressed to Ferdinand and Isabella, May 1499. Gil Varela Cartas, Carvajal's letter to Columbus, May 15, 1499. Las Casas Historia, vol. 1, chap. 162. Las Casas Repertorium, chaps. 157, 158, 162. Las Casas Repertorium—2nd, 4th Voyages, secs. 5.2, 5.4. Libro Copiador, letter 5 (October 15, 1495). Parry & Keith, Roldán Letter. Varela Gil Textos, letter of Columbus to Ballester, May 21, 1499.

S, prev. cit.: Deagan; Fernández-Armesto *Himself*; Floyd; Márquez; Pons *Colón, Española*; Sauer; Varela *Caída, Estudios*.

All agree that tribute failed regardless of Columbus's effort to reimpose it, but—other than the journeys to the sites depicted—primary and secondary sources don't describe in detail his effort, the chieftains with whom he parleyed, or their reactions thereto. I have speculated the parleys depicted given the importance and prominence of the chieftains to tribute's reinstitution and the coexistence arrangements later prevalent at Concepción, as apparent in the Bobadilla Investigation Testimony.

Niana was a fictitious person introduced in *Columbus and Caonabó*.

CHAP IV: REPLACEMENT AUTHORIZED, EXPANDING HORIZONS

Patience Lost, Isabel, Fernando, and Fonseca, April–May 21, 1499

P, prev. cit.: Benzoni, bk. 1. Bernáldez, chap. 131. CDDD docs. 298 (sovereigns' order that Fernando de Guevara and Miguel Moliart be returned to Spain, June 1, 1495), 421 (Bobadilla's commission as judicial investigator, May 21, 1499), 422 (proclamation naming Bobadilla governor, May 21, 1499), 423 (order to turn over forts, May 21, 1499), 424 (letter for Columbus introducing Bobadilla, May 26, 1499). Ferdinand Columbus, chap. 85. Hojeda Pesquisa. Las Casas Historia, vol. 1, chaps. 163, 170, 179. Las Casas Repertorium, chaps. 139, 161, 176–178 (which contains English translations of the sovereigns' May 1499 orders). Martyr, decade 1, bks. 6, 7, 10. Oviedo Repertorium, secs. 3.19, 3.35. Parry & Keith, Aguado Instructions; capitulations between the crown and Vicente Yáñez Pinzón, June 6, 1499 (also CDDD doc. 426). Pleitos, docs. 13.3, 13.5, 15.7, testimonies of Alonso de Hojeda, Rodrigo de Bastidas, Pedro de Soria. Santa Cruz, chap. 50.

S, prev. cit.: Ballesteros; Fernández-Armesto *Amerigo, Conquest, Ferdinand Isabella*; Gould; Morison *Admiral, Southern Voyages*; Navarette; Ortega; Saco; Sauer; Subrahmanyam; Thomas *Rivers*; Varela *Caída*; Vingeras.

Martyr relates that Bobadilla was appointed as governor, and Ferdinand Columbus relates the appointment was merely as a judge who would become governor if he found Columbus guilty (i.e., Bobadilla was self-interested in finding that guilt). Many historians have followed one version or the other. The story follows the sovereigns' proclamations and Las Casas's explanation of why they were drawn. Based on Navarette, some historians date the sovereigns' commission to Bobadilla as March 21, 1499, but I've followed Las Casas, Ballesteros, and others in dating it May 21, 1499.

Hojeda and Niño's capitulations with the crown have been lost, and I have assumed they were the same as Pinzón's, executed within weeks of their sailings, except I have followed Las Casas, Oviedo, and some historians in stating the prohibition on sailing to Columbus's "discoveries" applied 50 leagues distant therefrom. I have followed Gould's analysis that Niño didn't sail on Columbus's third voyage.

As for Vespucci, I've mostly followed Fernández-Armesto's analysis of his life and controversies and the Vespucci letters presented as genuine in Vespucci Letters.

Anacaona, Behecchio, and Bartolomé, Counterplotting and Courtship, June 1499

P, prev. cit.: Ferdinand Columbus, chap. 84. Oviedo, vol. 1, bk. 3, chap. 1, bk. 5, chap. 3.

S, prev. cit.: Gil; Granberry *Americas*; Oliver *Pané*; Restall *Myths*; Varela *Caída, Estudios*.

Some secondary sources relate or suggest an intimate relationship between Bartolomé and Anacaona and that Bartolomé traveled to and lived in Xaraguá to pursue that. But Ferdinand Columbus is the primary source dating Bartolomé's visit to Xaraguá depicted herein and doesn't attribute Bartolomé's purpose or relate what happened—either intimacy or the counterplot depicted. I doubt Bartolóme lived in Xaraguá during Roldán's ascendancy there, and I speculate his principal motive in visiting was the shrewder objective depicted.

Oviedo relates that Anacaona slept with Christians dissolutely after Caonabó and Behecchio's deaths, but not before. Whether true or not, I speculate that her and Behecchio's principal purpose in receiving Bartolomé at this time was equally shrewd.

Possession of Paria, Niño, Hojeda, Guevara, and Vespucci, June–August 1499

P, prev. cit.: Hojeda Pesquisa. Las Casas Historia, vol. 1, chaps. 163–166, 170. Las Casas Repertorium, chap. 139. Martyr, decade 1, bks. 8, 10. Oviedo Repertorium, sec. 3.35. Pleitos docs. 13.2, 13.3, 13.4, 13.5, testimonies of Andrés de Morales, Alonso de Hojeda, Nicolás Pérez, Rodrigo de Bastidas. Vespucci Letters, ltr. 1 (to Lorenzo de'Medici, July 18, 1500).

S, prev. cit.: Ballesteros; Boomert; Fernández-Armesto *Amerigo*; Herrera; Morison *Admiral, Southern Voyages*; Sauer; Thomas *Rivers*; Varela *Caída*; Vingeras.

Historians disagree on the number of Hojeda's ships, Vespucci's role on Hojeda's voyage, the portions of the voyage in which Hojeda's and Vespucci's ships sailed together or apart, and whether Hojeda or Niño arrived at Margarita first. I generally have followed the Hojeda Pesquisa and Morison as to Hojeda's ships and voyage, and I read the Pleitos testimony (other than Hojeda's) as suggesting Niño arrived first, as Vingeras maintains.

CHAP V: REPARTIMIENTO

Repartimiento's Inception, June–October 1499

P, prev. cit.: Bernáldez chap. 131. CDDD, doc. 434 (Roldán's letter to Columbus re: Hojeda, October 1499). Ferdinand Columbus, chaps. 83, 84. Hojeda Pesquisa. Las Casas Historia, vol. 1, chaps. 119, 163, 167, 168. Las Casas Repertorium, chaps. 154, 157–159. Martyr, decade 1, bks. 4, 7.

S, prev. cit.: Bakewell; Ballesteros; Deagan; Fernández-Armesto *Conquest*; Floyd; Guitar; Hanke; Márquez; Morison *Admiral*; Pons *Colón, Española*; Raccolta Letter Notes; Sauer; Tudela; Varela *Caída*; Varela Gil *Pané*.

Primary and secondary sources do not relate how Roldán informed Behecchio and Anacaona of repartimiento's inception or the awards granted; this and the following story are my speculations thereof.

Many historians trace repartimiento's origin to doctrinal influences of the Reconquista, but I have followed other historians who view it more as an event organic to the circumstances on Española.

Repartimientos Awarded, October–November 1499

P, prev. cit.: Ferdinand Columbus, chaps. 83, 84. Las Casas Historia, vol. 1, chaps. 159, 167, 168. Las Casas Repertorium, chaps. 155, 159–161. Martyr, decade 1, bk. 7. Parry & Keith, Roldán Letter.

S, prev. cit.: Ballesteros; Deagan; Errasti; Fernández-Armesto *Conquest, Himself*; Floyd; Guitar; Hanke; Herrera; Kulstad; Márquez; Morison *Admiral*; Pons *Colón, Española*; Raccolta Letter Notes; Sauer; Thomas *Rivers*; Tudela; Varela *Caída*; Varela Gil *Pané*.

Although not indicated by primary sources, I speculate that Columbus agreed with Roldán that Columbus's loyalists wouldn't live in Xaraguá, which is consistent with subsequent events.

Following Varela, I believe that Leudelle and Tisín departed Española on the two ships depicted rather than earlier, as some historians believe.

Carlos is a fictitious person.

CHAP VI: MORE REBELLIONS, SPAIN AND ESPAÑOLA

Surrender Terms Obliterated, Granada, Autumn 1499–January 1500

P, prev. cit.: Bernáldez, chaps. 158, 159. Harvey, translation of 1491 surrender capitulations. Las Casas Historia, vol. 1, chaps. 170–173. Las Casas

Repertorium, chaps. 161, 176. Martyr Epistolario, docs. 212 and 215 (letters of March 1 and July 16, 1500). M. Ladero Quesada, docs. 84 (Ferdinand's letter to Tendilla, December 22, 1499), 86 (sovereigns' letter to Tendilla and Cisneros, late December 1499), 87 (sovereigns' order of January 3, 1500), 89 (letter of Cisneros, January 16, 1500). Santa Cruz, chaps. 44, 47. Zurita, bk. 3, chaps. 39, 44, 45.

S, prev. cit.: Ballesteros; Carroll; Fernández-Armesto *Ferdinand Isabella, Himself*; Harvey; Ladero Quesada; Liss; Pérez; Prescott; Rubin; Sauer; Subrahmanyam; Tarsicio; Thomas *Rivers*; Tremlett; Vilar Sánchez; Vigneras.

Historians differ on the sequence and severity of the Granadan events depicted, and I've mostly followed Vilar Sánchez's exhaustive study of the sequence and Zurita's characterization of severity.

Hojeda's Rebellion, Haiti (Quisqueya), November–December 1499

P, prev. cit.: Ferdinand Columbus, chap. 84. Fernández-Armesto *Himself*, Fragments of Letters to the Monarchs of 1498–1500, extracted by Las Casas. Jane, Letter to Juana. Hojeda Pesquisa. Las Casas Historia, vol. 1, chap. 168. Las Casas Repertorium, chaps. 154, 156. Libro Copiador, letters 7 and 8 (February 3, 1500). Vespucci Letters, ltr. 1 (to Lorenzo de' Medici, July 18, 1500).

S, prev. cit.: Ballesteros; Cervantes *Conquistadores*; Fernández-Armesto *Amerigo, Columbus, Himself*; Herrera; Morison *Admiral, Southern Voyages*; Sauer; Thomas *Rivers*; Varela *Caída*; Vingeras.

I'm unaware of primary or secondary sources indicating that Hojeda met with Anacaona and Behecchio. I have speculated that the three did so when Hojeda remained at the Bay of Port-au-Prince, and the conversation is fictionalized based on what primary sources indicate Hojeda told Christians and/or Taínos at the time. Vespucci indicates his ships were repaired on Española over two months, but not by whom, where, or when; I've speculated it would have been by Behecchio in that bay commencing mid-December, two months prior to Hojeda's eventual departure from Española.

Historians disagree whether Columbus's flight to a caravel was real, a hallucination, or simply made up. Columbus and his son Ferdinand relate that the caravel went to sea, but there is no independent evidence that Columbus was then in physical danger. I have speculated as presented in the story, that the caravel was real but actual flight not.

Mohammedan Uprising, Granada, February–March 1500

See "Surrender Terms Obliterated, Granada, Autumn 1499–January 1500" above.

Higueymota's Engagement, Xaraguá, January–April 1500

P, prev. cit.: Ferdinand Columbus, chap. 84. Jane, Letter to Juana. Las

Casas Historia, vol. 1, chaps. 168, 169. Vespucci Letters, ltr. 1 (to Lorenzo de' Medici, July 18, 1500).

S, prev. cit.: Ballesteros; Cervantes *Conquistadores*; Fernández-Armesto *Columbus*; Galván; Herrera; Mira Caballos *Armada*; Varela *Caída*; Vingeras.

Ferdinand Columbus indicates Roldán restrained Guevara from taking Higueymota as wife. Las Casas suggests the marriage occurred, an unidentified cleric was summoned to baptize Higueymota, and that Guevara's belief Anacaona voluntarily had given him Higueymota as wife due to his nobility was credible (an atypical observation for Las Casas), although Guevara might have "taken" her. The Bobadilla Investigation Testimony doesn't mention either the marriage or baptism, despite Columbus's refusal to permit Spanish/Taíno marriages being an investigation focus (as depicted hereafter). Guevara left no writing. Secondary sources conflict as to whether a marriage actually occurred. The record is clear that, with or without marriage, Higueymota and Guevara had a sexual relationship. Some historians and considerable tradition cast that relationship as romantic on behalf of both persons and Guevara's motivation for marriage as love. Other historians believe the betrothal was just another instance of abuse, imposed by a conqueror on Anacaona and Higueymota against their will.

I've followed Ferdinand Columbus that the marriage was prevented. I believe Guevara's isolated circumstances left him without the authority or command in Xaraguá to force marriage upon Anacaona and Higueymota— particularly when Roldán opposed it. As depicted in the story, I suspect Anacaona desperately but volitionally agreed to marry her daughter to a conqueror for the motive portrayed, her ability to identify and choose a true nobleman within the alien society of the conquerors she'd met both remarkable and confirmatory of that intent. I don't see love as motivating either Guevara or Higueymota.

It is problematic to identify a cleric then remaining on the island who would have risked both Roldán and Columbus's anger by performing the baptism and Christian marriage.

Gold Mining, January–May 1500

P, prev. cit.: Bernáldez, chap. 131. Ferdinand Columbus, chaps. 84, 85. Friars' Letters to Cisneros. Jane, Letter to Juana. Hojeda Pesquisa. Las Casas Historia, vol. 1, chaps. 119, 121; vol. 2, chap. 1. Las Casas Repertorium, chap. 176 (including alternate translation in Parry & Keith). Las Casas Repertorium—2nd, 4th Voyages, secs. 5.4, 10.1. Libro Copiador, letters 7 and 8 (February 3, 1500). Martyr, decade 1, bk. 4. Morison Documents, Columbus's Memorial to Sovereigns on Colonial Policy, 1493(?), and Varela Gil Textos, Columbus's Memorial to Sovereigns on Population of Indies,1501(?). Nader, sovereigns' license to settle or trade in the Indies, April 10, 1495. Oviedo, bk. 5, chap. 3. Oviedo Repertorium, sec. 3.19.

S, prev. cit.: Ballesteros; Fernández-Armesto *Columbus*; Floyd; Herrera; Raccolta Letter Notes; Sauer; Subrahmanyam; Thomas *Rivers*; Varela *Caída*; Wilson.

The historical record indicates that a miner's share of gold mined changed over time and that Columbus had the authority to adjust it, but it's often unclear what the share was from time to time. The sovereigns' order of April 10, 1495, had then specified a share of one-third; Bernáldez confirms some amount was paid (chap. 131); Ferdinand Columbus indicates that miners kept two-thirds (chap. 84); and, as previously depicted, Las Casas reports that, when dispatching Carvajal's two ships in 1498, Columbus instructed Bartolomé that miners be allowed to retain gold mined exceeding a quota (vol. 1, chap. 119). Las Casas also indicates that Bobadilla favored miners by allowing them to retain 10/11ths (vol. 2, chap. 1). See Chap. IX, "Bobadilla's Governorship, October 1500–1501," and Chap. X, "Knight Commander Ovando's Orders, September 3–December 1501" below.

The question is largely unimportant prior to gold's discovery in 1499, as its procurement was intended to be largely through barter until 1495 and through tribute thereafter. I've speculated that Columbus altered the miners' interest from quota-based to two-thirds when the New Mines were developed, the percentage Columbus indicates in the Letter to Juana. The estimate of Columbus's wealth is an extrapolation of the amount accumulated months later indicated in that letter.

CHAP VII: ISABEL'S CONQUEST AND DYNASTY REORDERED

Bobadilla's Dispatch, Manumissions and Enslavements, Seville, March–June 1500

P, prev. cit.: CDDD, docs. 444 (list of Indians repatriated, April 1500), 454 (proclamation ordering manumission, June 20 and July 1500), 550 (information regarding Indians sold, 1501). Duke d'Alba, sovereigns' order to pay salaries, May 30, 1500. Friars' Letters to Cisneros. Las Casas Historia, vol. 1, chaps. 168, 170–173; vol. 2, chap. 2. Las Casas Repertorium, secs. 176, 178. Martyr, decade 1, bks. 7, 8, 9. Parry & Keith, Manumission Order. Rumeu de Armas *Tenerife*, doc. 37, order liberating guanches, March 29, 1498. Santa Cruz, chap. 50. Symcox *Italian Texts*, letter of Giovanni Mateo Cretico, 1501. Vespucci Letters, ltr. 1 (to Lorenzo de' Medici, July 18, 1500).

S, prev. cit.: Crowley; Fernández-Armesto *Amerigo, Canary*; Floyd; Forbes *Africans/Native Americans*; Gibson; Gil; Herrera; Liss; Manzano; Morison *Southern Voyages*; Mira Caballos *Conquista, Española, Indígenas*; Ortega; Pagden; Reséndez; Rubin; Rumeu de Armas *Indigenista, Tenerife*; Sauer; Stone; Subrahmanyam; Thomas *Rivers*; Tudela; Universidad Rábida; Varela *Caída, Estudios*; Vilar Sánchez.

I'm unaware of a primary source indicating what the sovereigns first instructed Pedro de Torres or how he went about finding and collecting all or selecting (i.e., excluding war captives) Taínos for manumission. Las Casas is internally inconsistent whether the collection included Taínos shipped to Spain in both 1498 and 1499. It's problematic to reconcile the terms of the decree with the Taínos actually manumitted, i.e., some were possessed by the original settler grantee and hadn't been sold. The story reflects my speculative reconciliation of Las Casas, the decree's terms, and analysis of lists of those manumitted and Indians sold.

Many histories depict a proclamation of a grander scope. Although a report hasn't been found, many historians believe a committee of theologians and lawyers had rendered a conclusion at this time.

While the sovereigns had decided to manumit Indians well prior to learning of Hojeda's enslavements, primary sources don't indicate whether they knew of Hojeda's enslavements by the time of the decree. As depicted, I speculate discussion between the sovereigns and Fonseca regarding Hojeda's enslavements occurred after the decree and had no effect on the decree.

There's no evidence that Isabel met those manumitted, but I speculate she would have wanted to and did, having previously reviewed Indians in audiences, as depicted in *Encounters Unforeseen* and *Columbus and Caonabó*.

Southern Landmass, Vespucci, de la Cosa, and Cabral, April–July 1500

P, prev. cit.: Hakluyt Cabral, letter from Manuel to Ferdinand and Isabella, July 29, 1501. Las Casas Historia, vol. 2, chap. 2. Symcox *Italian Texts*, letter of Giovanni Mateo Cretico, 1501. Vespucci Letters, ltr. 1 (to Lorenzo de' Medici, July 18, 1500).

S, prev. cit.: Crowley; Fernández-Armesto *Amerigo*; Morison *Southern Voyages*; Raccolta Letter Notes; Subrahmanyam; Vigneras.

Plots and Destinies Frustrated, Haiti (Quisqueya) and Spain, June–August 1500

P, prev. cit.: Bernáldez, chaps. 154, 164. Bobadilla Investigation Testimony. Ferdinand Columbus, chap. 84. Jane, Letter to Juana. Las Casas Historia, vol. 1, chap. 169. Las Casas Repertorium, sec. 177. Martyr Epistolario, doc. 216 (letter of July 29, 1500). Santa Cruz, chaps. 49, 52. Zurita, bk. 4, chaps. 5, 8, 13, 27.

S, prev. cit.: Ballesteros; Fernández-Armesto *Columbus, Ferdinand Isabella*; Floyd; Herrera; Liss; Morison *Admiral*; Rubin; Thomas *Rivers*; Varela *Caída*; Vilar Sánchez.

I've speculated Múxica's motives for his rebellion, which aren't clear in primary sources. Columbus's orders to capture him and others are taken from the Bobadilla Investigation Testimony and Las Casas, rather than Columbus's explanation in the Letter to Juana.

CHAP VIII: CRISTÓBAL'S DEMISE

Bobadilla and Cristóbal, August 23–September 14, 1500

P, prev. cit.: Bobadilla Investigation Testimony. Ferdinand Columbus, chaps. 85, 86. Friars' Letters to Cisneros. Jane, Letter to Juana. Las Casas Historia, vol. 1, chap. 177. Las Casas Repertorium, chaps. 177–179. Martyr, decade 1, bk. 7. Oviedo Repertorium, sec. 3.19.

S, prev. cit.: Ballesteros; Fernández-Armesto *Columbus, Conquest*; Floyd; Gil; Herrera; Morison *Admiral*; Phillips; Sauer; Thomas *Rivers*; Varela *Caída*.

The description of Bobadilla's arrival is based on Las Casas, with some of the dialogue extrapolated from Las Casas and the Bobadilla Investigation Testimony. I have speculated some of the information-gathering steps I believe Bobadilla, as investigator, would have taken and his tactical motivations.

Submission and Investigation, Santo Domingo, September 15–October 12, 1500

P, prev. cit.: Benzoni, bk. 1. Bobadilla Investigation Testimony. Bernáldez, chap. 131. Duke d'Alba, Columbus's response to Bobadilla's command to pay salaries, September 15, 1500. Ferdinand Columbus, chap. 86. Gil Varela Cartas, Friars' Letters to Cisneros. Jane, Letter to Juana. Las Casas Repertorium, chaps. 179, 180. Martyr, decade 1, bk. 7. Ortega, undated memorial of Fray Ruiz, 1515 or later. Oviedo Repertorium, sec. 3.19. Santa Cruz, chap. 50.

S, prev. cit.: Altman; Altman/Wheat; Ballesteros; Canedo; Cervantes *Conquistadores*; Fernández-Armesto *Columbus, Conquest*; Floyd; Gil; Herrera; Morison *Admiral*; Ortega; Pérez; Raccolta Letter Notes; Rumeu de Armas *Indigenista*; Sauer; Thomas *Rivers*; Tudela; Varela *Caída, Estudios*; Varela Gil *Pané*.

Consuelo Varela's *Caída* and Isabel Aguirre's Bobadilla Investigation Testimony, first published in 2006, analyze and present only a partially preserved record of the evidence Bobadilla took to transmit to the sovereigns, and the portions of the testimony not known today might well contain additional witnesses and different information. Nevertheless, what is preserved contains substantial information not factored into older biographies of Columbus or histories of the events and—as depicted in this and the prior two stories— results in a narrative regarding Bobadilla's treatment of Columbus different than that previously taught.

The testimony contains prefatory information relating the events from Bobadilla's arrival on Española through September 23, including the two audiences between Bobadilla and Columbus depicted; the dialogue for those audiences is speculated from this prefatory information and Columbus's Letter to Juana. The prefatory information doesn't indicate that Bobadilla met with Roldán; but Oviedo says they did, and I've speculated such meeting based on the outcome known.

In its entirety, the testimony is partisan and conflicted, as are the other principal primary sources—Columbus, Ferdinand Columbus, and Las Casas. As if a juror, I've weighed the likelihood and credibility of the testimony, usually favoring testimony against interest or contra-loyalty, and other primary sources to reach a composite portrayal. Other jurors may favor other interpretations.

Anacaona and Behecchio, Guamiquina's Departure

P, prev. cit.: Las Casas Historia, vol. 2, chaps. 9, 10 (including Collard Translation). Oviedo, bk. 3, chap. 12.

S, prev. cit.: Altman; Altman/Wheat; Canedo; Herrera; Oliver; Pérez.

Neither primary nor secondary sources relate the scene depicted. The Bobadilla Investigation Testimony establishes that Behecchio ruled Xaraguá past Bobadilla's arrival on Española; and Las Casas and Oviedo establish Anacaona was Behecchio's successor. For discussion of Behecchio's death, see Chap. XI, "Anacaona's Ascension (Early 1501)," below.

I am unaware of primary or secondary sources discussing the subsequent Christian worship of the two to three thousand Taínos baptized in the prior story. My speculation that few (if any) of them genuinely converted to Christianity is based on (i) that silence (tangible worship thereafter likely would have been noted) and (ii) the history later depicted herein (and in the next sequel) of the Spanish crown's unsuccessful effort to convert Española's Taínos (other than members of cacical families) as their population continued to decline over the next few years.

The Guaorocuyá mentioned is Anacaona's nephew, so identified by Las Casas, Oviedo, and Herrera, an adult at the time of this story. It's possible that Guaorocuyá was Behecchio's son. The Guaorocuyá who became the rebellion leader Cacique Enrique, an infant or toddler at the time of this story, will be introduced in the next sequel.

Cristóbal, Isabel and Fernando, Voyage Home and Audience,
October 13–December 17, 1500

P, prev. cit.: Benzoni, bk. 1. Bernáldez, chap. 131. CDDD, doc. 463 (fragment of Columbus letter to couriers, 1500). Ferdinand Columbus, chaps. 86, 87. Fernández-Armesto *Himself*, Fragment of a Memorandum apparently addressed to the Council of Castile, late 1500? Isaiah, 65:17. Jane, Letter to Juana. Las Casas Repertorium, chaps. 181, 182. Las Casas Repertorium—2nd, 4th Voyages, sec. 8. Libro Copiador, letter 7 (February 3, 1500, with addenda November 20, 1500). Martyr, decade 1, bk. 7. Oviedo Repertorium, sec. 3.19. Revelations 21:1. Santa Cruz, chap. 50.

P: Letter of Bobadilla to Cisneros, October 12, 1500, contained in Boletin del Archivo de la Nacion 8, nos. 38, 39 (January 1945), pp. 72, 73.

S, prev. cit.: Ballesteros; Canedo; Carroll; Fernández-Armesto *Columbus, Conquest, Ferdinand Isabella*; Floyd; Gil; Herrera; Hillgarth; Liss; Lunardi; Morison *Admiral*; Ortega; Pérez; Raccolta Letter Notes; Rubin; Rumeu de Armas *Indigenista*; Thomas *Rivers*; Varela *Caída, Estudios*; Vilar Sánchez.

Primary sources don't indicate whether the sovereigns had reviewed Bobadilla's investigation report or learned of the friars' letters to Cisneros before their audience with Columbus. The delivery of Columbus's memorandum to the Council of Seville is unverifiable. Secondary sources, most written prior to publication of the report in 2006, often (but not Morison) depict the sovereigns as rushing to free Columbus from inappropriate incarceration by an unworthy Bobadilla.

But Santa Cruz indicates the investigation report and its find of guilt was transmitted to the sovereigns, and Bernaldéz, Martyr, and Oviedo shy from criticizing Bobadilla; as depicted, I speculate the sovereigns were aware of the basic conclusions of the report and the friars' letters before the audience, including (consistent with Floyd) meeting Fray Ruiz prior thereto.

CHAP IX: ANACAONA'S ASCENSION,
OTHER TRANSITIONS

Bobadilla's Governorship, October 1500–1501

P, prev. cit.: Benzoni, bk. 1. Bernáldez, chap. 131. Ferdinand Columbus, chap. 86. Italian Reports Repertorium, account of Angelo Trevisian, chap. 17, 1504. Las Casas Historia, vol. 2, chaps. 1, 3 (including Collard

Translation). Las Casas Repertorium, chap. 160. Martyr, decade 1, bk. 7. Oviedo, vol. 1, bk. 3, chap. 6. Oviedo Repertorium, sec. 3.19.

S, prev. cit.: Deagan; Fernández-Armesto, *Columbus, Conquest*; Floyd; Márquez; Morison, *Admiral*; Oliver; Pons, *Colón, Española, Historia*; Raccolta Letter Notes; Sauer; Thomas *Rivers*; Tudela; Varela *Caída*.

Anacaona's Ascension (Early 1501)

P, prev. cit.: Martyr, decade 3, bk. 9, decade 7, bk. 9. Las Casas Historia, vol. 1, chap. 169; vol. 2, chaps. 1, 3, 9 (including Collard Translation). Las Casas Repertorium, chap. 160. Oviedo, vol. 1, bk. 5, chap. 3.

S, prev. cit.: Altman; Granberry *Americas*; Keegan *Myth*; Lovén; Ochoa/Guengerich; Oliver; Oliver *Pané*; Priego; Sauer; Sued Badillo *Mujer*.

Primary sources don't indicate the date or cause of Behecchio's death. Primary sources establish Anacaona ruling prior to the arrival of Bobadilla's successor and do not attribute Behecchio's death to Spanish actions. Like some others, I believe he died naturally—which I have speculated by the European-introduced disease typhus.

Historians and anthropologists debate whether Taínos were ruled occasionally by cacicas prior to 1492, some believing they weren't and that rule by cacicas came only after traditional male rule had been disrupted by the conquest. Based on Las Casas, Oviedo, and some secondary sources noted above, I believe Anacaona rose—after a decade of conquest—to rule Xaraguá as its supreme cacique. Others, while not denying her power, caveat that she might not have held it as supreme cacique.

The burial description is based on Martyr and Oviedo. Martyr writes that Anacaona forced Guanahattabenecheuá to be buried and an unnamed Franciscan friar intervened to prevent Anacaona from so forcing more wives. Oviedo says that two wives were forced. Sutteeism sometimes was part of caciqual funerals on Haiti, and I have speculated that: according to Taíno custom, both wives did so voluntarily, and Anacaona didn't attempt to force more wives to join in; and the unnamed friar was ignored, as depicted.

Primary sources don't attribute the names Mencia and Ana de Guevara as originating with the friar or another identified person; as the story reasons, I doubt they were proposed by Taínos, and I have fictionalized the friar as doing so. The next sequel will revisit these names.

Cristóbal Discarded, Book of Prophesies, January–June 1501

P, prev. cit.: Bernáldez, chap. 165. Book of Prophesies, including the Prophecies Memorial. CDDD, doc. 470, Columbus's letter to Gorricio, May 24, 1501; docs. 471 and 473, Hojeda's capitulation and appointment as Coquibacoa's governor, June 8 and 10, 1501. Martyr Epistolario, doc. 221, letter of June 9, 1501. Nader, doc. 59, anonymous legal opinion re: Columbus's rights under Santa Fe Capitulations. Parry & Keith, doc. 24:1, license for Hojeda's second voyage and governorship, June 8, 1501. Rumeu de Armas *Indigenista*, doc. 110 (list of Spaniards indemnified for Indian slaves manumitted, May 28, 1501). Santa Cruz, chap. 58. Zurita, bk. 4, chaps. 31, 32.

P: Matthew, 24:14. Revelations, 21.

S, prev. cit.: Carroll; Cervantes *Conquistadores*; Fernández-Armesto *Columbus*; Liss; Mira Caballos *Indígenas*; Morison *Admiral*; Nader; Rubin; Rusconi; Vilar Sánchez; Vingeras.

Following Rusconi and others, I doubt Columbus ever delivered the Book of Prophecies or the Prophecies Memorial to the sovereigns.

Paolo Emilio Taviani believed that Columbus lived in the convent of Zubia outside the city of Granada during this period. That's possible, but it was some distance from the Alhambra, and I speculate he would have lived in the Alhambra's monastery, if only to be closer to his sons.

Historians disagree whether additional Indian slaves were manumitted on May 28, 1501, and if so, whether they included Indians enslaved by explorers other than Columbus. My speculation is that additional manumissions occurred then, but only of those Columbus had enslaved.

Isabel, Catalina, and Juana, Summer 1501

P, prev. cit.: Bergenroth, vols. 1 and 2, docs. 203, de Puebla's letter to sovereigns, July 17, 1498; 241, report of nuptials celebrated in abstention, May 19, 1499; 246, Arthur's letter to Catalina, October 5, 1499. Bernáldez, chap. 164. Martyr Epistolario, docs. 221, letter of June 9, 1501; 222, letter of June 30, 1501. Santa Cruz, chaps. 59, 61. Zurita, bk. 4, chaps. 28, 40.

S, prev. cit.: Aram; Carroll; Downey; Fernández-Armesto *Ferdinand Isabella*; Hillgarth; Liss; Rubin; Thomas *Rivers*.

Southern Landmass, Xaraguá, Summer 1501

P, prev. cit.: Bernáldez, chap. 196. CDDD, docs. 469, Hojeda's license to cut brazilwood, March 10, 1501; 471, Hojeda's capitulation, June 8, 1501; 475, Guevara's license to cut brazilwood, July 24, 1501; 657, delivery of a Bastidas slave, March 6, 1504. Jane, Mendez Testament. Las Casas Historia, vol. 2, chap. 2. Martyr, decade 1, bk. 10. Oviedo Repertorium, sec. 3.21. Parry & Keith, docs. 17:7, license of Rodrigo de Bastidas, June 5, 1500; 17:9, crown's judgment in lawsuit against Bastidas, January 19, 1504; 24:1 license for Hojeda's second voyage and governorship, June 8, 1501. Symcox *Italian Texts*, letters of Alberto Cantino and Pietro Pasqualigo, October 17 and 18, 1501.

S, prev. cit.: Herrera; Mira Caballos *Indígenas*; Morison *Northern Voyages*, *Southern Voyages*; Navarette, vol. 3; Sauer; Vigneras.

No primary or secondary source relates the conversation depicted between Isabel and Guevara; the historical record indicates Isabel was informed of Anacaona, and I've speculated that Guevara's licensing would have been an occasion for that.

Primary sources do not: identify Bastidas's first landfall on Española or his debarkation site on Haiti's southeastern peninsula; identify the caciques with whom Bastidas met while in Xaraguá or mention meetings with Xaraguá's Spanish settlers; or explain why Bastidas felt it necessary to burn and bury the ships' weapons and artillery, given the Spanish settlers' presence near modern Port-au-Prince. Bastidas was sailing from a layover on Jamaica, and I've speculated that his landfall was at the closest point thereto, the tip of Española's southwestern peninsula (following Morison), where settlers wouldn't have resided, not Port-au-Prince (Navarette). I've speculated Anacaona's knowledge and involvement (which to me seems certain, given Bastidas's extended stay in Xaraguá) and use of Haniguyabá as emissary. There is no record of Bastidas's thoughts depicted, and I've speculated he had the same perceptions of Xaraguá as Diego Mendez, who debarked on the peninsula three years later.

Isabel and Fernando, Grand Designs, July–September 2, 1501

P, prev. cit.: CDDD, docs. 479, appointment of Ovando as governor, September 3, 1501; 484, appointment of Pinzón as governor of his discoveries, September 5, 1501. Ferdinand Columbus, chap. 87. Hakluyt Cabral, letter from Manuel to Ferdinand and Isabella, July 29, 1501. Las Casas Historia, vol.1, chap. 77; vol. 2, chap. 3 (including Collard Translation). Las Casas Repertorium—2nd, 4th Voyages, sec. 8. Oviedo Repertorium, sec. 3.20. Parry & Keith, doc. 20:01, Columbus's memorial on settlement and gold mining, 1501(?). Santa Cruz, chap. 60. Varela Gil Textos, undated letter of Columbus to Isabella, August–September 1501.

S, prev. cit.: Aram; Ballesteros; Crowley; Floyd; Lamb; Liss; Mira Caballos *Ovando*; Morison *Admiral*; Pons *Colón, Española, Historia*; Rusconi; Rubin; Subrahmanyam; Thomas *Rivers*; Tremlett; Tudela; Vilar Sánchez.

While some historians believe Columbus was considerably involved in the sovereigns' decisions regarding Española's resettlement and governance, as the story reflects, I have followed historians who believe otherwise. A significant number of Columbus's writings likely composed during this period are undated, permitting alternative interpretations of the order of their composition and his concurrent state of mind, and the story reflects my speculation as to their order consistent with that noninvolvement. For example, historians disagree whether Columbus's undated memorial regarding settlement and gold mining was written before the second voyage (Las Casas Historia, vol.1, chap. 77, and Morison), before the third voyage (Ballesteros), or before his fourth voyage (Tudela, Gil, Varela). As to the memorandum itself I have favored Las Casas (and so presented in *Encounters Unforeseen*), but I believe the sovereigns repeatedly requested the substantive advice the subject of the memorandum, including before the third voyage and—as presented in the story—the fourth.

There is no record of the audience between Isabel and Columbus depicted, but I speculate she would have given him forewarning of Ovando's appointment rather than leaving it to rumor.

Cacique Diego and Guarionex, Concepción
No primary or secondary sources.

CHAP X: VISIONS, ISABEL'S ESPAÑOLA AND ANACAONA'S XARAGUÁ

Knight Commander Ovando's Orders, September 3–December 1501
P, prev. cit.: Book of Prophecies, Columbus's letter to Gorricio, September 13, 1501. CDDD, docs. 479, appointment of Ovando as governor, September 3, 1501; 483, Luis de Arriaga's capitulation, September 5, 1501 (translated in Parry & Keith, doc. 20:3); 486, Fray Trasiera's summons to court, September 7, 1501; 488, memorial re: royal participation in armada to repopulate Española, September 12, 1501; 492, sovereigns' instructions to Ovando, September 16, 1501 (translated in Parry & Keith, doc. 20:02); 497, sovereigns' order to reverse Bobadilla's gold award, September 16, 1502; 498, sovereigns' order prohibiting arms sales to Indians; 501, sovereigns' response to questions posed by Ovando, September 20, 1501; 505–508, sovereigns' orders re: Columbus's residence, Carvajal's appointment, Columbus's one-eighth interest, and Columbus's brothers' restoration, September 27 and 28, 1501; 517, memorial re: Columbus's request for fourth voyage, c. June–October 1501 (also translated in Raccolta Letters); 522, 523, 532, instructions re Cristóbal Guerra's slaves, November 10 and 11 and December 2, 1501; 528, sovereigns' instruction to treasurer, November 18 and 25, 1501; 600, instructions for government of Indies, March 20 and 29, 1503 (translated in Parry & Keith, doc. 20:4, but misdated 1501). Ferdinand Columbus, chap. 87. Las Casas Historia, vol. 2, chap. 3 (including Collard Translation). Las Casas Repertorium—2nd, 4th Voyages, sec. 8. Santa Cruz, chap. 67. Rumeu de Armas *Indigenista*, doc. 115 (sovereigns' order re: Indian gold tribute, December 2, 1501). Symcox *Italian Texts*, doc. 28, papal bull Eximiae devotionis, November 16, 1501. Zurita, bk. 4, chaps. 49, 55.

S, prev. cit.: Aram; Bakewell; Ballesteros; Cervantes *Conquistadores*;

Fernández-Armesto *Columbus, Conquest*; Floyd; Gil; Guitar; Herrera; Lamb; Liss; Mira Caballos *Conquista, Española*; Morison *Admiral*; Mörner; Pons *Colón, Española, Historia*; Rubin; Rumeu de Armas *Indigenista*; Sauer; Thomas *Rivers*; Tudela; Vilar Sánchez; Vingeras.

Some historians depict Columbus's fourth voyage as being authorized in tandem with and by the time of Ovando's appointment. As the story reflects, I have followed historians who believe the sovereigns then remained uncommitted to Columbus but recognized the voyage might benefit Spain.

Supreme Cacique Anacaona

P, prev. cit.: Las Casas Apologetica, chaps. 5, 197. Las Casas Historia, vol. 2, chap. 9 (including Collard Translation). Las Casas Short Account, "The Kingdoms of Hispaniola." Pané, chaps. 12, 22, 23.

P: Matthew, 6: 9–11, 22: 35–40.

S, prev. cit.: Bakewell; Stevens-Arroyo.

No primary or secondary source relates the caciqual council or visit to the unnamed friar's church depicted (the above sources relate only to incidental information). The next sequel will address Ovando's charge in 1503 that Anacaona and her vassal caciques plotted rebellion.

Primary sources don't relate that Anacaona adopted Christianity for herself or recommended it for her people generally, from which I have speculated—as culminated in this story—that she outright rejected it (it likely would have been trumpeted had she embraced it) for reasons similar to Guarionex's rejection thereof (as depicted in *Columbus and Caonabó*). The next sequel will address Higueymota's decisions regarding Christianity for herself and her daughter.

Primary sources discussing missionaries in this period don't relate their views of repartimiento or the de facto encomienda depicted herein. I've speculated that the unnamed friar shared the supportive or at least uncritical views of the churchmen who accompanied Ovando in 1502, as will be depicted in the next sequel.

Grand Colonizing Fleet Sails, Cristóbal's Exploratory Fleet Authorized, December 1501–March 1502

P, prev. cit.: Bernal Díaz, bk. 2, chap. 1. CDDD, docs. 483, Luis de Arriaga's capitulation, September 5, 1501 (translated in Parry & Keith, doc. 20:3); 528, sovereigns' instruction to treasurer, November 18 and 25, 1501; 536, 537, and 538, sovereigns' orders to depart promptly, December 6, 1501; 540 and 544, sovereigns' orders re: repatriation and boarding sick manumitted Indians, December 9 and 12, 1501; 571, sovereigns' permission for Portuguese, January 17, 1502; 574, sovereigns' order to depart promptly, February 2, 1502; 576, notices re: armada and Franciscans extracted by Muñoz, 1502; 577, Alonso Vélez de Mendoza's license, February 14, 1502; 578, Columbus's letter to Pope Alexander VI, February 1502 (translated in Fernández-Armesto *Himself*). Ferdinand Columbus, chaps. 87, 88. Fernández-Armesto *Himself*, letter to Pope Alexander VI, February 1502. Gómara, chap. 1. Jane, Fourth Voyage Letter. Las Casas Historia, vol. 2, chaps. 2, 3, vol. 3, chap. 27 (including Collard Translation). Las Casas Repertorium—2nd, 4th Voyages, sec. 8. Morison Documents, Fourth Voyage Instructions. Raccolta Letters, Columbus's memorial re: fourth voyage requisitions, c. June–October 1501; Columbus's letter to sovereigns, February 6, 1502. Santa Cruz, chaps. 61, 67. Zurita, bk. 4, chaps. 54, 55.

S, prev. cit.: Álvarez; Bello León; Aram; Ballesteros; Cervantes *Conquistadores*; Crowley; Fernández-Armesto *Columbus, Conquest, Himself*; Floyd; Friede/ Keen; Gil; Lamb; Mira Caballos *Armada, Conquista*; Morison *Admiral*; Restall *Meeting*; Rubin; Thomas *Conquest, Rivers*; Vilar Sánchez; Vingeras.

As most historians, I have followed Las Casas in relating that 2,500 persons sailed on Ovando's fleet, and while there isn't uniform understanding, I believe that number to be all-inclusive, i.e., including crews, crown appointees and soldiers, all other passengers (including servants and slaves), and Arriaga's 73 families. Mira Caballos's exhaustive study of the armada concludes that the "rounded" 2,500 is a considerable overstatement of the actual number; while I haven't abandoned the 2,500, the description of the armada's organization and who sailed is based largely upon his analysis.

Columbus's letter to the sovereigns of February 26, 1502, is lost, and the discussion of it is based on deduction from the sovereigns' reply and order and other primary sources.

The evidence that Bartolomé de las Casas and Juan de Esquivel participated in Sevillian militias organized to subdue the Granadan rebellion is uncertain. I speculate they did, finding such service consistent with their background and social status; quite a few historians agree as to Las Casas, and Mira Caballos agrees as to Esquivel.

CHAP XI: INVASION RENEWED

Higuanamá and Cotubanamá, Cohoba Ceremony (March 1502)
P, prev. cit.: Las Casas Apologetica, chaps. 3, 20, 197. Las Casas Historia, vol. 2, chap. 7 (including Collard Translation). Las Casas Short Account, "The Kingdoms of Hispaniola." Oviedo Repertorium, sec. 3.18.

S, prev. cit.: Floyd; Herrera; Oliver; Priego; Sauer; Sued Badillo *Mujer, History*.

Las Casas is inconsistent about the relationship between Higuanamá and Cotubanamá, and my speculation is based on one of the possible interpretations.

Primary sources don't discuss the two caciques' approval of the arrangements made by the Adamanay caciques or the cohoba ceremony, and the origin of the arrangements is unclear; I speculate (as Sauer) the arrangement was to forestall occupation, the caciques' approval would have been necessary, and the ceremony would have been invoked to validate seeking revenge.

Grand Invasion Arrives, April–May 1502

P, prev. cit.: CDDD docs. 480, sovereigns' order that Ovando assume Bobadilla's residence, September 3, 1501; 496, sovereigns' order that Ovando investigate Bobadilla, September 16, 1501; 499, sovereigns' order that Bobadilla return to Spain, September 17, 1501; 505, sovereigns' order re: return of Columbus's personal property, September 27, 1501. Las Casas *Historia*, vol. 2, chap. 3, vol. 3, chaps. 21, 27 (including Collard Translation). Oviedo, bk. 3, chap. 12. Oviedo *Repertorium*, sec. 3.20.

S, prev. cit.: Ballesteros; Canedo; Deagan; Floyd; Friede/Keen; Herrera; Lamb; Kulstad; Mira Caballos *Armada, Española, Ovando*; Pons *Colón, Dominican Republic, Española, Historia*; Reséndez; Sauer; Stone; Thomas *Rivers*; Tudela.

I'm unaware of preserved communications by Ovando during the first months of his rule; few primary sources indicate what he then did or ordered, and historians don't have a uniform interpretation of these months. The story's fictionalized meetings and dialogues are based largely on analysis of events that transpired thereafter and my synthesis of other historians' interpretations.

Caciques Guarionex and Diego Colón, Summoned to Santo Domingo (May 1502)

S, prev. cit.: Altman; Ladero Quesada; Márquez; Mira Caballos *Conquista, Española, Indígenas*; Pennock.

No primary or secondary source relates the process of transfer of Guarionex to Santo Domingo or the meeting with Ovando depicted. I've speculated that (i) Ovando's approval would have been required before Guarionex's transfer from Concepción and Ovando would have demanded Guarionex's submission before dispatching him to the sovereigns and (ii) Cacique Diego Colón's years of ongoing services for Ovando— as discussed by Mira Caballos and others—commenced at the time of transfer.

CHAP XII: PRAYERS AND PUNISHMENTS

Isabel and Cristóbal, April–May 1502

P, prev. cit.: Bernáldez, chap. 164. CDDD, docs. 585, Columbus's letter to son Diego, March 1502; 684, Diego de Porras's relation of Columbus's fourth voyage and territory discovered, November 7, 1504. Dotson, docs. 156, Columbus's letter to Oderico, March 21, 1502; 157, Columbus's letter to Bank of St. George, April 2, 1502. Ferdinand Columbus, chaps. 88, 102. Jane, Fourth Voyage Letter. Las Casas Repertorium—2nd, 4th Voyages, sec. 9.1. Martyr, decade 3, bk. 4. Morison Documents, Fourth Voyage Roster. Oviedo Repertorium, sec. 3.20. Pleitos doc. 14.11, Testimony of Francisco de Porras. Santa Cruz, chaps. 61, 67. Testamentos, Isabel's will, October 12, 1504, and codicil, November 23, 1504. Zurita, bk. 4, chaps. 55, 59.

S, prev. cit.: Álvarez; Azcona; Aram; Ballesteros; Cervantes *Conquistadores*; Fernández-Armesto *Columbus, Conquest, Himself*; Floyd; García Oro; Gil; Liss; Morison *Admiral*; Nader; Pérez; Raccolta Letters Notes; Rubin; Thomas *Rivers*; Vilar Sánchez; Vingeras.

A few historians believe that Columbus intended to return to Spain—after finding the passageway to the Indian seas—by circling the globe west. As depicted, while at voyage outset Columbus certainly believed he could and might do that, I don't find that positive intent expressed in primary sources and believe other perspectives compelled an intention to return east.

Ovando, Cacique Diego, Guarionex, and Anacaona,
May–June 27, 1502
P, prev. cit.: Benzoni, bk. 1. Bernáldez, chap. 196. CDDD doc. 684, Diego de Porras's relation of Columbus's fourth voyage and territory discovered, November 7, 1504. Ferdinand Columbus, chap. 88. Jane, Fourth Voyage Letter. Las Casas Repertorium, chap. 180. Las Casas Repertorium—2nd, 4th Voyages, sec. 9.1. Morison Documents, Fourth Voyage Roster. Las Casas Historia, vol. 2, chaps. 1–3, 6, 11 (including Collard Translation). Oviedo Repertorium, sec. 3.20. Pleitos docs. 14.01, 14.11, Testimonies of Diego and Francisco de Porras.

S, prev. cit.: Ballesteros; Deagan; Fernández-Armesto *Columbus, Conquest*; Floyd; Herrera; Kulstad; Lamb; Mira Caballos *Armada, Ovando*; Morison *Admiral, Southern*; Pons *Colón, Española*; Sauer; Stone; Thomas *Rivers*; Vingeras.

Ovando's investigation reports on Bobadilla and Roldán haven't survived. With respect to Ovando's treatment of Roldán and other significant rebels, (i) following Las Casas and many historians, I conclude they were exiled, (ii) following some historians, I conclude their Indians were freed from their control, and (iii) based on what is known to have occurred later, I speculate their repartimientos were also undone, all as depicted in the story. The story relies mostly on Las Casas's *Historia*, including the avoidance of informing Taínos of their freedom and the explanation of why they fled.
    Some historians believe Columbus exaggerated the unseaworthiness of the *Santiago* to fabricate an excuse to detour to Santo Domingo. Las Casas reports seeing both Roldán and Fernando de Guevara in Santo Domingo at this time, but other sources (noted herein) show Guevara was elsewhere during the period presented.

Primary sources and historians vary as to the number of ships that would depart and the amount and value of gold shipped. Pesos of gold have been converted to maravedís at a rate of 450:1, based on Las Casas and Floyd.

Hurikán, June 28–July 2, 1502

P, prev. cit.: Bernáldez, chap. 196. Ferdinand Columbus, chap. 88. Pané, chap. 23. Jane, Fourth Voyage Letter. Las Casas Historia, vol. 2, chap. 2. Las Casas Repertorium—2nd, 4th Voyages, sec. 9.1. Martyr, decade 3, bk. 4. Santa Cruz, chap. 67. Oviedo Repertorium, sec. 3.20.

S, prev. cit.: Ballesteros; Cervantes Conquistadores; Gould; Leguina; Mira Caballos Armada, Ovando; Morison Admiral, Southern; Raccolta Letter Notes; Thomas Rivers; Vingeras.

Primary and secondary sources don't relate the hurricane preparations of Taíno caciques or their subjects, and the story's depictions thereof are my speculation.

As for the Europeans, primary and secondary sources conflict considerably regarding the numbers of ships departing, sinking, returning to Santo Domingo, and reaching Spain in 1502, as well as the numbers of persons departing and perishing. The story reflects my reconciliation of sources, relying principally on Morison's analysis of the course of the hurricane, Mira Caballos's study of the identity and fate of the ships, and my own speculation on how the participants reacted.

Some historians (including Ballesteros) believe Roldán survived to live out his life in Spain. See Chap. IX, "Southern Landmass, Xaraguá, Summer 1501," above for sources re: Bastidas's slaves.

The Repartimiento de Alburquerque of 1514 (Márquez) records a cacica Catalina Ayahibex in Santo Domingo. Whether this Catalina is the same Catalina that cohabitated with Miguel Díaz is unknown; if not, to my knowledge, the Catalina cohabitating with Díaz disappears from history with the hurricane. I speculate that Díaz and she never married, as Díaz later married a Spaniard.

Isabel and Anacaona, Early July 1502

P, prev. cit.: Benzoni, bk. 1. Ferdinand Columbus, chap. 89. Las Casas Repertorium—2nd, 4th Voyages, sec. 9.2. Oviedo Repertorium, sec. 3.20. Rodriguez Valencia, vol. 3, letter of Ferdinand to Isabella, July 30, 1502. Santa Cruz, chap. 62. Zurita, bk. 4, chap. 68.

S, prev. cit.: Carroll; Liss; Rubin.

No primary or secondary sources relate the conversations or prayers depicted.

ACKNOWLEDGMENTS

As with my prior books, research for this novel included visiting museums, libraries, and sites in the Dominican Republic and Spain, which added to my appreciation of events depicted (unfortunately, I couldn't revisit Haiti). I wish to thank those who assisted.

In Spain, at Madrid's Naval Museum, José María Moreno Martín, head of the museum's cartographic and scientific instruments collection, educated me about the Juan de la Cosa world map in the collection and gave me a tour of the other fifteenth and sixteenth century maps and instruments exhibited. In Toledo, Inma Sáuchez Bernardo explained where Isabella prayed in the city's great Cathedral and the Church of San Juan de los Reyes and guided me through the archaeological remains of the fifteenth century alcazar where she likely resided. In Granada, Conchi Fernández Cueto provided a tour of streets where the Mohammedan uprising likely began and the Alhambra palace room where Isabella would have informed Columbus he'd been replaced. In Seville, José Alfonso Muriel showed me the Admiral's room in Seville's alcazar and led me past the royal shipyards and through the Triana neighborhood where statues of and plaques to mariners who sailed with Columbus are found today.

In the Dominican Republic, Carlos Mercedes resumed as my driver, guide, and companion as we explored sites along the Ozama River in Santo Domingo and west to Puerto Viejo (south of Azua), north to the northern coast at Sabaneta de Yásica, and east to Higüey and the island of Saona, all with the logistical assistance of Richard Weber, the founder of Tours, Trips, Treks & Travel. Raymond Mateo guided me in Santo Domingo's Museum of the Dominican Man, and Ivelisse Castillo gave me access to its library. Francisco Ramirez gave me a tour of rooms and walls presently part of the Hotel Nicolás de Ovando in Santo Domingo's colonial zone, where Ovando began European construction on the Ozama's west bank. Domingo Abreu, the Dominican archaeologist and speleologist, took me to the area of the New Mines along the upper Jaina River and explained "Española's" early gold mining. Juan Carlos Maldonado Coste showed me the remains of Fort Concepción and its nearby church. Rosa María Peña assisted me in Santiago de los Caballeros's library Amantes de la Luz. Captain Luis Carlos Lopez Sanchez and mate Hector Roldolfo Contreras Castro took me on a boat ride to explore Saona's coast. Yerenmy Rosario guided me about the fortified residence of Juan Ponce de León near the Bay of Yuma. Diógenes Alcalá E. of the Regional Museum of Archaeology at Altos de Chavón provided useful insight into the events relating to Cotubanamá.

I remain indebted to L. Antonio Curet, Francisco V. Coste, and Pauline M. Kulstad-González, esteemed archaeologists specializing in Taínos. While not consulted for this book, themes depicted herein have been influenced by my prior discussions with them.

For literary editing, I thank Joie Davidow, Davy Kent, Ann Mason, and Marla Markman.

Last (but not least), I thank the team assembled for *Columbus and Caonabó* for returning to work on this sequel: Glen Edelstein, book and cover design; Robert Hunt, cover illustration; Boris De Los Santos, newly drawn maps and illustrations; Neil Rosini, my lawyer; and Jerome McLain, webmaster.

www.ingramcontent.com/pod-product-compliance
Lightning Source LLC
Chambersburg PA
CBHW020242120726
47904CB00001B/67